Contents

A

PRAIRIE

Christmas

COLLECTION

9 Historical Christmas Romances
from America's Great Plains

A
PRAIRIE
Christmas
COLLECTION

Tracey Bateman, Tracie Peterson, Deborah Raney,

Pamela Griffin, JoAnn A. Grote, Maryn Langer, Darlene Mindrup, Janet Spaeth, Jill Stengl

BARBOUR
PUBLISHING

Print ISBN 978-1-62416-261-9

eBook Editions:
Adobe Digital Edition (.epub) 978-1-60742-884-8
Kindle and MobiPocket Edition (.prc) 978-1-60742-885-5

Cover image: VEER Alison Shaw/Photonica/Getty
Interior illustrations: Mari Small

Published by Barbour Publishing, Inc., P.O. Box 719, Uhrichsville, Ohio 44683, www.barbourbooks.com

Our mission is to publish and distribute inspirational products offering exceptional value and biblical encouragement to the masses.

Member of the
Evangelical Christian
Publishers Association

Printed in the United States of America.

Take Me Home

by Tracey V. Bateman

Dedication

To my sister, Linda Devine.
I love you dearly.

Chapter 1

Coon's Hollow, Iowa—1887

A frigid wind assaulted Kathleen Johnson the second she stepped off the train onto the boardwalk in front of the Coon's Hollow station. A shiver began at the base of her spine and worked its way to a full-bodied shudder. Apparently Pa's prediction of an unusually frigid winter was coming true. Here it was barely mid-October and the gray clouds overhead seemed suspiciously plump. She wouldn't be surprised if it snowed overnight. Gripping her valise tight with one hand, she pulled her scarf closer about her head with the other and braved the few feet of cold wind until she reached the depot.

The smell of sawdust hung in the air, tickling her nose and throat. She gave a little cough and glanced about, looking for someone who might be looking for her. The telegram from Reverend Nelson had promised that someone would be at the station to collect her upon her arrival. But though she received numerous curious glances, no one seemed inclined to offer her a ride.

With a sigh, she made her way to the ticket booth and placed a gloved hand on the tall counter. "Excuse me, please."

The man glanced up. His brow rose, and his face split into a leer at the sight of her. "Well, well. How can I help you, little lady?"

Barely containing her revulsion at the lecherous tone, she swallowed hard, wishing that Pa or one of her four brothers were here to put this man in his place. The fact that she was on her own now for the first time ever washed over her with startling clarity.

She forced the deepest frown she could muster and raised her chin. "I am looking for someone—"

"Look no farther, beautiful girl," he shot back, his eyes traveling over her face and neck. Kathleen had never been more grateful for her petite height, which in this instance kept everything below her shoulders hidden from his view.

"No, I'm not looking for someone like that." Her face burned, and she wished she could think of a crushing retort, thereby reducing his cocky exterior to a puddle of shame. But as usual, when faced with conflict, words failed her.

He leaned on the counter, his elbow supporting him. His hand shot out and covered hers before she could anticipate the move and pull back. "Don't break my heart, honey. I'm looking for someone just like you."

A gasp escaped her lips at his boldness, and she snatched her hand away. He was bordering on more than rudeness. Before she could conjure a thought, rescue came in the form of a puff of smoke and a declaration. "Abel Coon, I've half a mind to tell your pa what I just overheard. Bet your ma'd beat the tar outta ya, iffen she was still kickin', God rest her soul."

"Mind your own business." The man scowled over Kathleen's shoulder.

Kathleen whipped around and nearly passed out at the sight of her savior. The woman—at least she guessed it was a woman—wore a man's overcoat that hung open, revealing an ill-fitting brown dress. A fat cigar hung from thin lips, and a wide-brimmed hat rested on her mop of gray hair. Her broad forehead and large nose made her look rather masculine, and sagging jowls reminded Kathleen of her family's bulldog, Toby.

Abel gave a loud, pointed cough. "No smoking in the depot, Mary."

"It'll take someone a lot tougher than you to stop me, you little pip-squeak."

Though Kathleen was a bit taken aback by Mary's habit as well, she couldn't help but be glad the woman didn't obey the despicable flirt behind the counter.

Mary snatched the cigar from her lips and held it between her fingers as she sized Kathleen up. "You the new teacher?"

"Yes, ma'am."

"Thought so." She gave a curt nod. "The reverend sent me to take you over to the school, though why I do favors for the likes of him..."

Relief coursed through Kathleen. "Oh, thank you, Mrs...."

Without asking, the woman reached out and took Kathleen's valise. "*Miss* Bilge, for now."

"Oh, are you soon to be wed, Miss Bilge?"

Abel's laughter echoed through the station. "In a pig's eye."

Miss Bilge's manly face turned scarlet, and she scowled at the ill-mannered young man. "Shut up, Abel. I don't see no gals takin' you up on any offers lately."

He reddened, and Mary Bilge nodded her satisfaction as she turned her attention back to Kathleen. "I ain't engaged, formally. But that don't mean I ain't willin' if the right fella came along. That's why I said I'm a *miss* for now."

"I see." Bewildered, Kathleen left her response there. Fortunately, Miss Bilge seemed ready to move on. She glanced about the floor, then looked back to Kathleen. "This your only bag?"

"Yes, ma'am."

She gave a loud snort, adding to her already unladylike demeanor. "Must not be plannin' to stay very long."

Kathleen once again felt her cheeks grow warm. "Well, I was..." What could she say? The astute lady was pretty much right. Her presence in Coon's Hollow was a trial run. First time teaching. First time away from home. Biting her lip, she fought the approach of hot tears.

Thankfully, Miss Bilge nodded in understanding, making it unnecessary for Kathleen to elaborate. "Ya want to make sure a town like Coon's Hollow is where you want to hang your hat permanently before you bring anything more than can fit in this here bag? Can't say as I blame a young thing like you. The last gal barely stayed a month."

Well, that explained the need for a quick replacement. The head of the Rosewood school board happened to be brothers with a member of Coon's Hollow's school board. Coon's Hollow had need of a teacher to fill in for the rest of the term. Kathleen's father, who sat on the Rosewood school board, had approached her with the suggestion. Though she hated the thought, she'd agreed to take the teacher's exam and left the results in God's hands. Two weeks later, here she was, shaking from head to toe from nerves and cold, feeling for all she was worth as though she'd bitten off more than she could chew in a million years.

Kathleen swallowed hard as Miss Bilge tossed her valise into the back of a wagon and offered her a hand up.

"Thank you."

The woman walked around to the other side of the wagon and swung herself up, forcing Kathleen to avert her gaze at the flash of a hairy calf as the patched skirt hiked. "Oops." Mary sent her an embarrassed grin and quickly righted her skirt. Kathleen couldn't help but return the smile.

Slapping the reins, Miss Bilge nodded in approval. "You'll do just fine. Don't worry about that Abel Coon. He's all talk. I'm thinking his pa regrets ever teaching him to speak."

Gathering all the bravado she could muster, Kathleen sat up a little straighter. "He didn't bother me. I was just about to put him in his place when you walked up."

"Sure you were. But I'm right proud of you for trying to be brave." She waved to a passerby. "The last gal nearly fainted every time she saw a mouse."

"M–mouse?"

"You scared of those furry little critters, too?"

Kathleen cleared her throat. "I should say not." She should say *so*! "A–are there any in the teacherage?"

"Tons of 'em. They come in from the field out back of the building. But don't worry. They ain't gonna hurt you. Just trying to get out of the cold."

Kathleen shivered as the wind whipped up and shook the wagon. "Well, I certainly can't blame them for that. I wouldn't mind getting out of this cold myself. Are we almost there?"

"It's just at the edge of town."

Kathleen followed the point of Miss Bilge's cigar. Her heart sank as she observed the clapboard structure. She'd expected a whitewashed building with a bell and a porch, like the school in Rosewood. She was sorely disappointed. The roof was straight across over one portion of the building, then slanted downward as though in an afterthought another room had been added. She assumed the afterthought would be her quarters.

Another gust of wind shook the structure, and Kathleen felt her spirits plummet further. It must be freezing inside with walls so thin. How would she ever stay warm? And it was only October. The term ended in two months, so she'd be home for Christmas. She could be brave that long. She hoped.

"Looks like someone built a fire." Miss Bilge's gruff voice broke through Kathleen's thoughts.

"Huh?"

"There's smoke comin' from the chimney."

"Oh, that's a mercy. My fingers are nearly frozen off."

The woman chuckled as she halted the team and hopped down. After wrapping the reins around the hitching post, she grabbed Kathleen's bag from the back. Kathleen stared. "Need help getting down?" the woman asked.

Heat warmed her cheeks. "I–I can do it."

She climbed down, careful to keep her skirt covering her legs. She stumbled a little as she touched the ground. Kathleen gathered her composure and followed Miss Bilge, who was almost to the door.

Suddenly, she was very glad that she'd decided against bringing a trunk. She'd already made up her mind. Coon's Hollow wasn't the town for her. She most definitely would not be accepting a certificate for another term. Lecherous train station men, crazy women who looked and talked more like men, mice in the schoolhouse. She shuddered.

How she wished she'd never agreed to this venture. Mama had warned her that she'd regret it, and as usual, Mama was right. Why had she ever listened to Caleb? Her favorite brother had been wrong in this instance. "Kat," he'd said. "Don't make the same mistake I did. You might find that you don't want to stay in Rosewood forever." At her gasp, he'd hurried on. "Now, don't think I'm not happy with Deborah and my girls, because I am. But maybe I would have liked the chance to make a choice. You have that chance. Take it."

And against her better judgment, Kathleen had taken his advice. Now she missed her family so fiercely it was all she could do to keep herself from bursting into tears. Though they'd said good-bye only this morning, her stomach tightened at the thought of them. Ma would be starting to fix supper, and the two younger boys would be finishing up chores while the two older boys helped Pa in the family-owned livery stable.

"Ya comin', gal?"

Kathleen jerked her gaze from the frigid ground to find Miss Bilge filling the doorway, her cigar a mere stub between her lips.

"Yes, I'm coming."

"It ain't much to look at, but we can get it fixed up in no time."

Kathleen couldn't stifle a gasp at her first sight of the schoolhouse. Every desk, including hers, was overturned, and many were broken. Dirt and mice droppings layered the floor, along with scattered books and tablets.

"What on earth happened?"

"Ain't no tellin'. My guess is a pack of ornery young 'uns with too much time on their hands since there ain't been no school. You can straighten 'em out in no time."

A sigh pushed from Kathleen's lungs. She would need at least a week to ready this room for school, and how would she ever control a group of students who were rowdy enough to cause this sort of damage?

Miss Bilge clucked her tongue and snatched up her valise once more. "Come on, gal."

"Wh–where are we going?"

"Back to the train station. This town ain't for the likes of you."

Chapter 2

At his first sight of the new teacher, Josh Truman nearly dropped the armload of wood he carried. He gaped at the young woman who followed quickly behind Mary Bilge, taking two steps to every one of the older lady's.

The teacher reached forward and took hold of Mary's arm. "Miss Bilge, please wait. I haven't said I want to go back."

A puff of wind caught the teacher's scarf, pushing it back from her face. Josh caught a glimpse of a lovely rounded face and enormous blue eyes. He sucked in a breath and tried to remember where he was. She reminded him of one of those store-bought dolls that Auntie Stell had brought back for his little sister, Flora, when she and the preacher returned from their honeymoon last summer. Only this living, breathing doll was a lot prettier.

He blinked. They sure hadn't made teachers like that when he went to school. As a matter of fact, most of his instructors looked more like Miss Bilge. Except they were all men.

He smiled at his own joke, then frowned as he realized the two women were moving away from the school rather than toward it. Where did that crazy Mary think she was taking the new schoolteacher? "Hey, where are you going?"

Mary snatched her trademark cigar from her mouth and tossed it to the ground, crushing it beneath the toe of her clunky men's boot. "New record for shortest time a teacher stayed. Looks like Wayne Sharpton wins the bet. He said Miss Johnson here would take one look at the schoolroom and hightail it home."

"Bet?" The young teacher's voice squeaked, and she stopped dead in her tracks. "Everyone's gambling about me? But that's. . .that's sinful. Besides, I never said. . ."

Feeling like he'd been kicked in the gut by her distress, Josh hurried to reassure her. "No, miss. Not everyone. Only the most disreputable characters in town."

Mary drew herself up and pinned him with a scowl fierce enough to scare a mama bear away from her cub. "There ain't no call to be insultin'."

Warmth flooded Josh's cheeks. "Sorry, Miss Bilge."

With a disgruntled snort, she hefted the valise she carried to the back of the wagon. "Not as sorry as I am. I lost two bits to that Wayne Sharpton." She shook her head in obvious disgust. "I gotta give up gamblin' on these teachers 'fore I end up in the poorhouse. I figured this one would stay for sure. Just had me a feelin'."

Miss Johnson gathered her dignity and squared her shoulders. "Pardon me for being the cause of your debt, Miss Bilge."

The young woman's offense was lost on Mary. "Debt? Naw, this is cash on the barrel. No one can bet lessen they got the money right then."

"Oh. Well, anyway, I never said I wanted to leave."

Mary squinted. "Don't ya? I thought sure it was all over for ya the second ya saw that wrecked building."

The young teacher hesitated. "While I admit I was a bit taken aback, I am not so easily deterred. I promised my father and the school board that I would teach until the end of the term."

Josh's heart soared. "Bravo, Miss Johnson."

Her eyes widened, and a dimple flashed in her cheek, sending his heart racing faster than at a log-splitting contest. "Thank you," she said, her tone velvety soft.

By the time he found his voice, she touched him lightly on the arm, and he lost it again.

She focused those beautiful, ocean blue eyes on him, nodding toward the wood in his arms. "Are you the one who built the fire in the schoolhouse?"

Josh nodded. "I was just about to go inside and start cleaning up the mess. I'd be honored if you'd allow me to continue with my plan and help get the room ready for classes." He hesitated. "Unless, of course, you've decided not to stay in Coon's Hollow."

"That's very kind of you." She turned to Mary and smiled. "Miss Bilge, I despise gambling as the devil's sport; however, you may just win that bet after all."

~

Soapy water sloshed onto the plank floor as Kathleen pushed the bucket forward, then crawled after it to the next filthy spot in the room. Mary Bilge lit another cigar—her second in an hour—and stared at Kathleen, her lined face scrunching together as she appeared to be pondering.

Kathleen's face flooded with warmth. She knew the woman suspected that her quick turnabout was in response to Josh's presence. But that wasn't true. The least she could do was stay after the generous man had given of his time to chop firewood and offer to clean. Besides, it wasn't her idea to go back home in the first place, and she had been trying to tell Miss Bilge that very thing when Josh showed up.

Her reason for staying had nothing whatsoever to do with Mr. Josh Truman or his lovely brown eyes that reminded her so much of the dark trunk of the maple tree in her backyard. After all, she had no interest in courting a young man from another county. Mama would just about die if she even considered it. All five of the Johnson children knew they were expected to stay in or around Rosewood when they married, and of the two that were married already, they had, without fail, obeyed. Pa joked that Mama's expectation was similar to God instructing the children of Israel—absolutely no foreign marriages. Mama's word was law in their household.

Another puff of smoke wafted into the air, pulling Kathleen from her thoughts.

"Miss Bilge, things might go much faster if you'd consider lending your assistance." Kathleen hated to be rude, but the woman was making her nervous as she watched and smoked and made silent assumptions.

"Well, la-de-da, missy. I ain't here to work; I'm here to chaperone. If I get myself too wrapped up in cleanin', I might miss something between you two young people."

Kathleen's cheeks warmed. "I assure you, Miss Bilge, you have no need to concern yourself about that. I've no intention of allowing anything between Mr. Truman and myself."

"That so?" The skepticism in her tone grated on Kathleen.

"Yes, it most certainly is."

"Then how come your voice changed when you spoke to young Josh? And how come you flashed those dimples when you smiled at him? And how come—"

"Why, I did no such thing." Only outrage could have caused her to rudely interrupt her elder, but Kathleen refused to stand by and be falsely accused of. . . flirting.

"Did too." Mary's cigar hung from her mouth as she folded her arms across her chest, stubbornly making a stand for what she believed.

"Okay, fine. Have it your way. But you're mistaken."

"We'll see. . . ."

Kathleen was about to argue further, but the blast of cold air blowing through the door silenced her. Josh stomped into the room, carrying a box of tools.

"Here we go," he said breathlessly. "I'll get started repairing the desks."

"That's very thoughtful of you," Kathleen said, making a conscious effort to keep her voice normal. Instead, it had a ring to it that sounded downright fake.

That Mary Bilge had the audacity to chuckle. Kathleen's ire rose. She sent the woman a glare that served only to make her laugh out loud.

"What's so funny, Mary?" Josh asked, shrugging out of his coat. He held his hands over the stove to warm them.

Kathleen sent Mary a silent plea not to further humiliate her.

"I reckon that's my own business," Mary said with a grunt.

Releasing a slow breath, Kathleen gave a grateful smile. Surprise flickered in Mary's eyes, and the hard lines of her face seemed to smooth a bit. She stomped to the door and tossed out her cigar stub, then turned back around. "Well, what are ya standing around gawking for? This here school ain't going to clean itself."

Affection surged through Kathleen. *The old softy.*

Josh brushed his hands together and stood, stretching his back. "That'll have to do for now," he said. He surveyed his handiwork with a sense of satisfaction. He'd repaired four of the damaged desks. The rest were beyond repair and would require rebuilding from the ground up. But he didn't mind. Not if it gave him a few more days to get to know the new teacher.

She smiled at him through a dirt-smudged face. "What a wonderful carpenter you are!"

Pleased embarrassment swept through him. "Thank you. Let's just hope they're sturdy enough."

"I'm sure they are." And to prove her point, she sat in each one and bounced. She grinned up at him. "See?"

Josh laughed out loud. Mary harrumphed. The woman had long since given up trying to help and now sat in the corner, her sharp eyes taking in every move he made. Why she had set herself up as Miss Johnson's watchdog, Josh wasn't sure. But it was apparent the two women held an instant affection for each other.

"Looks to be about suppertime," he mused.

"Oh, I'm sorry I kept you so long, Mr. Truman." Miss Johnson stepped forward and offered her dainty hand. He clasped it gladly, enjoying the smooth warmth of her slender fingers. "Thank you for your assistance. I don't know what I'd have done without you."

Miss Bilge snorted.

Miss Johnson glanced over her shoulder. "I don't know what I'd have done without either of you. You were both sent by God, and I'm truly grateful."

Miss Bilge stood to her full height. "The Almighty would not be sendin' the likes of me to someone such as yourself."

"Of course He would, and He did," the teacher retorted. She grinned and met Miss Bilge across the room. She slipped her arm around the woman's thick shoulders and gave a squeeze. "You're my very first friend here in Coon's Hollow and just like an angel unawares."

For the first time since Josh had known her, Mary Bilge blushed. It wasn't a pretty sight. Rather, she looked like a rabid dog. Her face screwed up, and Josh could have sworn she was about to cry. Instead, she scowled and shook off Miss Johnson's arm. "Angel, my foot." She pinned Josh with her stare. "You takin' her home for supper?"

"Yes, ma'am. If she'll accept the invitation."

"I wouldn't want to impose."

"Mama's expecting you," he assured the girl. "You'd be more than welcome as well, Miss Bilge."

"Thankee kindly, but I got plans. You comin' tomorrow to work some more?"

Josh nodded. "I planned to."

"Fine. I'll be here by nine. Don't come any earlier. Ain't no sense in compromising the girl."

Miss Johnson gasped.

Heat crept up the back of his neck. "Yes, ma'am."

"Well, get on outside and wait in the wagon whilst Miss Johnson cleans up."

Josh couldn't resist a glance at Miss Johnson. Her face was scarlet, and she didn't quite meet his gaze.

"I'll be waiting," he said softly, trying to put her more at ease. "Take all the time you need."

She nodded, and he exited the schoolroom. He whistled a lively tune as he headed toward the livery to pick up the team. He certainly anticipated the drive home. It would be nice to chat with Miss Johnson without the constant glaring from Miss Bilge.

❧

As the wagon jostled up the pocked lane leading to Josh's house, Kathleen surveyed the white two-story home. A large oak tree stood next to the house, its branches encircling one side of the roof as though they were arms of protection.

"Home, sweet home," Josh said, breaking the silence.

"It's lovely." And it reminded her of her own house back in Rosewood. Loneliness clutched her heart.

Josh reined in the horses and hopped down. He walked to her side of the wagon and reached up to her. "May I?"

She nodded. Her stomach lifted with butterflies when Josh's warm hand closed around hers. He kept a firm grasp as she carefully climbed down. When her feet touched the ground, she looked at him, expecting him to release her hand. But he didn't. Instead, he caught her gaze and smiled. "You have the most beautiful eyes I've ever seen, Miss Johnson."

"I–I don't know what to say."

He placed his finger beneath her chin, the slight pressure encouraging her to return his gaze. "I didn't mean to embarrass you."

They were so close, she could feel his warmth. She'd never stood so close to any man other than family members, and her heart began to race. He smelled of wood smoke and fresh air, and she longed to lean closer. Feelings she didn't understand churned inside her. A wish that he would keep hold of her hand, that he would speak to her in that rich voice, that he would keep looking at her as though he never wanted to look away.

Too soon the moment ended as the door flew open. Kathleen jumped, snatching her hand away.

"Josh! You're finally home!" A little girl hopped off the porch, her brown braids flying behind her as she ran toward them. "Mama was just about to send Pa looking for you."

"Well, we're here. Time got a little away from us."

"I'll say." She turned to look at Kathleen. "I'm Flora Truman. Josh is my brother. You the new teacher?"

Kathleen smiled and held out her hand. "Yes, I am. Pleased to meet you, Flora. I'm Miss Johnson."

"I hope you like it here, Miss Johnson." She heaved a sigh. "Most teachers don't."

"All right," Josh said, taking the little girl by the shoulders and gently turning her toward the house. "Let's go inside."

He offered Kathleen his arm. "Don't let her discourage you. Coon's Hollow isn't so bad once you get used to it."

Unable to resist his boyish grin, she slipped her hand through the crook of his arm and smiled. "I can't help but wonder why your teachers seem to leave. It's not unusual for women to fall in love and marry, thus leaving their positions to be wives, but for someone to just leave for no reason, especially in the middle of the term. . ." She shrugged. "I don't know. It seems a little odd to me."

"It's not unusual for women to fall in love with a local man, eh?" He waggled his eyebrows. "Maybe you'll be a one-term teacher, too."

Kathleen's eyes widened, and she gaped as he opened the door and nudged her inside ahead of him.

Chapter 3

Flopping onto her stomach, Kathleen tried desperately to find a comfortable spot on the straw tick mattress. She grabbed her feather pillow and hugged it into a ball beneath her head. Only the ping of ice balls hitting her window and the occasional *scritch-scratch* coming from the mouse population inside the building penetrated the vast silence.

After a lovely evening at the Trumans', she had enjoyed her ride home with Josh and Flora. But as they approached her teacherage, dread had clenched her stomach. They'd said a hasty good-bye so that Josh could get Flora home and out of the cold. Then the loneliness had set in, and there seemed to be nothing better to do than go to bed.

But sleep never came. Tears rolled down Kathleen's cheeks, soaking her pillow. She'd never spent the night alone before. Silence permeated the darkness. How she longed for the sound of her brothers' snoring from their respective rooms. The solitude was almost more than she could bear. Mama's words of warning rang in her ears: "Without family around you, Kathleen, you're going to be one miserable young woman. Mark my words."

"Oh, Mama," Kathleen whispered, "you were so right. I should have stayed home where I belong. How will I ever make it here until Christmas break?"

The two months loomed ahead of her as though they were two years. Gentle tears gave way to choking sobs, and finally, just before dawn, only shuddering breaths remained of her sorrowful night.

Despite the gentle light seeping through the cracks in the walls, she was just dozing off when a knock at her door startled her fully awake. Shivering in the cold of the poorly built room, she stepped onto the icy floor and grabbed her dressing gown. She opened the door just a crack.

Miss Bilge stood outside, her arms loaded down with a crate as wide as she was. "Thought you might need some supplies."

Kathleen pulled her wrapper close and peeked at her through the sliver of an opening she'd made when she opened the door. "Good morning, Miss Bilge."

"Well? Ya going to ask me in? Or didn't your ma teach you any manners?"

If it hadn't been so frigid, Kathleen's face would have been hot with embarrassment.

"Yes, ma'am. Come in, please."

Mary shivered and stomped inside. She set the crate on the table and looked about with a scowl Kathleen was beginning to get used to. "Ain't much warmer in here than it is outside. Don't you know how to make a fire?"

"Well, yes, but I haven't had a chance to yet. I just got up."

The woman's gaze swept over Kathleen's attire, and she nodded. "Never been much of a late sleeper myself. Always get up before the chickens."

Defenses raised, Kathleen could just imagine the whole town thinking their new teacher was a stay-a-bed. "I always get up early, too. I just didn't sleep very well last night."

"Why not?"

"I'm just not used to being alone in a new place."

"Well, go on and make yourself decent while I build up the fire," she commanded, waving Kathleen toward the sleeping part of the room. Kathleen ducked behind the curtain. She dressed quickly and made up her bed. By the time she emerged, Mary's fire was already beginning to warm the room, and the table was set with fresh bread, a jar of milk, and a jar of preserves. Mary had pulled out a skillet and stood over slices of ham sizzling on the stove. She turned when Kathleen emerged.

"That's more like it."

Kathleen's curiosity got the better of her, and she peeked inside the box on the table. Flour, sugar, yeast, a crock of butter, fresh eggs, a slab of salt pork, and a pail of lard were packed together. Also, she'd included some apple butter. "Thank you for the provisions, Miss Bilge. Mrs. Truman was kind enough to fill a crate as well, so between the two of you, I'm all fixed up for a while."

"Weren't me, missy. That Mrs. Nelson sent it over."

"The reverend's wife? How kind. I look forward to meeting her on Sunday."

Mary harrumphed. "Not much to look forward to iffen ya ask me."

Picking up on the fact that she'd struck a raw nerve, Kathleen pushed the issue to the back of her mind to discuss with Josh later and broached another topic.

"How long do you suppose it will take before the schoolhouse is ready for the children?"

Mary forked a slice of ham and lifted it to a plate. She shrugged and reached for the second. "Near as I can tell, you oughtta be havin' school by Tuesday or Wednesday of next week. There's holes in the wall that needs to be patched up. Window's got a crack in it and has to be replaced. I reckon someone'll drive into Taneyville and pick one up. Ain't got no ready-made windows 'round here." She glanced at Kathleen. "I reckon young Josh'll be comin' every day to help out."

Kathleen's stomach jumped at the sound of his name. "He's very kind. But I don't want to impose."

"From the looks of it, you'd have to be rude to get rid of him. It's a funny thing. He's never been smitten before, leastways not that I can recall."

"Smitten? Oh, Mary, really. We've only just met."

Mary cracked an egg into the skillet and nodded back at her. "Well, I've known him since he was born, and I say he took a shine to you from the second he laid eyes on ya. And I don't think he's the only one who's sportin' a shine." Setting a plate in front of Kathleen, she cast a sidelong glance.

"I'm sure I don't know what you mean, Mary."

"Ha! I'm sure ya do."

Kathleen was just about to argue further when Mary silenced her with an upraised hand. "No sense denying it to me. I spent the day watchin' ya yesterday. I wouldn't be a bit surprised if he doesn't come courtin' and the two of you end up at the altar before the school term ends. Guess we'll be losin' another teacher after all."

The delicious picture Mary's words conjured up made Kathleen pause and dream—but only for a minute, as the memory of her lonely, sleepless night returned with aching clarity.

Mary's sharp gaze scrutinized her. Kathleen squared her shoulders and forced a firm tone. "You are mistaken. I do not intend to become entangled with anyone in Coon's Hollow. I am going back home in two months. And I'm never leaving home again."

Chapter 4

Sunday morning dawned with warmer temperatures, a brilliant sun, and a return to more fall-like conditions. Kathleen woke much too early from a fitful night's sleep and was ready and waiting a full two hours before Josh arrived to escort her to the worship service. She could feel the stares searing her back as she followed him down the center aisle of the church. The whispers gave way to something akin to a buzzing hive of bees by the time the pair made it to the third row of pews where Josh's family sat.

A man with graying hair and blue eyes, whom Kathleen recognized as Josh's pa, stood and offered his hand. "Nice to have you here, Miss Johnson."

"Thank you." The sight of the large family packed into the pew pinched Kathleen's lonely heart, making her all the more forlorn. Her lip trembled as she smiled at Mrs. Truman. The tiny woman had a kind face, and her returning smile seemed tinged with sympathy. "Are you all settled in, Kathleen?"

"Yes, ma'am. The curtains you gave me last night at dinner spruced the place right up. Thank you."

"I'm so glad." Warmth exuded from her, and Kathleen began to relax. Mrs. Truman turned to the younger boys sitting on the pew. "Alvin, you and Joe move back a row so Josh and Miss Johnson can sit with us."

Kathleen placed her hand on the woman's arm. "Oh, no. I can sit somewhere else. I don't want to put anyone out."

"Nonsense. They don't mind moving." Mrs. Truman waved toward the boys, who were already vacating the pew. "And you two best behave yourselves, or else."

"Yes, Mama," they replied in unison.

Mrs. Truman sat and moved her legs aside so Kathleen and Josh could slide into the seat. Flora sat next to her mother, and Kathleen took the spot next to the little girl. Josh squeezed in on the other side of Kathleen. His warm shoulder pressed against hers, causing her stomach to jump and her pulse to quicken. She pressed her hands together on her lap, reminding herself that Josh could not be the man for her.

Relief washed over her as Reverend Nelson walked to the wooden podium and greeted the congregation.

Kathleen's face grew warm when he singled her out and introduced her as the new teacher. The townsfolk shifted and murmured but didn't seem all that impressed. She had to wonder what was wrong with being the teacher in this town that they couldn't keep one for a full term.

She didn't ponder the question long, however, as the pastor invited a man to the front to lead the congregation in song. Mrs. Nelson's accompaniment on the piano was as beautiful as any music Kathleen had ever heard. The tinny chords seemed to flow outward from her very soul. Indeed, when the preacher's wife played "Blessed Assurance," tears choked Kathleen's throat, and she couldn't sing along.

Reverend Nelson preached a heartfelt message on the subject of contentment, and even with the distraction of Josh's warm shoulder pressed against hers, Kathleen bowed for the closing prayer more moved spiritually than she'd been in a long time.

Though guilt pricked her at her disloyalty to her own pastor, she had to admit Reverend Nelson's gentle delivery and transparent love for God were more inspiring than Rosewood's eighty-four-year-old pulpit-pounding preacher, Obadiah Strong.

After the benediction and subsequent dismissal, Mr. Truman turned to Kathleen. "I hope you'll come to the farm for Sunday dinner, Miss Johnson. My sister, Estelle, and the pastor will be joining us as well."

Relief washed over her. Her greatest dread had been what she would do with herself for an entire Sunday afternoon alone. She felt a gentle squeeze on her elbow and turned to meet Josh's gaze. He smiled. "Please join us. It would be my honor to escort you home this evening."

"Well, of course she's coming." Mrs. Nelson seemed to have appeared out of nowhere. "If we hadn't accepted Susan's invitation to dinner, I would have insisted the new teacher come have dinner with us. So, Miss Johnson," she said firmly but with a smile, "you must say yes."

"Then yes it is. And thank you for your kind invitation, Mr. and Mrs. Truman." She turned to the preacher's wife and grinned. "And Mrs. Nelson."

As had been the case the previous two nights, dinner at the Truman farm proved to be a noisy, fun affair. Only Josh's younger brother Alvin ate in silence while the rest of the family spoke above one another, laughing and reaching until Kathleen couldn't help but feel right at home.

When the last bite had been eaten, Flora hopped up and tugged at Kathleen's sleeve. "Eliza had puppies. They're so cute. Do you want to see them, Miss Johnson?"

"I suppose so, if it's all right with your ma and pa."

"Not so fast, little girl," Mr. Truman spoke up, placing a restraining hand on the child's arm. "First you have to help your ma clean up."

"I'll help, too," Kathleen offered, seeing the little girl's expression plummet. "Then maybe we can go see the puppies afterward."

Mrs. Truman stood and picked up the empty platter that had been laden with fluffy biscuits an hour earlier. "You'll do nothing of the kind," she said firmly. "As a guest in this house, you are not allowed to lift a finger to help. Josh, please escort Kathleen to the barn and show her the new puppies. Flora, honey, grab a towel and get ready to dry the dishes."

Flora scowled but looked down quickly before her mother noticed. "Yes, ma'am," she mumbled.

Kathleen's heart went out to her, and when Flora ventured a glance, she couldn't resist a wink at the child. Flora's expression brightened considerably, and she scurried off toward the kitchen.

Josh stood. "Shall we go and see the wiggly bunch of mongrels in the barn?"

Mindful of the vast interest coming from the family members still seated around the table, Kathleen felt her cheeks warm. "You don't really have to show me the puppies," she said.

His smile fled. "You don't want to see them? Or you'd prefer to wait for Flora?"

Was it her imagination, or did he seem deflated?

"Oh, no. I'd love to see them."

"With Flora?"

"Or you. I just didn't want you to feel obligated."

"It would be my pleasure to escort you to see the new puppies, Miss Johnson."

His adolescent brother, Joe, snickered. Josh's face tinged with pink, then deepened a shade when even tight-lipped Alvin joined the laughter. Soon, even the pastor couldn't hold back a smile.

Mr. Truman stood and slapped Josh on the back. "If you two don't head on out to the barn, those pups are bound to be weaned and having pups of their own by the time you finally get around to it."

"Yes, sir." His brown eyes seemed to entreat her to hurry and get him out of the humiliating situation.

With a nod, she rose and placed her napkin on the table. "Please excuse me," she murmured to the family without making eye contact with any of them.

She could feel Josh's relief match her own when they were outside, away from the amusement-filled room.

"Your family is quite nice," she said, if for no other reason than to break the heavy silence.

"Thanks. Sometimes they're a bit much. I'm sorry if they made you uncomfortable."

Kathleen laughed. "Being the only girl in a house with four brothers, I'm used to teasing. As a matter of fact, I miss it. So in a way, your family's ribbing helped ease my homesickness a bit."

Josh reached out to lift the latch on the barn door. "Are you very homesick? You've only been here two nights."

"I've never been away from home before."

He nodded, stepping aside so that she could precede him into the barn. "I suppose I can understand that. Are you sorry you didn't take one look at the school and hightail it home like Mary suggested? Please don't say you are. I'll be completely crushed if you do."

He grinned, and Kathleen nearly melted into a puddle. She chuckled at his crooked smile but answered honestly. "When I'm around people, I know I made the right decision. But it's difficult for me to be alone. The funny thing is that growing up I always longed for privacy. I often take a book and go down by the little creek that runs through our property and just sit for hours and hours reading and being alone with my thoughts. But now the solitude is almost painful."

As soon as the last sentence left her lips, Kathleen regretted it. She hadn't meant to be so transparent, but Josh's obvious concern combined with her need for conversation had brought the admission tumbling out. Before he could answer, she wandered away from his side and followed the sound of whimpering until she found a scruffy black-and-white mama dog surrounded by wiggling pups.

Approaching cautiously, Kathleen expected the dog to growl. Instead, the animal gave a welcoming whine. Kneeling on the hay, Kathleen reached out and stroked the mama dog's head while the blind puppies whined and nuzzled, trying to find a place to nurse.

"I don't believe it. Only Flora's been able to get anywhere near that dog since she had those pups day before yesterday."

"Well, she knows a friendly soul when she sees one. Don't you, sweet girl?" she crooned. "May I hold one of your babies?" Gingerly, she eased her hand under one of the milk-rounded bellies and lifted a shiny black pup. It trembled until she snuggled it close, speaking in soft, reassuring tones. "Oh, you're just so precious."

Kathleen could feel Josh watching her. She glanced up. Tenderness shone from those wonderful eyes, and his full mouth curved into a smile. "Sort of makes a fellow wish he was a puppy," he said, his voice husky and barely above a whisper.

She blinked. "I beg your pardon?"

"The way you're holding the puppy makes me wonder what it would be like to have your arms around me."

A gasp escaped her lips, and she set the dog down, then scrambled to her feet. Tossing out a look of utter disdain, she stomped past him toward the door.

"Wait, Miss Johnson." He caught up to her and took her firmly but gently by the arm, turning her to face him. "Kathleen, I'm sorry I offended you."

"I do not know what sort of woman you think I am, sir." Kathleen's lip trembled as it always did when she was angry.

"I think you're a fine young lady. And I can't help but admire you. Is that so wrong?"

"In so much that you are imagining my—my arms about you, it is quite wrong." Her voice cracked under the embarrassment. Her mind conjured the lecherous smile from the man at the train station, and her ire rose even higher. "I have never met such ill-mannered young men before in my life. And that's no affront to your ma's raising of you, either. I'm sure she did her best."

Rather than apologizing, Josh planted his feet, releasing her arm. A muscle twitched in his square jaw. "I don't know what sort of men court you back home, but if they don't admit to wondering what it would be like to hold you in their arms, they're just not being truthful."

"Wondering it and saying it are two different things, *Mister* Truman."

"Well, saying it and *doing* it are two different things as well."

He took a daring step closer. Kathleen's pulse sped up like a runaway train. Her thoughts jumbled together. Was he going to try to kiss her? Surely she couldn't allow such a thing. She moistened her lips. Josh's hand slid around her waist, and he pulled her close. A warm woozy feeling enveloped her, rendering her unable to think straight. She barely registered his head descending. Oh, Ma would be mortified. But how could Kathleen resist?

She was just about to close her eyes and surrender to her first kiss when the creaking of the barn door jolted her back to her senses. She leaped from his embrace as Flora skipped into the barn.

"Did you see the puppies? Aren't they adorable? Ma said I can keep only one. But I can't decide which one I like best. Which one do you like best, Miss Johnson?"

"I, um, I don't really know. I only held one." She tried to concentrate on the little girl's words, but Josh's nearness and the memory of what had almost occurred between them had her so rattled, she barely remembered her own name.

"Which?" Flora pressed.

"Um, a black one, I think."

"Oh, I like the black ones. There are two of those."

"Are there?" Why couldn't she take her gaze from Josh's? There was no triumph in his eyes, as one might expect from a young man who knew he'd almost been successful in his quest to steal a kiss. Rather, the look in his eyes nearly stole her breath away. His eyes spoke his respect for her, and only a quick glance to her lips and back to her eyes betrayed his regret that the kiss had been interrupted before it began.

Kathleen felt her own regrets at the moment. Later, however, after Josh, accompanied by Flora and Joe, had escorted her home and she sat alone drinking a cup of tea, she remembered Ma's edict. The Lord knew quite well where Kathleen lived. He was quite capable of sending the right young man to Rosewood. She didn't need to go off looking elsewhere.

Shame infused her. The guilty knowledge that she'd been on the verge of actually allowing a kiss made her squirm. She and her friends had a word for girls who teased the boys: *fast*. The only thing was that it didn't feel like she was being forward. It felt like a cozy fire on a cold day. Like the warm promise of spring as green grass pushed through thawed earth, the budding flowers after a dreary, colorless winter. That's what it had felt like when Josh held her close.

Kathleen shook herself from her thoughts. She had no intention of allowing herself to become infatuated with a boy living outside of Rosewood. How could she bear to be separated from her family permanently when two days away from them seemed like an eternity? She chewed her lip as she pondered the thought. Perhaps Josh would move to Rosewood. He could join Pa and the brothers at the livery.

Kathleen laughed into the empty room. She'd known him for two measly days, and already she was planning his future for him.

That night, as she crawled into bed, she resolved to banish all romantic thoughts of Josh Truman. She had a job to do, and she would do it well. When her term was up, she'd return home and never, ever leave Rosewood again. If only she could convince herself of that fact. Instead, her traitorous brain insisted on replaying the scene in the barn over and over until finally she drifted into a dreamless sleep.

Chapter 5

Kathleen rubbed her arms vigorously, trying to generate heat in the cold schoolroom while she waited for the newly built fire to warm the chill in the morning air. She glanced about with a satisfied nod.

It had taken her, Josh, and Mary Bilge the better part of a week—with the exception of the Lord's Day—to make the school presentable. Now the odor of fresh paint hung in the room, and the walls shone white without a smudge. The single window sparkled, and not a speck of dust could be seen on the desks or floor. And she'd already swept up this morning's traces of mouse droppings.

Kathleen knew pride was sinful, but as she surveyed their handiwork, she couldn't hold back a smile. They had taken a room filled with broken desks and scattered materials from messy to ready in such a short time. She glanced at the watch pinned to her dress and felt her heart pick up a few beats. The children would be arriving soon. Her palms dampened at the thought.

Despite her nervousness, she hoped to discover the reason Coon's Hollow couldn't seem to keep a teacher for more than half a term. From her admittedly limited experience, the townsfolk didn't seem overly friendly, but neither were they rude—with the exception of the man in the train station upon her arrival. So she had to wonder why there was such a turnover of teachers that the seedier citizens had a running pool every time a new teacher arrived.

A wide yawn stretched her mouth. At least the nervousness served to keep her from dozing off. Sleep still eluded her at night. She had taken to heeding David's psalms. *In the night his song shall be with me, and my prayer unto the God of my life.*

What else was there to do but sing and pray to God when one was completely alone and wrestling insomnia? Sleeplessness was doing wonders for her spiritual life. Unfortunately, her physical body was running down.

Twenty minutes before school was set to begin, the door opened. Kathleen gave a startled glance up. Mary stomped in, her cigar hanging from her lips.

Kathleen scowled. "The cigar, Mary."

"What about it?"

"The children will soon begin arriving. I would rather they not be subjected to the sight of anyone smoking. It sends the wrong signal."

"Smoke signals? Ain't been no Injuns 'round these parts for quite some time.

29

Leastways, none that'd be inclined to send up a signal." Mary cackled at her own joke.

Holding back a smile so as not to encourage her, Kathleen shook her head.

With a sigh, Mary straightened up. "Oh, okay. What sorta signal?"

Kathleen hesitated. She was loath to offend the woman, but neither could she take a chance on one of the children walking in to find Mary smoking in the school. She chose her words carefully. "I'm sure you understand that I can't allow it to appear as though I condone the practice. To children that would send a message that I believe it's all right for them to do the same. I am in charge of this classroom of students, and I must be morally upright."

"Well, la-de-da." Mary snorted but tossed her cigar out the door, then let it bang shut.

Somewhat surprised by the easy compliance, Kathleen gave her a thankful smile. "What can I do for you this morning, Mary?"

"Thought I'd come see how your first day's going."

A smile tipped Kathleen's lips. "Hmm, let me see. I got up, made my bed, and dressed. I ate a little bread for breakfast and wiped off my table. Then I came in here to build the fire. And that's about it so far."

Mary smirked, obviously appreciating Kathleen's humor. "Guess it is a bit early. I best get me on to the preacher's house. That missus of his wants me to scrub down the walls today." She shook her head in disgust. "I think she just does it to see me workin' hard. Like she's lording it over me just 'cause the reverend married her 'stead of me. Ya want to know why he picked her?"

"Why?"

" 'Cause I'm too much woman for him, that's why." She gave a decisive nod. "I just don't know what to say about a man that settles for a woman like that." With a heavy sigh, she clomped toward the door. "I best get on over there before she takes it as a reason to let me go. If they didn't pay so good. . ."

Kathleen stared in bewildered silence. Josh had told her that Mary worked for the preacher and his wife. And that the woman had once locked Mrs. Nelson in the cellar, but no one could prove it, and Mary wasn't confessing.

When she reached the door, Mary turned. "Now don't worry about anything today. If them rapscallions get out of hand, you give 'em a good smack. I'll be around at noon to check on ya and see how things are going."

Affection surged through Kathleen. Now she understood what had prompted Mary to stop by. She knew Kathleen would be a bundle of nerves at the anticipation of the children's arrival. "Thank you for the suggestion. Let's hope it doesn't come to anything more forceful than a stern word or at worst a few minutes in the corner."

"Harrumph. That last teacher didn't believe in corporal punishment, either. And look where she is now. Sometimes a good whack on the behind is the only thing a child understands. Spare the rod and spoil the child. And all that Bible stuff."

The word *Bible* reminded Kathleen of Mary's absence from church on Sunday.

Though today was Wednesday, she'd forgotten to ask the woman about it. "Were you feeling poorly on Sunday, Mary?"

"Poorly? Me? No, ma'am, I'm as fit as a fiddle." She narrowed her bushy brows. "Why'd ya ask?"

"I missed you in church."

To Kathleen's surprise, Mary flushed, and pleasure lit the slightly yellowish countenance. "Go on, now. You didn't miss me."

"No, I really did. I don't have many friends in town, and I was looking for a familiar face."

"Well, I don't go in for religion much. I gave it a try about a year ago. But that was before. . ."

Before the preacher got married. Though Kathleen was aware of the woman's crush on the preacher, she would no more have humiliated Mary by letting her know than she would have admitted her own crush on the preacher's nephew-in-law Josh.

"It's a shame you stopped going. But it's never too late to return to the house of God."

"So you really missed me, did ya?"

"Yes."

"I might show up on Sunday. If I don't got nothin' better to do."

"That would be wonderful. I'll save you a seat."

A rare smile split the woman's face, showing a surprisingly healthy set of teeth. "You'd do that? Sit next to me and all?"

"Why, Mary, you have a beautiful smile. You should display it more often. And yes, I would be honored to sit beside you during the service."

Mary turned four shades of red, cleared her throat, and frowned. She slapped her man's hat onto her head. "Well, don't get your heart set on it. I said maybe." Without giving Kathleen another chance to speak, she opened the door and paused. "You look out for that Myles Carpenter, now. We think he's harmless enough. But you just never can tell with crazy people."

Before Kathleen could ask what she meant, Mary slipped through the door, slamming it shut behind her.

Kathleen didn't have much time to ponder Mary's warning, as two minutes later the first of a steady stream of students arrived. Boys and girls ranging in age from five to fifteen—a total of twenty-four in all.

Her legs trembled a bit as she called the school to order and the children took their seats, silently watching her. . .waiting for her to speak. She spotted Flora sitting in the second row of desks. Her glossy brown braids were tied with two blue ribbons that matched her eyes. Kathleen smiled, amazed at the difference a friendly face could make in such a nerve-racking situation.

Clearing her throat, she looked from left to right, including each child with her smile. "Good morning."

A scattered mumbling of "good mornings" came in reply. Not a very friendly group. But she'd warm them up in no time. She hoped.

"Let's begin the day by saying the Lord's Prayer. Please stand and remain next to your desks."

The sound of chairs scraping the floor followed as the children rose. Kathleen closed her eyes and took a deep breath as she started the prayer. When they'd finished with "for thine is the kingdom and the power and the glory forever, amen," she opened her eyes, ready to start her first day as a teacher.

By noon, she wished she'd gone back to Rosewood while the getting was good. Now it was too late, despite the unresponsive, disinterested children who barely knew the material. To make matters worse, they were unruly. Jonah Barker had yanked on Flora's braid hard, eliciting a howl from the girl and a retaliatory smack in the face. Kathleen had been forced to stand them both in the corner for thirty minutes. Snickers from the students during arithmetic had confused her until she realized Jonah was making faces at her. She'd commanded him to stand in the back corner where she could keep an eye on him after that.

Now she sat alone eating her lunch of leftover ham between two thick slices of bread. She finished her sandwich all too quickly and stuffed her napkin inside the pail, then glanced at her watch. The children were allowed a full hour for lunch; forty-five minutes remained. She ventured to the window and smiled at the sight of her students playing baseball in the schoolyard.

Wandering back to her seat, she yawned. Her eyes felt gritty from lack of sleep. The desktop looked so inviting that she folded her arms over the desk and rested her head. What could it hurt for just a few minutes? She closed her eyes and felt powerless as she slowly drifted to sleep.

ornament

Josh frowned as he heard the sound of children's laughter. He knew it was half past two because he'd just checked his watch a moment earlier. Why were the children outside?

He pulled into the schoolyard. Flora gave him an uncertain smile. He motioned her over.

"Hi, Josh. How come you're in town? It isn't time to pick me up yet, is it?"

"No. Ma sent me for some sugar at the dry goods store. Why are you outside playing instead of inside learning?"

Flora shrugged. "Miss Johnson never rang the bell after lunch, so David Kirk said we should just keep playing until she came out. Only she never did. I looked inside a little while ago, and her head is down on top of her desk. Sarah Thomas said she might be dead. I'm too scared to go find out." Flora's blue eyes implored him. "You don't think she's dead, do you?"

"Of course not, honey." Concern knotted his stomach. He wrapped the reins around the brake and hopped down from the wagon seat. "You stay outside while I go check on her, okay?"

Flora nodded. Josh recognized the look of worry in her eyes. He patted her shoulder. "Don't worry, sugar. I'm sure Miss Johnson is just fine."

He reached the door and slowly stepped inside. As Flora had said, Kathleen was at her desk with her head resting on her arms. With no attempt to keep his boots from making noise on the wood floor, he clomped up the aisle. His heart nearly stopped until he saw the rise and fall of her shoulders. Then it nearly melted. Tenderness such as he'd never before experienced washed over him. He reached out and caressed her silken cheek with the back of his hand. Still she didn't budge.

"Kathleen," he said, keeping his voice soft so as not to startle her. He squatted beside her. "Kathleen, honey, wake up."

With slow movements, she shifted, sighed, and nestled back into sleep.

Josh smiled and gave her shoulder a gentle shake. "Kathleen."

She moaned and shifted. Then her eyes became slits. In a beat, they opened fully. She gasped and sat up. "Josh!"

"Good morning, sleepyhead."

"Morning? What time is it?" Without waiting for an answer, she grabbed at her brooch watch. "Oh no! The children. Lunch was over an hour and a half ago. Where are they?"

"They're still outside playing baseball. They thought you were dead."

First her eyes widened in horror, but as she observed his laughter, her own lips curved upward. She lifted her eyebrow. "Baseball, huh? My untimely demise must not have weighed too heavily on their little minds."

He chuckled. "Flora wanted to check on you, but she was too scared to take the chance, just in case you really were dead. You know how young 'uns are."

With a moan, she pressed the heels of her hands against her forehead. "How could I have fallen asleep like that? The school board will be sure to send me packing now."

"I don't think you have to worry about that. It's not as though they'll likely get yet another replacement this term."

A frown puckered her brow, adding to the lines still imprinted from her dress sleeves. "Josh, can I ask you something?"

When she gave him that beguiling, innocently confused look from beautiful blue eyes, she could ask him anything. He swallowed hard and tried to focus. "Sure."

"Why does Coon's Hollow have such a hard time keeping teachers? Pa said no teacher has ever stayed for a second term. And I know I'm taking over for the last one."

Josh stood and shrugged. "I guess a town like this isn't exactly too enticing for a young woman. Plus. . ." He hesitated.

"What?"

"Well, I take it Myles Carpenter didn't show up today?"

"Mary Bilge mentioned him as well, but I don't recall a child by that name."

"Myles isn't a child, except in his mind. He's about seventy."

"Then why would you ask if he showed up at school?"

"Sometimes he gets a little confused and thinks he's the teacher."

At her look of alarm, he hurried on. "He's a little strange but harmless.

Unfortunately, he doesn't seem to value cleanliness, so he doesn't look or smell too great."

She wrinkled her nose and shook her head. "That's a shame, but what does it have to do with Coon's Hollow's inability to keep a teacher?"

He took a breath. "Apparently, Myles was once a schoolmaster. Then the War Between the States started, and he left to fight. When he came back, he wasn't the same. His wife welcomed him home, but they never had children. She died about ten years ago. The old-timers say Myles lost what was left of his mind when she passed on."

Pity clouded Kathleen's eyes. "How sad."

"Yes, and most of the teachers feel that same compassion until he orders them from his classroom three or four times." Josh smiled. "The board goes to him, and he promises to behave, but he always ends up back at the school. I've never thought him to be crazy, to be honest. Personally, I think he drinks too much."

"Oh, my. Does he frighten the children?"

"Naw. They're used to him."

"Well, I'll be on the lookout. Thank you for giving me advance warning."

"I suppose I should have told you sooner. But I was afraid you might not stay."

A smile curved her full lips. "I might not have."

He gazed speechless into her eyes, and it was all he could do not to finish the kiss he'd almost started a few days ago in the barn. Obviously, she realized his train of thought, because her eyes grew wide, and she shifted back. "Josh," she said, her voice faltering. "You need to know something."

"Yes?" He couldn't concentrate on anything when she looked at him that way.

"I'm not. . .free to become attached to anyone." Her eyelashes fluttered downward as she studied her hands in her lap.

Feeling like a bull had kicked him right in the gut, Josh winced. "I see. You're already spoken for by someone in your hometown?"

She glanced up quickly. "Oh no. Nothing like that."

Relief shattered the sick feeling of defeat. "Then you're free to be courted properly. You don't have to worry. I can restrain myself as long as we don't spend too much time alone. I won't try to steal any more kisses."

Her face turned several shades of pink. "It's. . .I mean I am free in that I'm not being courted by anyone." She gathered a long breath. "What I meant to say is that I cannot allow myself to become attached to a man who lives so far away from my family. I don't want to live apart from them."

That sick feeling stole over him again as he realized she was saying he had no chance. "I see."

"Do you?" Her beautiful blue eyes implored him to understand.

He was trying. Smiling, he pressed her hand. "Then we'll be good friends? Deal?"

Hesitation shone across her features, and Josh swallowed hard and hurried to add, "You don't want to go to the dance next month all by yourself."

"Dance?"

"Fall dance. We usually hold it earlier in October, but with the teacher leaving so suddenly and all, no one had the heart. It'll be the second Saturday of November."

"I see. Maybe I'll just stay home."

"A girl like you doesn't stay home from dances. Besides, it's held in the schoolhouse." He grinned.

Her lips twitched in amusement. "Maybe I'll go alone."

Josh knew they were playing a game, and he played along. "All right. But without an escort, all the fellows will buzz around and try to court you. You'll be doing an awful lot of explaining about how you're not to court anyone not from Rosewood."

She narrowed her gaze. "Are you teasing me or making fun?"

Tenderly, he knelt beside her and took her hand and pressed it to his heart. "I promise you, I will never make fun of you."

Tears sprang to her eyes, making them look like two clear pools. It was all Josh could do not to move in for a kiss. But she'd made her position clear. He had no intention of letting her go if there was any way to change her mind. But he'd let her get to know him. If he had to be her protector, her friend, until she realized he was the man for her, then so be it. He'd finally found the woman of his dreams, and he'd be a no-good disappointment to generations of Truman men if he didn't try his best to win her love.

Flora took that moment to burst into the schoolroom. "Josh! Come quick! Jonah's beating up Andrew Coon. We can't get them to stop."

Chapter 6

Kathleen fought tears as a paper wad zinged past her ear and smacked the wall behind her. She surveyed the unruly room—proof of her utter failure as a teacher—then allowed her gaze to settle on Flora. The girl stared back, her wide blue eyes clearly asking her why she was putting up with such shameful conduct from the boys.

The answer was that they were big. At fifteen, Andrew Coon was the size of a grown man. She was clearly at a disadvantage, and he knew it. Therefore, ever since the first humiliating day when she'd fallen asleep—had that really only been two weeks ago?—Andrew had essentially run the class. No one was learning, and she could barely hear herself think above the chatter and shouting.

A glance at her clock revealed a depressing one-thirty. Too early to dismiss. *Oh, Lord. What am I going to do?*

Outside, the wind howled, shaking the place, and she found herself almost wishing for a blizzard to close the school down for a few days.

"Ow, Miss Johnson, help!"

The sound of Melissa Sharpton's pain-filled cry pulled Kathleen from her fog, and she leaped to her feet. "What is it, Melissa?"

Tears pooled in the eight-year-old's eyes.

Behind her, Andrew cleared his throat. . .loudly.

"Well, Melissa?" Kathleen asked.

"N–nothing."

Kathleen turned to Andrew. Triumph shone in his eyes. Indignation lit a fire inside Kathleen. Clearly the bully was terrorizing the smaller children.

"Andrew, I would like for you to stand in the corner."

"What for, teacher? I didn't do nothin'."

He had a point—she hadn't absolutely caught him. Still, she couldn't back down now. Not if she were ever to have a prayer of regaining control of her class. She planted one hand on her hip and pointed with the other. "In the corner. Now!"

The room became deathly silent. Andrew sneered. "I ain't doin' it."

Out-and-out defiance. Exactly what she'd been afraid of and the very reason she'd failed to confront Andrew thus far. Now what was she supposed to do? "You will obey me, or you will not return to my classroom. Is that clear?"

"Ain't nothin' you can do about it. I'm a Coon."

"I don't care if you're a squirrel. You'll do as I say."

The children snickered at her joke.

Andrew's face deepened to a dark red. "Shut up!" he bellowed. The room fell silent once more.

A gust of wind jolted them from the intensity of the moment. All eyes turned toward the open door. Kathleen gasped as a man—who could only be Myles Carpenter—walked regally into the room. Though layered in filth and crowned with a thick head of uncombed gray hair, Mr. Carpenter owned the room from the moment he appeared.

"What can I do for you, sir?" Kathleen walked cautiously toward him.

"What can you do for me, young lady? You can control your students, that's what."

At least for the moment, he recognized that *she* was the teacher.

"What was that hollering I heard coming from in here?"

What did she have to lose? If she was going to be criticized by the town crazy man, how long was she going to have her job anyway?

She gathered a deep sigh. "I'm afraid that was Andrew Coon. He is disobedient, rude, and refuses to be disciplined."

The man's gaze narrowed. Then he turned to the classroom. "Which one of you, may I ask, is Andrew Coon?"

Every set of eyes in the room turned to stare at the culprit, but Andrew averted his gaze. Clearly his pride in his name had all but vanished.

But Mr. Carpenter got the hint. His odor trailed behind him as he sauntered across the room, his back straight as an English butler's.

Kathleen gathered the sides of her skirt into the balls of her fists to keep from pinching her nose.

"Stand up, young man," Mr. Carpenter ordered.

With a nervous laugh, Andrew turned his head and stared at the window as though he hadn't heard the man speak. In a flash, Myles's hand shot out. He grabbed Andrew by the scruff of his collar and lifted him to a standing position, knocking his chair back in the process.

"Hey! Turn me loose, old man! Wait 'til I tell my pa."

Despite Andrew's size, Mr. Carpenter had a good three inches of height on him. His strength seemed amazing as Andrew's attempts to free himself failed. "You have a deplorable lack of manners, boy." Keeping a firm grasp on Andrew's collar, Mr. Carpenter turned to Kathleen. "What would you have me do with the lad, miss?"

Kathleen blinked and fought to regain her voice. "I. . .in the corner, please."

"There are four of them; please specify."

Remembering the ridicule from Jonah the first day of school, she knew better than to stand Andrew in the corner behind her desk. She pointed to the back of the room. "Over there."

Mr. Carpenter nodded his filthy head, and Kathleen cringed at the layers of dirt encrusted on his neck. "Good choice," he said.

Laughter buzzed about the room as Myles walked Andrew on tiptoes to the corner. Kathleen looked about and shook her head for them to hush. They complied. Apparently no one wanted to be Mr. Carpenter's next target.

When he reached the corner of choice, Mr. Carpenter simply let Andrew go. "And stay there until your teacher says you may return to your seat. Is that clear?"

Obviously startled into submission, Andrew nodded without turning around. But Mr. Carpenter wasn't finished. "When school is dismissed, you will stay afterward and clean up the mess. It is disgraceful."

Perhaps his last comment was a bit like the pot calling the kettle black; still, Kathleen couldn't help but be grateful to the gentleman.

She expelled a pent-up breath, then wished she hadn't as she was forced to breathe in at the same time Mr. Carpenter returned to confront her. Fighting to contain her nausea, she offered a wobbly smile.

Her cheeks flooded with warmth at his look of utter contempt.

"You must show them who is in charge or you are wasting their time."

Their time?

Though he dwarfed her, she gathered herself to her full height, raised her chin, and looked him in the eye. "Thank you for your help, Mr. Carpenter. I'm sure I can take it from here."

His disparaging look told her more than she cared to know about his opinion of whether she could handle the situation. Nevertheless, he scowled and walked to the door, his shoulders squared. Such a show of dignity touched Kathleen's heart.

He turned when he reached the door. Though his face was caked with grime, his hazel eyes pierced her. "These children have precious few years to learn anything at all before their Neanderthal fathers stick them in the cornfields and squash the greater portion of all that wonderful knowledge from their heads. You must pack as much into their brains as possible, so that perchance they will retain what is most relevant."

He slipped through the door and was gone as quickly as he'd come.

Dread gnawed Kathleen's gut as she glanced toward the corner. At the very least, she expected Andrew to lean against the wall. But to her delight, he stayed put. Perhaps he was afraid Mr. Carpenter was watching from a window somewhere. Or perhaps the stench had rattled his brain. Whatever the case, after thirty minutes, she took pity and quietly suggested he return to his seat. He obeyed, sitting while the rest of the children took their turn at reciting their spelling words.

It was ten minutes after three before Kathleen realized they were over the time for school to be let out. "School is dismissed," she announced. In subdued silence, the children rose, gathered their belongings, and left in an orderly fashion.

She leaned her elbows on her desk, closed her eyes, and rested her forehead in the heels of her hands. Taking a few deep breaths, she willed herself to relax.

When the door opened again a minute later, she looked up and gasped. Andrew stood, hands stuffed into his pockets.

She swallowed hard. Was he planning his revenge? Whatever the case, she couldn't show her fear. "Did you forget something, Andrew?"

"Yes." He sauntered up the aisle. He hesitated then scowled. "That crazy ol' Myles told me to clean the room after school."

She'd completely forgotten!

"Thank you for coming back, Andrew. The place is quite a mess."

"Yeah."

"How about if we clean it up together?"

He shrugged but remained silent as they spent the next fifteen minutes removing wads of paper, chalk, pencils, and even crusts of bread from the floor.

"I think that about does it," Kathleen announced.

"Fine. I'm leavin' then."

"All right. And Andrew?"

"Yeah."

"You know we're putting on a Christmas program the week before school gets out."

"What of it?"

"I was hoping you'd consider playing Joseph."

Interest sparked in his eyes, and Kathleen proceeded before she lost her nerve.

"Yes, Rebecca Dunn has already agreed to play Mary."

His face turned three shades of red. "Rebecca?"

A bit of guilt nipped her insides like a troublesome pup. She'd caught Andrew staring at an oblivious Rebecca more than once. She figured he might have a chance if he'd simmer down.

"Yes. I thought the two of you would make a handsome Mary and Joseph. What do you say?"

He kicked at the floor with his boot and shrugged. "Ain't got nothing better to do."

"I take it that's a yes?"

A sigh lifted his chest. "I guess."

"Wonderful. We start rehearsal Monday after school. Please tell your pa to come speak to me if he has any problems with you remaining after class."

"He ain't gonna care." He slipped through the door before Kathleen could press further.

Kathleen stared at the closed door for a few seconds. After one last look at her tidy schoolroom, she adjourned to her quarters for another lonely evening.

❧

"Then he stayed in the corner until Miss Johnson told him he could sit down."

Josh listened to Flora's recounting of her afternoon with a combination of concern and amusement.

"And he didn't order her from her classroom?" Ma asked, setting a platter of ham on the table.

"No, ma'am. He didn't seem all that crazy to me. Just stank real bad."

"Flora! Don't be rude."

"Sorry, Ma. But he did. Bad." She grinned at Josh. "Miss Johnson looked like she might faint. Everyone said so."

Ma cleared her throat, a clear sign that Josh was not to encourage the child.

"Paul, perhaps we should speak to Frank about this. After all, he is the preacher. If anyone should talk to Myles, it should be him."

"How do you figure? Myles hasn't darkened the doorstep of our church in longer than I can remember—not since Frank asked him to kindly take a bath." He winked at Flora. "So that the ladies didn't faint at the smell of him."

Flora giggled, and Ma frowned at them both.

"I suppose you're right about Frank. All the same, someone should talk to him about not interrupting Miss Johnson's class. After all, the young woman is doing us a kindness by taking over at the last minute. How many more teachers are we going to let that man run off?"

"Miss Johnson didn't seem to mind him too much." Joe spoke with a mouthful of potatoes.

"Mercy, Joe," Ma admonished. "Swallow first."

He swallowed hard, then washed down the bite with a gulp of milk. He wiped his mouth with the back of his hand, forked another bite, and held it in front of his mouth. "Miss Johnson was a lot nicer to him than the other teachers ever were." He shoveled the bite inside.

Josh listened to this news with tenderness. Her kindness was only one reason he was falling for Kathleen Johnson.

Still, Ma didn't seem convinced. "Well, the girl's obviously been raised with better manners than some, but that doesn't mean she'll put up with constant interruptions, especially if he gets confused. Someone had better give him a good talking to before he runs her off like all the others." She gave Pa a pointed look, but Josh judged from Pa's scowl that he had no intention of butting into the situation.

Her gaze shifted to Josh.

He nodded. He only had a few weeks to prove to the girl of his dreams that he was the man for her, even if he did live fifty miles away from her family. There was no way he would let an outside influence like a crazy former schoolmaster send her running home even one day earlier than absolutely necessary.

Chapter 7

Kathleen shot straight up, unsure why she'd awakened so suddenly. Outside, the wind howled and shook the thin boards. The fire had died down, and the air inside the room bit through her, chilling her to the bone. She pulled the quilt up to her neck and shivered in an attempt to warm herself. Finally, she pushed the covers aside and tiptoed across the icy floor to the stove.

Moments later, wood crackled as the glowing coals caught. Another gust of wind shook the little room.

She shuddered. The clock on a shelf over the stove clearly showed four o'clock. Too early to get up. Yawning, she headed back to her bed.

Thump, thump.

Footsteps? Cold fear swept through Kathleen as the sound in the schoolroom came closer. She eyed the door that separated the two rooms and was suddenly aware of the absence of a lock. She spun around, searching for anything with which to defend herself. Hesitating only a second, she snatched up a large kitchen knife and inched toward the door.

Crash!

Kathleen jumped, her heart nearly beating from her chest. Clutching the knife firmly with both hands, she listened for more sounds. Anything that might mean someone was about to burst through her door. Numbness crept into her feet as she remained barefoot on the icy floor.

Muscles knotted, stomach tight, she waited, and waited. . .and waited until, finally, the fire died again, and she was forced to hang on to the knife with one hand and add wood to the stove with the other. Muted light slowly expelled the darkness from the room, and when Kathleen dared to take her gaze from the door, she noted the clock read seven-thirty.

The children would be arriving for school in less than an hour. How could she cower in her room and allow any one of them to step into a possibly dangerous situation?

Lord, give me courage.

Reaching out with trembling fingers, she grabbed the latch, gathered a deep breath, and flung open the door. A split second seemed like an eternity as she

41

waited for her attacker to strike. When all remained calm, she took a cautious step across the doorway.

A body lay atop the remains of one of the newly repaired desks. She couldn't make out a face, but the stench was unmistakable. Her heart beat a rain dance within her chest as she approached. She grimaced at the thought of having to touch his filthy chest to ascertain whether or not he was breathing. He moaned, and she jumped back.

Relief like a fresh summer breeze washed over her, and her wobbly legs refused to hold her another second. She made it to the last desk and sank into the seat, dropping the knife to the ground.

The clatter woke her intruder.

"What on earth is that racket?"

Kathleen blinked as he sat up, brushing away the splintered wood.

He was asking *her* about racket?

"Well? Speak up!"

"I–I dropped my knife."

"Why, pray tell, do you have a weapon inside the school? You are not fit to teach these children. I knew that from the first moment I saw you."

Tears pricked her eyes, and her throat clogged. What could she say? The man had a point.

She stood, offering him her hand. Ignoring the gesture, he averted his gaze. "Miss, I must insist you go at once and do not return until you are properly attired."

With a gasp, Kathleen realized she was in her nightgown. No dressing gown or house shoes—she'd been too afraid to remember either.

"Oh, my. I am so sorry. Of course. I'll just go and get dressed."

Not until she had changed into her gown and hooked her boots did she realize the irony of Mr. Carpenter scolding her about her appearance. She grinned as she headed back into the schoolroom.

Warmth met her from the fire Mr. Carpenter had built in the stove.

"Why, Mr. Carpenter. Thank you."

"You are most welcome. The desk was beyond repair, I'm afraid."

"I see." She gathered her courage and took a step closer to him. "May I ask why you came to the school at such an hour?"

He looked away. "I beg your pardon, miss. I succumbed to my weakness and visited the saloon."

Kathleen's eyes widened. "Well, you should be ashamed of yourself. But that doesn't explain your presence here."

He shrugged. "The wind was extremely cold, and it was snowing so hard I could scarcely see where I was going. I knew I couldn't make it home, so I came here."

"Oh, it snowed? I best clear a path for the children."

"Don't bother. No one will be coming today."

"What do you mean? It's Tuesday. Of course they'll be here. It's a school day."

"Look outside."

Crossing to the window, Kathleen peeked through a circle Mr. Carpenter had wiped in the frosted glass. "Oh, my. I'm afraid you're right." Not only was the ground covered but heavy snow still fell from the sky.

"Naturally."

With a sinking—and slightly nauseated—stomach, Kathleen realized one more thing: If the children couldn't come to school, Mr. Carpenter couldn't leave.

By noon, the stench was beginning to waft into Kathleen's own living quarters, and she'd had all she could take. The ham she'd sliced for lunch sizzled in the skillet, the smell turning her stomach.

She tossed aside her book and flung open the door. "Mr. Carpenter, we need to talk."

He sat in *her* chair holding *her* book in his dirt-caked hands.

"Yes, miss?"

Her courage faltered, then revived as she thought ahead to the possibility of days and days with this man. "I haven't all day, Miss Johnson. I would like to get back to this perfectly delightful book." Kathleen recognized Edgar Allan Poe's name on the spine and rolled her eyes. She shook herself to get back to the matter at hand.

"Mr. Carpenter, I–I am afraid I must ask you—no, I must insist that you. . ."

He frowned. "Yes?"

"Sir, I beg of you to fill the tub and take a bath."

His eyes sparked as he jumped to his feet. "What?"

Kathleen shrank back from his anger.

"What right have you to insult me, young lady?" He glared down at her.

"I–I meant no insult."

He seemed not to have heard. "I was born and bred in Boston, the son of a wealthy merchant. I attended the finest schools and served as a schoolmaster in this very town until the war." He banged his fist on her desk, and Kathleen jumped, tears filling her eyes. "I am entitled to respect. I *will* be treated with decency!"

Fearing the wild fury in his eyes, she turned and fled the room. Once she was safely inside her quarters, she leaned against her closed door and willed her racing heart to return to a normal beat. Fat tears rolled down her cheeks. How could she have been so insensitive? From their first encounter, she had known that beneath Mr. Carpenter's exterior was a great man. She couldn't begin to fathom why on earth he would choose to live as he did, but wasn't she called to love him regardless? Would Christ have insisted he take a bath without taking the time to have a proper conversation?

Dear Lord, You brought Mr. Carpenter stumbling into the schoolroom as a blizzard roared. You knew we'd be trapped together, and You know how vile he smells. Please give me Your grace, compassion, and love for the man.

She walked to the stove and removed the slightly burned slices of ham from the skillet. She brewed a pot of strong coffee. When it was finished, she poured two mugs full, piled ham between two slices of bread, and returned to the school.

Mr. Carpenter sat in her chair, reading as before. He didn't look up. "I'd like to apologize, sir."

Still no response. Kathleen set the mug and plate before him on her desk. She took a gulp of her own coffee and nearly choked as it scorched her throat. "B–be careful. The coffee's hot."

He glanced up at her, curiosity in his eyes.

There. At least he was responsive. She began again. "I had no right to speak to you as I did. You are a full-grown man of more intelligence than anyone I know, and you have the right to decide whether or not to bathe."

With a grunt, he eyed the sandwich and mug, then turned his attention back to his book.

Heat flooded Kathleen's face. "Well, I guess I'll. . .I guess you don't want company. I can drink my coffee back in my room." Turning, she swallowed back her humiliation.

"Wait, miss."

She turned back. "Yes, sir?"

"You brought only a cup of coffee for yourself. Are you not eating?"

So heavy was the stench, her stomach revolted against the thought. "Uh, no. I'm not very hungry."

He scrutinized her a moment, nodded, and then returned his attention to the book. Feeling dismissed, Kathleen returned to her quarters and picked up her knitting. Her lonely evenings had afforded her plenty of time to stockpile knitted gifts for her family and friends. Now she was determined to knit a stocking cap for each boy in her class and a scarf for each girl—something for them to remember her by when she went back home.

She had just finished another scarf when a knock at her door nearly sent her through the roof.

Mr. Carpenter handed her the mug and plate. "Thank you kindly for your generosity," he said regally. "Now if I may trouble you once more."

"Of course. What can I do for you?"

"I'd very much appreciate the use of a pot with which to collect snow. And the washtub. And one more thing. Might I trouble you for a blanket to wrap around myself while my clothes are drying?"

Kathleen collected the items he requested and threw in a chunk of lye soap.

"Thank you." He gave her a stern glance. "You must not enter the schoolroom until I return your items. I'm not entirely sure this is appropriate as it is. But for the sake of your appetite, I see no alternative."

Heat scorched her face and neck. "Of course."

She spent the afternoon listening to the door opening and closing more times than she could count as presumably Mr. Carpenter crammed pot after pot with snow to melt and warm on the stove. Thumps and sloshes were her music while she filled another pot with chunks of meat and canned vegetables—the Trumans' latest contribution to her welfare. She whiled away the afternoon, reading off and on, knitting, checking her pot frequently, and watching the clock. Curiosity nearly overwhelmed her at the thought of what Mr. Carpenter would look like absent the grime, though she was highly dubious as to whether he could successfully remove years of dirt.

The sun had set, and the stew filled the room with a tantalizing and most welcome aroma by the time Mr. Carpenter knocked on the door once more.

Kathleen gasped at the sight of him. He handed her the pot. "I apologize for not returning the rest of your items, Miss. The blanket you so generously supplied is soaking in the tub. And the soap is. . .well, I was forced to use the entire block."

"Oh, Mr. Carpenter. You look wonderful!" And she meant it. His skin, though red where he'd obviously scrubbed and scrubbed, was devoid of dirt. His gray hair hung to his shoulders, thick, with just a touch of wave. His clothes, though ragged and damp, were clean. She couldn't help the tears filling her eyes, and she quickly looked away, so as not to humiliate either of them.

"Won't you come inside and join me for supper, Mr. Carpenter?"

"Now, Miss Johnson. Have you no sense of propriety? Bad enough we must share two rooms. A grown man does not enter a young lady's sleeping quarters."

"Of course. M–may I join you for supper in the school?"

He scowled but gave a jerky nod. "Under the circumstances, I believe that would be acceptable. But only because I am old enough to be your grandfather."

Kathleen beamed at him. "I'll dish up our supper and bring it in there lickety-split."

He turned away and headed away from her door, but Kathleen heard him mumbling, "Lickety-split. It's no wonder children today have such an appalling vocabulary when their teachers use such common speech."

She grinned as she filled their bowls. Who would have thought two unlikely people stranded together in a blizzard would turn out to be such a blessing?

Chapter 8

The blizzard stranded Mr. Carpenter in the schoolhouse for three days. During that time, Kathleen learned a great deal about the man. The torments of war had caused him to retreat into a shell. By the time he had come to his senses, he'd lost all credibility with the town. He sank into despair. Even before her death, his wife had grown so cold, life was nearly unbearable. Mr. Carpenter bore all the blame himself.

One thing she knew for sure: Mr. Carpenter's love of teaching was nothing less than a holy calling. He adored sharing knowledge. Kathleen had made up her mind to discuss his placement as the town schoolteacher next term. She felt certain if the school board spent time with him they would see him as she did—particularly if he resisted the urge to allow himself to go without bathing and abstained from even an occasional visit to the saloon.

By breakfast time on day four, Kathleen and Mr. Carpenter had pretty much run out of things to talk about, so it was with great relief that Kathleen responded to a knock on her door just as she returned the dishes to her quarters.

Mary and Josh stood outside. At least two feet of snow blanketed the area, with drifts as tall as Flora in some places.

"Mary! Josh! Come in. I'm so glad to see you."

Mary grinned, her face red from the cold. She stomped over to the stove and held out her large, rough hands. "Thought that ya might be gettin' powerful lonesome."

Kathleen turned to Josh and smiled. "What are you doing in town?"

He smiled back, but his eyes held a serious look that made Kathleen want to run away, to hide from the temptation of falling in love with Josh Truman. It would be so easy to do just that. His kindness and humor drew her, and she'd never known a man to be so self-assured and yet vulnerable, as when he'd professed to having feelings for her so soon after they met. Josh was a rare man, and she knew someday he was going to make a woman very happy. She was almost jealous of whomever that woman would be.

"I hooked the team up to the cutter."

Mary harrumphed. "Rode those horses too fast, if you ask me. Downright dangerous."

Josh grinned, and Kathleen couldn't help but return it. "Sounds wonderful," she said.

"How would you like to go for a ride? I imagine you're just about crazy being cooped up for three full days all by yourself."

A knock sounded on the door between her quarters and the schoolroom just as she was going to explain about Mr. Carpenter. "Miss Johnson? Is everything quite all right in there? I thought I heard voices."

"Who in the. . . ?" Mary flung the door open. Mr. Carpenter gave a little scream and jumped back, fists up ready to defend himself.

Undaunted, Mary advanced. "Who are you? Whad-darya doin' in the schoolhouse, and what have you done to our little girl?"

Mr. Carpenter gaped. "I beg your pardon? I wouldn't lay one finger on that child, and I highly resent the implication."

Mary squinted and peered closer. "Myles?"

"Most certainly. Who else would I be?"

"Well, I'll be. . ."

Kathleen stepped between the two. "Mr. Carpenter came into the schoolroom to get warm just before the blizzard hit. He graciously accepted my invitation to sleep in the school and has been a godsend. If I had not had his stimulating conversation these three days, I would be stark raving mad."

"Well, I'll be. . ." Mary stared at him. "I sure did forgit you was such a good-lookin' fellow, Myles." She glanced back at Kathleen. "How'd ya ever talk 'im into takin' a bath?"

"Why, Mary!"

"Sorry. But we been stayin' upwind from this fellow for years, and here he is in the middle of a snowstorm, smellin' like a dandy. I never would have believed it."

"For your information, Mr. Carpenter asked me for the loan of all things necessary to accomplish a bath, and I merely handed them over and stayed out of his way. The decision was entirely his."

Josh joined the three of them in the school. "You two stayed together for three days?"

Mr. Carpenter drew himself up with all the dignity he could muster considering his scarlet face—compliments of Mary's loose tongue. "We most certainly did *not* stay together. Miss Johnson stayed in her quarters behind closed doors, and I, a man old enough to be her grandfather, stayed as far back from her door as possible. However, if you feel she has been compromised, I will do my duty and marry her properly, lest her name and reputation be tarnished."

Kathleen gasped as horror tingled between her shoulder blades. Josh placed an arm about her and pulled her away from Mr. Carpenter. Mary scowled. "For pity's sake. That girl ain't been compromised. Now if it had been young Josh on the other side of that door 'stead of you, old man, we might have something to talk about. 'Sides, when this town gets a load of you in your new clean state, there ain't gonna be no other topic of discussion."

47

Mr. Carpenter looked as relieved as Kathleen felt at the cancellation of possible nuptials. Still drawn into the circle of his arm, Kathleen turned to Josh. Her face was inches from his, and she could feel his breath warm on her face. She swallowed hard in an attempt to compose herself and stepped out of his embrace. "Would you mind giving Mr. Carpenter a ride home in your cutter? He can't walk in this snow."

"I'd be happy to." Josh smiled—the gentle, intimate sort of smile reserved for a man in love. He stole her breath away, and she felt the heat rush to her cheeks.

"Thank you," she whispered.

"Yes, thank you." Mr. Carpenter's voice held just a touch of amusement. The first hint of humor Kathleen had ever detected in the man.

Josh broke eye contact and shifted his gaze to the former schoolmaster. "I'll wait while you get your coat."

The older gentleman cleared his throat. "I am quite ready when you are."

"You're crazy as a loon," Mary said. "It's at least ten below out there. Where's that army coat you been wearin' since '65?"

"The coat has been properly destroyed, as it should have been years ago."

Kathleen realized now what he'd been doing when he built a bonfire during a letup in the falling snow on the second day of their confinement. She walked to her quarters and hesitated only a moment before she peeled back her quilt. She folded it, then hugged it to her chest. As she walked back to the schoolroom, her mind argued with her nostalgic heart. Could she truly bear to part with her quilt? Perhaps Mr. Carpenter could simply cover with it on the way home and then give it back.

As soon as the thought came, she rejected it. In all likelihood, his blankets at home were as filthy as the coat had been. A new quilt would remind him of the dignity he'd acquired during the past three days and possibly discourage him from going back to his old ways. She had other blankets. But she wanted him to have something special to mark what she hoped was a new beginning.

A sudden image flashed across her mind of the beautiful quilt layered in grime. She shook the troubling thought away as quickly as it had come. She was only responsible to be generous. It wasn't up to her to judge what a person did with her gift. She had only to give it cheerfully as unto the Lord.

Mr. Carpenter's brow furrowed when she handed it to him and mentioned it was his to keep. "I'd like you to have this as a token of my appreciation for keeping me company during the storms. God knew I needed you here. I would have been petrified alone."

Tears misted in his eyes. Reaching forward, he cupped her cheek in his palm as though caressing a beloved child. "It is I who needed you, dear child. You have aptly spoken, in that God sent me here, but it is I who shall forever be grateful."

Impulsively, Kathleen hugged him. He patted her back awkwardly. Miss Bilge blew her nose loudly. "Well, if that ain't the nicest thing. . .well, I just don't know what is."

Josh grabbed Kathleen's hand and squeezed it. He, too, seemed moved by the scene, and Kathleen could almost feel God's stamp of approval as though He had put a period on a well-constructed sentence.

Mr. Carpenter glanced at Josh. "If you are ready, I must be going, young man. My home needs considerable work, and I'd like to get to it."

"Yes, sir. I'm ready when you are." Josh squeezed her hand again. "I'll be back later to take you home, Miss Bilge. And to take you for that ride," he said, his gaze settling on Kathleen in a way that made her pulse leap.

When the men had left, Mary Bilge stared at Kathleen for a long second. "That offer to save me a seat in church still standin'?"

"Of course, Mary!"

She moved her head in a jerky nod. "I guess iffen the Almighty can change a fellow like Myles, there might just be hope for me after all."

Kathleen's lips curved into a smile, and delight rose in her chest. *Oh, Lord, Your ways truly are so much greater than mine.*

School remained closed for the rest of the week, and each day Josh arrived by noon to take Kathleen for a sleigh ride. On Saturday she packed a picnic lunch. They sat together under a warm lap blanket in the cutter. The sun's rays shimmered across the frozen lake and danced off the icicles hanging from the barren tree branches.

"I'm sorry we missed the November dance." Josh's voice broke a long silence. Each knew this would be their last sleigh ride for a while as school would be back in session on Monday. The mood between them had been somewhat subdued.

"I don't suppose they'll reschedule since the blizzard caused it to be canceled."

Josh shook his head. "Pa said the recreation committee decided two failed attempts were enough, and God must not want it to go on this year for some reason."

Disappointment crept over Kathleen. "I would have enjoyed dancing a waltz with you before I go home, Josh Truman." She tried to keep her voice light, but even she could hear the false gaiety.

He stretched his arm across the top of the seat and cupped her shoulder, pulling her to him. "I would have enjoyed a waltz, too, Kathleen Johnson."

As his face grew closer, Kathleen fought a battle inside. As much as she craved his embrace, she knew it wasn't fair to either of them. She placed her palm against his chest and pushed slightly. "Josh, please. I've already told you that I have to go home in three weeks. Don't make me take the memory of your kiss with me. If I do, how will I ever fall in love with a man in Rosewood?"

A plethora of emotions seemed to cross his face as though he struggled with his next course of action. Finally, he squeezed her shoulder and released her. Kathleen struggled against the feelings rising in her. All the emotions she'd felt over the past few weeks came to the surface, and tears pricked her eyes.

"Ah, Kat, don't cry."

"Kat?" Only those nearest and dearest to her had ever called her by her pet name.

"You don't like it? Kat suits you so well."

She smiled without elaborating. "I like it." Especially when it came from his lips.

As though reading her thoughts, he raised her gloved hand to his mouth. He kissed each finger, then pressed her palm to his cheek. He closed his eyes. "I want to remember this moment."

"W–we have three weeks. . . ."

"My heart can't take being alone with you and knowing you'll never be mine. Every time I'm with you, I fall deeper in love."

Oh, how she knew what he meant. But it would be so lonely without him for the next three weeks. The last day of school was only one week before Christmas. Then she'd go home and never see Josh again.

That night as she lay in bed listening to the sound of the mice scratching inside the walls, Kathleen remembered her brother's words to her. "Kat, don't make the same mistake I did. You might find that you don't want to stay in Rosewood forever."

Not stay in Rosewood? The thought had never occurred to her. Not in a million years. But now. . .

Was it possible?

Chapter 9

The next weeks moved frighteningly fast but at the same time crept along. Fast because Kathleen was busy with last-of-term grading and Christmas play practice. Slow because her sleeplessness had returned. She tossed and turned at night, her mind racing over and over with scenes from the moments she had shared with Josh. She had seen very little of him since the day at the lake, and she missed him. No longer did she lie awake weeping for her family in Rosewood, though she still longed to see them, as well. Now she wept for Josh. Precious Josh. Josh, who would never belong to her.

The night of the Christmas play arrived with a chill in the air and a dampness that caused the old-timers to predict a blizzard was coming. There hadn't been one flake of snow since the last blizzard, and everyone laughed off the predictions.

The children buzzed with excitement. Kathleen pulled a visibly nervous Andrew Coon aside.

"You're going to be wonderful, Andrew. Thank you for being our Joseph."

The teen had been a model student since the encounter with Mr. Carpenter and had even taken the initiative with the other unruly children. He'd become another gift from God. "My pa came. Said it was about time I did somethin' he could be proud of."

Andrew tried so hard to please the man—to make him proud.

She patted his shoulder. "We're about to start. Are you ready?"

"Yes, ma'am."

Kathleen smiled and moved back to the front of the room.

"Good evening, ladies and gentlemen," she said, smiling at the crowd. A few returning smiles warmed her. Mr. and Mrs. Truman; the pastor and his wife; Mary Bilge, who sat beaming next to Myles. Much to the shock of the town, Myles had done an almost instant about-face and had stayed clean against dire predictions. He hadn't missed a church service, nor had Mary Bilge, and they'd recently taken up courting. Two more unlikely people Kathleen couldn't imagine, but according to Mary, he was teaching her etiquette and proper speech, and she was teaching him to laugh. Perhaps God had sent two lonely souls to one another.

Kathleen's gaze landed on Josh standing in the back of the schoolroom, leaning against the wall. Her pulse quickened at his crooked smile. But there was no time to ponder her feelings; she had a play to oversee. "I would like to introduce our narrator for the evening—a truly brilliant man with a gift for literature—Mr. Myles Carpenter."

He seemed ill at ease as he stood and came to the front. When the idea had occurred to Kathleen that Mr. Carpenter's beautiful deep voice and eloquence of speech would make him the perfect narrator, she'd approached him with caution. She needn't have worried. He agreed to her request without question, and she had grown to love him more each day. At Kathleen's encouragement, he often showed up during afternoon sessions and read portions from Shakespeare, Charles Dickens, Tennyson, and even Edgar Allan Poe. The children adored him, and he rarely had occasion to reprimand.

"Glory to God in the highest, and on earth peace, goodwill toward men." Kathleen came back to the present as Myles's voice accentuated the words. She peeked at the audience to see if they were equally affected. The spellbound looks on their faces convinced her that Myles had a captive audience.

Not a dry eye remained as he finished the story with Simeon and Anna's blessing over the baby Jesus.

Mary and Joseph smiled at each other and held their "baby," which was actually made of straw.

"And that, my friends," Myles said, his voice shaking with awe, "concludes the wonderful story of the birth of our dear Lord."

For a long few seconds, no one moved, then slowly people began to clap, then stand. Kathleen had never been so moved by a Christmas play.

The pastor shook her hand afterward. "I'm so pleased by all you've accomplished these past two months, Miss Johnson. Can't we convince you to stay on another term?"

As much as she'd considered staying for Josh, the thought of teaching left her cold. "These children are wonderful, as is Coon's Hollow, Pastor, but I'm afraid teaching isn't the profession for me."

"But you've done so well."

"Pastor, may I be honest?"

He grinned. "I wouldn't have it any other way."

She returned his smile. "Of course you wouldn't. I would like to suggest that you hire Myles to teach."

Alarm shone in his eyes. "Myles?"

"The children are thriving because of his influence in my classroom. Myles comes most afternoons. The students adore him. I don't believe you'd be sorry."

"Well, I certainly never would have thought of him, but perhaps you're right. I will look into it."

"Thank you, sir."

The pastor smiled again and looked over her shoulder. Instinctively, Kathleen turned. Her pulse thumped in her throat. "Hi, Josh."

"Hi, Kat." His gaze perused her face. "Your play was very nice."

"Thank you. I can't take much credit."

They stood at a loss for words. Finally, Josh broke the silence.

"You're leaving tomorrow?"

She nodded, gloom descending. "My train leaves at ten in the morning. Will you come see me off?"

"Won't you change your mind? Say you'll come back after Christmas and marry me."

"Oh, Josh, my mother would be so hurt. My family stays in Rosewood. I just can't go against that."

"Then you're robbing yourself of happiness with the man you love."

He spun around and stomped away, leaving Kathleen's heart shattered on the wooden floor.

✥

With aching heart, Josh watched the train pull away from the station. He expelled a heavy sigh. *Well, Lord. That's that, I guess. I tried. I felt sure she was the one for me.*

The snow was falling with more force, and he turned his collar up to ward off the icy blast of wind. A sliver of unease crept through him as the wind howled. With a frown, he nudged Shasta. Rather than turning and heading home, he found himself in front of the school almost without memory of how he'd gotten there.

His memory played in his head like a picture book. His first sight of Kathleen's blue eyes and sweet dimple. The musical sound of her laughter. Her kindness to Mary and to Mr. Carpenter. There would never be another girl like Kathleen Johnson.

He went home and moped for a good four hours while the snow continued to blanket the area. Alarm seized him when Pa entered the barn near suppertime.

"What's wrong, Pa?"

"I'm not sure, but I'm afraid the train to Rosewood might be in trouble."

Josh's mouth went dry. "What makes you think that?" he choked out.

"A rider came into town. Said it's been snowing that direction for a full day longer than we've had it. Snow's piling up. If it's over the track, the train could be in for some problems. I figured you'd want to know."

Josh had already moved into gear. He grabbed a harness and headed for the horse stalls.

"Josh!" As chaos and panic struck the passengers inside the tipping train, his was the only name Kathleen could remember, and she screamed it over and over as she fell. It all happened so fast that it took awhile for Kathleen to realize the train had derailed and she was falling. Pain hammered her right shoulder. And hip. When the car finally stopped moving and groaning, she tried to stand, but the shape of the train and the benches was too awkward for her to walk on with unsteady legs. So she crawled.

Her head felt light, as though she might faint. Oh, how she'd give anything if

Josh were with her right now.

"Is everyone all right?"

The sound came from somewhere outside the train. It couldn't be Josh. He was back in Coon's Hollow. "I'm going to need someone to go to the lever and open the door. I can't get it open from out here." There was no mistaking the sound of that voice.

"Josh? Josh? Is that you?"

"Kathleen? Honey, are you all right?"

"I think so. Just a little bruised."

"Oh, thank God. Can you get to the lever?"

"I'm almost there."

In a moment, she opened the door and felt herself being pulled up. He sat on the side of the train and gathered her in his arms. "My love. Are you sure you're all right?"

"I am now."

"Is everyone all right down there?"

"I don't know. I think so."

He called down, and when no one reported anything but minor injuries, he promised they would send help back.

Since they were several hours closer to Rosewood than Coon's Hollow, Josh turned his team toward Kathleen's hometown. After they spoke with the mayor about the train, Josh headed toward Kathleen's house, then stopped before they got there.

"Kathleen." He looked into her eyes, and the intensity of his gaze nearly clouded her senses. "I can't let you go."

Tears filled her eyes. "I know. I feel the same way. But my family. That is. . . my mother especially. They expect us to stay in Rosewood."

"Sweetheart, I can't move here, if that's what you're thinking. I have a family, too, and my own squared-off piece of land that I've been clearing this winter."

"I know, Josh."

"I want to ask you something. I can't go all of my life knowing I didn't at least ask."

Kathleen closed her eyes, then opened them again.

Josh took her hand in his and pinned her with his gaze. "Kathleen, I've fallen in love with you. From the moment I saw you, I felt you were the girl for me. I want to ask you to be my wife. Will you marry me?"

"Oh, Josh." The negative response was on her lips, but she realized she couldn't say no. She just couldn't. She didn't even want to. "I will marry you."

His eyes widened. "You will?"

"Yes. I will."

He crushed her to him, taking her breath away. "Are you sure you can leave home?"

"Coon's Hollow is home now. I miss Mary and Myles, Flora and the boys, and even Andrew Coon. I want to go back and be a part of their lives."

"I'm so glad." He lowered his face, and this time Kathleen didn't resist. His mouth pressed against hers, soft and warm and filled with promise. Josh pulled away and looked deeply into her eyes. "I love you."

"I love you, too, Josh."

When his lips descended, Kathleen knew without a doubt that she'd finally come home.

Epilogue

Christmas morning

Abel Coon sneered at the two of them.

"Don't worry about him, Josh," said his wife of three days. "We'll beat him by a mile."

After meeting Kathleen's parents, Josh had asked for her father's permission to marry her. Kathleen had stood strong against her mother's protests, and Josh had returned to Coon's Hollow with Kathleen as his wife.

This beautiful Christmas morning had dawned bright, a perfect day for the Coon's Hollow Christmas sleigh ride—and Josh and Abel's yearly race. Josh hadn't lost one yet, and he'd informed Kathleen he didn't intend to start now.

She nestled beside him, feeling the muscles in his arms tighten with anticipation.

The gun sounded, and they were off, each cutter sliding through the snow. After a minute, Josh got a margin of a lead and knew the race was all but over. Sandy and Chester weren't going to let Abel Coon win now that they'd had a taste of being ahead. The horses were more competitive than he was.

"Oh, Josh. There's our lake."

Trying to stay focused on the race, Josh didn't comment.

"Our lake. Where you almost kissed me. Where we admitted our feelings for the first time."

With a sigh, Josh slowed the cutter. Abel dashed ahead, a grin splitting his face.

"What on earth are you doing, Josh Truman?"

"I'm letting Abel have the race." He nudged the horses to the right and pulled them to a stop in front of the lake. The frozen crystals shimmered.

"But, Josh, you always beat Abel."

"Some things are just more important. Like a man kissing his wife next to a beautiful frozen lake."

There was no time for her to respond as he pulled her close. He kissed her thoroughly until all thoughts of Abel Coon's first-place finish in the race fled from Kathleen's mind.

"Let's go home," he said.

Kathleen nodded. "Yes, let's go home."

One Wintry Night

by Pamela Griffin

Dedication

A special thank you to all the wonderful women
who helped me by critiquing this book—
Maryn L., Jill S., Paige W. D., Lena D., Anne G.,
Candice S., Erin L., Mary H., and, of course, Mom.
Also thanks to Meredith E., Pamela K. T. (O.),
and Mary C. for helping with the Nebraska and Welsh information.

To my loving Guide, my Lord Jesus,
who's always been the Light to lead me
through the sudden storms in life.

*Charity suffereth long, and is kind; charity envieth not;
charity vaunteth not itself, is not puffed up.*
1 CORINTHIANS 13:4

Chapter 1

Leaning Tree, Nebraska—October 1871

Hiya, Boston." With his forefinger and thumb, Craig lazily tipped the brim of his hat toward the pretty brunette.

Indignation shot through her blueberry-colored eyes. Pink stained her cheeks. Instead of answering him, Ivy Leander tossed her dark curls with a little huff and walked right past where he stood on the weathered boardwalk in front of Johnson's feed store.

Old Mr. Meyers rasped out a chuckle before she was out of hearing range. "Might as well forget that one, Craig. She's about as friendly as a pork-ee-pine with all-over body aches. And she don't seem to like you much neither."

The former cobbler from Tennessee might be right about that—for now. But Craig wouldn't let that stop him. He stared after the woman in the gray store-bought dress with the shiny ribbons. He knew the dress was store-bought because of all the gossip flying among the town's old hens ever since Gavin Morgan married Ivy's ma and brought the woman and her daughter to Leaning Tree, Nebraska, this past spring. Then, too, no store-bought dress could be found at the general store, so it must be from Boston. Under Ivy's stylish hat, out of place in this rugged town, spirals of dark curls hung, bouncing along her neck. Most women he knew wore their hair wrapped in two braids around their head or in a bun. Craig liked Ivy's way of doing her hair better.

"She sure is a feisty one," he agreed as he went back to the task of foisting the cumbersome feed sack into the rear of Mr. Meyers's wagon. He shoved the large canvas sack into place next to the farm supplies the old man had purchased.

"Thankee much, Craig." Mr. Meyers rubbed his white-whiskered jaw. "Don't know what I woulda done if you weren't here. Never woulda reckoned that young giant Tommy woulda gone and busted his leg."

"Glad to have helped," Craig said with a sincere smile. Mr. Meyers looked about as brittle as an ice-coated twig and close to being as skinny. Craig hoped the man's nephew Tommy was up to par soon.

A burst of giggling sailed across the muddy road. Craig looked to see two young women, Beth and Sally, strolling along the boardwalk. They whispered behind their hands, staring Ivy's way. Craig also turned to look. A wagon had just rumbled past where Ivy walked, spraying muddy water on the bottom of her gray dress. She stamped her kid boot, her fists pumping once at her sides, and glared at the retreating wagon.

"I hate this town!" The small growl left her throat, but it was loud enough for Craig to hear. She marched forward several more steps and turned to enter the general store. As though she sensed Craig's stare, she looked in his direction.

He dipped his head her way, tipping his hat again. She broke eye contact, slipped her hand to the top of her feathered bonnet to pat it, as if to make sure it was still in place, and marched through the door.

"Yessiree," Mr. Meyers said with a low whistle. "I sure enough do pity the poor fool who takes her for a wife."

Craig eyed the closed door of the general store a few seconds longer, then turned, the grin going wide on his face. "I reckon that'd be me, sir."

"Pardon?" Mr. Meyers pulled at his thick earlobe as if he had wax in his ear and couldn't hear well, though the man was reputed to hear a sneeze in the next county.

"I'm the one who's going to marry Ivy Leander."

Surprise shone from Mr. Meyers's eyes, then pity. He let out a loud guffaw. "The sun must've gone to your head, boy!"

"No, sir. By this time next year, I plan to make Ivy my wife. Or my name isn't Craig Watson." He adjusted his hat, gave a jovial farewell nod, and headed toward the general store.

"Nice knowin' ya, Jim," Mr. Meyers's amused voice came from behind. "Wonder what Ivy'll think of your little plan. Care to make a wager on its success?"

Craig kept walking—not that he had any doubts concerning his claim. He just wasn't a betting man. And even if he were, Jebediah Meyers didn't usually have more than two coins to rub together after a trip to town. It would shame Craig to take money from the old man.

⚭

Ivy eyed the sparse selection of goods in the cramped store with distaste. Even the nicest ribbons and combs and whatnots for sale were a pale comparison to the quality of those found in Boston. Everything in the East was nicer, with more variety from which to choose. The stores were cleaner, too. She skirted a couple of muddy boot prints on the plank floor, scrunching her nose in disgust.

Could the fifty dollars her wealthy grandmother secretly presented to her before she left Boston even be spent in such a place? The dear woman had known how much Ivy dreaded prairie life and told her to use the money for some "little extravagance" but not to tell her mother about the gift. Yet what of that nature could be found here?

Why Mama had to go and fall in love with an uneducated farmer who chose to make his home in the prairie wilds lay beyond Ivy's scope of reasoning. Her young stepsisters certainly didn't add honey to the pot, either. Crystin and Gwen couldn't keep their hands off Ivy's things, despite Ivy's frequent complaints to her mother to have a talk with them and set them straight. Mama quietly explained to Ivy that, being so new a family, there were bound to be disturbances and issues needing to be ironed out, and Ivy should just be patient and let time run its course to fix things.

Ivy had been patient—up until yesterday when she found her gold-filigree garnet brooch with the seed pearls, a gift her beloved grandmother had given her, tromped into the hay-strewn ground near the pig's smelly trough. A tinge of remorse unsettled Ivy at the way she'd lit into eight-year-old Crystin, and she couldn't help but remember the tears that made the child's big blue eyes glisten.

The door opened, and Craig Watson strode inside. A blacksmith by trade, he had the strong arms and hands to prove it. Tall, well-built, with his nutmeg brown eyes often dancing in amusement—no doubt at her expense—he had an annoying habit of calling her "Boston" rather than using the appropriate title of "Miss Leander," as the Bostonian gentlemen of her acquaintance had done. To their credit, a few of the male settlers in this town also addressed her properly, though most just called her "ma'am." But not Mr. Ill-mannered Blacksmith. Oh no. Not him.

"Good morning, Craig," the plump Mrs. Llewynn said from behind the counter.

"Mornin', ma'am." The timbre of his voice poured out like wild honey, smooth and warm. He caught Ivy's stare and tipped his hat, that ever-present, rakish, close-lipped grin on his tanned, all too attractive face. "Mornin'."

Ivy's heart ran a foolish little race in her bosom as it often did when he smiled her way. She snapped her focus back to the bolts of sprigged material lying on a nearby weathered table. Calico. Only poor country folk wore calico. She might as well cut holes in a feed sack and wear that.

She heard his boots clomp toward the counter at the front. Curiosity propelled her to lift her gaze a few inches. From the back, under his hat, thick clumps of wheat-colored hair brushed the bottom edge of his collar. The man was in dire need of a haircut. And a bath. Though the odors weren't exactly offensive, the smell of smoke and raw iron permeated his clothing, and fresh sweat dampened his shirt.

"What can I do for you today?" Mrs. Llewynn asked him with a wide smile, looking up from thumbing through a magazine.

"I need to get a caldron if you have one. Mine sprung a leak this morning."

"Oh, my. I sure don't, but I do have an old washtub you can use."

"I'd appreciate it." Craig tipped his hat back from his forehead. "That your latest issue of *Godey's*?"

"Yes. It just arrived yesterday."

"Excuse me?" Ivy moved forward. "Did I understand correctly? You have a recent copy of the *Godey's Lady's Book*?"

"That I do," Mrs. Llewynn said with a nod before she again looked at Craig. "I'll just go get that washtub." She left her place behind the counter and bustled to the back room. Craig nudged the corner of the magazine with two fingers, pushing it at an angle. He looked down sideways, tilting his head as if to peer at the cover but not wanting to seem too interested.

Ivy stepped up beside him, almost knocking into him in her haste. "Pardon," she breathed as she slid the magazine the few inches her way for a better view. Excited, she thumbed to the first page and soon became engrossed in the illustrations, rapidly shuffling through the pages. Her hand stilled, and she sighed. "Oh, what a simply lovely gown this would make for a Christmas ball."

"I surely wouldn't mind seeing you in it," Craig's amused voice came back.

Ivy's hand froze at the top corner of the next page before she could turn it. Heat flamed her cheeks, and she snapped her gaze from the illustrations of velvet and ribbons and bustles to Craig's laughing eyes.

"Oh, my" was all she could think to say. She wasn't sure which embarrassed her more—his highly personal and improper remark or the fact that in her great excitement to find a link with civilization, she had acted like a hoyden and pushed him aside to snatch the magazine away. Miss Lucy Hadmire of the elite ladies' academy Ivy once attended would be shocked to have witnessed her prize pupil's performance.

"I do apologize," she murmured, snatching her hand from the magazine. "I didn't mean to be rude."

His thick, neat brows lifted in wry amusement, as if reminding her of the irony of that statement, and another wave of embarrassment swept over her. Ever since she'd stepped off the wagon that first day in Leaning Tree, she'd been nothing but rude to this man. Yet such rudeness developed from the dread that he might one day become interested in her, as his looks toward her implied. She could never stoop so low as to marry a farmer, much less a blacksmith! Her husband would be an educated man of considerable means, as her doctor-father had been.

"Well, now, Boston, ladies' magazines aren't exactly of interest to me," he said with another of his irritating grins. "So look as much as you'd like."

That name again. *Insufferable man.*

She turned on her heel. "I'll come back another time." Before he could let loose with another teasing remark, she flounced out of the store.

Chapter 2

Two days after his encounter with Ivy, Craig brushed at the sweat dripping from his brow with the back of one forearm, then set the glowing yellow iron over the horn of the anvil and resumed pounding it into a horseshoe shape. Regardless of the fact that the huge doors of the smithy were rolled open as far as they would go, it was still muggy and unseasonably warm.

He whistled a tune, though the jarring strikes of the hammer ringing off metal blocked most of it. Whistling helped him relax, and he did it for that reason alone. As he worked and the sparks flew, he thought about Ivy. His mind jumped back to the first day he'd met her.

Plump and pretty, she had just stepped off a dusty wagon that rolled to a stop not far from where Craig worked. A thinner woman stepped to the parched ground behind her. She had the same blue eyes and was older by about twenty years. Then Gavin Morgan stretched his short, compact build from the wagon and helped a petite elderly woman to alight. Ivy had stood eyeing her surroundings with a mixture of frank despair and cold disdain. As Craig approached, he could almost feel the thick frost coating her, though the day was about as hot as bacon fat sizzling on a griddle.

"Afternoon, ladies." Craig tipped his hat to the women, then shook his friend's hand. "Gavin, good to have you back." His gaze again settled on Ivy. "Welcome to Leaning Tree."

The younger woman gave what Craig thought might be considered a nod. It was so slight, he wasn't sure.

Gavin presented his new wife, Eloise, and his mother, also referring to Ivy as "Eloise's daughter," then he walked into the general store with the two older women following. Before Ivy could join them, Craig thought up something to say. "So, where are you from?"

She looked down her nose at him. "It really isn't proper for us to converse without first being *formally* introduced. But to answer your question, I'm from Boston. That's in Massachusetts, incidentally."

"Really. You don't say." He felt a grin curl up his mouth at her high-handed approach toward what she considered his ignorance, and he pushed back his hat from his forehead, deciding to play along.

"Well, now, ma'am, 'round these here parts, the most formal interductions sound something like, '*Here, soooo-eeeeee!*'" He let the words loose in a squeal similar to the one he'd heard Mrs. Llewynn use when calling her hogs to their meal.

Ivy's blueberry eyes widened in surprise, and she took a quick step back, almost tripping over the warped boardwalk. She put her gloved hand to the nearby hitching post to steady herself.

"'Course, that approach only works when you're socializin' with the hogs," Craig continued matter-of-factly. "When you wanna talk to the chickens, you should say, 'Here, chick, chick, chick, chick, chick, chick!'" He let the phrase jump from his mouth in a rapid stream of bulletlike words, then feigned a look of innocent realization. "But I reckon what you actually was meanin' was a formal interduction with the people 'round these here parts."

"Of course I meant the people," she snapped. "Why should I wish to socialize with the pigs?"

"Hogs, ma'am. They's different than pigs, but prob'ly a whole lot more sociable than mosta the folks here in Leaning Tree." He leaned in close as though about to reveal a secret. "Smarter, too," he confided in a low voice. "Why, ole Stony Jack's hog can count to ten while most people 'round here cain't even read nor write."

She crossed her arms over her frilly, lace-covered blouse, her reticule dangling from one wrist. "Oh, really! Surely you don't expect me to believe such nonsense?"

He crossed a hand over his heart. "Sure as I'm standin' here and the day is warm. Where'd you say you was from again?"

"Boston." She frowned. "Must I write the name on my forehead for you to remember it?"

Craig held back a chuckle. "Oh no, ma'am. I think I can remember it next time around."

And he had—calling her "Boston" from that day on. It fit her, from the top of her sassy, feathered hat to the leather soles of her fancy kid boots and all points between. Still, there was something about Ivy Leander that aroused more than his curiosity. She intrigued him; he'd never met a woman like her. All spit and fire but with a noticeable softness touching her expression when she didn't know she was being watched. And Craig had done his share of watching these past months.

At the harvest dance, he'd even asked her to take a spin with him around the huge wooden platform built just for the occasion. She had snubbed his invitation with a brisk "No, thank you," looking away as if he were no more than a pesky horsefly buzzing about. Yet Craig had made up his mind that he wouldn't let that deter him from his plan to court her. He'd caught Ivy doing her share of watching him when she didn't think he was looking. She didn't fool him one bit; Ivy appeared as interested in Craig as he was in her. Underneath all that lacy froth and those fancy ribbons, he imagined he'd find a woman with a tender heart. At least he hoped so. Everyone from Mr. Meyers to the old doc thought him foolish in his persistence to try to win her affections. Maybe he was, at that.

Seeing that the metal had lost most of its color, Craig stopped his pounding and whistling and twisted around in a half-circle, intending to poke the iron back into the fire blazing yellow in the forge, to get it to the right temperature again. To his surprise, he heard the next notes of his tune faintly whistled behind him before cutting off abruptly.

He spun around in the direction from which he thought the notes were coming in the dim light of his three-walled shop. No one stood there. One hand still wrapped around the handle of his hammer, the other around the tongs, he made a slow circle of the room. In a dark corner, he noticed one of his work aprons crumpled on the floor—then saw it move. Craig thought about the recent theft of one of Gladys Llewynn's chickens.

"You come on out from there," he said, tightening his grip on the hammer. "I don't want any trouble." He took a step closer. "Come on out, I said."

A stiff rustle of cloth was followed by the sight of a small girl popping her head up, her eyes wide with uncertainty. Beads of sweat trickled down her temples, and wisps of damp hair stuck to her skin. As stifling hot as it was in the smithy, that was no surprise.

Craig relaxed. "Amy Bradford, what are you doing hiding in that corner? You come on out from there. Do your parents know you're here?"

Amy hurried to stand and shook her head, her two corn silk–colored braids swishing against her brown calico dress. "Miss Johnson let us out early today. I'm hidin' from Wesley."

Once classes were dismissed, the brother and sister often played such games on the rare occasions they did attend school. Yet Craig wasn't sure he approved of them playing in his workplace. Before he could answer, a young boy's voice called from outside.

"Amy Lamey, I know you're in there!"

The girl's mouth compressed at the nickname her brother used. "Don't tell him where I am," she whispered, putting a finger to her lips before diving back under the apron and curling into a ball.

Craig blew out a lengthy breath and shook his head. He couldn't find it in his heart to begrudge the two a little fun. Coming from a family of fourteen kids, Amy and Wesley were the middle children, responsible for a good portion of the chores. They barely found time to play. Of course, that was the lot of most prairie children.

"I heard you talkin', so's I know yo a're in here." Nine-year-old Wesley, with his carrot top of curly hair, moved into the smithy as if he owned the place. "Howdy, Mr. Watson."

Craig nodded in greeting. Accustomed to customers milling about the place while they waited on orders to be filled, he heated the horseshoe again, forged a turned-up clip at the front to protect the horse's hoof, then bored eight holes into it with his pritchel tool to hold the nails. After rounding the ends, he doused it in Mrs. Llewynn's nearby washtub filled almost to the brim with cool water. A loud *hisssss* escaped, and steam sprayed his face. With the iron now cooled so that he could handle it without burning himself, he hung it over the anvil's horn to join the other three horseshoes there.

"Guess who I saw mailin' a letter today?" the boy asked, reminding Craig of his presence.

"You still here?"

"Aw, come on, Mr. Watson. Guess."

"I wouldn't have the vaguest idea." Craig wiped the sweat and grime from his hands down the front of his leather apron. At present, the schoolhouse shared its space with the postal office—Mr. Owen taking over one corner of the building to conduct his business there.

"Miss Uppity from Boston," the boy announced.

Craig bit back the grin that wanted to jump to his mouth at the boy's nickname for Ivy. He hung his tools on their spot near the bellows. "You shouldn't call her that, Wesley. It's not nice to call people names."

"That's what Ma calls her when she's talking about her to Pa." The boy headed to a hitching post several feet away, where a skittish horse waited to be shod, and hoisted himself up to sit on the wood. The bay whinnied a greeting, and Wesley looped a chubby arm around its neck in a brief hug. " 'Sides, she is uppity. She comes to town 'most every week to look through those fancy ladies' magazines of Mrs. Llewynn's, but she doesn't talk to hardly no one."

"Maybe she doesn't know what to say. You ever talk to her?"

Wesley scrunched up his mouth in a guilty expression. "Naw, but Amy tried today durin' lunch. Miss Ivy got all funny lookin', like she didn't want nobody knowin' her business. She was mailin' a letter but kept lookin' behind her, like she was afraid someone would see. Amy walked up to her and asked her who the letter was for, but she didn't pay Amy no mind."

Craig tucked the words away to ponder later. He donned his hat, picked up his toolbox, and walked out in the sunshine toward the boy. "There's no law that says she has to tell two bean sprouts her business."

Wesley chuckled and began swinging his short legs, as if daring gravity to keep him upright. Craig wondered how come the boy didn't fall, balanced as he was on such a narrow beam.

"Is it true what Mr. Meyers said?" the boy asked. "That you told him you're gonna marry up with Miss Ivy someday?"

Surprised, Craig set his tools down with a bang. "Where'd you hear that?"

"Just around."

Craig grimaced. He never should have told Mr. Meyers his plans. The last thing he needed was for Ivy to hear such news through the town's busybodies. "Know why God gave you two ears and one mouth?"

Wesley shook his head.

"So you'd spend more time listening to the teachings of your elders and less time talking about matters that aren't any of your business." Craig released a long breath. "As long as you're here, put yourself to use. That horse seems to like you, but I've been having trouble with it all morning. When I took the old shoes off, she almost bit me. I need you to hold the halter and talk nice and easy to her while I shoe her."

Wesley's face brightened as he slid off the hitching post. "Does this mean I can be your apprentice?"

Craig's eyebrows lifted. "Where'd you learn such a big word?"

"At school. We was studyin' on colonial times when they had them apprentices. Some of us even had to learn us a poem about a village blacksmith. I'd like to be a blacksmith someday. I learn real fast. So can I be your apprentice?" he asked again.

"Don't know about that. You're a mite small yet." At the boy's downcast eyes, Craig relented. "Give yourself a few more years to fill out, and I'll consider it. That is, if your ma and pa agree. Now hold the horse steady. While I'm pounding these nails in, I don't want her suddenly getting skittish so that I end up missing the horseshoe and hitting my leg instead."

The boy was as good as his word and held the horse while Craig drove the short nails into the holes of the shoes, fastening them to the horse's hooves. The studs on the bottom would give the horse traction over icy roads once the snows hit. Craig had already fitted his own horse with similar shoes and was surprised the town hadn't received any freezing weather yet.

"All done." He removed the hind hoof of the horse from his lap, straightened from his bent position, and turned to face the bay and the boy who held her. "You get on home now, Wesley. Your ma will be worried."

Wesley scratched the back of his curly head. "She does worry an awful lot, don't she? Pa says she's fractious 'cuzza the twins. Bye, Mr. Watson."

Before the boy walked more than five steps, Craig called out. "Wait! Aren't you forgetting something?"

Wesley turned and lifted his shoulders in a shrug. "Uh, don't think so."

Craig raised his eyebrows. "Your little sister?"

"Oh, Amy," he said as if just remembering her name. "I forgot about her."

"That's what I figured," Craig muttered, heading into the smithy. He wondered why Amy hadn't made her presence known before this. Wesley had been at the smithy for the better part of an hour. When he hunkered down in the corner where he'd found her, Craig had his answer. The girl lay fast asleep under the leather apron.

For a moment, he studied her rosy cheeks and the tendrils of light-colored hair sticking to her face. Her expression was peaceful, like an angel's. He hoped to have a little girl like Amy someday—several of them. And a passel of boys, too. He wondered if Ivy liked kids.

Craig put his hand to the girl's bony shoulder and gently shook it. "Amy? It's time to wake up and go home now. The smithy's no place for little sprouts like you."

She blinked her eyes open, then sat up and rubbed them. "Oh, hi, Mr. Watson," she said sleepily. "Is it mornin'?"

"I hope not. Actually, you've been here for almost an hour, since the schoolmarm dismissed you from school anyway."

"Oh!" The girl threw off the apron and scrambled to a stand. "I have to get home and help Ma with the ironin' and cookin'. Bye, Mr. Watson!" She raced out of the smithy, soon catching up with her brother, who was waiting for her on the road. Ivy came into view, walking in their direction. She looked at the children, then darted a glance toward the smithy.

Craig smiled and tipped his hat her way.

Hurriedly she refocused on the road. Skirts a-swaying, she increased her pace and hotfooted it in the direction of her stepfather's soddy. Bottling his irritation at the latest snub, Craig watched her awhile longer, shook his head, then turned back to finish his long list of tools needing forged or mended.

Morning sunshine appeared to illuminate the white-painted, timbered house at the far end of town. Ivy turned wistful eyes upon the two-story structure as she walked past. Modest in size, it was still a lot nicer than any of the other six buildings that made up Leaning Tree. And certainly a great deal more refined than the house of sod belonging to her mother's new husband. Still, it was nowhere near comparable to her grandmother's stately home in Boston, looming at the end of a tree-lined street.

Ivy halted her steps and further studied the building before her. Lace curtains at the windows. A stone chimney at the side. At least the white timbered house belonging to the Pettigrasses was respectable. People were meant to live in sturdy buildings with wooden floors and pretty rugs. Not underneath earth and grass like bugs and animals.

A petite, brown-haired woman stepped onto the porch and began to shake out a blanket in the direction the wind was blowing. Catching sight of Ivy, she smiled.

"Hulloa, Ivy! You come to town often, indeed," Winifred Pettigrass called in the lilting Welsh accent that all the Morgans and a few other families in town shared.

"Yes," Ivy called back. With nothing better to do after the morning chores her mother assigned her, she often preferred to spend time thumbing through the pages of the ladies' magazines and perusing the items at the general store, though she still hadn't found anything appropriate to buy. Since her stepfather's home-stead was close to town, the walk was short, less than two miles.

"Can you come inside and sit with us for tea?" Winifred called out.

Ivy would like nothing better than to sit in a real chair and drink from a fine china cup, but she shook her head. "I can't. I promised Mother I'd be home to help her with the noon meal."

"Another time, then, while the weather is nice. Go you and tell that dada of yours he must come, too. Never will I understand that man and how his mind thinks."

Her words were cheery. Ivy had been in Leaning Tree long enough to realize what the woman's mood meant. Winifred Pettigrass wanted something from her brother, Ivy's stepfather. How different the two siblings were! Winifred had married a wealthy man who worked for the railroad and originally had come to town as a surveyor, where he'd met Winifred. The spry woman appreciated the finer things in life, as did Ivy, while Ivy's new stepfather was content to live like a mole and toil the earth to produce wheat and corn.

Winifred's mother came through the open door. "Good day to you, Ivy," she said. "You be certain and tell that son of mine I said to come. Three weeks now, I see nothing of him."

"I'll tell him," Ivy called back and continued down the road. Gavin's mother was the initial reason her stepfather had gone to Boston this past spring. Weak from the voyage to America years ago, Bronwyn Morgan stayed with a relative while Gavin settled his claim and built his home in Nebraska.

How unfortunate for Ivy that Gavin chose this past year to collect his mother—and that Ivy's mother had been the one strolling down the sidewalk when Gavin approached asking for directions. Two weeks later they married—scandalous to Ivy and her grandmother's way of thinking, but necessary since Gavin had to return to his homestead and needed a wife and a mother for his two daughters. Eloise Leander had been only too happy to comply, dragging along her only daughter with her.

When Ivy begged to remain in Boston with her grandmother, her mother flatly refused, stressing they were a family and would remain one. And so, one minute Ivy was dancing at a ball with the cream of Boston society. The next she was whisked away and picking up cow patties for fuel with the same gloves she'd worn to the ball.

Ivy sighed at the memory of those chaotic first few months in learning a new way of life. She focused on the road before her. A sea of undulating grass higher than her head flanked both sides of the muddy lane. Skirting the holes filled with rainwater, Ivy was glad she'd given in to common sense last week and had bought the clunky but serviceable footwear at the general store. Her soft kid boots never would have withstood this! At least, underneath her long skirts, the ugly new shoes couldn't be seen.

Hearing a child softly crying, Ivy lifted her gaze off the puddles and spotted Amy Bradford kneeling at the edge of the road. A bunch of cracked eggs littered the ground in front of the fair-haired girl. Yellow yolks mixed with the clear pool of liquid, which seeped near Amy's threadbare dress.

"Oh, Ma's gonna be so mad at me!" The nine-year-old lifted pale green eyes to Ivy and wiped the backs of her fingers over wet cheeks. "I walked all the way from home and was so careful. But this puddle was deeper than I thought, and I twisted my foot."

Ivy decided not to ask why the child would deliberately step into a puddle. "Are you hurt?" She bent down, careful not to ruin her dress.

"No, but the eggs are. What am I gonna tell Ma? She's already mad at me for stayin' so long at the smithy's two days ago and comin' home late. She needed to stay with the twins—they's awful fractious with the teething—and she told me to take the eggs to Mrs. Llewynn this morning. Ma wants to get Clarence a warm coat before the snows come. And Wesley needs shoes. They ain't got none that'll fit, and Ma's been takin' eggs every morning so's she can save enough money to buy some."

Ivy knew that, with fourteen children to raise, the Bradfords barely had enough to get by. Their sod house was even smaller than the one Ivy was forced to live in with her mother, stepfather, and two stepsisters, and Amy's home contained only one window with a cracked pane.

"How many eggs did you have with you?" Ivy asked.

"Fifteen. One's okay, though." Amy reached in the basket beside her and held up a brown oval that had somehow missed destruction.

Ivy held out her hand for the lone egg and inspected the shell. It bore a faint, hairline crack. She reached inside her reticule and withdrew a coin. "There you are."

Amy stared at the shiny dime in Ivy's hand as though puzzled. "What's that for?"

"Your egg. I'm buying it."

"But"—Amy's light brows sailed up—"that's more'n Mrs. Llewynn pays for the whole basket!"

"That's all right. I'm fond of eggs."

"A whole dime for one egg?" Amy sounded as if she still couldn't believe it.

Ivy shrugged. "If you'd rather not sell it. . ."

"Oh no." Amy grabbed the dime with dirt-stained fingers. "I wouldn't want ta deprive you of your egg, Miss Leander." She used a version of the saying Ivy had often heard Mr. Bradford use.

Ivy carefully set the egg at the bottom of her reticule. "Good. Then it appears we've struck a bargain."

The child seemed to consider before a sly smile lifted the corners of her mouth. "Anytime you want more, you let me know, and I'll be sure and save you some."

Ivy laughed, the sound trilling through the air. "I'll do that, Amy." The grin was still on her face as she watched the girl gather her empty basket and head for home. Suddenly Ivy noticed a wagon coming her way. As the rider neared, her heart plummeted, then lifted, almost soaring above the clouds like an eagle. She pressed her hand to her bosom in a futile effort to quell the rapid beating and averted her gaze past the wagon.

"Mornin', Boston," Craig said, pulling his horse to a stop beside her.

Despite her desire not to pay him any heed, she darted a glance his way. He tipped his battered brown hat, giving her that lazy smile.

She offered a brief nod in an effort to be polite.

"Can I give you a ride home?"

"We're going in opposite directions."

"It won't be any trouble for me to turn my horse around. And your father's claim is close to town."

"Stepfather, you mean. He's not my real father."

Craig didn't reply. Feeling flustered and wishing she hadn't blurted out what she had, Ivy looked back down the road. "Thanks for the offer, but I'd rather walk."

"You sure?" His voice was gentle.

"Yes. As you pointed out, it's not far, and I enjoy the exercise."

"Okay. If you're sure." His warm brown eyes never left her face, and she felt the blush rise to her cheeks. His look reminded her that she was an unmarried woman and he was an unmarried man. A rather attractive unmarried man, even with that slight bend in his nose and his untamed hair, which grew a little long over the ears.

"I–I have to go now," she said quickly, moving away as she spoke. She set off at a walking-run for the first several feet, then slowed to a more moderate pace. However, her heart didn't slow one bit.

What was she thinking? She could never be interested in anyone from this godforsaken little town tucked away in the middle of nowhere! Even if the man wasn't a farmer and did hold what her mother had informed Ivy was one of the most respected trades in the township, Craig Watson still lived like a pauper in one cramped room adjoining his shop. He didn't even own a decent home—not that she could think of the soddies that most people from these parts lived in as decent. Yet they *were* houses with windows and doors.

With each step she took, Ivy's resolve strengthened. She would keep as far away as she could from the town blacksmith.

Chapter 3

The wind howled outside the soddy as Ivy concentrated on helping her mother hang the wash over the clothesline extending from one end of the dirt-brick wall to the other. Cold weather had hit with a vengeance, and this week's washing needed to be done inside the crowded front room. The family's faithful guard dog, Old Rufus, snoozed at his usual place near the cookstove, and Ivy had to step over the old hound more than once as she went about her task.

"'*Under a spreading chestnut tree, the village smithy stands,*'" Gwen suddenly quoted as she scrubbed a shirt on the washboard. "'*The smith, a mighty man is he, with large and sinewy hands; and the muscles of his brawny arms are strong as iron bands. . .*'"

"Must you recite that now?" Ivy asked her stepsister, perturbed when an image of Craig Watson breezed past the shuttered door of her mind. It had been difficult to bar invasive thoughts of the man ever since she'd last seen him, when he offered her a ride home in his wagon. Now the poem brought vivid pictures to mind.

The eleven-year-old turned solemn blue eyes Ivy's way. "I'm supposed to know Henry Wadsworth Longfellow's poem by tomorrow, when Mr. Rayborne will make me stand up in front of class to recite it. I have to practice." She began scrubbing again. "'*His hair is crisp, and black, and long, his face is like the tan; His brow is wet with honest sweat, He earns whate'er he can. . .*'"

"I'm going outside to get some air," Ivy muttered, grabbing her woolen cloak.

Her mother's gentle gaze met hers from across the room, where she stirred lye-water in a kettle heating over the fire. "While you're out, please gather more fuel, Ivy."

"Yes, Mama." Ivy grimaced in distaste but wrapped a scarf around her head, pulled on her discolored ball gloves, and reached for a nearby basket. She despised this chore above all others, but the fire was getting low, and she was the only one available to do it.

A bitter, cold wind chapped her face and bit into her, almost sweeping her the rest of the way outside. She struggled with the door to close it. Searching the frozen ground for the brown lumps, she walked a short distance until she found some. Scarcity of trees in the area made this type of fuel a necessity. Wrinkling her nose in distaste, she picked up the hardened cow patty with gloved fingers and quickly dropped it into the basket. She'd kept her old ball gloves for just this purpose. She wouldn't dream of touching the disgusting things with her bare hands as her stepsisters did!

Soon her basket was filled, and Ivy straightened. Her lower back had cramped from bending over so much, but she wasn't about to rub the ache out with the glove she'd just used. As she trudged against the wind and back to the sod house built of "Nebraska marble," as the locals were fond of calling the earthen bricks, she critically appraised it. Even prettying the name didn't change its appearance, making Ivy certain that the man who had coined the phrase did so out of a warped sense of humor. Their home was dirt with dead, brown grass growing on its roof. And the fuel for their fire was dried cow manure. If her grandmother could see the depths to which her only granddaughter had fallen, she would likely have a fit of apoplexy.

"Well, I think she's horrid!" Gwen's voice coming from around the other side of the soddy brought Ivy up short. She hesitated at the rear of her stepfather's home, wondering if she should make her presence known or keep quiet.

"I hate her," Gwen added, her words emphatic. "She thinks she owns the world and everyone's supposed to wait on her."

"She does do her part of the chores," Crystin reminded. "And Dada says it's not right to hate."

"Maybe. But just by looking at her face, you can tell that she clearly thinks all work is beneath her. And she doesn't do half of what she should. Miss Ivy, queen of Boston society." Her voice took on an affected tone. "You, girl, iron my gloves and darn my stockings. *I'm* going to the ball!"

Crystin giggled. "You can't iron gloves, Gwen."

"I know. But if she had her way, she'd probably give the order to have it done. She's so mean and bossy. The way she yelled at you when her stupid old brooch went missing is proof."

"But I did take it to look at it." Crystin sounded both repentant and puzzled.

"Yes, but she has so many fancy things. She could share instead of flaunting them in our faces like she's better than us. Not everyone has a mother or grand-mother who has pretty things to give."

"You mean us?" Crystin's voice was solemn. "Was our mama poor when our dada met her?"

"She had the riches that counted. Inside beauty is what Dada called it. Sweetness of spirit."

"Do you remember her?"

"Some. Not a lot."

"Me, either." There was a short pause. "Gwen, do you like our new mama, even if she is from Boston where the rich people live?"

"She's a lot nicer than Ivy. Yeah, I like her."

It was a moment before Crystin spoke again. "Is our dada poor?"

"No, leastways not poor like we were in Wales when we lived in the mining camp. But you were too young to remember those days. Now then, cheer up,

Crystin. Who needs Miss Uppity's old Boston things anyway?"

The girls' voices grew stronger, and Ivy ducked around the opposite corner before they came into view. From her hiding place, she saw that between them they held a large pail and were headed in the direction of a nearby stream. Probably to get more rinse water.

"I think she's sad," Crystin said. "Because she don't fit in. That's what Maryanne says."

"She could fit in if she wanted to," Gwen shot back. "She just doesn't want to."

Although the words were accurate, they cut Ivy to the quick. She never entertained any doubts that her new stepsisters held anything but dislike for her, though the little one seemed to like her a bit. She'd taken up for her, anyway. Yet why should Ivy care?

She stiffened her back and walked to the front of the soddy, against the wind, letting it dry the few unexplainable tears that teased the corners of her eyes. The girls were right. She did not belong. So maybe it was time to go back to where she did.

Craig worked the lever of the huge bellows, fanning air over the fire to get it hot enough to repair a plow. His mind went to thoughts of Ivy. Weeks ago when he'd seen her on the road, after delivering an order to an old farmer who didn't get around as well as he used to, Craig had been touched to watch the encounter between her and Amy. It didn't take a lot of figuring to realize what must have happened. Craig had perfect vision and hadn't been so far away that he couldn't spot the cracked eggs and overturned basket at the side of the road. He had watched Ivy take an egg from Amy's outstretched hand, then give her something in return.

The girl's jubilant face afterward as she turned in his direction and ran for home—like a shining sunbeam parting the gray sky—made it obvious that Ivy had paid a handsome price for the hen offering. Ivy *did* have a good heart underneath all those ribbons and furbelows. He'd known it all along. And hearing her laughter caress the chill air, Craig's own heart had soared within his chest. Her laugh reminded him of small tinkling bells and produced a smile on his face, a smile that stretched his lips even now.

Seeing by the white color of the fire that he'd made it too hot, Craig stopped fanning the flames and grabbed his washer. He immersed the bundle of tied-together twigs in water, then flicked the drops over the blaze to bring it down to a steady yellow glow. Thinking about Ivy was breaking his concentration, and that could prove dangerous. Besides, he had another busy day ahead.

Craig had finished up five of his orders when young Wesley ran into the smithy. "Mr. Owen said to tell you something came for you today by freight wagon," he blurted, out of breath. "I have to get home now, or Pa'll tan my hide."

Before Craig could respond, Wesley was gone. Craig eyed the sawhorse table along one wall, holding the orders still needing to be filled, then looked at what he'd accomplished that afternoon. Deciding it wouldn't hurt to take a short break, he put his tools away, exchanged his leather apron for his coat, and settled his hat firmly on his head.

Once outside, he moved against the cold wind toward the opposite edge of town that held the school and post office. The sky was blue and clear, and the sun gleamed off the windows of the modest-sized building. Inside and to the right, a colorful blanket hung from the ceiling. Through the gap, empty benches revealed that school was out, though the young teacher still sat behind her desk. To Craig's left, a customer stood in front of Mr. Owen's counter, and Craig's stomach did a little rollover when he saw who it was.

"Miss Leander," Mr. Owen patiently stated, "you should cut some words from that telegram to make it shorter. I charge by the word, you know."

"Yes, I know. However, every word is essential to the message."

"I understand that, ma'am, but, well, for example, this part: 'It is imperative that I hear from you before the snows begin to fall and travel becomes difficult. I am most eager to return to Boston within the next two weeks.' Well, now, ma'am. That's repeating something you said in the first sentence."

Craig's heart dropped to his boot tips. Ivy was leaving?

He shuffled his foot, unintentionally gaining her attention. She looked over her shoulder. Her eyes widened when she saw him, and her face paled.

"Hello, Boston," Craig said quietly.

"How much of that did you hear?" Her blue eyes were anxious.

"Enough to know that you plan on breaking your poor ma's heart."

Her mouth thinning, Ivy faced Mr. Owen. "I want the entire message telegraphed. I can pay for it."

The bearded man shook his head but didn't pursue his arguments. "There's a package over there for you, Craig. For some reason, it got dropped off here instead of at Mrs. Llewynn's."

Craig nodded his thanks and went to retrieve what he saw was a crate. His new caldron must have arrived. Seeing it was too big to carry, he decided to come back for it with a wagon later. He'd already settled all accounts with Mrs. Llewynn, so the caldron was his. After giving a solemn nod to Mr. Owen along with a brief explanation that he'd be back soon, then a nod to Ivy, who hesitantly turned to glance at him, Craig exited the building.

❧

Ivy concluded her business with the postal clerk. Taking a deep breath, she stepped outside. She'd half-expected Craig to be waiting for her, so she wasn't at all surprised to see him leaning against a hitching post, his arms crossed. What did surprise her was his somber appearance, so much different from the usual one with the expression lines ready to stretch out in amusement.

She moved down the road, intending to ignore him.

"Why are you leaving us, Boston?" He straightened as she walked past, his long legs easily matching her stride.

"I don't see that it's any of your business."

"Maybe not. But you're going to hurt a lot of people by your decision to go."

"I do not belong here. This isn't my home and never has been."

"Do you really think you've given it a decent enough try?"

Needled by his words, she stopped walking and spun to face him. "Just what difference does it make to you, Mr. Watson? I should think you'd be glad to see me go. I haven't exactly been sociable toward you—toward anyone here."

A boyish grin lifted the corners of his mouth. "Not even to the hogs or the chickens?"

She felt her own lips lift upward in a smile, surprising her. She wanted to remain annoyed with this man but found it difficult to do so. "No, definitely not to them. Incidentally, I discovered you were right about Mr. Stony Jack's hog being able to 'count.' Although my stepfather explained away the incident as Mr. Stone teaching his animal to fetch objects rather than the hog itself being intelligent. Still, I suppose I do owe you an apology for that first day we met. I was upset and weary from the train ride, and I, um, acted rather supercilious toward you."

"Oh, now I wouldn't have gone and called you conceited, exactly. More sure of yourself and everybody else than anything." His grin widened.

The man was a scholar? Amazing. Ivy hadn't reckoned on him having enough schooling to possess any knowledge of the word she'd used to describe her bad behavior. "Then I'm forgiven?"

"I don't hold grudges."

"Thank you." She hesitated. "About what happened in there just now—I would appreciate it if you'd keep this our little secret. I don't wish for anyone to know of my plans."

"You planning on running away in the middle of the night?"

"Of course not! I simply want to approach my mother with the news when I feel the timing is appropriate."

He studied her a long moment. Uneasy, she glanced away from the steady look in his eyes. "I'll keep your secret," he finally said, "but on one condition."

A sense of misgiving made her gather her brows. "What condition?"

"That you let me take you to the church meeting next Sunday and go on an outing with me afterward."

"Church meeting?"

"You hadn't heard? A preacher is coming through here next week. We'll meet in the schoolhouse for services."

"No, I hadn't heard." Ivy thought quickly. A few hours with the man seemed a small price to pay for his silence. "All right, I'll go with you."

The warmth of his smile took her breath away. "I'll be looking forward to it, Boston. Well, I should get back to work now. I have orders to fill. Afternoon." With a quirky tip of his dusty hat in farewell, he headed down the road to his smithy.

Ivy continued to stare after Craig until he reached the huge doors of the building, then she realized what she was doing. With a frown, she shook herself out of her trance and walked in the direction of her stepfather's claim.

Chapter 4

I doubt he'll come. The snow is too much like ice for a wagon."

At Crystin's solemn words to Ivy, she looked out the window again, all hopes fading. The light from the morning's gray skies revealed a world clothed in a blanket of white stretching as far as the eye could see. Crystin was right. It was doubtful Craig would show. Ivy smoothed the skirt of one of her best dresses, a rich maroon brocade embellished with black ribbons matching the one she'd woven into her hair. Around her neck she wore her garnet brooch on another black velvet ribbon, and her fingers went to the stone, tracing its square outline. She told herself that she was relieved Craig hadn't shown, that this released her from their agreement. Yet the feelings coursing through her were not those of gladness.

"Never mind, Ivy." Her mother's soft voice broke through her thoughts. "We have each other, and we can read from the Holy Bible as we always do."

Ivy glanced at her mother, and concern replaced disappointment. She didn't look at all well. Her face was drawn, and her eyes had lost the luster that usually made them shimmer like precious sapphires.

Ivy went to kneel beside her chair and took her hand. "Mama, aren't you feeling well?"

"Of course, I'm fine. Just a little stomach upset. Hand me my Bible, dearest."

Ivy did so, and her mother opened the gilt-edged book she'd brought with her from Boston, reverently touching the pages as she skimmed through them. Her stepfather couldn't read English, though he spoke it, but he also often spoke in Welsh to his girls to keep their language from dying. Still, Ivy noticed that he seemed to derive great satisfaction from listening to Mama read the English words in her soothing voice.

" 'Behold, how good and how pleasant it is when brethren dwell together in unity....' " As her mother continued to read the passage from Psalms, Ivy inwardly squirmed, though outside she remained as still as she'd been taught. Afterward, her mother closed the book, and no one spoke for a moment.

"Dada, when will Uncle Dai come to see us?" Gwen asked.

The question surprised everyone and seemed to hang in the air. Ivy knew the girls had been taught not to speak unless they were spoken to. She glanced at her stepfather to gauge his reaction. His face grew red, and he looked away toward the cookstove. "He chose the road to take. No one forced it upon him."

"But can he not just come see us?" Gwen insisted softly. "Nana says the same thing Mama does—family is important. Won't you write a letter to Uncle Dai and ask him to come, like Nana wants? He can stay with Aunt Winifred, since they're making their home into a boardinghouse."

"Gwendolyn! That is enough. I will have no more talk on the matter."

Ivy jumped. Even Old Rufus lifted his head off his paws to look at his master. Ivy had never before heard her stepfather raise his tone in anger, and she studied him curiously. Just what kind of man was this Uncle Dai to get such a rise from Gavin?

"I'm sorry, Dada." Gwen's lower lip trembled, and her eyes grew moist. Gavin held out his hand to his daughter, and she went to hug him.

Before Ivy could dwell more deeply on the subject of Uncle Dai, the sound of faint bells came from outside, growing louder. Old Rufus pricked his ears and padded to the door, fully alert, his tail wagging. He let out a bark. Crystin darted to the window.

"It's Mr. Watson!" she cried. "And he's in a sleigh!"

Ivy quickly rose to see, Gwen right behind her. Sure enough, Craig sat inside a sleigh being pulled by his dark gray horse. Bells rang from the harness, and Ivy wondered if Craig had made them.

Crystin turned excitedly. "Can we go, Mama? Can we?"

Ivy's mother smiled and nodded. Amid many squeals, the girls grabbed their coats and shrugged into them, pulling scarves about their necks and hats over their ears. Ivy also went about the ritual of preparing to face the outside cold, but she did so more sedately than the girls.

Inside, her heart mocked her with its rapid beats.

Ivy met Craig at the door. "Hello," she said, feeling at a strange loss for words. She motioned to Gwen and Crystin, who appeared at her side. "My sisters are coming with us."

"Of course they can come." The smile he gave them was genuine. He bent down to scratch Old Rufus between the ears. "There's room, but you two children might have to snuggle close like fox cubs."

At this, Crystin giggled. To be on the safe side, Ivy planned the seating arrangement so that the slight Crystin was sandwiched between her and Craig, and Gwen sat behind them. The ride to town was filled with the little girls' excited chatter and Craig's patient answers to their questions.

Due to the nasty weather, the schoolhouse wasn't crowded, but Ivy was surprised to see among the townsfolk there a family who owned a claim a few miles away. The Reverend Michaels was young with bushy red eyebrows, long sideburns that swept down his jaws, and a decidedly Irish accent. He had a way of spearing a person with his intense blue eyes, and his words were full of something that convicted Ivy's heart. The passages he read from 1 Corinthians about love seared her conscience, and she thought back to what her mother had read earlier.

Perhaps Ivy never had tried to exhibit Christian charity or goodwill toward anyone while living in Leaning Tree and only expected to be treated kindly by others. Yet had she truly expected even that? She wasn't sure what she'd expected; she'd been so angry with her mother and new stepfather those first few months after she'd moved here. Yet the anger had begun to subside at some point without her realizing it. When had that happened?

After the rousing service, which lasted all morning, the people visited. Winifred pulled Ivy aside and asked how her parents were. Ivy explained that her mother wasn't feeling well, and both Winifred and Bronwyn shared a smile. "It will soon pass," Winifred said. "Give her tea with mint. It has helped me." She blushed.

By their reactions and words, Ivy felt a stab of dread. Oh no. Her mother couldn't be in a family way!

"It is the way of things," Bronwyn said, her blue eyes wise. "She is still young and strong. She will be fine."

Ivy nodded, though inside she felt like a newly broken wheel cast aside from the stagecoach whose destination promised a better life. How could Mother do this to her? How could Ivy leave Leaning Tree now?

"Are you all right?" Craig asked when they returned to his sleigh. Both Gwen and Crystin ran ahead and jumped in back, leaving Ivy no choice but to sit beside Craig. She did so stiffly, and he pulled up the bristly fur lap robe over their legs. She shivered when his arm and leg inadvertently pressed against hers in the confined space.

"Cold?" He pulled the lap robe up farther before taking the reins.

The warmth surging through her blocked out most of the chill.

"How did you get this sleigh?" she asked, raising her voice above the wind that resulted from the vehicle's movement once it was in motion. If they talked about inconsequential matters, she might be able to concentrate on those issues and not on the man sitting so close to her.

"A customer asked me to fix it for him last year, but he ended up moving back East. When I reminded him about the sleigh before he left, he told me that if I could fix it, I could have it. It was in bad shape when he brought it to me. It had hit a tree, and the runners were twisted."

"Did you make the bells on the horse's harness, too?"

"My cousin did. He's a silversmith who I'm trying to convince to move here. He's considering it. The town is growing, and by this time next year, I'd be surprised if the population hasn't doubled. We even have our own doc now."

Doubt edging her mind, Ivy looked at the ramshackle town. Either Craig had high aspirations or she was blind.

"Still doubt that Leaning Tree amounts to much?" he asked.

She shrugged, deciding it best not to comment. When he didn't steer the sleigh left at the turnoff leading to her stepfather's soddy, Ivy looked at him. "Where are you taking me?"

"To a little piece of the future."

"Where?" Her brows shot upward.

"You'll see. Relax, Ivy. You did agree to an outing after the service, and we do have the girls along as chaperones."

Some chaperones. A glance over her shoulder revealed that Gwen and Crystin had their heads tucked underneath their lap robe. Occasionally, a giggle would escape from beneath the fur.

"All right. I suppose," she gave her grudging consent.

Craig steered the sleigh by a copse of trees growing along the stream. White coated any remaining leaves and branches, and the water lazily trickled under a thin crust of ice.

"See that?" Craig pointed to a tree whose trunk leaned at an angle toward the water. "That's how the town got its name."

Ivy was interested despite her resolve not to be. She'd never been in this area before. Where her stepfather lived, there wasn't a tree in sight, though a scant few grew on the outskirts of town. She'd recently heard her stepfather and Winifred's husband discuss a man named J. Sterling Morton, who'd proposed an idea for everyone in Nebraska to plant a tree next spring. He felt the economy would benefit from the wide-scale planting. Ivy looked over the vast land of untouched white that the sleigh now faced. It would take a great many trees to make that happen! She tried to imagine all that empty white being broken up by forests of trees or even a small wood.

"What do you see?" Craig's voice caught her attention.

What did she see? "Um, snow, and a lot of land. Gray skies above."

"Know what I see?" She shook her head, and he continued, "I see opportunity. A land that's ready for growth and is just waiting to be farmed or used in other ways for the good of the community, even the nation. Miles and miles of rich, fertile soil ready for the first touch of that plow."

She turned her head to look at him. "Are you planning to trade in your anvil and become a farmer?"

He chuckled. "No. But where there are farming tools, mules, and horses, there's a need for a blacksmith. And where there's virgin land, there's a need for people with enough courage to carve out a promising future. People who won't say no to a challenge, who keep on when all they want to do is quit." His gaze briefly swept the land again. "And I believe you're one of those people, Boston. I believe you've got what it takes."

Ivy jerked in surprise. "Surely, you're teasing me."

"No. You've got gumption. I noticed that the first day we met. While it's true you weren't happy to come here and felt forced into it, you made do and adjusted the best you could. I have a feeling that if you'd also adjust your thinking and try to see some good in this town, you might find that this could be more of a home to you than Boston ever was."

"I sincerely doubt that."

He shrugged. "Just don't close your mind to the possibility. It may be that you coming here was all part of God's plan."

His words irritated her, and she looked away to the sweeping vista. "Please take me home, Mr. Watson."

"Don't you think you could learn to call me Craig?"

"Only if you'll stop calling me Boston!" The words shot out of her mouth before she could stop them.

Craig laughed, a rich, exuberant sound that warmed her clear through and brought two small heads from beneath the fur lap robe. "I can't promise I'll always remember," he said. "But I like the name Ivy, so I'll surely try."

That wasn't what she'd meant—she'd meant for him to address her properly by her surname. She opened her mouth to tell him so, then snapped it shut. Oh, what was the use? From what she knew of the man, Craig Watson would likely do as he pleased. Moreover, she did notice that the people in Leaning Tree weren't big on formality. So maybe no one would make anything of it.

Another pair of giggles brought her sharp focus to the girls, who quickly ducked their heads back underneath the blanket.

Ivy watched her mother pull the flat iron from the top of the cookstove and continue to press the wrinkles out of Gavin's shirt. She turned back to her own task of kneading bread dough. Since Winifred and Bronwyn had spoken to her after Reverend Michael's message three weeks ago, Ivy had kept a close eye on her mother. Mama hadn't told her she was expecting, but that was little surprise. Such things weren't discussed in polite society, and her mother had been raised in Boston, too. What had happened to make Mama forget that? Why would she wish to leave behind a life filled with every luxury imaginable to marry a poor farmer?

At the other end of the table, Crystin painstakingly used a pencil nub to write out a short essay on the discarded brown paper that had been wrapped around a parcel from the general store. By the light of a kerosene lamp, Gwen read the book on colonial life her teacher had lent her. Outside, the night was still and not as cold as it had been. December proved to be milder than Ivy expected, with few scattered snows. Yet she'd been warned that January had the teeth of a wolf—and being snowbound for days or weeks wasn't an improbability.

"What are you working on so diligently, Crystin?" Ivy's mother asked.

Crystin looked up from her paper. "We must write an essay on what we like most about Christmas and then tell what's most important." She looked in the direction of the sleeping quarters of the two-room soddy. "Will we go to Aunt Winifred's and pull taffy, Dada?"

Gavin walked into the room and sat at the opposite end of the table. He pulled a handmade pipe from his mouth and turned his blue eyes to his youngest daughter. "Much will depend on the weather."

"I hope we do," Crystin said wistfully. "That's one of the things I like best about Christmas."

"I like the *Mari Lwyd*," Gwen said, putting down her book. She turned her gaze toward Ivy, who stood less than a foot away. "That's where a big horse's skull knocks on your door to ask a question, and if you get it wrong..." She mashed her elbows together, hands wide apart, then brought her palms to connect with a loud smack directed Ivy's way. Startled, Ivy jumped.

"Snap!" Gwen continued gleefully, a smug look in her eye. "Off with your head."

"Gwendolyn, I will have no more of such foolish talk," her father said sternly. "Or perhaps you shall not get the pink sugar mouse in your stocking this Christmas. You are too young to remember the customs practiced in the old country."

"Did the horse's skull really bite people's heads off?" Crystin's eyes were wide.

"No." Gavin directed another severe look at Gwen before explaining. "The *Mari Lwyd* was an ancient ritual for luck the townsfolk played among one another, a game of wits. No one was hurt."

"What's your favorite Christmas memory, Dada?" Crystin asked.

Gavin's eyes grew misty. "I remember going with my brother, Dai, to the *Plygain,* since the time we were young men. It is a service where the townsmen sing carols and songs and read from the Bible. Always, it takes place in the dark hours of Christmas morning before the dawn."

"While the women pull taffy!" Crystin inserted eagerly. "Nana told me that."

"Yes." Gavin's word came softly. He stared into the distance, and Ivy wondered if he was thinking about his brother.

"What about you, Ivy?" Crystin suddenly asked. "What's your favorite thing about Christmas?"

Ivy stopped kneading the dough, surprised the child would ask but heartened that she had. She thought back to happier Christmases. "In Boston my grandmother gives a festive party and a grand ball during the Christmas season. Everyone of importance is invited, from the mayor to the wealthy ship merchants to the doctors and their families. People come from miles around to enjoy one of her affairs. There's dancing until all hours of the night and lavish banquets with roast goose and plum pudding. Among the many pastries she has her chef make are ladyfingers, since she knows how much I fancy them."

Crystin looked horrified. "You eat ladies' fingers?"

Ivy shared a smile with her mother. "They are thin white cookies the size of a woman's finger. That's how they got their name, I suppose. You dip them in chocolate, or they have chocolate spread over them. I've eaten them both ways."

"A cookie with white sugar? I can't remember the last time I had white sugar."

"Brown sugar is just as good, Crystin," Gwen said, a sting in her voice. She ducked her head back toward her book before her father could see, but the look she shot Ivy spoke volumes.

Ivy knew the white variety was expensive because it was scarce. Most settlers used brown sugar instead. Seeing Crystin's wistful expression, Ivy wished she hadn't spoken.

She pounded the dough, placed it in a pan, then covered it with a towel and left it near the warmth of the stove to rise. Thankfully, this time she hadn't forgotten the yeast. Last time she'd made bread, her thoughts had been centered on Craig instead of the contents she mixed in the bowl, and she had omitted that most essential ingredient. Gwen had teased her mercilessly about her flat bread, and Ivy had bitten her tongue so as not to respond sharply.

She recalled the last time she'd seen Craig, in late November when he'd taken her for another ride in his sleigh before that first snow melted to mush. He'd told her then that he also had a stepmother and stepsister, and adjustments had been difficult for him, too, at first. None of them were able to get along, so he could sympathize with Ivy's plight.

Then he'd said something to make her think. He told her that one day his stepsister went missing. During the search, Craig realized he didn't actually want her gone, as he'd often thought after one of their rows. The dread he'd felt until they found her safe in the tall grasses helped to dissolve the distance between them, and he was able to open his heart and see that his stepmother and stepsister weren't quite so bad as he'd thought. In fact, according to Craig, they had formed a caring relationship before the women had moved with his father farther west to California.

Ivy wondered why Craig hadn't also gone but was glad he'd decided to stay. To her amazement, she'd found him good company.

Ivy looked at Gwen and Crystin. They could be a trial at times, especially Gwen, but Ivy wouldn't wish evil upon either of them. Again, memory of Craig's words during that first sleigh ride revisited her—that if she would only adjust her thinking, she might find some good in Leaning Tree. Ivy pondered the idea and recalled the past months of living on the prairie.

She hadn't been fond of the inch-long worms that appeared on the walls, ceiling, and floor after a hard rain months ago. Nor did she like the dirt that sifted down and once landed in her bowl of fried corn mush. And she detested the snakes that liked to hide in tall grasses—and the one that preferred the soddy this past summer and had suddenly dropped down from the inside wall, landed at the foot of her cot, and frightened her silly. She had jumped out of bed and run outside screaming, while Gwen had doubled over laughing. Still, Ivy had to admit that the little sod house stayed warmer in winter and cooler in summer than a wooden one, and since her stepfather had plastered and whitewashed the inside walls, the place even seemed somewhat cheerful.

She enjoyed the huge canopy of sky that was often a rich, robin's egg blue and stretched on endlessly without any buildings or trees to mar it. Wildflowers in spring dressed the grass with abundant splashes of crimson, gold, and purple, pleasing to the eye. And when she stood outside and looked in all four directions at the miles of windswept grassland, an exhilarating feeling of freedom sometimes surged through her.

That was the sole thing about Boston that Ivy didn't like. Sometimes she'd felt confined. Here, anytime she felt the need to leave the cramped soddy, she could walk outside for miles with nothing but the constant, whispering wind for company—and Old Rufus, when the hound chose to trot beside her. The hard work that resulted from living on the prairie and all the walking she'd done had trimmed her figure and given her muscles a strength they'd never before had. Town wasn't so far away that she couldn't visit, and often she did, though she had yet to make friends. Unless she could count Craig Watson as a friend. . .

A rush of warmth tingled through Ivy, and she attributed it to standing so near the cookstove. She stepped over to the window and parted the curtains made of flour sacks embroidered with green flowers. A thick frost covered the ground, and a half moon provided little light. She might not want to admit it, but she was growing accustomed to living in this place.

"Gwen, Crystin, come with me to tend the animals," Ivy's stepfather suddenly said.

"Yes, Dada," they both replied.

Once the three left the soddy with Old Rufus trotting beside them, Ivy watched their trek to a smaller soddy that her stepfather had made to house the cow, the horse, and the chickens in winter.

"Ivy, a word with you." Mother's soft voice bore a trace of sobriety, and Ivy knew she must have signaled Gavin to leave with the children so that the two of them could speak privately. She turned to face her mother.

"I know life has been difficult for you here and that you miss Boston a great deal," her mama began. She sat down on the bench and laid one work-worn hand over the other on the table, then stared at them. "To understand why I wouldn't allow you to stay with your grandmother, as you asked of me, I would have to recall the past and speak of issues I long to forget. Suffice it to say, my mother and I had opposing views as to what was important, and I didn't want you under her sole influence."

Ivy took a seat across the table, waiting for her to go on.

"I love my mother, but we see things differently. She wasn't pleased when I married your father. She wanted me to wed someone wealthier, though your father wasn't poor. When he died, I was devastated and chose to move in with her. You were only six at the time."

Ivy knew this already but nodded in acknowledgment.

"Wealth and position are of paramount importance to my mother. It's true that I enjoyed many luxuries while growing up in my parents' home, but your father helped me to see that there were more important matters in life, such as God and family." Her mother reached across to take hold of Ivy's hand. "I wanted you to learn this, too. Your father would have wanted it."

"I know, Mama," Ivy said, her voice a wisp.

"You will soon be seventeen," her mother said. "A woman of marriageable age. I know I cannot keep you with me forever if you wish to go, but I ask that you remain here until early summer. You see," a faint blush touched her face, "I am expecting and will need your help. Mother Morgan told me that you knew."

Ivy looked at her lap and nodded. She'd never spoken of that first telegram she'd sent to Grandmother but wondered if Mama might have somehow learned of it. Once Ivy found out about her mother's delicate condition, she'd sent another telegram, this one telling her grandmother that she would have to delay her travel plans until after the baby came.

"I only want what's best for you, Ivy, and I considered it best to bring you with us to Nebraska. I wanted us to be a family. If I erred in that respect, forgive me. I don't want us to drift apart as Gavin and his brother have done."

Ivy's head snapped up. "Oh no, Mama!" She moved off the bench to hug her mother. "I could never feel any ill will toward you. I know that you love me."

Her mother smoothed Ivy's hair, much as she had done when Ivy was a child. "I spoke to you of this because you're old enough to understand such matters now. You've matured in the months we've lived here, and I thought it time that you know the lay of things. However, your grandmother loves you as well, Ivy. It is not my wish for you to bear any ill feelings toward her."

"I don't, Mama." Ivy thought about the money her grandmother had given her with explicit instructions not to tell her mother. Grandmother often did things like that, allowing Ivy to have anything she wanted against her mother's wishes and without her knowledge. As Ivy grew older, she'd felt uneasy about the duplicity. Perhaps she should tell Mother of the fifty dollars.

"Well, then!" her mother exclaimed, her voice light, signaling an end to the serious discussion. "If I'm to learn how to make a pink sugar mouse, I must find a way to do so with the ingredients I have. I shall make one tonight once the girls are asleep."

Ivy pulled away. "A pink sugar mouse?"

"A Welsh custom. I don't want Gwen and Crystin to be disappointed on Christmas morning when they look into their stockings."

"Can't Winifred or her mother do it, since they likely know how and we plan to be at their house on Christmas Eve?"

"Winifred has enough to do preparing for the social that she plans to hold for anyone who will come. It will be the last gathering before she turns her home into a boardinghouse this spring."

"Still, Christmas is a week away."

"Yes, but I need the practice. I've never made anything remotely like a sugar mouse." Her mother smiled. "Will you help me?"

"But, Mama, you know I haven't yet learned to cook without burning what I do make!"

"I know. Yet this can be something we learn together. We can help one another. Mother Morgan told me some of how it's done, but I've no idea how to make the mouse pink! Berry juice from preserves perhaps? What do you think?"

Ivy smiled. "That might work." Suddenly she felt lighthearted and looked forward to the event. Who would have thought the idea of making a pink sugar mouse with her mother could give her such joy?

"Will all the townspeople come to Winifred's on Christmas Eve?" she asked.

"All have been invited. Whether they will come or not is another matter." A gleam lit her mother's eye. "Was there anyone in particular you were inquiring after?"

Ivy rose from the bench to sort through the freshly pressed laundry and collect her things. "Of course not." Yet when thoughts of Craig visited, she realized that wasn't entirely true.

Chapter 5

Christmas Eve arrived cold and windy with a few inches of new snow. Yet the weather wasn't bad enough for Gavin to cancel their outing to his sister's place. They bundled up for the ride in the wagon. Before they could leave the soddy, Old Rufus barked and ran to the door. Soon the jingling of bells alerted them to company. Ivy hurried to the window to see, as did Gwen and Crystin.

"It's Craig, and he's in his sleigh!" Crystin announced.

Gwen threw open the door. "Hulloa!"

For a moment, Craig seemed uncertain. "Hello. I came to ask permission to take Ivy to the social."

Ivy felt her face warm while her stepfather seemed to mull over the request. From the twinkle in his eyes, Ivy wondered if this was the first he'd known about Craig's invitation. "I think you'd best ask Ivy," Gavin instructed.

"Ivy?" Craig looked her way, his brown eyes hopeful. "Will you accompany me?"

She hesitated, not wanting to seem too eager, then nodded and walked toward his sleigh. She did enjoy his company, even if considering him for a husband was out of the question. Instantly he scrambled from the conveyance to help her into it.

"Can we go, too, Dada?" Ivy heard Crystin ask from behind.

"Not this time. There is a pout; now then, I'll have none of it," he said a little more sternly. "Or you will have no taffy pulling this night."

"Oh no, Dada, I'll be good," Crystin hurried to say.

As though afraid he might indeed change his mind, both Gwen and Crystin scampered in the direction of the wagon, which sat hitched up and waiting by the barn. Gavin chuckled and nodded to both Craig and Ivy before he and Ivy's mother set off in that direction.

The sleigh whizzed over the snow the short two miles to Winifred's, while the wagon bumped over small drifts at a much slower pace. Ivy noticed that the Bradfords' wagon was coming from the east, from the direction of their claim, and also headed toward town. All sixteen of the Bradfords appeared to be packed inside.

"I'm surprised they're taking the time to go to something like this," Ivy mused.

"A social is good enough reason for everyone to put off work for a few hours," Craig explained. "They're few and far between, especially this time of year. I worked extra hard this week at the smithy getting orders filled so that I would have today to enjoy with my neighbors."

Despite the chill air blowing on parts of her face not covered by the woolen scarf, Ivy's skin and insides warmed with embarrassment. She hadn't reckoned on Craig hearing her observation about the Bradfords. The man must have the hearing of a hound! Yet she was glad that he would be there—just as a friend, of course. Ivy certainly had no other reason for desiring his company.

Sleigh bells ringing, they soon arrived at the white timbered house. A curl of gray smoke rose into the sky from the chimney. Craig took care of the horse and sleigh, while Ivy hurried up the wooden steps. Thankfully, they weren't coated in ice.

Winifred met her at the door. "Hello, Ivy. I'm glad you could make it! But. . ." Her brow creased, and she looked behind Ivy in the direction of the road. "Where are my brother, your mother, and my nieces?"

"They took the wagon. Craig brought me." Too late, she realized the slip of using his first name in public.

Winifred smiled. "Come in and get warm."

Ivy did so, though she left her cloak on. It was cold inside even with the fire to warm the parlor. From what Ivy knew, the Pettigrasses were the only people in Leaning Tree to own a genuine parlor, but then, Winifred's husband was wealthy, though not as wealthy as Ivy's grandmother. As Ivy drew nearer to the blaze, she noticed wood didn't burn there but the usual "Nebraska coal," as her stepfather chose to call the cow refuse. She looked toward the corner where someone had chopped down a wild plum bush to use as a Christmas tree and had decorated it with strings of popcorn.

"Greetings, Ivy," Bronwyn said, coming from another room, a fine china cup and saucer in her hand. "Have some wassail to warm yourself." She offered the steaming cup to Ivy, who gratefully took a short sip. Piping hot apple, cloves, and cinnamon teased her tongue while delicious warmth filled her.

The door constantly opened as more people arrived. A few were Welsh immigrants who'd also settled in Leaning Tree like the Morgans. It appeared that everyone who lived nearby was making a showing, and the parlor soon felt cramped and warm. Men and women talked and visited. Older children rushed outdoors to amuse themselves, while the younger girls sat in a circle to play with the corncob dolls they'd brought from home.

As the afternoon progressed, some of the families left the gathering early. Mrs. Llewynn's husband, Milton, brought out his fiddle, and lively music filled the place. A few men, including Craig, circled the baldheaded fiddle player. They clapped their hands and stomped their feet to the frenetic melody while the women flocked together and chattered away like magpies who hadn't seen each other for an entire season. The topic was the second theft of one of Mrs. Llewynn's chickens just that morning.

"Well," Mrs. Johnson, the feed store owner's wife, said, "I think it's just horrendous. And on Christmas Eve, besides. Whoever would do such a thing? A definite ill-bred churl, if you ask me." Her gaze speared Mrs. Bradford, and Ivy felt the look was deliberate. Did Rowena Johnson suspect one of the Bradford children of being a chicken thief?

"I'll be thankful when we get a sheriff for this town," Mrs. Llewynn said. "As well as a preacher." Suddenly she was all smiles. "I hear, dear Winifred, that the men of Leaning Tree asked your husband to act as our first mayor."

"Yes," Winifred said. "It is all so exciting."

"Then he has agreed?" the doctor's wife, Adella Miller, asked.

Ivy's attention was diverted to Bronwyn, who offered each of the guests their choice from a platter layered with fancy iced cookies and sliced fruitcake. Ivy had never seen Crystin's eyes go so round as they did when her grandmother held out the tray toward her. The child moved her small hand in the air over each item, as though uncertain of which to take, then opted for a slice of fruitcake. Ivy took a cookie. It was brittle, but it wasn't bad.

"Your mother tells me of the pink sugar mouse and your attempts to make one for my granddaughters," Bronwyn said, eyes twinkling.

Ivy felt the blush rise to her face and was thankful no one was within hearing distance. Crystin had taken her cake and moved toward one of the Bradford children. "Yes, and sad attempts they were, too. They crumbled to nothing."

Bronwyn chuckled. "Tonight, after the girls sleep, I will show you both how it is done. Pleased I am that your mama tries so hard to be a good mother to Gwendolyn and Crystin. The Lord smiled the day Gavin met your mama. Before she came, lonely were the girls to have no mother."

Ivy saw the truth of what the elderly woman said, though her poetic way of speaking was a bit difficult to follow at times. Ivy's mother was kind and unselfish, wanting only the best for her family. She had adapted to this wild prairie life and was a good wife to Gavin, too.

"It is also well to have you as part of our family, Ivy," Bronwyn continued. "There is kind, you are, to be a good sister to the girls. To you as an example they look."

If Ivy wasn't well trained in social etiquette, she might have gawked or allowed her cup to clatter to the saucer. Gwen definitely didn't regard her as a friend!

Bronwyn seemed to read her thoughts. "Gwendolyn is like my youngest son, Dai. Stubborn he is, with a strong will. The voyage to America and losing her mother years later to fever made troubles for Gwendolyn. She was made to tend Crystin much, and she, only a child herself. She is angry but does not dislike you. Many times I see her watch and imitate what you do. As she does now." Bronwyn smiled and barely nodded to a corner of the room.

Ivy's gaze followed. Gwen stood, adopting the same well-postured stance as Ivy, with her little finger in the air as she sipped her tea and smiled politely at those nearby.

Suddenly Ivy heard raised voices, and she looked to see that the Bradfords were leaving. Mr. Bradford, his face flushed, said something to Wesley. The boy grabbed the hand of one of his young brothers and hurried outside. Two of his sisters followed. Had Mrs. Bradford been offended by Mrs. Johnson's remark or the taciturn look she'd given? She didn't look happy. Nor did Mr. Bradford.

Bronwyn rushed toward the couple to offer her farewells, Ivy assumed. As the front door swung open, she noticed that the sky had grown murky and a heavy snow fell. The Johnsons and another couple gathered their outer wraps, making for home as well.

"Will you also need to leave since the weather's taken a turn for the worse?" Craig's voice came from near her elbow.

Ivy managed to keep her grip on the saucer, though her cup gave a telltale clatter. She hadn't heard him come up beside her. Perhaps there was a disadvantage to having a carpet cover the floor.

"No," she said. "My mother and sisters and I plan to stay and take part in the late-night taffy pulling. My stepfather will return to the soddy to tend the animals. He'll come back for us in the morning."

Craig nodded. "I imagine this isn't anything like the fancy socials you're used to. But admit it, Ivy—you did have a good time today, didn't you?"

Why his words should irk her so, especially since there was a ring of truth to them, she didn't know. She raised her chin a notch. "Why should you think that?"

"Because your cheeks are glowing like summer-ripe strawberries, and your eyes are sparkling like blueberries after the rain." His grin was teasing, his gaze admiring.

Ivy felt the hot blush spread toward her ears and down her neck. She lowered her voice to a whisper so only Craig could hear. "If my face is glowing and my eyes are shining, it's due to annoyance regarding your improper behavior, Mr. Watson. Kindly desist from further talk of comparing my features to fruit."

Craig let out a loud laugh, bringing a few glances their way. He shook his head, still grinning. "Boston, you are the only woman I know to get offended by a compliment. But in the future, I'll keep your wishes in mind."

"Miss Ivy." A child's voice spoke to her right.

Ivy swung her gaze in surprise to see Amy Bradford standing there.

"Do you know where my mama is?"

Alarm filled Craig as he looked at Amy, whose tousled golden hair and heavy-lidded eyes suggested she'd been sleeping. "I was hidin' from Wesley, but he never came and found me. I don't see none of my family here, neither."

Craig quickly bridged the distance to the door and opened it. Behind him the fiddle playing stopped. The wind blew the snow harder, and some of it swirled inside. He could see the Bradfords' wagon in the distance, slowly making its way home. He closed the door and strode to the fireplace. Winifred had joined Ivy, who had an arm around the girl's shoulders. Amy now looked wide-awake, her eyes uncertain and a little afraid. Apparently she'd just learned that she'd been left behind—again. Why the Bradfords couldn't keep track of their children, Craig didn't understand. Fourteen kids was a lot for any couple, but this kind of situation happened far too often to be called accidental. More like negligent.

He hunkered down in front of the child and smiled. "Ever ride in a sleigh, Amy?"

She shook her head no.

"Would you like to? We can catch up to your folks in no time."

Her eyes began to shine. "You mean that sleigh with all those pretty ringin' bells? Oh yes, Mr. Watson. I'd like that awful much."

"Then let's hurry."

While Craig shrugged into his outerwear, Ivy buttoned Amy's threadbare coat, which looked a size too small. "Is this all you have to wear, Amy? Have you no hat or scarf?"

The girl shook her head.

"I'll just go upstairs and get a quilt to wrap her up in," Winifred offered.

The wind raised its voice, an angry foe, and now Craig could hear it shrieking through the eaves. "Better make it fast, ma'am. I want to get back before the weather gets worse."

"You think it will?" Ivy asked, concern edging her voice. "Are you certain you should risk it then? I'm sure Amy's parents will know that she's here and safe with us."

He grinned. "You worried about me, Boston?"

"Me worried? About you?" Pink stained her cheeks. "I've never heard of anything so vain. Why would you think such a thing? My concern was solely for Amy."

He chuckled. "Methinks the lady doth protest too much," he teased under his breath so Amy couldn't hear. "Shakespeare. *Hamlet*. And yes, I can read, too."

The pink swept up to cover Ivy's entire face. Winifred returned with the quilt, and Ivy quickly claimed it, kneeling down to wrap the child inside. "Merry Christmas, Amy. Mr. Watson will see that you get to your family safely."

"Thank you, Miss Ivy," the little girl whispered.

"I will be back shortly," Craig said to Ivy. Maybe he shouldn't have teased her, but he hadn't meant the words in a negative way. He had only positive feelings with regard to Ivy. Yet he was beginning to wonder if she would ever feel anything for him. Eight months of trying to win her favor was a long time. Maybe such an effort really was wasted, as he'd been told often enough, and he should just give up.

Craig bent to scoop the bundled child in his arms. He could feel her tremble against him.

"Still cold?" he asked as he headed for the door.

"No. I'm just hopin' Pa won't be mad about this fix I'm in."

"It'll turn out all right. It wasn't your fault you got left behind." Sensing that she was still upset, he added, "Know what I do when I'm nervous or scared?"

"Pray to God to make it all better?"

"That, too. I also whistle. It relaxes me. Shall we whistle?"

She grinned and nodded. Yet, as they stepped outside, the angry wind snatched their cheerful notes from their pursed lips, and Craig fought the wintry beast all the way to the sleigh.

Staring out the window at a world of white, Ivy stood with folded arms and rubbed them. Craig had left with Amy some time ago. Not long after his sleigh took off in the direction of the Bradfords' homestead, the wind increased to gale force, whipping snow first one way and then the other. Only for periodic snatches of time had Ivy been able to see farther than a few feet past the porch. A short time ago, the storm calmed some, though the snow still blew in whirls. At least she could see for a much greater distance than before.

Why had she snubbed Craig yet again when he'd asked her if she was worried about him? True, she'd been embarrassed that he'd so accurately discerned her thoughts. Regardless, she shouldn't have treated him so shamefully.

"Ivy, come away from that window," her mother gently commanded.

Ivy turned. "He should have been back by now."

"Perhaps he went home. The smithy is only across the road."

"No, he told me he'd be back shortly. Something's happened. I just know it." She glanced toward the window again, as if by doing so she could summon Craig back.

"Worrying won't help matters, dearest. All it will do is put wrinkles in that pretty forehead of yours. Now come here and let's pray."

Ivy did so, and her mother took her ice-cold hands in her own. "Father, we ask that You protect all Thy children out there. Help everyone to reach safety, and—"

Her mother's prayer was cut off as Ivy's stepfather and Winifred's husband walked into the room. Doc Miller and Mr. Llewynn were right behind them. All the men wore coats, hats, and mufflers. "We've talked it over, and we're going to look for them," Gavin explained quietly. "There is no way the Bradfords could have reached home in time. And Craig cannot have gotten far."

Ivy's mother rose to hug Gavin, and Bronwyn did the same to her husband. Mrs. Llewynn wrapped the scarf a second time around her husband's neck and fussed with his coat. Then they watched the men walk outside into the dancing snow. Ivy moved to stand beside her mother and slipped her hand into hers, both to take comfort and give encouragement. "Heavenly Father," she said, taking up the prayer where her mother had left off and trying not to let her voice shake, "we earnestly ask that Thou wouldst be a guiding light and protect our husbands and fathers and friends so that they may find and help any who are in need."

Ivy's mother squeezed her hand gently. "Amen," she whispered.

Chapter 6

Minutes after Craig left the Pettigrasses, the blizzard had started in earnest. Though he wore thick gloves, he had ceased feeling his hands long ago. The unforgiving wind whipped stinging particles into his eyes, the only part of his face exposed to the blinding snow. He couldn't tell if the constant, faint ringing he heard was in his head or from the sleigh bells. The wind drowned out most other sounds. He should have listened to Ivy. If he had, Amy would be safe by the fire right now instead of curled up in fear under the lap robe beside him.

If only he could sense direction; if only he could see something around him besides a curtain of white. He hadn't driven that far before the storm worsened, so he'd turned back in what he assumed was the direction of town. Now they were struggling against the wind.

Father, my own stupidity got me into this mess. I was so sure I could beat the storm. Please don't let a little child's life be lost because of me. Show me where to go.

Traveling blindly on in a foreign world of nothing but white, Craig urged the horse forward. If they stopped, the horse might freeze. He might freeze. With that thought, he moved his limbs to try to keep the blood flowing while taking care not to drop the reins. Amy's thin arms suddenly clutched him tight around his waist. He couldn't blame her for being scared.

"Help, please."

Craig blinked. Did his ears deceive him? Had that been a human cry for help? He strained to hear against the forceful wind.

"Help."

Sensing the call was coming from his right, Craig directed the horse that way. He pulled down his muffler from his mouth. "Call again so I can find you." The wind snatched his words from him the second they reached the air, and he doubted he could be heard.

"Over here!" The reply came, stronger this time.

A shift in the wind made the dancing snow seem to stop and swerve. In that instant, Craig spotted a sod house with light coming from inside. He remembered it as belonging to a family who'd moved back East two summers ago after a prairie fire destroyed their crops.

Craig guided the sleigh less than a foot from where a boy stood in the open doorway. A lamp glowed inside the rundown one-room house, devoid of all furniture except for a small bed and table. Craig questioned the intelligence of leaving Amy in the sleigh, even for a short time, but he did not know what he would find when he entered the soddy.

"I hear the bells and know help has come." A boy of perhaps eleven with shoulder-length black hair, brown skin, and liquid-dark eyes looked up at him. "Please to help my mama," he implored in broken English. "She very sick."

Craig stepped inside. No fire burned, though a flame steadily shone in the lamp's glass globe. Chicken feathers littered the earthen floor and table, and what was left of a stew sat in a pot. Craig would guess that he'd just discovered the identity of the chicken thief. Across the room a smaller boy sat on the cot, upon which a young woman lay stretched out, fully clothed. A baby nestled beside her.

"I am Roberto, and that is my brother, Paulo," the boy at the door said. "Mama sick many days, since my sister, Carmelita, come two months ago."

"Where is your father?" Craig asked.

"He died when we come West. We find this place, me and Mama, and stay here now."

Craig moved forward. "Are you all right, ma'am?"

The huge, dark eyes of the beauty surveyed him, but she didn't answer.

"Mama speak no English."

"How is it that you do?"

Roberto smiled. "Boys in wagon train teach me some. Other words I learn after we leave our band."

Gypsies. That explained it.

"And did you learn to steal chickens, too?"

The boy's eyes glittered in defense. "The store owner has many birds. My mother and brother are hungry. I am head of family now." He puffed his small chest out. "My duty is to feed them."

Craig decided this wasn't the time for reprimands. Realizing the situation wasn't dangerous, he went to collect Amy from the sleigh. Roberto's eyes widened when he saw the girl in Craig's arms, and his fascinated gaze focused on her snow-covered fair hair. Craig set Amy down, shut the door, and searched for fuel to make a fire. He must get the place warm. Then he would figure out what to do next.

❧

"Put a table by the front window," Bronwyn ordered a few minutes after the storm worsened and the wind increased again. "Fill it with every candle and lamp in the house. Do the same with the upstairs window, Winifred."

Her directives caused the women to hurry into action. Soon a yellow blaze lit up the rattling pane from the inside, and the aroma of honey from many beeswax candles filled the room. The rest of the house was dim, but if sacrificing light with which to see might help bring the men home safely, Ivy wasn't going to complain.

She prayed nonstop for Craig and the Bradfords, for the search party, and for her stepfather. She was surprised that she felt so strongly about her stepfather's safety and realized she didn't dislike him at all. Now that she was being honest with herself, she silently admitted that she approved of her mother's husband even though he had chosen to make his home on the prairie. He took care of Ivy and never ceased to treat her as one of his daughters despite how she behaved. She burned with shame when she thought of the caustic remarks she'd flung his way upon her arrival in Nebraska. He wasn't her own dear papa, but he was a good man, a strong man, and he obviously loved her mother. Ivy owed him her respect.

When her thoughts returned to Craig, she forced her hands to any task that presented itself to help her forget. She couldn't think of him right now or she might cry. It had taken a blizzard to make her realize she loved the man. She didn't know what she would do if Craig were killed, if she never saw his sunny smile or heard his warm, teasing words again. How she wished she could retrieve every occasion on which she'd acted indifferently toward him or ignored him outright.

As they waited, Bronwyn took the chair beside Ivy and began to speak of her son Gavin and of how proud she was of what he'd achieved. Her reminiscences brought up the conflict between Gavin and his brother, something about which Ivy often wondered. Ivy's heart ached for the brothers and their mother, who felt torn by the anger between sons. Gavin, the oldest, strongly felt the responsibility for his family and had worked hard to keep them together. Upon reaching America, his brother had other ideas. Gavin assumed Dai would help him stake his claim during the five years necessary to possess the land, but Dai had not wanted to be a farmer. Harsh words arose between them, ending in fisticuffs, before Dai stalked off, angry. That had been seven years ago, and to this day, Gavin and Dai had not seen one another or written to each other.

"I pray for them, every night, to end their quarrel," Bronwyn admitted, tears trickling freely from her eyes. "I miss my Dai. There it is. Only the Almighty can work in my sons' stubborn hearts."

Ivy thought about Bronwyn's words as she took her mother some tea with mint. "Winifred said this will help ease the sickness, and it might help to calm your nerves, too."

Her mother took the saucer. Ivy noticed how her hand trembled and the small amount of liquid that sloshed from the teacup.

"Mama, please don't be upset. We've prayed, and now we must trust. We mustn't worry, as you said. My stepfather is an intelligent man; I've seen this. He's not one to make foolhardy decisions."

Her mother laid a palm against Ivy's cheek. "Bless you, dearest. Thank you for being such a comfort to me."

Ivy took her mother's hand—a hand that had once been so smooth and pale but was now rough and brown—and kissed the inside of her callused fingers. Then she moved around the room to serve tea to the other women. She found that she enjoyed helping by doing what she could; it gave her a sense of purpose and helped to keep her thoughts off Craig.

"Ivy," Winifred said, "in the spring when the weather warms, the women will meet for a quilting bee each week. We would like for you to join us."

"Thank you, but I don't know how to quilt." She felt embarrassed to admit it.

"We will teach you," Winifred said with a faint smile. "It will be a time for us to encourage and pray for one another's needs also. As we are doing this day," she said more softly.

Ivy felt tears prick her eyes at the sense of unity she suddenly felt toward these women. "I'd like that."

"Listen!" Adella Miller lifted her head of tight curls higher. "Do I hear bells?"

"It must be Craig!" Forgetting etiquette, Ivy set the platter holding the tea pitcher down with a bang and rushed to the door, throwing it open. The snow didn't swirl as heavily. The icy wind sucked the breath from her lungs, but its effect didn't compare to the breathlessness she felt at the sight of a sleigh drawing closer.

"Craig," she whispered, clutching the doorframe.

He awkwardly exited the conveyance and picked up a long bundle. As he drew closer, Ivy could see he carried a woman. Amy and two other children hurried behind them, bent over as the wind half blew them to the porch.

"Hiya, B–Boston," Craig said stiffly from between blue lips as he moved across the threshold. "Miss me?"

The gripping emotion of wondering if he were dead, then seeing him alive—with a strange woman in his arms—was almost Ivy's undoing. She couldn't respond. She stared at him for a few quick heartbeats, then gave a short, abrupt nod and switched her focus to Amy and the two boys.

Ivy helped to get the children out of their snow-encrusted coats, hats, and mufflers and noticed Bronwyn and Winifred doing the same for Craig. Ivy's mother and Adella were tending to the woman, whom Ivy could now see clutched a baby to her chest. Mrs. Llewynn took the child. When Ivy felt she could face Craig again, she shifted her gaze to where he'd taken a seat in a chair nearby. He was wrapped in a quilt, and icy particles of snow still clung to his eyebrows, hair, and eyelashes. His skin looked pale, his brown eyes serious.

"You really d–did miss me," he said, his words still stilted from the cold. They didn't contain any of their usual teasing but were filled with amazement.

"Drink your tea," she ordered, noticing that he held a cup someone had given him.

As he lifted the steaming cup to his blue lips, Ivy decided to be honest with him. After her telling actions upon his arrival, she couldn't very well pretend differently. Nor did she want to. "Yes, I did miss you. I was worried about you and continually prayed for you—and the others."

Craig frowned. "What others? The B–Bradfords?"

Ivy nodded. "And the men who went searching."

Craig clumsily set his cup and saucer on the floor. "I must help them."

To his obvious amazement—and hers—Ivy pushed him back in the chair with one hand. "Oh no, you mustn't! You might get lost again, out there all alone. Look at you! You resemble a walking snowman. And your teeth are still chattering. You must get warm before you can even think about going back out there. How ever did you find your way?" She switched the topic, hoping to detain him.

He drained his tea. Winifred appeared, quickly refilled his cup, and moved away again to tend to the woman. Craig then related to Ivy what had happened and how he'd found the gypsy family. "When the wind stopped blowing so strong, I kn–knew I had to get Juanita to the doc."

"Juanita?"

"Roberto's mother. I prayed I was d–doing the right thing and took the risk once the storm died d–down, figuring out which direction to go from their s–soddy. I knew that town was to the w–west. While I was still a ways off, I saw a light and was sure God was leading me home. That was a smart thing you women did, putting those c–candles and lamps in the windows."

"It was Bronwyn's idea." Ivy hesitated. "Is Roberto's father away? Is that why he didn't come?"

Craig took another large swig of tea. "He died on their journey West."

"Oh. Then Roberto's mother is a widow." Ivy glanced her way. The exotic-looking woman was wrapped in a colorful blanket and seated before the fire. The baby was nestled at her bosom. "She's quite lovely."

"Not as lovely as you."

Craig's low words sped up Ivy's heartbeat. She blinked his way. The steady look in his eyes sent warmth trickling through her, and suddenly she didn't mind the cold so much.

"Miss Ivy," Amy said, walking up to her. She still trembled. "Are my m–ma and p–pa going to be okay? And my brothers and sisters?"

Ivy hugged the girl close, rubbing her arm to help warm her. "We can pray that God will keep them safe, as we've been doing since this started." Noticing the concern on Gwen's and Crystin's faces as they kept casting glances toward the door and window, Ivy came up with a plan.

"Bronwyn, didn't you tell me that one of your traditions is to put on a Christmas play?"

"Yes, every year in the old country we hold a play of Christ's birth."

"Then let's have one now." Ivy ignored the shocked looks sent her way by the rest of the women. She thought that if they engaged in such a play, it might help lighten the atmosphere as they waited for their men to return.

Winifred looked at Ivy and nodded, lending her support. "Yes, this will be a good thing."

Ivy smiled her thanks at her stepfather's sister. "Amy, you be Mary. And Crystin, you can be the angel. Gwen, you shall be the wise man, since you're the eldest."

"Who will be Joseph?" Crystin asked.

Amy pulled on the older boy's arm. Ivy had noticed how he tried to edge out of the room during her announcement of the play. "Roberto can be Joseph—and we even have a baby to play Jesus!"

"But Carmelita's a girl!" Roberto protested.

"That's okay," Ivy assured him. "No one will be able to tell. If it's all right with you?" Ivy looked at Juanita for permission.

Roberto spoke in rapid Spanish to his mother. The woman looked mystified but nodded. She handed the baby to Roberto, then with another uncertain nod accepted the tea Winifred handed her.

"Perfect." Ivy smiled at her small cast of characters. "We shall need costumes."

Winifred smiled. "I will help. I have dresses I can no longer wear." She blushed, then hurried upstairs. Soon she returned, her arms full of ivory-, blue-, and peach-colored dresses, sheets, and a gold-topped walking stick that belonged to her husband. She handed the contributions to Ivy, then excused herself to make coffee.

Roberto folded his arms across his thin chest and absolutely refused to wear a sheet for his costume. However, he did accept the fancy walking stick to use for a staff. Crystin looked adorable in a white satin dress, though it was much too big for her; Winifred was petite like her mother, yet the dresses still hung on the girls.

Someone fashioned a "halo" from a ring of lace and set it atop Crystin's dark curls. Amy's thick, golden hair shone against the oversized, pale blue gown. The glow on her face and the brightness of her eyes as she stared at the baby in the manger—the cradle that would be used for Winifred's child—made her appear peaceful and awed, much like the Virgin Mary must have been. Ivy noticed how often Roberto stared Amy's way.

"Are we ready to begin?" Crystin asked. "Shall I make my announcement to the shepherd now?" The shepherd was Paulo, and he looked lost wrapped up in a white sheet with only his nut-brown face showing.

"Not quite," Ivy said. "There's one item we've overlooked." She undid the velvet ribbon from around her throat that held the garnet brooch and approached Gwen. "Why don't you wear this, since a king—or in this case a queen—would wear jewels?"

Gwen's mouth opened, but no words came out. Crystin gasped.

"Here," Ivy said, "I'll fasten it around your neck." Once she did, she stepped back to look. "Perfect." She smiled.

"Thank you," Gwen whispered, awkwardly fingering the square jewel and seed pearls.

The old irritation rose up, but Ivy squelched it. Her sister's fingerprints couldn't harm the brooch, nor could she hurt it if she squeezed the stone too hard. The truth was, Ivy had thought up that and any other ridiculous notion as an excuse to be self-ish with her things. *Dear God, forgive me for being so self-centered*, she prayed when she saw Gwen's joy at wearing the brooch. The genuine smile the girl sent Ivy did her heart good. Perhaps they really could be friends someday.

The children began their rendition of Christ's birth. Roberto walked with Amy from the top of the stairs to the parlor to reenact the journey into Bethlehem. Carmelita gurgled from her place in the wooden cradle off to the side, awaiting her debut appearance.

"I am tired and hungry, Joseph," Amy said, putting one arm across her stomach and draping her other hand across her forehead. "I need rest."

"I will find us a chicken," Roberto proclaimed.

"That's not what you're supposed to say," Amy hissed.

Mrs. Llewynn raised her brows, and Craig leaned toward her. "I have something I need to tell you later," he whispered, the effects of the cold no longer affecting his speech.

"I think I know." The woman looked at the skinny boys, then at their sickly mother wrapped in quilts and leaning weakly back against her chair. A smile replaced Mrs. Llewynn's frown. "Never mind. I'm sure we can work this out to benefit everyone. I could use a strong boy like Roberto to help at the store. As you said, we will discuss this later."

Ivy decided that she also wished to discuss a matter with Mrs. Llewynn when she could get the woman alone—the purchase of a doll with a real china face for Crystin and of a leather-bound book of children's stories for Gwen. She remembered seeing such items in the general store. Add to that the beautiful oak cradle she'd also noticed—a cast-off from a family who'd returned back East—that would make a perfect gift for a new baby sister or brother. She should have enough of her fifty dollars left over to buy several yards of material for both her and her mother to have spring dresses. And gloves. She simply must buy herself new gloves.

Ivy mentally created her Christmas list. Hopefully the gifts would impart the message she wished to convey: that she now considered them all her family.

"You look like the cat that got away with the mouse," Craig whispered to Ivy as Gwen, the wise man, moved forward bearing a plate with an iced cookie and a piece of fruitcake to use as a gift for the baby. Roberto eyed the offerings hungrily.

Ivy winced and glanced at Craig. "Please, don't talk to me about mice," she whispered. "Not after our failure with the pink Christmas mouse."

"That sounds like it could be an interesting story," he mused. "A pink Christmas mouse? Still, I have to wonder what would cause your face to glow like that, as if you'd just swallowed one of those candles. Pleased with yourself and the play, maybe? A great success, by the way. The women's minds are off their worries for the time being. And the children are having the time of their lives."

Ivy smiled. It was true. "I just came to the realization that this is where I belong. Being here finally feels right, as if I fit in now."

A couple of heartbeats passed before Craig spoke. "Ivy, look at me." His tone was serious.

She turned to stare into his steady brown eyes.

"Are you telling me that you've decided to stay in Leaning Tree?"

"Yes, Craig. This night has helped me to discover what's truly important, as well as shown me how foolish I've been."

Before she could explain further, the door blew open. Four white-crusted figures stiffly clomped inside, followed by fifteen more shivering forms.

"Ma!" Amy cried, abandoning her role when she caught sight of her mother. She almost tripped over the borrowed dress in her haste to get to her. The women jumped up from their chairs to embrace their frozen husbands and help them and the others out of icicle-laden coats and mufflers. Roberto dove for the slice of cake and crammed the entire thing into his mouth, his smile wide.

"It w–was a miracle we f–found the p–place before we f–froze to death," Ivy's stepfather said, his teeth chattering. "Their w–wagon was stuck. W–we had to w–walk, and I th–thought all w–was lost when the s–storm started up again. Then, w–we saw that light in the w–window."

"Thank God you're safe," Ivy's mother said, briskly rubbing on the blanket that she'd draped around his stocky form. "Come closer by the fire."

Mrs. Bradford hugged Amy, and her father put a hand on her shoulder.

"Miss Ivy took care of me and helped us put on a play," Amy enthused. "I'm Mary. Will you watch me, Ma? We can start over."

The woman's grateful gaze met Ivy's. The look in her pale green eyes said what words couldn't. Ivy smiled and nodded in understanding. "I'll just go and get some coffee for everyone."

"I'll come with you." With the quilt wrapped around his shoulders, Craig stood to his feet.

Ivy darted a glance at the others as he walked on ahead of her. Everyone was so wrapped up in their loved ones' return and getting them warm again that Ivy didn't think she or Craig would be missed. Laughter, tears, and thanks filled the parlor, and she silently added her own prayer of gratitude. Strange as it might seem, this Christmas had been one of the best—and most challenging—she'd ever known.

In the kitchen, a cookstove burned, and the coffeepot simmered. Sweet spice scents of cinnamon and cloves lingered in the air, along with the aroma of rich coffee beans.

Craig abruptly turned Ivy's way. She jerked in surprise, her skirts brushing the wall. Her heart began a lilting cadence at the intense look in his eyes.

"Tell me again," he said. "I'm not sure I heard right the first time. Do you plan on staying in Leaning Tree?"

"Yes."

"For good?"

"Yes."

He raised one brow. "Do I dare hope your decision might have something to do with me?"

At least two-thirds of it does. "It might," she said. It was one thing to be remorseful for needlessly slighting him in the past; it was quite another to throw herself at the man.

A slow grin curled his mouth. "I've got enough money saved up to build a house come spring—the kind you like with wooden walls and floors and a roof. If you'd consent to be my wife, Ivy, you'd make me the happiest man in all of Nebraska."

"Craig Watson!" Exasperated, she shook her head, though her heart beat triple time at his words and she couldn't prevent the smile that stretched her cheeks. "Before introducing the subject of marriage, don't you think you should at least ask to court me properly?"

"Would you agree?"

A sudden case of shyness hit. "I might."

"To both?"

"Yes," she whispered.

Craig whooped in delight and cast the quilt from his shoulders. Sliding his large hands about her waist, he twirled her once around the confined space. She squealed when his leg knocked against the table. Dishes clattered, silverware clinked, and she laughingly protested that he put her down before someone came into the room and saw them. He set her gently on her feet, his brown eyes rich with amusement and warmth.

"I'll always love you, my proper Boston girl. I knew it from the first day I saw you stepping off that dusty wagon with your chin a mile high in the air."

Before she could think to be indignant about his teasing remark, Craig dipped his head and tenderly kissed her, and Ivy forgot all else but him.

Boston's Ladyfingers

Adapted from an old prairie cookbook, this recipe is for thin, biscuit-like chocolate-frosted cookies—perfect for a Christmas tea or small party.

3 egg whites	½ teaspoon vanilla
5 tablespoons	½ cup flour
powdered sugar	¼ teaspoon salt
2 egg yolks	Powdered sugar
(well beaten)	for coating

Beat egg whites until stiff. Add powdered sugar. In a separate bowl, beat yolks. Fold into mixture. Add vanilla. Fold in flour and salt until batter is well blended. Line a cookie sheet with waxed paper. Press the batter through a pastry bag and onto cookie sheet, forming strips approximately 4 inches long and 1 inch wide. (I use a plastic freezer bag with one tiny section snipped off at a bottom corner for a pastry bag.) Sprinkle with powdered sugar. Bake at 350 degrees for 10 minutes. Edges should be light golden brown. Remove from oven. After a minute, while cookies are still warm, slide spatula underneath to loosen them from waxed paper. Frost or dip in chocolate when cool. Makes approximately 24 cookies.

Chocolate Frosting/Sauce:

Stir over low heat 1 cup powdered sugar, ½ cup semisweet chocolate chips, and ⅛ cup water until rich and creamy. As it cools, it thickens and makes a sweet frosting to spread over cookies. Or put back on low heat and add several drops more water until thin enough to use as a dipping sauce.

Image of Love

by JoAnn A. Grote

This is my commandment,
That ye love one another, as I have loved you.
JOHN 15:12

Chapter 1

Minnesota, 1869

Mantie Clark stood at the schoolhouse door, smiling as she watched the children don their winter coats. She shivered and drew her green shawl more closely about her shoulders. Winter had arrived early this year, even by Minnesota standards. The wool coats and colorful mufflers and mittens were welcome against the bite in the air.

The children's chatter and laughter filled the cloakroom. Their energy contrasted sharply with the quiet discipline they portrayed in the schoolroom.

She wished each child good-bye as they hurried through the doorway and into the chill outdoors. Each returned the farewell, most with a mittened wave, though their attention was on the freedom beyond the door.

"See you at home, Jesse and Jenny." Mantie patted her nine-year-old nephew and ten-year-old niece on their shoulders as they passed.

A six-year-old girl with blond braids tugged at Mantie's skirt and held up hands encased in black mittens. "My fingers don't work. Will you tie my hat?"

"Of course, Susannah." Mantie smiled and knelt beside the banker's daughter. Swiftly she secured the black knit hat. "There you go."

"Thanks, Teacher."

Five minutes after she dismissed school, only one child remained. Eight-year-old Nathan Powell stood silently beside her in the doorway, watching the street. He held his floppy brown felt hat in mittened hands, respectful of the rule not to wear hats inside.

"Do you remember how to find your home?" Mantie broached the question gently. Nathan was the only child in town she didn't know. Today was his first time at school.

"My brother said to wait. He said he'd come get me when school was over."

"Then I'm sure he'll be here soon. Doesn't your brother go to school?"

The look he gave her indicated he thought her comment stupid, but his voice remained properly respectful. "He doesn't have to go to school. He's a man."

"I see." She wondered how old the brother was. Any male over twelve seemed a man to an eight-year-old.

Nathan continued to watch the village lane, which led past a scattering of log and clapboard homes to the short, straggling business street. The only movement on the street was the children laughing and teasing each other on their way to their homes, their winter clothing splashes of moving color against the snow-covered ground. Books swung from leather straps at the children's sides. Snowballs arched through the air.

Jesse scooped up a handful of snow, hurried up behind his sister, Jenny, and stuck snow down the back of her coat. An indignant yell resulted. Jesse ran off laughing amid loud but meaningless threats from Jenny.

Mantie shook her head, still smiling. *Things haven't changed much from when I was their age,* she mused. A bittersweet memory of Colin Ward bombarding her with snowballs at the ripe old age of ten whisked her into the past. Colin had been the new boy in town. She'd been too young to know the attack and the gleam in his brown eyes meant he found her attractive.

She touched the cameo locket at her throat, sighed, then closed the door on both the winter scene and the past. "Why don't we wait inside where it's warm, Nathan?"

He walked with her into the schoolroom, rather reluctantly, she thought. He kept his brown wool jacket buttoned up and his darker brown mittens on. Instead of standing beside the stove at the front of the room, he moved to a window and stared out.

"How many people are in your family besides you and your brother?" Mantie sat down on a desk near him and tried to draw him out.

"None."

Her heart twisted. His parents must be dead, like Jesse and Jenny's parents. She hated that any child needed to live through that.

Her gaze slid over his clothes. The jacket, corduroy pants, and high-buttoned black boots looked new. They weren't fancier than the other children's clothes but were in better shape than most. His brother must make enough money to provide well for Nathan. She searched her mind for the newcomers to town. "Is your brother the new blacksmith? Everyone is excited to finally have a blacksmith in town."

He shook his head. "No."

"What does your brother do? Is he a farmer?" New farmers still flooded the area, enticed by the rich soil that until seven years ago had belonged to the Sioux. Former soldiers, tired of the war between the North and South, embraced the land that the Homestead Act offered them for nothing but the sweat of their brow.

"He bought the livery stable."

She hadn't realized the stable had a new owner. The boy didn't seem eager to discuss his family. Perhaps he'd open up on another topic. "What do you think of our schoolhouse? It's only three months old." To Mantie, it still smelled of newly planed wood and fresh paint.

The boy shrugged.

Mantie smiled. "I suppose boys don't get excited over new school buildings like adults do. Until now, the children in town went to school in a room over the general store, so you see why I think this building is special."

He continued to stare out the window.

Was he reticent because he was terribly wounded over his parents' deaths? *Please find a way to heal him, Lord.* She wondered how long ago he'd lost his parents—and how. Apparently there wasn't a sister-in-law to help raise the boy, since the family was made up of only Nathan and his brother. Or perhaps Nathan didn't consider a sister-in-law family.

"Did the other students tell you that I'm not the teacher? I'm helping out today because the teacher is down with the croup."

"They said the teacher is a man." His voice announced he didn't particularly care.

"Yes, Mr. Wren. I think you'll like him. He loves children and loves to teach."

Silence.

The door opened. Nathan turned, hope written large on his wide face.

Mantie stood and turned around to greet the newcomer. A tall young man entered the room, his gait quick without a sense of rush. Like Nathan, the man held his beige hat in his hands. The friendly gaze from blue eyes beneath pale brown hair swept over her to the boy. "I'm sorry I'm late, Nate. I was helping a customer." The gaze moved back to Mantie. He nodded, smiling. "I'm Lane Powell, Nathan's brother."

"Mantie Clark."

Nathan moved quickly to stand beside his brother. Mantie noted with approval that Mr. Powell rested a hand on his younger brother's shoulder.

The man's clothes were shades of brown and tan, like Nathan's. Unlike Nathan's, the older brother's clothes showed signs of wear. A patch covered one corduroy knee. Sweat stained the broad-brimmed hat. He brought a scent of horses and hay and leather, but it was mild next to the animal smells on some of the farmers she knew.

Nathan looked up at his brother. "She's not the teacher. The teacher's sick."

Mantie bit back a laugh. "That's right. I hope Mr. Wren will be back Monday. The croup caught him."

"He's not alone in that, I hear."

"No. A number of students stayed home today. Nathan tells me you bought the livery stable."

"Yes. The new blacksmith, Abe Newsome, is my good friend. When he decided to move here, Nate and I decided to join him."

He isn't as secretive as Nathan, she thought. "I hope you'll like it here."

"I'm sure we will. Town's new, but not so new as the towns to the west. That's where Mr. Frank, the former livery stable owner, headed. You probably knew that."

"No. I'm surprised to hear he left. Usually news in this small town is common knowledge before the weekly newspaper comes out on Fridays."

"Mr. Frank said he's itching to try business in one of the towns on the prairie. This is far enough west for me. Peace is older than those prairie towns, but it shows lots of promise. It's nice to see people so excited about building it together."

"Yes, I think so, too." People were eager to leave behind the miseries of the war that had ended four years earlier and look ahead to a more promising future. She didn't correct him by saying people thought of the rolling lands around Peace as prairie. Descriptions of prairie to the west told of flatter lands with trees only along rivers. Here much of the land was treeless, but the hills north of the river, where she lived, reminded her of the Big Woods to the east. "The town still needs an assortment of skilled tradesmen. We've not a cabinetmaker or shoemaker or milliner, for instance."

"Is the town offering free lots to people with those skills? Have to say, that's what convinced my friend Abe to move here."

"The town fathers consider a blacksmith more important than most trades, evidently. I know of no other trades for which free land is offered."

"Certainly not for the livery. What does your husband do?" Mr. Powell's inflection hinted at the simple curiosity of a newcomer rather than interest in her as a woman.

She lifted her chin slightly. "I'm not married. I live with my brother, Walter Clark, and his wife, Alice. He has a position with the railroad here."

His eyes lit with recognition. "Oh, yes, I met him briefly."

Silence fell between them. Nathan shifted impatiently, his boots scuffing against the wooden floor.

Mantie returned to the business required of her as schoolmistress. "I noticed Nathan brought his slate today." She smiled down at him and looked back at Lane. "He'll need to purchase a reader and an arithmetic book. You can find them at the general store. The proprietor will know what Nathan needs."

"Thank you kindly, but Nate brought a reader and an arithmetic book along from Wisconsin. That's where we moved from. Guess Nate forgot to bring the books with him this morning."

She smiled at Nate once more. "It's easy to forget things in the excitement of starting at a new school."

Nate flushed and looked at the floor, but Mr. Powell beamed at her. Appreciation for her understanding of his brother shone from his smiling eyes.

"There's no school tomorrow, Nathan," she reminded him, "so don't forget to bring your books on Monday."

He looked up at his brother. "Tomorrow's Thanksgiving. We had a play today about the first Thanksgiving and the Pilgrims and the Indians who helped them. I didn't have a part since I'm new."

"Next year you'll have a part," Mantie assured him. "The women will make Thanksgiving dinner for the town tomorrow. Everyone is invited. It's a tradition." She didn't reveal the reason for the dinner. Bachelors outnumbered married men two to one. The married women felt it their obligation to ensure the bachelors ate at least one good home-cooked meal each year. "The children will give the play for the town tomorrow." An idea struck her. "Nathan, would you like to help by introducing the play? It's an important job. You'd only need to learn a few lines."

Nathan didn't look eager. "In front of the whole town?"

"You won't be alone. I'll be there and so will all the other children. You can wear the black paper hat and collar Jesse wears in the play. When you're done with your speech, you can return them to him."

"What do you say, Nate? I'll help you with your lines," Mr. Powell encouraged.

"All right, I guess."

Mantie clasped her hands lightly in front of her. "Thank you. You'll be a big help to me."

In small letters she wrote a few sentences, which took up both sides of his slate. He read the words aloud, slowly.

"Perfect." She beamed at him. "Be careful carrying the slate home so you don't brush the chalk off."

Mr. Powell frowned slightly. "Miss Clark, where is this play going to be given?"

"Here, at the schoolhouse."

"Here?" He looked around.

Her gaze followed his. No wonder he looked doubtful. The room held no tables—only desks and a few benches along the walls. "I assure you, tomorrow there will be tables. We'll set boards across the desks and use the benches. People may need to eat in shifts, but that only adds to the fun. It gives people more time to visit." She laughed. "It may seem unusual, but it's better than meeting at the saloon, which is where public meetings were held before the school was built. Church meetings are held here, too."

Mr. Powell grinned. "Sounds like the school needs a carpenter more than a livery stable."

She laughed with him. "I hope you and Nathan will join us for both the play and dinner."

Immediately she regretted her words. Would he think them a personal invitation? Her intention had been simply to extend welcome to a new member of their small community. "We're all like family here." Would that sound to Mr. Powell like the lame afterthought it was?

If so, he didn't show it. Instead he looked pleasantly surprised. "Thank you. We'll be there with bells on. My cooking is good enough for everyday, but a holiday demands something better, don't you think, Nate?"

Nathan shrugged but grinned.

"Good. We'll see you tomorrow then." Mantie began briskly picking up papers from the simple, handmade teacher's desk.

Mr. Powell seemed to hesitate, but she kept her attention on her work.

"Come on, Nate. We're keeping Miss Clark from her duties. Likely she's eager to get home after a day herding you youngsters. Good-bye, Miss Clark."

"Good-bye." She didn't look up until she heard the door close behind them. Lane Powell seemed a nice enough man, but she didn't want to give a hint that she might like him to show her anything but friendly interest. Romance wasn't in her future.

Chapter 2

Lane shut the schoolhouse door and followed Nate down the steps. It was a beautiful day, but his mind remained inside the school. There was something about that schoolmarm-for-a-day that appealed to him. He liked that she found a way to make Nate feel a part of the school by including him in the play at the last minute. He liked her intelligence, liked that she smiled easily, and liked her pretty green eyes. He especially liked that she was friendly without being flirtatious or shy. *Is she the one, Lord?*

Lane cleared his throat. "Miss Clark seems like a nice lady to start your school days with here."

Nate shrugged. "I guess."

"Meet any boys your age?"

"No."

Lane swallowed a sigh of exasperation. He'd hoped the move to Peace would be good for Nate. Instead, Nate grew quieter every day. "Thought I saw a couple kids pass by the livery stable after school who looked about your age."

"No one is eight like me."

"Close?"

"One boy is nine."

"What's his name?"

"Jesse."

At this rate, it was going to take the entire walk back to the livery to get two full sentences out of the boy. "Does this Jesse seem friendly?"

Another shrug. "I guess so. He didn't tell me he's going to beat me up."

Lane chuckled. "That's a good sign."

"Two older boys said they're going to beat me up."

"Why?"

A shrug. "Jesse said they want to prove they're tougher than me." A look of disgust crossed Nate's face. "Isn't that stupid? They're ten. Of course they're stronger than me."

"Sounds like you're smarter than they are."

Nate looked pleased at that.

Lane was tempted to ask what Nate planned to do if the boys bullied him to

111

a fight. He decided against it. Boys hadn't changed much since he was young. Sometimes a fight was hard to avoid. Some kids seemed born bullies.

"Jesse says the boys who want to fight me think they're tougher than everybody else and are always trying to prove it. Nobody else likes them much."

"What else does Jesse say?"

Shrug. "He lives on the other side of the river."

"Does he have brothers and sisters?"

"Only a sister. She's ten. Her name is Jenny. Miss Clark lives with them. She's their aunt."

Now there's some worthwhile news, Lane thought. "What about their parents?"

"They're dead. Their dad died in the war. So did Miss Clark's beau. He and Jesse's dad died in the same battle, fighting side by side."

"I see."

Was that why she was still Miss Clark instead of Mrs.? A lot of women lost brothers and beaus in the war, but it would be especially difficult to lose both in one day. Sounded like she might be helping raise her brother's children, too. Maybe that's why she wasn't married. Many men didn't like taking on a ready-made family along with a wife. He'd never thought much about the issue one way or another.

Strange that he hadn't. Any woman who married him would have to not only accept but also love Nate. Lane couldn't imagine refusing to do the same for any children dear to the heart of a woman he loved.

He'd been barely more than a boy when he'd entered the war. When the war was over, his first responsibility had been to find a way to support himself. He knew he couldn't support a wife right away.

Besides, he hadn't met anyone he wanted to marry. For the last two years, he'd been asking the Lord to bring into his life the woman God meant for him. He wanted more than someone to help him with the everyday chores and to bear his children. He wanted a woman for whom he would be a special blessing and who would be a special blessing to him.

Miss Mantie Clark's green eyes smiled in his memory.

Is she the one, Lord?

❦

The small white clapboard house smelled of baking pies and wood smoke when Mantie entered. The warmth in the house felt good to her chilled cheeks. She hung her fox-trimmed, hooded, gray wool cloak on the pegs on the entry wall, set her books and gloves on the trunk beneath the pegs, and hurried into the kitchen.

"I'm sorry I left you alone with all the Thanksgiving baking, Alice." Mantie reached for an apron while apologizing to her sister-in-law.

"I don't mind as long as you're up early tomorrow to help me with the turkey." Alice grinned and brushed a dark brown lock of hair behind her ear. "Or perhaps the most diligent work will be keeping the family away from the baking tonight.

We'd hate to go to the dinner tomorrow without dessert."

Mantie slipped the gray-and-blue-plaid apron over her head and tied it behind her back. The colors clashed with the navy-and-green plaid of her dress, but as long as the material was protected, it didn't matter. She picked up the quilted potholders, scorched from use, and lifted the cover from the deep pot on top of the cast-iron stove. Simmering vegetable soup, thick with barley, set her stomach protesting in hunger. "I didn't even smell the soup for the pies when I entered. Soup always tastes especially good on a cold evening like this."

"I'm sure Walter will complain we aren't having meat and potatoes, but I didn't think it necessary with the large meal tomorrow."

"You always feed him well. He's put on a few pounds since you married last summer. It must be your good cooking. Or perhaps it is that he is so content with you."

Alice stopped beside the oven, about to open the door with the hot pad Mantie had set down. Pleased surprise filled her deep blue eyes. "Do you truly think he is content?"

"Absolutely. There's a restfulness about him when he's with you that wasn't there before."

A smile played on Alice's lips as she removed two maple syrup pies from the oven and set them on wooden slats to cool.

Twenty-year-old Alice sometimes acted the mother to twenty-five-year-old Mantie. Normally, Mantie didn't mind. She'd been the homemaker for her brother Walter and their late brother Howard's children, Jesse and Jenny, for more than five years. It was sometimes difficult handing control of the household over to Alice, but Mantie knew it was only right for Alice to be allowed that place in her husband's home.

Mantie's thoughts turned from her brother's marriage to Lane Powell's news. "Did you know Mr. Frank sold the livery stable?"

"Yes. He's moving farther west. Walter told us at dinner last night. Don't you remember?"

"I must have been woolgathering." She frowned. Likely Colin had filled her thoughts. In the five years since he'd passed, she'd thought of him almost every waking hour. She forced her attention back to the present. "I met the new owner today."

"Of the livery stable? Where?"

"He came by the school to walk his brother home."

Alice dipped a long-handled wooden spoon into the soup pot. "His brother? Don't you mean his son?"

"No. Evidently it's only the two of them. The rest of their family is dead. His name is Lane Powell. His younger brother is Nathan."

Alice grinned. "Another bachelor. Maybe this one will catch your heart. You've turned down all the others in town."

"You're exaggerating."

"Mm." Alice blew on a spoon filled with soup. "Those who haven't asked to court you are afraid to. You're chillier than a Minnesota blizzard toward the poor bachelors."

"I'm not breaking any hearts. The men aren't interested in me because I'm me. They are only interested because so few single women live in the area."

"A fact for which most of the single ladies are thankful. But not you."

Mantie touched the cameo locket pinned at her throat. "Those women are welcome to the men in this town. There isn't one man here who lives up to Colin."

Alice stared at her a moment, then put the lid back on the soup kettle and laid down the spoon. She walked slowly to Mantie's side and rested her hand on Mantie's arm. "Sometimes," she said gently, "I wonder if you're building your memories of him into something no man can live up to, memories even Colin could never have matched."

Pain jabbed at Mantie's chest. Though gentle, the words were still a reproach. Mantie seldom allowed herself the luxury of speaking of her continued love for Colin. She well knew that her family believed the five years since Colin's death had provided ample time for her to put her love for him behind and start a life and family with another. Alice's comment, however, was the closest anyone had come to putting that sentiment into words.

"Colin isn't replaceable like a china plate that's been broken."

"I'm sorry. I didn't mean—"

"I know you didn't." Mantie walked to the open shelves built into the kitchen wall to retrieve bowls for the evening meal, glad for a reason to walk away from Alice's touch. She tried to calm the anger that roiled in her chest. *Alice doesn't know anything about losing the man she loves,* Mantie reminded herself. *She doesn't know what it's like falling asleep every night remembering his kiss and waking every morning remembering you won't see him that day. How can I expect her to understand?*

❧

Mantie and Alice arose Thanksgiving morning before daybreak. It was pleasant working near the stove. The winter night had chilled the house as usual. They prepared stuffing while the oven heated. By the time Walter, Jesse, and Jenny awoke, the aroma of roasting turkey filled the house.

When the dinner preparations were almost done—long after the breakfast of eggs, bacon, and oatmeal sweetened with maple syrup—Alice and Mantie left the kitchen to change from their working dresses.

"Wear that beautiful emerald-green swirled silk you made last month," Alice urged. "It brings out the green of your eyes."

"I planned to save it for Christmas."

"Why? There's no one who will see it at Christmas who won't see it now."

"But it's always nice to have something new to wear for Christmas, and this is the only fancy dress I made. The other two are practical wools."

"All the more reason to wear it now. There aren't many special days to wear it."

"I guess you're right."

The prospect of wearing the emerald green cheered Mantie considerably. She poured cold water from the pitcher on her washstand into the matching porcelain bowl. The water refreshed her after the hours spent around the hot kitchen stove.

To keep her hair out of the way when she worked in the kitchen, she'd left it in the braid in which she'd bound it before going to bed the night before. Now she released her hair with quick fingers, brushed it out, and swept it up into a figure eight at the back of her head. She anchored the hair with tortoiseshell pins.

Slipping into her silk dress, Mantie checked her reflection in the walnut-framed mirror above the washstand. Alice was right. The color of the dress did make her eyes look greener. It was the prettiest dress she'd made since Colin died. Clothes hadn't seemed important after losing Colin and her brother Howard in the war. But when she saw the emerald-green swirled silk at the general store, a desire to wear the beautiful material leaped within her.

Mantie wrapped a narrow black velvet ribbon around the dress's lace neck and tied it in back. Turning, she looked over her shoulder at the mirror and smiled at the long ribbons hanging down her back, ending below the level of the mirror.

Finally she picked up the locket lying on the stand. The locket had belonged to her mother. Inside Mantie had placed a picture of Colin. Wearing the locket made her feel closer to them both. She touched the hidden button, and the locket sprang open. Colin's broad face stared back at her.

Would she ever stop missing him? Had God placed her in this town with so many single men because He wanted her to marry, to help someone build a family? She pushed away the thought and the guilt that accompanied it. She was so horribly lonely, but she couldn't imagine loving anyone but Colin.

With a sigh, she closed the cameo locket and pinned it at the neck of her dress. Some might think the pale blue background against which the cameo was set clashed with the green dress, but she didn't care. She wore it always. The townspeople were accustomed to seeing it. If anyone other than family knew it carried Colin's image, they didn't say so.

Her fingertips rested against the cool ivory of the cameo. "I love you, Colin," she whispered.

Chapter 3

Lane Powell's gaze swept the crowded schoolroom. He grinned at Nate and Abe. "Seems Miss Clark's prediction that the entire town would be at the Thanksgiving dinner was accurate." So many people filled the room that the warmth was stifling.

"Sure smells good. My stomach's growling," Nate complained.

"Mine, too. Smells like turkey and ham." The aromas were strong, in spite of the fact the meals had been cooked elsewhere. Lane spotted a makeshift table where there might be room for three more if the men didn't mind squeezing together a bit. He made his way through the crowd, nodding at the few faces he recognized. Nate kept close on his heels, and Abe followed.

Lane tapped the shoulder of a man whose brown hair was graying at the temples. "Excuse me. Room for a few more here?"

"Sure thing. More the merrier." The man dug an elbow into his neighbor's side. "Scoot over."

Lane and Nate sat down beside the man. Abe made his way to the other side of the table. The men looked askance at Abe's wide chest and huge arms but made room for him, to their own crowded discomfort.

A high whistle screeched through the room. It brought everyone's attention to a tall, skinny man in a black suit who stood on a chair at the front of the room. A grin split his long, narrow black beard. "Greetings, everyone."

"Greetings to you, Pastor."

"Howdy, Reverend."

The pastor rubbed his hands together. "Let's thank the Lord for His bounty."

All heads bowed. At the end of the pastor's prayer, "amens" rumbled through the room.

"Remember, men," the pastor warned, "no snoose and no cigars. This is a schoolhouse. There'll be a church service here tonight, and I expect to see all of you. Let's show the Lord you meant it when you thanked Him for the food these women have prepared."

A burst of energy followed as women bustled about the room with plates and bowls heavy with food. Silver clanked against china. Men's voices rose in conversation and easy joking with the women.

Lane caught sight of Mantie moving between the closely spaced benches, a bowl of mashed potatoes carried high above the heads on either side of her. In her dress of shimmering green, she looked more beautiful than he remembered.

She set the bowl down on the table in front of him, reaching between Abe and his neighbor to do so. Straightening up, her gaze met his. Her smile blazed, setting his heart aglow.

"You made it." Her smile shifted to welcome Nate. "Hello. Are you ready to introduce the play after dinner?"

Nate nodded and returned her smile with a shy one of his own.

Lane indicated Abe with a wave of his hand. "This is the friend I told you about, the new blacksmith." He introduced them.

Abe nodded at her greeting, his gaze not quite meeting hers.

Lane was accustomed to his friend's bashful nature around women. Abe only spoke to members of the fairer sex when he couldn't find a way around it. The man whose strength and size intimidated other men was as timid as a hare when it came to women.

"Hey, Miss Clark." The man beside Lane vied for Mantie's attention. "You decide to marry me yet?"

Lane's breath caught at the man's bold comment. Mantie Clark was a lady, not the kind of woman one spoke to in such an uncomely manner.

A blush covered Mantie's cheeks, but she smiled gamely. "Tom Morrison, if I said yes, it would frighten you so, you'd skedaddle out of town before sundown."

Tom joined the other men in laughter. He waved his fork back and forth and lifted his eyebrows in a teasing manner. "One of these days, Mantie Clark, I'm goin' to quit askin', and then you'll be sorry."

She didn't reply but kept her smile as she turned away.

A man with curly red hair who looked to be in his mid-twenties stopped her after two steps. "How about marrying me? I could sure use some good home cooking like this every day."

A chorus of "Me, too" went up from the table.

Mantie shook her head. "And what's the benefit in that to me? I'd be better off opening an eating establishment and feeding the lot of you for money."

Chuckles mixed with groans.

Lane watched Mantie with admiration. She threw back the men's teasing comments with charm, though their comments obviously embarrassed her.

"Hush up, you men." A young woman with black hair grinned from behind Mantie. "The women in town have decided there'll be no more marriages in this town until there's a proper church building to perform the ceremonies in."

A roar of protests greeted her announcement.

"Alice Clark, you take that back." A girl with red hair that waved in glorious color down her back stood with hands perched on narrow hips. "I'm to be married next week, and I'm not waiting for any church building."

Lane grinned as the bachelors visibly and audibly relaxed.

Alice handed a gravy bowl to a man seated near her. "That'll be the last marriage until you men pitch in enough money and labor for the church."

"No need for us to worry, Mrs. Clark," Tom Morrison spoke up. "You up and married Walt on us last summer. Torey here," he indicated the red-haired girl, "has agreed to wed young Spangler. Mantie won't court any of us. Hardly any women left for us poor old bachelors and widowers to marry."

"Notice you didn't come up with this church-first-weddings-later idea until you married Walt," the man beside Abe challenged.

Alice laughed with him. "I wasn't about to give the best-looking man in town a chance to back out of marrying me."

The women headed back to the front of the room, where platters and bowls covered the teacher's desk.

"Lack of women in this town's not such a joke," Tom Morrison informed Lane between forkfuls of turkey. "Single women are snatched up almost soon's they hit the county."

"That's right." The young man with red hair agreed. "Torey there, she's barely turned seventeen. Moved here with her ma and pa two months ago."

"Now, Mantie Clark, she's different from the rest." Tom emphasized his point with a shake of his empty fork. "She and her brother have lived here for three years. She's turned down every man in town who's had the courage to ask to court her."

"Good woman, too," the redheaded man assured. "A man'd be lucky to have her for a wife."

Lane tried to avoid being obvious about his interest in Mantie, but he watched her throughout the meal. Most women he knew eagerly anticipated marriage. Many snatched up the first man who asked, especially after the war killed off so many young men. Why wasn't Mantie Clark interested in marriage? Was she still holding on to the pain of losing her beau?

Or had the Lord been keeping her for him? He was probably being fanciful, but he was attracted to her more than any woman he'd ever met. Had to admit, though, it didn't look likely she'd return his interest; and if what these men said was true, moving to Peace might not have been wise for a man looking for a wife.

Lane discovered he liked the easy bantering among the townspeople. Mantie's description had been correct: The people here were like one big family. Warmth filled his chest. Maybe he'd made the right decision following Abe to this young town.

As Mantie had warned, men continued to crowd into the church. Those fortunate enough to find seats at the first serving gave up their places to others as soon as they completed the main course. Pie was eaten standing up along the walls or in the cloakroom.

After the meal was over, dirty dishes were piled into baskets to be taken home and washed, and the few leftovers were stored temporarily. While the baskets were carried out to wagons and buggies, the men removed the planks that had made up the tables.

The children, their eyes shining, assembled in the cloakroom with Mantie. The adults took their places on the backless wooden benches and waited, sitting shoulder against shoulder to make room for as many as possible. Some men cheerfully offered to stand against the walls or sit on the floor.

Lane was pleased when Mantie's brother, Walter, sat down beside him. Walter introduced the black-haired Alice as his wife. Her pretty young face lit up when Lane was introduced as the new stable owner. "Walter told us about you. Welcome to our little town. You and your brother must come to dinner with us some night soon. I simply won't hear otherwise."

"Thank you, Ma'am. We'd be honored." The prospect of dinner at the home of the elusive Mantie pleased him. He wanted to know the woman who turned away most of the single men in town.

"Perhaps this Sunday?" Alice inquired. "You do close the livery on Sunday, don't you?"

"I only accept business on Sundays when it can't be helped," he replied cautiously. It often couldn't be avoided. People needed stables and transportation when they needed them. However, he didn't go out of his way to work on the Lord's Day.

The audience quieted as Nate made his way to the front of the room through the men seated on the floor. A tall black paper hat rested on his ears and hid his brown hair. A round black-and-white collar embraced his neck and stuck out over his shoulders. When he reached the front of the room, the audience broke into applause.

Lane shifted in his seat as he watched Nate's face grow red. Would the boy have the courage to say his few lines?

"Ladies and gentlemen, we, the students of Peace school, invite you to join us in reliving the first Thanksgiving in this bount. . .bounti. . .bountiful land."

Lane held his breath. *Keep going, Nate. You can do it,* he urged silently. Nate's panicked gaze met his. Lane smiled and nodded.

Nate pressed his lips together before starting again. "The Lord. . .the Lord led the Pilgrims to the shores of this great land. The natives welcomed them with kind and generous hearts." His voice grew stronger and the words came quicker. "Together they shared the bounty of the fer. . .fertile land. Celebrate that day again with us now."

He kept his gaze on the floor as he made his way back to the cloakroom amid a spattering of applause.

Lane knew the rest of the play was as important for the parents of the other children as Nate's presentation had been to him, but he could barely wait for it to be over. He wanted to tell Nate how proud he was of him.

When the play ended, Lane made his way to the cloakroom. It was filled with parents and children finding each other. The children still carried or wore their simple aprons and paper and feather hats that made up most of the costumes.

Lane rested his hand on Nate's shoulder. "You did a fine job. I'm proud of you." Nate stuffed his hands into the pockets of his corduroys and kicked at an unseen pebble. "I stammered, and I almost forgot part of it."

Suddenly Mantie stood beside him. "Anyone could stammer over some of those big words. And you didn't forget anything. You were wonderful."

Lane could have hugged her for her kind words. "See there? If the teacher says so, it must be true."

"She isn't the real teacher," Nate grumbled. But Lane noted the twitch of Nate's lips and knew the boy was struggling not to smile.

He winked at Mantie. "Nope, but she does pretty well in a pinch, don't you think?"

Nate shrugged.

A girl and boy stopped by. Mantie introduced them as her niece and nephew, Jenny and Jesse. Lane remembered Mantie had said that the hat Nate wore for the play was Jesse's. The boy wore it now and carried the paper collar. Nate's gaze lingered hungrily on the hat. Lane glanced about. All the other children appeared to be taking their simple costumes home with them. Nate hadn't a costume of his own, of course. Lane's heart sank. He should have anticipated that.

"You did good, Nate," Jenny said.

"Thanks."

Jesse grinned. "My hat was almost too big for you. Good thing Mantie stuffed that handkerchief inside it to make it fit better."

Nate colored.

"Here." Jesse held out the collar. "You should have part of this costume since we shared it."

Pleasure followed surprise on Nate's wide face. "You mean it?" He took the collar before Jesse could reply.

"Don't think that collar will fit beneath your jacket," Lane said. "Why don't you let me hold it while you get ready to go?"

Nate handed it over with obvious reluctance.

"Say," Jesse started, "a bunch of us boys are going skating down by the mill. Do you want to come, Nate?"

"I don't have any skate blades."

"That's all right. Come anyway. Lots of the kids don't have skates. It's just as much fun to slide around in your boots and pretend you're skating."

"It's too early for the ice to be hard enough to skate on the river yet." The very thought of the children out on the ice tightened the muscles in Lane's stomach.

"But winter's been here forever," Jesse protested.

Lane grinned. "It just seems like forever. I don't think it's been cold enough for the ice to be safe."

"Mr. Powell is right," Mantie agreed.

Jesse screwed his face into a scowl. "Aw, Mantie."

She shook her head. "You must stay off the river."

"Why don't you go sledding instead? If you do that, I promise to check the ice every day and let you know when it's safe for skating," Lane promised.

Jesse's scowl deepened. "I don't have a sled."

"I do," Nate piped up.

Jesse looked at Nate. "That all right with you?"

"Sure. I have a toboggan."

"Oh, will you let me ride on it?" Jenny's eyes were wide with eagerness.

Nate glanced from her to Jesse. "I thought only boys were going."

Jenny groaned. "Mantie, make them let me play."

"Why don't you see if you can talk some of the other girls into going with you?" Mantie suggested.

The corners of Jenny's lips drooped, but she didn't protest.

The children moved away, Jenny to look for a playmate, the boys to retrieve Nate's jacket from the other end of the cloakroom.

Lane smiled at Mantie. "Thank you."

"For what?"

"For making Nate feel welcome here."

"I think Jesse is the one making him feel welcome."

"It isn't only Jesse." As he spoke the words, Lane ruefully thought, *I wouldn't mind if Miss Mantie Clark went out of her way to make me feel more welcome here, too.*

Chapter 4

Mantie bowed her head slightly to the slender man with the long, narrow black beard. "Good Sunday to you, Reverend."

"And to you, Miss Clark."

She slid her gloved hands into her fur muff and followed Alice through the schoolhouse door and down the wooden steps, moving cautiously. The steps were swept free of snow, but they were still slippery. Safe after the last step, she allowed herself to look up and drink in the beauty around her.

When they'd arrived for the church service, fog had covered the ground like a shade drawn tight down against the night. Now it was lifting, leaving behind bare tree limbs and pine trees encased in ice. Horses, blanketed against the cold, their white breath blending into the white landscape, waited at white wooden hitching posts.

"Morning, Mrs. Clark, Miss Clark." Lane Powell's greeting pulled Mantie from her reverie. A gentle smile reflected from the gray eyes that met her gaze.

Beside him stood Abe, whom Mantie remembered from the Thanksgiving dinner. Lane quickly introduced his friend to Alice.

To Mantie's surprise, Alice responded with bright enthusiasm. "Mr. Newsome, I'm pleasured to meet you. My husband told me he'd met you. Won't you join us for dinner today along with Lane?"

Abe shifted, looking uncomfortable. "Thank you for the invitation, Ma'am, but I won't be able to make it. One of the farmers who came to church this morning needs new shoes for his horses." His voice wasn't loud and booming as Mantie had expected. There was a rumble to it, to be sure, but the voice was quiet and unassuming.

"Surely he doesn't expect you to work on the Lord's Day." Alice sounded shocked.

"I hate to ask him to make an extra trip into town, Ma'am. Hate more to let a horse go longer than necessary without proper shoeing. Don't expect the Lord minds much when our work relieves a bit of pain for another, even if the other is an animal."

Mantie wasn't sure whether the reverend would agree, but she liked Abe Newsome's consideration for a creature's pain.

"You'll be wanting to put the horses in the livery stable, I expect," Lane said.

"Feel free to do so."

Abe nodded. "Hooves need to warm up before shoeing after being out in weather like this. Always hate to shoe horses in winter."

Mantie suspected from Abe's demeanor that he was glad for an excuse to avoid the dinner. But why? Most bachelors jumped at the chance for a meal cooked by a woman and leaped faster when it meant spending time in the presence of an unmarried woman such as herself. Curious, she watched Abe as he lumbered across the snow toward a farmer who stood beside a wagon set on runners.

Walter stopped beside them, only to lead Lane away to introduce him to the local banker.

As soon as the men were out of earshot, Mantie turned to Alice. "So that's why you swept pine needles over the parlor carpet this morning. You invited the town's newest bachelors to dinner without telling me. How could you?"

"Walter and I want to make them feel welcome here." The twinkle in Alice's eyes confessed the incompleteness of her answer.

The Clarks hadn't ridden to church. As the little group started home, Jenny, Jesse, and Nate ran ahead. Walter and Alice walked together, so Mantie hadn't a polite reason to refuse when Lane Powell fell into step beside her. To her relief, he kept their conversation friendly but impersonal, asking many questions about the young town.

The stone bridge near the mill was slippery. His gloved fingers touched her elbow as they crossed, ready to support her if needed, but he removed them when the river was behind them. Mantie knew from experience that a number of the bachelors in town would not have acted in such a gentlemanly manner. She appreciated both his concern for her and his restraint.

"Walter, do go build a fire in the parlor stove," Alice insisted as soon as they entered the house. "We'll want it warm and cozy for visiting after dinner."

Alice had prepared a pot roast early that morning before church. Though she'd made sure the fire was no longer burning when the family left for the service, she'd left the roast and vegetables warming in the oven while the family was gone.

As Mantie and Alice completed the meal preparations, the men visited in the kitchen because the parlor wasn't yet warm. Mantie made sure Jesse sat between her and Lane during the meal, frustrating Alice's plans. Alice wrinkled her nose at Mantie as their gazes met across the table.

Everyone welcomed the raisin pie Mantie had made the night before. The children gobbled up their portions, in spite of Alice's gentle reprimands to eat slowly, and were done before the more manner-conscious adults.

"Can we go outside and play?" Jesse asked eagerly as soon as he swallowed the last bite of piecrust.

Mantie touched the tip of her napkin to her lips before replying. "We have company, Jesse."

Jesse clasped his hands in his lap and pressed his lips together. Mantie could barely keep a smile from forming. *The energy of youth is so difficult to contain,* she thought.

Jenny sought Lane's expertise. "Do you think the ice is ready for skating?"

"It looks pretty thick to me." Jesse's voice held only a small waver of doubt as he looked at Lane for confirmation.

"Well, I don't know." Lane methodically folded his napkin and laid it beside his plate, the children squirming all the while. He rubbed his chin with his index finger. "Rivers don't usually freeze hard enough for skating before Christmas. Might be you'll need to wait until then."

A groan rose from the three children.

A grin burst across Lane's face. "I spoke with the local ice cutter yesterday. He says the ice is plenty thick for skating as long as you stay a safe distance from the dam."

"Yeah!" Jesse's chair scraped across the wooden floor as he pushed back from the table. Jenny and Nathan followed suit.

"Did anyone say you could leave the table?" Alice asked.

Jesse's excitement dropped from his face, replaced by disbelief. "But. . ."

Walter rested his hand on Alice's. "Won't harm any great world plan to let them leave the table early this once, will it?"

Mantie's stomach turned over at the sweet smile he gave his wife and the way Alice easily capitulated to him. Mantie touched the locket at the neck of her gray wool gown. She and Colin would never again share tender glances.

The children noisily donned their coats. Jenny and Jesse hurried to their rooms to retrieve their skate blades.

Alice smiled at Walter. "Why don't you and Lane visit in the parlor while Mantie and I clean up the kitchen?"

Lane looked a little uncomfortable. "I hate to appear unappreciative, but I'd like to head to the river with the children. It being Nate's first time there, I'd like to check it out."

"But I thought the ice cutter said the ice is fine," Alice protested.

Mantie allowed herself a small smile. It appeared Alice's attempt to bring Lane and Mantie together for the afternoon was crumbling, and this time Mantie wasn't the one avoiding the situation.

"I trust the ice cutter's knowledge," Lane said. "After all, he knows how thick the ice is. Still, I'd feel safer if I were there this first time. I can check out some of the areas where the current might make the ice thinner and warn Nate and the others to stay away from unsafe spots."

"Why don't we all go?" Walter looked from Alice to Mantie.

"We don't have skates," Alice protested.

Mantie suspected her sister-in-law was thinking more of the defeat of her matchmaking plans than of her lack of skates. Outside in the snow and cold, with Lane's attention on the children, the atmosphere would not be as conducive to budding romance as it would be in the parlor.

"It might be fun to watch the children," Mantie said. "And now that the fog's lifted, it's beautiful out."

Alice conceded with an exaggerated sigh. "All right."

Mantie smiled. She truly liked her sister-in-law. Alice was beautiful, animated, and very good for Walter. In the past she'd honored Mantie's desire to avoid encouraging the town's single men. She hoped Alice's broken plans would discourage her from trying again.

By the time the adults left the house, the children were out of sight. Their laughter drifted back along the road to the river.

Tall jack pines covered the hills. Their greenery was still encased in shimmering ice, as were the winter-barren limbs of deciduous trees. With the brilliant blue sky for a background, the ice-encrusted trees reminded Mantie of the ivory cameo set against blue.

When the group rounded a bend in the tree-lined road, Mantie could see the stone bridge spanning the river at the bottom of the hill. On one side of the bridge stood the mill, its wheel frozen into the millpond ice. Bright scarves and mittens highlighted the more muted colors of jackets as boys moved about on the ice, shovels and brooms pushing back the snow. The sound of metal scraping ice drifted up the hillside alongside children's calling voices.

When they reached the riverbank, Lane scanned the area. "It seems they've selected a good spot." He and Walter went out on the ice, stopping every few yards to sweep away snow and check the ice for cracks and depth.

When the men returned, Lane said, "The ice looks good here."

Walter agreed. "Think I'll gather some wood and start a small fire up on the bank. The kids will want to warm up after a bit."

Already the children were setting aside their shovels and brooms and fastening the leather straps of their skate blades over their boots.

Lane reached his hand out toward Mantie. "Would you like to check out the ice along the river's edge with me, Miss Clark? Just for a short ways. We can count on some of the kids wandering. Too tempting to check out what's around the bend."

Mantie hesitated, then removed one of her gloved hands from her muff and allowed him to clasp it. Footing could be tricky on the uneven ground along the riverbank.

As she and Lane started down the bank, she caught Alice's triumphant look. Frustration squiggled through Mantie. Alice obviously thought her attempt to push Lane into Mantie's life was progressing in spite of the change in plans.

Around the bend the noise of children's laughter and skates against ice diminished. Soon the quiet of the woods surrounded Mantie and Lane. He stopped and looked up at the jack pines towering above them, closed his eyes, and took a deep breath. "I love the silence of snow-covered woods in winter."

"I do, too." She spoke softly, as he had, not wanting to disturb the peace that filled the forest.

He squeezed her hand and smiled. "Hard to believe Peace is such a short distance away." He pointed at a snow-shrouded bush beside the river. "Look."

A rabbit quivered beneath the branches, its nose twitching.

Together, they watched it for a few minutes. Finally they proceeded with their duty, and the hare raced across the ice and into the woods above the opposite shore.

Lane pointed out tracks of deer, raccoons, squirrels, foxes, and wolves. "The deer are the road builders in winter."

"What do you mean?"

"They make paths in the snow that shorter-legged creatures follow."

Mantie's gaze slid along one of the snow paths from the river's edge until she lost sight of it up the hill. "God must provide path makers for us when we need them, too."

"I expect He does." The smile in his eyes told her he liked her thought.

"I think we don't always recognize our path makers or the paths."

For a few moments he studied the path he'd shown her. "Maybe we don't recognize them because they don't look the way we expect."

When they'd checked the ice along the bank far enough to satisfy Lane, he tested the ice farther out himself before allowing Mantie to cross with him to the opposite side. They followed the bank back in the direction of the skaters.

She wondered what Alice was thinking. A quizzing regarding the time spent out of sight of the others likely lay ahead this evening. What would Alice think when she discovered Lane had spent the time pointing out animal life and their habits instead of romancing her? The thought brought a smile.

Alice's plan to treat the blacksmith to dinner had failed, too. "I'm sorry your friend wasn't able to join us today."

"Abe?"

"Yes. It was kind of him to help out the farmer on a Sunday." She smiled. "Most of the single men in town beg and cajole for an invitation to a dinner made by a woman."

He laughed, shaking his head. "Not Abe. He avoids women like they carried the plague."

"Why?" She snatched back her curiosity. "I'm sorry. It's not my affair."

They walked on for a few more steps. She was surprised when Lane spoke, answering her question.

"Women never seem to care for Abe. Maybe his size intimidates them. Or they don't like the smell of the forge that hangs about him or the soot beneath his nails. Maybe they don't think a blacksmith is gentlemanly enough for them. Or maybe it's that he's a bit shy around them. Whatever the reason, they don't like him. Rather, they don't give themselves a chance to find out if they might like him."

"I suppose some women might be put off by the appearance of a man like Mr. Newsome."

Lane grunted.

"I'd like to think," she continued, "that most women would get to know him before deciding he is undesirable. He's obviously a hardworking, responsible man. Since he's your friend, you must recognize other good attributes in him. In the end, it's a man's heart that's important."

Lane stopped and turned to face her. His gaze searched her eyes.

She gave a nervous laugh. "What?"

"I've been warned that you don't allow any man to court you."

Embarrassment surged over her. Did that mean he'd asked about her? Did he want to court her? She pulled her gaze away and began walking. "I can't see what that has to do with Mr. Newsome."

He fell into step beside her. "I thought since you have the same aversion to romance, you might understand Abe better than most."

"Are you trying to play matchmaker, Mr. Powell?" First Alice and now this man who'd been a stranger only a few days ago. Really, it was more than a woman should need to bear.

"Not for Abe, Miss Clark. Not for Abe."

The laughter in his voice spurred her to increase her pace. She focused her attention on the bend just ahead. Her foot struck something and she stumbled. "Oh!"

Lane grabbed her arm with one hand and grasped her about the waist with his other. "Steady there."

"I'm quite all right." She pulled away from him.

He kicked at the snow where she'd stumbled. "Here's your culprit. A twig caught in the ice."

She started again toward the bend.

"Miss Clark, I apologize." His hand at her elbow urged her to stop. "It wasn't my intention to insult you."

She lifted her chin and looked him directly in the eye. "If I don't want to court and marry, it's no one's business but my own."

"You're right."

His quick agreement only incited her anger. "If you must know, I loved someone once. He died."

"I know." His voice, like the look in his eyes, softened. "I'm sorry."

She stared at him, stunned. Where had he heard about Colin?

He squeezed her arm gently. "I spoke out of turn. I was wrong to compare your situation to Abe's. Please forgive me."

Her anger receded in the face of his sincerity, but at a loss for words, she simply nodded and turned away.

Her thoughts were in turmoil as she and Lane walked back to join the others. Realizing he knew of Colin made her feel exposed and vulnerable. She'd told no one in Peace but Alice about the love she'd lost. Certainly Alice wouldn't breach good manners so far as to reveal her loss to a comparative stranger. Walter must have told Lane of Colin; and if Walter had told of Colin's death, what else had he revealed?

Chapter 5

L ooks like the whole town's out to skate," Lane observed when they arrived back at the millpond.

He exaggerated, but not by much. The area of shoveled ice had been enlarged during their absence. At the far end, Jesse and Nate played with boys who were hitting a large flat rock along the ice with sticks and brooms. Parents and older children held the hands of little ones who were learning to maneuver on the ice. Jenny skated close to the river's edge with a girl about her own age. Mufflers and skirts floated on the breeze their owners created by skimming over the ice. Husbands and wives skated arm in arm. As always, seeing happy couples caught at Mantie's heart with memories of Colin and the knowledge they'd never again be together.

Lane touched Mantie's elbow and nodded toward a little girl who wobbled on shiny skate blades a few feet from them. Mantie recognized the banker's six-year-old daughter, Susannah. Golden braids hung below her black knit hat, framing a round, rosy-cheeked face. As they watched, Susannah's skates skidded out from under her. Undeterred, she pushed herself up and tried again.

Whomp! Her bottom hit the ice. Pressing her lips firmly together, she struggled once again to her feet.

Plunk! Back down. The front of her blades curved in front of her boot toes like smile lines. Susannah's mittened hands formed into fists. "Oh, my!"

Mantie and Lane shared a laughing glance.

"Shall we help?" Lane took Mantie's answer for granted and started toward Susannah.

Mantie followed, walking carefully on the ice. "Hi, Susannah."

Lane smiled at Susannah and held out his hands. "Need a hand up?"

Susannah let him take her hands. He lifted her in one swift movement to her feet.

"How about if Miss Clark and I each hang onto one of your hands while you skate between us?"

"Only for a little bit." Susannah lifted one of her hands toward Mantie. "I'm trying to learn to skate by myself."

Lane nodded solemnly. "Of course."

Susannah's skates thunked rather than rang against the ice. Mantie realized the girl was walking on her blades. "Try pushing your blade across the ice instead of stepping on it, Susannah."

Susannah tried. One foot moved out in front. Farther. Farther. "Help."

Lane and Mantie lifted the girl's arms until both feet were underneath her again.

Mantie tried once more. "Push your foot like this, Susannah. Just a little way at a time." She shoved the toe of her right boot forward. "See?"

Susannah nodded.

Mantie pushed the toe of her left boot forward. "O–oh!"

She thrashed about with her free arm. It was no use. She fell to the ice, pulling Susannah and Lane with her.

"Oh, my!" Susannah pushed herself off Mantie. "I think I'll skate by myself, thank you very kindly."

Mantie's gaze met Lane's over Susannah's head. They burst into laughter.

Susannah levered herself with her hands against Lane's legs and stood up. A second later she sat between them again.

Laughter shook Mantie's voice as she inquired whether Susannah was hurt. Before Susannah replied, a man asked whether Mantie was all right.

She looked up to see Susannah's father. "Quite fine," she managed before breaking into another peal of laughter. She pulled her disarrayed skirt over her boots.

Susannah's father lifted the little girl into his arms. "I think we've had enough skating for one day, Susannah. Thank you for trying to help her, Miss Clark, but she's determined to do it herself, as you can see."

Susannah's protests drifted back to Mantie and Lane as the girl's father carried her toward the shore.

"The girl is pioneer stock for sure: stubborn and tough." Lane stood and with a grin helped Mantie to her feet. "You never learned to skate?"

"Whatever gave you that impression?" Mantie attempted a haughty expression but couldn't keep it up. She grinned back at him. "I haven't skated since I was a girl back in New York. My old skate blades now belong to Jenny."

He steadied her with a hand under her elbow. "Doesn't the general store sell skate blades? Or perhaps you didn't care for skating."

"I'm not sure whether the general store sells blades. I liked skating when I was young. I guess I haven't thought about it for quite awhile." Life's everyday duties had filled her days for so long. Spending time at things such as skating seemed frivolous. Caring for the children and Walter, moving across the country after the war, and existing each day with the pain of losing Colin and her brother had taken all her strength.

Lane pointed to the riverbank. "Looks like Walt got the fire going."

The pleasant scent of wood smoke drifted on the air. A small group gathered about the flames with Walter and Alice. Nearby, boys lying belly-down on wooden sleds sailed down the smooth riverbank and out onto the ice.

Mantie became aware of skaters watching her and Lane. She didn't mind people laughing at her fall on the ice, but she didn't want them thinking she and Lane were courting. With a sinking feeling, she realized it was already too late to stop such speculation.

When they arrived at the fire's welcoming warmth, Mantie immediately moved away from Lane to stand beside Alice. While Lane answered Walter's questions about the ice downriver, Alice nudged Mantie. Black brows lifted above eyes dancing with excitement and curiosity.

Mantie frowned at her and shook her head slightly, then pointedly looked away.

Jesse and Nate came up the slope from the river, red-cheeked and panting. Jesse's progress to the fire, made on his skate blades, was slower than Nate's.

"They must be exhausted," Mantie said to Alice. "They'll sleep well tonight."

Nate stopped beside Lane, waiting with obvious impatience for his brother to stop speaking to the adults. He broke in as soon as he politely could. "Can I go get the sled, Lane?"

Lane laughed. "Sure, if you think you have enough energy to use it."

"We're not tired, are we, Jesse?"

"Not a bit of it." Jesse dropped to the ground. "Wait for me to take off my skate blades, Nate."

"Looks like you were wrong," Alice said as they watched the boys race toward town.

"Yes," Mantie agreed. "I'm glad to see Jesse and Nate get along so well. I wasn't sure Nate wanted to make new friends at first."

She felt someone's gaze on her and glanced about. Lane was watching her with a smile. She realized he'd heard her comment and sensed his thankfulness for her concern for his little brother. His gratitude filled a place inside her with warmth, a place untouched by the fire before them.

Nate and Jesse's shouts announced their arrival with the sled.

"I've never seen such a fine sled," Mantie marveled to Alice.

It didn't look like the sleds with which Mantie was familiar. Instead of the usual lengths of wood that completely filled in the space between the sled's bed and the snow, these runners were made from metal and gave the sled the more delicate, graceful image of a sleigh.

Townspeople surrounded the sled. Men wanted to see how it was made. The boys merely wanted to ride it.

Nate took it for the first run. It whizzed past the crowd, down the bank, and onto the ice. Instantly the other children crowded around Nate, begging for a chance to ride.

"Nate looks like he's grown three feet, he's so proud," Lane confided to Mantie. "Just hope he realizes that this doesn't mean those kids want him for a friend."

"I think it's nice he's sharing it with them. It seems to ride more smoothly than the shovels and sleds with wooden runners."

"Have you ever ridden a sled?"

"No."

He reached out his hand. "We can remedy that."

She stepped back. "Oh, no." The town already thought they were courting. She wasn't going to cement the idea, tempted though she was to sail down the hill. Besides, she couldn't imagine a less elegant position for a woman than lying on her stomach racing headfirst down a snowy riverbank.

Lane gave in without a fight.

She wished he hadn't and was immediately disgusted with her contrary attitude.

She turned her back on the sled and shovels and walked down by the ice. Colin wouldn't have given in as easily as Lane. He would have badgered and teased and insisted until she rode down the hill whether she wanted to or not. In the end, she'd have loved it. She always loved everything they did together. He'd been so full of energy and fun and laughter. Her stomach tightened at the memory. He'd brought so much joy into her otherwise quiet days.

The longer Mantie watched the sledders, the more she wished she'd accepted Lane's challenge. The children's laughter, giggles, and shining eyes told of their fun. The way they ran up the slope, their sleds bouncing behind them, spoke of their eagerness to experience the exhilarating run again. Soon snow encrusted the clothing of all the children, but they didn't seem to notice.

With a bit of a swagger, Nate agreed to give little Susannah a ride. She sat in front, her eyes wide with excitement. "Hold on to the sides," Nate commanded. He sat behind her, reaching in front of her to grasp the sled's rope in both hands. She let out a squeal of delight as the sled gained speed, closing her eyes hard against the flying snow, bringing laughter from the crowd.

Jesse condescended to give Jenny a ride next. The other girls weren't as fortunate. "Sledding is for boys," Nate announced solemnly. Jesse nodded in agreement. Disappointed, the girls went back to the river to entertain themselves.

The brightness of the winter afternoon dimmed as the sun neared the horizon. The number of skaters and sledders dwindled as they headed toward home and warmth and dry clothes and supper before the evening church service. Alice left to begin preparing the family's meal. "Stay for a while if you want," she urged Mantie.

Walter made sure the fire was out, spreading the embers and covering them with snow.

"Do we have to go? Can't I have just one more ride?" Nate begged.

"I think Miss Clark should have the honor of the last ride." Lane smiled at Mantie. "What do you say? Changed your mind yet?"

The temptation was too great. Most of the townspeople were gone. She grinned. "All right."

Nate sat down on the front of the sled. "You can get on behind me, Miss Clark."

Mantie shook her head. "I don't think there's room for both of us."

Nate relinquished his sled with obvious reluctance.

Rejecting the idea of lying on her stomach, Mantie knelt on the sled and grasped the sides.

"That might not be the best position," Lane warned. He explained how lying down kept the weight more evenly distributed over the length of the sled and showed her how it was easier to grasp the sides while lying down. "And of course, if you need to avoid a rock or tree, it's not as frightening to roll off if you're already lying down."

"Cheerful thought." She darted him a look of disgust and didn't change her position.

He chuckled.

"Will you give me a push, Jesse?"

Jesse obliged.

She barreled down the slope at a speed that felt considerably faster than when she'd watched others. The sled seemed to leap when it went over a slight bump in the path. Mantie's heart dropped from her chest to her stomach. Her weight pitched to one side. The next moment she lay in the snow, the sled on its side next to her.

She sat up and reached to brush snow from her eyes. Instead, she made it worse. Blinking, she looked down at her gloves. They were covered with snow. Her wrists stung from the cold of snow jammed into the top of the gloves.

Jesse, Jenny, and Nate raced up to her. "Are you all right?" Jenny asked, panting slightly.

"Did you like it?" Jesse asked. "Isn't it grand?"

"Yes, to everything." Mantie struggled unsuccessfully to find a way to get up with a modicum of grace. Jesse and Jenny each grasped one of her arms and tugged.

By the time she was standing, Lane had reached them. "You're going to try again, aren't you?"

She had the juvenile desire to stick out her tongue at his teasing tone and laughing eyes. Instead she righted the sled and pulled it back up the hill. He fell into step beside her. "How do you steer this thing?" she asked when they arrived at the top.

"You lean. It doesn't make sharp turns, of course, just kind of veers to the side you lean toward. Of course, it's better sometimes to try to find a straight course and keep the sled on it."

"Do tell. And where on a hillside does one find such a perfect course?"

He had the grace to smile sheepishly. "Why don't you let me go down with you once and show you how it's done?"

She wasn't sure whether that was a good idea, but she obligingly made room for him at the back of the sled. "Pull the rope tight and hold it with both hands," he instructed. When she'd done so, he reached his arms forward and grasped the rope, too. His breath was warm against her cheek, and she caught her breath at his closeness.

The intimacy was forgotten a moment later in the exhilaration of racing down the hill, flying past trees and shrubs. The bump that had thrown her earlier threatened to toss the two of them. She felt the sled start to lean to one side. "Lean!" Lane's yell sounded in her ear at the same time his arms pressed against hers. Together they shifted their weight. The sled shifted, too, and they hit the ground and continued their descent. Then they slid across the ice. Lane stuck out his feet and dug in his heels until they slowed to a stop.

It happened in a flash, but Mantie was aware of it all and exuberant at having mastered that silly lump of land, even though it took Lane's help to do it.

They stood up and she turned to him, smiling. "Thank you. It was wonderful." She felt as carefree as a child.

"Maybe next time you'll want to try it alone again. I think it's getting too dark to sled now."

She hadn't noticed how deep the shadows had grown. He was right, of course.

As she walked home with Jenny, Jesse, and Walter, Mantie relived the afternoon in wonder. She couldn't remember when she'd last had so much fun that she'd lost track of time.

Chapter 6

"Mantie, it's time to get up."

Jenny's voice broke through Mantie's sleep. "I'm awake," she mumbled.

Light, Alice and Walter's voices, the smells of oatmeal and bacon, and too little heat rose through the grated opening in the floor near the bed. The room was still gray in the early morning. Through half-opened eyelids, Mantie watched Jenny, with whom she shared the room, grab her dress and high-buttoned shoes.

Jenny opened the door and stopped. "Don't go back to sleep," she warned before hurrying downstairs to dress beside the kitchen stove.

I can't believe I slept this late, Mantie thought. Usually she was up early, helping Alice prepare breakfast for the family while Walter milked the cow and broke the ice in the water for the farm animals. At least she didn't need to be at school this morning. Mr. Wren had attended church services yesterday, hale and healthy.

She stretched, then drew the quilt back up beneath her chin. Its heaviness and warmth were so enticing. Just a minute or two longer couldn't hurt.

Images from yesterday afternoon at the river filled her mind: Lane pointing out animals and tracks in the quiet forest around the bend; Susannah's determined chin as she tried out her new skate blades; the color and sense of life the skaters brought to the river and millpond; the children's laughter; the excitement of skimming over the snow with Lane on Nate's sled.

Lane. She liked the way he played and laughed with the children. She'd enjoyed his friendly, but not too friendly, company. If only men could remain friends and not always try to court a woman.

She pushed the quilt back, sat up, and swung her feet over the side of the bed. Even through her stockings, the floor chilled her feet. She dressed quickly, pulling the warm but itchy wool stockings over her knees, donning her brown wool housedress and high-buttoned shoes. She left her braid. She'd brush her hair out downstairs. Looking in the mirror, she pinned the locket above her heart.

Shocked, she stared at the locket's reflection in the mirror. This was the first morning in years that she hadn't awakened with her first thought being of Colin. Troubled, she walked downstairs, yesterday's joy-filled memories smirched.

Clothes still draped over the rope Walter had strung across the kitchen the night before. Everyone but Alice had returned from the river wet to the skin and had needed a complete change of clothes for the evening service. Alice had scolded good-naturedly, warned they would all come down with croup, and heated apple cider to warm them.

Jesse and Jenny were ready to leave for school by the time Mantie entered the kitchen. The children's coats and accessories were still damp from the previous day. Mantie lent Jenny a dry pair of gloves, and Jesse wore the stained pair he used for chores.

Walter left with the children, he for work and they for school. Mantie couldn't avoid seeing the affectionate look and squeeze of the shoulders Walter gave Alice at the door before leaving. Although she was glad for her brother's happiness, the signs of their affection were a painful reminder of the life she would never share with Colin.

Mantie filled a bowl with oatmeal from the pot on the back of the stove and sat down at the table. As the children often did on cold winter mornings, they'd pulled the table closer to the stove. Mantie was glad they had. The extra warmth was especially welcome after the cold blast of air let into the kitchen with their leave-taking.

She checked the white porcelain pitchers on the table. The children and Walter hadn't emptied them. She poured warm maple syrup on the oatmeal to sweeten it and covered it with cream.

"Are you going to join me, Alice, or have you already eaten?"

"Mm." Alice set a cup of coffee beside Mantie's plate and seated herself across the table.

Mantie tilted her head and studied her sister-in-law's face. "Are you all right?"

Alice rested her elbows on the table and waved one hand in dismissal. "I'm not hungry, thank you."

Mantie shook her head. If Alice were a student, the teacher would accuse her of daydreaming. "I'm sorry I overslept this morning and left you to feed everyone and get them off to school and work."

"I didn't mind. Did you have a good time with Mr. Powell yesterday? You do like him, don't you?"

So that was it. Alice's mind wasn't on breakfast and Monday morning chores. She wanted to know whether her matchmaking attempt had succeeded.

"He seems to be nice," Mantie conceded.

"Did he ask to see you again?"

"No."

"Oh. That's too bad. Of course, he still might ask you. Maybe he's scared off by your reputation."

"I hardly think—"

"Didn't he hint at liking you, even when you were alone together down the river?"

"No. I mean. . ." The memory of his laughing response when she'd asked whether he was trying to make a match between her and Abe flashed through her mind: *Not for Abe.*

Alice didn't seem to notice her hesitation. "I have something to tell you."

"Yes?"

"That is, Walter and I have something to tell you, but Walter thought I should tell you." Alice looked uncharacteristically embarrassed.

"Alice, you are not making any sense this morning."

Alice rested her hands in her lap, took a deep breath, and met Mantie's curious gaze. "We're going to have a baby."

Mantie blinked. "A baby? I mean, that's wonderful."

Alice smiled. Her shoulders lifted in a nervous shrug. "We think so. Walter is very excited about it."

"Of course he is. Are you feeling all right?"

"Oh, yes. I was sick when I got up this morning, but I'm fine now."

"Don't worry about getting up to take care of anyone for a while. I can see to getting breakfast and all. When is the baby due?"

"The end of June." Alice rested her hand on her stomach. "My dresses are beginning to feel tight already."

"We'll need to make you some new clothes."

Alice reached across the table and clasped one of Mantie's hands. "I'm so glad you're here. I'm excited about the baby, but I feel safer knowing I have you to depend on."

Mantie smiled and squeezed Alice's fingers. "I'm glad I'm here, too. It will be fun to have a baby in the house, won't it?"

But later, cleaning soot from the kerosene lamp chimneys while Alice heated water for the weekly laundry, Mantie wondered how long Alice would welcome a sister-in-law in her home. At the moment, Walter's home was large enough to easily house his sister, nephew, and niece. He and Alice were only starting their family. Would Alice soon feel Walter's extended family was crowding her and Walter's family?

What else can I do but live here, Lord? I can't support myself, let alone Jesse and Jenny.

The young town desperately needed skilled people, but it didn't need any of her skills. She could teach, but neither the town nor the surrounding townships needed teachers. Men filled the available positions. The salaries the male teachers demanded cost the townships more than female teachers, but everyone agreed men needed the jobs more than women, especially women like herself who had relatives to support them.

She could sew, but the town already had a tailor, and a number of women took in sewing. She doubted she could make enough money to pay for room and board from sewing, even if she added laundry and ironing. Those needs were also already met by others.

She was a good cook, but she hadn't the funds to open an eating establishment. Men served as clerks at the few businesses in town.

I'm letting my fears run away with my senses. Walter and Alice aren't kicking me and the children out of their home.

But the niggling fear remained, and her thoughts struggled with it while she and Alice performed the hot, heavy work of washing linens and clothing. Mantie couldn't imagine Walter and Alice actually asking her to leave. Still, things might grow uncomfortable between them. She wouldn't want to stay if she weren't genuinely welcome.

But where could I go, Lord? The question returned.

A number of unmarried men in town would gladly offer a solution. Her heart cringed from the thought. It was unbearable to consider spending her life as the wife of any man other than Colin.

Besides, she'd need to find a man who wanted not only her and her skills as a housekeeper, but Jesse and Jenny. Many men didn't care to take on the responsibility of children other than their own.

For that matter, she hadn't raised Jesse and Jenny by herself. She and Walter had raised them together. If she left Walter's home, would he want Jesse and Jenny to stay? Would Alice?

The thought chilled her heart. Jesse and Jenny had been the center of her life since their father and Colin had died. The prospect of life without them at its core was as bleak as a windswept prairie on a winter day.

Of course, she couldn't expect the children to spend the rest of their lives with her. One day they would leave to establish homes of their own. That was how it should be. One way or another, the day would arrive when she must live without them. She'd never allowed herself to face that fact before.

What am I going to do, Lord? I need to start building my own life. I can't expect Walter or the children to take care of me for the rest of my years. I know You must have a path for me. Please, make it clear.

The image of the animal paths in the forest flashed across her mind. She'd told Lane that we didn't always recognize God's paths and path makers. What had been his reply? She furrowed her brow, searching her memory. Oh, yes. He'd said, *Maybe we don't recognize them because they don't look the way we expect.*

Leaving Walter's home certainly didn't look like a path she expected, but she must be prepared for the possibility.

The morning had started with such joy-filled thoughts, and Walter and Alice's baby was marvelous news. But her own fears brought clouds that were missing from the bright winter sky.

❧

Walter and Lane recognized a friend in each other. Often during the next weeks, Lane and Nate joined the family for supper and Sunday meals. Once, Abe came along, though Lane confessed that it took a bit of arm twisting.

Mantie heard Abe talking and laughing when he visited with Lane and

Walter in the front room while she and Alice cleaned up the kitchen after dinner. But if she and Alice were near, Abe was quieter than the proverbial church mouse, and she could see the guarded look in his eyes.

"Is that the way I am around men?" she asked Alice. "Like I've built a fence around myself that says 'no trespassing'?"

Alice nodded. "Yes, I'm afraid so."

"That's why you said I'm colder than a Minnesota blizzard around them. I didn't realize how off-putting my manner is. I don't mean to be unfriendly with the men. I just don't want to encourage their romantic attentions."

"Lately, I thought I'd sensed a thawing. Is Lane Powell beginning to interest you?"

"Absolutely not."

Alice gave an exaggerated sigh. "Well, I can hope, anyway."

Mantie's fears of one day being unwelcome resurfaced. "Are you hoping to marry me off to get me out from underfoot?" She kept her tone light, hoping Alice wouldn't know how important the answer was to her.

"I'm hoping you find someone to fill your life with love and joy the way your brother does mine. I only want you to be happy."

Mantie slid her arm about Alice's shoulders and gave her a quick hug. "There's lots of love in my life."

"Not the kind I mean."

No, Mantie thought, *not that kind of love. There'll never be room for that kind of love in my life again.*

Chapter 7

O
ne night when Abe had refused another invitation to join them for supper, Alice asked Lane about him.

"I feel guilty coming over here without him so often," Lane confided. "He lives with Nate and me. This part of the country's been without a blacksmith for so long that Abe can't keep up with the work. Works into the night, most every night."

Nate had told Mantie he preferred time at their house to hours spent in the two rooms he and Lane and Abe shared at the back of the livery stable. "Lane says we'll have a house of our own one day."

The first couple evenings Lane spent at their home, Mantie was wary. Would he press to court her? She treated him politely but made certain Alice didn't succeed in placing her beside him at meals or leaving them alone where an opportunity might arise for him to speak as a possible suitor.

Soon Mantie admonished herself that her fears were unfounded. Lane was friendly but appeared uninterested in pursuing a romantic involvement. Before long, Lane's and Nate's presences in the house felt as natural as her brother's and Jesse's. She began to miss Lane on the evenings he didn't come.

Walter and Lane established a pattern of challenging each other to checkers after dinner while the children studied under Alice and Mantie's watchful eyes at the kitchen table. But if Nate or Jesse or Jenny needed help with their sums, Lane always gave it without complaint.

Whichever boy finished his lessons first received the reward of a game of checkers with whichever man won the first game. Mantie couldn't remember when Jesse had completed his lessons so quickly and with so little complaint.

"We're learning a new poem at school," Jenny announced one evening. "Abe would like it. It's called 'The Village Blacksmith.' "

"Longfellow's poem. A good one," Lane commented.

Mantie glanced at him in surprise. She hadn't thought of him as a man who read poetry.

Jenny nodded. "I like it, too. Mr. Wren says we need to memorize the whole thing, and it's very long."

Lane grinned at her. "You can do it. You're smart."

Her face brightened, and she stood a little taller. "Do you really think so?"

"I know so."

Alice leaned close to whisper in Mantie's ear, "That man would make a good husband and father."

Mantie smiled blandly back at her. "Yes. Won't some woman be glad?" She didn't admit she admired his way with the children. So many men preferred children be seen and not heard.

Nor did she admit that the thought of Lane married, his life centered around a family of his own, struck a chord of anticipated pain. *He is only a friend,* she hastened to reassure herself, but she suspected she'd miss him when he married.

As Christmas grew closer, days and evenings were filled with pleasant tasks and whispered, shining-eyed secrets. "Don't come in until I say so," became a common command from the children as they worked on Christmas gifts. Mantie and Alice worked on their gifts during moments stolen from other duties while the children were in school or after the children were in bed at night. Tempting odors elicited pleas for tastes as Alice and Mantie built up an assortment of cookies, pies, and sweetbreads.

When weather permitted, the family spent part of Sunday afternoons at the millpond and river. The Sunday before Christmas was no exception. Shadows grew long in the late afternoon as Mantie stood beside Alice, laughing at Lane and Walter playing crack the whip with Jesse and some other boys. Nate, having no skate blades, was sledding.

"I'm glad Walter has found such a good friend in Lane," Alice commented.

"He's been good for Walter," Mantie agreed. "Walter's always been a wonderful uncle to Jesse and Jenny, but Lane seems to have brought out Walter's lighthearted side. He's been so immersed in the responsibility of providing for the children all these years that he forgot how to play with them."

Alice grinned and patted her stomach discreetly. "He'll be well prepared to play with this little one."

Mantie smiled at Alice's anticipation.

Fun-filled shouts came from the ice as the human whip cracked and three boys tumbled. One of them landed beside a wooden sign Mantie hadn't noticed before. "Who put up that thin ice sign?"

"Lane. Walter told me Lane takes time away from the livery stable every day to check the ice. Lane says he doesn't want any of the village's children losing their lives to the river."

The men and boys ended their game. Mantie studied Lane's face as he and Walter headed toward the bank. *He is a fine man,* she thought.

Alice smiled up at Walter. "Look at your red cheeks. I suppose it's time I head home to prepare something warm for our skaters."

"I'll go," Mantie offered.

Lane smiled at her. "Mind if I join you? I'm ready to get in out of the wind and cold, but Nate wants to sled awhile longer."

As they crossed the bridge, they looked out over the river. Watching the skaters weave gracefully or dart with spirit about the ice, Mantie wished she had skate blades. Her childhood blades on which Jenny now skated were too small for Mantie.

Lane seemed to recognize her thoughts. "You enjoy watching the skaters. Why don't you buy blades?"

"I'd love to skate again, but spending money on skate blades seems frivolous. I haven't much money beyond the little I earned helping at school last month. Walter never complains about supporting me, but I try to buy as many of my personal needs as possible. Then, too, there are Christmas gifts to consider. I make most myself. They don't cost much, but when money is in short supply, each penny counts."

When they reached the house, Lane lit a kerosene light against the encroaching evening darkness while Mantie stirred up the embers in the kitchen stove and added wood to hurry the heat along. A pot of beans that had been baking since morning would soon be warm enough for supper.

She put apple cider on to heat. Cinnamon sticks filled the air with a spicy aroma.

A sense of pleasant familiarity in performing simple home tasks together heightened Mantie's awareness of Lane. It made her feel good and uncomfortable at the same time, and she pushed the feelings away.

From the small pantry, she brought a plate of sugar cookies and placed it on the table before sitting down across from Lane. "You're receiving company treatment. The family eats only broken cookies before Christmas."

Lane chuckled. "My mother did the same with our family."

"You've never told us about your family."

He told briefly of his parents and life growing up in Pennsylvania, of moving to Wisconsin, of his parents' death after he'd returned from the war, and his decision to move to Peace along with Abe.

"With the war, the move from Pennsylvania, and my parents' death, I felt Nate and I had lost enough people in our lives. I didn't want to lose another friend if I could avoid it. Some people, when they lose someone they love, draw away from others. The risk of losing someone again is too painful to face, I guess. I do the opposite. I figure since it's inevitable we lose people we love—not everyone, but some of them—the only thing that makes it bearable is to love them as much as we can while we're here."

"Yes." Mantie touched the cameo locket pinned at her shoulder. "I don't know what I would have done without Walter, Jesse, and Jenny when my brother and Colin died."

"Was Colin the man you told me about, the man you loved?" His tone was soft, almost apologetic.

"Yes."

"Walter said Colin died in the war."

Mantie stared at him, shocked.

"I wasn't asking him about you," Lane hurried to assure her. "He said he lost his brother in the war and that your beau died in the same battle. War's been over four years. That's a long time to love someone." His voice gentled.

"Is it? Love doesn't end because someone isn't with us anymore. Love is too strong. Once it's born, it just goes on forever, don't you think? We don't stop loving people just because we can't see them." She kept her gaze on his, allowing him to search her eyes. She wasn't ashamed of loving Colin, even if most people would have set aside the love after so many years. "When Nate goes off to school, you don't stop loving him until he gets home in the evening."

Lane didn't respond for a minute. "I was going to say it isn't the same, and it's not, in most ways. But maybe in a sense you're right. We expect children to come home from school at the end of the day. In the same way, at the end of our life here, God is waiting for us to come home." He smiled.

"Have you lost a woman you loved?" Mantie asked the question gently, a bit uncertain whether it was appropriate. Would he think the question too personal, too invasive?

"No. I never loved a woman the way you speak of loving. Colin was an especially blessed man to know a love like yours. Tell me about him, will you?"

She began haltingly. Lane listened, attentive, smiling, nodding. The words came more easily as his interest appeared genuine. She told how she and Colin met, of his love for life, the way he brought laughter into her quiet world.

"I've heard people say they began to forget what the person they loved looked like after awhile."

Lane nodded.

"I never forget. I remember everything. He was short, with wide shoulders." She held out her arms. "Like so. He was stocky and strong. He had wide cheekbones and laughing blue eyes and black hair with curls that fell over his forehead. I remember the sound of his laughter and the way he threw his head back and laughed robustly, loud and uninhibited. I remember—"

The sound of feet stamping on the porch and laughter outside the door cut off her reminiscences.

Mantie pushed her chair back. "I'd best get cups out for everyone. Will you and Nate join us for a supper of baked beans and bread?"

"And broken cookies for dessert?" Lane's eyes danced.

"Or maybe a whole cookie if you behave very well."

Happy chatter filled the kitchen as the family entered. Mantie smiled and nodded as they spoke, but her mind remained on her memories of Colin.

I remember the timbre of his voice, the way it dropped and grew husky when he said, "I love you." Most of all, I remember that.

⁂

The next afternoon, Mantie stopped at the general store for crochet thread. She was eager to get started on the collars she planned for Jenny and Alice for

Christmas. The clerk was busy helping Lane when she entered the store. She looked in surprise at the large order of red ribbon the clerk was cutting for him. She lifted her eyebrows in curiosity. "Are you planning to dress up the horses at the livery with red bows for Christmas?"

His face turned almost as crimson as the ribbon. "It's a surprise. I mean, what I plan to use the ribbon for is a surprise."

"I see." She didn't, of course. What use could a man possibly find for red ribbon? If he had a sweetheart, she'd suspect the ribbon was for the woman's hair. But no woman needed the yards of ribbon he was purchasing. She was certain he wasn't buying it to trim an outfit. She refused to pursue her rampant curiosity with more questions.

The clerk completed measuring the ribbon for Lane. "Anything else, Sir?"

"Some red paint if you have it. Otherwise, brown will do. And candles. I need a lot of candles. A couple dozen, I'd guess."

Red ribbon, red paint, candles. It was a riddle to Mantie.

While the clerk wrapped the candles and ribbon in brown paper and tied the package with cheerful red twine, Mantie waited beside Lane.

"Beautiful weather today," Lane said. "Crisp air, no wind, no clouds, not too cold but cold enough to keep the snow and ice from melting."

"Yes, beautiful." Weather was always a safe conversational item.

"Would you like to go sleighing?"

It was on the tip of her tongue to refuse. A negative response to a man's invitation was habitual. He spoke again before she could answer.

"It would be a shame to waste an evening like this. I have a great sleigh at the livery."

A smile tugged at her lips. "Red, I suppose."

"How did you know?"

"Oh, just a suspicion." What could it hurt to accept his invitation? After all, he acted almost like a brother toward her. "I haven't been sleighing in years. It might be fun."

"Wonderful. I'll come by with the sleigh about eight. Late, but we want the benefit of the moon."

Mantie watched him as he left the shop, still wondering about his strange combination of purchases.

The clerk discreetly cleared his throat.

She turned about with a bright smile, embarrassed to have been caught watching Lane. She selected her threads and left the shop.

Lane was right. The weather was perfect for sleighing. Her spirits lightened at the prospect.

Chapter 8

Lane hung lanterns at the front of the sleigh and walked around the vehicle for a last check. He'd taken time to polish it this afternoon after Mantie's unexpected agreement to go sleighing. It didn't matter that by the time he got to her house the polish would be smudged. It didn't matter that it was night and Mantie wouldn't see his effort. He'd wanted to polish it; a symbol, he supposed, of how important this evening was to him.

A buffalo robe covered the leather seats. Another robe was folded and lying on the seat. The metal foot warmer filled with warm coals sat on the floor. Was he forgetting anything?

He patted the dapple gray and adjusted its blanket, making sure it was secure and wouldn't fall off or get tangled in the harness as they traveled. He'd selected his favorite, most trustworthy horse for this duty. "You ready, Jeremiah? Be on your best behavior tonight. You'll be pulling precious cargo."

The horse snorted and shook its mane, setting the sleigh bells a-jingling.

Lane chuckled. "You're right. I'd better be on my best behavior, too. Knowing Mantie Clark, I won't have a second chance to put my best foot forward."

His thoughts raced to the evening ahead as he drove toward the bridge over the river and the road to Mantie's house. He could barely believe she'd said yes. From the day less than a month ago when he'd met her at the school, he'd had the impression this was the woman God intended for him. This was the woman who was the answer to his prayers for a wife.

"Is this faith, God?" he spoke into the winter night. "Or am I deluding myself because I'm tired of living without someone to love and someone to love me? The way she talked of Colin yesterday, it's hard to imagine she might ever love anyone else." Even if she was a little interested, he'd need to take it slow and easy, building up to keeping steady company with her.

But she said yes to going sleighing tonight.

Maybe it's sleighing she likes and not the company. Maybe it's best not to get my hopes up.

But they were up, no denying; they were up high.

❧

"Don't forget, you and Nate and Abe are spending Christmas Eve with us," Alice

144

reminded Lane as he and Mantie headed out the door. "Don't you let Abe sit home, you hear?"

"Yes, Ma'am." Lane grinned. "I'll make sure he's here, if it means carrying him myself. Thank you for the invitation."

Mantie waited while he placed the foot warmer she'd prepared next to his own on the floor of sleigh. He helped her up and climbed in beside her, then settled a thick buffalo robe over their laps. With her gloved hands in her fur muff and the fur-trimmed hood of her cape covering her ears, she felt snuggled in warmth.

"Ready?"

She nodded. "I'm excited. I haven't gone sleighing in years."

They started slowly, for the road led downhill to the river. Jeremiah's hooves crunched in the snow. The lanterns danced from their brass hooks on either side of the sleigh, sending golden streams of light shimmering across the snow to banish blue shadows cast by the moon. An owl hooted overhead, startling Mantie and Lane, and they laughed together at themselves. Lantern light briefly silhouetted a deer at the forest's edge. It stood as if frozen, staring toward them, then turned and darted away.

Skaters moved like shadows along the river as the sleigh passed over the bridge. With the cloudless sky, the moon's light made the skaters' way clear. Flames from a small warming fire on the riverbank waved orange and welcoming.

Here the road became flat as it headed into the village. Lane urged Jeremiah to a faster pace. The runners hissed against the snow and the bells' song quickened. The sleigh slipped into a gentle rocking motion.

They passed other sleighers and called and received cheerful greetings. Lamplit windows added a friendly sense of welcome to the town. The crisp air carried the scent of wood smoke, which rose in straight columns from every chimney.

The wood smoke was left behind when they headed out of town, down the road that ran along the river where the land was flat. Only the moonlight and their lanterns lit the road here, but that was sufficient. The silence was broken only by the bells, the singing runners, and Jeremiah's hooves.

Mantie remembered the feel of the cool breeze created by the ride and the way it tugged at her hood. She remembered the way her cheeks felt chilled even while the rest of her body was snug and warm beneath the lap robe. She remembered the sounds and the pleasant rocking.

She'd forgotten how sweetly intimate it felt to ride through the beauty of a quiet, moonlit night with her shoulder rubbing against a man's.

Lane's conversation didn't tend toward romantic intimacy. He asked about the town's short history and queried about her childhood and her life in New York. He shared stories of his own childhood, some which made her laugh, some which made her wish it were possible to hold and comfort him without his misinterpreting her concern.

Sleigh bells announced another sleigh coming up behind them. When it drew alongside, Mantie saw the occupants were red-haired Torey and her new husband.

"How about a race?" the recent groom challenged.

"No, thanks," Lane called back.

"More important things to do?" The challenger and his wife grinned.

Embarrassment swept through Mantie, but Lane only smiled and waved.

The other sleigh picked up speed and was soon out of sight around a bend.

Lane looked at her. "I hope you didn't want to race. I don't cotton much to racing, especially at night. A horse could take a nasty spill."

"I don't like racing, either." She did like the way he cared for his horse; liked that he kept it blanketed against the cold; liked that he didn't use a whip.

There wasn't much she didn't like about Lane Powell, she realized.

She was enjoying the evening so much that a sliver of disappointment ran through her when Lane turned the sleigh around and headed back toward town. Her gaze fell on his gloved hands, which held the reins firmly but gently. What would it feel like to be held by this man?

The image shocked her. She hadn't thought in such terms about any man but Colin. What was happening to her that an evening in a sleigh could make her so unfaithful to Colin's memory?

Lane kept up a friendly but impersonal conversation, and before they reached town, Mantie's emotions relaxed once again.

Lane pulled Jeremiah to a stop on the bridge. "Still a few skaters braving the chill," he observed. The sound of blades scratching against ice was audible in the winter quiet.

"The scene is beautiful in the moonlight, isn't it?"

"There's something about bridges that appeals to me. During the war, one bridge in particular became special to me."

She studied his profile. "You haven't spoken about your war experiences before."

He shrugged, still watching the skaters. "Not much to tell. Not much different than the experiences of other soldiers. Too much blood. Too much death. Too much sorrow." He breathed in a deep, shaky sigh.

Mantie rested a hand over his. "I'm sorry." She slid her hand away.

"It seemed too much for a while. One summer night when the moon was full, I stood on a bridge like this talking to God. I told Him how weary I was of the fighting. I asked how man could be so evil to his own kind." He shook his head.

"Did He give you an answer?" She didn't blame God for the deaths of Colin and her brother, but no answer ever seemed sufficient for the war and evil that caused their deaths.

He nodded. "In a way. I carried two books with me through the war. One was the Bible. The other was poems by Longfellow."

Mantie still found his love of poetry unusual. She smiled but didn't interrupt him.

"Standing on that bridge, the words of Longfellow's poem 'The Bridge' came to me. Do you know it?"

"No."

"It ends like this:

> *'And forever and forever,*
> *As long as the river flows,*
> *As long as the heart has passions,*
> *As long as life has woes;*
>
> *The moon and its broken reflection,*
> *And its shadows shall appear,*
> *As the symbol of love in heaven,*
> *And its wavering image here.'*"

Mantie swallowed the lump that swelled in her throat at his words. "That's beautiful."

"When I remembered those words, it was like I understood them for the first time. They gave me hope. Man isn't perfect; that's no secret. The best love we're capable of is only a 'wavering image' of God's love, a symbol of His love. And I suddenly realized that both God's love and man's love are always around us."

"Even in war? Even on a battlefield?"

"Even there: soldiers risking their lives for each other, women who needn't be there at all coming to help wounded soldiers, soldiers sharing the last of their food with each other." He turned toward her, and their gazes met. "Then there are people like you."

"Me?" Mantie blinked in surprise.

"Yes, you. You and all the other people who raise children orphaned by the war."

"I never thought of that as anything special. How can a person not love the children?"

"That's the answer God gave me on the bridge that night." He smiled at her and lifted his hand to her cheek. "As awful as war is, it hasn't the power to destroy love."

It seemed the most natural thing in the world when his lips touched hers in a kiss that was gentle and warm and filled with reverence. When it ended, he pressed his lips against her forehead. His voice was gruff with emotion when he said, "I'd best get you home."

He slid his arm about her shoulders. She allowed herself to be pulled closer until her head rested against his shoulder. She was glad Jeremiah walked the rest of the way, pulling the sleigh up the winding road. She was glad, too, for the time to spend close in Lane's embrace, without the need to look into his eyes. What would she see there, and what would he see in hers?

Amazement filled her that she'd welcomed a man's kiss. She wanted to push away questions and doubts and relax in the beauty of the moment. Of one thing she was certain. Only Lane Powell could have broken through her defenses. She would never have allowed another man such intimacies.

Lane pulled Jeremiah to a stop in front of the house and wrapped the reins around the terret to keep Jeremiah still. All the while Lane's arm remained around Mantie's shoulder. Her heart raced, but she stayed in his embrace. His lips brushed her cheek, and when he tentatively kissed her lips, she yielded completely and joyfully.

Neither of them spoke while he helped her out of the carriage and walked with her to the door, his arm around her waist. At the door he set the foot warmer on the porch. Then he kissed her again, and she wondered at how right and safe and good it felt to be in his arms.

"Good night, sweet Mantie," he whispered.

Their gazes met. Mantie dropped hers after a brief instant. It was still all too new. She knew her eyes shone with joy and awe and was afraid they were making promises her heart wasn't ready to keep.

She was torn between relief and yearning when the door closed between her and Lane Powell.

Lane's thoughts were a jumble as he climbed back into the sleigh and started down the hill. He hardly dared examine the evening. Mantie had let him kiss her. More than that, she'd seemed to welcome his kiss, had rested in his embrace.

His heart soared with joy. He lifted his gaze to the sky. Was it possible the Lord was answering his prayer so quickly? He wanted to stand up and yell out his thanks.

Yet one small corner of his heart warned him to wait, warned him that Mantie Clark's heart would not be so soon and easily won.

He didn't want to listen.

Instead he wrapped himself in the memory of the feel of her lips, warm and yielding and sweet beneath his own. And he hoped.

Chapter 9

Mantie went to sleep remembering the enchantment of Lane's arms. His arms were her first thought on waking.

The chill set in to her bones and her heart as soon as she stepped out of bed and onto the cold bedroom floor. How could she have been so foolish? A little moonlight, a kind man, and she allowed herself to enjoy his kisses. No matter how much she liked Lane Powell, she couldn't love him. It simply wasn't possible to love anyone as much as she loved Colin. Of course kisses and hugs felt good to a woman who'd lived without the kisses and hugs of the man she loved for over five years. That didn't mean she was ready to give her heart away to another.

At breakfast, she avoided the family's teasing questions as best she could. With a smile firmly in place, she told them she'd enjoyed the ride and scolded them for trying to make something romantic of it. "You know Lane and I are friends."

The children and Walter let it go with a laugh, but Alice's expression made it clear she wasn't certain Mantie was being entirely forthcoming.

That afternoon Mantie and Alice collected pine boughs and cones from the surrounding woods. They piled the collection on the kitchen table and worked together to form garlands. It was fun hanging swags around the parlor and kitchen walls. They tucked fragrant boughs behind the tortoiseshell-framed portraits of Alice's parents in the parlor and the print on the kitchen wall by Currier and Ives titled "Skating Scene—Moonlight." The picture brought tears to Mantie's eyes. She'd always loved it. Now it raised memories she didn't dare face.

Mantie wasn't happy to discover Lane and Nate were again invited to supper. "Really, Alice, do you think that's necessary? They'll be here tomorrow night for Christmas Eve, after all."

Alice's eyes registered surprise. "That's not at all like you, Mantie. Did you and Lane argue last night?"

"No. I just think our family should be able to spend a few nights by ourselves."

"We do."

The truth of Alice's reply only sparked Mantie's impatience. "Lane and Nate shouldn't depend so much on our family. They can't spend their evenings here for the rest of their lives."

Alice shook her head. "I hope you never go for another sleigh ride. Sleighing obviously doesn't agree with you." She tied a strip of red patterned calico about the bottom of the kerosene lamp in the middle of the kitchen table. "There. Doesn't that look festive?"

The red bow reminded Mantie of Lane's purchase of red ribbon. *Isn't there anything that won't remind me of that man?* she wondered. She headed for the stairs and the sanctuary of her room. "I still have some Christmas gifts to finish."

That evening when Lane arrived, Mantie saw his gaze immediately seek her out. She recognized the thinly veiled joy at seeing her. She shifted her gaze away and answered his warm greeting with a cool hello.

During the meal she continued to avoid his gaze and responded to his attempts at conversation with stiff politeness. She could feel his confusion at her attitude but did nothing to dispel it. Speaking frankly in front of the family wasn't to be considered.

After the meal, as Mantie gathered dishes into the wash pan, Alice whispered, "Brrr. I can feel the blizzard is back."

Mantie shot her an angry look. "It was never gone."

"Wasn't it? My mistake."

Across the room, Lane cleared his throat. "Nate and I will be heading home now. Thank you kindly for supper, ladies. It was delicious as always."

"Aw, Lane, can't we stay awhile?" Nate pleaded. "You and Walt haven't even played checkers yet."

"Big night tomorrow, Nate. Christmas Eve. You want to be rested up."

Mantie kept her back to the door and her hands busy, all the while listening to the good-byes. She tried to forget the hurt, pleading look she'd seen in Lane's gray eyes in the last glance of him she'd allowed herself.

Later, when the others were in bed, Mantie sat beside the kitchen table, a soft warm shawl about her shoulders, putting the finishing touches on the collar she was crocheting for Alice's Christmas gift. Her thoughts stubbornly refused to stay on her work. They drifted instead to Lane.

When the last stitch was made, she studied the collar. In spite of her wandering thoughts, the collar looked just as it should. Mantie rested her head against the back of the rocking chair and closed her eyes.

Why am I letting this man slip into my heart, Lord? I don't want to stop loving Colin. I never want to forget the beautiful love we shared.

Abe's face appeared in her mind.

She frowned. Why had she thought of him? Alice had accused her of being as cold toward men as Abe was toward women. Yet she certainly hadn't been cold toward Lane. That was the problem.

But Lane had said something else about Abe. She struggled to clear the memory in her tired mind. Lane had said when some people lose people they love, they try to stop loving people so they won't risk the pain of loss again.

Is that what I've done, Lord?

No. She wouldn't believe it. She wouldn't believe her love for Colin was an illusion she'd clung to in order to keep at bay the possibility of loving and losing again. Her love for Colin had been real and strong.

But he was gone, and Lane Powell was here. Last night her heart had been light and filled with wonder and joy. It had felt good to be happy again because a man liked her. All day she'd fought that happiness and her guilt. Tonight, she was tired, weary to her very bones.

Lane lay awake long into the night. His heart felt bruised by Mantie's cold rebuff.

How could I have been such a fool, Lord? I knew I needed to work up slow to asking her to keep steady company. To kiss her, to actually kiss her... Lane groaned and buried his face in his pillow. Her kisses had been wonderful, and she'd offered them willingly, he had no doubt of that. But he knew her heart still belonged to Colin.

Will she ever allow me another chance, Lord, or have I destroyed any opportunity that she might grow to love me?

Chapter 10

Mantie and Alice banked the fire in the kitchen stove before leaving for church the next evening. They'd eat supper following the service. Pots and kettles and roasting pans covered the top of the stove and filled the oven. The food would stay relatively warm even with the fire banked. It wouldn't take too long to have the meal ready when they returned.

Jesse and Jenny could barely contain their excitement. Gifts wouldn't be opened until the morning, but Christmas Eve was still special. Their excitement was contagious. Mantie's spirits lifted, even knowing Lane would be spending the evening with them.

Alice spoke of that point while she and Mantie put on their capes and gloves. "I hope you can find it in your heart to be kinder to Lane tonight than last night. After all, it is Christmas. You might make an effort not to take the joy out of the evening for him."

Her words stung, but Mantie was in no mood to let down her defenses. What if she couldn't build them up again?

The early evening was crisp, but the family was too excited to mind. There were no skaters to watch as they crossed the bridge. Everyone in town would be at church. Even Peace's three saloons were closed in honor of Christ's birth.

The road was filled with sleighs, wagons on runners, and people walking. Every group carried lanterns, the light swinging in merry golden squares on the snow. Cheerful greetings of "Blessed Christmas to you" were offered and received again and again.

The school bell was bonging when the family arrived at the schoolhouse, reminding stragglers the service would soon begin. They were among the last to find room to sit down, but those who stood didn't complain. Like many people, the Clarks extinguished their lantern lights upon entering the church. A few lanterns remained burning, but there was no need for everyone to waste their candles.

Mantie's gaze swept the crowd. She saw Lane and Nate seated near the front on the opposite side of the room and felt a tug at her heart. Frightened by the attraction she felt for Lane, she looked away.

What is happening to me, Lord? she prayed silently. *If I truly loved Colin, how can that love be swept away so suddenly?*

The service began with a hymn. Mantie turned her mind to God's gift. She wished there were a piano to accompany the group but was grateful for the reverend's fiddle. Certainly the lack of a piano didn't dampen the joy in the congregation's hearts and voices.

The reverend led everyone in prayer, then read the beautiful Christmas story, telling of Christ's birth.

"A new member of our community has a gift for you tonight," he announced after the reading. "Mr. Lane Powell told me of a Christmas Eve tradition in a church back in Pennsylvania where he grew up. He asked if he might share it with you tonight. I was pleased to say yes. Would everyone extinguish their lanterns, please? And all the children under twelve please come to the front."

Whispers and shifting feet filled the room with a sense of confusion. Lanterns were extinguished. Only one lantern, on the teacher's table at the front of the room, remained lit. Children made their way to the front. An occasional "Ouch" and "Sorry" marked their paths.

Lane reached into a basket near the lit lantern and took out a candle. Lifting a window of the lantern with a candlesnuffer, he lit the candle, then extinguished the lantern. The candle he held cast light on his hand and his chin, but not much else.

A little light emanated from the stove in the middle of the room. The drapeless windows were pale gray, as the moon wasn't yet shining in its glory.

"When Christ came to earth as a little baby," Lane began, "He was like this little candle flame. This one candle doesn't cast a very big light, does it?"

The children answered with a chorus of timid no's.

"What do you think Christ's light was?" Lane asked.

None of the children ventured a guess.

"I'm sure you know," Lane encouraged. "What did Christ bring us?"

"Forgiveness," Nate suggested.

"Why did He bring us forgiveness?"

"Because He loves us," another boy replied.

"Why does He love us?"

Silence. Then Jenny piped up. "Because He's God's Son, and God is love."

"That's right. So what do you suppose is the light baby Jesus brought to the world?"

"Love. God's love," the children eagerly answered.

"How did the little light of God's love, which the baby Jesus brought, grow large enough to light the world?" Lane touched another candlewick to the flame. It flared into light. He held the candle out. "Here, take it."

One of the children held the candle.

"How did the little light grow?" he asked again.

"He gave it away," Jenny answered.

"He shared it," another said.

"That's right," Lane agreed. "Jesus said, 'This is My commandment, that ye

153

love one another, as I have loved you.' "

In the candlelight, Mantie could just make out Lane picking up the basket from the table and holding it out toward the children. "Nate, would you pass these out?"

From the movement and shadows, it was obvious Nate did as he was asked.

Lane whispered something Mantie couldn't hear. In a moment another candle flamed. Then another. Soon all the children held lighted tapers.

"See how bright the light shines when we share it with another?" Lane asked. "Take your candles back to your families, and light your families' lanterns."

The children did as he asked. As they returned to their seats, the light that had been concentrated around the teacher's desk spread throughout the room. When the lanterns were lit, few shadows remained.

Wavering image. The phrase from Longfellow's poem flickered through Mantie's mind as she looked about the room at the many candle flames—wavering images symbolizing God's love.

Mantie glanced down at Jenny's candle. A smile tugged at Mantie's lips. A red ribbon tied low around the candle in a bow protected Jenny's fingers from dripping wax.

Thank You, Lord. Mantie's heart swelled in gratitude. Her prayer was answered.

Lane, Abe, and Nate walked to the Clarks' house with the family. Mantie was anxious to speak with Lane but not with the family around. She did walk beside him long enough to say without the others hearing, "I'm sorry I acted so snobbish last night. I hope you can forgive me."

He looked wary but nodded.

Relieved, she fell into step beside Jenny. Lane's cautious look made Mantie a little uneasy. Perhaps he wouldn't find it possible to forgive her to the extent he'd trust her enough to keep company with her, but at least things should be more comfortable between them among the family this evening. All she could do was offer that bridge of peace and trust the Lord to work the rest out as He saw best.

The scent of pine from the decorations mixed with the cooking aromas as the family entered the house. Mantie, Alice, and Jenny bustled to get supper ready. The women donned their best aprons. The fire in the kitchen stove was stirred. The table was set with the best china and napkins.

Walter had milked the cow and checked on the horses before leaving for church, so there was no need to change out of his church suit. Alice shooed the men into the parlor, where Walter lit the stove to warm the room for family gathering later.

So many serving platters and bowls filled the table that Walter observed as he sat down, "Hardly room for our plates." Oyster stew started the meal. Roast turkey with oyster stuffing centered the main course. Sweet potatoes, carrots in cream sauce, boiled onions, ruby jelly, and sweet rolls filled it out.

Mantie was disappointed to find herself seated on the same side of the table as Lane, with Nate between them. It afforded her no opportunity to show him by her smiles that she wished to return to friendlier times.

"Where do oysters come from?" Nate asked.

"The ocean," Lane told him.

Nate gave Lane a look of disgust. "No, they don't. The ocean is far away." His observation brought a chuckle from the adults.

"You're right," Mantie assured him. "The ocean is far away. The oysters are sent to Minnesota by boats on the Mississippi River or the Great Lakes, or across land on the railroad. Some are packed in buckets with ice on top so they don't spoil. Others are canned. It takes a lot of work to get oysters to Minnesota."

"Do you believe Mantie?" Jenny challenged.

Nate heaved a sigh. "I guess so. Even though she isn't a real teacher, she teaches sometimes, so she must be pretty smart."

His comment set the others laughing again, but beneath the laughter, Mantie heard Lane murmur, "That she is, Nate." She missed much of the rest of the conversation. Her mind was filled with arguments for and against allowing Lane into her life as a suitor.

Fruitcake and apple pie left everyone content at meal's end. "We'll serve coffee and cookies in the parlor," Alice informed everyone.

The children's coffee was liberally doctored with milk and sugar. Jenny sat on the edge of her chair in the parlor, balancing her china cup and saucer in a masterful attempt at imitating a lady. At Jenny's urging, Alice shared stories of her childhood Christmases. Then the children insisted on Lane's Christmas stories, and Abe's and Mantie's and finally Walter's.

While Walter regaled the children, Mantie took the almost empty china cookie platter to the kitchen to replenish it. When she came out of the pantry, Lane was waiting for her beside the kitchen table.

"Alice sent me out here to help you." His voice was more guarded than usual.

She set the platter down on the table, hoping he wouldn't see how her hands trembled. Her smile trembled, too, as she looked up at him. "I don't need your help, but would you wait here for me a moment?"

His brows drew together in a mystified frown, but he nodded.

Mantie hurried up to her room, retrieved a small package, and hurried back down. Her heart pounded wildly. Would he think her unseemly in offering him this gift?

"Since you won't be here tomorrow, I'd like you to have this now." She handed him the package. It was about as long as her hand, thin, and wrapped in a piece of the emerald-green silk from her favorite dress. A length of black ribbon tied it closed.

Light kindled in his gray eyes. For a moment Mantie thought he was going to hug her, but he didn't.

His wide fingers struggled with the ribbon, but eventually he freed the package and unfolded the material carefully. Inside was a crocheted ivory bookmark. His gaze examined it carefully, then shifted to meet hers. Wonder shone from his eyes. "You made this for me?"

She nodded, feeling shier now than before he'd opened it. "It's for your Bible. Or your poetry."

"I'll cherish it. Thank you."

The sincerity in his voice warmed her.

He grinned. "I've something for you, too." He removed a leather bag from the pegs beside the door and pulled a package from it. The package was wrapped in brown paper and tied with red twine. "Not wrapped so fancy as the gift you gave me, but that doesn't diminish the thought."

She knew from the weight and feel what it was as soon as she took the package. Excitement sparked through her. She couldn't hold back a grin. She pulled off the paper with such speed that it brought a laugh from Lane. "Skate blades. Oh, they're the perfect gift. Thank you, Lane. Thank you."

"What do you say we try them out? I brought my own blades along, just in case I could convince you."

Mantie glanced at the door to the parlor. "We probably shouldn't go right now." Everything within her hungered to leave immediately for the river.

"They won't miss us much."

That was all it took to convince her. They hurried into their outer garments, giggling like children. They were just leaving when Mantie heard Alice say, "Mantie, are the cookies ready yet? Mantie? Lane? Where are you going?"

"Skating," Lane called and closed the door firmly behind them.

Only half a dozen other skaters were enjoying the crisp night on the river. Mantie and Lane sat on a fallen log and strapped on their skate blades. When they were ready, Lane stood and held out his hand toward her. She placed her hand in his, smiling, and slid her other hand into her muff.

"Let's try a few laps around the millpond first, where the ice is smoother," Lane suggested.

She stepped onto the ice with caution. Her first strokes wobbled. Her grip on his hand tightened. "It's been such a long time."

"We'll take it slow. You'll get the feel of it again before long."

"It might not be much fun for you skating with me. If you'd rather go off by yourself for a while, I won't mind."

He slid an arm around her waist. "I'm not going anywhere. We have all the time in the world."

She wondered whether he was referring to skating or romance.

She forced her mind away from his nearness and concentrated on leaning into the outside edges of her skates and keeping her balance over the ball of her foot. Before long her strokes were easy and smooth alongside Lane's.

"There, see? You haven't forgotten how," he encouraged.

Their blades sang in unison as he matched his strokes to hers. They moved well and easily together. "Ready to try the river?"

"Yes."

They skated beneath the arch of the stone bridge. The moon lay a golden path before them. Trees cast blue shadows across the snow-covered banks. Stars burned brightly in the sky overhead. Mantie sighed in contentment.

He grinned. "Your eyes are shining with excitement."

"It's more perfect than I remember. Thank you so much for the blades."

"You are so welcome." He shifted his weight slightly, drawing her nearer to his side.

Her heart picked up its beat. She heard him clear his throat.

"Mantie, when you asked me to forgive you earlier. . ."

"Yes?"

"I'm the one who should be asking your forgiveness."

"Mine?" Surprise poured through her.

He nodded. "You told me how devoted you are to Colin. I had no right kissing you."

Was he sorry he'd kissed her? Mantie's thoughts and emotions tumbled into a mess. Surely he must have realized how she'd welcomed his kisses. But he'd properly interpreted her coldness last night. Now what was she going to do? "I liked your gift to the church tonight."

He didn't say anything for a few strokes. "Aren't you changing the subject?"

"Not exactly. I liked what you said about Christ's love being like a candle flame, how it grows when it's shared."

Lane chuckled. "I can't exactly take credit for the idea."

"I've been hanging onto my love for Colin like. . .like it was a shield. I didn't realize it until last night. I was using my love for him to keep the risk of loving someone else away. It's not that I didn't love him," she rushed to explain. "I did love him, truly."

"I know that." His voice was quiet and low.

"During your candle parable tonight, I understood. . .oh, I don't know if I can make it clear to you, but. . .when a person lights one candle and then blows the original candle out, the second candle still burns."

"Yes."

"I know the sermon was about God's love, but. . .it's like that with Colin." It was terrifying to share this. What if Lane thought her a fool? But she didn't know any other way to tell him. "Colin's love touched my life deeply. When he died, what I learned about love from him remained. Tonight it was as if God were showing me it's time to take what I learned about love from Colin and share it." Her chest hurt from fear Lane would reject what she was offering.

Lane's skates hissed against the ice as he stopped. He gripped her shoulders and looked into her face. "Mantie Clark, are you saying you might be willing to share what you've learned about loving with me?"

She swallowed hard. "If. . .if you want it."

"If I want it?" He caught her in a hug that pushed her hood back on her shoulders. "My dear girl, I assure you I want nothing more."

She slid her arms around his neck and laughed softly. "It's not perfect, you know. Only a 'wavering image.' "

He pulled back just far enough to look into her eyes. "It's all I have to offer, too."

"That's enough."

"You dear girl." He lifted her about the waist and swung her around.

"One more thing."

He set her back on her blades, keeping her within his arms. "Anything it's in my power to give."

Mantie's cheeks heated. "About that apology for your kisses. . ."

He chuckled and whispered close to her ear, "May I trade it for more of the same?"

"I was hoping you would."

In the moonlight's golden path, he joyously complied.

His kiss felt as beautiful and right as the first one. With a little sigh, she leaned against him. He touched his lips to her temple, then kissed her dimple before claiming her lips again. "Blessed Christmas, precious one."

A flame leaped within her heart, wavered slightly, then settled into a steady glow. "Blessed Christmas, Lane."

The Christmas Necklace

by Maryn Langer

Dedication

With gratitude to the talented writers
who helped me in so many ways with this book:
Pamela G., Patti D., Terry M., Sandy S., Robin H.,
Michael M., Nicole C., Shirley P., and always, Ken.
Also thanks to Ray B. and Loraine and Gayla A.
for giving the Christmas story the right setting.

To my beloved Savior, Jesus Christ,
whose birthday this story celebrates,
for being my Comforter and loving Teacher.

Now therefore put away. . .strange gods
which are among you, and incline your heart
unto the LORD God of Israel.
JOSHUA 24:23

Chapter 1

Chicago—October 8, 1871

A rumble like the sound of an approaching train rolled through Lucinda Porter's dream, growing louder and louder until the roar enveloped her. It continued to roar, not lessening, not moving on. Lucinda rolled onto her back and worried herself awake. *Trains never sound that loud for this long.*

She jerked off her sleeping mask and sat up, puzzled by the crimson light filtering into her canopied bed. She tore open the brocade bed curtain and stared in disbelief through the wall of windows across the room. Flames licked at bare branches of the ancient sycamore. Black smoke seeped in around the window frame.

From outside her room came a rattling, a pounding on the door. "Mistress! Mistress!" The lock gave way and Pearl, nanny of her childhood and now beloved personal maid, rushed in with two serving girls. Lucinda bolted out of bed, grabbed a velvet dressing gown, and struggled into it.

"Hurry, Mistress," Pearl pleaded. Strong hands rammed satin slippers onto Lucinda's feet.

The sycamore exploded into a giant torch of white light. Windows blackened and cracked. Smoke came from everywhere and filled the room. Coughing and with eyes streaming, they stumbled toward the hallway. Blistering heat enveloped the room, and the roar of red-yellow flames swallowed up all other sound.

Terror muted her, muted them all. They gripped hands to make a human chain and rushed, stumbling, choking, into the hallway. Lucinda, Pearl, and the loyal serving maids staggered half seeing down the grand staircase to the foyer. They stepped onto the marble tile and fumbled their way through the smoke across the foyer, down the back passageway, and out the servants' entrance into the cool October evening. Lucinda took her first deep breath and stopped. Pearl wrapped her arm around Lucinda's shoulder and guided her to safety.

Lucinda twisted about in time to see the home of her childhood, sanctuary in her widowhood, haven after the sudden loss of both parents, and one of the most beautiful houses in Chicago collapse into a great bonfire. She searched for voice to scream her pain but found none. Her lungs burned, her heart hurt, her legs buckled.

A heavy hand shook Lucinda. "Lady, wake up," a weary voice said. "It's mid-morning and train's about to leave Peoria. You ain't got a ticket to go beyond."

Lucinda Porter jerked awake and blinked up into the furrowed, mocha-colored face of the uniformed conductor. "What? Who?" *How dare he speak to me in such a familiar manner.*

"You almost missed your station."

Where is Pearl? I can't miss my station. Why didn't she wake me? Lucinda shook her head to clear the confusion. Slowly, the heartbreaking reality of Pearl's leaving settled in again. She had departed two months ago, but Lucinda still couldn't fully accept that she wasn't there. Forcing the painful memories back into hiding, she sat up and slid forward on the wooden bench. She pulled her ill-fitting, second-hand coat tightly about her and glanced down at serviceable, over-the-ankle brogans. Impoverished and alone, the finality of her situation sent a chill that rattled her bones.

During this past week, she had been reduced financially to a class lower than that of the conductor. She felt ill at ease in his presence, but she forced a tremulous smile. "Thank you for your concern. I must have been exhausted to fall asleep so soundly," she managed to say.

Apprehension registered in his eyes as he waited.

"My experiences of the past two months have left me fatigued." Her words were mumbled, hurried. The conductor raised his eyebrows. "The great Chicago fire destroyed my home and everything in it."

Why should he care? Their lives would likely never touch again. Daily he would keep his train on schedule, and she, by early afternoon, would become a kitchen maid at the Tillotson mansion outside Peoria. At least there, though she was not of that world any longer, she would be tucked away in familiar circumstances. She could lick her wounds and try to put her life back together.

"Ohhh, I see," the man said. "Mrs. O'Leary's cow what kicked the bucket burned ya out, so you've come to Peoria to spend Christmas with relatives, have you?"

Lucinda gathered her worn carpetbag and stepped into the aisle. "I have no relatives, here nor anywhere. I've come to Peoria as a domestic at Judge Marshall Tillotson's country estate." *There, you have my pathetic story in one sentence.* Hearing her own words forced her to finally accept the hard truth of her new station in life. She couldn't pretend anymore that this new life was a bad dream and would go away.

"I'm sorry that you have to go out in the storm. It's comin' straight across the prairie. Nary a tree to break the wind." Gently, he held her arm and moved her along the aisle and down the steps to the platform. "This storm's gonna be a real humdinger. You got someone to meet you?"

She looked up and studied his eyes, his face. He knew little about her situation yet seemed genuinely anxious for her welfare. *Amazing. Why should he give me a second thought?* It had never occurred to her that, with the exception of Pearl, her servants and others of the serving class truly cared about her comfort and well-being. This notion needed some more pondering.

"I'm sure my transportation to the Tillotsons' will be along." At her weak smile, the conductor's face relaxed somewhat, and he climbed the steps. Over the clanking and grinding of the train into motion, he shouted, "Have a merry Christmas."

His well-meant words stabbed her heart. This Christmas would not be merry. No magnificent tree in a foyer that was larger than many homes, no welcoming candles lighting twenty-three sparkling windows. There would be no teas, no balls, no banquets, no Christmas Eve service with her parents in the family pew, no expensive gifts spilling from under a tree whose top star reached the second-story balcony. This Christmas she would not accompany her mother in directing the preparation and delivery of baskets heaped high with food and clothing for the unfortunate.

A year ago she had become a widow before she reached her twenty-first birthday. Last July she was orphaned, and this December she was left completely without means. Even Pearl was living a pampered life with her wealthy sister while Lucinda had become one of those unfortunates.

Shivering in the oversized coat and ugly blue and yellow striped cap, she watched the caboose sway off down the tracks. Not until the train became a distant blur did she remember that her small trunk had not been put off. Except for her sweater and nightgown in the carpetbag, everything she owned was in that trunk.

Her heart lurched, and her hand flew to her chest. Hidden beneath her navy wool dress, the precious antique necklace with flawless emeralds the color of her eyes was still there. It was the first and last Christmas present from her late beloved husband, the seventh earl of Northland. Lucinda pressed her hand against the precious gift and fought back tears, thankful she had fallen asleep wearing it on the night everything burned.

Hopeful, she looked around the platform. Except for the stationmaster in his little box of an office, the station was deserted. Remembering her new class in life, it dawned on her that a servant of such lowly rank wouldn't likely have someone waiting to convey her. Those charged with the transport of common serving maids weren't known to be prompt or polite. Sent on more errands than one, picking up the new kitchen help was probably last on their list before they left for home.

She crossed the street in front of the station and stood where she would be visible to any passing conveyance. The street corner offered no protection from the wind; gust after gust swept over her, biting through her coat. Shivering, she pulled the collar tighter about her throat and moved back into a warehouse doorway, looking up and down the empty street. At last, the smart *clip-clop* of horses' hooves broke the silence.

"Oh, thank you, thank you," Lucinda whispered. A large enclosed sleigh came into view. She rushed into the street where she could more easily be seen. The sleek team drew alongside. The driver gave her nary a glance and raced on, leaving a miniature blizzard behind. Fine snow settled over Lucinda and marked the departure of the only transportation to have traveled that way.

"They aren't coming for me." She wilted against the building, her courage draining. "Maybe they don't expect me. Maybe I don't even have a position." A tear she couldn't contain slid down her cheek and froze. Lucinda found a clean handkerchief and wiped her nose. "Oh, Pearl, I miss you so. You would know what to do." It then occurred to Lucinda that she should have asked the stationmaster for advice before she stepped into this freezing, awful wind.

She limped on numb feet back across the street to the little building and related her situation to the old man. The stationmaster shook his head. "Mistress Tillotson don't furnish transport coming or going. You get out there the best way you can, and it's mighty hard to leave once you're there."

"But I'm expected to arrive by early afternoon, or I shan't have a position. What am I to do?" She blinked back threatening tears.

"Best I can suggest is you go over to Main Street. Maybe you can catch a ride on a farm wagon. They come along that way all the time. With it being the last Friday before Christmas and a storm coming in, if you hurry, you might find one."

Lucinda thanked him. Fighting against a blend of panic and misery at being so helpless, she limped away through the blowing snow toward Main Street.

Chapter 2

David Morgan stood in the hall outside the sitting room of Mistress Rosella Tillotson's townhouse and adjusted his cravat. He removed his mouton Cossack hat and ran a hand along the sides of his blue-black hair in a futile attempt to smooth it. Calling on Mrs. Tillotson before noon probably wasn't the wisest thing he had done in his life, but time was running out. The Tillotsons were leaving in two weeks for an extended trip to Paris for the winter season.

I must find the good judge today. Remind the kindly old man to write the referral letter he promised.

He shucked off his overcoat and knocked with a firm rap on the ornately carved door.

"A pox on your generations. It's not yet ten," called a woman's voice, deep and gravelly. "Who's the degenerate cur who can't tell time?"

"David. David Morgan, Mistress Tillotson."

"David?" Her harsh voice changed to beckoning satin. "Since when have you started knocking?"

What is that supposed to mean? I always knock.

"Come in this minute and explain why you've been neglecting me, you naughty boy."

An unremarkable girl in a gray uniform opened the door. David entered the sitting room and handed her his hat and coat.

Though professional decorators had tried to create elegance, Rosella's taste for heavy furniture upholstered with bold textured fabric overpowered the classic objects of art the Tillotsons had collected from around the world.

Rosella fit with the surroundings perfectly. Society matron of Peoria, wife of renowned Judge Marshall Tillotson, she reclined in a regal pose on an elaborately carved chaise lounge. She was robed in a white satin dressing gown and propped amid plump pillows in burgundy satin cases. Mistress Tillotson laid aside a large hand mirror and smiled a coquettish welcome to David. "Come. Sit and tell me what is happening in the outside world." She sat up and patted the foot of the burgundy velvet chaise.

He ignored her command. "I've come hoping the judge was here."

"I suspect he's in the country. We are having a Christmas party this evening, you know." She patted the chaise again.

He deliberately walked to the fireplace. Nodding toward the newly hired maid hovering in the doorway to the bedroom, he asked, "What happened to Gigi?"

"Gigi, that ungrateful wench! She ate her way into a waddling, shiftless mountain of fat. Cost me a fortune to keep her in uniforms. Three days ago, without a second's notice, she up and left. Disappeared. Vanished without a trace." Rosella's eyes, an unusual autumn green with gold flecks, glared at him as though this disaster were his fault.

David shook his head. *The woman is impossible. No wonder Judge Tillotson stays away.*

She picked up the mirror and pursed her lips. "What a pity I don't rouge my lips. I could wipe them clean and add another touch to my invalid's ruse." She looked over the top of the mirror at him, eyes twinkling. "Can you not see, David, how very ill I am?"

He folded his arms. "Why, may I ask, are you playing the invalid?"

"I must look sick enough to convince Marshall that I am unable to attend that wretched dinner he insists on having in the country this evening."

"Why did you agree to have it if you didn't want to attend? I fail to understand the need for the charade. There's a storm predicted for today. And coming in on this *particular* day, you could just say that you don't feel well enough emotionally to cope with such an affair."

Her eyes narrowed. "You remember what day this is?"

"How could I forget? You've reminded me every December twenty-second for the past five years. But you've never gone to this extreme to celebrate your grief."

Rosella drew back her hand and flung the mirror at the wall. David jumped out of the way of scattering shards that fell like ice crystals onto the oriental carpet. "Mistress Tillotson, throwing things is going too far."

She didn't acknowledge his scolding. "I wonder why Marshall doesn't remember? Meghan was his daughter, too. The fact is, the way he doted on her sickened me."

"Of course he remembers, but he needs friends to help him through the pain."

Rosella's expression softened. "Meghan would have been twenty-two today." Her voice trembled. "She's been gone twenty years—a lifetime." Rosella reached for her linen handkerchief and blotted the tear threatening to streak her powder. "To this day, I cannot believe someone could creep into the house and snatch a sleeping child from her crib without leaving a trace. Not a clue could the Pinkerton detectives find. Two years of searching and they never found how she left Peoria." Rosella buried her face in the handkerchief.

David watched the performance and felt a churning start in the pit of his stomach.

Rosella dabbed around her eyes and snapped her fingers. "Girl, get me another mirror."

The maid quickly handed a replacement to Rosella, who ignored David and checked her makeup for damage. David pulled out his pocket watch. The morning was slipping away. "I must—"

"I'm really glad you dropped by this morning. I'd like for us to have a little visit before lunch." Rosella stood and walked slowly toward him.

He edged away from the fireplace. "What do you want to visit about?"

"Your going to Paris."

"Paris! I don't want to go anywhere close to Paris," he said bluntly. "What I want is to go west, not east."

She shuddered. "West? Have you lost your senses? The West is unfinished. Nothing but sagebrush, Indians, and other wild things."

"The far West is new territory. A man can get a foothold. Become anything he wants to."

"That's nonsense. What is it you want to become that you can't achieve right here in Peoria? After we get back from Paris."

He was amazed at how innocent her smile appeared, how convincing her eyes. "Before *you* get back, I shall be gone."

Rosella's mouth took a cunning twist into a half-smile that he had learned spelled danger.

"David," she said ever so sweetly, "I've given the past five years to turning you, a raw Welsh immigrant, into a gentleman with the savoir faire to be my escort in Paris. And I just spent a king's ransom on my wardrobe and yours."

"Rosella, you've been telling everyone you and the judge are going."

She wasn't listening. *She's already plotting her revenge.*

Her thin smile sent a shiver down his spine. "That is no way to repay the kindness I have extended you. That makes me very unhappy. And Marshall won't be happy, either."

"That sounds like a threat, Rosella. I repeat, you've told—"

"About a month ago, Marshall decided he couldn't go. Too many court cases on the docket, or so he says. So, David dear, because I am going and I will not go without an escort, you *are* going."

"No, Rosella, I'm not." He turned to the maid. "Please bring me my coat."

Fury darkened Rosella's face. "Hear me well, my young friend." Her eyes sparked a look he had seen turned on others. Never on him.

Her hand shot out, lightning fast, and grabbed his wrist. Rosella stared hard into his face. "If you think you can run away on a whim, think again. If you even consider such a thing, I shall tell Marshall you took advantage of my disturbed state during this upsetting time of the year—Meghan's disappearance—and you forced yourself on me."

"You would be lying and would have to prove those accusations in court, Mistress Tillotson." David clamped his jaw tight, revealing none of his own rage.

"Ha! Don't you worry about court. Have you any idea what Marshall would do to you? You'd be ruined!" Her evil smile suddenly turned sweet. "But enough of this. Look over there, dear." She waited until he looked. "See the lists on my desk? I have a million things to attend to."

He started to speak, but she cut him off with a wave of her hand.

Her mood shifted, and her voice was now light and happy as a child's. "Your wardrobe is ready at the tailor's. Pick it up, and I'll send word so you can accompany me to the country."

David grabbed his hat and coat from the maid and left without a word. He stormed down the stairs, jamming his hat on his head and his arms into his coat as he went. Propelled by fury, he scarcely noticed the storm or the stately homes he passed as he stalked toward Peoria's downtown and his boardinghouse across the tracks.

Rounding the corner of Jefferson and Main, he came face-to-face with an ill-dressed waif. They collided, and she went spinning toward the street. He grabbed for her, managing to get a grip on her coat, stopping her fall. Angry and frustrated, David forgot both when he looked down into her eyes—clear green with flecks of gold, framed by long, smoky lashes. Her eyes. . .they reminded him of someone.

Little else of her face showed between the striped woolen cap pulled down to just above her eyes and the large coat collar covering her cheeks. But the eyes: He couldn't help staring. They held him captive, nearly drowning him in the sorrow reflected there. Only once before had he seen such deep sadness. When his father was killed in the coal mines of Wales, his mother's eyes never lost that look. *What has happened to you, little mud lark, to scar you so?*

He let go of her coat and stepped back. "I'm so sorry. Are you hurt?" She shook her head, and an auburn curl escaped from her cap. Her coat was soaked, and snow spilled over her shoe tops. "You are not properly dressed for such weather. You must get inside at once."

"Indeed, I shall avail myself at the first opportunity."

He smiled. She might look like a poor waif, but her speech was that of a lady. Interesting. He wondered what she looked like without that unsightly cap. He gestured at the three-story brick structure across the street. "The Pinkney Building is a good place to get warm. The bakery there is the best in town."

She thanked him, and he watched as she slipped and slid her away across the street. The bakery would be warm. They would give her a free sample of the day's special. Once in front of the three-story building where Judge Tillotson had his offices, she looked back at him, nodded, then disappeared inside.

Alone on the empty street, David's frustration returned. With every step, he seethed at Rosella's cunning entrapment. Indeed he had escorted her through five years of social events, but it was at the insistence of her husband who never seemed to be available. *Now I know why. She's demented,* he thought.

By the time David reached his room at the boardinghouse, he could see no way to gracefully disentangle himself except to flee far and fast. He knelt before the steamer trunk given to him by his mother. Taking out the little coffer locked away inside, he counted the money he had saved. Eighty-four dollars, after the payment of his room and board. Enough to take him west if he guarded his spending.

He decided to accept the suit Rosella promised him. The tailor shop was in his neighborhood, so he hurried over. There, to his chagrin, he found a complete wardrobe waiting. A month ago when he went in to be fitted for one suit, he had no idea what Rosella had planned. It took two trips for David to carry his new wardrobe to his room.

From the mountain of items laid neatly on his bed, he chose the tuxedo for the dinner at the Tillotsons' prairie mansion. His mind raced as he carefully folded the items of clothing into his soft-sided leather case. "I know one thing. I am not going to the country with Rosella. Or anywhere else."

David snapped the case shut and changed into his riding clothes. "I shall stop over at the judge's office and write the referral letter. Then all he'll have to do is sign it, and I'll be out of Rosella's clutches before tomorrow dawns."

Chapter 3

Inside the spice-scented bakery, Lucinda sat thawing her nearly frozen extremities and sampling immodest amounts of oatmeal cookies, lemon custard pie, and cherry cobbler the owners urged on her. Business was brisk, but in the dim corner where she was seated on a crate near the ovens, no one paid her any mind. While she ate, she took stock of her situation.

For the first time, she allowed herself to review the events of last Wednesday. Was it only two days ago that she had still thought of herself as the wealthy Countess Lucinda Porter, fresh out of widow's weeds? Though her house and buildings had burned to the ground, she did own the ground. Her father's business partner, whom she called Uncle, took care of the legalities. After the fire, she had stayed in his lavish home and been treated with great kindness but not allowed to look at the books. Wednesday last, he had sat her down and told her the whole story.

Papa always assured Lucinda and Mama that they would always be well cared for. Never did anyone dream he would be temporarily deep in debt and both parents would die in a carriage accident before the debts could be paid. Uncle tried everything he knew to save her estate, he said. But even with the infusion of her inheritance, there was only enough money to pay off half the loans. However, he assured her he would gladly assume her debt if she would marry him. Uncle was a man twice her age, pompous and demanding. She quickly understood she would become his hostage until the debt was paid. She signed over her property to him.

Having chosen poverty, here she was in Peoria.

Lucinda's reverie was interrupted when a tall, thin woman dressed in calico and moccasins walked into the bakery from the interior darkness of the back hallway. Long dark hair pulled into double braids down her back framed her furrowed bronze face. Taking no notice of Lucinda, the woman began checking the contents of the ovens. When she finished, she straightened up and walked over to Lucinda.

Lucinda blushed at having been caught in her silent examination. Clear, nearly colorless blue eyes stared at her with an intensity that felt to Lucinda like they pierced her soul. She felt a deep connection to the old woman and, with it, a tremor of anticipation.

"I am known to all as Yarrow Woman. You are a stranger here." Her voice enfolded Lucinda like a warm blanket. She hadn't felt this safe since before the fire.

"Yes. I'm seeking transportation to the Tillotson estate. I'm expected this afternoon to assume duties as a kitchen maid."

The old woman looked deep into Lucinda's eyes. "I have been prayerfully searching for some answers about my future, and I now have the feeling you and I are going to be bound together somehow." Taking Lucinda's hands, she examined them. "You have never served."

Lucinda looked and saw what Yarrow Woman saw—hands soft and manicured. She shook her head.

Yarrow Woman let go of Lucinda's hands and continued to study her. "You will serve the Tillotsons scarcely any time at all and then never anybody else." Her words were soft, her tone reassuring.

Lucinda felt the blood drain from her face. *I cannot fail in my first position. Where will I turn?*

Yarrow Woman's expression softened. "I apologize for upsetting you, but God moves in unexplained ways, and on occasion I receive impressions about a person's future. I give all praise to the Lord and take no credit unto myself." She waved a work-hardened hand in a gesture of helplessness. "I am not usually this forthright, but I could not seem to contain this message."

Lucinda's heart skipped a beat.

The woman stood quietly, her eyes fixed on Lucinda. "I have never been to such a place, but I see beyond great mountains of granite, across a desert of death, to a city built by silver."

Lucinda shivered and closed her eyes.

"Do not let your necklace be seen. Keep it hidden and in your possession at all cost."

Lucinda's eyes flew open. She felt for the outline under her dress. "Ho–how do you know these things?" she stammered.

"From childhood I have been gifted with second sight. It is not a thing I control. In the Sioux tribe, I was a wise woman. Now that I know Jesus as my Savior, I receive only that which He chooses to give me." She turned and started back toward the shadows.

Lucinda jumped up. "Do you see when I shall go to that far-off land?"

"You will begin the journey tonight, of course." The words were spoken matter-of-factly as she entered the dim hallway.

"Surely not tonight. How will that happen?" Lucinda called, but Yarrow Woman continued down the hallway.

Lucinda felt warmth deep in her chest, yet at the same time she shivered at Yarrow Woman's words. To consider that she could be out of work by tomorrow was frightening. She had no place else to go. Her fingers trembled as she dusted crumbs off her clothes. She wouldn't consider the possibility of being let go. *I must work hard to please and make myself so useful that they will find me irreplaceable.* She thanked the bakery owners and let herself out, vowing to waylay any conveyance that might be moving upon the prairie toward the Tillotson mansion.

Lucinda walked along Main Street's crowded sidewalk, clutching her valise in one ungloved hand and the collar of her coat tightly about her throat with the other. She mulled over her experience in the bakery and decided that people of the working class were kind and honest. She liked them. Surely one of them would give her a ride.

She approached several kind-looking shoppers, but they gave her sharp looks and continued on their way. Desperation drove her to walk in the street, where she hailed sleighs, carts, wagons, any conveyance moving and some that were parked, but all she received were blank stares or curses for her trouble.

The wind picked up, building the drifts ever deeper until the shoppers gave up and vanished, leaving the streets deserted. "Oh, please, dear Jesus, help me find a ride. Please."

Before the noon church bells chimed, the storm retreated inside low-slung gray clouds. Still, she trudged up and down Main Street, around and through the drifts, battling mounting despair. She kicked at a drift of snow blocking the sidewalk. The more discouraged Lucinda became, the more she clung to Yarrow Woman's words. *She said I would serve scarcely any time at all. But she did say I would serve. That must mean I will get to the Tillotson mansion somehow.*

She walked into the middle of the street and looked both ways but saw no wagons. Not even a rider. What was she to do? She turned her back to the wind and began to cry, no longer able to hide her despair. It was then she heard hoofbeats pounding hard and fast. Before she could move from the center of the street, he was upon her.

He reined the charging horse to a skidding stop. "Excuse me," a deep voice said, "are you or are you not going to cross the street?"

She whirled around and found herself staring up into the face of the fine-looking man who earlier that morning had directed her to the bakery. Now he sat astride a magnificent chestnut stallion that refused to stand still.

With eyebrows knit together, he asked, "Why are you still out in this weather?"

"Ahh. . .my. . .the train left with my trunk on it. I only have what is in that carpetbag." She gestured at the shabby bag resting on the curb. "And I must. . .I am trying to. . ." *Lucinda, you're babbling.* She took a deep breath. "I have the promise of work as a domestic at the Tillotson estate, but I can find no transportation to take me there."

She said a silent prayer of thanks that her voice sounded strong and clear. "I must be there by early afternoon if I'm to claim the position." She kept her unwavering gaze on his face. His skin was a weathered brown common for farmworkers and did not match the gentleman his riding habit and coat suggested. His eyes focused on her with a force that made her uncomfortably aware of how common she must look. Covered with a dusting of snow, peering out from under a boyish woolen cap, the rest of her buried inside the giant coat, she must look awful.

Swallowing hard, she continued to stare at him. His broad shoulders were covered in a stylish long coat layered with a cape buttoned high around his throat. He had a regal tilt to his head, accented by a Cossack hat that gave him the appearance of an English nobleman, a scowling English nobleman. Then he flashed a wide smile that lit his face.

Even in her misery, Lucinda smiled back. Was he as kind as he looked? Had her prayer for a ride been answered? "I would pay you to take me to the estate." Her voice filled with hope, and she opened her palm to show twenty-five cents. "I know this isn't much, but perhaps we could work out an arrangement where I might pay you later. . . ."

His laugh cut her off. "You're not familiar with money, are you?"

She shook her head. "I was served by a woman who took care of all the details of my life."

"You have offered far too much." The horse tossed his head and gave an impatient stamp. "Kambur says it is time we were off. My name is David Morgan, and you are. . . ?"

"Lucinda. Mrs. Lucinda Porter, late of Chicago."

He nodded at the introduction. "You are fortunate, Mrs. Porter. I'm traveling to the Tillotson estate. Put your money away. I shall be happy to deliver you to your destination if you have no objection to riding astride and double."

Dumb with gratitude, she shook her head and picked up her carpetbag. He removed his foot from the stirrup and reached out his hand. "Let me have your satchel." She handed it up to him, and he hung it from the saddle horn opposite his own fine case. She hiked up her skirt, slid her square-toed brogan into the empty stirrup, and let herself be pulled up behind him. Ladies generally rode side-saddle, but she wasn't going to point that out.

"Put your arms around my waist and hang on," he ordered. "I don't relish being out in this weather longer than necessary."

Gingerly, she reached around his waist.

"My dear lady, this is no time to be shy. I mean to ride hard, and if I cannot feel your arms, you'll probably land in the road at the first corner. Now slide closer so your face rests against my back, and lock your hands together in front." His brusque voice left no room for argument.

Lest she be left behind, Lucinda positioned herself tight against his back and clasped her hands around his waist. Even from the back, this man radiated power, someone to be reckoned with.

"That's better," he said and flicked the reins. The horse leaped forward. They whirled away up the steep incline and out onto the prairie.

As they flew along, she silently repeated his name, David Morgan, an important name she must not forget. When she was sure she would not forget his name, she began to wonder just how much twenty-five cents was. It must be a goodly sum. She must learn about money.

All she had to her name was contained in the small trunk left on the train and the well-used carpetbag—and of course, her necklace and the clothes on her back. She reminded herself that she was probably going to be known as Lucy Porter, household servant, hoping to arrive at the Tillotson estate in time to serve other people's lavish Christmas parties.

She sighed and let her thoughts drift to this man she was clinging to. She was certain that the likes of David Morgan would not normally give the current version of Lucinda Porter a second glance. That he did said much about him. But such a man was bound to have a beautiful lady waiting at the Tillotsons', most likely his wife. *If he isn't married, Lucinda, he's far above your station now.*

The sky lightened the farther into the country they rode. Lucinda studied the beautiful homes on expansive grounds. A majestic redbrick house, clearly visible at the top of a rise, caught her fancy. It cheered her when they turned up the wide road that led toward the front entrance guarded by thick white columns—the Tillotson mansion. However, they veered to the left onto the tradesmen's narrow lane that ran alongside the house. She had never entered a house through the servants' entrance. Once more she was reminded of who she had become.

A hedge of tall yew, pruned to unnatural perfection, screened the lower windows of the house. At the back, the lane widened into a cobblestone yard that separated the kitchen wing from the carriage house and stables. David stopped at the kitchen door. Lucinda held still as he swung his leg over Kambur's neck and landed on the ground at her feet. He offered up his hand. She took it, and their gazes locked for a moment. Quickly, she came to her senses and concentrated on getting off the horse with some degree of grace.

David carried her satchel and ushered her up the steps. "With the dinner hour drawing near, there's such chaos in the kitchen that a cannon blast would go unnoticed. They'll never hear you knock." Handing her the carpetbag, he pounded on the door with no success. He shrugged and said, "Just go on in."

He looked intently into her eyes. "I hate to leave you like this, but three days ago, the good Andy Henderson, head groomsman, and his wife left in the middle of the night. I'm sure the stables are in a muddle since most of the guests are already here. I owe it to the judge to set things straight." He gave her hand a slight squeeze and, with easy grace, swung onto Kambur.

"Thank you," she called and waved. David returned her wave before he rode on to the stables.

He didn't really squeeze my hand, did he? You're imagining things. A combination of emotions raced inside—unexpected attraction to Mr. Morgan and pure terror of facing an unfamiliar kitchen from the servant's side of the fanning doors.

Cautiously, Lucinda tried the latch. It lifted, and the heavy door swung open on silent hinges. A rush of hot air filled with a mix of savory aromas swept over her as she stepped inside.

Chapter 4

How she wished for Mr. Morgan's comforting presence as she stepped into an unfamiliar kitchen for a job she had never done. She stared in disbelief at the sea of humanity running in all directions. To keep from getting trampled, she huddled in the corner and surveyed the kitchen. At the far end of the room and up seven stone steps were the fanning doors that separated the main house from the kitchen and service pantry. Serving maids wearing toadstool-shaped hats bustled in and out through the doors, carrying linens, trays of flatware, and condiments.

They would be bringing in empty plates and carrying out the next course if the meal had begun. Relief surged through her; she had made it in time. Very soon she would be one of those servants, indistinguishable from the others unless someone looked closely. No one probably would unless she did something inappropriate.

Lucinda had never studied formal dinner preparations in the detail she did now, but she knew these girls would keep their harried pace until long after the dinner hour. Guilt sprang up when she remembered her uncaring attitude in the past toward those who served her. Especially Pearl. *I was so ungrateful. I took her for granted. Now she's gone, and I have to fend for myself. I deserve this fate. I truly do.*

The kitchen was almost as large as the one in her English manor house, and the floor and the walls were tiled bright red. Against the outside wall stood a copper sink with water piped directly into it. The Tillotsons must truly be rich to afford such a luxury. Young servant girls stood on stools before the sink, elbow-deep in dishwater, scrubbing endless stacks of pots and pans. From the wood range, Lucinda caught the aromas of burning fruitwood and tantalizing spices. It had been many hours since she had eaten, and her mouth watered.

The kitchen was sweltering. The large cook, autocratic ruler of her domain, mopped the sweat from her face with a Turkish towel round her neck. She was in the process of hoisting a huge baron of beef from the oven onto the chopping block in the middle of the room.

She looked up from testing the roast and spotted Lucinda. She pointed at one of the maids. "You, Molly! Come." Molly came running down the stairs. "See who's hiding in the shadows by the door. If it's a dirty tramp begging food, lay this frying pan across his back." She grabbed up a heavy black skillet and thrust it into Molly's small hands.

Lucinda hadn't thought of herself as looking like a tramp, and she wasn't going to cower in the corner. She moved out of the shadows and watched Molly cross the kitchen.

At a safe distance, she stopped. "Mrs. Kidd, do I. . ."

"Get on with it, girl."

"Yes, Mrs. Kidd." Molly straightened to her full five feet and raised the pan over her head. "Get out, you ruffian! Get out afore I split yer skull." Her voice squeaked like an adolescent boy's and made a mockery of the threat.

Clutching her satchel, Lucinda pushed back her cap and began walking toward Molly, never taking her eyes from the skillet. *If I don't assert myself right now, I'll become the goat for the entire staff.* She brushed by Molly and said in a firm voice, "I am the new maid Mr. Button engaged. Please let him know I have arrived."

Not used to such boldness, the other servants stopped in their tracks and gawked at Lucinda. *Good. They shall not know how frightened I am. Let them think I'm a trusted colleague of the mighty Mr. Button.* From managing her own house, she knew that the butler was the person to watch out for. He ran the staff upstairs and was absolute dictator below.

Mrs. Kidd was first to recover her composure. "Well, goose, go fetch him," she thundered.

Still clutching the frying pan, Molly fled past Lucinda, up the stairs, and through one fanning door as Mr. Button entered the kitchen through the other. His cherubic face remained calm, but round eyes, partially obscured by bushy black brows, narrowed as he drew closer to Lucinda. "Ah, you are Mrs. Porter?" he asked in an adenoidal voice.

The effect of the imperious Mr. Button bearing down on Lucinda caused her to stand tall and tip up her chin. Then she remembered her position and lowered her eyes as became a domestic servant.

"So you have deigned to finally honor us with your presence. Early afternoon, as you promised, would have been much preferable. However, we're a bit short of help, so I won't throw you out with the chickens just yet."

They needed her, so she could afford to establish herself a bit higher in the pecking order. "Circumstances prevented an earlier arrival." She spoke firmly.

"I see," said Mr. Button. "I understand your experience is limited."

"I have had no experience in this country. In England, however, I spent two years with the earl of Northland." She stopped short of mentioning that she spent it as his wife. "I worked with the staff of a very large manor house. I am capable of serving in any area where I am required."

He cast a jaundiced eye over her from head to foot.

Lucinda knew her worn coat and cap certainly did nothing to validate her claims. "All I had in this world was destroyed in the great Chicago fire last October. I have been forced to accept the generosity of others for my needs."

He sniffed and nodded. "Are you sensible and literate as your papers state?"

His left nostril twitched in time to his words.

"The papers are correct," she said, giving an autocratic lift to her words. "I am both sensible and literate. Trained by the royals of England, I remain today on the most intimate terms with Lady North."

"Yes, yes, you come highly recommended. Have you brought sufficient aprons in good repair for housework? And suitable apparel for your afternoon off, if you are found worthy to be granted one?"

"I did. However, my trunk was not put off the train."

"Late and no aprons. Not an auspicious beginning. What are you called?" he asked sharply.

"My name is Lucinda. Lucinda Porter, sir," she said over the steady chug of the water pump in the background. When she pulled off her cap, auburn curls tumbled over her shoulders. She lowered the collar away from her face and bobbed a curtsy.

His eyes widened, and his left nostril twitched violently. "Yes, well. . ." He cleared his throat. "A bit pretentious, I'd say. Lucy seems more appropriate."

Lucinda debated with herself but a moment. "Perhaps Lucy is more appropriate for a serving girl, sir, but Lucinda is my name, and I prefer it."

Mr. Button smiled. "A girl with spirit has a place. However, I hope, Lucy, you know the time and place."

He turned toward Mrs. Kidd. "Though the mistress has not yet arrived, Judge Tillotson says we are to serve dinner. And you, Lucy. . ."

Lucinda winced at the name but held herself in the best servant stance. "Yes, sir?"

"You will be assigned a post in the dining room. We shall assess the quality of your work while you serve dinner. Molly, take Lucy into the press for a fresh white apron and cap and show her how they are to be worn."

Lucinda followed Molly down a dim hallway and into the laundry press. Her back to the entrance, a lone woman stoked wood into the small, cast-iron range. Half a dozen irons of different sizes heated on the top of the stove, and a wrinkled sheet lay on the ironing board to press. Molly walked over and placed her arm around the woman's shoulder. "I've brought the new girl in for an apron and hat."

The woman straightened and gave Molly a tired smile. "You know where they're kept. Help yourself." Molly scurried away. The frail woman wiped her hands on a towel and returned to the ironing board with a fresh iron.

Lucinda studied the piles of laundry neatly arranged by color near the washtubs. *I hope I never have to work here. This has to be the hottest, hardest work in any house.* "Do you do all this work alone?" she asked.

The woman looked up. Her face paled. "Oh, my," she gasped and rushed to shut the door into the linen keep.

"Pearl?" Lucinda cried out in disbelief, and they flew into each other's arms. "Oh, Pearl, I can't believe it's you. What are you doing here? You told me you were going to live with your rich sister."

"Lucinda?" Pearl stepped back; her expression looked as though she would faint. "Is Molly getting the uniform for *you?*"

Lucinda touched Pearl's cheek. "Why are *you* here in the laundry press? Where is the rich sister who needed you to come be with her?"

"I am living in my rich sister's house. But no matter. I want to hear about you, my dearest child. Why are you here?" Pearl studied Lucinda. "You look. . ." Her eyes filled with tears. "What has happened to you?"

All that Lucinda had bottled up came out in a tumble of words. "Wednesday last, Uncle announced it was his unpleasant duty to tell me that I was no longer wealthy. In fact, I was deeply in debt. Papa had unfortunate financial reverses, so he took on many loans. When Mama and Papa were killed, all that indebtedness fell on Uncle's shoulders. He said he must repay these huge loans or the business was doomed. And there was no hope of rebuilding my home. Uncle assured me that my only option was to declare bankruptcy."

"But what happened to your settlement from Lord North's estate?" Pearl asked. "That was substantial."

"It all went to pay off loans, according to Uncle."

Pearl's brow creased. "But if it was your money that cleared the loans, shouldn't you own the land?"

"I did own it, but there's no money to pay off the other loans. Uncle handed me sheaf after sheaf of papers. After I scanned them, I signed away everything."

Pearls eyes widened. "Not your necklace." She spoke in a whisper.

Lucinda shook her head and put hand over her heart. "Uncle finally let me keep it." She glanced anxiously at the door into the linen keep, certain that Molly would be returning soon. "He said he had to sell his house and all he could scrape together to put against the debt or the business would fail. He had no money and suggested that I visit an intelligence service to find work as a domestic. So here I am."

Pearl wrapped Lucinda in her arms and crooned, "Your papa was a fine businessman, but I knew there had been financial reversals. I had no idea they were so severe. Only a few days before. . .the Fourth of July, I heard him tell your mama he had made an exceptional sale that would clear all their debt and permanently assure their financial future. Oh, my poor girl." She released Lucinda. "Hurry, tell the rest."

"I must have looked stricken, because Uncle offered me money to tide me over until I could locate work. I thanked him and told him that I would get on just fine."

Pearl caressed Lucinda's cheek. "So you went to the intelligence office and found work with the Tillotsons. But how did you get from the train station to here?"

"Mr. David Morgan was kind enough to bring me." The mere mention of his name made her glow inside.

Pearl nodded. "A fine young man." She held Lucinda at arm's length. "Is the mistress home?"

"I don't think so. I overheard it said that we are to serve dinner without her."

"Then some quick words, my dear. Listen carefully. Stay out of sight as much as possible. Never turn your back on your betters, and never meet their eyes. Speak clearly but only as much as is necessary."

"Thank you, Pearl. I will be respectful in all ways, but I don't plan to spend the rest of my life as a domestic—"

Molly threw open the door and bustled into the press. "Land, Pearl, you had the aprons on the top shelf, and I liked never to have found one her size. Come, Lucy, take off that coat, and I'll help you with the apron. Thank goodness you have a decent dress on." Molly worked as fast as she talked, helping Lucinda don the apron and hat. "Now you look like a proper servant. Step lively, now. We're to be in the serving pantry."

Pearl glanced toward Molly. "I need a moment with Lucin. . .Lucy. She'll be right out."

Molly shrugged a shoulder and hurried down the hall.

Pearl tucked a copper curl inside Lucinda's mushroom-shaped hat. "For your own sake, keep your head down, your hair covered, and remain in the background. If the mistress arrives, stay as far from her as you decently can. Now hurry off. You'll do just fine."

Reluctantly, Lucinda left the comfort of Pearl's company. Fighting back tears, she walked slowly down the hallway, mindful of each step that took her farther from her predictable past into an unpredictable future.

"Lucinda? We seem to have a tendency to run into each other," a deep velvet voice said.

She turned quickly, her gloom lifting. "Mr. Morgan? Whatever are you doing in the servants' wing?"

"I needed to see if you were all right. I dumped you off like a sack of potatoes and left you to fend for yourself. I've felt guilty ever since. The least I can do is apologize for not seeing you safely inside."

With a faint smile, she asked, "What exactly is your position here, Mr. Morgan?"

He laughed. "You're a courageous one, aren't you?"

"Are you avoiding my question?"

"On the contrary, I was buying time while I tried to determine what exactly my position is. First of all, please call me David. I am uncomfortable with being Mr. Morgan to you."

That wouldn't be difficult since she had been thinking of him as David all evening. "David it is. And I'm Lucinda, even though Mr. Button has christened me Lucy. He feels Lucinda is an uppity name."

David laughed again. "Yes, Button, as he is called on this side of the fanning doors, would consider that a threat to his dominion."

"Your position, David?" she reminded. She was desperate to know more about him. Even in the short time she had known him, she had become acutely aware that he was a mighty man. It showed in the way he moved, quick and powerful as the horse he rode. It showed in his eyes, bright and respectful—a rich navy blue she could see now in the light of the corridor. He seemed to know what she was thinking even when she did not speak her thoughts. It showed in his voice, deep, full, to match his speech. He was not given to needless words or courtly phrases but came to the point of things. Yes, she very much wanted to know more about this man.

"Well," he began with some hesitation, "during the past five years I've been a law clerk in Judge Tillotson's office, read for the law with him, escorted Mistress Tillotson to various social events when requested to do so, and shoveled out the stables when the need arose." He pursed his lips. "That pretty much sums up my position."

"You will be a lawyer one day?"

"I think that day may be upon me very soon."

Lucinda's heart sank. "Does that mean you'll be leaving?"

He studied her as though reading her story. "Yes, right away. But now it won't be by choice, and I shall regret having to go."

"You will?"

"I will. Very much."

Molly's worried face appeared behind David. "Lucy, please come. You're going to be in terrible trouble if Mr. Button comes back and you're not in the serving pantry."

David took her hand. "I know this is unacceptably sudden, but I can't bear to think of leaving you just when I've found you. Perhaps later this evening when you have finished your duties. . ." He paused and looked deep into her eyes. "Could we talk? I feel I must know more about you."

"Lucy! Come!" Molly was running toward them.

"Yes, David. You will find me?"

"I will find you."

Molly grabbed Lucinda's arm and guided her away. She looked back before she was propelled through the fanning doors. David stood in the middle of the hall, his eyes focused on her.

Chapter 5

D avid arrived outside the drawing room as Button was ushering the men from the library into the Tillotsons' elegantly appointed drawing room. The ladies, resplendent in low-cut evening dresses, greeted them. David slipped inside and mingled with the assemblage. The men brought with them the fragrance of bay rum and the pungent scent of smoke from the thick cigars and cheroots that most in the library had smoked. Mixed with the women's heady perfumes from Paris, the aroma was unusual but pleasant.

Then, as was his habit, David retreated to an inconspicuous corner to observe. Though the women wore different colors and fabrics, all wore long skirts drawn back, bunched into an elaborate arrangement at the hip and, over a supporting bustle, draped into a train that swept the floor. No doubt the latest Paris fashion. He imagined Lucinda in such a gown.

He jerked himself up short. He must keep his wits about him if he was to get the judge's signature tonight. He forced himself to stay in the present by studying the gentlemen's attire. They wore flowery waistcoats, impeccably tailored. Most were embellished with watch chains from which jeweled charms dangled. Precious stones anchored wide, colorful cravats. Black or dark blue swallowtail tuxedo jackets, the rage this winter, hung over fawn-colored pantaloons. He couldn't help but notice that in most cases they stretched across ample stomachs.

David ran his hands over his own black frock coat. Thanks to Rosella's excellent tailor, it fit perfectly. He imagined Lucinda next to him, promenading gracefully across the room. A waltz played in his head, and he could feel her in his arms as they pirouetted around the floor. He became so lost in his fantasy he almost missed Judge Tillotson motioning him to join a small group of community leaders.

The judge was short and ruddy of complexion. He had one badly squinting eye, which he habitually kept closed, and his head was oversized for his body. His thick white hair was his best feature. Tonight its sheen glowed in the lamplight like a halo. On the judge, however, the halo effect missed being regal because he had been forced since birth to hold his head stiffly inclined toward his left shoulder. His detractors said his head was askew like a cow with horn-ail. David, on the other hand, thought that Judge Tillotson had a fine presence, giving the impression of a successful and happy man. That is, until one caught him off guard and looked deep into his eyes. Behind the judge's pleasant, summer blue eyes lurked a chained darkness writhing to break free. David had only looked there once.

He came to stand with the group. "Good evening, Judge Tillotson," he said and nodded to the other gentlemen.

"Glad you could join us, my lad. I want the boys to meet a first-rate new lawyer. You'll be hearing of this young man, gentlemen."

David could feel heat rise above his cravat to his cheeks. He clasped his hands behind his back and squared his stance, ready to listen to the judge's current monologue.

Instead, the judge said, "Please excuse us, gentlemen. Business never takes a holiday." He put his strong hand around David's back and guided him to the side of the room. "David, I must admit, I've never worked with a lad that I've enjoyed as much as you." He took a long swallow from his glass of sherry. The judge usually drank nothing stronger than watered wine. Was this his attempt to ease the pain of this day?

The judge continued. "You know that I've come to care about you. Your quick wit and diligence have touched a chord in me. You're a young man with a future."

David flushed again, realizing that praise was harder to handle gracefully than criticism. "Thank you, sir."

"I'm sad to think you'll be moving on soon."

His words caught David off guard. He started to protest, but the judge held up his hand. "Nothing to be ashamed of, son. Be ashamed if you didn't want to strike out for yourself. Besides, you're ready. Where is it you're thinking of going?"

"Well, sir, I do have an article about the possibilities." He pulled a newspaper clipping from his tuxedo pocket, but before he could unfold it, the dinner gong sounded. The judge glanced around the room and then gave David a pat on the back. "I don't believe Mistress Tillotson has arrived yet, but we will be dining without her. Excuse me, David, perhaps we can talk later. Right now I must claim my dinner partner."

"Of course." David mumbled something about finding his own partner. Without Mistress Tillotson, the table would be short one lady. This was not the first time he had waited at the back of the line, ready to escort a neighbor hastily invited.

The double doors to the dining room swung open. Under the scrutiny of the well-organized Mr. Button, the judge and his lady led the guests in to dinner. The table, set for twenty, created a forest of French crystal and English bone china. Holly and evergreen cascaded down from a regiment of tall silver cones spaced along the center. Kerosene lamps on the sideboard, along with rows of candles down the center of the table, gave off a romantic glow. A pair of footmen hired for the occasion stood at attention at the head and foot of the table.

David's dinner partner had a difficult name he never seemed able to recall, a great many large teeth, not to mention arthritic fingers that occasionally gripped his arm or twisted a long rope of pearls. David braced himself for an evening of her nonstop conversation. She immediately launched into the intimate details of how she came to be unmarried.

The woman seated on the other side of David managed to engage him in conversation. But each time David's dinner companion sensed the slightest break, she skillfully turned his attention back to her story, beginning precisely where she had been interrupted. She did not require answers, making it possible for him to contemplate Lucinda. She had the most unusual eyes and a square chin with a delicate cleft. She was captivating yet with a disturbing resemblance to Rosella Tillotson as she must have looked in her early years. That connection gave rise to all manner of speculation.

Thinking about Lucinda was not wise. She so completely took over his concentration that David lost track of the table conversation. He must keep an eye on the judge and anticipate when he would be approachable to sign the referral letter.

To occupy his thoughts, David tried to plan the best route across the prairie in the morning. He tried to think what to take with him. He tried to envision all the things he had to do. He tried, and all he saw was Lucinda's face, Lucinda's smile, and the sadness in her eyes. He could easily drown in the emerald depths of those eyes. He longed to let his fingers trace her delicate forehead and high curving cheekbones, the straight nose, and her full mouth. His hands flexed with the urge to feel her chin with its intriguing cleft and the smooth line of her throat. *Is she the woman for me?* He thought about the circumstances of their meeting. *Is there a divine plan behind this day?*

He scolded himself. This was not the time to be thinking such things.

Just at that moment, across the room from David, a door opened noiselessly. Half-hidden by a carved wooden screen, a maid emerged wearing one of those absurd English caps. She delivered a large silver tray into Button's hands. He in turn passed the tray to the footman to begin serving.

David forgot all else when he recognized the maid. It was only a glimpse before Lucinda vanished behind the screen, but he knew well that intense, pale face with a copper-bright lock of hair escaping from the cap. His heart leaped, and he remembered the feel of her small, soft hand in his. *She speaks like a lady; her hands are soft and manicured. What is she doing here? Why is she a serving maid?* Questions reeled in his head.

"Excuse me, sir."

Dazed, David blinked up at the footman who served the fruit compote, then discreetly slipped a piece of paper into his hand and moved on.

David excused himself politely and left the table. Once in the hall, he read the note. *Meet me at the servant's entrance immediately.* No signature. He burned with curiosity as he hurried along the hallway. How very odd. Was it Rosella? No, she would never step foot near the servant's door. Lucinda, perhaps? David reached the back hallway. In the dim light he could see a figure in the shadows.

A frail little woman stepped forward to greet him. "Thank you for coming. I apologize, but this is a desperate situation. I have no one else to turn to, and they say you are a just man." The woman bowed her head. "My name is Pearl. Lucinda told me that you brought her from town this afternoon. I am Rosella's sister."

"Rosella's sister? I can assure you, madam, all between us has been most proper in every respect."

"I am in no way suggesting otherwise, Mr. Morgan."

"Then may I inquire how it is that you know Lucinda?"

"All I can say at this moment is that I am Lucinda's friend. I apologize for taking you from dinner, but time is of the essence. You are a stranger to me and Lucinda, but I understand you are well thought of by the judge and my sister. Lucinda is in danger, and I am helpless to do anything."

David came to full attention. "Danger? How? She arrived not two hours ago."

"The story is long and tragic. I shall try to give you only the briefest details. Please understand, sir, that Lucinda knows nothing of what I am about to tell you. For years, I thought it best she never know. Now my deceit could cost Lucinda her life."

She took a breath and hurried on. "Rosella and Marshall had a daughter, a beautiful child named Meghan that Marshall was so taken with he failed to give Rosella the attention she demanded."

The frail woman looked stricken. "Twenty years ago today, at Rosella's insistence, I secretly spirited that child away to New York to a wealthy family who was desperate for a child. The couple paid a huge sum of money for her. They made Rosella a rich woman, so rich she didn't mind not knowing any details of the transaction. I became nanny to that child, Meghan. The couple renamed her Lucinda. As she grew, she looked more and more like Rosella. Certainly you have noticed the strong resemblance. Twelve years ago, the family moved to Chicago, and for Lucinda's safety, I told them the truth. It frightened them, so they took Lucinda to England. She married the earl of Northland, and just over a year ago, he died. Lucinda and her parents returned to Chicago."

Pearl paused and wiped the tears streaming over her cheeks. She hastily summed up the story of the fire and Lucinda's financial situation. "Left with nothing, Lucinda chose to make a new beginning. Do you understand the danger of her being here? If my sister recognizes her..." She looked up, pure terror reflected in her eyes.

David stared. He most certainly understood the peril. If Rosella so willingly sold her child, then how far would she go to keep her secret? "What do you want from me?"

"I have no plan, sir. But Rosella is no fool. Even disguised in that horrid uniform, Lucinda's identity will be obvious. Rosella loves Marshall, but she is beauty to his beast. She will not allow anyone or anything to come before her. Lucinda inherited her mother's great beauty, and Rosella will make certain Marshall does not see his daughter. Ever."

Icy fingers of dread squeezed David's heart. The torment hiding in the judge's eyes finally made sense. So did the melodrama Rosella had staged on this date every year since he had known her. David's first inclination was to dash into the serving pantry, grab up Lucinda, and flee far and fast.

He spoke in an urgent whisper. "A new storm has begun. I can't take her away tonight without someplace to go. So how do we keep her hidden until morning?" David chastised himself. Ordinarily he could solve any predicament with a logical plan. But he had never faced a problem of this magnitude. His thoughts tumbled over each other and refused to be ordered.

Pearl's look told him she had no answers. "You must get back, now." She touched his arm before she scurried along the hall and disappeared through the fanning doors.

David started back to the dining room, his mind churning. What if the judge wasn't as drunk as he pretended? David was a successful lawyer because he seemed to have a sixth sense. Maybe he felt the unrest in the house. He had been uneasy all evening but had chosen to ignore it. Now he had to get Lucinda hidden. But where? How?

Entering the dining room through the serving door, he returned to his seat. At the end of the table, the judge was deep in conversation; he didn't look up, but David had the distinct feeling he had been missed. His dinner partner immediately turned to him and launched into a new story as though he'd never left. David glanced toward the drawing room. *Please, Rosella, don't come through those doors.*

Lucinda spotted David halfway along the table, sitting with a coquettish older woman who never seemed to stop talking even while eating. The princeliest man at the table, David had on a beautifully tailored tuxedo that showed his broad shoulders to their best advantage. Though Lucinda tried subtly to attract his attention, he seemed unaware of her efforts. His faraway look told her that his thoughts were elsewhere. Reluctant to leave, she picked up a tureen and backed through the door to the hall, only to bump into Molly. "Lucy, you best get a run on. Cook's screaming for your scalp." She rolled her eyes.

Lucinda rushed toward the kitchen, the aromas of food filling the hall. Unexpectedly, hunger overwhelmed her. Her knees started to buckle; she caught her balance against the wall inside the fanning doors. In a lightheaded moment, she saw herself seated as David's dinner partner. Felt his eyes warm and loving as he lifted a spoon of soup to her lips. Their gazes linked and the warm soup trickled onto her tongue. . .

"You, be quick with this platter of lamb!" Mrs. Kidd screeched, shattering Lucinda's dream. She deposited the tureen on the mountain of dirty dishes and, under Mrs. Kidd's eagle eye, raced to lift the enormous silver platter. Concentrating, Lucinda picked up the platter without sending the slightest shimmer through the delicate rope of mint jelly decorating its edges. She caught the cook's slight smile of approval.

"Now hurry along," Mrs. Kidd added in a much kinder voice, but Lucinda had already cleared the top of the stairs, rushing as fast as her burden allowed toward the dining room. There, David waited to be served. And after dinner they would meet. Quivers of anticipation lightened her spirits.

Chapter 6

M r. Button took the tray from Lucinda. "That will be all in the dining room tonight, Lucy. Molly will show you the way to the card room. Polish the furniture one last time. Then see that the tables are prepared for playing whist." He looked hard at her. "You know about whist?"

Lucinda curtsied. "Yes, Mr. Button," she said and groaned silently. She hadn't eaten since this morning, but there was no mention of food. She remembered those who had served her so faithfully and lamented that she had been raised to think of servants as having few needs. When she was again in a position to be served, she vowed to be a different mistress.

While she polished the Chippendale tea table until it gleamed in the candle-light, she thought of David. How, when, where would they meet? She placed whist cards and score sheets on each of the five gaming tables and arranged the chairs into more suitable conversation groupings. She surveyed her handiwork and, satisfied that all was in readiness, pulled the bell cord that signaled Mrs. Kidd in the kitchen. Soon Molly arrived with a Sheffield tray of teacups and a heavy silver teapot. She dashed back to the kitchen, leaving Lucinda to set out the tea service. That done, she scanned the room once more. Numerous candelabra and wall sconces cast a warm glow over the brocades and velvets, all in shades of golden peach. The fire in the large marble fireplace burned in silent and smokeless perfection. The slight fragrance of oriental incense added a hint of mystery. Everything was as ready as she knew how to make it.

In the Florentine mirror, Lucinda reviewed her appearance and looked carefully at her apron to be sure it was still clean. At least she had been allowed to wear her blue wool dress instead of a gray, shapeless maid's frock. She tucked the stubborn lock of copper hair under the giant mushroom cap and made sure her hidden necklace didn't show. Satisfied she was presentable, she turned from the mirror. Were those lights in the lane? Mistress Tillotson's coach perhaps?

Hurrying to the window, she pulled aside heavy lace curtains and stared into the dark. *Oh my, that coach is having a sorry time in this snow and wind.* The coach and four, battered by the storm, drew up before the house. Down from the driver's box vaulted a dark figure carrying a ship's lantern to light the way. He leaned into the wind and struggled to reach the broad front steps of the baronial house.

Disregarding the driving snow, a woman called from the coach window. "Button! Where are you? Is there no one to answer the door?" Her voice shrilled above the wind.

The staff was busy serving dessert, so Lucinda went to answer the summons. She had survived dinner without being thrown out with the chickens. Could she now please a mistress who came late and screamed for assistance? She set her face in a smile and, with quick, efficient steps, hurried down the stairway to the front door. All the while the mistress was caterwauling at the top of her lungs.

Lucinda held the oversized door open enough to see the footman leap from the box. He opened and steadied the coach door against the wind. A second footman lifted Rosella Tillotson from inside the coach. Carrying her, he staggered against the driving snow and deposited her at the top of the steps.

Judge Tillotson came hurrying down the hall and pulled the door wide open. The wind swept inside, blowing out the lamps and casting everything in darkness. Stepping into the doorway, the man with the lantern held it high to furnish light. The judge braved the storm and stepped outside to meet his wife. The wind flapped the tails of his long black coat and rearranged his cravat and hair. Mistress Tillotson, standing erect and as tall as her husband, presented her cheek for his kiss. His lips brushed the general vicinity as he reached to take her arm. She pushed him away.

His expression remained pleasant, but Lucinda noticed a muscle working along his jaw. He ushered Rosella into the foyer, but it was so shadowed Lucinda could see little of the large woman except for a square chin under the bill of the bonnet.

David came striding along the dark hallway with Mr. Button and Molly at his heels. Immediately, the butler ordered the candles in the wall sconces relit. He looked straight at Lucinda.

David stepped beside her. "I'll show her where the safety matches are, Mr. Button." With the briefest of nods at David, Button turned his full attention to the Tillotsons.

Taking Lucinda's arm, David set a breathtaking pace down the hallway and into the dimly lit drawing room. He sat her in a large wing-backed chair facing the fireplace. "Stay here while I take the matches to Button." And he was gone.

Lucinda stared in the fire. What in the world made David whisk her away like that? If he didn't have a good reason, they were going to have words. Just because she was a servant girl didn't mean she would allow such treatment. She had been assigned to the game room, and she was going to be on duty there whether David liked it or not. Dinner would soon be over, and the guests would be adjourning to the game room. What would Mistress Tillotson do when no one was there to serve? As Mr. Button threatened, Lucinda would be out with the chickens for sure. She was ready to leave when the door opened and closed.

"Lucinda?" David whispered.

She leaned around the chair so he could see her. "I'm here, but now that you're here, I must leave."

"I've brought Pearl to see you."

"Pearl?" Lucinda started to stand.

"Please, sit down." David's words were gentle as he pulled up a chair for Pearl and knelt beside Lucinda. "Pearl has something she needs to tell you. It will help you understand many things."

"What is going on? David, I won't be ordered around like this."

Pearl took Lucinda's hand and gave her a weak smile. "I'm so sorry. I should have told you years ago, but I never imagined anything like this would, could ever happen."

Chills ran up Lucinda's spine. "I don't think I want to hear this."

Pearl looked deep into Lucinda's eyes. "And I don't want to tell you, but you must know." When Pearl finished her story, Lucinda sat silent. "I hope you can forgive me." She hung her head and stepped back beside the fireplace.

Lucinda felt as if she had been pitched off a cliff and sent spinning toward huge rocks at the bottom. She gasped, but her lungs refused to fill. David rubbed her back. "Breathe in," he said softly. "That's right, another breath." She heard his voice as from a distance until her breathing stabilized and she could speak. "This is going to take time to sort out, Pearl. But I love you and hold nothing against you."

Pearl kissed Lucinda and held her for a moment. "I must get back to the laundry. David is a good lad. He'll see to your safety."

The door clicked shut, and David moved to the chair Pearl vacated. "The problem is keeping you safe through the night until we can put together a plan for getting you away from here."

"No matter if Rosella does recognize me, she'll be as shocked as I am. I'll be safe for a while yet." She slumped back in the chair. "Could I rest just a minute before I go upstairs?" Her eyes drooped from weariness.

He nodded, and her lids closed.

When voices filtered into the room from the hall, Lucinda woke. She felt brittle, as though if she were touched she would shatter into myriad slivers of glass. She felt the urge to scream and to go on screaming until she broke. Instead, she stood, her hands balled into fists at her side, and willed herself to complete the task at hand. "They are on the way to the game room. I must go."

"Come with me," David said. "I'll show you a way to the card room that will keep anyone from noticing your arrival."

Holding her hand, he led the way to a large mirror on the fireplace wall. He touched the heavy gold frame, and the mirror swung open. Lucinda gasped. "What, how...?" she stammered.

"This house was used to hide runaway slaves during the War between the States. This is the hidden stairway they used." He helped her through the opening, closed the mirror, lit a small lamp, and led her up stairs that eventually came out at a panel in the library next to the card room.

"You go in. Busy yourself like you've been there all the time. I'll go back down and come up the main stairs."

When Lucinda arrived in the card room, Mistress Tillotson was waiting across the room at the top of the main stairway. She had changed clothes and wore a peignoir of white satin, flounced at the throat and covered with heavy lace at the waist. A double rope of pearls and diamonds lay across her ample bosom. Her amber hair was locked in a careless chignon held in place by a white net. *So, that is my mother.*

Thankfully, the mistress couldn't see her. Lucinda picked up a tray of champagne, and, staying as far from the woman as possible, began passing it to the guests. Mixing among them, she felt safe until she felt a tap on her shoulder. Keeping her head down, Lucinda turned. Rosella tipped her face up. The attempt to stifle her gasp failed. She continued to stare with a look of unclothed astonishment little different from those registered by David Morgan and Mr. Button. *She recognizes me!*

Lucinda kept her face frozen. "Champagne, mistress?" Her voice sounded normal, the English accent firmly in place.

Rosella, on the other hand, turned deathly pale, and her chest heaved for breath. "What is your name?" she gasped through trembling lips.

"Lucinda, ma'am." She carefully balanced the tray and curtsied. Over Rosella's shoulder, she saw David's eyes widen. He turned as pale as Lucinda felt.

Rosella's eyes narrowed. "Come," she said in a shrill voice and led the way to a card table. Her hand trembled as she picked up the deck of cards. "Now, my dears," she said to the three men present, "if you don't mind playing with my personal maid and secretary, we can begin."

Lucinda gasped. "Mistress, I–I . . . ," she stammered.

"You do play whist, do you not?" Her tone was sarcastic.

"I have played some," she said quietly.

"I do not wish to play this evening," Rosella announced. "You will be the fourth at my table."

The looks on the men's faces told what they thought of the idea. "Really, Rosella, this is too much," one of the men objected. "We came to play with you." The others at the table echoed his sentiments.

Mistress Tillotson ran an unsteady hand over her brow. "Very well, gentlemen, but don't expect much of me. It has been a long and most trying day." She looked squarely at Lucinda before she sat down and began shuffling the cards. "Lucinda, put that tray down."

"Yes, ma'am." Lucinda curtsied and handed off the tray.

"Make yourself useful in the library." Rosella began dealing the cards expertly, watching Lucinda all the while. "There are newspapers there. Find some bits of scandal to amuse me tonight when you prepare me for bed. See if you can find a novel, a love story, something set in India." She had regained her color and her voice, but her smile was brittle, her eyes hard. "And David, you are a poor player. Sit at my elbow and learn."

He sent Lucinda a look of resignation and seated himself beside Rosella.

Lucinda managed to stuff the feelings aroused by knowing that Rosella was her mother, but her movements were too sharp, too quick. She smiled at the right times and answered politely, but she was off-key, like an out-of-tune piano. She could tell David was worried. His eyes were overly bright and, to the detriment of his attention to the card game, he often gazed after her. That made her task more difficult because she wanted to look at him, but she forced herself to concentrate on the black print. In the *Peoria Review* and *Chicago Democrat* she found items she thought might interest Rosella. She finished her task, but the card party showed no sign of ending. After building up the fire in the card room's fireplace, Lucinda again moved to the library and examined the shelves for a novel to fit Rosella's description. Attracted by the title *The Ganges by Moonlight,* she drew a volume from its place. As she did so, a leather pouch hidden behind the books slid out, scattering its contents.

Lucinda stood stock-still, staring at the floor. "What is this?" Her heart leaped at the sight.

A handful of cut, unset jewels—emeralds, sapphires, two large rubies, and diamonds of various shapes and sizes—splattered over the Persian carpet. She stooped and was gathering them up when Rosella Tillotson came into the room with David at her heels, his face creased with concern. Rosella's eyes instantly focused on the sparkling stones in Lucinda's hand.

The briefest of smiles brushed Rosella's lips, then the expression vanished and her face became unreadable as she walked with firm steps across the room to where Lucinda stood, her trembling hands cupped around the jewels.

"How fortunate that you found my little gems. I had quite given them up for lost." Rosella's hands closed like icy claws over Lucinda's and grasped the stones. Her red mouth smiled, but her eyes were dark and hard.

Chapter 7

It was well past midnight before the guests were bedded and Lucinda was able to light her own candle to carry up to her attic room. The flame flickered in the sudden drafts and sent writhing shadows over the unfamiliar stair walls. She closed the door at the foot of the attic stairs and slid the little lock into place. Her room under the eaves was directly above Rosella's dressing room.

Though there was a bell to call for service, Rosella insisted on this arrangement because she preferred to rouse her maid during the small hours of the night by throwing a shoe at the ceiling, Lucinda had been told. She was ordered to listen for the thud beneath her bed and consider her position at the mansion to be dependent on her instant response to such a summons.

From kitchen maid to personal servant to the mistress—her mother. So much had happened this day.

Lucinda stumbled with weariness on the last step and pitched the candle forward onto the splintered floor. It guttered out. The storm had passed for now. Through a single dormer window set in the slanted roof over her bed, moonlight flooded into the tiny cubicle and fanned across the tied patchwork quilt. Kneeling on the bed made from a knotty plank, she let the moon bathe her in white light. Warmth from an unseen source seemed to envelop her, bringing with it a longing for the way things were before catastrophe became an almost constant companion.

Thoughts of Rosella tried to rise, but Lucinda forced them away. She was far too weary to examine the latest blow to her life. *I never dreamed I would be grateful for such poor lodgings, but tonight I am. I am gifted with my own room.* The other maids slept in a long room under the eaves of another wing of the house. There were two rows of beds and no privacy.

Lucinda sat on the bed and caressed the platinum heirloom fastened around her neck. This was her only physical tie to her past. The memories it kindled would help her through the rough places. Surrendering to a consuming weariness, she scarcely managed to hang her apron and hat neatly on the peg beside her coat and cap. She brushed out her hair but chose to sleep in her dress in case she was summoned in the night.

Just when exhaustion should have sent her slipping under the quilt, she became caught up by a strange sensation she could neither capture nor dismiss. In that moonlit moment, Lucinda knew that she would not be a servant all her days. One day she would again have her own mansion filled with servants. And she would be waited on as she had served others tonight. *Is this the vision Yarrow Woman had of me?*

She eased her aching body under the quilt and onto a harsh covering over a thin horse blanket used for a mattress. The narrow bed might have been as soft as eiderdown for all she noticed. Staring up into the night through the window, her mind drifted away to mingle with the stars that shone like the jewels she had held in her hands. One day she would again have piles of beautiful gemstones. She thought about how Mistress Rosella, her mouth twisted, her eyes hard, had snatched the jewels and clutched them to her bosom. Lucinda would not clutch her jewels. She would have so many she could be, would be, generous.

Her thoughts turned to David Morgan sitting beside Rosella in the card room. *He was looking at me, only me.*

Lucinda's mind slipped further into the stars and saw that David stood alone on the veranda of a silver mansion glittering in the noon sun. She advanced toward him, bearing a heavy ornate tray. On it, instead of drinks, was a lumpy sack of silver and a neat stack of papers, stark white with black writing and large official seals. He helped himself to a stack and motioned to her to do the same. She set the tray down and took a few papers. He shook his head and handed her the whole stack. She fanned the sheets. They turned to silver coins falling like snow on the floor until she stood in a knee-deep drift. For no apparent reason, she woke up.

Her heart altered its pace and pounded a different rhythm in her ears. Her eyelids would not stay closed, fluttering instead like insistent moths. Nothing in the house below suggested an intruder, yet she believed someone to be about. She thought of the door at the bottom of her stairs. The simple lock would keep no determined soul out, but it would sound its own rattling alarm were someone to set hand to it.

Lucinda tensed and listened and knew with an unexplainable certainty that somewhere in the bowels of the sleeping house someone was awake and abroad. She slid from beneath the quilt and rose to her knees, searching for the latch on the slanted window over her head. Her fingers found and flipped open the latch. She broke the seal on the frame and tried to avoid the shower of dislodged grit and dead flies. Standing on her bed, she thrust back the window and straightened into the opening.

The air, tinged with the smell of evergreens, hung unmoving. Chimney pots belching occasional wisps of smoke stood over the house in rigid ranks like guards. Yes, she could climb out onto the roof and escape if it became necessary.

Relieved, she slid back through the window. Her feet, freezing now, found the bed below. She pulled the window closed and twisted the latch shut. Brushing off the debris and curling into the quilt, she shivered, not so much from cold as from the disturbing feeling that would not leave. At last, exhaustion overtook her and she slept.

For the second time that night, Lucinda sat bolt upright. A thud beneath her bed had wakened her. She struggled to remember where she was and finally realized Rosella had summoned her. Still caught in the web of a dream she could not remember, she moved as if in a trance across the cold, splintery floorboards toward the stairs. In the blackness of the stairway, her bare feet found their footing.

Loosed from its efficient knot, her curly hair tumbled over her shoulders and down her back. At the foot of the stairs, she twisted the lock, tripped the cold latch, and pushed open the door. Her bare feet sank into the oriental carpet runner along the hall leading to Mistress Tillotson's bedroom suite. Her hair blew across her face as air currents from the hallways below rose past her and into the attic.

A beam of moonlight struck the face of a floor clock. The time stood at three.

Lucinda turned the corner and entered an unlit hallway. She moved slowly along the corridor until she felt the door frame and realized that she faced Mistress Tillotson's sitting room door. Her heart pounded in her throat, and her mouth dried with fear. She reached for the knob.

Someone came unheard from behind, and a hand gripped her shoulder. Lucinda's mouth opened to scream, but only a pitiful whimper escaped. *I shall be murdered,* she thought with terrifying clarity as the soft hand with fingers like steel bands tightened on her shoulder near her throat.

The black hallway seemed rent by screams, but when the man spun her around, she realized the sounds were all in her head. The dam in her throat prevented any communication. His hand easily held both of hers in a vise behind her back, and he pulled her to him, half-smothering her against his chest.

The sleeve against her throat was silky, and he smelled of sweet pipe tobacco. His cheek rested against her temple. "Oh, my beautiful one," he whispered. "Please don't fight me. I only want to hold you. I would never hurt you. Never. I will protect you. Care for you. Love you." A hand closed behind her neck, beneath her flowing hair. "Such magnificent hair, such perfect features." He caressed the flowing strands. "Do not be afraid. No one will hurt you. I promise."

Who was this man? Lucinda could not force her eyes open to look, shut tight in terror as they were. *None of this is happening.* Her exhausted mind and body refused to function further. She sank into a stupor, too stunned for thought or prayer, too frightened to call for help.

Then, as suddenly as he came, he vanished without a sound.

Tears flooded her cheeks. Lucinda's shaking hand gripped the chair molding along the hallway, and soundlessly she started back along the corridor. Before she turned the corner, she looked back. In the deep shadows, she watched a short man open the door to Rosella's bedroom. He stood for several seconds silhouetted in the glow cast by fire from the hearth of the bedroom fireplace. Then, as though having been invited, he stepped across the threshold into Rosella Tillotson's bedroom and carefully shut the door.

Lucinda fled up the narrow stairs to her attic and curled into her bed. With cold, trembling fingers she sought the comfort of her necklace.

It was gone.

A sob escaped, and a stupefying emptiness swept over her. Yarrow Woman's words drummed in her head, *"Never* take it off or let anyone else take it from you." Yet Lucinda could not bring herself to go back down those stairs. Even though her mistress summoned her, she could not go. A deep moaning sob escaped, shook her body. She knotted her fist at her throat and cried over her loss until she fell into a deep sleep.

Chapter 8

Lucinda woke with a startled cry, roused violently from more violent dreams. Strong hands muffled her mouth as someone ripped the quilt from her trembling body. She struggled against her assailant and fought for breath.

"Hush, Lucinda!" a strong, deep voice pleaded urgently. "It's David Morgan come to save you. Stay still!" The hovering form removed his hand from her mouth.

Shouts and the clatter of the bolted door at the foot of the stairs rent the night.

"What are you doing here?" she gasped. "What do I need to be saved from?" It was then that the scene in the hallway spun up through her exhaustion-fogged brain. Was that awful person trying to get at her again? How would David know?

The sound of wood splintering meant the door was giving way under the assault. He shoved her feet into the brogans. "Hurry! Up through the window. Those shoes are bound to be slick. Watch your footing on the roof."

His voice was rough as he helped her into her coat and hat and hoisted her through the opening. Far below, the yard was still darkly quiet, but footfalls pounded on the stairs behind them. David crept out onto the roof and stood beside her. Lucinda burrowed into his sheltering arms and pressed her face hard into his chest as though he could make the terror go away.

"Stay low," he said softly. Hugging the shadows, he steered her along the roof. Her shoes slipped on the cold tiles, but David held her tight and kept her moving.

"Watch your step on the ladder," he whispered. "I'll go first and guide your feet onto the rungs." He pried her hand from his, and the parting wrenched her heart. With the greatest care, he placed each foot on the rung, but still she never felt more gratitude than when she stepped onto the ground. He pulled her into the deep shadows of shrubs next to the house. "Wait here."

Taking down the ladder, he laid it against the foundation and came back to her.

Lucinda fought tears. "David, can't you tell me what's going on? Who are those men? Why are they chasing us?"

He motioned her to silence and rushed them through the shadows along the side of the house.

A horse whinnied.

He pulled her to her knees and knelt before her, shielding her body from any eyes. "Catch your breath. I know you didn't do anything, but we have to keep you from that pack of ruffians the judge has set on you. Do you understand that?"

"No, I don't understand any of this, but I trust you." She set her lips in a line and swiped two large tears tracking down her cheeks. David stood, wrapped her in his great arms, and pulled her to her feet. "The entrance to the secret stairs is inside the yew hedge." He glanced right, left, and behind like a cornered fox. "All right, run!"

They fled across the lane and inside the thick hedge. He took a branch and swept away their footprints, then lifted the trapdoor. Once inside the tunnel, he struck a safety match and lit the small oil lamp. "This is used often by servants returning late." He grinned. Making sure the trapdoor was secured, he led the way through the tunnel and up the hidden stairway inside the house.

It seemed an eternity before she was once again sitting in the drawing room, now dark except for what was left of the fire's faint embers casting a glow on the area directly before the hearth. David spread a lap rug over her. "I'm hoping this is the last place anyone would think to look for you. I need to get my letter and money."

"Please, David, I don't understand any of this."

"I'll be right back and will tell you everything."

Lucinda heard the door latch click shut, and her heart sank. Too tired and frightened to think, she stared into the embers of the hearth for what seemed hours until once more the door opened and someone—no, more than one—came into the room. She held her breath. Footsteps came toward the fireplace. *Dear Father in heaven, help me, help me,* she prayed over and over.

"It's David," he whispered. "And Pearl." He set his leather case beside the fireplace.

"Did you say 'Pearl'?"

Pearl came into view and set two small bags beside David's. She bustled over to Lucinda. "You need looking after, and I don't want to spend the rest of my days in the laundry press. I'm coming with you." She stood bundled inside her coat.

Lucinda looked at the bags. "Where are we going? Please tell me what's happening. I can't imagine why I'm being pursued."

David knelt beside her. "Earlier this evening Mistress Tillotson was found assaulted in her dressing room. The gemstones she took from you are missing. The judge said she was clutching a shoe in one hand and your antique necklace in the other. Thus, my dear Lucinda, it is you they are seeking."

Lucinda's hand flew to her throat. Panic rushed over her. "I had it on," she cried. Her heart raced, and she felt sick. "How did the judge get it?" Then, she remembered the man who accosted her in the hallway. She told David the story.

"Your account of the man who waylaid you describes the judge. He must have taken the necklace from you and later placed it in Rosella's hand. I wondered how he even knew about it." David reached in his pocket and laid her necklace, the emeralds gleaming, on her lap.

Lucinda caressed the jewels. "David, how did you get this?"

"It was on my bed wrapped in a silk handkerchief like the ones the judge carries."

"I don't understand."

"I think he figured out that Rosella arranged for you to be kidnapped twenty years ago. He confronted her with his suspicions. Whatever she said or did made him so angry that he grabbed the poker and hit her, though he didn't kill her. Afraid for you, he planted the necklace he took, knowing that would force you to flee. She is still unconscious, but Pearl overheard Rosella tell the judge she'd take care of you herself this time and know the job was done right. Since he saw us talking together earlier in the salon, I suspect he counted on Pearl and me helping you to get away. It's snowing hard, and our tracks will soon be covered." He checked his watch. "Things are finally getting quiet, but dawn will soon be here. We don't have much time."

Lucinda's thoughts were spiraling. "Where are we going?"

"To Yarrow Woman."

"Why to her?"

"Her name is Mary Margaret Mason," David explained. "She was captured by the Indians when she was fifteen. The Masons moved heaven and earth and spent a fortune to get her back. She fought returning to her old world, having become more Indian than white. Now she lives on the edge of the Mason property. She dresses as an Indian, talks their language, and has little to do with anyone but the prairie settlers. Hers is the perfect place to hide until we can figure out what to do." David looked outside. "I'll get the sleigh and Kambur. You and Pearl wait at the tunnel exit. I'll come back for you shortly."

And he was gone.

Chapter 9

From Illinois to Kansas the prairie stretched miles without number, a gray wasteland filled with empty silence and boundless cold. A hard wind from the northwest pushed across the flatland, but in this deep fold of earth, it was calm. David pulled the sleigh to a halt in front of Yarrow Woman's cabin. He had heard many stories of this strange woman, but he tried not to believe them.

The slab door creaked open, and David hoped they weren't going to be looking down the barrel of a shotgun. Showing no signs of surprise, Yarrow Woman motioned them in. "Hurry, all of you."

David didn't need a second invitation. He helped the two women out of the sleigh, and they entered the dusky interior, a small room that served as Yarrow Woman's kitchen, parlor, and dispensary. Shelves lining the walls were filled with bottles and vials. A blend of aromas wafted from bunches of dried herbs hung from the rafters. In the kitchen area a small cooking stove occupied the corner next to the copper sink, which had an indoor water pump. Kerosene lamps on the windowsills and the round oak table gave off a yellow glow. Yarrow Woman sat Pearl and David at the table and Lucinda in a willow rocker near the fireplace. Two gray cats on the hearthstones stirred and coolly examined Lucinda with their green eyes.

Yarrow Woman also studied Lucinda. "You arrived at the Tillotsons' in time."

Lucinda managed a wan smile. "I did, and as you predicted, I served a very short time."

David wondered how much Yarrow Woman had already guessed but told her the whole story, anyway.

"I've been waiting for you." She smiled. "The hens are laying well. I will whip us up an omelet." Without waiting for a response, she busied herself at the kitchen counter.

"We apologize for placing you in such danger, but we had nowhere else to turn," David explained.

She brought them steaming mugs of coffee. "I have been thinking of what we can do. I have spent far too many years baking scones and listening to the troubles of settlers. My bones tell me it is time to go home." The room grew silent. "Come, Lucinda, you must eat. I doubt they fed you at the Tillotsons'."

David bounded to his feet and helped her to the table. His heart ached when he looked at her. She was pale, and dark circles ringed her eyes.

Yarrow Woman came carrying a silver serving tray. After the blessing, they feasted on the omelet and generous slices of bread.

"Lucinda, you are almost asleep," Yarrow Woman said when they finished the meal. "Let me tuck you into bed while we pack the sleigh." She guided the exhausted girl to the bed in the adjoining bedroom.

While Yarrow Woman filled boxes with food and bottles with water, she directed Pearl in filling several gunnysacks with herbs. David laid fresh straw over the bed of the sleigh and stacked up bales of hay for the horses. The food and water he padded with quilts and pillows. Finished, they sat down for a last cup of coffee and some elk jerky.

A mighty crash thundered against the door.

They leaped out of their chairs.

The door exploded open.

David stared into cruelty: A middle-aged man with a red beard on a skeletal face glared at them from behind a Remington shotgun. A white scar zigzagged down his cheek, pulling his mouth into a perpetual sneer. Nothing in his expression suggested goodness or mercy. Cold, black eyes raked the room.

David, his insides knotted, forced himself to stay calm. "Who?"

"Don't try to stall me. I ain't stupid. Where is the new maid that tried to kill the judge's wife? The judge wants her real bad."

"I don't know about a new maid trying to kill anyone."

"Word's spread over the county. New maid hired yesterday disappeared from the Tillotson place sometime after midnight. Old judge is paying a thousand dollars silver for her return alive, no questions asked."

David couldn't believe the judge would post a reward. He knew Lucinda was his daughter and would want her safe. Tillotson servants must have seen easy money in the return of Lucinda, David guessed, and exploited the situation. "Do you have a wanted poster or anything to prove your story?" David stepped toward the antsy gunman.

He shifted the weathered shotgun and pointed it directly at David's midsection. "Word I got is straight from someone at the mansion. Countryside's crawlin' with bounty hunters. Nobody's thought to look here yet."

This fellow probably wasn't a bounty hunter. Under the brim of his greasy hat, sweat beaded on his forehead, and his hand holding the gun twitched nervously. His desperation and lack of experience, however, made him more dangerous.

His ugly bearded face took on a sly look. "I says to myself, I says, I'll just have a look around the squaw's place." He brandished the gun at Yarrow Woman, but she didn't move a muscle. "And look what I find. A sleigh at the front door and three innocent-looking people with nothin' in common, getting' ready to leave." He pointed his gun at the boxes and sacks stacked in the corner. His laugh was low and coarse. "Wonder where the fourth one is?" Keeping the gun trained on them, he began a thorough search of the room, including looking through all the drawers and cupboards and tapping the walls and floors for signs of hidden closets or trapdoors.

David spoke up. "As you can see, there are no hiding places here."

The ruffian looked toward the bedroom. "That must mean you got her stowed away in the other room." His heavy boots thumped on the floor as he walked to the door.

David's heart turned over. There was no place in that room to hide. *Think, David, think. You have to do something.* He turned toward the fireplace and the poker resting there. The man whirled and leveled the gun. "See the notches on the butt?" David could. "You wanna be another one?"

He would be no good to anyone if he were dead. David froze, but his heart raced.

The old hunter unlatched the door and eased it open with the toe of his boot. Silently the door swung open to reveal a single bed spread with a tan Indian blanket in the corner of the small room. On the opposite wall stood an ornate mahogany armoire with a large mirror beside it. A small table next to the bed and a single willow chair completed the furnishings. The floor was bare pine slabs; a large rag rug lay rolled up in front of the armoire. The thug pulled open the muslin curtains covering the single window and looked out over the snowy yard.

Oh, dear God in heaven, don't let him look down, David prayed. A small scrap of blue fabric hung from a nail on the side of the window. *Lucinda! She has more courage than anyone I know. But where is she hiding out there in the wind? She'll freeze.*

Apparently convinced Lucinda was still in the house, the ugly man looked under the bed and poked the mattress with the gun barrel. Nothing. He turned his attention to the armoire. After checking every drawer, he then gave the rug a solid kick with the side of his boot, thumped it with the butt of his gun, shrugged, and went about tapping walls and floor for hollow sounds. He found nothing. He rested his foot on the rug and snarled, "I know ya got her stashed somewheres." He bent down and started to unroll the rug.

David clenched his fists and wished he hadn't packed his pistol away in the wagon. Pearl turned her back and clamped her hand over her mouth. Yarrow Woman's face remained stoic, but her black eyes sparked rage.

The rug flopped open. Nothing. He swore his disappointment. "Well, folks, she cain't stay hidden ferever. I'll just wait it out."

David stormed through the doorway, his hands working, his breath coming hard and fast. "Your search is over. Get out!"

The man thrust the gun in David's face. "Lucky fer you I'm feelin' generous, or you'd be dead. But shoot you I will. It'll give me pleasure to let you stew not knowin' when." His look included them all. "I'll be watchin'."

He tromped outside, waved his fist in the air, and yelled obscenities at David, who stood in the doorway with Yarrow Woman's gun trained on the man. The old scoundrel mounted his horse and rode out of range. He stopped and hung his leg around the saddle horn, making it plain he was prepared to wait out their departure.

They rushed to the window and threw open the sash. "Lucinda," David called softly. Her face appeared around the corner of the house. "Come, we'll help you in." She grasped the rope David lowered and hung on tight while he hoisted her up and into the room. "Lucinda, oh, Lucinda, are you all right?"

She looked up into his eyes, and he caressed her face and hair. "How brave you are. That's a long drop to the ground. Are you hurt?"

"I don't think so. Just terribly cold."

Yarrow Woman pushed David out of the way. "I'll tend to Lucinda. You finish with the sleigh."

David tied Kambur to the rear of the buckboard sleigh and checked the traces of Yarrow Woman's gray Percheron. Satisfied that all was well, he took off his oilskin and climbed into the sleigh. Yarrow Woman appeared, and they quickly stretched a canvas top over a frame to keep out the worst of the storm and block the view of the front door.

"Pearl, you get in. We'll get Lucinda."

They wrapped her in the rug. David picked up one end and Yarrow Woman the other. Gently they carried her to the wagon. Pearl guided the burden inside until it rested on the straw.

"Can you breathe all right?" David asked. He was thankful to hear a muffled yes. He leaned the front door in place and climbed up on the seat beside Yarrow Woman. A mewing caught his attention. Beside her on the floorboard was a basket containing her two cats. *She's such a softy under that rough exterior.*

"I'm glad you know the way," he said to Yarrow Woman.

She nodded and slapped the reins, and they were off. When they reached the prairie, David looked back. A solitary horseman followed close enough to be seen.

Minutes later, David looked back again. *He's still there and drawing closer. He's going to do exactly as he said. We're all going to be dead before nightfall except Lucinda.* He couldn't even think about what would happen to her.

By mid-afternoon, David realized the man was not going away. Up the road, another snow squall stalled and waited for them to drive into a whiteout.

They were almost out of time, but David still had no idea what to do. After they drove into the whiteout, he had Yarrow Woman stop. He crawled into the back and got his gun. He untied Kambur and mounted up. "Go on. I'll catch up," he shouted over the wind.

He rode to the edge of the whiteout and waited. It wasn't long until the hunter rode by, his head bent against the blizzard. He had let down his guard. David waited until he passed, then followed him. The wind carried away all sound. David rode up beside him. He cocked his pistol and pointed it at the man's head.

"Hands in the air!" he shouted. David reached over and lifted the shotgun out of the old man's raised hands. He pitched it far out into the whiteness. Searching through the man's pockets, he found a pair of handcuffs. David cuffed his hands, turned the horse around, and with a solid boot to the rump, sent the horse galloping back the way it had come.

David felt no remorse as he turned around and again faced the wall of white. The bounty hunter wouldn't die, and he couldn't hurt Lucinda anymore. David sat very still, with no idea of which way to go. Letting the reins go slack and with a prayer on his lips, he allowed Kambur to move forward on his own.

The storm had stopped by the time David spotted Yarrow Woman's sleigh before a sod house with an attached stable. Another sleigh stood in the yard. David leaped down from Kambur and made his way to the door, realizing that this must be the "inn" Yarrow Woman had referred to earlier. Tacked there was a sign: DIPHTHERIA. His heart sank.

"Hey, there," a voice called from near the stable. "Praise be to God! We're having a baby. Your friends are inside the stable helping my wife."

David turned and recognized Andy Henderson, the Tillotsons' former head groomsman.

Chapter 10

T he stable was quiet. Lying on beds of fresh straw and wrapped in buffalo robes, the weary travelers encircled the makeshift fire pit. Andy kept watch over Gigi and baby Gabriel asleep in her arms. The animals rested in stalls beyond the flickering firelight.

Unable to sleep, Lucinda sat up and stared into the fire. "This is the most amazing Christmas I've ever had, but I feel as though something more will happen," she said to no one in particular.

"It has been a sacred experience," Pearl agreed and rolled to a sitting position.

David roused up and looked puzzled. "It does seem incomplete, somehow. I, too, feel like I'm waiting for something more."

"Maybe that's why I don't want the night to end." Lucinda felt David's loving eyes on her, and they smiled across the fire.

Soft drumbeats sounded from a dark stall at the back of the room. With great dignity, Yarrow Woman in her white buckskin dress with its heavy beaded designs, her dark hair in two thick braids down her back, came to the fire. She pulled up a log stump and sat. "Before we sleep this night, we must give thanks for this lowly stable as refuge from the storm and protection from the disease in the cabin beyond. Please bow your heads."

Lucinda closed her eyes and listened intently to the prayer. Yarrow Woman expressed all that was in Lucinda's heart and warmed her with peace and gratitude. When Yarrow Woman pronounced the amen, Lucinda and the others echoed it.

Again Yarrow Woman softly beat the little drum. "It is now Christmas Day. Would you like to hear the legend based on the birth of our Savior as told by my people?"

Lucinda's breath caught. Was this what they had been waiting for? "Yes. Oh yes." Her voice chimed in unison with the others.

"In the country north of us," Yarrow Woman began in her firm but soft voice, "there is the *he sapa*, a range of pine-covered mountains so green that from a distance they look black. At the foot of the *he sapa* are the mysterious *mako sica*, or Badlands, a mass of buttes and spires that stretch as far as the eye can see. The Badlands end at the sweeping prairie, long and wide and rolling. To the Northern

Plains tribes who live there, all of creation—animals, birds, insects, plants, and humanity—are part of the sacred hoop. The Lakota express this as *mitakuye oyasin.*

"A very long time ago, the people who had been full of goodwill and generosity of spirit began to lose those virtues. The wise men were much concerned and fasted and prayed diligently to the Great Spirit for help. He heard their prayers and told the grandfathers to bring the people together on the longest night in the month of the moon.

"Out of curiosity, they came, hard of heart, selfish and arrogant, to wait and watch. They were not disappointed, for as the light darkened, they saw an eagle. It soared in high, wide circles above the Black Hills and out over the mysterious Badlands until the setting sun struck fire upon its wings. This was the signal, the grandfathers said. For what, they refused to say.

"The night settled like black velvet, and the people lit a huge bonfire. They encircled the fire and sat, watching the sparks rise among the stars. The air, cold and crisp, was scented with the sweet smoke. The night sky was radiant, the silence vast, peaceful, expectant.

"When the hush became so deep the titmouse could be heard, the representatives for *mitakuye oyasin* began to arrive—Those Who Fly and the Four-Leggeds—and take their place in the circle. They sat together around the glowing coals until all their heartbeats were as one.

"Then the snow goose stepped forward. 'The people have gone astray from the cycles of their journey and are lost. I will teach them the patterns of the seasons.'

"The chipmunk came to the fire. 'The Two-Leggeds wander, hungry and without purpose. I will teach them to gather and store the harvest. I will share my store of nuts.'

"The great buffalo lumbered up and stood with lowered head. 'The people waste what they take and share nothing. I will give my flesh to feed them and, to warm them, my coat. I will give myself away.'

"The eagle flew up and landed in the forming circle. 'The Two-Leggeds are blind. They do not see the aftermath of their actions. Perhaps if I give them my eyes, they will see beyond the present.'

"Each representative moved to the circle to tell of a gift, the most precious portion of themselves, that they wished to share until all had spoken and the night was silent again.

"When the very air quivered with anticipation, from inside the night came the deep, sad voice of the Creator. 'Those Who Fly and Four-Leggeds, you waste yourselves. They will accept your gifts and take the credit unto themselves.' There was heavy silence. 'It is I who must give myself. I will come, innocent and small.'

" 'How is that possible?' asked the relations. 'A Babe will be born, the Son of the Great Spirit. He will be born among the Four-Leggeds and Those Who Fly. He will give hope where there is hopelessness. He will bring love where there is hate. His name will be great among the people of the world.'

"And the people's hearts grew soft and loving. They looked at themselves and asked what they could give to the Small One. They were told they were free to give anything, anything at all, as long as the gift required the giver to make a great sacrifice.

"So the people went in search of perfect gifts to lay at the feet of the Small One. Some found their gifts at once; others searched longer; but many searched most of their lives before they found gifts perfect enough. Some never found a gift, because once more they strayed far from the virtuous life, the Red Road. The Small One was sad about that.

"On the longest night in the month of the moon, each gift was honored and the giver given a blessing and a promise. And for a little while, the people were once again full of goodwill and generosity of spirit.

"And so it is in our time, on the longest night in the month of the moon, we bring a perfect gift to somebody and give it in the name of the Small One. Tonight I give my gift—this drum given to me by the grandfathers, that I have cherished for many years—to Baby Henderson, in the name of the Small One, our Savior and Lord, Jesus Christ."

A holy silence filled the stable and was disturbed only by an occasional snap of an ember.

Lucinda remembered all the lavish Christmas celebrations and presents of her past. Nothing had stirred her heart like the message of this simple story. She fingered her necklace and thought how she had counted on it for her strength. It had become an idol to her! This knowledge came with a shock. *Do I have the faith to give it away?* It was a perfect gift and would help the young couple. She herself could never sell it for money. Giving it was truly a sacrifice.

She looked at David and found him studying her, his eyes filled with a love she had never known. As though he read her mind, he smiled and nodded.

Slowly, Lucinda returned the nod and sent her love to him. She understood. *I must trust God to take care of me and not depend on things.* With a prayer for strength to release the necklace and the past it represented, she slid from beneath the robe and knelt before Gigi. "In the name of the Small One, I give this necklace, cherished by generations of the House of North. It is the last tangible object from my past. It will become the foundation of the future for the House of Henderson." And she fastened the necklace around Gigi's neck.

Lucinda entered into the silence that once again settled over the stable as the gift was honored and the spirit of the season entered each heart.

Then David rose from his bed and walked to Kambur's stall. He returned with the bridle and saddle blanket, knelt, and laid them at Andy's feet. "Lucinda and I will be traveling west by train. We'll go as far as Nebraska, where I have something I must settle with my brother. After witnessing all that Lucinda has been through, all that she has suffered, I realize I have some fences I must mend. I need to find work and let Lucinda get to know me and my family."

"I would like that," she said quietly.

A broad smile lit his face, and he turned back to Andy. "You have a gift with horses, so I know you will treasure Kambur and take good care of him. If you choose to breed him, the charge for his services will support your family well. Kambur is a choice animal, and I give him to you in the name of the Innocent One who left His heavenly home to come to earth and sacrifice Himself for us." He moved to sit beside Lucinda, cradling her in his arms.

Again the silence descended and deepened. Lucinda, safe now, felt the very air change. God's presence seemed to come into the stable to watch with approval. Soft tears streamed down her face, and her heart burned with joy.

The fire burned low. David stirred the coals and added a log. The smoke carried sparks up through the smoke hole in the roof and left the scent of apple wood inside the stable. He returned to his place beside Lucinda, and she leaned her head on his shoulder. He again put his arms around her and held her close. "You realize that all we have in this world is eighty dollars."

She smiled and dug into her coat pocket. "I have twenty-five cents. We are rich. Very rich."

They both looked over at Yarrow Woman. David then looked back at Lucinda and framed her face with his hands, kissing her gently, tenderly. "We are indeed rich beyond our grandest fantasies."

The straw rustled as Pearl pushed back her robe and stood. All eyes focused on her. "I have been praying to know what I should do. I have raised Lucinda from babyhood, and she is like my own. But she is grown now and has found a wonderful man to love and who loves her. I need to let you go and make your own way."

Lucinda felt stricken. It had never occurred to her that Pearl would not want to be with her and David. "You're not leaving us for good, are you?"

"Never that." She smiled, kissed Lucinda, and crossed to where Gabriel lay. Dropping to her knees in front of the baby, she said, "I have no worldly possessions to bring, but I can give myself in service to the Lord by serving Gabriel and his family. Will you accept my gift?"

Andy and Gigi gaped at Pearl, and disbelief filled their eyes. Gigi finally found her voice. "*Oui, oui.*"

"Then I shall see David and Lucinda safely to their destination in Nebraska and return to you by the time you are ready to travel."

Andy wiped away a tear and nodded. "We will love you, and you will have a home with us all the days of your life." He turned to David and Lucinda. "Earlier we discussed this. Gigi and I would like you to be godparents to our firstborn."

David and Lucinda nodded, unable to speak. Pearl hugged them and then moved her bed next to the baby.

Yarrow Woman stood and raised her arms. "The circle is complete. We recognize that the true meaning of Christmas is Christ's sacrificial birth, life, death, and resurrection for us. These gifts are our poor attempts to remind us of His great sacrifice and to show our gratitude for it. May the Spirit of the Lord abide with us this day and every day during the coming year. Amen."

Easy Fruit Cobbler

½ cup butter
1 cup flour
1 cup sugar
1½ teaspoons
    baking powder

¾ cup milk
2 cups fruit
1 cup sugar

Preheat oven to 350 degrees. Melt butter in oven in 9 x 9-inch pan. In bowl, mix flour, 1 cup sugar, baking powder, and milk. Blend well. Pour batter into pan with melted butter; don't stir. Pour fruit over the top and sprinkle with remaining 1 cup sugar. Bake 25 minutes. Serve hot with vanilla ice cream.

A Christmas Gift of Love

by Darlene Mindrup

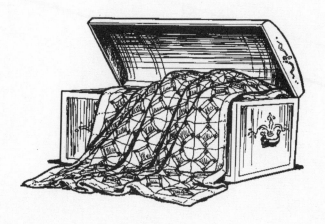

Chapter 1

Rose Johnson clutched the edges of the rough plank table and stared out the window at the bleak November landscape. A brisk, chill rain was pelting rhythmically against the glass pane that was the kitchen's sole source of light. Perhaps she should light the lantern on the table and dispel some of the gloom, but her lethargy wouldn't allow even that much effort.

Sighing, she allowed her thoughts free rein as they pushed insistently against the forced shield of her mind. For the first time in days, the tears came as relentlessly as the precipitation outside.

Papa was gone, and she was alone in the world. What was she to do now? She had nowhere to go, no one to care. If she had any relatives, she didn't know about them. For the last twenty years, it had been just Papa and she; and before that there was Mama.

She smiled as she remembered her mother's gentle face. Mama had died when Rose was just fifteen, and Rose had thought the pain would never go away. But it did. Slowly. Inevitably. Just as this pain would pass, too; but from experience Rose knew it would take time. Lots of time.

She could see her own reflection in the darkness of the glass. Her wide blue eyes were her only good feature. Her brown hair looked almost black against the darkness of the pane. Papa had named her Rose, but she bore no resemblance to the beautiful flower. She had never had a beau, and she knew now that she never would. At thirty-five years of age, she was well past her prime here on the prairie of the Dakota Territory.

She could hear conversation reverberating from the other room and knew that she would have to return soon. But not just yet. She needed time to herself. Time to grieve.

Since tomorrow was Thanksgiving Day, Rose had decided to forego the more formal wake that would last all night. It was well past four o'clock already and several of the others were preparing to leave, to return to their homes and their lives celebrating a national holiday established in 1863, less than six years ago, by the then president, Abraham Lincoln.

She thought about this Thanksgiving, so different from the past few years that she had spent with her father, and more recently with Ward Taylor, a good friend of her father's. This year there would be no cooked venison with savory stuffing, no wild berry pies, no celebrating of thanks to the Lord.

Well, that was not entirely true. Although Papa was gone, she knew that she still had much to be thankful for. God had given her thirty-five wonderful years with the best papa a girl could have. Now, he was with her mother and she was truly thankful for that. The future without them she refused to consider, for it seemed terribly bleak.

Last night she had lain down to sleep wishing that she could join her parents during the night, but she had awakened this morning before the sun was up, as usual, and knew it was a fruitless wish. God must still have a purpose for her, but right now she couldn't even begin to know what it might be. Her tired mind refused to function properly, and concern for her future continually twisted her mind with worry.

She could hear Ward's deep voice rumbling in the outer room. Rose was always uncomfortable in his presence, even though he and her father had been friends for several years. When he came to visit she usually found an excuse to absent herself. That he knew it was obvious. Still, he hadn't let it affect his friendship with Papa.

Frowning, she tried to think what it was that stirred that sense of panic she felt whenever he was near. He had been only kind to her. Perhaps it was the fact that he was such a large man, and when he spoke she felt he would surely rattle the walls of the small shanty where she lived. He seemed such a powerful man, such a contrast to the other men she had known. Men like her quiet, gentle papa.

And Ward's eyes were the most incredible color of green that she had ever seen, like the shifting prairie grass in the spring, yet they seemed so vacant of any emotion. Almost cold. At least it had always seemed that way to her, but when she mentioned it to Papa, he had vehemently disagreed with her.

She shook her head slightly and tried to banish thoughts of the man from her mind. Going to the cupboard in the corner, she tried to reach the extra mugs she kept stored on the top shelf. Papa usually fetched them for her, but Papa was not here to do so now. Well, at least his body was, but not his spirit. That had been freed from the pain of the last several days.

She closed her eyes against the anguish of that memory. Papa's twisted, broken body that had been brought to her after his horse had spooked and he had been thrown from it. He had lived for three days in excruciating pain before his spirit had finally been put to rest.

She shuddered as she thought of her present company keeping watch on the now cold body of her beloved father. She had always hated the custom of wakes. Why couldn't they just have buried him yesterday and have done with it? If they thought he was merely unconscious and might waken at any moment, she could tell them otherwise.

A small moan escaped her and she leaned her head against the cupboard. She had heard the stories before of people being buried alive, thence the custom of wakes, but nothing would bring her papa back again, no matter how much she might wish it. If only it could be so, she would gladly let the others keep watch forever.

"Here, let me get that for you."

Rose tensed at Ward's voice, the timbre of it sending little chills skittering down her spine. He reached around her, pushing against her back as he stretched to the top shelf. Rose stiffened against him, turning slowly when he moved away.

Quietly, he handed her the tray of mugs, his eyes never leaving her face. Rose felt the color spread across her cheeks and unconsciously she lifted a hand to her hair to make sure her bun was still in place. Drawn back from her face so tightly, her hair only added to her wan appearance, but of this she was unaware.

Rose turned away from him and began readying the coffee, pouring the steaming brew from the blue-speckled pot she kept on the back burner of her woodstove. She pulled some sugar cookies from the jar on the counter and added them to the tray.

Feeling his eyes on her, she grew suddenly clumsy, her fingers failing to do what she required of them. When she snapped a cookie in two, she sighed with exasperation.

"Sugar cookies are my favorite," he told her, his kindness twinkling in those green eyes. A small sound escaped from her throat before she could stop it.

Ward reached to take the tray from her, and set it on the table. When he pulled her gently into his arms she stiffened, and then suddenly she collapsed against him, her tears releasing her of the past hours of stored-up grief. He drew her closer still as he murmured soothing words of comfort.

Rose acknowledged to herself the warmth and security she felt in Ward's arms as he rocked her gently back and forth, and while she longed to remain just where she was, a part of her told her it was not a very good idea. Finally, Rose pulled away, rubbing angrily at the wetness on her cheeks. She refused to look at Ward. "They were Papa's favorite, too," she told him, as though that explained everything. Lifting the coffee tray from the table, she hurried from the kitchen, Ward following close on her heels.

The shanty, though small, still boasted four separate rooms: kitchen, living area, and two bedrooms. For many of the people living here on the prairie, this house would seem palatial. To Rose, it was just home. Other neighbors were seated in the main living area, while Papa was laid out in his own bedroom, awaiting burial the next day.

Rose handed mugs of coffee to those present, passing the cookies among them. When she sat down, she found herself across from Ward. His veiled eyes seemed to be watching every move she made.

Shifting uncomfortably, she dropped her eyes to the black band around his forearm. Every person in the room was wearing such a band, their symbol of respect to her deceased father. Except for a sprinkling of gray throughout his tresses, the color of the band was as dark as the hair on Ward's head. At forty years of age, he was still a striking man where looks were concerned. He had the lean fitness of a man who spent many hours out-of-doors.

Thankfully her attention, and his, was diverted by several people rising to leave. Rose handed them their coats and thanked them for coming. Soon there were only herself, Ward, and Emily Haskins left.

Closing the door against the fast-approaching night, Rose turned to the elderly woman and almost choked at the soft look of sympathy she saw reflected in the older woman's gentle brown eyes.

"I'm not leaving you alone here tonight, Rose. Ward has agreed to stay and take me home after the funeral in the morning."

"That's really not necessary," Rose told her, her own voice tinged with dismay.

Ward gave her a sharp glance. "It's no trouble," he answered her. "Emily and I would be traveling back in the morning anyway, so with the weather being like it is, we thought we would just as well stay." His green eyes roved her features slowly before being caught by the troubled look in her own blue eyes.

Rose was relieved when Ward released her from his mesmerizing gaze and turned instead to Emily. "I am at your command," he told her, his face splitting into a grin.

Emily had a penchant for organizing things, and Rose had no doubt that she was about to do that very thing now. It was quite possible that Ward had suggested it, thinking that Rose would be in no fit state to do much of anything.

Rolling up her sleeves, Emily headed to the kitchen. "Bring me some more wood from the lean-to, and don't forget to feed the livestock. Oh, and Rose, help me find the flour so that I can bake you some bread. I'll not leave you here without the basic necessities."

Rose found Ward smiling at her and couldn't help but smile in return. Shaking her head, she followed Emily into the kitchen. Already the older woman was bustling about finding the items she needed to concoct her famous honey wheat bread.

Rose's eyes fastened on the jar with the honeycomb smothered in honey. A small smile touched her lips as she thought of Papa and her finding the hive this summer. Together they had managed to smoke the bees and retrieve the sweet liquid, though she had received three stings for her effort and had ached for days. Papa, on the other hand, had not been stung at all. He had laughingly told her that the bees knew she was afraid of them.

"It's amazin' how we women tend to think so much alike."

Rose shifted her wayward thoughts and focused on the woman before her. "What did you say?"

"I said it's amazin' how much women tend to think alike. I could find just about everything in your kitchen 'cause it's pretty much in the same place as mine."

Rose pinched the bridge of her nose, closing her tired eyes. She appreciated

Emily's concern, and Ward's, but she would much rather be alone. Papa's body might be lying in the next room, but there was nothing about that to frighten her. If anything, it offered her a slight measure of comfort.

Pulling out a chair at the table, Rose slowly lowered herself into it. She watched Emily working the dough and realized that the older woman had been right. Rose was so tired, she would never have bothered to fix anything for herself to eat.

Ward brought the wood in and dumped it in the bin by the stove. Taking off his dripping sheepskin jacket, he hung it on the hook behind the door. He stretched his muscles tiredly, his gray flannel shirt rippling across his broad shoulders with the movement. Rose swallowed hard and quickly turned her eyes away.

"What else?" He spoke to Emily, but his eyes were once again centered on Rose.

"The animals taken care of?" Emily asked him.

"I did that earlier." His look swung again to Rose. "You look just about done in. Why don't you get some sleep? Emily and I will see to things here."

Rose was already shaking her head. "I couldn't do that."

Hands placed firmly on her rounded hips, Emily scrutinized Rose with a knowing eye. "Why ever not? You're not much good to us like you are. You're already half asleep on your feet. Good Book says to do unto others as you would have them do unto you. Now, if the shoe were on the other foot, what would *you* say?"

Rose blinked tired eyes up at the elderly woman standing before her. Truth to tell, having someone take charge was a blessing for which she should be thankful. She glanced at Ward and found his lips twitching with amusement. Emily Haskins had always had the last word about anything for as long as Rose could remember. She couldn't think of a time when the spry woman hadn't gotten her own way.

"All right," she relented, rising to her feet. "You've convinced me. I'll go to bed."

Emily's face broke into a broad smile. "I knew you were a woman of good sense."

Ward followed Rose from the kitchen. "I'll just see that the fire in the fireplace is still going strong, then I'll go back and help Emily."

Rose only half-heard Ward placing another log on the still-crackling fire as she sluggishly made her way across the room to her bedroom door. She had her hand on the latch, but stopped just short of lifting it.

When she turned to go to the other door, Ward barely made it there before her. He placed his hand over hers as she was about to pull the latch.

Startled, she jerked her hand back and lifted her face to his in question.

"Don't," he told her softly. "Not tonight. You're too tired. Wait until the morning."

She wanted to argue, but she knew he was right. Still, something about him made her want to do everything opposite to what he suggested. Could it be because everything he said always came out sounding like an order?

As though he could read her mind, he touched her face gently with a curled finger. "Please."

His touch set off an explosion of feelings she had no hope of interpreting. Ward could see the trepidation return to her eyes as she quickly moved away from him. "You're probably right," she told him breathlessly. "I only wanted to see him one more time before the others come again tomorrow. One more time, just he and I alone."

Ward said nothing, merely watching as she quickly crossed to the other door and let herself into her own bedroom.

Closing the door behind her, Rose leaned back against it, pressing a hand to her heart. Never in her life had she been so unsettled by a man's touch. It sent feelings twisting through her that she had never experienced before, made her want things she had long ago considered impossible.

Brows puckering in confusion, she made her way across to her bed and began to disrobe in the dark. The chill temperatures had her hurrying, and quickly climbing beneath the quilts on her bed she curled herself into a ball, shivering against the cold sheets.

How could a man affect her in such a way? A man she barely liked. And now, of all times, with her father lying mere feet away, lost to her for the rest of this lifetime. She was overly tired. That had to be it, for no other explanation offered itself to her fatigued mind.

Huddling beneath the covers, she felt the chill lessen and her eyes grew drowsy. As she drifted off to sleep, she resolved to free herself of Ward's unwanted presence at the earliest opportunity.

&

"Does she know about the farm yet?"

Ward lifted tired eyes to the woman before him. Slowly, he shook his head. "I didn't want to burden her with that tonight. She'll know soon enough."

Emily pulled out a chair and joined him at the kitchen table. "I agree, of course. It just amazes me that Gabel kept such a thing to himself."

Ward nodded. "He was that kind of man. Willing to help others in any way he could, but not willing to let others do the same for him."

"A lot like someone else I know, Ward Taylor. Maybe that's why you two got along so well."

Grinning, Ward didn't deny it. He lifted the steaming mug to his lips and blew softly. Actually, he hated coffee; but he wouldn't for the world let Emily know that, because to Emily, coffee was a panacea for all kinds of evils. Grimacing when her back was turned, he reached for the sugar bowl and ladled a heavy spoonful into the dark, aromatic brew.

"So what will you do now?"

One dark eyebrow winged its way upwards. "What makes you think I will do anything?"

A very unladylike snort followed his question. "Ward Taylor, you gotta do somethin'. That little girl in there can't take care of herself, you know. She needs a good strong man to look out for her."

Ward had to smile at Emily's reference to a woman of thirty-five years of age being a "little girl." The smile disappeared quickly when he realized what she had said. "Why, you old matchmaker, you! You can just get that notion out of your mind, real quick."

Innocent brown eyes didn't fool Ward for one minute. He knew he had to do something to help Rose, and he didn't need anyone like Emily pointing it out to him. But she was suggesting—no, that couldn't be what she was suggesting. Surely he was being paranoid.

When he looked at her again, his eyes narrowed in suspicion. "What did you have in mind?"

"Well. . ." she drawled. "You could use a good wife and Rose could use a good husband." He rose quickly to his feet, but Emily continued undaunted. "If you had a wife, you wouldn't need to pay me to do your baking, and Maudie to do your laundry, and—"

"Okay, okay," he told her in exasperation, lifting a hand as though to stem the flow of words. "I get the picture. But I thought you enjoyed the extra money, and if it doesn't bother me, why should it bother you?"

"Now don't get ornery," she huffed. "I *do* like the extra money, but I think you could put *yours* to better use."

Ward was shaking his head. "Emily, you never cease to amaze me."

"Did you know Rose ain't got no place to go?"

He collapsed back into the chair. "I know."

"Well?"

Ward stared at Emily several minutes before he realized that he was actually considering what she had suggested. Gritting his teeth, he jumped to his feet, grabbing his coat from the hook on the back of the kitchen door.

"I'll just go check on the animals," he told her.

She gave him a "you don't fool me" look, but she remained quiet as he escaped through the door.

As Ward made his way to the barn he stole a glance at the sky. Clouds blocked out the cold night moon and he knew there would be more rain come morning. What a miserable day for a funeral it was going to be, not that any day was a good one.

Throwing some more hay in the manger, he patted the old milk cow's neck and checked once again to make sure everything was all right. There was very little hay left, but he doubted Rose was even aware of it. He sighed. If only these torrential rains had come this past summer when the farmers needed it instead of now. He hadn't realized just how badly Gabel had been affected by the drought.

Making his way back to the cabin, he made sure he entered through the front door instead of the kitchen. He could hear Emily moving around, humming faintly to herself.

Leaving his muddy boots beside the door, he made his way quietly to Rose's door and pressed an ear against the portal. No sound came from within, so he assumed she was fast asleep. What would she say when he told her everything tomorrow? What would she do? Where would she go? The questions kept circling round and round in his mind. One thing was for certain, Emily's idea was positively out of the question.

Chapter 2

Ward's prediction of rain hadn't materialized as of the time set for the funeral, and he knew Rose was thankful. Hovering clouds to the north spoke of a winter storm approaching and everyone knew that with that storm, winter would set in with a vengeance.

The minister hurried the ceremony, and surrounding neighbors quickly made their way back to their horses and wagons. It wouldn't do to be caught out in a blizzard.

Out of necessity, Gabel's body was buried close to the shanty on the land that he loved. Ward walked beside Rose back to the house, wondering how he could broach the subject of Rose's future. He was relieved of that obligation when Rose spoke first.

"I want to thank you for everything you've done." She glanced at him, but quickly turned away. "Both now and in the past. Papa. . .Papa was grateful for your friendship."

There was a catch in her voice as she said the last and Ward knew she was struggling with tears held tightly in check. He took a deep breath, but before he could say anything she continued.

"It was nice of Pastor Hoover to offer to take Emily home."

He gave her a quick glance, but made no comment.

"I know you must be anxious to get home yourself, but would you like a cup of coffee before you go?"

Ward wrinkled his nose slightly. "That would be nice," he lied.

When they reached the shanty, Rose disappeared into the kitchen to fetch them each a cup of coffee. Ward followed her, watching her without appearing to do so.

He seated himself at the table and Rose pushed a cup in front of him. She sat down across from him and hastily lowered her eyes.

Ward noticed the traces of Rose's tears and felt suddenly very protective toward her. Both she and her father had been good friends to him over the past several years, though he knew that with Rose it was a somewhat reserved friendship. For some reason he seemed to alarm her, but as yet he hadn't found the cause. It had never bothered him overmuch, seeing as how it was her pa he came to see. She had always seemed to just melt into the background whenever he was around.

He had been unfailingly courteous to her whenever they came in contact, but each time he could sense the wall she erected between them. He had never felt as free with her as he had with Gabel, her father. Now, suddenly, he wished it had been different. Then he might know what to say to her now, what comfort he could offer, though from experience he knew there was really nothing you could say to a person who had just lost someone held dearer than life itself. And now he had to give her more bad news.

"Rose, there's something I need to tell you."

When she looked at him with those innocent blue eyes, Ward found himself momentarily rattled. How was he ever going to manage this? It was hard to think straight when confronted by such liquid pools of misery.

"Yes?"

Ward pushed his cup away, rubbing at his face in agitation. "This house—I mean this land—"

"I know what you're going to say. A woman alone can't take care of the land and the crops. I've heard it all before. But other women have staked claims and worked to prove 'em up. I can too."

Pursing his lips, Ward began to draw circles with his finger on the table. He didn't look at her when he said, "There's no claim to prove up."

She frowned across at him. "What's that supposed to mean? Papa has had this claim for over six years now. It's his, free and clear. It was tough, but we did it. We even stayed through the Santee Indian uprisings when most other folks left. This is *our* land."

When Ward captured her look, his eyes were serious. "Your pa mortgaged this land to buy seed for crops. This land isn't yours. It belongs to the Yankton Bank."

Rose's already pale face became even paler. "I don't believe you."

"It's true," he told her. "What's more, I think you know it."

Rose sagged back against her chair. "You're right. I've known something was wrong for a long time now. When the rains failed to come this past spring Papa was more worried than I can ever remember seeing him." Her eyes met his. "Why didn't he tell me?"

"He was hoping to recoup his losses by selling a piece of his land, but—"

"But he died before he could do it," she finished for him tonelessly.

"Yes."

For the first time, Ward noticed a spark of interest in her eyes. "Then I could do the same. Sell some of the land, I mean." The sudden, irrelevant thought occurred to him that her eyes were the very color of a summer sky.

He shook his head slowly. "It's already too late. The bank intends to foreclose by the end of this week."

She rose quickly to her feet. "Then I haven't time to lose. I'll saddle Baron and leave straightway. I should be able to make it to Yankton in two days."

Ward stared up at her in openmouthed amazement. He rose to his own feet, his six-foot-six height towering over her by a good nine inches. "Of all the stupid— don't be ridiculous! For one thing, you'd never outrun that storm." He motioned toward the kitchen window where the morning light already resembled dusk.

"I could try!"

"And for another thing," he went on, "the bank already has a buyer for this property at twice the rate of your father's mortgage. There's no way they're going to give you more time, and especially not to sell off part of the land which would detract from its value."

Rose slowly sank back to her chair. She buried her face in her hands. "There has to be a way," she muttered. "I *have* to keep this property. I have nowhere else to go."

Ward knelt beside her, pulling her hands away from her face. The abject misery in her visage reminded him of a wounded fawn he had come across this past spring.

"There is a way," he told her softly.

Hope brightened her features, and she smiled at him with a smile that seemed to dispel some of the gloom from the darkened interior. "There is?"

Her childish faith disturbed him. He swallowed twice before he could get the words out. "You could marry me."

Her smile disappeared and such a look of horror crossed her face that Ward was momentarily offended.

Rose couldn't have looked more surprised if the floor had opened up beneath her. She stared at Ward with a look that surely doubted his sanity. Neither one spoke for a long moment.

"Just listen to me a minute," he urged. "I'm not suggesting a regular marriage. I know you don't love me, and I don't. . .well, I don't love you either. But we *need* each other."

If she could have gotten past him, Ward had no doubt Rose would have left him kneeling there. She really had no option but to listen to everything he had to say.

"I can't promise you love. All of that died in me seven years ago. But I can promise you that I will care for you. All I ask in return is someone to meet my needs. I know you're a fine cook, and you have a knack of making even the roughest dwelling seem like home."

The anger seemed to drain from her face as she considered his proposal.

"I need time to think, Ward. Time to sort things through."

"I can't give you that time," he declared roughly. "The minister only stayed for your father's funeral and he intends to leave within the next hour. He's going to try to reach Mitchell before the snow flies, so he would have to marry us now. I can give you five minutes to decide."

With that, he got up and left the room.

⬤

Rose sat there, her mind totally blank. Five minutes to decide her future. Of all the nerve! Of course she would decline his offer. In fact she would take perverse delight in doing so. But what *would* she do with her future?

Her mind wandered round and round in circles until Rose thought she would scream, but no matter which way her thoughts turned, she always came back to the same conclusion. She had *nowhere* to go. Marrying Ward offered her a solution, but what kind of woman would she be if she accepted such an arrangement?

Of course, others before her had accepted such a proposal, but that certainly didn't justify Rose's doing the same. Still, Ward had said that he *needed* her. A man alone on the prairie was about as useless as a woman alone on the prairie.

For the first time Rose considered the sacrifice Ward was willing to make for her. After several moments of such reasoning, Rose finally convinced herself that she would be doing Ward just as big a favor as he was doing her.

Not willing to be found waiting for him, Rose got up and went in search of Ward. He was kneeling next to the fire slowly stirring the hot coals with the fire iron. His brow was furrowed in thought and from that distance he seemed quite unapproachable. Rose had to take her courage firmly in hand before she could get her feet to move.

He glanced up as she stopped beside him. Green eyes studied her thoughtfully, their look inscrutable.

"Why?"

He didn't pretend to misunderstand her. "I owe you and your father a lot. It's the least I could do."

Rose blew out through tightly clenched lips. "We owe you just as much, if not more."

He stood and crossed the room, returning the iron to its place by the fire. When he turned back to Rose his expression was carefully veiled. He took her by the shoulders, studying her face carefully. "I need a wife. You need a husband. It's as simple as that. Don't look for something more when there *is* nothing more."

Rose struggled with the desire to say no, but she held herself in check. She needed more time to decide what to do, but her time was rapidly running out. It was clear Ward expected an answer.

"What do you want from me?" she asked in an unsteady voice.

"Only what you're willing to give."

"If I say yes. . .will you. . .do you want. . . ?" Her tongue tripped over the words.

"I expect nothing from you except to care for my home, cook my meals, and possibly help with the land. In time. . .in time, maybe we could learn to care for each other. I don't know. As I said, my heart died a long time ago. I don't know if I have any heart left to give."

Rose lay a hand against his gray flannel sleeve. "You have a heart, Ward. You proved that just now."

She walked away from him and went to the window. Rose knew putting in glass panes was an extravagance, but Papa had wanted it so much for Rose. He had tried to make everything easier for her.

Ward cleared his throat. "Rose, there's something else you need to know."

She glanced over her shoulder, waiting for him to continue.

"My place is nothing like this." He motioned with his hand, indicating the shanty's interior. "I had no need to fix my place up special since. . .since I had no woman to care."

Rose saw the brief look of grief that crossed his features. Ward had lost his wife on the trip out to the Dakota Territory, that much she knew. Something to do with fever. How he must have loved her to feel the pain of loss even after seven years.

"Please don't tell me you live in a soddie," she whispered.

Surprised, he blinked at her before breaking into a soft chuckle, his eyes suddenly alive with devilment. "Nothing like that. I just want you to know that I only have a one-room cabin with a dirt floor. If you decide to marry me, I will immediately begin to change that."

"Only one room?" If anything, her voice was fainter than before.

He nodded. "After the storm passes I can begin to bring logs from the river to add on. It'll take time, but I have nothing else pressing since winter has set in."

Rose turned back to study the outside and saw the first soft flakes begin to fall against the panes. Snow!

Ward noticed too. He came to stand beside her, his attention focused outside. "You have to give me your answer now, Rose."

It seemed an eternity before Rose could bring herself to answer him. She sent up a quick prayer for the Almighty's blessings on this seemingly unholy contract. She couldn't get the words past the lump in her throat, so she settled for nodding her head.

She felt more than saw Ward relax. "You'll have to get your coat and come with me to the Haskins'. Pastor Hoover is waiting for us there."

"You were so sure I'd say yes?" she asked quietly.

"Let's just say I *hoped* the answer would be yes," he answered just as quietly.

❧

Ward watched Rose cross the shanty to her room. When she disappeared from sight his shoulders slumped, and he let out a long breath. What on earth had he gotten himself into now? Of all the stupid notions, this had to top them all. When Emily had first suggested he marry Rose, he had thought it ludicrous, but after a fitful night with no sleep and images of Rose's less than rosy future, the idea had seemed not only possible, but necessary.

Rose returned and Ward helped her into her coat. He took the blanket she handed him and followed her outside to his waiting wagon. A fine layer of white covered the horses from head to tail.

After tucking the blanket securely around her, Ward climbed into the wagon beside her and taking up the reins clucked to the horses. The silence hung between them, almost deafening in its completeness.

Emily was waiting for them when they arrived. Although the trip was only two miles, snow now covered the ground to a depth of several inches. If the wind should pick up, it would become a full-out blizzard.

Pastor Hoover hurriedly performed the service, smiling at them both when he gave his blessing. In a short time Ward and Rose found themselves on their way back to Rose's shanty. Emily had wanted them to stay for a celebration supper, but prudence dictated otherwise. There were animals to attend to. Besides, neither Ward nor Rose felt that there was anything much to celebrate.

Rose climbed down from the wagon and hurried inside while Ward took the horses to the barn. Her hands were shaking so badly she could hardly undo the buttons on her coat.

She threw the coat on the hook behind the front door and slowly made her way into the kitchen. She went to the window and looked out, not even bothering to light the lamp. Anguished blue eyes reflected back to her from the darkened panes. *Oh Papa! What now? Would you have wanted this?*

There was no answer, only the keening howl of the wind as it began its trip across the prairie.

Chapter 3

The morning dawned bright and clear, almost as though the previous night's storm had never been. It had left behind a reminder, however, and the flat prairie was covered in white for as far as the eye could see.

For Rose, the past twenty-four hours had seemed like a surrealistic dream or, depending on one's opinion, a nightmare. She twisted the gold band Ward had placed on her left hand only last night. Where he had obtained it she had no idea, nor was she about to ask. She had this horrible feeling that it might have belonged to his first wife, Elise, and that he had carried it around with him for the past seven years. Such morbid thoughts made her shiver with distaste.

Now Ward was hitching his team of horses to the wagon in preparation for returning to his own cabin. She could see the frown furrowing his brow and realized that he was concerned for his livestock since he had been unable to make it back last night, the storm having effectively stranded them here. Her own milk cow and Papa's horse were tied securely to the back of the wagon.

She drifted to the front door, opening it and leaning against the jamb. Ward glanced up briefly but continued with what he was doing. The winter landscape shone so brightly it stung the eyes just to look at it. The wind had scattered the snow, piling it up against small obstructions until there were little hills all around.

"I'll be back by sundown. It would help if you had the place cleaned out and your things ready to be moved." He retraced his steps to the other side of the team and began tightening the harness on Big Ben, Old Blue's teammate. "You can leave the bedding since it will be too late to make it back to my. . .*our* place this evening. We'll stay the night here again."

Would she ever feel comfortable around this man? She certainly didn't feel married, though never having experienced that state before, she wasn't quite sure what "feeling married" entailed. "I'll. . .I'll have supper ready when you get back."

Nodding his head, Ward climbed into the wagon. He gave Rose a long, searching look before lifting the reins and clucking to the team. As the wagon moved forward, Rose heard the cackling of the chickens that Ward had crated up to take back with him. They seemed as unhappy with the situation as she was.

Closing the door, she began wandering from room to room, lifting a pot here, moving a blanket there. She stood in Papa's room a long time before shaking her head, and finally pulling herself together. This was getting her nowhere. She knew what she had to do, so it was best to pull herself out of the doldrums and get the job done.

Since she had no crates or barrels, she used her clothes and blankets to pile dishes and supplies into, leaving only those blankets and sheets necessary for their sojourn here tonight. She gathered her breakables next to her storage chest beside her bed and lifting the cover peered inside.

Her heart seemed to lodge somewhere in her throat when she spotted the colorful quilt to one side. She had forgotten. Now, she carefully lifted it out, spreading it across her lap. Tears began to pool in her eyes as she moved her hand softly over the covering.

This quilt had been a labor of love, worked on for months now. She had taken materials left over from worn-out clothes belonging to Papa and Mama, and even her own, and fashioned them into this beautiful spread.

That blue piece was from a shirt she had made for Papa when she was but fifteen, shortly after Mama had died. Mama had taught her to sew, but the shirt had proven trickier than she had expected and somehow she could not get the sleeves to set right. Still, Papa had worn it proudly.

There were pieces from the dresses her mother had made for her as a child. There was even a beautiful piece of faded white satin from Mama's wedding gown.

Rose had been saving these pieces for ages, and it was the one thing Papa had not left behind them when they had come west. Most people would have considered a crate of material pieces a foolish waste of space, but not Papa. He had known just how much they meant to her.

It had only been this past summer that the thought of making a special quilt for him had occurred to her. She had created her own intricate pattern and worked long hours to complete it in time for Christmas. The tiny, even stitches spoke well of Rose's ability with a needle and she felt a little thrill of pride in herself and her mother who had taken such pains to teach her the finer art of quilting.

Since she had finished the quilt before Thanksgiving, she had put it away until later to give to Papa. It had been all she could do to keep it from him until Christmas. Now, it was too late. He would never see it.

Tears crowded close in her throat and she gently lay the covering back in the chest, arranging her breakables among its soft folds. She shut the lid firmly.

Well, the quilt was hers now. All that was left of Papa and Mama. Even the farm was no longer hers, but no one could take away her memory quilt, especially not some greedy bank. Let them have the land, the shanty, and even the livestock if they so desired, but the quilt belonged to her, and her alone.

It didn't take long for her to empty the shanty of their few possessions. She hadn't realized just how much trifles added to the warmth of a home, but now, with the barrenness, the shanty seemed less friendly somehow. Again she experienced that feeling of living in a dream. She moved listlessly about, unable to set her mind to anything.

Finally, she made her way into the kitchen and checked on the stew she had started earlier. Thanks to Emily, there was bread to go with it, but little else. Still, it would have to do.

The day seemed to drag, and although she was unaware of it, Rose sighed with relief when she heard the returning wagon.

Ward opened the door, stopping on the threshold to scrape off the mud and ice caked to his boots. He glanced briefly at Rose before closing the door behind him and hanging his coat on the peg behind it.

"How were your animals?" she asked him, busying herself with setting the table so that she wouldn't have to look at him. Every time she was in his presence, she felt such acute shyness that it was hard for her to form a coherent thought.

"*Our* animals were fine," he told her, deliberately stressing the pronoun. "Hungry, but none the worse for their unexpected fast."

He joined her at the table, breathing into his cupped hands to free them of their cramping cold. "Smells good," he told her, his nose twitching appreciatively.

Rose ladled him a bowl of stew, adding a buttered slice of bread. She kept wracking her brain trying to think of something to say. Ward seemed equally as uncomfortable.

After fixing her own bowl, she slid into the seat across from him. Giving him a brief look she bowed her head and asked him to say grace.

There was a long silence in the room, and just as she was about to look up to see what the problem was, she heard Ward clear his throat and hesitantly offer thanks for the food.

Rose frowned. Hadn't Papa told her once that Ward was a man of God? If that were so, then why such hesitation over a simple grace?

She kept her gaze focused on her own plate and decided not to worry about it. Let the Good Lord handle Mr. Ward Taylor; she had enough troubles of her own.

After supper, it didn't take Rose long to wash the few dishes and pack them away in one of the crates Ward had brought back with him. She made one more check through the house to assure herself that nothing had been left behind. Ward had told her that the furniture could be stored in the barn temporarily, but otherwise there was no room for it right now in his—their cabin. She was beginning to really fret about this cabin that was soon to be her new home.

When she closed her eyes that night, Rose tried hard to pray and leave things in God's hands, but no clear thoughts would come. Her mind seemed to have gone blank. Finally, she allowed her musings to roam in a wordless appeal that she knew the Lord would be able to untangle and set right. Only He could possibly have any idea of what she was really trying to say. She only knew one thing. God had been with her all of her life, and she was sure He wouldn't abandon her now.

❧

Conversation was nonexistent for the first two miles of the trek to Ward's cabin. Both he and Rose were busy with their own thoughts, both trying to adjust themselves to their sudden change of circumstances.

Rose wondered just how far the cabin was. She couldn't remember ever discussing it with Papa, but it must be quite a distance since it took the better part of a day for him to reach their place. She really wanted to know, but she was too nervous to ask and draw his attention to her.

"Our place is about ten more miles that way," he told her, motioning to the northeast. His look swung briefly her way. "Are you sure you're warm enough?"

She nodded. Now was the time to strike up a conversation and relieve them both of this tense situation, but her tongue was simply too tied.

As though he read her thoughts, Ward began a rambling monologue of the countryside around, how he thought it was going to be a long hard winter, and what to expect when they reached his place. Rose was trying to prepare herself for the worst.

About halfway to their destination, they rounded a bend in the road which was little more than dug-in wagon tracks. Rose assumed that most of them must have come from Ward and his frequent trips to her cabin.

There was a house nestled back from the road, if one could call it a house. In actuality, it was nothing but a small soddie. Probably the occupants were either too lazy to haul logs from the Missouri River close by, or they had been here too short a time to make other arrangements.

She was surprised when a man hurried out to intercept them on the road. He had a short, neatly clipped beard and although his clothes were little more than patched rags, he was clean.

Ward pulled the wagon to a stop, setting the brake. He reached down to the man, a smile lighting his features.

"Howdy, Adam. I'd like you to meet my wife, Rose." Ward nodded toward the other man. "The Comptons are our nearest neighbors."

Brown eyes sparkled with friendliness as the man reached out a hand. "Howdy, ma'am."

Rose returned his smile. "Mr. Compton."

"How's the family?" Ward asked him.

"See for yourself."

Over his shoulder, Rose could see a woman and two children hurrying their way. The woman stopped beside the wagon and shyly handed Rose a bundle. "For you. A wedding present."

Rose was stunned. She knew that news here on the prairie traveled as fast as a wildfire, so she shouldn't have been surprised. But she was.

Taking the bundle, Rose unwrapped it, revealing a small loaf of bread. She could feel Ward's eyes on her. When she looked his way, there was something indefinable in his eyes.

"Thank you." She acknowledged the woman's friendliness with a smile that brought a quick one in return.

"This here's Alice," Adam told her, the pride evident in his voice. "She's my missus. And this here's Alicia and Andrew. Twins." He ruffled the boy's hair good-naturedly, but Andrew pulled away.

"Aw, Pa!"

Adam grinned at his son. "Thinks he's too growed up, now that he's turned six."

Rose smiled at the play between father and son. It was obvious that this was a very close and loving family. Her gaze settled on little Alicia, a perfect replica of her mother. Blond ringlets cascaded down the child's back in abundance, and her periwinkle blue eyes smiled timidly at Rose.

"Won't you come in and have a bite to eat? You must be hungry after traveling so far."

Rose was about to answer the woman when she felt a sudden pressure on her knee. Turning startled eyes on Ward, she found his hand gripping her knee but his look was fixed on Alice.

"We can't today, Alice. We still have a long way to go. Besides, Rose fixed us something to eat for the trip."

That was certainly true, Rose thought, *but Ward was being unneighborly to say the least.* Everyone on the prairie shared with each other, helped each other, and looked forward to each other's company.

She opened her mouth to disagree with his statement, but he suddenly fixed her with a steely eye. She snapped her lips together, turning back to Alice and smiling with regret.

Ward made as if to leave, but suddenly stopped as though he had just thought of something. He turned to Adam.

"Adam, I was wondering if you might be willing to help me gather some logs from the river. My cabin is much too small now that I'm a married man." Both men exchanged amused glances. "I thought since it was winter and all, you might have some free time to help me. If so, I thought since we would be cutting and hauling logs for my cabin, we might just as well do so for you, too. Now, I can't pay you, but I figured if you helped me, I could help you and we could call it even."

A sudden light entered Adam's eyes and he straightened his shoulders. When Rose looked at Alice she saw the same shine reflected in her eyes.

"I reckon that'd be a fair trade," Adam agreed. "When do you want to start?"

"Is tomorrow too soon?"

Adam grinned. "I'll be there at first light."

Nodding, Ward lifted the reins again and clucked to the horses. They hadn't traveled far when Rose rounded on Ward.

"I can speak for myself, you know. It would have been nice to share a meal with the Comptons."

Ward's lips lifted slightly in an amused smirk. "I wondered how long it would take before you launched your attack."

"I'm not attacking," she huffed, "but you weren't being very neighborly."

When he turned her way, his green eyes were serious. "You're right. I wasn't being very neighborly, but for good reason." He motioned to the loaf of bread that Alice Compton had handed her. "That bread was probably their allotment for the week. Since the drought this past summer and the grasshoppers the year before, Adam hasn't fared very well. He still has three years left to prove up, and if things don't change, he'll lose his claim. You saw the condition of their clothes. They can barely afford to feed themselves, much less clothe themselves. But they're a very proud family. Adam feels if he can't make things work, then they just weren't meant to be. He won't accept 'charity.' "

Rose considered the loaf of bread in her lap. What a sacrifice! "Why didn't you say something? I wouldn't have accepted this."

He turned away from her, studying the white prairie around them. Puffs of frost billowed out of his mouth and nostrils and he pulled his hat lower on his head to ward off the cold. "I wouldn't hurt Alice for the world. I'll find a way to make it up to them."

He remained quiet after that, and Rose observed him silently. Ward, it would seem, had a far larger heart than he gave himself credit for. Her first thought had been to condemn. She dropped her chin and stared at her fingers. If the Lord had wanted to teach her humility, He had certainly found an effective way of doing it.

She had never known hunger herself. Papa had brought money with him when he first settled here on the prairie, so when the crops were scarce, the money had been there. It only now occurred to her that he must have been using that money little by little to make her life more comfortable. She felt ashamed of herself for not seeing it sooner.

She wrapped the loaf of bread gently, as though it were some great treasure, as in a sense, it was.

Chapter 4

Adam showed up as he said he would, at first light. Ward had been awake for hours and had already taken care of the chores and fed the livestock.

The cabin itself hadn't been nearly as unsatisfactory as Rose was expecting, but it was only one large room with very little in the way of furniture. The fact that there was only one bed had caused her serious qualms until Ward began making himself a pallet on the floor next to the fireplace.

Feeling guilty, but relieved nonetheless, Rose had prepared an elaborate supper to make amends. The whole evening had been an ordeal in itself, but one lighthearted moment had occurred at supper time that had relieved Rose of much of her dread of her husband, though at the time it had caused her a moment of panic.

She had poured him his third cup of coffee and was just turning away when he cleared his throat. Turning back, one eyebrow raised in question, she noticed Ward's nervousness. Suddenly, she began to feel rather nervous herself.

"Rose, there's something I need. . .I have to. . .well, we're going to be married a long time, God willing, and you just gotta know."

When he stopped, Rose waited expectantly, not realizing that she was holding her breath.

His chin lifted in determination, his eyes intent. "I'm sorry, Rose, but I just can't abide coffee."

Her breath rushed out of her in a gasp. Is that what this was all about? And here she had been expecting. . . what? She wasn't quite sure, but suddenly her relief lent a sparkle to her eyes, and she grinned at him.

"I'm not offended, Ward," she told him lightly. "Fact is, I can't stand the stuff myself."

His shoulders relaxed, and his mouth curled slowly into a heart-stopping smile. "The way you continually fed me the stuff, I never would have guessed." He shook his head, grinning. "Well, we should save a good deal of money on *that* commodity, then," he finally told her.

Rose shook her own head as she began clearing the table. "And all this time you've been forcing yourself to drink it whenever you came to our place. You should have told me. I thought all men drank coffee. Papa certainly loved it."

His smile was sheepish. "My pa taught me to *never* say anything against a woman's cookin'."

Rose shook her head again, just thinking about it now as she watched Ward hitching the team to the wagon. With Adam's wagon, they would be able to haul twice as much wood and wouldn't have to make as many return trips. It should save time all around, and the sooner the other rooms were added, the better it would be in her opinion. She hated the fact that Ward had to sleep on the cold, dirt floor.

Ward returned to the cabin to retrieve his leather gloves. He paused beside Rose on his way back out the door. "You sure you're gonna be all right here by yourself?"

She nodded. "I'll just unpack some of my things, if that's okay with you."

He lifted a hand and pushed a stray lock of hair behind her ear. His voice was so soft, it sent shivers of awareness throughout her entire being. "This is your place now, too. Remember?" When he bent and kissed her cheek softly, Rose thought her heart would surely come to a standstill. "Make it into a home," he continued. "I haven't had a real one in a long while, and I know you have the knack."

With that, he left her standing there gaping at his retreating back.

By the time Ward had returned, Rose had unpacked most of her possessions, though there was little room in the small cabin to accommodate them. On the mantle above his fireplace, she placed her parents' anniversary clock, surrounding it with her own pair of silver candlesticks that Papa had bought for her twentieth birthday.

She had thought of adding her memory quilt to Ward's spartan bed, not only for the warmth but to add some cheerful color to this otherwise drab cabin. In the end, she had thought better of it. Perhaps there would be a time when she could look at the coverlet without feeling so much pain, but now was not that time. So she had carefully folded the quilt and returned it to her chest.

Over the next few days, Ward and Rose grew accustomed to each other's presence. Their conversation became less stilted, more natural, and before long they were conversing together as though they had been friends a long time, as indeed they really had, though they had not considered it so at the time.

In the evenings when Rose would pull out her Bible for her daily devotions, Ward would continue with his own work. He would clean the halters and oil them against the weather, or sharpen the tools he would need come planting time. Eventually he asked her to read aloud, and though she was surprised, she nonetheless readily agreed. It became an evening ritual that Rose looked forward to.

Ward still slept on his pallet by the fire, and Rose felt guiltier and guiltier about making him do so, especially when he spent such long, hard hours felling trees and she did so little. But when she had suggested switching beds, she had been met with such a cold look of outrage that she didn't dare suggest it again.

It was now a week into December, and suddenly Christmas loomed largely on Rose's horizon. The holiday didn't strike the same chord of joy that it usually did, however, and she wondered just how she and Ward should spend it. It was the day set aside to remember Christ's birth, but Rose didn't think her Lord would really mind if she didn't celebrate just this once. After fretting about it several more days, she decided that she would just ignore Christmas this year. She was fairly certain Ward would agree with her.

In this she was wrong. When she suggested it to him, Ward told her that he had already invited the Comptons to spend Christmas with them. "I'm sorry," he told her, although he didn't look it. "I didn't know you felt that way."

Peeved, Rose told herself that he had no way of knowing *how* she felt since he was never around to talk about such things. She stopped in her tracks, realizing just how much she had been missing him when he was away. Of course, that was logical. It was lonely out here on the prairie, she reasoned, ignoring her heart when it tried to presume otherwise.

As she was preparing for bed that night, she happened to catch Ward's regard fixed intently on her as she brushed her long hair her usual one hundred strokes. Her fingers grew clumsy as they always did when he looked at her in such a way, and she dropped the brush.

Cheeks filling with color, she lifted it from the dirt and shook it out. Reluctantly, she looked at her husband again only to find him stirring the logs in the fire in preparation for the night. She curled down among her covers and tried to get her heart to steady into its normal rhythm. It was a long time before sleep found her.

⬡

The cold breeze from the cabin door closing roused Rose in the middle of the night. Sitting up, she tried to rub the sleep from her eyes, wondering what time it was and what had disturbed her.

She could barely make out the hands on the anniversary clock in the dying light from the fire. Twelve-twenty. Ward's covers were thrown back and his bed was empty. Heart jumping in alarm, she hastily climbed from her own warm cocoon and slid into her robe.

Opening the door, she scanned the area to see where Ward could have gone. A light glimmered faintly from the barn, and closing the door behind her, Rose headed in that direction.

By the time she reached the barn she was shivering with cold. She opened the door, swiftly closing it behind her. When she turned around she found Ward staring at her in surprise.

"What are you doing out here? Get back to the house! You'll freeze in that getup."

Ignoring him, she moved forward to where he was kneeling. "I thought something might be wrong."

He shifted his position next to his mare, Beauty, who was lying on her side, her flanks heaving. Rose's eyes widened in surprise. "Is she foaling?"

The look Ward focused on the mare was grim. "Yes," he told her shortly. "Now go back to the house."

"Is something wrong with her?"

"She's breech," he told her through gritted teeth. "Now, for heaven's sake, get out of here."

Rose looked from the heaving mare back to Ward. She could sense his desperation. Not only was the foal valuable, Ward truly cared for his animals.

"No," she answered him firmly, moving closer to his side. "I want to help. Just tell me what to do."

He looked as though he were about to argue when Beauty whinnied in pain. Giving Rose brief instructions, he turned his full attention back to the mare.

They worked together, side by side, until the first fingers of dawn were spreading across the sky. Just when she thought all hope was lost, Ward managed to turn the foal slightly, enough to allow it to pass through the birth canal.

Only moments later, a wet and bloody but triumphant colt struggled to get to his feet.

"It's a boy!" Rose exulted. "A beautiful baby boy!"

Ward shook his head slightly as he wiped his hands on a rag, his lips turning up into a reluctant smile.

Now that the excitement was over, Rose found herself trembling with the below-freezing temperatures. Although the barn was relatively warm compared to the great outdoors, it was much too cold for someone standing in her nightgown and robe.

Ward noticed her shivering and came quickly to her side. Pulling his own sheepskin jacket from the stall where he had left it, he wrapped it securely around her. His eyes found hers and held. "Thanks for your help. I couldn't have done it without you," he told her softly.

Rose swallowed hard against his fingers where they clutched his jacket together at her throat. Her eyes were drawn to his as they darkened in response to hers. He leaned forward and lifting her chin with his thumbs he pressed his lips warmly against hers.

Rose went from freezing to feeling as though her entire being were on fire. When Ward wrapped his strong arms around her, she leaned her full weight against him, knowing that her own legs would be useless as support.

She thought the moment would never end, in fact hoped that it wouldn't, but Ward pulled away when he heard Adam's wagon entering their yard.

He dropped his arms, stepping back from her, something undefined in his eyes. Rose shivered against the returning cold, her mind filled with a mixture of wonder and confusion, and turning, she fled back to the cabin.

❧

For the next several days Ward took pains to avoid being alone with Rose as much as possible. She jumped whenever he entered a room, and she sensed he knew it had to do with that moment in the barn. The friendly rapport they had established had vanished, but she realized that what was done couldn't be undone. She would have to do something to make him comfortable again.

Ward was clearly surprised when Rose followed him out to the wagon the next day.

"Do you think I can ride with you to Alice's today?"

Since he and Adam had accumulated enough logs to build a cabin, Ward had insisted that Adam have first priority. Pride battled stubbornness, and stubbornness had won out. Rose had had no doubt of the outcome. Ward had a tendency to have his own way, one way or another.

The two men working together should have most of the cabin raised by that evening, barring unforeseen circumstances. Alice would be ecstatic.

Ward studied Rose a moment as she quietly awaited his answer. Her coat was buttoned tightly against the bitter cold and she was clutching a bundle in her arms. He hesitated, but she knew he really had no reason to refuse her.

"Sure. Climb up."

He helped her into the wagon, reaching into the back to grab the blanket he kept there. He dropped it over her knees, fitting it snugly against her sides. When his eyes met hers, Rose felt there was a moment when it seemed as if the entire earth held its breath.

Turning quickly away, Ward picked up the reins and snapped them against the horses' flanks.

When they reached the Comptons' soddie, Alice met them outside, her face wreathed in smiles of welcome.

"Howdy! I'm so glad you came," she told Rose, her voice filled with pleased expectation. Little Alicia stood shyly watching from the doorway, but her brother Andrew pushed his way forward to stand beside the wagon.

Climbing down from her seat beside Ward, Rose followed Alice inside while Ward went to find Adam.

Alice's soddie was small as it was, but when Rose's presence was added along with the two children it became quite cramped. How could she stand it? The claustrophobic feeling such a tight space engendered would make even the sturdiest soul run mad.

"Can't I go outside and help Pa, Ma?" little Andrew whined.

Alice glanced quickly at Rose, her face filling with color. "It's too cold son, and you haven't a warm enough coat," she told him quietly. Sighing in disgust, Andrew flung himself down next to his sister and began playing with the wooden blocks their father had made for them.

Surveying the room, Rose noticed only one bed in the soddie and wondered where the children slept. Her question must have been reflected on her face because Alice hastily assured Rose that they all slept together since it was warmer that way. There was only one thin, faded quilt on the bed and Rose's heart went out to this family. They tried so hard to give the impression that all was well. No wonder Ward had invited them for Christmas.

Settling her pack on the table, Rose addressed Alice. "I hope you don't mind, Alice, but I brought some things to add for lunch. I so wanted to have some company today, but it hardly seemed fair for me to just wish myself on you and your family without bringing something along to feed that giant of mine."

Tears came to Alice's eyes as Rose unloaded her pack. "I fixed too much chicken last night, 'cause Ward found a bunch of prairie chickens and brought them home for me to cook. I guess he forgets there's just the two of us."

Alice didn't bother to suggest that Rose could have put them in her cooler pit and frozen them, and Rose was certainly not about to mention it herself.

"I also tried a new recipe for cookies that Emily Haskins gave me, but I don't think they turned out as well as Emily's, so I think I'll try again. Do you think Alicia and Andrew might like some?"

Rose wore such a woebegone look, her voice tinged with just the right shade of anxiety, that Alice hastened to assure her that Andrew and Alicia would be pleased to try some. As for the children, although their manners kept them from saying much, their eyes spoke volumes.

When the men came in for lunch, they both stopped short at sight of the heavily laden table. Besides the chicken and cookies, Rose had brought potatoes, squash, and bread. If Ward was surprised by the great quantity of food, he didn't say so. His eyes rested thoughtfully on his wife, and when she chanced a look at him he smiled at her. Her cheeks filled with guilty color and his smile widened into a full grin.

Adam said nothing, but there was a suspicious sheen in his solemn brown eyes. When he said grace, Rose felt a lump rise in her throat at his fervent thanks.

When they were on their way home that evening Ward was unusually silent. He stopped the wagon suddenly and turned to Rose. Circles of frost puffed around his face almost hiding him from view.

"That was a wonderful thing you done. I'm right proud of you for thinking of it." He landed a kiss on her surprised mouth, and lifting the reins, clucked to the horses.

Rose's astonishment turned to a pleased feeling of accomplishment. She felt warm all over, but of course that had nothing to do with Ward's kiss. Nothing at all.

Chapter 5

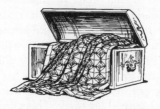

T hat's a mighty fine woman you got there, Ward."

Ward glanced up from notching the log between his feet and smiled at Adam. "That she is, Adam." He thought again of how Rose had come with him again, bringing an old coat of hers for Andrew. She had made it sound like Alice would do her a favor by taking it since it was too small for her, and could Alice manage to use it? Yes, Rose was a manipulator all right, but she always did it in such a nice way.

"How'd someone as ornery and cantankerous as you get such a fine woman out here so far from civilization, anyway?" Adam teased.

Ward lifted the log, motioning for Adam to take the other end. "Same way a *pigheaded* old coot like you managed to get someone like Alice, I reckon."

Adam laughed, lifting his end of the log. They moved as one, hoisting it and dropping it into place. Adam stepped back, brushing his hands together. He nodded his head in satisfaction.

"Looks like one more should do," he told Ward. They moved toward the logs still piled a few feet away. Lifting one away from the others, each man began to notch his own end.

"Truth to tell," Adam continued, "I think it must have been the Good Lord looking out for me. Seems He's been lookin' out for me right well."

Ward stopped chopping, resting the head of the ax against the ground and leaning on its handle. "You can say that after all that's gone wrong the past two summers? You may lose your claim."

Adam snorted. "Pshaw, that ain't nothin'. I still have my family, and good friends like you. Didn't God send you to me just when I was about at the end of my rope? Now I won't have to worry about my family this winter. They'll be snug as a bug in a rug."

Smiling, Ward continued notching the log. "Adam, you've given me something to think about."

Yes, he did have something to think about. It was amazing how much had happened in so little time. It was almost as though the Almighty had allowed Gabel Johnson to die so that Ward could step in to take care of Rose, so that Rose could in turn help the Comptons. Of course it was foolish to suppose that one knew the mind of God, but sometimes it was simple to see how things might have been arranged.

He knew Rose, though sad, had no worries about her father's death. She was absolutely certain where he would be in his afterlife.

And what about Ward, himself? He hadn't had nearly as strong a faith as Rose, because when Elise had died he had turned his back on God. Before her death, he and Elise had talked often about the possibility of one of them being taken from this life. Elise had showed him in the book of Hebrews that Satan had the power of death. He knew that to be so; then why had he blamed God?

Because God was stronger than Satan; he knew that, too. Yet he was angry with God for allowing his beloved Elise to die. Thinking back on it now, he realized that it had been *his* idea to move to Dakota Territory. Elise was one of those women who would follow her man anywhere, but he knew she would never have survived for long on the prairie. The solitude alone would have killed her. Guilt over his own selfishness shuddered through him. A thought crossed his mind that deepened his guilt. Where would Rose be now if Elise hadn't died?

To shake away such gruesome thoughts, he threw himself into his work so that by the end of the day, the Comptons' cabin was finished except for the caulking that Adam could do on his own.

The women came out to admire the men's work and the children ran excitedly in and out of the open space that would be used as the door. The structure stood solidly against the ever-present prairie wind.

"Oh, Adam." It was all Alice could say as tears pooled in her eyes. They worked so hard trying to make a home out of this inhospitable territory. For Alice to have lived in a soddie as long as she had gave credence to the woman's remarkable ability to adapt. Ward knew it came from the great love Alice had for Adam, wanting nothing but to assure her man's happiness, just as Elise had for him. And now Rose was doing her best to adapt to his harsh life.

As Ward began gathering his supplies together, Adam came up and slapped him on the back. "We can start on your place tomorrow."

"If you don't mind," Ward told him, keeping his face averted, "I'd just as soon wait a day. I need to figure where I want to build, and how many logs it'll take. Why don't you go ahead and chink your cabin and make your door?" He lifted his head enough to catch Rose's eye and give her a wink.

Dawning comprehension brought a quick smile to her lips. "What a great idea! That means I can have you all to myself for one whole day."

Ward's heart jumped at this pronouncement. If he didn't know better, he'd think she actually meant it.

Alice and Adam exchanged knowing smiles.

"Well, if you're sure," Adam told Ward. He turned to his wife. "Then, woman, you should be snug in your own house by tomorrow evening."

On the ride home, Rose suddenly turned to Ward. "Ward, how come you haven't been affected by the drought and the grasshoppers?" She had seen the barn and knew that it was full of supplies for both the animals and himself.

He glanced at her briefly. He took a long time answering, almost as though he had to choose his words with care. "When I lived back East I had a good paying job, a nice home, and a pretty good nest egg in the bank. After we decided to come out here, I sold the house for a fair price and added to my nest egg. Elise and I decided not to bring too much with us. We figured that since it was easy enough for boats to travel up the Missouri, it should be easy enough to get goods from the East by way of Yankton."

He stopped, his thoughts obviously far away. "I still have most of that money. After Elise. . .after Elise died, I didn't need much for myself. I've tried to use some of my money to help others, but it's hard. These are a proud people."

His look returned to her, one dark eyebrow lifting high. He nodded to her hand. "Even your ring."

Rose felt her heart drop. "My ring?"

"Didn't you ever wonder where I got it?"

Her face turned so red, Ward's other eyebrow rose to match its counterpart. He grinned, but turned his attention back to the road. "Someday, you'll have to tell me just exactly what you did think. I got it from Emily. The Haskins have had almost as hard a time as everyone else. Emily mentioned to me a long time ago that she had her grandmother's wedding ring, and if she could find a way she'd sell it. I remembered."

Rose wasn't exactly sure how she felt about this revelation, but it made her glad that Ward had been able to help the Haskins. Secretly, she was also relieved that the ring hadn't belonged to Elise, though why it should matter so much she wasn't sure.

They rode the rest of the way in thoughtful silence.

*

It was just two weeks until Christmas and Rose began to fret about what to serve for Christmas dinner. She was growing more excited just thinking about sharing with the Comptons. It had been so much fun to make them happy with just the little she and Ward had done. The Bible was right. It *was* more blessed to give than to receive.

Ward had absented himself from the house in the evenings, not coming in till long after dark. It bothered her that he spent all day chopping logs for their cabin and then spent so much time doing she knew not what out in the cold barn.

It was below freezing tonight and still he hadn't come in except for a quick bite to eat. Lips setting into a firm line, she pulled on her coat and went in search of him.

When she first opened the barn door, she couldn't see Ward anywhere. Thinking he might be someplace else, she was about to close the door when she heard a faint scraping in the corner. Following the direction of the sound, she found Ward in the end stall surrounded by shavings of wood. He glanced up in surprise.

"What on earth are you doing?" she asked warily.

Ward went back to carving on the piece of wood he held in his hand. Rose could see the beginnings of a rifle barrel forming from the wood he was shaving.

"I'm making a toy for Andrew. For Christmas."

Her mouth dropped open. "A toy?"

Rose's eyes went beyond Ward to the corner of the stall and she could see something covered with a burlap sack.

"What's that?"

"Something for Alicia."

Rose pushed past him and lifted the cover, gasping in surprise. Color came to Ward's cheeks, but he didn't stop his work.

"Oh, Ward! It's beautiful!" Rose stroked her hand softly over the toy cradle, sliding a finger gently around the intricate design carved into the headboard. "How did you do it?"

He shrugged, lifting the rifle for inspection. Closing one eye, he pulled the toy to his shoulder to check that the barrel was forming in a straight line.

"I used to be a carpenter."

Amazed, Rose could only stare at him. She hadn't known that about him! Of course there was very little about her husband she did know. She watched him work several more moments. Periodically he would stop, blowing into his hands to relieve them of the cold.

"You should come inside. It's much too cold out here," she told him.

He shook his head. "Can't. Gotta get this done by Christmas."

She frowned at him. "Well, bring it inside then. It's warmer by the fire."

He glanced up at her in astonishment. "It would make too much of a mess. Elise hated having wood shavings all over the house."

Rose felt a slight pang at mention of his first wife. "Well, I'm sure she didn't have a dirt floor either. How's a few shavings of wood going to hurt that? Besides," she reasoned, "you can always sweep them up."

He studied her pensively. "You sure?"

She nodded. "Course I'm sure. Come inside now."

⬥

It was two days later as she watched Ward whittling away at the wood that she came up with an idea. From what she could see, Alicia had no doll to play with. Being a man, Ward had probably never considered that fact.

After supper, she hesitantly approached him. "Ward, do you think Alicia would like a new doll to go with her cradle?"

His eyes brightened at the suggestion. "Why, I think that'd be a great idea. I never thought about a doll." Rose hid a smile.

"Do you have the stuff to do it?"

"I still have some scraps left. . .left from before. I think I have enough for a doll and a small quilt."

"Well, if you don't, give me a list. I plan on going into Yankton tomorrow."

240

He went back to his whittling. Surprised, Rose continued to stare at his down-bent head.

"But, that will take you four days!"

He scrutinized her tense face, his eyes unfathomable. "You scared to stay alone?"

She pressed her lips tightly together. "Course not, but this isn't exactly the time of year to be making such trips. What if you get caught in a blizzard?"

He rose to his feet, placing his hands on her shoulders and staring solemnly into her worried eyes. "There's settlers between here and there. If I have to, I can take shelter."

Hearing the determination in his voice, Rose knew it would do no good to argue. When Ward made up his mind to do something, nothing could sway him from his purpose.

Sighing, Rose turned away. "I'll make the list."

Ward studied the sky along the northern horizon. This didn't look good. He was caught on the open prairie and a storm was rapidly approaching. He knew it had been foolish to try and make the trip to Yankton at such a time, but he wanted to pick up something special for Rose as a Christmas present.

He knew how much she loved to read, and her own books were already dog-eared from use. Probably she could recite the books verbatim.

He glanced at the crate behind the wagon seat. It had been unwise perhaps, but it was something he had been determined to do.

As a man, he had a lot to occupy his time. There were barely enough hours in the day to get all his work done, even in the winter. But for a woman, it was different.

Course, he knew women weren't idle. Far from it. They filled their hours with hard work and all the little details that made a house a home. But women felt the solitude more. To Rose, reading was like visiting with a neighbor.

She had been so patient with him, waiting for all the things that would make his cabin more the home she was used to, and never complaining. In fact, she had encouraged him to put the Comptons first.

He shook his head. She was nothing like his Elise. Elise had been like a beautiful fairy, flitting through her life with gay abandon. Rose, now she was different. Rose was more like the wild prairie rose that her name brought to mind. Sturdy, dependable, a spot of beauty in a rugged landscape.

He frowned. Just exactly when had he started thinking of Rose as beautiful? The frown deepened as he tried to reason it out. Maybe when she had first sat cross-legged on the bed combing her long, dark hair with the fire reflecting off of it in shimmering particles of light.

He had wanted to go to her then. It had taken all of his willpower to turn away. Had love been creeping up on him unawares, only he hadn't recognized it as such? Could she tell? Probably if she knew his thoughts and feelings, she would freeze him out as she had after that first kiss in the barn. The cold December landscape had been nothing in comparison.

As the wind picked up and feathery flakes of snow began to fall, he wondered if he would ever have the chance to find out.

Rose watched the huge snowflakes as they drifted to the icy ground. This was the day Ward was supposed to have returned home. She went back inside, praying that the wind would hold off and that this would just be another snowstorm instead of the blizzard the howling wind could make it.

For the first time, she felt frustrated at the dark interior of the cabin. In her own shanty, Papa had placed purchased glass for windows. Ward had not, and now with the shutters closed the dim interior seemed full of foreboding as she heard the soft breath of wind turn into a whirling gale.

So much for prayers. She switched her petitions to asking for Ward's safe-keeping. If anything should happen to him, she didn't know what she would do.

Sitting down hard on the chair next to their eating table, Rose put her face in her hands. *How, God? How had this happened? How could I possibly be in love with my husband? When had it even started?*

She had always been a little afraid of him, but not because she thought he would hurt her. No, it had more to do with the way he made her feel. Had she been falling in love all along only hadn't realized it?

She picked up the small sticks lying on the table and began to tie them together with cord. Ward had given her several carved figures: Mary, Joseph, Baby Jesus, several wise men, and several shepherds. There were even tiny sheep, cattle, and a donkey. He had been whittling them over the past several years. His ability to carve such intricate, beautiful things still filled her with awe. What an incredible gift God had given him. Did he recognize it as such?

Her part was in making the crèche where they would sit. Funny, she and Ward seemed to complement each other well as they worked together.

As she worked, she tried to ignore the ever-rising wail of the wind. Placing cut pieces of hay among the crèche, her petitions to the Lord grew more fervent. What would she do if something happened to Ward? To have finally found love and then to have it snatched away so suddenly was incomprehensible. Surely God could not mean for such a thing to happen. She needed time to make Ward love her in return.

Setting Mary next to Joseph, she allowed her thoughts to wander. Did Joseph love Mary, or had Mary had to contend with a marriage such as Rose's? Joseph was a good man, that was evidenced by the fact that he wanted to put Mary away quietly instead of making her face her shame. But did he love her?

Restlessly, she got up from the table and opened the door to look out. The portal was flung back against the interior cabin wall with the force of the wind. It took everything Rose could muster to be able to close it again. She leaned back against it, her breathing ragged.

What would happen to the animals? They were safe in the barn, but Ward had forbidden her to go to them if there were a storm. Not that she was crazy enough to do so anyway.

She wandered restlessly around the cabin, not able to settle to doing anything. Even little Alicia's doll that she had started lay forgotten on the bed.

When darkness came, Ward still had not returned. It seemed the hands of the clock on the mantle ticked slowly by, dragging each hour to its fullest.

Supper sat untouched on the table. It had been something to occupy her time, and at least she had the hope that Ward would be home soon and hungry. But he hadn't come.

Finally, Rose could take the strain no longer and flinging herself to her knees beside the bed she began to pray loudly, trying to block out the sound of the wind. Before long, her voice turned hoarse with the exertion and trying to suppress her tears. Giving in to the inevitable, she allowed the tears to come. Great, wracking sobs tore at her body.

Suddenly, the door flung open and Rose sat staring at what seemed like a huge, hulking polar bear.

Rose came quickly to her feet and was across the room, flinging herself into her husband's arms.

Chapter 6

Rose glanced periodically at her husband thawing in front of the fire as she walked over to get him dry clothes and a blanket. Steam rose from his wet clothes as he tried to huddle closer for warmth, a hot cup of tea clutched in his shaking hands. She had been so glad to see him, so relieved that he was alive, that she had thrown herself into his arms.

She worried about that now. Had she given away her feelings with that action? She certainly hoped not, because although she may have discovered her own love for him, he had shown nothing that would give her hope that he felt the same. Hadn't he told her that his heart was dead?

"How did you ever manage to get home in this blizzard?"

He looked at her briefly, his teeth still chattering as he took off his wet outer clothes. "I just decided to let the horses have their head. Animals have a pretty keen sense of direction, even in a storm. I was hoping they would find their way home, and they did."

Bless Old Blue and Big Ben. She would give them an extra portion of oats to show her appreciation.

Rose handed Ward his nightclothes. "Put these on and get into bed," she scolded. "We'll be doing good if you don't catch pneumonia."

She turned her back as he fumbled out of his heavy, wet clothes and into his dry night things.

"Where's the blankets for my pallet?"

Not looking at him, Rose began laying his wet clothes over the chair to dry. "You're not sleeping on the floor. I'll not have you catching a chill."

The room grew so silent, she could hear the logs pop in the fireplace. When she finally turned his way, he was staring at her somberly. "Just what are you saying, Rose? 'Cause I'll have you know that I won't allow *you* to sleep on the floor."

She continued to flit about the cabin, straightening things here, fixing things there. Her face was the color of a ripe apple when she told him, "I figured as much. I'm willing to share the bed."

Although she couldn't see him, Rose could feel his eyes upon her back. His stillness reminded her of a cougar she had seen once, just before it had lunged at his prey.

244

Ward hesitated. Fatigue and confusion crossed his face. Without saying anything, he finally climbed into the bed. "Are you coming?"

Shaking her head, Rose picked up Alicia's doll. "No, not yet. I think I'll work on this for a while."

She wasn't fooling him and she knew it, but there was no way she could crawl into that bed next to him right now. The way she was feeling. . .

⌘

Sighing, Ward cuddled down under the covers. He appreciated Rose's concern, but this was a volatile situation. Could they ever go back to the way things had been after sleeping together? Even if nothing happened, it was still sure to change things. Still, things couldn't continue the way they had been, either. He thought he could sense a subtle change in Rose's attitude toward him, but his mind was too foggy with fatigue that he couldn't even begin to figure it out now.

There were many times in the last couple of days that he had longed to be in this bed, but he hadn't imagined it being this way. In his dreams he had imagined himself telling Rose of his love for her and her throwing her arms around him and telling him she felt the same way.

Well, she had certainly thrown her arms around him, but dealing with her sobs was not part of his fantasy. Nor was having her order him to bed as though he were a child. If he were a betting man, he'd wager she'd sit up all night in that chair by the fire just so she wouldn't have to share his bed.

He considered going to her now and telling her how he felt, but his eyes were already becoming heavy, his body succumbing to its ordeal. Besides, she had offered to share the bed with him, nothing more.

⌘

Before long, Rose could hear Ward's soft snores. The poor man was exhausted. The doll lay forgotten on her lap as she watched him sleep.

Getting up, she crossed to his side and stood observing him, her eyes tender with the love she felt. Reaching out, she pushed the dark hair from his forehead, bending and placing a kiss there.

He was definitely out. Nothing, including an earthquake, would wake him now. Feeling safe, she changed into her own nightclothes and blowing out the lamp, crawled into bed next to him.

For a long time she lay tense, listening to him breathe. Finally, she was able to relax and turning, she curled herself against his side, determined to share with him her body heat. The fear of pneumonia was never far from her mind.

Eventually, with an exhausted sigh, she too succumbed to sleep.

⌘

A thumping on the door brought them both wide awake. Ward tried to scramble across Rose just as she was trying to get from the bed. They wound up in a tangle of arms and legs. Ward propped himself up with his arms and gazed down into Rose's still sleep-laden eyes. A smile tugged at his lips and before they knew it, both were filled with paroxysms of mirth.

He quickly kissed her lips before climbing from the bed and opening the door a crack.

"Morning, Ward." Adam's voice sounded loud and clear in the bright morning sunlight slitting through the opened door. "Sorry I'm late, but there are some pretty big drifts out here."

Surprised, Ward hastened to assure him. "I'll be right with you."

Rose hustled out of bed once the door was closed. "You can't go out today! You need to rest. Stay in bed."

Sitting on the chair pulling on his boots, he threw her a wicked grin. "What are you suggesting, Mrs. Taylor?"

Her face colored hotly and she began stammering in her confusion. "I. . .I didn't mean—"

Taking pity on her, he stood up and crossed to her side. "I was only teasing. I'll be back later. This should be our last load of logs and then we can start on the bedrooms."

The look he gave her was searching in its intensity, but Rose was too distraught to notice. Was he that anxious to have the bedrooms done that he would be willing to risk his health? Surely Adam would understand if he knew the situation. She lifted a hand to her temple, rubbing against a fast-approaching headache.

Bundling into his coat, Ward strode to the door. "See you later. I'll take care of the animals before I leave."

The door closed behind him.

For the next several hours Rose gave herself a good talking to. As she embroidered tiny even stitches to make the doll's mouth, she lectured herself on being a fool. When she began sewing scraps together to make a small quilt for the cradle, she admonished herself to be more careful to hide her feelings in the future.

It was only as she was sewing together some old pieces of leather for a musket case for Andrew that she stopped to think about that brief kiss this morning. She felt warmth creeping into her cheeks as she wondered what would have happened if Adam had not come this morning and they would have awakened on their own.

Was it possible that Ward might harbor some slight feeling for her? As impossible as it seemed, that little bud of hope refused to die. Such thoughts had her feeling as prickly as her pincushion by the time Ward was due home.

When Ward came in that evening, he carried a small tree he had brought from the river. "How's this for a Christmas tree?"

Rose's eyes lit up, and forgotten were those moments from this morning that had caused her such worry all day long. "Oh, Ward. What a great idea!"

He grinned back at her, tired lines radiating from his eyes. "It's the reason I insisted on going today. I wasn't sure when I'd get another chance."

Rose frowned as she looked about the room. Although the room was large enough, there really was very little furniture and the tree was so small it would need to be situated on a table. If they used the table in the kitchen area, they would have no place to eat.

"I was thinking," Ward suggested, "that maybe I could bring in that table of yours from the barn. Since it's larger than this one, we could move this one to the corner for the tree and then use yours for eating. It will give us more eating room when the Comptons come for Christmas."

Gripping her hands together, Rose placed the nails from her two index fingers against her teeth. Squinting her eyes, she tried to "see" how things would look in her mind's eye. "That'll work."

They shifted the table to the corner and Rose found a bowl for the tree. Laying the tree on the floor, Ward took the bowl and headed for the door. "I'll get some dirt from the barn. Outside's too frozen. It would take me all day just to chip out enough dirt to fill this bowl."

When he came back, Rose helped him move the table and fix the small tree. They found themselves giggling like children when the determined thing tipped first one way and then another.

Finally, Ward leaned back sighing. "We need something to wrap around the base for support."

They both searched the cabin with their eyes. When Ward lifted an eyebrow at Rose, she just shrugged. "I don't know. What do you suggest?"

"I have some burlap in the barn. We could use that."

Rose wrinkled her nose. "I don't think so. The whole cabin would soon smell like the barn." She thought a minute and then her eyes lit up. "I know. Look in my trunk there by the bed. There's an old white blanket. We could use that, then it would look like snow."

Ward rummaged through the chest while Rose held the tree steady. It was a moment before Rose realized just how quiet the room had become. Turning to see where the problem lay, she found Ward holding her memory quilt across his lap. His eyes went to hers.

"This is beautiful. Why don't you use it?"

The color that had drained from her face now came rushing back. She opened her mouth to explain, but no words would come.

Ward crossed the room to her side, the white blanket clutched in his hands. He handed it to her without comment. Together they wrapped it securely around the base of the little tree.

"That should hold it," Ward told her.

She agreed, and though it was nothing like the pine trees back home, still it would do. She stepped back to get the full effect, smiling her pleasure. Ward was such a thoughtful man. Why had she never seen that before?

"It looks great. I'll decorate it tomorrow."

Smiling, Ward told her, "I'll help."

Rose turned to him in surprise. "That's right, you're finished chopping trees. Aren't you and Adam going to start building tomorrow?"

The look he settled on her was disturbing in its intensity. "I'm in no hurry," he told her quietly.

Unsure what to make of his attitude, Rose decided to leave him to his own thoughts and go fix supper. Ward's fingers closed softly but inexorably around her wrist when she turned away. "Tell me about the quilt," he commanded softly. "It upset you to see it. Why?"

Rose's eyes met his and she found herself unable to look away. She began to tell him of the quilt without quite realizing what she was saying. His nearness was doing funny things to her insides.

When he suddenly released her, she felt curiously bereft. He returned to the chest and pulled the quilt from it. Laying it across the bed, he motioned for Rose to come to him. Reluctantly, she moved to his side.

Ward motioned to the spread. "Tell me about the material."

Uncertain as to his reasons for wanting to know, Rose still found herself telling him little stories about the various pieces. He laughed with her over her tales, and grew somber when she told him of the piece that was from the last dress her mother wore before she died.

He gently folded the covering and replaced it in its position in the chest. When he looked her way, his face was solemn. "Perhaps you will use it one day, perhaps not, but it's great that you have so many memories. What a unique way of making sure that those memories are around for a long time."

Ward was silent throughout supper, his thoughts far away. Rose assumed that in sharing her own memories, she had resurrected his own recollections of Elise. She picked at her own meal, pushing the stew around on her plate.

After washing the dishes, Rose decided to search through her things and see what she could use to decorate the tree. She hadn't much, but she had a lot of ingenuity.

Ward settled himself beside the fire to put the finishing touches to Andrew's gun. Although it wouldn't actually shoot, Rose knew the boy would be thrilled with it.

Taking out some scraps of material, Rose held them against the tree. Their bright colors added a bit of cheer to the drab interior. Yes, she would tie various colors of bows to the branches. That would be a start.

"Ward?"

"Hmm?"

Rose watched as he expertly smoothed the gun barrel with a piece of sandpaper. "We don't have a gift for Alice and Adam."

He looked up at her then. "I'm sure they won't expect one." He went back to sanding. "If I'd thought about it, I would have picked up something in Yankton."

"Why *did* you go to Yankton?"

Without looking up he answered her. "I needed some supplies."

Rose had no idea what he could have possibly needed, but then she knew very little about the running of his farm. Shrugging, she sat down to cut some of her scraps into small enough strips to use as bows.

Although Ward said nothing, Rose could see the tired droop of his shoulders.

He had battled a blizzard half the night and then rose at first light to go finish chopping logs for their cabin. It was obviously catching up with him, but for some reason he seemed reluctant to go to bed.

Rose put her things away and began to prepare herself for bed. After brushing her hair its required one hundred strokes, she crawled beneath the covers. Ward still sat next to the fire working on the gun.

"Aren't you coming?" Rose asked him.

She could see him swallow hard before shaking his head. "Not just yet. I'm almost finished here."

Rose lifted herself on one elbow. "Andrew will love that. And Alicia will love her cradle. You do beautiful work, Ward."

"Thanks."

The one clipped syllable brought a frown to Rose's face. Ward seemed almost like a stranger tonight. Cold. Aloof. Like he had been before their marriage. Sliding back under the covers, Rose turned her back on him, feeling unreasonably hurt.

It was some time later before Ward banked the fire and prepared himself for bed. Rose pretended to be asleep, waiting to see if he would take up his pallet on the floor again. She thought she would die if he did, thinking that he would be rejecting what she had so shyly offered.

Ward blew out the lantern and Rose held her breath until suddenly she felt the bed dip as Ward climbed in beside her. He lay staring up at the ceiling for a long time before finally he rolled toward Rose's back.

Wrapping one strong arm around her waist, Ward pulled her back against his chest. He made no move to do anything else and Rose sighed with relief when after several moments she heard his even breathing. Feeling safe for the night, she allowed herself to relax back against his body and even in his sleep, he cuddled her close.

Goodness only knew how they were going to handle this situation in the morning.

Chapter 7

The morning light didn't penetrate the dingy interior of the cabin, so it was late when Rose opened her eyes. Sometime in the night she had curled herself into Ward's arms and now felt her face flame with color.

She made a move to get up, only to find herself pulled back and Ward's handsome face grinning down into her own.

"Where you going?"

"I. . .I have to fix breakfast."

He shook his head slowly and a lone curl dropped tantalizingly down across his forehead. "Not yet. There's something we need to discuss."

Feeling her heart begin to pound, Rose swallowed hard. "What?"

Ward stared down into her blue eyes as he traced a finger across Rose's flaming cheek, his eyes dark and serious. "Rose, I think I'm in love with you."

He waited for her reaction, and a long moment passed as Rose tried to believe her ears.

"What. . .what did you just say?" Her voice came out as little more than a croak.

"I said that I think I'm in love with you. I guess I have been for some time, only I didn't realize it."

Rose could only stare up at him, stunned into a lack of speech. Ward frowned. "Well, say something."

"I. . .I think I love you, too."

The frown eased from his features. "You're not sure?"

"You're not, either?"

Ward hesitated. "I've only had one experience with love, Rose, and it was nothing like this. I'm beginning to believe there are different kinds of loving between a man and a woman."

Rose could only nod.

"I want to be with you," he continued. "And when I'm not I find myself thinking about you. You're kind and loving, stubborn and proud. You make me feel. . . strong."

Rose knew he was having trouble putting his thoughts into words. For Ward, actions would speak more loudly than any words he could ever hope to utter. She smiled in understanding and he kissed her softly on her lips.

The moment his lips touched hers, Rose felt all her doubts vanish. She would gladly give her life for this man, and she knew without any more uncertainties that she loved him with her entire being.

Wrapping her arms around his neck, she tried to show him of her love in the oldest way known to women.

Christmas day dawned bright and clear. Much of the snow had disappeared from the area, blown by the ever-present winds.

There was a spring in Rose's step as she set about making the cabin ready for their guests. She and Ward had spent the last several days getting to know one another better, and her love for him grew daily. She didn't think it was possible to love a man as much as she loved Ward. As they went about their duties, they found themselves eager to be together, to touch.

Ward had been hunting and had brought home a deer for their Christmas dinner. Now it roasted over the open fire as Rose prepared the vegetables.

Ward came in the door, his eyes searching for and quickly finding Rose. Setting down the crate that he carried, he smiled and held out his hand to her and she quickly went to him. He wrapped his arms about her and kissed her lightly on her nose.

"Before company gets here, I have something for you. A Christmas present."

Surprised, Rose could only stammer. "You shouldn't have. Oh, Ward, I didn't get you anything."

"You've given me the greatest gift a man could ask for. Your love."

Rose wrapped her arms around his neck and smiled. "You say the nicest things."

His return smile was wry. "Not always."

Rose's eyes began to glow. "What do you have for me?"

"You mean besides me?"

"Ward!"

He grinned, turning her loose so that he could lift the crate and carry it to the table. Using his hammer, he pried the top from the box and then moved aside so Rose could see what was inside.

Pushing back the paper, Rose found the crate filled with books. Her eyes grew wide with excitement. "Oh, Ward!"

She pulled out the first book and turned it gently in her hands. "Charles Dickens. I love Dickens! How did you know?"

"I think you can just about recite *A Christmas Carol*. I thought you might like something else."

"I've never read *The Cricket on the Hearth*, though I have heard of it." She rummaged in the crate again. "Alexandre Dumas' *The Three Musketeers*. You should like that," she told him.

"I will if you read it to me."

Rose wrinkled her nose at him, but her attention was more on the jewels she was uncovering in the crate. Not since her move from the city had she seen so

251

many books. She pulled the last one from the box and set it with the others. "I heard about Louisa May Alcott before we left Boston. I don't know where you were able to find all of these books, but I thank you with all of my heart."

Ward wrapped her back in his arms. "You're welcome. Now thank me properly."

Grinning, Rose reached up and kissed his chin.

Ward shook his head. "Nope, that won't do it."

Reaching up again, Rose kissed his cheek.

He shook his head again. "Nope. Wrong again. I guess I'll just have to take the books back."

Rose tried to push away. "Never!"

One dark eyebrow winged its way upward. "I'm waiting, then."

Rose sighed. "Well, if I must," she teased.

She would have given him a peck on the lips, but Ward captured her lips with his own and suddenly, all humor fled for Rose. She kissed him back with abandon, wondering at herself and her ability to lose her restraint with a man that just a few short weeks ago she hadn't even thought she liked.

Ward finally pulled away, his voice husky. "Enjoy your present, Rose. I'm glad it pleases you."

He took the now empty crate and made his way back outside to break it into kindling for the fire.

Rose picked up the copy of *Little Women* and hugged it to her, her eyes sparkling. What a wonderful gift. If only she had something as nice to give Alice.

She went to her chest and rummaged through it, sighing when she found nothing suitable to give as a gift. Her eyes lighted on the quilt, and she rubbed the cover softly, thinking how happy her papa and mama would be for her.

With a determined sparkle in her eye, Rose quickly pulled the quilt from the trunk holding it up to the light. Firmly, she blanked her mind and refused the memories access as they tried to rush upon her.

She took the paper that the books had been wrapped in and some string, and quickly wrapped the quilt and placed it with the other gifts under the tree.

If only she had something she could give Ward. Remembering how he said he was happy with her love brought a flush to her face. Next year, maybe she could give Ward a son. The thought pleased her.

The Comptons arrived shortly thereafter. The children oohed and aahed over the tree, their eyes growing large at the sight of the presents under it.

Rose exclaimed over Alicia and Andrew's coats. Alice's face flooded with color. "I hope you don't mind, Rose," she stated quietly. "The coat you brought for Andrew was too big for him, so I took it and made it into two, one for Andrew and one for Alicia."

"What a good idea. And you've done it so beautifully. You must be a wonderful seamstress."

Alice shrugged, her head ducked shyly.

After everyone was in the cabin it suddenly seemed a lot smaller, but no one seemed to mind. Children and adults alike were willing to overlook the cramped confines of the small structure just for the joy of being together.

It was a happy time for everyone. The roast deer was devoured and pronounced a success. Squash, potatoes, corn cakes, boiled eggs, cake, and pie were consumed until everyone declared they hadn't feasted so well in years.

Ward announced that it was time for everyone to open their gifts, and Rose could see how relieved Alice was that she had been able to contribute. She handed Rose a small package wrapped in brown wrap.

"Oh, Alice. You shouldn't have."

Alice's face filled with color and she dipped her head shyly. "It's not much."

Rose exclaimed over the beauty of the fine stitching Alice had used to turn an old sheet into a beautiful tablecloth.

Ward handed the twins their presents and with a small smile watched them rip them open.

Alicia squealed with delight. "A baby! A baby, Mommy! Look!"

Adam's eyes found Rose's and in their shimmering brown depths she read his thanks.

"Wow!" Andrew pealed. "A gun! My very own gun!"

"I hope it's all right?" Ward questioned Alice.

She only nodded, her own eyes glimmering with unshed tears.

Finally, Rose handed her package to Alice. "For you and Adam."

Ward glanced at Rose in surprise, watching as Alice unwrapped her gift. Alice sucked in her breath, her eyes going wide. She pulled the quilt from its wrap and Ward quickly rose to his feet, his protest checked on his lips.

The tears in Rose's eyes matched those of the other woman as both embraced. "Oh, thank you, Rose. It's beautiful. Thank you so much."

The rest of the day was pleasant and Rose watched the Comptons climb into their wagon with a warm feeling of having done what was right. Papa would have wanted her to do just what she had done.

After their guests drove away, Ward followed Rose into the cabin. He pulled her gently into his arms. "Why did you do it?"

She sniffed into his chest. "Papa would have wanted it. The quilt was doing no one any good sitting in that chest. The Comptons needed it."

Ward rested his chin on her head, staring at the ceiling. "But your memories."

"I'll always have my memories," she told him. "And with you, I'll start to make new memories."

Ward sighed and Rose finally pulled away.

"Can we read the Christmas story now? That was always my favorite part of Christmas with Papa, when he would read the Christmas story from the Bible."

She handed Ward her Bible and waited while he settled himself in his chair. She curled up at his feet prepared to listen.

At first, Ward's voice came out hesitantly, but as the story progressed it grew stronger with the feelings the story inspired. Rose wiped the tears from her eyes when he finished.

"I never get tired of hearing it. How God sent His only Son to die for people who openly mocked and ridiculed Him."

Ward was quiet for a long while. "He did it for the same reasons you gave the Comptons your special quilt. They needed it, and He loved them enough to sacrifice that which was most precious to Him. That's what makes a true sacrifice."

Rose climbed up into Ward's lap, laying her head on his shoulder.

Ward's voice was husky when he nuzzled her ear. "Just like you gave me a gift of your love, so God gave us a gift of His love. I've forgotten that. I've lived my life the last several years without Him, but not anymore."

He pulled her face back so he could look into her eyes. "When I saw the sacrifice you were willing to make, knowing how much that quilt meant to you, I wanted so much to say something. To take it back. But it wasn't mine to deny.

"Just like sometimes I wish I could take back God's sacrifice. Make it never have happened. But then, the world would have been condemned to an eternity without God. I can't imagine a life without God," Rose told him.

"I can't imagine a life without you," Ward answered back.

Rose sighed. "I am so thankful that God brought you into my life."

"That makes two of us, because if not for your unshakable faith, I don't know if I would have ever realized just how much I needed God. How much I needed you. I've been selfish."

He kissed her with all of the love stored in his heart and Rose returned the kiss in kind. For a long time the only sound in the cabin was the soft murmuring of the words of love.

Later, Rose went with Ward to feed the animals. A million shimmering lights glimmered from the dark sky above. As they watched, hand in hand, a shooting star left a fiery path across the sky and disappeared in an instant.

Just like that star so long ago had led the wise men to the Savior, so God had led Ward and Rose to each other.

Rose continued to stare at the night sky. She had found unexpected happiness after adversity. She had lost one precious man and found another. She smiled slowly and Ward had to bend close to hear her say, "Thank You, Father. Thank you, Papa."

God Jul

by Tracie Peterson

Chapter 1

OSTKAKA
(Swedish Pudding)

2 eggs
1 cup cream
½ cup flour
¼ tsp. salt

2 quarts milk
½ rennet tablet
½ cup sugar

Beat eggs and ½ cup cream together, add flour and mix until smooth. Add salt. Heat milk to lukewarm and add mixture. Soften rennet tablet in a spoonful of water and add to mixture, stirring slowly until evenly mixed. Let stand for 10 minutes then bake in hot oven at 400°F for 30 minutes. Then turn oven down to 350°F and bake for 1 hour. Take out of oven and pour remaining ½ cup of cream and sugar over it and bake at 350°F for an additional 20 minutes. As the pudding is formed, the whey (milky liquid) may threaten to run over, so use a deep pan. Serve with sweetened berries.

Lindsborg, Kansas

Sigrid Larsson stared in stony silence at the pine casket. Inside, her mother's body lay in final rest and even now as the pastor spoke of the resurrection to come, Sigrid felt a terrible loss. She had built her life around her mother's needs and now she was gone, and at twenty-seven Sigrid felt she was far too old to start a new life.

Even if I wanted to start over, she chided herself, *what would I do? Who would have me, an old spinster with nothing to offer?*

She looked around the circle of mourners to find friends and family whom she cherished dearly. She was alone. They had each other. They were husbands and wives and children, and together they made up families. Her family had started out to include a mother, father, sister, and brother, but now they were gone. Father had died fifteen years ago in a railroad accident, and with that one stroke of fate, her life had changed. At twelve she had been forced into adulthood in many ways.

"Let us close by singing together," the pastor stated, then boomed out the words of a well-known hymn in a deep heavy bass.

Sigrid mouthed the words, uncertain that she could actually sing. How could you sing when your heart was so heavy? She glanced up to find Erik Lindquist staring at her with a sympathetic, yet otherwise unreadable expression. His blue eyes were the same shade as her own, a rather pale, icy blue. His blond hair, straight as string as her mother would have said, was parted down the middle and slicked back on either side. He looked most uncomfortable in his "Sunday-go-to-meeting" clothes and Sigrid would have laughed had the circumstance not weighed so heavy on her heart.

Erik had been her mother's hired man for the last twelve years. He owned the property next to theirs and when he learned of the Larsson women's struggles to survive and keep the farmstead running, he had gone to Bothilda Larsson, or Tilly, as most folks called her, and struck a deal. He would farm their land, as well as his own, and split the profits down the middle. Bothilda and Sigrid would care for the dairy cows, pigs, and chickens as was in keeping with Swedish traditions. American men might take the reins of caring for the animals, but Tilly thought it funny to see a Swedish man trying to milk a cow.

The arrangement worked well for everyone, including Sigrid's brother, Sven, who had a new family and land of his own to worry about. He seemed more than happy to turn over the responsibilities of his parents' homestead to Erik. Sigrid had been the one to protest, but she knew it was of little use to argue. She couldn't very well farm the land herself, yet she had resented the interference of an outsider. Even if that outsider was a rather nice-looking, young Swedish man.

The singing had concluded and people were coming up to offer her their condolences.

"Tilly will be missed for sure," Mr. Anderson told her.

"*Ja,* t'ings won't be the same without her," another man assured Sigrid.

Mrs. Swanson and Mrs. Moberg both took hold of her hands at the same time and tearfully lamented the loss of their dear friend. Sigrid tried not to notice that her mother's casket was slowly being lowered into the ground.

"Come along," yet another of her mother's friends announced, "we've laid food at your house, Sigrid."

Sigrid nodded and allowed the women to herd her along to the awaiting carriage. She thought it funny that she should ride when so often she had walked the distance from church to home. But the women insisted she ride, in spite of her own longing to be left alone. *Grief and mourning make folks do strange things to offer comfort,* she thought.

The Larsson farmstead was situated on the east side of Lindsborg, just far enough away to make a walk into town a good stretch of the limbs. Her father had managed to secure a prime tract of land when they'd first come to the area in 1869, and in her entire life, Sigrid had never ventured any farther than a ten-mile radius from the tiny town.

She loved her home, and her heart swelled with pride as they approached the narrow drive that marked the property. Sigrid stared at the white clapboard house and felt a real sense of peace. Her mother might be gone from her in a physical sense, but she would live on in this house and in the things that surrounded Sigrid. She would simply remain here the rest of her days, living as best she could, and always she would remember the good times she'd known when her family had all been together.

The carriage came to a halt and before she actually realized what was happening, Erik Lindquist had appeared to help her down. She felt small beside his six-foot-two frame. He towered over her by nearly a foot and his big, callused hands betrayed signs of hard work. Farming in Kansas was at worst a practice in futility, and at best a labor of love. Her mother used to say that Job's patience had never been tested to the extent of trying to grow crops in Kansas. Sigrid smiled at the thought and Erik seemed taken aback.

"Someone tell a joke?" he asked, leaning down to whisper in her ear.

She startled at the warmth of his breath on her neck. "No, I was just remembering something *Moder* used to say."

"If you were remembering Tilly's words then I'm sure I understand."

He offered her a gentle smile and stepped away just as Sven approached.

"Sigrid, Ina and I want to talk to you."

Sigrid sighed and nodded. She could well imagine that neither her brother nor sister wanted to worry about her grieving on her own. They were no doubt going to suggest she come spend a few months living with one or the other of them. And, frankly, most folks would expect her to do something just like that. But Sigrid didn't want to leave the house. She wanted to stay on and think about her life. She wanted to watch another spring blend into summer and then autumn.

She followed her stocky, blond brother into the house and was surprised to find Ina standing alone while her husband, Clarence, herded their five children outside.

The sisters embraced and nodded at each other with stoic expressions securely fixed in place. Their family had never been given to public spectacles of grief and as was true of many of their Swedish friends and extended family, they weren't ones for showing much emotion.

"So, what is it you wanted to talk about?" Sigrid asked, looking from Ina to Sven and back again. In the background, the clatter of dishes and women's chatter caused Sven to motion the sisters to one of the side bedrooms off of the main living area.

"Ina and I have discussed it and we both agree that the house should be sold immediately," Sven said, as though the matter was settled. "I've talked to Olga and she said it would be a great help to have you around the place."

"You want to sell *Fader* and *Moder's* house?" she asked in disbelief.

It was as if no one had heard her, however, as her sister picked up the matter.

"I'm happy for you to come and stay with us part of the time, as well. You could sleep with Bridgett in the loft bedroom. You know how she adores you."

Sigrid stared at them both as though the meaning of their words had eluded her. "I don't know what to think."

"That's why I figured on taking care of the matter for you," Sven said, with the authoritative air of an older brother. "I'll put up a notice and—"

"No!" Sigrid said, suddenly finding her voice. "I don't want to sell."

Ina looked at her with wide blue eyes. "What do you mean? Surely you don't want to stay on here alone. *Moder* wouldn't want you to be here alone."

"Of course, she can't stay here," Sven said, quite seriously.

"I'm a grown woman, Sven. There is no reason why I can't stay here. I'm fully capable of doing what work needs to be done. Erik is taking care of the farming, and the rest of the work was pretty much my responsibility anyway." She paused to settle her nerves. With only the tiniest hint of emotion in her voice, she continued. "Erik already has the ground turned and the planting will be finished within the week. I've got peas and potatoes planted and you can't expect me to just up and let someone else reap the benefits of my labors."

"I've got plenty of peas and potatoes at my place," Sven countered. "Be reasonable, Sigrid. Ina and Clarence need the money and so do I. Last year's crops weren't that good and—"

"I don't want to move. This is my home. I stayed behind while you both married and went your ways," Sigrid protested in uncharacteristic anger. "I think I deserve to live out my days here."

"You could marry," Ina suggested. "You aren't so very old that a bachelor or widower wouldn't see the use in having you around."

Sigrid felt as though her sister had somehow just insulted her. It wasn't that she didn't know the odds were against her finding a love match and marrying. It wasn't even that her sister spoke aloud the sentiments that Sigrid had already considered many times. It was…well…it was just more than she wanted to have to deal with at that precise moment.

"We can talk about this tomorrow," Sven said, opening the bedroom door. He looked out into the living room as if seeking someone. "Olga's going to wonder what's keeping me."

"Come stay with us tonight," Ina said softly as she turned to follow Sven.

"No," Sigrid stated firmly. "I'm not going anywhere."

Ina shrugged, while Sven rolled his eyes and grunted something unintelligible before leaving the room. Sigrid closed the door behind her sister and leaned back against it to calm herself. *How dare they try to force me from the only home I've ever known!* She felt somehow betrayed and the only thing she wanted to do was hide away in this room until everyone else went home.

She glanced around and sighed. *Am I being foolish? Is it completely unreasonable to want to stay here, even if it means staying alone?*

A light rap sounded on the door. Sigrid bolstered her courage and turned to open it. Ella Swanson, Sigrid's lifelong friend, stood holding a bowl of ostkaka and lingonberries.

"I thought your favorite dessert might help," Ella offered.

Sigrid smiled and nodded. "You always know just how to cheer me up." The ostkaka looked most appealing and Sigrid realized she was quite hungry. "Thank you, Ella."

"*Ja*, sure. You'd do the same for me."

Sigrid's smile faded. "This day has been so hard."

Ella's countenance mirrored the way Sigrid felt inside. It was a blend of confusion and sorrow. "*Ja*," Ella whispered. "Your *moder* was a good woman. I miss her too."

Sigrid thought how strange she should have to struggle with such a riot of emotions in one single day. The sorrow over losing her mother was enough to keep her drawn within herself, but her anger at Sven's insensitivity to her needs threatened to burst forth without warning.

"Everything okay?" a masculine voice questioned from behind Ella. It was Erik.

Sigrid shook her head. "No. I don't think anything will ever be okay again."

"What's the matter?" he asked. Ella seemed eager to know the problem as well, but just then her mother called her away leaving Sigrid to awkwardly face Erik alone.

"Sven wants to put the property up for sale right away," she finally managed to say. She refused to say anything else as she was desperately close to tears. Cradling the bowl in her hands, Sigrid tried to focus on the pudding and berries instead.

"I hope you won't sell it off without giving me first chance to buy it," Erik said.

Sigrid's head snapped up and she knew without needing to see for herself that her face clearly registered her anger. "Erik Lindquist, I have no thought to see this place sold to anyone. This is my home. I have nothing else now, and I'm tired of people trying to separate me from the only thing left me."

Erik seemed notably surprised by her outburst. Unable to bear up under his scrutiny, Sigrid pushed him aside and made her way into the living room. *I'm not going to deal with this today*, she thought, lifting a spoonful of ostkaka to her lips. The dessert seemed flavorless to her, and what would normally have been a rare treat was now souring on her stomach. *Would this day never end?*

Chapter 2

SKORPOR
(Swedish Rusks)

1 cup sugar	½ tsp. soda
½ cup shortening	½ tsp. salt
1 egg	1 tsp. baking powder
1 cup sour cream	1 cup nuts
3 to 4 cups flour	
(enough to make dough stiff)	

Mix all ingredients together and pour onto a long sheet pan. Bake 1 hour at 325⁰F. Take out of oven and turn oven to 200⁰F. Then cut skorpor into strips about 1 x 4" while still in the pan and put back in the oven to dry until hard and light brown (about 1 hour). These make great dunkers for coffee.

Sigrid's week went from bad to unbearable. Sigrid remained firm as Sven continued to nag about selling the property, but when a town meeting was called to discuss the railroad moving into the area, she had second thoughts about maintaining her life in the quiet town of Lindsborg. Building the railroad had brought her parents from Illinois to Kansas in the first place, but the railroad had also cost her father his life.

"The railroad is bringing new life to your community," an older man in a black suit assured the crowd. "The railroad will bring new people to settle the area and with them will come new industry and growth. A community like Lindsborg needs the railroad and," he paused to play up to the crowd, "the railroad needs Lindsborg."

The townsfolk murmured amongst themselves while Sigrid found an inconspicuous place for herself at the back of the meeting hall.

"Excuse me," a soft masculine voice whispered over her shoulder. "You aren't leaving, are you?"

Sigrid turned to find a handsome, dark-haired stranger eyeing her with consuming interest. "I'm not very interested in the topic," she managed to reply.

"Oh, but you should be." The man's brown eyes seemed to twinkle and a broad grin was revealed beneath his thick, handle-bar mustache. "I'm Ruben Carter. I work with this railroad." He said the words as though she should be impressed with such an announcement.

Instead, Sigrid dismissed herself and went outside to wait for Sven and Erik. Both were enthusiastic, or so it seemed, to at least hear what the railroad was offering the community.

"Wait, Miss..." Carter called, following her.

"I'm sorry, Mr. Carter," Sigrid said, rather stiffly. "The rail holds nothing but bad memories for me. My father was killed in a railroading accident near Salina."

"I'm sorry to hear that, Miss. . ." Again he paused, waiting for her name.

"Larsson," she replied flatly.

He gave her a sweeping bow and pulled up with a grin. "Miss Larsson, it is a pleasure to make your acquaintance."

Sigrid smiled in spite of herself. "Thank you, Mr. Carter. Now, if you'll excuse me—"

"But we've only just met," he interjected. "You can't go now. Why don't you tell me what happened to your father?"

Sigrid smoothed the dusty folds of her dove gray skirt. "He was pinned between two cars. He died soon after they were able to free him."

"I'm sorry. But you know, that doesn't make the railroad evil."

"No, I suppose it doesn't," Sigrid admitted. "But it does make me wary of having it in my town."

"Where do you live? Perhaps the railroad will be far removed from your daily routine."

Sigrid shook her head. "No such luck. We've already received a notice saying that the railroad will pass over a corner of our property. No one asked me if I wanted it there. We were simply told that it will be placed there and we will be given a modest amount of money to compensate the taking of that which never belonged to the railroad in the first place." Her words were delivered in a stern, unemotional manner.

Ruben nodded sympathetically. "I can understand, but you mustn't fret so over it."

"I believe we've adequately discussed this issue," Sigrid said and turned to go. She was barely halfway down the street when Ruben caught up with her.

"At least allow me to make a suggestion," he offered. "We will be looking for ways to feed our workers. Perhaps you would care to assist us by cooking for the railroad?"

Sigrid shook her head and continued walking. She had absolutely no desire to be responsible for aiding the railroad's entry into Lindsborg. She might not be able to stop its arrival, but she certainly didn't have to assist it.

"Wait, Miss Larsson," Ruben called out again, then joined her matching her stride.

Sigrid said nothing for several moments. She wondered who this man really was and what his part was with the railroad. Perhaps he had a great deal of money tied up in the development of Lindsborg, and maybe all of that hinged on the successful presentation of the railroad to the citizens of the small town. But most folks were quite excited about the railroad, so surely talking her into a favorable response wasn't all that important.

"Please just hear me out. If nothing else, do it for the sake of Christian charity," Carter said with a pleading expression.

Sigrid felt helpless to argue with the man. *Moder* had always said that God expected folks to treat one another as they would if Jesus Himself was standing in their place. "All right," she replied, looking Ruben Carter full in the face. "I'm listening."

Ruben smiled. "Would it be possible for you to have me to coffee?"

"Swedes are famous for always having a pot on the stove," Sigrid said, warming to his smile. He seemed like such a gentle-natured man and his soft-spoken words were methodically relaxing her prejudices. "I suppose the men will be along directly," she said glancing back at the main street of town.

"Yes, they were very near to concluding their discussion," Ruben agreed.

"All right, Mr. Carter, I will give you coffee and hear you out," Sigrid said.

"So you see," Ruben told her as she poured steaming black coffee into his cup, "the railroad likes to work with the folks of the community. We have a great many workers who set the rails in place and bring in supplies. We rely upon good folks like you to help us with the feeding and sometimes the housing of our workers." He took a drink of the coffee and nodded approvingly. "This is very good."

Sigrid smiled and brought a plateful of skorpor to the table. "These are for dunking in the coffee." She paused as his gaze seemed to roam the full length of her body before resting on her face.

"I think I've died and gone to heaven," he said, taking one of the skorpor.

Sigrid, not used to open flirting, felt her face grow flushed. As she turned quickly away, she saw out the open kitchen window that Erik and Sven were coming up the lane. Their heated discussion seemed to indicate a problem and Sigrid could only wonder if they were discussing the sale of her home.

"So now that I know exactly where you're situated," Ruben began again, "and I know you can cook, what say you to the possibility of hiring on to fix my men breakfast each day? You'd be well paid."

Sigrid immediately thought of her brother's need for money. *What if I were to find enough or make enough money to buy out Sven and Ina's shares of the property? Would that satisfy them?*

"How much would I be paid?"

"Oh, it depends," Ruben said, looking up to the ceiling as though to mentally calculate the matter. "If you were to provide a full breakfast, and remember those are hardworking men with hearty appetites, it could be a very satisfactory sum."

"I assure you, Mr. Carter, farmers are hardworking men with hearty appetites as well. I've fed plenty of farmhands and I know how men can eat. What I don't know is what the railroad considers satisfactory."

"Enough to cover your expenses and then some," Ruben replied. "Look, if you'll consider this, I promise to make it well worth your time and trouble. The men need to be fed before first light every morning so that they can be to work by sunup. There will probably be about twenty or so in number, and you only have to worry about the morning meal. I'll arrange other plans for the noon and supper meals."

Sigrid finally felt intrigued by the idea. She could easily feed twenty men, and making money from the railroad seemed a promising way to keep Sven from forcing her to sell the homestead. "How long will you need to keep this arrangement?" she asked, glancing back out the window to find Sven and Erik stopped at the gatepost. They appeared to be in no hurry to come inside.

"Probably six or seven months, maybe less," Ruben replied.

Sigrid turned back to find him dunking yet another skorpor into his coffee. "All right," she said, taking the chair opposite him at the table. "I will consider doing this thing, but only if you put all the details in writing. I don't want the railroad cheating me for my efforts."

"You certainly have a low opinion of us, don't you," he more stated than questioned.

"You would too, if you'd lost your father and found your family forgotten and destitute by the very organization that took his life." She knew her words sounded pain filled, yet Sigrid couldn't stop herself from continuing. "Frankly, I'm grateful that my mother won't have to see the railroad come to this town. It would break her heart and make it seem like losing my *Fader* all over again."

"I'm truly sorry for your loss, Miss Larsson. My own parents are still alive, so I cannot possibly know your pain. Please believe me when I say the railroad will be honor bound in their arrangements with you. You need not fear that you will be cheated in any way."

For a moment, Sigrid lost herself in his compassionate expression. His brown eyes seemed to reach inside her with a comforting assurance that every word he spoke was true. She wanted to do nothing more than listen to his promises and know that she wouldn't have to leave her home, but the slamming of the back porch screen door brought her out of her reverie.

Sigrid jumped to her feet to get two more coffee mugs. With emotions fading and senses returning, she called over her shoulder, "I'll do the job, but I still want it in writing."

Chapter 3

RAGMUNKAR
(Swedish Potato Pancakes)

3 cups grated raw potatoes 2 T. flour
½ cup milk 1 ½ tsp. salt
1 egg, slightly beaten 1 T. onion, finely
chopped

Beat egg into the milk and immediately add potatoes. Sprinkle in flour, mixing well and add salt and onion. Fry in greased skillet, as you would regular pancakes, until golden brown.

Sigrid went to work immediately to prepare her house for the railroad workers. She cleared the living room of its normal furniture, with exception of the piano and wood stove, and brought in tables and chairs from every other corner of the house. Ella had even managed to loan her an extra table, and with that, Sigrid was able to put five men to a table with enough space to accommodate them all comfortably.

She rose every morning at three-thirty in order to have the stove hot and the food ready for the workers. It caused some havoc with her normal routine, but after a week or two Sigrid had worked through all the minor problems. Her supplies had used a fair sum of her funds, but she was already turning a profit. Not to mention that her jelly jar was now rapidly being filled with money. Not only was the railroad paying her to feed the men, but some of the men paid extra for things like cookies, pies and biscuits. Sigrid was finally seeing a way to satisfy Sven, although he'd been none too impressed with her method of earning the money.

Erik was even less impressed.

As a hired hand, Erik had made a routine of sharing the morning and sometimes the evening meal, with Tilly and Sigrid. He seemed to resent having to share his sanctuary with fifteen to twenty rowdies every morning. Sigrid ignored his scowls and comments that the men would just tear up the place. She was happy to have something to focus on other than her mother's death and her brother's insistence that she move. She'd even managed to make a small peace with the railroad. She would never embrace this mode of transportation as being of particular importance in her life, but she could overlook their intrusion so long as it meant she could keep her parents' home intact.

"My, my, but aren't you the sun in the sky," Ruben said, as he joined the men who were filing into the living room for breakfast.

Sigrid said nothing, but glanced down at the yellow calico gown. It was worn, yet serviceable, and she'd put it on with the intention of brightening her own day. She was tired of the dark woolens she'd worn all winter and tired of feeling a sense of loss for her mother every time she reached for something black. Spring was a time of colors and Sigrid wanted to bring such color back into her life.

"Smells mighty good in here, ma'am," a burly man with a matted black beard announced. "Hope you're servin' them thar Swedish pancakes again."

Sigrid smiled. "There are whole plates of them already on the tables, and I'll be in directly with ham and eggs."

Ruben followed her into the kitchen and reached out to touch her arm. "I meant what I said. You are about as pretty as a picture today. I like what you've done with your hair, too."

Sigrid reached a hand up to the carefully pinned blond bun. She usually just braided her hair and pinned it up at the nape of her neck, but today she'd felt like something different. With a surprising flair of artistry, Sigrid had woven her hair atop her head, leaving wisps to fall around her face. In a moment of pure vanity, she'd even taken a fork and heated the tongs to carefully curl each wisp until it conformed to her desired style.

"It really makes you look much prettier," Ruben said. "Not that you weren't already quite pretty to start with."

Sigrid felt her cheeks grow flushed and turned in a panic to check on the biscuits. Bent over the open oven door, she hoped that the redness of her cheeks would be explained away by the heat.

"You shouldn't find my praise so embarrassing," Ruben whispered as she straightened up. "I'm quite sure any of these men would agree with me."

"You do go on, don't you?" Sigrid said, busying her hands with slicing additional pieces of ham. "You'll have to excuse me, I need to get these on the table." She lifted two large platters of ham and eggs, but Ruben took them from her and leaned close to her ear.

"Perhaps you would honor me with a walk later?"

Sigrid jumped back, startled at the way his hot breath made her skin tingle. "I. . .ah. . .I have too much work to do."

"It can wait," Ruben said with a roguish smile. "But I can't."

He left her standing there cheeks flushed and heart racing, to stare after him. Sigrid had no idea how to deal with his attention. She'd never allowed herself to enjoy the attentions of any man, and now Ruben Carter was putting her resolve to the ultimate test.

But why not enjoy it? she thought. *I'm twenty-seven years old. It's not like men are beating down the door to court me.*

✧

Erik watched from the doorway as Ruben wooed Sigrid with his smiles and words. A pang of bitter jealousy coursed through him, and he didn't like it at all. He'd known Sigrid for what seemed an eternity, but more than this, he'd loved her for nearly as long. And, he'd come to think of her as belonging to him.

He remembered the first time he'd seen her at a church youth function. At least, it was the first time he'd seen her as anything other than a child. She was fifteen and the new pink gingham dress that she wore more than showed off her womanly charms. She had just started to pin her hair up and looked so very grown up that, for a moment, Erik had wondered who she was. It wasn't long until he realized that this was the little Larsson girl. And, she wasn't so little anymore.

As Ruben passed by with the ham and eggs he gave Erik a sideways glance. Erik, feeling rather embarrassed, realized that he was scowling. He was even more embarrassed when he found Sigrid staring at him with a questioning look.

"Something wrong, Erik?" she asked, before turning to pull biscuits from the oven.

Erik crossed the small kitchen amidst the noise of the railroad workers' hearty approvals. "This is wrong, Sigrid," he said flatly. "You have a house full of rowdy men and no chaperone to keep you from their attention should somebody get out of hand. You know what they're saying in town, don't you?"

She straightened and put the pan of biscuits on the counter. "No, I'm sure I don't. I scarcely have time to lounge around town listening to gossip."

Erik's conscience smarted, but not enough to leave the thing alone. "You're risking your reputation here, and I think that Carter fellow is way too familiar with you if you ask me."

"Well, I didn't. Stop playing big brother to me and stay out of it."

Erik wanted to pull her into his arms and tell her that being a big brother was the furthest thing from his mind, but instead he crossed his arms against his chest. "So you don't care what people think?"

"Not when they are misjudging me without bothering to learn the truth," she said rather defiantly.

Erik wondered if he was included in that group. Had he misjudged the situation? Was it mere jealousy that fanned his concern? He waited while Sigrid took out biscuits and coffee and tried to think of what he would say next.

When she came back into the kitchen, she looked up at him for only a moment before heading to the back door.

"Where are you going?"

"I need more wood," she said, motioning to the empty bin beside the stove.

"Let me get it," he offered.

She looked at him hard for a moment, then nodded. "All right, but you must promise no more lectures."

He smiled. "I have to promise good behavior in order to haul wood?"

He watched her fight back a smile before rolling her eyes. "No, but if you want breakfast then you must mind your manners."

He went outside into the darkness of the morning and noted that the faintest light was now touching the eastern horizon. They followed the well-worn path around the side of the house and Sigrid began picking up logs.

"Here," Erik suggested holding out his muscular arms, "just load me up." Sigrid did as he told her and they worked silently for the remaining time.

After making three more trips, the bin was full and the coffee perked cheerily atop the stove. The day was dawning, and with it, the railroad workers were taking their leave. One by one they filed out the front door, stopping only long enough to leave bits of change in the jar by the door. Ruben seemed reluctant to leave, but Erik made it clear that he was staying on and in no hurry to go about the farm's daily chores. Returning Erik's look of unspoken challenge, Ruben finally donned his hat and bid a busy Sigrid good day.

"I'll stop by later," Ruben assured her, "with a railroad check. Maybe you won't be too busy to take that walk then?"

"Thank you, Mr. Carter, and we shall see," she called over her shoulder, her arms filled with empty plates.

When Carter had let the screen door slam behind him, Erik picked up a stack of plates and followed Sigrid into the kitchen. He wanted to question her about Carter's mention of a walk, but he knew she'd only take offense.

"You really shouldn't wear yourself out doing this," Erik began. He wanted to plead a case that would appear entirely sympathetic to her own condition. "Getting up at three-thirty and adding this to your other chores is taking on way too much."

Sigrid laughed at his concern. "Erik, I need the money, and you know as well as anyone that a little hard work never hurt a body."

She was plunging the greasy plates into soapy water, but Erik took hold of her arm anyway and pulled her with him to sit at one of the empty tables. "I want to talk to you about all of this."

She wiped soapsuds onto her apron and shook her head. "There's nothing more to be said. You heard Sven. He wants this place sold or he wants the money entitled him. I can work hard and give him the latter, but I can't lose this place. Not yet." Her expression softened and her gaze traveled the interior of the room. "I'm not ready to say good-bye yet. I know it might sound foolish, but that's just the way I feel."

"I'm not asking you to say good-bye, nor to sell the house, unless of course you want to include me in on the deal." He held up his hand as she started to protest. "You've got to understand, in many ways, I'm just as tied to the place as you are. After all, I've been helping to farm it for almost thirteen years."

"I know all of that," she said, her voice edged with irritation. "That's why you should understand how I feel."

"But I do," he softly replied. He studied her confused expression. Her blue eyes seemed to search him for answers, and he wondered if he could go through with what he planned to do.

"Then why can't you understand my feeding the workers?" she asked flatly. "Why can't you see that by the end of autumn the railroad will be finished, and I'll have saved enough money to buy out Sven and Ina. It's the only way."

"No. It's not the...*only* way," Erik said, hesitantly.

"Then what do you suggest?"

"You could marry me. I'd be happy to pay Sven and Ina whatever they thought fair."

Sigrid's mouth dropped open. She stared at Erik with such a look of alarm that he wondered if he'd actually offended her.

"*Marry you*? You must want this land bad to offer me marriage." She got up from the table and Erik could read the anger in her eyes. "You've treated me like an unwanted little sister all of my life. When you ran around with my brother you ignored me or else teased me unmercifully and when it was just *Moder* and me you. . .well you—" She stopped mid-sentence, her face reddened from the tirade, eyes blazing in accusation. "*Uff da!*" she exclaimed in exasperation. "Why does everyone suddenly seem intent on putting me out of my home?"

She ran from the room before Erik could offer a single word of explanation. Not that he was entirely certain that he would have even tried to speak. She was more angry than he'd ever seen her, and yet he couldn't help but smile. *Little sister, indeed,* he thought. *I've seen you as something more than a little sister for a great long while.* But this thought only frustrated him more as he remembered that Ruben Carter obviously looked upon her in other than brotherly fashion.

Leaning back in exasperation, Erik ran a hand through his hair and contemplated the situation. *How can I convince her that it isn't her land I love?*

Chapter 4

SWEDISH RYE BREAD

1 cup potato water	2 cups rye flour
(water from a boiled potato)	1 T. salt
½ cup all-purpose flour	1 package of yeast
1 potato	2 cups water
(boiled and mashed)	(or buttermilk)

Mix and leave to rise until double in size.

Boil together:

½ cup sugar	¼ cup orange peel,
¼ cup shortening	finely grated
½ cup molasses	

Cool and put into doubled bread mixture. Work this well with 5 to 6 cups of flour to make a dough that doesn't stick to the board. Form into 2 or 3 medium-size loaves and let rise until double. Bake at 375⁰F for 1 hour.

A week later, Sigrid found that there were still no easy answers to the questions that plagued her mind. Erik made himself her constant companion so long as the railroad men were in the house. He was also more than attentive when Ruben Carter chose to spend time with her, and Sigrid felt great frustration with his interference.

Even now, as she pounded out those frustrations on the bread dough she was working, Sigrid found Erik staring at her from over the rim of his coffee cup. He went later and later into the fields these days, and Sigrid knew that it was because of Ruben's attentions. *He's appointed himself my guardian,* she decided, and the thought of answering to yet another "brother" left a completely sour taste in her mouth.

"Aren't you worried about rain?" she asked, patting the dough into a ball.

Erik glanced at the window, as if contemplating her question, then shook his head. "It won't rain today. Maybe tomorrow. I've got time."

"Well if you've so much time on your hands you could fix that section of fence my cows keep escaping through. I did my best, but it won't do much to keep them in if they get very determined to seek greener pastures."

"You want me out of here for a reason?" Erik asked, eyeing her seriously.

She looked at him for a moment, thought of an angry retort, then bit it back and turned away. She couldn't very well tell him that he made her uncomfortable. Everyone made her uncomfortable these days. She couldn't even go to church without getting an earful of how scandalously she was behaving. It didn't matter that she was working herself to death in order to save her home from being sold.

"Well? Is that the reason? Is Mr. Carter headed back to fill your head with more nonsense?"

Erik was referring to a conversation he'd come in on earlier that morning. Ruben had been telling her about his home in Kansas City. Well, home seemed a paltry description, compared to the glorious details Ruben had offered. Anyway, it wasn't any of Erik's business, she reminded herself.

"Sit here all day, if that's what you want," she snapped and glanced out the window in time to see her brother coming up the walkway. "Oh, great. Now I'll have two of you to deal with."

"What?" Erik said, getting to his feet. "Carter *is* back, isn't he?"

Sigrid turned angrily. "It's Sven, if you must know. Now sit down and finish your breakfast. You might as well talk with Sven, because I have nothing more to say to either of you."

She covered the rye dough with a clean towel and went into the living room to pick up the last of the dishes. Sigrid could hear Erik greet her brother with an offering of coffee. She felt herself tense, wondering why she couldn't understand Erik's protective nature. He'd never been one to watch over her like this. Then again, *Moder* had always been alive to keep watch over her. *But I'm twenty-seven*, she thought with a sigh of exasperation. *I don't need someone to look after me.* Then she thought of a prayer she'd been taught by her mother.

Gud som haver barnen kar, Se till mig som liten ar.

"God who holds the children dear, Look after me so little here," she whispered.

Tears came to her eyes. "Oh, *Moder*," she whispered. "I miss you so. I do need God to look after me. I know that. But I don't need—"

"Well, Erik said you were hard at work," Sven boomed, coming into the living room. "I don't suppose you're ready to put an end to this foolishness?" He didn't bother to wait for her to answer. "I'm tired of hearing the talk about you in town."

Sigrid gave him a casual glance of indifference. "But I suppose you aren't too tired of it to repeat what you've been bothered by."

Sven's broad face tightened at the jaw, but otherwise he showed no other expression of emotion. "Those men seem to have a right good time taking their breakfast here."

"Good," Sigrid replied and went back to wiping down the table.

Erik had joined Sven by now and added his own thoughts on the matter. "I heard your name bandied about by that Carter fellow. He's taking an awful liberty if you ask me—"

"Well, I didn't," Sigrid replied and gathering up her things, whipped past both men before either one could respond.

Sven was first to follow, and when he caught up with her he took her by the arm and made her come to sit at the table.

"You're going to talk about selling the land," he said. "I know several people who are interested in buying—"

"No!" Sigrid interjected. She crossed her arms and glared at both Sven and Erik. The men took seats opposite her and waited for her to calm.

"Sigrid," her brother began.

"No, Sven. I don't want to leave. Maybe next year. But not now. I need this house. I need to feel *Moder's* presence. It gives my heart peace. I need to think about what I want to do. Where I want to go. Is that so hard to understand?"

"No, but as I've already said, Ina and I could use the extra money."

"I'm planning to buy you both out," Sigrid announced, surprising her brother. "That's why I took on the job of feeding the railroad workers. Ruben, that is Mister Carter," she added after noting the look on Erik's face, "has seen to it that I'm amply paid."

"You think you can make enough to buy us out?" Sven asked with a look of disbelief.

"How much are you expecting to make?" she asked, happy to at least have his attention turned in a direction she could deal with.

"Well, I figured there would be at least fifty dollars for each of us. Tom Anderson said the place is worth at least one hundred fifty dollars, maybe more."

"I know I'd pay you that," Erik threw out quite casually.

"Fifty?" she asked, her voice faltering. "Each?"

"*Ja*, that seems more than fair."

Fifty to each, she thought. That was one hundred dollars, not counting her own share. It might as well be a million for all the good it would do. She did a quick mental calculation and realized that if the railroad stayed in the area until November, she could amass the money needed. Maybe even by then, she could sell extra vegetables from her garden, as well.

"Give me until Christmas," she finally said.

Sven rubbed his chin and exchanged a glance with Erik. "It would be mighty hard to wait."

"Well, I can give you part of your share now, and if Ina can wait, I'll have the rest by then."

"How much are you talking about?" Sven questioned.

Sigrid could see that she had his interest. "Twenty dollars."

"Twenty?" He perked up at this and rubbed his chin again. "I suppose I could wait until Christmas."

"Good," Sigrid said, jumping to her feet. She rushed to her room and took out twenty dollars from the money she'd saved back. It didn't leave her much, but in a few weeks she would make it all up. Hurrying back, she thrust the money into Sven's hands before he could change his mind. "Now, I have work to do."

Going back to the sink, she ignored the hushed talk between her brother and Erik. *Please God, let it be enough to make Sven go in peace*, she prayed. She understood her brother's need for cash, but it hurt her that he couldn't understand her reluctance to leave the home of her birth.

"Well, I'll go then. Olga will wonder why I've been so long to town."

"Don't lose your money," Sigrid called out, turning to watch him go.

When Sven had gone, she could see that Erik had more to say. Wiping her hands on her apron, Sigrid came to sit down once again and folded her arms. "All right, speak Mr. Lindquist, and tell me what I've done to offend you now."

Erik shook his head. "You haven't offended me. I just wish I could explain some things to you. I wish you'd let me help."

"Help do what? Buy the farm?"

"I could help you in that way. You know I wouldn't expect you to move. Letting me help you would be a whole sight easier than working yourself into an early grave."

Sigrid could see that he was genuinely concerned and that his words were given in an attitude of sincerity. She felt her resolve crumble. He had been good to her and *Moder*, and to turn her back on him now would be cruel.

"Erik, you are kind to offer, but I don't think I could live here with you owning the land. I could never afford to pay for my keep and it wouldn't be right to expect you to let me live here for free."

Erik smiled. "Like I said before, we could get married. I'd be happy to pay Sven and Ina their fifty dollars, and we could even live on here if you wanted to."

Sigrid was touched more deeply than she could express. That Erik would offer himself up in that manner seemed to say that her welfare was of more importance to him than his own. "That's very kind, Erik," she murmured. "Kind, but not very practical for you."

"I don't want you thinking that it would just be an act of kindness," Erik said, seeming to struggle for words. "I mean…well—"

"You don't need to explain," Sigrid interrupted. "I know how you cared about *Moder* and you probably feel obligated to see me cared for, for her sake. I think, too, that you understand why I want to stay on. But, I'd like to accomplish this myself. I don't want anyone marrying me out of pity, all so that I can keep a parcel of land and a run-down house."

"Sigrid—"

"No, hear me out, Erik. It's important to me that you know how much I appreciate your offer. It shows what a good friend you really are. I'm sorry I got so mad at you earlier, but you have to understand I'm a grown woman. I can't have you telling me who I can and can't talk to, and I don't want you worrying about the men coming here to eat. God watches over me, and He knows my heart in this matter."

Erik's expression seemed almost pained. Sigrid thought it would be better to put the matter behind them. "I've got to get to work, whether you do or not," she said, trying to sound lighthearted. She got to her feet and went back to the sink. "God will work out the details."

⬥

Erik left the Larsson house feeling more frustrated than ever. God might know Sigrid's heart, but he sure couldn't figure it out. Had she fallen in love with that Carter fellow? Why couldn't she see the trouble Carter could be? She was too naive, too sheltered. He wanted to explain all of those things to her, but she'd only see it as interference.

Kicking at a rock, Erik looked up at the sky. Wisps of lacy white clouds were strung out against the brilliant blue. It would rain tomorrow or the next day for sure, and he still had work to do in the fields. Maybe he would give Sigrid another day to think about things and then he would bring up the subject again. *Only this time*, he thought, *I'll find a way to tell her how I feel about her.* Surely that would make a difference.

Chapter 5

SMORBAKELSER
(Swedish Butter Cookies)

1 cup butter	2 cups flour
2 egg yolks	1 tsp. almond extract
½ cup sugar	1 tsp. vanilla extract

Cream butter, egg yolks, sugar, and extracts together until light and fluffy. Add flour and mix well. Dough will be soft, but not sticky. Roll out (don't overflour) and cut with cookie cutter or use in cookie press. Bake at 400°F for 8 to 10 minutes. They burn easily, so be careful.

The September wedding of her widowed friend Ella Swanson gave Sigrid something else to focus on other than work. Ella, with her three fatherless boys, was quite happy to accept an offer of marriage from Per Anderson. The thirty-five year old bachelor seemed overly quiet and reserved for Ella's rambunctious bunch, but Sigrid could see that the boys adored the man. And, Ella seemed quite satisfied with the match.

With the weather cooperating perfectly, the wedding supper was held outside in picnic fashion on the church lawn. Sigrid had baked several dishes to bring to the supper, including one of Ella's favorites, *smorbakelser*, little butter cookies so light and rich that they instantly melt in your mouth. *They appear*, Sigrid thought with a smile, *to be one of Erik's favorites as well*. Seeing him make yet another trip to the dessert table, she watched him grab up a handful of the cookies and plop them down on his plate in a rather possessive manner.

"Oh, there you are," Mrs. Moberg said, coming up from behind Sigrid. "I hoped to talk to you. I heard it said that the railroad is planning to buy your land for a depot. Is that true? What will you do then? Are you going to live with Sven and Olga?"

Taken aback by the rapid interrogation, Sigrid shook her head. "I don't know anything about a depot, but I don't plan to sell the farmstead to the railroad. Where did you get such an idea?"

The robust woman jutted her chin in the air. "Mr. Moberg told me, and where he heard it from, I can't say."

"Well someone obviously has their facts wrong."

"Wrong about what?" Mrs. Swanson questioned and before waiting for an answer, added, "Don't Ella look nice?"

They all agreed that Ella made a radiant bride before Mrs. Moberg relayed her information on the railroad.

"*Ja*, I heard there was talk of a depot and roundhouse for the engines. Your farmstead is a good place for these things."

"That's not my opinion," Sigrid said. "I intend to get down to the bottom of this gossip right away." Leaving the two old women to stare after her in stunned silence, Sigrid went in search of Ruben.

Weaving her way through the crowd, Sigrid felt disheartened at not being able to immediately locate Ruben. She knew he'd been invited to the celebration, and she had counted on seeing him here. It was funny the way he made her feel. Sometimes she welcomed his visits and other times he made her feel like a creature misplaced in time. He laughed at her crude lifestyle and told her that with the coming of the new century, her way of life would rapidly become obsolete. Still, he made her feel like a woman, all feminine and girlish. She found herself wanting to impress him, and she wanted him to take notice.

Spying him watching a game of horseshoes, Sigrid slipped up from behind and pulled on his coat sleeve. "Can we talk for a moment?"

He flashed her a grin that suggested she'd just made his day, and with a hand to the small of her back, he led her away from the crowd to a nearby stand of trees.

"What would you like to talk about?" he asked, rubbing one of the handlebars of his mustache between his thumb and finger. "I've known weddings to bring even the shyest girl out of her shell."

Sigrid felt her cheeks grow hot. Ruben seemed to imply that she was interested in some kind of romantic tryst, and while she could easily see herself in the role, she had to know the truth about her property.

"I've been told by some of my friends that the railroad intends to try to build a depot on my land. Maybe even take the entire farmstead for a roundhouse and such. Is this true, Ruben?" She searched his face, particularly his dark eyes, and waited for some sign that would reassure her.

Ruben took hold of her hand and kissed it lightly. Sigrid found herself trembling from the action and quickly pulled her hand away. "Is it true?" she pressed the question again.

"I have no knowledge of it, if it is," he admitted. "I would have been told if that were the plan, and I know nothing of it."

Sigrid relaxed a bit and sighed. "I hate gossip. It's always getting a person worked up for no reason at all." She felt him move closer to her and thought of moving away. But the thought quickly passed from her mind.

"Sigrid, you are so beautiful. I don't know why you let yourself worry about things. Trust me, I'll find out if there is any truth to the rumors. In the meantime, why don't we spend some time together? We could walk down by the creek and leave the others to their celebration while we have our own private party."

Sigrid stammered at his passionate expression. "I. . .ah. . .I don't think. . ." Before she could finish her words, Ruben pulled her into his arms.

"I don't want you to think about anything but me," he said and kissed her quite soundly on the mouth.

Sigrid stood absolutely rigid as he let her go. She had to remain fixed that way, because she was certain if she so much as took a single step, her knees would buckle from beneath her.

He gently touched the curl of hair that fell over one ear. "You are a magnificent woman, Sigrid. I think I'm losing my heart to you."

Sigrid couldn't look him the eye. The whole idea of being courted was so foreign to her. For so many years she'd kept her heart completely boxed off, knowing that as the youngest daughter she was required to care for her mother until the time of her death.

"Don't be afraid to trust your heart," Ruben said, softly. "Come with me."

Sigrid knew it would be impossible to go with him down to the creek. What little reputation she might have managed to keep intact would be ruined for certain if they were to slip away.

"I...I need to go," she finally said, and turned to walk briskly away.

Ruben did nothing to stop her, and a part of her was hurt by this. If he cared so much about keeping her company, why didn't he at least call after her? But another part of her was just as grateful that he didn't. She'd never been kissed on the mouth before, and it seemed such a glorious and wondrous experience that Sigrid wanted to find a way to go off by herself and contemplate what had just happened.

❦

"I just saw him kiss her," Mrs. Moberg was saying to a collected gathering of older women. "I think that more than suggests what I said was true."

Erik came upon this conversation as he made his fourth trip to the supper tables. His agitation at not being able to spend time alone with Sigrid had made him poor company for everyone else. She was ignoring him, and in the months that had passed since his offer to marry her, Sigrid had never allowed him to speak on the matter again. He'd hoped the atmosphere of a wedding might give him the forum to declare his love, but so far Sigrid had remained completely out of his company.

"You know I heard they were close to an understanding," one of the women continued the conversation.

"Bah!" exclaimed Mrs. Moberg, "I've heard it said that Sigrid has already accepted his proposal. Think on that, our Sigrid married to Ruben Carter. Why I don't imagine she would stay in Lindsborg long after that."

"No, indeed," a third woman countered. "I heard he is rich. Lives in a fancy mansion in Kansas City. No doubt she'd prefer spending the winter in luxury rather than on the prairie."

Erik's chest tightened as the words of the conversation permeated his brain. *Sigrid and Carter were engaged? When had this happened?*

"Well, from the looks of the way he was kissing her just now, I'd say they'd better do something in a hurry," Mrs. Moberg added in a rather haughty tone.

Erik left his plate at the table and walked away in a daze. *Carter had kissed Sigrid? And she'd let him?* Anger slowly welled inside. It seemed to pulsate to life from every part of his body, until there was a hard, black ball knotting up in his stomach. *She couldn't be in love with that two-faced, no-good.*

"Erik, have you seen my sister?"

Erik glanced up to find Sven coming toward him. "No, but apparently a good many other people have."

Sven stared at him with an expression of confusion. "What do you mean by that?"

Erik started to explain, then bit back the retort and shrugged. "I can't seem to locate her, but I've heard others mention having seen her. She must be around here somewhere."

"*Ja*, I suppose she's found some way to keep busy."

Erik grimaced. "Yes, I suppose she has."

He walked away quickly, lest he should open his mouth and let pour the anger inside. Hurrying away from the party, Erik found himself taking the long way back to his house. He realized that he wanted nothing more than to find Sigrid and force some sense into her head. And then, he wanted nothing more than to kiss her himself and show her that he meant business.

"I'm powerful angry, Lord," he said, looking skyward. "I don't mean to be, but I am and there's no use denying it. I've tried to be reasonable about things. I've tried to keep my hands and mind busy so that she'd have time to consider my proposal, but it isn't my proposal she's considering."

He slowed his stride as his anger spent itself in prayer. "I don't want to lose her, but how can I convince her that I love her?"

Just tell her, a voice seemed to say.

Erik stopped in his tracks and glanced around him. Nothing but a few buildings and cornfields greeted his gaze. Maybe God was trying to speak to his heart. Maybe he had relied too long on his own understanding, and now it was time to face doing things another way.

"Have I ignored You, God?" he asked suddenly. Shoving his hands in his pockets, Erik moved on down the lane. He tried to imagine what God would have him do.

"Tell her? But she already knows how I feel about her. After all, I asked her to marry me."

You asked her to marry you so that you could keep her on her land, his heart reminded him. *You said nothing of love.*

"Well, maybe it's time I did," Erik declared, suddenly feeling a bit of his self-confidence return. "After all, they aren't married yet."

Chapter 6

Egg Gravy

2 T. bacon or sausage drippings	2 egg yolks
4 cups milk	½ tsp. salt
2 T. flour	

Put meat drippings into a skillet over medium heat. Add flour as you would for gravy. Blend and leave to brown a bit. Mix milk, egg yolks (slightly beaten), and salt, and add to flour and grease. Mix this until thick, but don't allow it to curdle. Add more milk if you like thinner gravy. When mixture is the right consistency for you, remove from heat and serve over Swedish rye bread.

Harvest was a busy time of year for all of Lindsborg, but Sigrid found it especially trying. It was easy to see now how hard her mother had worked. Even though Tilly was unable to do much of the heavy work, she had prepared the vegetables for canning and helped with the livestock. Now that all of this fell to Sigrid's shoulders, her only saving grace was that the railroad had completed its line and she was no longer needed to feed the workers.

Still, she'd been up by four that morning to do her own chores, and throughout the course of the day, there'd been little opportunity to even pause for the briefest rest. Most of the morning had been spent in cleaning vegetables and the afternoon would be devoted to canning them.

Glancing at the clock, Sigrid was startled to find it was nearly one-thirty, and she hadn't fixed anything for lunch. During harvest time, Erik usually made his way to her house for the noon meal. Since she was already spending most of her time in the kitchen canning, making lunch for the both of them made sense. What didn't make sense was sending Erik back to his own place or even into town for a bite to eat. But now, she'd let it slip her mind completely and she feared he would show up starving, and she'd not have a single morsel prepared.

Staring at the cupboards trying to decide what would be quickest, Sigrid finally decided egg gravy would be the best solution. Her mother said there was always a meal to be had in egg gravy and rye bread. Sigrid hoped it would be filling enough to meet with Erik's hearty appetite. She fried up a panful of bacon to go along with it, then used the drippings for the base of her gravy. She had just finished adding the final ingredients when she heard a knock on the back door.

"Come on in, lunch is nearly ready," she called and hurried to slice tomatoes and rye bread.

"Well, I didn't know you were fixing lunch for me," Sven said, lumbering into the kitchen.

"What are you doing here?" she asked in surprise. "I figured you'd be cutting broomcorn."

"*Ja*, we've been hard to work on it, but something else came up."

Her brother's expression appeared a cross between anxious and hesitant. "So what is it that brings you here?"

"I want to talk to you about our agreement."

"You mean regarding the property?" she asked, turning back to give the gravy a quick stir before removing it from the stove.

"I know I told you that you could have until Christmas, but—" He fell silent as though trying to figure out how best to explain..

"Sven, what are you up to?" she asked flatly. "If it's the money, I can pay you now. I have enough put together to pay both you and Ina. So if that's what you're here for, I can accommodate you."

"No, Sigrid. Sit down."

She sat obediently as a sense of fear ran down her spine. Something had changed his mind. *He's come to break our deal.*

"The railroad has offered to pay double what we talked about," Sven announced. "They are willing to give us three hundred dollars for the farm."

"So they *are* trying to get this land for a depot and roundhouse. Is that it?" Sigrid asked. Why hadn't Ruben known about this yesterday when she'd asked him?

"I guess that's the idea," Sven replied. "I can't say for sure. Maybe they just want the extra space for a spur line to work on the cars."

"Well, they can't have it!" she declared firmly. "Sven, you've been taught to be a man of honor. *Moder* would expect you to keep your word, and so do I."

"Be reasonable, Sigrid. That's a hundred dollars apiece. I could use that money and so could Ina, especially now that the new baby is nearly here. She and Clarence barely have room as it is and a hundred dollars would go a long way to help them build onto the house and get some of the things they need. And, if you're still determined to live alone, a hundred dollars could buy you a little place in town. You wouldn't have to work nearly so hard. You could probably live off that money for a good long time."

"I don't want a place in town, Sven. I want this place. This is my home. Or at least I always thought it was. I love this place. It's a part of *Moder* and *Fader*, and I don't want to let that go."

"I'm your brother, and I'm the head of the family now. I'm sorry, Sigrid, but I'm going to talk to Ina about this. I'm sure she'll feel the same way I do." He got to his feet and walked to the back door.

Sigrid had no other choice but to follow after him. "You can't do this. If you love me, you won't do this." She knew the words cut him like a knife. She could see even with his back turned to her, that his shoulders slumped a little lower.

"I'm sorry," was all he could say.

Sigrid's vision blurred with tears. She watched Sven walk away and wished she could think of something to say in order to change his mind. She could never pay him and Ina both one hundred dollars. She barely had enough to pay them the fifty each.

"What did Sven want?" Erik asked, coming from around the corner of the house. His face and arms were still wet from having washed up at the pump.

"To ruin my life," Sigrid barely managed to whisper before fleeing into the house.

She wiped her eyes with the apron, not wanting Erik to see her cry, but he had followed on her heels and knew exactly what was happening.

"What is it? What did he do that would make you cry?"

Sigrid swallowed down a lump in her throat. "He plans to sell the farm to the railroad."

"He can't do that," Erik said, and his expression told Sigrid that he was every bit as upset at the prospect as she was.

"That's what I told him, but he doesn't care. They are offering him three hundred dollars, and I can't possibly match that." She sat down hard on the chair. A thought came to her, but she quickly pushed it aside. If she married Erik then perhaps they could combine their money and pay Sven and Ina. But no! That was no reason to marry. Besides, the haunting reminder of Ruben's kiss stood between her and Erik now.

"Ruben said he knew nothing about this," she said, mindless of the effect on Erik.

"Apparently he had other things on his mind," Erik said, not even attempting to hide his bitterness.

"What is that supposed to mean?" Sigrid asked.

"There's rumors about you two. I guess you made quite a spectacle of yourself yesterday." He looked at her seeming to dare her to deny his words.

"It's none of your business," she snapped and got up to bring the food to the table. "You'd better eat before this gets cold."

Erik surprised her by taking hold of her arm and forcing her to face him. "You can't trust Carter. He isn't one of us. He isn't from around here. He doesn't know the first thing about farming and you can bet your pretty little head, he doesn't intend to stay in Lindsborg for long."

"Stop it!" Sigrid said, pulling away. "You don't know anything about him. You're just mad because I won't sell you the farm."

"What do you know about how I feel? You haven't bothered to give me so much as two words at one sitting. I come here, you throw food at me, and then I leave to go tend the livestock or garden, or go to town. I know you're hurting over this, but you aren't hearing me."

"I've heard enough!"

"Then you don't care that people think you are playing fast and loose with Ruben Carter? You don't care that folks did more talking about you and Carter kissing yesterday, than they did discussing Ella's wedding?"

Sigrid felt the heat rise from her collar. She couldn't deny what he was accusing her of, and for reasons she couldn't understand, this only made her more angry. Jerking away, she waved to the food on the counter. "Eat or not, but I refuse to talk to someone who only wants to yell at me!"

She stormed off to her bedroom and slammed the door as loudly as she could to make her point. Turning the key in the lock, she hoped it made enough noise to leave Erik without a doubt as to how she felt about him at that moment.

Throwing herself across the bed, Sigrid began to cry in earnest because she really *didn't* know how she felt about anything. Especially Erik. Why did this have to be so difficult? She cared a great deal about Erik, but Ruben made her feel so excited and alive. Ruben had only to look at her a certain way, and she trembled from head to foot. Erik certainly never did that for her.

Or had he? She thought back on times when she'd caught him smiling at her a certain way. Her stomach had always seemed to do flip-flops when that happened, but she had always ignored it. *But he doesn't think of me the same way Ruben does*, she thought, and hot tears fell from her eyes. *Ruben desires me as a woman. Erik just thinks of me as a child. He only wants me for the land.*

Beating her hands against the pillow, Sigrid cried until there were no tears left to cry. It was only when she'd dried her eyes and rolled over on her back that she thought to pray.

"Oh, God," she mournfully whispered, "I'm so confused. I don't know what to do. I don't want to leave my home, but it seems that Sven has made up his mind. I have no choice but to do as others direct me to do. But I want You to show me what to do. I want You to guide and direct me. Please help me to know what's right in Your sight, and give me the strength to deal with this matter."

She sighed, feeling only marginally better. There was a kitchen full of work awaiting her attention, and yet all she really wanted to do was sleep. Just sleep and forget the rest of the world and all the problems that went along with it. The coming months would forever see her life changed, and Sigrid wanted to keep things still, if only for a little while.

Giving into her desires, she closed her eyes and fell asleep. Somehow, God would surely find a way to make it all work out.

Chapter 7

POTATISKORV
(Potato Sausage)

6 large raw potatoes
  (peeled and ground)
1 tsp. pepper
2 tsp. salt
1 tsp. allspice

1 cup milk
1 ½ lbs. ground beef
2 ½ lbs. ground pork
1 medium onion
  (ground)

Mix all ingredients together and stuff into sausage casings, being careful not to overfill as they will expand during cooking. Prick casing several times with a needle before cooking. Put into a pot of hot water and boil over medium heat for 1 hour. Then brown in a frying pan if desired. Makes six 24-inch sausages.

C old weather set in, and with it came a frenzy to finish up the harvest chores. Sigrid had scarcely seen anything of Erik or Sven since that dreadful day in the kitchen. She felt relieved to have been left to her own concerns, and yet she rather missed seeing Erik at mealtime. With the heavy work of harvest, Sigrid was used to Erik sharing all of her meals, but after that day, he had simply stopped coming.

Her conscience bothered her when she thought about having hurt his feelings. She didn't know where to fit Erik into her life. She knew she had feelings for him, but they certainly weren't the same kind of physical feelings she had for Ruben. On the other hand, she shared very little of common interest with Ruben. They talked on several occasions since he'd stolen the kiss at Ella's wedding, and each time Sigrid tried to imagine herself spending the rest of her life with him.

These thoughts continued to haunt her as she worked to stuff sausage casings with *potatiskorv*. The potato sausage would be a nice delicacy to have for the holidays, and Sigrid could remember what a favorite it was of her mother's.

"Oh, *Moder*," she whispered, "I miss you so. Nothing seems right with you gone. I've made such a mess of things."

The sound of the back door opening gave her start. Had her brother come to torment her with the signing over of her home? Or, had Erik returned to confront her with her behavior?

"Sigrid?"

It was Ruben.

Sigrid was surprised and more than a little bit embarrassed to have Ruben find her in such a state of disarray. Wiping the sausage from her hands, she put a hand up to her hair, hoping desperately that she wouldn't appear too much of a mess.

"I wasn't expecting you," she murmured, trying hard to steady her nerves.

He glanced around and smiled. "I hope I'm not interrupting."

"Only in a pleasant way," she said, beginning to relax. "I've been making sausages all morning and in truth, I could use a rest." She turned back to put a towel over the entire affair and felt a charge of electricity shoot through her when Ruben came to stand directly behind her.

His warm breath on her bare neck caused Sigrid to tremble. Ruben turned her gently and took hold of her shoulders. "I haven't been able to get you out of my mind. I miss coming here on a daily basis." He tilted her face up and studied her for a moment as though inspecting a rare flower. "I can't get this face out of my mind. When I sleep, I dream about you, and when I awaken, I long to see you and to hold you."

Sigrid felt her breath quicken. My, but this man could bring her blood to a boil quicker than anyone she'd ever known.

Ruben took her tenderly into his arms. "I want to kiss you again. May I?"

She was touched that he should ask. "I suppose so."

He lost little time. Lowering his mouth to hers, Ruben pulled her tightly against him. He kissed her with more passion than she'd ever imagined, and it so frightened her that she pulled away panting. Stepping away from him, she stared back, trying to reason inside her what it was that had caused her reaction.

"I'm sorry," he said, softly. "I didn't mean to frighten you. It's just that I can no longer fight the feelings I have for you. There's something I want to say, and hope you won't think me too forward." His words were methodically delivered and Sigrid found herself very nearly mesmerized by them.

"What…what…is it?" she barely managed to croak out.

"I want you to marry me."

She gasped. "What?"

His expression suggested he enjoyed the control he held over her. With a smug grin he repeated the proposal. "I said, that I want you to marry me."

Sigrid couldn't believe that he'd actually just proposed. She felt the warmth of his passionate gaze pierce her facade of indifference. He wanted to marry her!

"Just like that?" she questioned, forcing her wits to resurface.

"Well, of course. I want us to marry right away. We can take a wedding trip to Kansas City and stay in my parents' home. The place is massive and we won't be cramped for room."

"But Lindsborg is my home," she interjected.

"Lindsborg has been your home, but it doesn't have to stay that way."

Sigrid shook her head. "I must say, this comes at a great surprise. We scarcely know each other."

"We know each other better than most folks," he assured her. "Come sit with me and we can talk about all the things that are worrying you." He reached out for her arm, but Sigrid was unsure that she wanted him to touch her. Strange things happened to her mind when he touched her. Seeing her hesitation, Ruben held up his hands and backed away. "Please. Just come sit with me for a time."

Sigrid took a seat and stared at the wall over his head. "All of my family live in Lindsborg. My friends are here. My life is here. I don't want to live in the city. At least I don't think I do."

"But my dear, you've never seen the city. You've never been outside this tiny town in all of your life. You told me so, remember?" She nodded and he continued. "You have no idea what lies in wait for you out there. The opportunities are too numerous and too wondrous to even imagine. You can never grow bored there."

"I don't grow bored here," she countered.

Looking at Ruben with a new heart, Sigrid tried to honestly see herself in the role of his wife. He dressed immaculately in fine suits, and always looked the epitome of style and fashion. His hands were soft and clean, with perfectly trimmed nails and no calluses to mar their appearance. He would no doubt expect just such perfection from a wife.

"Family is very important to me, Ruben. The man I marry will have to understand that, and he will have to honor God, as well. God is the foundation for all I hold true and dear."

"I understand and completely agree with you." The words came without any appearance of discomfort.

She got up without warning and walked to the kitchen window. "I've grown to love this house and this land. My parents worked hard to make this a home, and now your railroad wants to destroy all of that and put in their depot and their roundhouse."

"So don't sell it to them."

His words were so matter-of-fact that Sigrid couldn't help but turn to look at him. "Just like that?"

He smiled. "Just like that. Don't sell it and they'll build elsewhere."

"But I thought this location was perfect."

Ruben rubbed his mustache. "It is, and it would make things go a whole lot better for all the people in this town. The railroad doesn't choose a site without weighing heavily the impact it will have on the townspeople. If the people aren't happy, the railroad is doomed to certain failure."

"I hadn't thought about making it easier for everyone else." Suddenly she felt very selfish. "I have to admit, I've only thought of my own pain. My own needs."

Ruben rose to his feet and slowly crossed the room. "As my wife, you need never worry about pain or comfort again. I can give you everything."

"But I have everything I want here."

He smiled tolerantly. "But there's so much more I want to give you. I want to show you the world, and I want to show *you* to the world. Will you at least think about my proposal?"

Sigrid swallowed hard and nodded. "All right. I'll think about it."

"Good. I'll expect you to give me an answer as soon as possible. After all, the holidays are nearly upon us and I know you'll be far too busy to give much thought over to a wedding then."

Sigrid nodded, but said nothing. Her mind was consumed with the weight of Ruben's proposal and all that it might mean to her.

He left without any further attempt to kiss her, even though for a moment Sigrid had feared that had been his definite intent. She turned back to the kitchen counter and sighed. How could she possibly keep her mind on work now?

She finished her tasks just before the last light of day faded into twilight. Lighting the lamps, Sigrid took down her mother's Bible and sat down to read. There had to be answers for the questions in her heart.

Her hand immediately opened to the tenth chapter of Matthew. Scanning down, she came upon verse sixteen which admonished, "Behold, I send you forth as sheep in the midst of wolves: be ye therefore wise as serpents, and harmless as doves."

Moder had often spoken of Satan's deception in appearing as one of the sheep in order to work his way into the flock.

"If you saw a wolf coming, you would shoot him, *ja?*" she could hear her mother question. "But when a stray sheep joins in, you think not so very much about it. You figure you will find the owner and return him, but he'll do no harm to graze with your own flock until that time. After all, he's just a sheep."

Erik had warned her that Ruben wasn't all that he appeared—that he wasn't one of them. He told her to mind herself around him, and his brotherly advice bothered her greatly.

Lord, I want to do the right thing. Selling the farm would help Ina and Sven in ways that I can't hope to help them. Giving this land up would benefit the town, and all of my friends and family would have a better life because of my sacrifice. She closed the Bible and laid her head atop it. *I don't mean to put a thing or place above the comfort and need of my loved ones. I guess I'm ready to let go, if that's what You want me to do. It doesn't feel good, or right, but if You want me to do this thing then please mark out the path.*

And as for Ruben and his proposal. She paused, trying to figure out what she should pray. *You know what he's asked of me, and You alone know if he's the one for me. I just feel so confused. There's Ruben, and then there's Erik. Ruben has asked me to marry him, and he seems to genuinely love me. Erik has asked me to marry him, and he seems to genuinely care about me, but I'm not so sure he loves me.*

And whom do you love? her heart seemed to ask.

"I wish I knew," she answered aloud.

Chapter 8

JAST KRANS
Yeast Wreath

1 package yeast	4 cups flour
3 T. sugar	1 tsp. salt
3 egg yolks	1 cup butter
1 cup warm milk	

Dissolve together yeast, sugar and ½ cup warm milk; set aside. Next, beat together egg yolks and ½ cup warm milk; set aside. Mix together flour, salt, and butter (this will be like pie crust). Add the yeast and egg yolk mixtures and mix well. Set in a cool place overnight.

3 egg whites	1 tsp. cinnamon
½ cup sugar	
Handful of nuts, dates, or raisins, if desired	
Oven at 350⁰F	

In the morning, divide into two portions and roll out thin. Mix 3 stiffly beaten egg whites with sugar and cinnamon and spread this on top of the dough. Sprinkle with nuts, dates, or raisins. Roll lengthwise and shape in a ring. Rise 1 hour or until doubled. Bake at 350⁰F for 20 minutes. Frost with ¾ cup powdered sugar blended with cream.

Erik sat in the cafe nursing his third cup of coffee. For longer than he cared to remember, he'd been coming here for meals instead of going to the Larsson house. He felt it was only fair to give Sigrid her head. She was going to have to decide for herself if he meant anything to her—anything more than friends and workers of the same ground.

Putting the cup down, Erik decided it was time to return to the fields. But just as he reached for his hat, the unmistakable voice of Ruben Carter sounded from the now open cafe door.

"Come on, Hank, I'll treat you to lunch and tell you where things stand."

Erik froze in place, wondering if he should confront Ruben with his concern for Sigrid. He wanted badly to warn the man to leave her alone, but it wasn't his place and so he held himself in check.

Ruben, clearly oblivious to anyone else in the cafe, took the booth directly behind Erik and continued his conversation. Never one to set out to eavesdrop, Erik couldn't help himself when Ruben brought up the subject of Sigrid and the farmstead.

"I figure if I can get her to marry me before Christmas," Ruben told his companion, "I can get her to sign over without too much difficulty."

"You mean you'll keep her so otherwise occupied she won't have time to worry about land, don't ya?" the man said with a dirty laugh.

Ruben chuckled. "Well, that will be one of the benefits of this whole scheme. She's not that bad to look at, although she's the same as the rest of these dirt-dumb farmers. She's actually happy to live here and wants to stay in Lindsborg."

"Maybe that'll change after you propose."

"I proposed yesterday," Ruben admitted.

Erik hadn't realized how hard he was gripping the coffee mug until his hand started to ache. He put the cup down and tried to refrain from jumping to his feet. He couldn't confront Ruben here. Not this way. Not now.

"Did she say yes?" the other man was now questioning.

"Not exactly, but I did my best to persuade her. If you know what I mean."

They laughed in a way that left Erik little doubt that Ruben had probably handled the matter in a most inappropriate way. But, he knew Sigrid, and he felt confident that she had probably put Ruben in his place in spite of what the man said to his friend.

"Sigrid will come around, and when she does," Ruben continued, "the land will be ours."

"I thought you had a deal with that brother of hers. Seems a sorry state of affairs that you should have to hitch yourself up with her in order to get the land."

"Her brother's willing to sell me the place, but he hates hurting Sigrid. I tried to play it smooth, let him think I understood his compassion. I let it drop and figured I'd work on Sigrid. If I can talk her into marriage, I shouldn't have any trouble getting her to give up the farm. After all, I made it clear that Kansas City could offer us both a great deal in the way of comfort and charm. After a couple of months there, I'll send her home to her brother. Then she can have her farm town and the railroad can have their depot and roundhouse."

"You mean divorce her?"

"Of course. I don't intend to stay married to someone like her," Ruben said in a voice that suggested how unthinkable such a matter could be. "Imagine trying to take her to New York. She could never hope to fit into my social circle. No, I've spent enough time listening to her stories of Swedish traditions and love of the land. I'll be glad to knock the dust of this town off my feet once and for all."

"But you'll have a good time with her first, I hope," the man said in a much lowered voice.

Ruben laughed. "Of course. I don't mind sampling country cooking, I just don't want it for the rest of my life."

The men laughed while Erik seethed. He wanted to punch Carter square in the nose, but more than that, he wanted to run to Sigrid and hide her away like a precious gem. How dare Carter talk of using her and then divorcing her! How would Sigrid ever live with the shame of such a thing?

The waitress came to serve the two men, and with her keeping them both completely occupied, Erik slipped out the back door of the cafe. He struggled to know what he should do. On one hand, if he went to Sigrid and told her the truth, she might not believe him. She might think that he was only speaking out of a jealous heart or worse yet, that he only wanted to keep her from giving Ruben the land.

"Lord," he whispered, stepping into the dusty alley, "this isn't an easy situation to be in. I don't know what to do to protect Sigrid." He paused and glanced heavenward with a smile. "But then again, I don't need to protect her when You're already on the job."

He walked down the alley and around the building, continuing to pray. *She needs to be kept safe, Lord. I don't know if I should tell her what I overheard, or leave it be. You know the answers, and You have a better picture of the truth than I do. What should I do?*

Erik paused beside the general store and looked down Main Street at their little town. He loved it here and he knew Sigrid loved it as well. The land and the community was as much a part of him as anything could possibly be, and he couldn't imagine his life in any way that didn't include living in Lindsborg.

Feeling his turmoil only moderately relieved, Erik sighed and made his decision. *If she asks me straightforward for the truth, I'll tell her. Otherwise, I won't volunteer anything.*

Moving down the street, another even more compelling thought came to mind. *What I need to do is ensure that she doesn't marry Ruben Carter.* He smiled to himself. *I just need to convince her that she should marry me instead of him.* Then his smile faded. Never having been one for romancing and courting women, especially given the fact that his eye had been on Sigrid for more than a decade, Erik wondered exactly how he should go about it.

As if on cue, Sigrid appeared—basket in hand—heading toward the general store. Erik swallowed hard. She looked wonderful. Her cheeks were rosy from the chill in the air and her eyes were bright and searching. He stepped out of the shadows and smiled, hoping she would smile in return—praying she wouldn't give him a cold shoulder.

"Erik!" she exclaimed, seeming surprised, but genuinely happy to see him. "I haven't seen you in forever."

The ease in which she spoke put Erik's pounding heart at rest. "I went to help Sven with the broomcorn."

"Oh," she said, nodding as if understanding some great mystery. "Have you finished?"

"Yes."

The silence hung between them for several moments. "Have you come to town for something in particular?" Erik finally asked.

"Oh, you know, the usual holiday things. With Advent, St. Lucia's Day, and all that goes with Christmas, I don't dare run out of sugar and flour. Not with all of my nieces and nephews to bake for. Oh, and I need some almonds. At least one almond," she said as if trying to burn it into memory.

Erik smiled. "Ah, making Risgrynsgrot?" He spoke of the favorite rice pudding that was always found at any Swedish Christmas celebration. The trick was to mix in one whole almond and whoever found it in their portion of pudding was said to be the next one to marry or have good fortune.

"Yes, that and about a hundred other things." She smiled and her blue eyes lit up as an idea appeared to come to her. "Say, if you aren't busy, why don't you come for dinner tonight. I'm trying out a new recipe for *jast krans* and I'd love for you to tell me what you think of it."

Erik felt his breathing quicken. It was as if their last meeting had never happened. She beamed her smile and talked as friendly and openly as she'd ever talked to him before. She was beautiful and charming and everything he longed for. Why couldn't she see that his love for her was sincere? "I'd like to come for dinner," he finally answered in a low, steady voice.

"Good. I'll see you at the usual time then." She turned to go into the general store, but Erik reached out to touch her arm.

"I...uh..."

"Yes?" She looked up at him, her eyes widening.

Erik felt unsure of himself. "It's just that, well..." What could he say? What should he say—that he missed her? That a moment didn't pass by during the day that he wasn't thinking of her? "Thanks for the invitation."

She nodded, and for a moment Erik almost thought he read disappointment in her eyes. Had she expected him to say something more?

He let her go and stared at the door to the general store for several minutes before ambling down the street. *Where do I go from here?* he wondered. He wondered, too, at her good mood and her pleasantries. Then a thought came unbidden to his mind. Maybe Carter's proposal had brought this about. Maybe her joy centered around contemplating a lifetime as the wife to Ruben Carter.

Erik frowned and his optimism faded. Maybe her invitation for dinner had been given in order to break the news to him. What if she announced that she planned to accept Carter's proposal? Erik felt his stomach tighten and begin to churn. There had to be some way to convince her that he loved her.

Tell her that you love her, his heart told him. Sit her down and tell her the truth? It was almost too much to think about, and Erik did the only thing that felt right and comfortable. He found his horse and went back to work.

❧

Later that night, after a quiet dinner with Sigrid, Erik found himself no closer to revealing the truth of his heart to her. She had presented him with a wonderful meal, but had gone to no special lengths to entertain him. She talked of her sister Ina and the baby that was on the way. She asked him if he would keep an eye on the house for her as she planned to spend the next few weeks with her sister.

"With the baby due," she had told Erik, "Ina isn't up to the usual holiday cooking. I promised I'd come lend a hand, and since she is on the other side of town, I thought I'd just as well stay on at her place."

Before he knew it, Erik had agreed to care for her livestock and watch over the house, but he hadn't found the right opportunity in which to share his heart. Kneeling beside his bed in prayer, Erik found a restlessness inside that would not be ignored.

"Father, help me," he murmured. "Help me to win her heart."

Chapter 9

LUSSEKATTER
St. Lucia Buns

2 pkgs. active dry yeast	1 cup milk, scalded
¾ cup sugar	6 cups flour
½ cup softened butter	2 eggs
1 tsp. salt	1 tsp. ground cardamom
½ tsp. powdered saffron	½ cup blanched almonds
(dissolved in 2 tsp. of milk)	(ground)
½ cup dark raisins	¾ cup lukewarm water
(optional)	

Soften yeast in lukewarm water. Dissolve thoroughly and add milk and sugar. Beat in 2 cups of the flour until mixture is smooth. Add butter, eggs, salt, raisins, almonds, cardamom, and saffron. Mix well. Add remaining flour and knead until dough is smooth and elastic.

Place dough in greased bowl, cover and let rise approximately 1½ hours. Punch down and let rise again for 30 to 40 minutes. Shape into various Lucia bun forms (description contained in chapter) and let rise for another 15 to 20 minutes. Bake at 350⁰F for 10 to 12 minutes. Makes 30 to 40 buns.

It was already December 12th, and with the celebration honoring St. Lucia being tomorrow, Sigrid would need to hurry to have the St. Lucia buns ready for the holiday. Pulling the dough from where it had risen, Sigrid began to form the buns into a variety of shapes.

First she made the priest locks or judge's wigs, as some called them. These were long thin strips, rolled in hand and shaped on top of each other until it resembled the old powdered wigs that magistrates wore in court. Each strip was curled up at the end to touch the curl above it. Next, Sigrid formed Christian crosses and Bethlehem stars. Then, just to keep with Swedish tradition, she made a great many buns in the shape of the *Julbock*, the Christmas Goat. Legend claimed that the goat would bring Christmas toys to good Swedish children. Straw replicas of the Julbock could be found in most of the Lindsborg homes during the Christmas season, and the children expected to find them on the Lucia platter.

The knock at Ina's kitchen door startled Sigrid for only a moment. Clarence was gone to town with the children in hopes of purchasing a Christmas gift for Ina. And, since Ina was sleeping, Sigrid had no other choice but to answer the door herself.

There stood Erik, with a light dusting of snow on his shoulders and head, his cheeks reddened from the wind and cold.

"What are you doing here?" she asked, mindless of her manners.

Erik laughed. "I came to see you."

"Well, you'd best come in then," she said, not understanding why she suddenly felt awkward in his presence.

Sigrid went back to the oven and checked on the buns. "Have a seat and I'll get you some coffee." Her heart skipped a beat and her stomach felt like a swirl of butterflies resided inside.

If it's possible, she thought, *he's more handsome than ever.* Then she pushed aside that line of thinking and tried to steady her nerves. Ever since she'd had him to supper the week before, he'd acted all tongue-tied and strange. She'd wondered what he was thinking, but it seemed rude to press him for an answer.

"Smells mighty good in here," Erik said.

Sigrid straightened and went to the cupboard for a cup. "I'm baking the St. Lucia buns," she told him and poured steaming coffee into the mug. "Ina's not feeling very good. I'm guessing the baby will probably come tonight or tomorrow."

She put the coffee down on the table before realizing that Erik held a wrapped package in his hands.

"This is for you," he said, holding out the gift.

"For me?" She knew her voice registered distress and disbelief. "It's too early for *Jul* gifts."

"It's not for *Jul*," he said quite seriously. "I've been doing a lot of thinking and there's some things that need settled between us."

She felt her mouth go down. "There are?"

"Just open the package and I'll explain."

She sat down at the table and pulled at the strings which held the paper in place. The paper fell away and inside she found two artfully carved wooden spoons. Tears came to her eyes.

"You know what these spoons represent," he more stated than questioned. She nodded but said nothing. "I figured it was time to speak my mind, Sigrid. I don't want to lose you to that Carter fellow. He's boasting all over town how he asked you to marry him, and I'm not giving you up without a fight."

Her head snapped up at this. "You want the land that bad?"

Erik slammed his fists down on the table. "It has nothing to do with the land.

I want to marry *you*. I know how you hold to tradition, so I carved the spoons for you and I'm here to ask you to be my wife."

Still she said nothing. She couldn't speak. Between the tears that were over-running her eyes and the lump in her throat, Sigrid was afraid to even try to talk.

"I know you think this is about the land, but it isn't," he continued. "Seeing that I have competition and that there's a real possibility you might slip away gave me cause to think. I don't want to lose you, Sigrid. I've loved you since you were a little girl."

At this Sigrid couldn't sit and face him any longer. All she'd ever hoped for was that he might actually declare his love for her. Why did he have to wait until now? Now, when Ruben was offering her the world. She walked away from the table, clutching the spoons to her breast. *What do I do?*

"Did you hear me, Sigrid? I love you. I want you to marry me." Erik came to where she stood with her back to him. He gently put his hands on her arms as if to turn her to face him.

This only caused Sigrid to draw her shoulders in tighter. She couldn't face him. She'd been such fool. Tears streamed down her cheeks. *He loves me. He wants to marry me because he loves me.* The wonder of it all was too much.

With a low groan that seemed something between anguish and anger, Erik dropped his hold and walked away. Sigrid thought he was taking his seat at the table until she heard the door open and close. She wanted to run after him, and had actually turned to get her coat when Ina called to her. Erik would have to wait.

❧

Throughout the night, Ina suffered in heavy labor to give birth to her sixth child. Sigrid stayed by her side, wiping her brow and praying. The breech-positioned infant girl was finally delivered by the doctor just after midnight, and Ina immediately bestowed the name of Bothilda upon the child. It was understood that she would be called Tilly, and Clarence thought it extremely good fortune that she had been born on St. Lucia's Day.

Sigrid's head had barely hit the pillow when Bridgett, the eldest daughter of the family, donned her white robe with the red sash. Yawning, Sigrid forced herself to get out of bed.

"I'll help you with the crown," she said, stifling a yawn.

Bridgett, taking her role as the *Lucia Bride* or *Queen of Lights* very seriously, nodded and positioned the wreath on her head and gingerly made her way down the loft stairs. Sigrid followed, finishing up the buttons of her dress as she went.

Bridgett arranged buns and cups on a tray while Sigrid made coffee.

"I love this day," Bridgett announced. "I always feel so special."

"I envy you," Sigrid said, and yawned once again. "I never got to be the Lucia Bride when I was growing up. In fact, as youngest, I didn't have a lot of privileges."

"*Moder* says you made a wonderful sacrifice to insure the happiness and well-being of your family."

Sigrid couldn't hide her surprise. "Ina said that?"

"Sure." Bridgett brought out the candles and handed them to Sigrid. "She said you did her a special favor by taking care of *Mormor*. She was afraid that since she'd just married *Fader*, she might have to take *Mormor* to live with them, and," Bridgett giggled for the first time that day, "she wanted to have *Fader* all to herself."

Sigrid smiled. "I can well imagine." She positioned the candles, thinking of Ina's gratitude and how she'd not only felt those things, but shared them with her daughter as well. It was rather like an honor, and Sigrid suddenly loved Ina more than ever.

Bridgett waited while Sigrid lit the last of the candles. She held the platter proudly and smiled. "Well, here I go." She took a deep breath and began to sing. "*Sankta Lucia, ljusklara hagring, Sprid i var vinter natt, glans av den fagring.*"

Sigrid smiled and thought of the words. *Santa Lucia, thy light is glowing, Through darkest winter night, comfort bestowing.* She thought of their traditions and how they honored this young martyr. Legend in Sweden held that Lucia, a young medieval saint, brought food to the hungry in southern Sweden. But Sigrid also knew the celebration to date back even further. The first Lucia was a young Christian girl who gave her entire bridal dowry away to the poor folk of her village. She was later accused of witchcraft and burned at the stake on December 13, in the year 304 A.D. But no matter which Lucia you considered, Sigrid knew that the celebration was a representation of sending light into the darkness.

"Lucia brings the symbol of the light to come," her *moder* had told her when she was very young. "Jesus is the light who comes to us and makes our darkest night to shine as day."

Sigrid wrapped her arms around her. She could hear Bridgett singing to her family, and the sound left an aching in her heart. She had no family to celebrate with. As the spinster aunt, she had to borrow upon her sibling's family. A tear slid down on her cheek and the only thing she desired in that moment was to find Erik and tell him that she loved him.

"I love him," she whispered. "How could I have ever doubted it?"

Suddenly, even the thought of kissing Ruben sounded less than appealing. How had she managed to get so completely swept away? Was she so desperate for affection and attention that she couldn't see how Erik's quiet love had been there all along?

Chapter 10

KOTTBULLAR
Swedish Meat Balls

½ lb. ground beef	½ lb. ground pork
2 eggs (beaten)	½ cup bread crumbs
½ cup cream	½ tsp. salt
(heated to a boil)	¼ tsp. pepper
¼ tsp. allspice	3 T. onion
	(finely minced)

Soak bread crumbs in cream and set aside. Blend the remaining ingredients together. Pour cream and softened bread crumbs into meat mixture and mix well. Roll into balls the size of walnuts and fry until outside is browned. Put into a baking dish with 2 T. oil and 1 T. water; cover and bake at 325°F for 1 hour.

Sigrid barely waited until the sun was fully risen before pulling on her coat and boots. With mysterious excuses delivered to Ina and Clarence, she made her way home in the pale pink light of dawn. Grateful that there was only a faint dusting of snow on the ground, Sigrid pressed toward town with only one thought in mind. . .Erik.

She had to find him. She had to tell him how she felt and how she'd ignored those feelings for most of her life. He'd always just been there: comforting, familiar, loving, although she couldn't see it for the nearness of it. Feeling a song in her heart, she hummed Santa Lucia and forced herself not to run.

Chilled to the bone, but warm in spirit, Sigrid crossed Lindsborg's Main Street and hurried in the direction of home. She'd just passed from town when Ruben came from seemingly nowhere.

"Sigrid! I was hoping to see you today. I was just on my way to your house."

She stopped and looked at him sternly, wondering what it was about him that had held her captive for so long.

"What?" Ruben questioned. "Isn't my hat on straight?" He reached up as if to adjust it.

"No, it isn't that." She smiled, not realizing how appealing she looked.

Ruben swept her into his arms, mindless of the very public scene they were making. "I've come for an answer to my proposal. You've put me off long enough." He tried to kiss her, but Sigrid turned her face away and pushed at his arms.

"Let me go, Ruben. I can't marry you."

Ruben dropped his hold and stared at her in surprise. "What do you mean, you can't marry me?"

"I don't love you, Ruben. I can't marry you, because I'm in love with someone else. I'm sorry." She didn't wait for his response but instead kept walking toward home. Home and Erik. She knew he'd be close by and whether he was caring for her livestock or working in his own barn, she would find him and declare her love to him.

"You can't be serious," he said, catching up to her.

She picked up speed and nodded. "But I am."

Ruben grabbed her and pulled her away from the road. Pushing her up against the thick trunk of a cottonwood tree, he glared at her. "You can't do this to me. I have plans."

"I'm sorry." His grip tightened. "Let me go, Ruben."

"No. You're being stupid. It isn't like something better is going to come along."

She smiled. "Something better already has come along. I just didn't realize that he'd been there all along."

"You're coming with me. We're getting married."

Sigrid's mouth dropped open as Ruben dragged her along behind him. She began protesting, yelling, almost screaming for him to leave her alone. Then suddenly, without warning, Sigrid felt her free arm being pulled in the opposite direction. Looking back, she found Erik.

"Let her go, Carter. You heard for yourself, she wants nothing to do with you."

Ruben dropped his hold, completely intimidated by the huge Swede. He opened his mouth as if to say something, then growled and took off in the direction of Main Street.

Sigrid looked up at Erik, not knowing what to say. Her heart was full to busting with the love she felt inside. He had come to save her once again.

Erik said nothing, but simply took hold of her arm and led her home.

❧

Once inside the warmth of her kitchen, Sigrid felt shy and uncertain. What if she declared her love and Erik no longer wanted her? She swallowed her pride and decided the best thing to do was be honest.

"I didn't expect to see you today," Erik said softly.

"I know." She tried to think of what to say next. "I had to see you."

"Why?"

She drew a deep breath and faltered. Lowering her gaze, she looked at her hands.

"Why, Sigrid?" Erik repeated.

"Because I love you," she whispered.

"What?"

She looked up and found him smiling. He'd heard all right, but he wanted to hear the words again. "I came home to tell you that I love you, and if you still think you want to marry me, then I'd love nothing more."

Erik laughed. "I suppose I could tolerate the idea."

Sigrid smiled and raised a single brow. "Only tolerate?"

"Well, I guess you've got me there."

He got to his feet and came to take her in his arms. Sigrid melted against him, feeling her heart pounding so hard that she was certain he could hear it. She looked up into his eyes and found all the love she'd hoped to find. "Do I really have you?" she whispered.

Just before his lips touched hers in a passionate kiss, Sigrid heard him whisper, "You've always had me."

After the Julotta services at church on Christmas morning, Erik and Sigrid joined the rest of her family at Ina's house. The smorgasbord was laid out with all of the traditional foods of their ancestry. Pickled herring, Swedish meatballs, lutefisk, ostkaka and, of course, rice pudding were among the many overflowing platters of goodies.

Sven offered a prayer at Ina's request, and as he finished, Erik requested everyone's attention to announce that he and Sigrid were to be married as soon as the holidays were completed.

"Oh, Sigrid!" Ina squealed in girlish delight. "I'm so happy for you."

Sigrid embraced her sister. "That's not all. Erik and I intend to pay you and Sven the same amount of money that the railroad is offering for the farm. We want to live on the farmstead. I want to raise our children where *Moder* and *Fader* worked so hard to make us happy."

Erik lost no time in pulling papers from his pocket. "I know it's Christmas, but this is to show you we mean what we say." He handed the papers to Sven. "I hope you will understand how much this means to both of us."

"Of course we understand," Ina said.

"But I struck an agreement with the railroad," Sven replied rather sheepishly.

"No money changed hands," Ina reminded him. "Besides, I never agreed to it. Erik talked to me some time ago, and I thought his proposal was much better."

Just then a knock sounded on the door and Bridgett went to open it. Ruben Carter didn't wait to be announced, but pushed his way past the girl and came to where Sven was still studying the paper Erik had given him.

"I want to finish our agreement," he told Sven.

"Sorry you had to come all this way, Mr. Carter," Ina said, before Sven could reply. "We aren't selling the land to the railroad. Sven had no right to make an agreement without Sigrid's and my approval."

"He's the man of the family, isn't he?" He glared at Sigrid as he asked the question.

"*Ja*," Ina replied, "but Swedish women are just as tenacious as Swedish men."

"Sorry, Carter," Sven offered apologetically. "I guess I'm outvoted."

"But we had an agreement."

"It wasn't a lawful arrangement, Carter," Erik said, moving in between Ruben and Sven. "But this is." He took the papers from Sven and held them up. "I'm buying the property with my wife."

Ruben threw Sigrid a sneering look of disbelief. "He's only doing this to get your land."

Sigrid didn't want to face him in an argument. "No, he did it because he loves me," she said as she turned and walked from the room to avoid any further confrontation.

Taking herself outside, Sigrid prayed that the matter would be concluded without her. She didn't like the way Ruben looked at her, and she didn't want to listen to his threats or foulmouthed accusations. Walking the full length of the wraparound porch, Sigrid had just come to the front when an angry Ruben bounded out of the house. He instantly saw her and stopped.

"I never wanted you for my wife. I wanted the land, just like Lindquist." The words were delivered with all the hate and bitterness that Ruben's face featured. "You aren't worth the trouble, Sigrid." He stormed off down the path and left her to stare after him.

His words should hurt, she thought. But they didn't. She only felt sorry for Ruben, and more sure of Erik. What did hurt, was that she had ever believed Ruben's flowery words of love.

Turning away, she found Erik standing at the end of the porch. He'd heard everything Ruben had said, and he seemed to watch her for any sign of regret in her choice. And then, Sigrid saw something more in his expression. He showed no surprise or alarm at the words he'd heard. Only patient compassion as he waited for her reaction. *He knew! He knew all along and yet he never told me!* Her heart swelled with love for him, and she smiled.

Erik held open his arms and Sigrid eagerly went to him, cherishing the warmth he provided against the cold of winter and Ruben's declaration.

"You knew, did you?" she whispered as he kissed the top of her head.

"Yes."

"And you never told me because you knew I wouldn't have believed you."

"Yes." He kissed her again.

"I was such a fool, Erik."

"Yes." This time he lifted her chin with his warm, callused fingers and kissed her on the forehead.

"*Moder* always said I could trust you. I should have believed her. . .and you."

"Yes." He kissed her right cheek.

"I guess love was so close I just couldn't see it. Forgive me?"

"Yes." His low, husky voice warmed her as much as the kiss he placed on her left cheek.

Sigrid smiled and pressed herself closer. "Love me?"

"Oh, yes," he half moaned, half whispered, and pressed his lips to hers.

Sigrid sighed and wrapped her arms around his neck. She returned his kiss with matched enthusiasm and felt the heat of passion radiate throughout her body.

He pulled away, and Sigrid opened her eyes to find him grinning as though he'd just won first place in a race. "*God Jul*, darling," he whispered.

"Merry Christmas to you." She strained on tiptoe and pulled his face back to hers. "The first of many." She kissed him gently.

"Kisses or Christmases?" he whispered as their lips parted.

"What?"

"The first of many kisses or Christmases?" he teased.

She didn't hesitate. Kissing him again, she pulled away to whisper in his ear. "Both."

Circle of Blessings

by Deborah Raney

Dedication

In memory of my beloved grandmothers,
Dorothy Teeter and Helen Reed,
and my dear great-grandmother, Stella Rankin.

Thy righteousness also, O God, is very high,
who hast done great things: O God, who is like unto thee!
Thou, which hast shewed me great and sore troubles,
shalt quicken me again, and shalt bring me up
again from the depths of the earth.
PSALM 71:19–20

Prologue

Dakota Territory, 1864

It was almost closing time, and in all of his seventeen years, James Collingwood could not remember being so bone-weary as he felt tonight. It seemed almost more than he could do to trudge one more time across the large dining room to the hotel's kitchen and lift yet another pot of coffee.

The Christmas crowd had kept all the staff hopping this week. He had put in more than ten hours himself today—and that with only five hours of sleep last night. Of course it was no one's fault but his own that he'd chosen to keep the candle burning and his nose in a book into the wee hours of the morning.

He ran a hand through his hair and mentally shook off the self-pity that threatened to take up residence in his mind. He knew all too well that he was lucky to be here, fortunate to be working long hours. If not for the mercy his employer had shown him, he might well be sitting under lock and key in the jailhouse across the street. He owed Mr. Browne more than restitution for his foolish offense. He owed him his life. Still, in spite of his gratitude that he was a free man able to provide for the needs of his mother and sister, his deep-held desire to continue his education consumed him. He wanted to attend the university and make something more of his life. He had begun to set aside a minuscule portion of his wages—after paying Mr. Browne the sum they'd agreed upon for restitution, of course. But he'd already missed the deadline for the new term at St. Bartholomew's Academy over in Clairemore, and if his savings didn't multiply any faster in the months ahead, it was doubtful he'd get in for the following term, either.

"Dear Lord," he prayed, weaving his way through the queue of waiters lined up for their orders, "if You desire for me to attend the university, I know You'll supply my needs. Help me to leave it in Your hands." It was not a new prayer. He'd bothered the Almighty with those words a dozen times in the past week. And he intended to bother Him as many times as it took to receive an answer. If that answer was no, he would accept it with grace; but until he heard otherwise, he would pray.

He took a steaming granite pot from the stove and carried it back out to the dining room.

"Care for more coffee, Sir?" he asked the gentleman seated at the head of a small corner table."

"Why, yes," the diner said, "I believe I will have one last cup. Thank you."

The family at this table was pleasant and undemanding. Unlike some of the hotel's patrons, who treated him like a lowly serf, this man and his wife had engaged him in polite conversation and had even inquired about his family. Throughout the evening, James had enjoyed watching their interaction. The couple chatted quietly yet were attentive to their children—an infant, who slept in a basket at their feet, and a talkative little girl of ten or eleven.

Yet something about watching the little family caused a deep ache in the region of James's heart. He could scarcely remember what it was like to be part of a real family. His father had died when he was a tot, and his mother could hardly *be* a mother when all her time was taken up being a nurse to his sister. He didn't fault Mama—or Sylvia. He'd lived long enough to know that they hadn't chosen their lots in life. And in spite of everything, he knew Mama loved him.

He poured coffee for the man's wife, checked on his other tables, and went back to the kitchen. Mr. Browne met him at the door.

"James, are you still here?"

"Yes, Sir."

The older man put a hand on James's shoulder. "Go on home. I'll finish up for you here. You've been putting in some long days."

"I don't mind, Sir."

Mr. Browne smiled and clapped him on the shoulder. "Go on now. I'll hold your gratuities for you."

"Oh, I'm not worried about the tips, Sir. They never amount to much anyway." He tried to make a joke of it, but the truth was, every copper that was laid on the table put him that much closer to the academy.

Ten minutes later, as James shoved his arms into the ragged sleeves of his coat, Mr. Browne came into the cloakroom and held out an envelope to him.

James questioned him with knit brows. But Mr. Browne merely thrust the envelope into his hands. James opened the loose flap and peered inside. A crisp bill with the likeness of Christopher Columbus engraved on its front stared back at him. It was a five-dollar note—one of the newly issued bank notes that James had seen pass through the hotel's cash register on occasion. In fact, there had been several of the bills in the till the night he'd foolishly helped himself to its contents.

He shook off the memory. "It's not payday, is it, Sir?" Even with the extra hours he'd put in, this was far more than he was owed.

"No, James, it's not payday. But this is yours. It has your name on it."

James turned the envelope over in his hands. Sure enough, his name was inked boldly on the front. "I don't understand," he told his employer. "What is this for?"

"One of your patrons left it on the table."

"Are you sure?" He inspected the envelope again. "There's no last name. There must be some mistake, Mr. Browne. I–I can't accept this."

"You can and you will, Mr. Collingwood. Apparently someone feels you offered exceptional service tonight."

"But. . ." He looked from the envelope to his employer and back. "Five dollars, Mr. Browne! My service couldn't have possibly been *that* exceptional. Do you know who left it?"

"I couldn't say, James. I couldn't say. But it could not be more rightfully yours. You take it and have a Merry Christmas. Go on home and get some rest now." Mr. Browne turned and disappeared into the dining room.

James stared after the man in stunned silence as realization washed over him. The envelope he held in his hands was the answer to the prayer with which he had long hounded heaven. Added to the small amount he had saved already, he was only a few dollars short of making tuition for next term.

It was all he could do not to sink to his knees on the cloakroom floor in humble gratitude.

And that was exactly what he *would* do the moment he arrived home.

Chapter 1

Dakota Territory, 1871

Stella Bradford hurried across the campus of St. Bartholomew's Academy, a stack of textbooks in her arms and a bulging drawstring bag looped over one shoulder. The petticoat beneath her long-sleeved cotton dress clung to her legs, and with her free hand she dabbed beads of moisture from her brow with a crumpled handkerchief. *One should not have to perspire in October!* If she didn't hurry, she was going to be late for class, and it would be the second time this week. She was having enough trouble with this infernal English grammar class as it was. It certainly wouldn't help matters to be late again.

The tower clock in the center of the campus quadrangle began to chime the hour, and Stella lifted her skirts above her ankles and broke into a very unladylike trot. She rounded the ivy-draped corner of Andrews Hall at top speed but was halted in her tracks when she bumped headlong into a broad masculine chest. The only thing that kept her from stumbling to the brick walk beneath her feet was the strong pair of hands that reached out to grab her by the shoulders.

"Whoa, Miss! Watch where you're going there." The voice was as deep as the brown eyes that looked down into hers.

"Oh, p–pardon me," she stuttered, "but I'm about to be late for class." She took a step back, out of the man's grasp.

The last chime of the carillon clock died away on the still autumn air, and Stella gave a little gasp of dismay.

"It looks to me as though you *are* late," the gentleman told her. "And at the reckless speed you were going, I'd venture to say you would have arrived so out of breath that you might as well not have bothered going at all."

"Please," she pled impatiently. "Let me pass. I simply can't miss this class again."

"Oh, I see," he said, a rather wicked gleam in his eyes. "So you make a habit of tardiness? And let me guess—you are not exactly a candidate for honors in this particular class?"

She stamped her foot and took another step back. *Of all the impudent—*

She did not have time for this. Donning her most patronizing smile, she told

310

him, "I do appreciate your concern, Mister. . ."

"Collingwood," he supplied, tipping an imaginary hat. "James Collingwood."

"I appreciate your concern, Mr. Collingwood, but I cannot waste my time standing here arguing about either my habits nor my grades—as if it were any of your business!"

"Or," he said.

"I beg your pardon?"

"The correct word is 'or.' *Either* my habits *or* my grades. It's 'either, or' and 'neither, nor.' "

Of all the nerve! How dare this complete stranger stand here and correct my grammar!

He folded his arms across a broad chest and stepped back to gaze at her. "And let me guess," he said. "English Grammar is the class you're tardy for?"

"For which you are tardy," she shot back.

He raised an eyebrow. "Pardon me?"

"The correct phrase is 'the class for which you are tardy.' It is not proper to end a sentence in a preposition." She bobbed her chin for emphasis, crossed her arms, and glared at him, pleased beyond words to have beat him at his own game.

The corners of his lips curled in a slow smile. "Touché, Miss. I stand corrected."

Recognizing his deference to her, Stella's smile became genuine. She turned, ready to continue on to class, but remembering her manners, she tossed an apology over her shoulder. "I *am* sorry to have bumped into you. And thank you for. . .for catching me."

Stella hurried on her way, her face flushed and warm—and from more, she feared, than the warm sun of an Indian summer.

The campus was nearly empty, and Mr. Collingwood's winsome smile still lingered in her mind when she stepped inside Voorhaven Hall a few minutes later. The heels of her shoes clicked on the tiled floor and echoed through the spacious corridor, tattling on her tardiness to anyone who was listening. Both doors to the classroom were closed, but Stella heard noisy chattering inside. Behind the frosted beveled glass in the front door, boisterous, flitting shadows testified that the session had not yet been called to order. She opened the door and was relieved to see that Dr. Whitestone had not arrived. She quickly made her way to her assigned desk at the back of the room. She slipped into her seat, pulled the drawstring bag open, and rummaged inside for her fountain pen and notebook.

A few minutes later, the door swung open and the class quieted immediately. Stella followed the other students' collective gaze to the door, but it was not Dr. Whitestone's profile she saw behind the frosted pane. Instead, the shadowy silhouette behind the door looked vaguely familiar. Recently familiar. She took in a sharp breath as the man she'd nearly bowled over on campus a few minutes ago stepped into the room and placed his small valise on the oak desk at the front of the room. Without looking up, he unfastened the latch on the case and took out a bulky textbook, then stepped behind the podium.

Clearing his throat loudly, he looked over the room, waiting until he had their undivided attention. "Good afternoon," he said. "Dr. Whitestone took ill suddenly, so I'll be substituting for him this hour. My name is Mr. Collingwood and I'm new to the English department here at the academy."

His gaze moved from student to student in the large classroom, and Stella thought she saw an amused glimmer of recognition when he noticed her shrinking in her seat at the back of the room. He turned and picked up a stubby length of chalk from the lip of the blackboard. "Please open your texts to page ninety-two, and copy the three sentences at the top of the page into your notebooks."

As they worked, the studious sounds of chalk on slate and pen nub on pad filled the otherwise quiet room. When the substitute had finished chalking the sentences on the board, the students went to work diagramming them.

Once nouns and verbs had been labeled, Stella was completely lost. She was far more concerned with the dangling hangnail on her left pinkie finger than with the dangling participle Mr. Collingwood was so intent on identifying. *Why does it matter?* she thought, allowing herself to be carried away on a daydream. She wanted to be an architect, not a grammarian. She loved the logic and precision of mathematics. She couldn't care less about the structure of the sentences on the board. But let her study the structural design of the historic buildings on campus. Now *there* was an interesting and worthwhile pursuit.

"Isn't that right, Miss Bradford?" a bass voice broke into her reverie.

"Um. . .I—I'm sorry. Could you repeat the question, please?"

The other students tittered like grammar school children, and Stella felt the blood rise to her cheeks.

Mr. Collingwood chose to ignore her and turned to another student who was waving his hand madly. "Yes, Mr. . ." The instructor referred quickly to his seating chart. "Mr. Granger?"

Peter Granger smugly answered the question—something about noun-verb agreement that meant absolutely nothing to Stella. She slunk a little lower in her seat. After forty interminable minutes, during which Stella prayed fervently that she would not be called upon again, the bell in the hallway finally sounded, and Mr. Collingwood dismissed them.

Stella attempted to blend in with the flow of students and sneak out the back door, but she was stopped short. "Miss Bradford?"

She turned to find James Collingwood beckoning her with a slender finger. "I'd like to see you for a moment, please."

She stepped back and waited for the last student to file out, then wove her way through the labyrinth of desks to the front of the room. "Yes?" she said, forcing her sweetest smile.

He gazed at her thoughtfully. "You don't much want to be here, do you?" he said finally.

"Here at the academy? Why, of course I do! I—"

"No," he interrupted. "I mean in this grammar class."

She had the decency to hang her head. "I'm sorry, Sir. I–I just don't understand it. It makes no sense to me. And frankly—" Suddenly feeling brave, she plunged in with her reasoning, gathering confidence like steam as she went. "Frankly, I see no reason why anyone needs to know whether a verb is active or inactive or whether a noun is proper or not. I mean, really, Mr. Collingwood, when you are on the street, how likely are you to strike up an intriguing conversation on the topic of dangling participles?"

He threw back his head and laughed. For a moment she was inclined to feel that he was laughing *at* her, but the warm gleam in his eyes assured her otherwise.

"Miss Bradford—I do have your name right, don't I?" he asked, running his finger down the seating chart again.

She nodded.

"You may be correct in your observation. However, I have not yet achieved a powerful enough position here at the academy to do away with the grammar requirement, and until such day as that has been accomplished, I'm afraid you shall be compelled to remain in Dr. Whitestone's class and learn enough to earn a passing grade."

She conceded with a slump of her shoulders.

He laughed again. "Oh, come now. It can't be that awful, can it? Dare I remind you that this class is meant to be merely a refresher course? Didn't you learn to diagram a sentence in your high school?"

"I could never make sense of it," she said flatly.

"Ahh. . .Well, Dr. Whitestone tells me he has suggested that you work with a tutor to get your marks to a more acceptable level in this class."

She nodded slowly, wondering how he could have known this. "Yes. I'm supposed to have my first session tomorrow, though I don't know what good it will do."

James Collingwood took a small appointment book from his inside breast pocket and leafed through it. "I don't know if he has mentioned it to you yet, but I feel it is only fair to inform you that Dr. Whitestone has appointed me to be your tutor."

As if he thought she would require proof, he pointed to a neatly printed notation in the logbook. Sure enough, there, beneath tomorrow's date, on the line reserved for four o'clock, was her name.

She gaped at him. "*You* are the tutor I've been assigned to?"

"I am the tutor *to whom* you have been assigned, yes. And one you are obviously in desperate need of," he said, with a sidewise grin.

Her mind scrambled to think of a comeback. True, he had ended his pathetic quip in a preposition; but she didn't dare argue with him, for she realized with dismay that his words were correct—in substance, if not in grammar.

Chapter 2

James Collingwood locked up the classroom and plodded down the hall, completely drained after a long day of filling in for Arthur Whitestone. As he stepped from the building, he shielded his eyes against the waning afternoon sunlight and started across the campus lawn. Though autumn had begun to paint the campus in its annual array of gold and scarlet and James looked forward to the chill air the season would bring, for now, he savored the warmth of the sun on his face.

He breathed a contented sigh and quickened his step. The ghost of what he had once been sometimes haunted his thoughts; but on days like this, the satisfaction he found in teaching managed to eclipse the unchangeable truth of his past. Working with Dr. Whitestone's students had reminded him all over again how greatly his life had been redeemed, how readily God could remake a worthless sinner into a willing servant.

Upon his graduation from St. Bartholomew's Academy the previous year, James had been offered a job as an assistant to his professor and mentor, Arthur Whitestone, the head of St. Bart's English department.

For this first year, his job mostly entailed grading papers and serving as a secretary of sorts to Dr. Whitestone. The work provided a modest income while he continued postgraduate studies at the academy. His ultimate desire was to become a professor himself. He had discovered the deepest fulfillment whenever he was given an opportunity to preside in the classroom.

And now, at his mentor's request, he'd taken on an additional assignment—one that would test his mind, not to mention his patience. Dr. Whitestone had asked him to tutor a student, the daughter of the department head's longtime friend Marcus Bradford. James had agreed without hesitation. He loved to teach, the extra money would be a blessing, and besides, how difficult could it be to help a first-year student with the basics of English grammar?

He smiled to himself, remembering the two exchanges he'd had with the young woman since then. Had he met Stella Bradford before Dr. Whitestone's proposition, he might have spent a bit more time in prayer before agreeing to the job—and he might have negotiated for a higher wage as well. Yes, he would have all he could handle, attempting to impart a grammatical rule or two into the brain of that little spitfire. But he welcomed a challenge, and the distraction would be good for him. With her halo of sunny curls and that engaging wit, James could see how Stella Bradford might, indeed, become quite a distraction.

Leaving the grounds of St. Bart's, he headed east. His sister's boardinghouse, where he lived, was almost a mile from the college. He didn't relish the thought of making this walk once winter set in. On a day like today, it was difficult to believe that blue skies would soon give way to snow flurries and bitter winds, but it would happen soon enough. This was the Dakota Territory, after all. He walked past the lumber mill on the edge of town. Here, at least, business seemed to be booming in the postwar economy; and James offered up a little prayer of thanksgiving. He knew too well the despair of financial hardship and what it could do to a man.

In front of him, the tattered slate shingles of the three-story boardinghouse rose through the trees, and he quickened his pace. He wondered how Sylvia was feeling. His sister worked far too hard. Since her husband's death two years ago, she hadn't had much choice. He would be glad when his tuition was finally paid and his first wages were in the bank so he could be of more help to her. How he would manage to get her to *allow* him to help, he wasn't sure. He knew Sylvia still felt guilty for the trouble he'd gotten into, though the Lord knew that his sister was no more to blame than God Himself. Why, she'd been a mere girl when it had all happened. Still, he'd committed his crime in an attempt to help her, and Sylvia seemed intent on making it up to him somehow.

As he opened the gate to the yard, he spotted his sister on the wide front porch. Wearing a light cotton dress and wielding a decrepit broom, she beat at the handful of prematurely fallen leaves that skittered across the whitewashed floor. The surface was already clean enough to eat from. She smiled when she noticed James coming up the walk, but Sylvia's smiles never quite reached her eyes.

"Hi, Sis." He bounded up the steps and planted a kiss on her smooth, pale cheek.

"Hi, Jimmy. How was school?"

He laughed. "You make me sound like a little boy just home from grammar school."

"If the shoe fits. . . ," she said wryly.

"And how was your day?" he asked, ignoring her joke. "Did Mr. Graves bring the rent money by?"

"Half of it." She sighed.

He shook his head and grumbled under his breath. "Well, that's something, at least." Unknown to Sylvia, he had delivered a stern lecture to Herbert Graves just last evening. How was his sister supposed to make a living—let alone pay for the medicine she needed—when her tenants refused to pay their rent?

"Well," he brightened, "you go ahead and see the doctor. I took on a tutoring job today. That'll tide us over."

Sylvia shook the broom at him. "There is no 'us' about it, Jimmy. That money should go to your tuition loan," she scolded. "I don't want you spending your hard-earned dollars on me."

Gently, James took the broom from her work-roughened hands and ushered her into the front parlor. "I'll spend my hard-earned dollars however I choose. And if I choose to spend them on my favorite sister, what business is it of yours?"

She rolled her eyes, but he heard the love and gratitude in her voice when she ordered him, "Go wash up for supper. It's just you, me, and old Mrs. Bellingham tonight."

❧

James sat facing the door of the small study hall in Robinson Library. For the third time in as many minutes, he pulled his watch from his vest pocket and inspected it. She was already five minutes late. Much as he hated to begin their very first tutoring session with a reprimand, he would not tolerate tardiness. Stella Bradford had demonstrated with their very first meeting that she had no regard for punctuality. Well, *his* time was valuable, even if hers was not.

A clatter in the hallway beyond the door interrupted his thoughts, and a few seconds later, as her perky countenance lit up the room, he quickly decided to let her tardiness go unmentioned for this one time. If it happened again, she would hear about it in no uncertain terms.

He rose from his chair. "Good day, Miss Bradford. Please, come in. Have a seat."

"Good afternoon, Mr. Collingwood. I do apologize for being late," she said, her breaths coming in labored, rapid gasps. "I confess, I don't know my way around the library yet."

He pulled out the chair beside his at the table. "Please, sit down. . .unless, of course, you'd like a moment to catch your breath."

She looked at him carefully, as though she were trying to decide if he was angry. He returned her gaze with a smile meant to put her at ease, and she took the chair.

"Thank you. I'm sure you must think that I am forever tardy."

He wasn't sure how to respond to that. What else *was* he to think? But she quickly relieved him of the need to reply.

"Well," she said brightly, opening her textbook decisively and resting her chin on one slender hand. "We'd best get started. I fear you have taken on a hopeless case in me, Mr. Collingwood, but I'm willing to give it a try if you are."

"All right," he said, amused by her brashness. "Let's begin with the sentences we worked on in class yesterday—since you seemed to be a bit lost. That was on page ninety-two, I believe."

While she copied the lines onto her notebook, he scooted his chair back a few inches so he could watch her discreetly. Her unruly curls were fugitives from the hairpins meant to hold them in place, and they formed a becoming halo about her fair face. He watched with amusement as she traced each letter simultaneously with pen and with tongue, like a first grader just learning to write. Surprisingly,

316

the resulting script was elegant and refined.

She glanced up and caught him watching her. "Yes?"

"You—you have lovely penmanship," he finally stuttered.

"Why, thank you. Shall we begin?"

"Of course."

He began to walk her through the process of naming the parts of speech in the sample sentences. But once past the basics of noun and verb, she floundered. He patiently defined adverbs and adjectives, but it seemed obvious from her blank stare that he was not getting through to her.

Finally, with exasperation in her voice, she laid down her pen and turned to him. "Why must we dissect this sentence as though it were a frog in the biology laboratory? I can see quite clearly that it is a frog and that it can jump. Isn't it enough to know that? Why is it also necessary for me to know that the slimy thing has a heart and lungs and muscles and other ghastly parts? Will the frog jump any farther once I know how to label its parts?"

James scrambled to think of a way to counter her charming metaphor, but before he could utter a word, she answered her own question.

"No, it will not jump any farther because the poor creature will be *dead!*"

He burst out laughing. She certainly had a point.

But she ignored his laughter, her voice rising an octave. "Truly, Mr. Collingwood, I see no use whatsoever in tearing apart a perfectly fine sentence when I can understand its meaning quite well *without* taking it apart."

An idea came to him. He placed his fountain pen on the table and leaned back in his chair. "What, might I inquire, is your field of study here at the academy, Miss Bradford?"

"I am going to be an architect." By the resolute tilt of her chin, he suspected that she'd had to defend her ambition on more than one occasion. It *was* a highly unusual aspiration for a young woman.

"An architect, eh? Well, that is a fine goal. But let me ask you: Do you take the same attitude toward the study of architecture that you seem to have taken with the study of the English language?"

"I don't understand."

"Do you believe it unimportant to understand how a building is constructed before you go about designing one yourself? Does it not matter a great deal that you know exactly how the beams and rafters should be secured? That the cornerstone be square and precisely placed?"

"Of course it matters," she said. "But I don't desire to build sentences, Mr. Collingwood. I desire to build buildings."

"Ah. . ." He held up a finger in triumph. "But whether you desire to or not, you *have* been 'building' sentences since you walked in that door"—he indicated the door to the study room with a slight tilt of his head—"and I must inform you that several of those sentences have been quite poorly constructed. Now—"

She opened her mouth, but he cut her off with an upraised hand.

"Please. Hear me out. When you are established in the business of architecture, do you not think it would be to your advantage to be able to communicate with your clientele in a grammatically correct fashion?"

"Certainly, but—"

He sighed and held up a warning hand. "Miss Bradford, I think it is clear that I am not going to convince you of the necessity of knowing how to properly diagram a sentence. But you must concede that passing this grammar class is a requirement for graduation from the academy. You will never become an architect without a passing grade in English grammar. Correct?"

He waited until finally she nodded in defeat.

"Perhaps, then, we should use that fact alone as our motivation for continuing: You must have a passing grade in this class; it is my job to see that you achieve it. Do you think we might be able to get somewhere with such an understanding?"

She thought for a minute, and a slow smile spread across her face. "That makes more sense than anything else I've heard this afternoon."

He returned her smile. "It's decided then. I will do my best to impart the knowledge you need to pass this class, and you will do your best to understand the material, regardless of how useless you believe it to be. Agreed?"

She nodded again, and they set to work.

For the next hour, he wrote sentences, and she struggled to—as she'd so aptly put it—*dissect* them. She was certainly bright enough, with an impressive vocabulary that seemed to expand in direct proportion to her frustration. And she did, indeed, grow frustrated as she struggled to comprehend and label the parts of speech represented in the increasingly complex sentences he invented.

Feeling she had reached her limit. He printed one last string of words on the notepaper in front of him: *Stella Bradford has successfully completed her first grammar lesson under the expert tutelage of James Collingwood.* He slid the pad of paper in front of her.

She read it and let out a little snort of laughter. "Oh, this is an easy one," she said. "Let's see. . ." She took her pen and underlined her name. " 'Stella Bradford' is the noun; 'has completed' is the verb." She glanced up at him with a mischievous gleam in her eyes and continued. " 'Successfully' is a questionable adverb, and 'under the expert tutelage' is a highly fictional qualifying clause."

He laughed. "Now you're making up entire new categories for the parts of speech."

"I'm sorry," she said coyly, "but your ridiculous sentence demanded it."

He gave an exaggerated sigh and closed the notebook. Pushing back his chair, he told her, "I can see that you have had all the expert tutelage you can handle for one day." He pulled the watch from his pocket. "And we've gone over our time as it is."

She stood beside him and gathered her things. "Thank you," she told him, turning serious. "I truly hope you don't feel you've taken on a lost cause."

"Not at all," he said encouragingly. "I believe we've already made some progress."

She left the room with a cheerful "Good day."

He straightened the chairs, closed the door behind him, and went into the main room of the library. As he approached the wide front doors, he saw that his student was just leaving the building also.

He held the door for her, and they walked out into the fresh air together. The sun was low in the west. "It will soon be dark," he said. "Do you live nearby, Miss Bradford?" St. Bart's had only recently opened its doors to women, and the campus housing was for men.

She shook her head. "I live with my parents a couple miles outside of town. But I am going to the mill to meet my father. I usually ride home with him each evening," she explained.

"Ah, Bradford Mills. Of course. I just happen to be going that direction. I'd be delighted to have your company as far as the mill."

She hesitated for the slightest of moments, then transferred her bag and books to her right arm and placed her left hand around the crook of his offered arm. "Why, thank you, Mr. Collingwood," she said.

They walked in silence for a few moments, and he wondered if he'd made her uncomfortable. After all, in spite of the fact that he was probably only four or five years her senior, he was an employee of St. Bart's—and her instructor.

"So tell me about this desire of yours to design buildings," he said, attempting to make conversation.

She looked up at him from beneath curly lashes, as if to determine whether or not he was teasing. Apparently deciding that his question had been sincere, she launched into her story. "Mama says I've been sketching houses and churches and shops ever since I could hold a crayon in my fist." She clenched creamy, white knuckles to demonstrate.

It was all James could do to resist wrapping that delicate little fist in his own large hands. He forced himself to concentrate on her words.

"Papa has been in the lumber business as long as I can remember, and I've always been fascinated watching houses and buildings arise from the flat earth. I guess you could say I was born to it."

"I suppose so," he conceded.

"Tell me about yourself, Mr. Collingwood."

He turned to her as they strolled along the walk on Main Street. "You know, Miss Bradford, if I'm going to be your tutor, I think you could call me James. Unless I'm teaching Dr. Whitestone's class, of course. A more formal title might be appropriate in front of the other students."

"Of course. Well then, please call me Stella."

"It's a very lovely name."

"Why, thank you. I'm named after my great-great-grandmother, Stella Mae Bradford."

"She would be proud."

"I'm told that I am a lot like her," Stella confessed. "Like my father, too."

"Oh? And how so?"

She gave an impish grin. "A little stubborn, a little tenacious, more than a little pigheaded, I'm afraid."

He reeled back in feigned surprise. "You? Surely not."

"I hide it well," she said, sounding quite serious.

He didn't have the heart to tell her that she didn't hide it nearly as well as she might think. Instead he said, "Rightly directed, those can be endearing qualities, you know."

"Endearing?"

"Charming, appealing." He defined the word for her.

She smacked his arm with a dainty hand. "I know what it means, silly. I was challenging the idea itself. I'm afraid not many people find my stubbornness charming."

Little do you know, he thought. "Maybe you are right. Perhaps 'beneficial' is a better word. Sometimes it pays to be stubborn and tenacious."

"I wish you'd tell that to my father," she said, a frown creasing her forehead.

"There are certainly worse qualities a child could have than a little stubborn streak," James replied.

She turned and peered up at him. "You sound as though you speak from experience, Mr. Collingwood. Did you cause your father as much anxiety as I've caused mine?"

"I don't know about fathers, Stella. Mine died when I was very young. But. . . well, let's just say that I gave my mother far more trouble than the good woman deserved."

"And is your mother living?"

"No. She died a few years ago. But I will be forever grateful that she lived long enough to see her son back on the straight and narrow path."

"I'm sure you made her proud," Stella said.

"I had much for which to atone," he told her, surprising himself with his honesty.

Stella looked at him, intense curiosity in her eyes, but she didn't voice the questions that were obviously in her mind. Instead, she asked, "And you live in a boardinghouse, you say?"

"Yes. Since her husband's death, my sister takes in boarders. If it were winter, you'd be able to see Sylvia's rooftop"—he pointed ahead toward a group of homes that rose above the trees in the distance—"just in front of that tallest gray roof to the south."

They chatted pleasantly all the way through town, and as they approached the mill, James fought to think of an excuse to continue their conversation, to see her again. "Have you lived in Clairemore long?" he asked.

"Since I was about twelve," she replied. "We moved here from Barton's Grove after Papa bought the mill."

Stella went on chattering about her family, but at the mention of the neighboring town, James felt his face grow warm and his heart begin to pound in his ears. He struggled to pay attention to what she was saying, but he wondered if there would ever come a day when he could be reminded of his past without flinching.

Chapter 3

S tella didn't know what had caused James Collingwood to turn suddenly sullen, but as the mill came into sight, her concerns shifted in another direction. She released James's arm and turned to him. "This will be fine. Thank you so much for walking with me."

He kept his arm bent, offering it to her again. "Please, let me take you to the door. I don't mind."

"No, truly. I'm fine."

But it was too late for her protests. From the corner of her eye, she saw Papa open the door of the mill office and step outside. He spotted her immediately, and even from a distance, she could see him craning his neck, trying to figure out the identity of this man who was harassing his daughter.

"You go on, Mr. Collingwood," Stella urged. "There's Papa now. I'll be fine."

James seemed to sense her unease and tipped his hat in farewell. "Good day, then. I'll see you for a lesson on Thursday?"

"Yes, of course." Stella was distracted, worrying that her father would try to detain her tutor and grill him without mercy, as was his habit where her suitors were concerned. But once James Collingwood started on his way, she saw that her father had ordered their rig brought around and was standing beside the wagon, waiting for her.

She hurried to meet him, took the hand he offered, and climbed up onto the wagon seat.

"Hello, there," Papa said, climbing up beside her and clicking his tongue at the team. The horses gave a low whicker and turned toward home as though they knew the way by heart.

As they headed west, Papa indicated James's retreating form with a backward flick of his thumb. "You had an escort, I see."

"Yes, Papa."

"A boy from the academy?"

"Yes. He graduated last year, that is. Now he's an assistant in the English department."

"He *teaches* at the school?" Stella heard accusation in his voice.

"He's Dr. Whitestone's new assistant, Papa," she explained. "His name is James Collingwood. He's working toward a professorship at St. Bart's."

"He's Arthur's assistant, you say?"

Stella nodded. "Yes. He's the one Dr. Whitestone assigned to tutor me."

"I see," her father said, stroking his silvered beard, obviously deep in thought.

For a moment, Stella dared to wonder if perhaps James would pass muster with her father simply because of his connection to Arthur Whitestone. Papa had the highest regard for the department head.

But she was mistaken. The interrogation had only begun. "And just how did this Mr. Collingwood come to walk you home?" Papa demanded.

"I finished my session with him—my tutoring session—and he. . .he noticed that it was beginning to get dark, so he offered to walk me home."

"Home? Did you tell him that you live a good distance in the country?"

It took every ounce of self-control she possessed to keep her voice steady. "I told him, Papa, that I was meeting my father at the mill. Mr. Collingwood lives at his sister's boardinghouse east of town." She pointed back toward the group of older homes beyond the mill. "Since he was going this way already, he offered to accompany me."

Papa grunted as though he didn't buy Mr. Collingwood's story. Stella could barely stifle the sigh that escaped her. For as long as she could remember, her father had scared off every young man who'd dared attempt to court her. Papa was a wonderful, generous, Christian man, and she knew that his intentions were fueled by deep love and a desire to protect his daughter. But if one more log were thrown on the fire of his intentions, she would end up a spinster for eternity. *Perish the thought!*

Until now, there had never been anyone who mattered enough for her to risk her father's ire. But something told her that James Collingwood might just change all that.

They rode the rest of the way in silence. But when the horses slowed and turned up the lane that led to the Bradford farm, Papa turned to her. "I never liked the idea of you going to the academy in the first place, Stella Mae." He shook his head in apparent exasperation, but the hand he laid on her shoulder was gentle. "You and this harebrained notion of yours—an architect! I don't know what you—"

"Papa—"

He hushed her, not unkindly. "All I can say is I hope you won't give me more reasons to regret the fact that I allowed you to go."

She turned to him, struggling to remain calm. "Papa, a very thoughtful gentleman walked me safely to the mill. I should think you would be grateful."

He reined the horses in and stopped the wagon in front of the house. Taking her hand briefly, he gave it an affectionate squeeze. "Go help your mama with supper. Tell her I'll be in shortly."

Stella managed a smile and jumped down from the wagon, dragging her books and bag off the bench behind her. She reached for the gate to the side yard, but before she could unfasten the latch, the back door flew open and her little sister raced into the yard.

"Stella's home! Stella's home!" Helen sang out merrily to no one in particular.

"Hi, there, Shortcake," Stella called, using Papa's nickname for the petite girl.

"We're having roast chicken for supper. Mama needs your help mashing the potatoes."

"I just got home, Helen. Give me a minute, will you?" She cringed inwardly. She hadn't meant to snap like that. It wasn't Helen's fault that Papa was so bullheaded.

"I'm just telling you what Mama said," the little girl pouted. "Was school hard today?"

"A little. How about your day? Did Miss Wickham like your drawing?"

Helen frowned. "She didn't get to see it. Timmy Hardtner tore it up before I got a chance to show it to Teacher."

"Why, that little—"

"Don't tell Papa," Helen breathed, her eyes wide. "He'll just make trouble. Timmy was only teasing."

Stella could scarcely suppress her laughter. Timmy must have fallen hard for Helen. As dark as Stella was fair, Helen was already a beauty. But the poor girl was barely eight years old, and already she was wise to Papa's fatherly sanctions against the masculine gender.

Stella put an arm around Helen and turned her toward the house. "I won't say anything. I promise. But you'll have to learn to stand up to Timmy. He shouldn't have torn your picture, even if he was teasing. That's just plain mean. Such a nice drawing—wasted!"

Helen smiled sheepishly, and love for her little sister welled up in Stella's heart.

"Come on, Shortcake," she said. "Let's go help Mama."

❧

Thursday morning Stella had a full day of classes, but as she sat through her world history lesson and worked the problems in her mathematics course, she realized that she was merely biding her time until her tutoring session with James that afternoon. She had been on pins and needles since Tuesday night, terrified that Papa might forbid her to walk with James again. Fortunately, her father hadn't said another word on the subject of James Collingwood, and Stella fervently hoped James might offer to walk with her again after today's session.

Finally four o'clock approached, and Stella hurried across campus to the library. This time she had no trouble locating the study hall where they'd agreed to meet. But even though she arrived several minutes early, James was waiting for her when she opened the door.

"Am I late again?" She sighed.

"Not at all," he said. "Right on time, in fact. I finished early in Dr. Whitestone's office and thought I could find a few moments of solitude here." He held up the book he'd been reading. *"Uncle Tom's Cabin,"* he explained, though Stella could easily read the embossed title on the book's cover for herself. "A fascinating novel. I hadn't read it before, but when I heard that President Lincoln had credited the author for starting the war, I decided I'd better see what kind of writing this was."

"And *is* Harriet Beecher Stowe a warmonger, in your opinion?" There had been a discussion of the book in one of her classes, though she hadn't read it herself. Papa and Mama didn't put much stock in reading works of fiction.

"Oh, no," James said. "I don't think that's what the president meant. To the contrary, I think his comment was a tribute to the author's skill with words. She managed to stir up some powerful emotions with her fiction."

For the next twenty minutes, she listened intently while James expounded on his impressions of Mrs. Stowe's novel. Stella was much relieved at the confirmation that James was a strong abolitionist. She had assumed so, given his friendship with Dr. Whitestone, who was a well-known supporter of the fight against slavery. But still, seeing this strong yet compassionate side of James's character only made Stella like him more.

Finally James gave her a guilty grin. "I've rattled on long enough. We'd best get on with the lesson."

As Stella opened her notebook and readied her fountain pen, he glanced at his pocket watch and took in a sharp breath. "Stella, I've cheated you of nearly half your allotted time. I am sorry. I promise to make it up to you. Perhaps you could come ten or fifteen minutes early for the next two sessions?"

"Certainly," she agreed. She looked forward with pleasure to any extra time with him.

They set about diagramming sentences, but each sentence James dictated seemed to remind one of them of a story, and when the clock in the library's entry chimed five o'clock, they were once again far off the subject, laughing and chatting about every topic *except* English grammar.

"I'm ashamed of myself," James told her, as they gathered their belongings and walked through the library stacks to the wide front doors. "I've wasted your time and your father's money."

"Please, James. Don't think anything of it. I did my share of the talking, too. Besides, I enjoyed every minute of our time together." Suddenly she felt rather shy with him. She hadn't meant to wear her feelings quite so obviously on her sleeve. "It was certainly more interesting than those silly grammar problems," she stammered.

"I'm afraid you'll feel differently when you fail your exam," he said solemnly.

"I'll work extra hard next time," she promised.

They reached the front doors and, as Stella had hoped, James issued an invitation.

"If you don't mind waiting while I stop by Dr. Whitestone's office to pick up some papers he asked me to mark, I'd be honored to walk you to the mill again."

"Why, thank you. I'd like that."

They stepped outside and were met by a blast of wintry air. "I believe the temperature has dropped by ten degrees," James said, perusing the sky. "I'm afraid our Indian summer has come to an end."

Stella shivered and pulled her wrap more tightly around her shoulders. She took the arm James offered, and they headed toward the building that housed the English department.

Arthur Whitestone was just locking up when they came down the main corridor of Voorhaven Hall. "Ah, James. There you are." He looked at Stella, an unspoken question in the tight knit of his bushy, snow-white brows. "Good day, Miss Bradford."

"Hello, Dr. Whitestone. We've just finished a tutoring session," she offered, knowing that her father would likely hear about her showing up at the office on James's arm. "James—um, Mr. Collingwood is going to escort me to the mill."

"I see," the professor said.

Stella imagined she saw a knowing glimmer in the older man's eye.

"Well, please give your father my greetings. It's been some time since we took tea together."

"I will tell him."

Dr. Whitestone disappeared into his office and came back with a thick sheaf of papers for his assistant. James secured them in the small valise he carried, and he and Stella waved to the professor and started across campus.

"I still feel awful about taking up all your time with my blather."

"Please, James." She gave him her sweetest smile. "You have nothing to be sorry for."

"Oh, but see there, you've just proven me right."

She raised an eyebrow in question.

"It's apparent that I have much *for which* to be sorry," he said pointedly.

She immediately picked up on the words he'd emphasized and put a hand to her forehead in mock distress. "Oh, I've trampled the English language once again, haven't I?"

He nodded, laughing. "Don't despair, Miss Bradford." He bent his head near hers, and his voice took on a conspiratorial tenor. "In truth, unless you are giving a dissertation before the faculty of the academy, you can often get away with in speech what would be inexcusable in print."

"That is good to know. Otherwise I wouldn't dare speak another word in your presence for fear of making a grammatical fool of myself."

He laughed again. James Collingwood was obviously easily entertained. She was glad, because she loved hearing his easy laughter, loved even more that she was the cause of it.

She barely noticed the chill in the air as they walked along, joking and talking together. As they neared the mill, Stella opened her mouth to insist again that James need not walk her all the way to the door, but before she could get a word out, he stopped abruptly in the street and turned to her. "Do you have classes tomorrow?"

"Yes."

"What if we meet again tomorrow afternoon at the library so I can make up the time I wasted? You wouldn't be charged for the extra session, of course," he added quickly.

She smiled to herself at his transparent excuse to spend time with her again, but she wasn't about to miss the opportunity. "I was going to be studying at the library anyway," she told him, "until Papa gets done at the mill. If you're certain you don't mind, that would be very nice."

She looked up to see Papa's team and wagon appear from behind the mill's warehouse. Stella could tell by her father's alert posture at the reins that he had been watching for her. When Papa spotted her with James, he nudged the horses forward and drove across the mill yard to meet them.

From his perch high up on the wagon seat, Papa tipped his hat politely in James's direction.

James returned the courtesy. "Good day, Sir."

"Papa, this is James Collingwood, the tutor I told you about. James, this is my father, Marcus Bradford."

"Pleasure meeting you, Mr. Bradford," James said.

"Likewise," Papa responded. He turned his gaze on Stella, and she recognized the tight wariness in his voice when he said, "We'd best be on our way, Stella. It looks like there might be a winter storm brewing, and we don't want to worry your mother."

Stella turned to her escort. "Thank you for walking me, James. I'll see you tomorrow."

James helped her into the wagon, and as they drove off, she gave a little wave, hoping that he hadn't noticed Papa's rudeness.

When the horses had trotted out of James's hearing, Papa leveled a one-word accusation at her. "James?"

Not understanding at first, she started to explain. "Yes, Papa. It's James Collingwood."

"And since when are students at St. Bartholomew's on a first-name basis with their professors?"

"Papa, I told you, he's not a professor. He's an assistant. He fills in teaching for Dr. Whitestone once in a while is all."

"He is your tutor, Stella, and therefore your superior. I don't think it's proper for you to be on a first-name basis with the man."

"He *asked* me to call him James, Papa. It would have been rude to ignore his request."

"Well, I don't like it. And what's this business about tomorrow? Perhaps I should speak to him."

"Papa, no! James—Mr. Collingwood didn't do anything wrong. Please, Papa."

They bumped along the country road in silence, Stella's mind churning. She would be mortified if Papa said anything to James. Suddenly she remembered her exchange with Dr. Whitestone.

"By the way, Papa," she started, trying to keep her tone casual. "I spoke with Dr. Whitestone this afternoon, and he said to tell you 'hello.' He mentioned that it's been some time since the two of you visited."

Papa thought for a moment. "Yes, it has been awhile. I suppose I should remedy that. Perhaps I'll pay Arthur a visit tomorrow."

Stella cringed. She knew exactly why Papa was suddenly so eager to visit with his old friend. Yet the more she thought about it, the more optimistic she grew. Dr. Whitestone knew James well. Perhaps her professor could serve as a liaison between James and her father. Perhaps he could put Papa's mind at ease about James. If anyone might be able to persuade Papa that there was no harm in her and James's friendship, it would be Arthur Whitestone.

Chapter 4

The encounter with Stella's father at the mill ate at James like a dog gnawing away at a dry bone. At dinner, over Sylvia's succulent roast beef, he barely said a word. Of course with Mrs. Bellingham at the table, one did not need to worry about a lack of conversation. The elderly widow expounded at length on every subject under the sun. Though he could usually tolerate the woman's well-intentioned lectures, tonight her high-pitched voice gave him a headache. He excused himself to his room as soon as he could politely do so.

Then when he should have been marking students' papers, he sat at the cramped desk in the tiny sitting room off his bedchamber and replayed the brusque meeting with Stella's father. He had gotten the distinct impression that Marcus Bradford was not at all happy about seeing James with his daughter. Maybe it wasn't personal. Perhaps Mr. Bradford was simply one of those overprotective fathers who never wanted to turn their daughters over to *any* man. But he worried that it was more than that. He knew that Dr. Whitestone and Marcus Bradford were friends. Was it possible that Dr. Whitestone had told Stella's father about him? And if so, was Marcus Bradford the kind of man who refused to forgive a man his past?

Guilt poured over James. It was one thing to mentally berate the man for having a judgmental spirit. But when Stella didn't know how much there was to forgive, he couldn't very well credit her for having a generous, forgiving spirit.

James knew that he had long ago been forgiven by the only One who mattered. Nevertheless, it wasn't fair to court a woman the way he wanted to court Stella Bradford without telling her the whole story. They could never have an honest friendship until she knew the truth about him and had an opportunity to decide for herself whether she could live with the ugly history that would always be a part of who he was.

He adjusted the wick on the kerosene lamp beside him and forced his attention to the compositions spread in front of him. If he didn't get to work, he would be up past midnight reading mostly dreadful freshman essays.

But before he set to work, he paused to bow his head and offer his worries to heaven. When he lifted his head, the flame in the lamp flickered, and a tender ember of peace glowed within his heart as well.

The Indian summer returned with surprising strength, and for a month and a half of Tuesdays and Thursdays, Stella Bradford spent her afternoons in Robinson Library with a handsome and fascinating tutor who was fast becoming her dearest friend and confidant.

James had taken to walking Stella to the mill each evening, even when he sometimes had to turn around and return to the academy for a meeting or to teach a late class. Papa had not said another word to her about James Collingwood. On the rare occasions when the two men encountered each other in front of the mill, Papa treated James with polite indifference. Stella was happy to leave well enough alone and was merely content that, for once, her father was not interfering.

In the early hours of a late November morning, Old Man Winter finally made his first appearance, dumping half a foot of snow on Clairemore and the surrounding area.

When the Bradford sisters awoke at dawn and discovered the blanket of white outside the farmhouse, young Helen danced around the cozy kitchen in delight. But Stella paced the hallway from front door to back a dozen times, wishing Papa would come in and tell her his decision about going into town. He had gone out to do the morning chores and to hitch the horses to the sleigh; but before he'd left the house, he had warned Stella that he doubted there would be classes at the academy after such a storm.

"Stella Mae, would you stop your pacing?" Dorothy Bradford said from her position at the stove, where she was frying bacon. "I never saw a child so enamored with school. You'd almost think there was another reason you were so anxious to get into town."

Stella looked suspiciously at her mother and detected a twinkle in the soft brown eyes. Though Stella usually confided in her mother, she hadn't yet dared to voice her growing feelings for James Collingwood.

She smiled coyly. "I don't know what you are talking about, Mama."

"Stella, Stella, what have we taught you about telling lies?" Mama teased.

Stella rushed to her mother's side and put an arm around the soft shoulder. "Oh, Mama. You have to make Papa let me go!"

Mama looked at her intently. "What is his name, Child? As if I couldn't guess, since I've heard the words of a certain handsome tutor quoted a dozen times over the past weeks."

Stella knew her smile betrayed her feelings. "Yes, it's James, Mama. Papa met him, you know—at the mill. Oh, Mama, he's wonderful. Did Papa tell you?"

"That James is wonderful?" She shook her head. "Hardly."

Stella smiled at her mother's attempt at a joke, and her heart overflowed with affection for this woman who had always been a buffer between a stubborn father and an equally stubborn daughter. "You have to make him understand, Mama," she begged again. "I'm supposed to meet James in the library this afternoon."

"But I thought your sessions with your tutor were on Tuesdays and Thursdays."

Stella blushed. "That's right. But. . .well, sometimes we meet there just to visit."

Mama walked to the dining-room window and pulled back a corner of the heavy drapes. "My sweet, silly girl, we are in the middle of a frightful storm. If you don't show up, I'm sure your James will understand that the weather detained you. And if he lets a little snowstorm change his mind about the prettiest girl in Clairemore County, then he wasn't worth pining over anyway," Mama declared.

Stella heard the door to the spring room open and the muffled sound of Papa stamping snow from his boots. She ran back to meet him. "How are the roads, Papa? Can we get into town?"

"I am going, Stella, but the snow is quite deep and there are branches down everywhere. It will be slow going. I don't think there is a chance that the academy will hold classes. And if they do, you won't be the only one absent. I think it's best if you stay home."

"But, Papa, I have an exam in history today. I can't be absent!"

The look he gave her made her feel as though her real reason for not wanting to miss class was written upon her forehead in India ink. She squirmed under his careful scrutiny, but she continued to try to convince him. "If we get there and find they're not having classes, I could come to the mill with you and help out in the office," she said hopefully.

Her father held firm. "Your mother will need your help here today. It will be all the two of you can do to keep the fires going, the snow cleared from the walks, and the animals cared for."

Stella recognized the resolve in his voice and knew that there would be no changing his mind. She went to her room and pouted for a while, then came downstairs to help her mother. Mama was right. James would understand why she wasn't there. But that wasn't the point. Though she had seen him only hours ago, she realized that she didn't want a day to go by without hearing that deep, gentle voice and that rumbling laughter she could so easily provoke in him.

❧

Another two inches of snow fell that night, and the wind drove the white stuff into drifts as high as horses' backs along the hedgerows. Many of the trees, still heavy with leaves, had broken under the weight, and the countryside was littered with broken limbs and splintered branches.

Even Papa stayed home the next day to deal with the havoc the storm had caused. Stella bundled up and went out to help clean up the mess in the farmyard, but when Papa forced her back inside after an hour, she thought she would go mad. She wondered what James was doing and whether he would go to the library for their regular Thursday session. She wondered if he was as disappointed as she to have lost two opportunities to spend time together.

Finally, on Friday, the sun came out, the winds calmed, and Papa hitched the horses to the sleigh and declared that Stella could accompany him to town. It was as though she'd been lying beneath a load of bricks for the past two days and finally, blessedly, someone had come and removed them from her body.

Papa let her take the reins, and as the horses trotted along the icy road into town, Stella's hands and face felt frozen, but her heart was toasty warm. Though she didn't have an appointment scheduled with James today, she had a feeling that she would see him anyway.

Sure enough, as she crossed the campus in the middle of the morning, carefully minding her footing on the snowy pathways, she heard her name called out. That masculine voice had haunted her dreams more nights than she could count, and as she turned toward the sound, her heart began to thump in her chest.

"Why, hello, James," she said, striving to effect a nonchalant air. "Isn't this something?" Her gaze swept the campus, which looked like a war zone. Though work crews had already picked up many of the limbs, the quadrangle was still littered with smaller branches and ice-encased leaves, and the sidewalks were lined with foot-high snowdrifts.

James had smiled when she'd first turned to greet him, but he ignored her question. There was a timbre to his voice that she couldn't interpret. "Stella, I–I'd like to speak to you."

She tilted her head, curious. "Right now?"

"Do you have a minute?"

"Well. . ." She turned to glance up at the tower clock behind her. "I have a class at eleven, James. I really can't be tardy again." She flashed him a coy smile at this blatant reminder of their first meeting, but he seemed not to notice. He appeared to be agitated and preoccupied.

"Is something wrong?" she asked, reaching out to put a hand on his arm.

"No. . .no." He shook his head and gave her a smile that didn't seem quite genuine. "It can wait. I–I just need to talk to you sometime. Will you be free after this class? I'd be happy to share my lunch with you."

She patted the bag that hung from her shoulder. "Thank you, James. But I brought my lunch. I'd like to eat with you, though."

"Good." He glanced around the grounds of the academy and pulled the collar of his coat up around his neck. "I guess it's not exactly picnic weather. Why don't we meet at the library at noon? Maybe our study room will be empty."

She nodded her agreement, only slightly reassured by his reference to "our study room."

Stella might as well have not been present in her history class. The professor had allowed them another week to study for the test, and now he droned on and on—something about the repercussions of the French Revolution on the economy. Stella scarcely heard a word he said, wondering why James had seemed so anxious to talk to her.

After her class was dismissed, she hurried to the library and went to reserve the room where they had enjoyed so many hours together. She sat at the little table, daydreaming of James's face, his voice, the sound of his laughter. But when he had not appeared almost an hour later, Stella ate her lunch alone. She finished, but still she waited in the room, getting up every few minutes to peer into the hallway to see if he was coming. Her thoughts were a tangled jumble, wondering why he hadn't shown up. She skipped her afternoon mathematics class, and by then, she didn't know whether to be worried sick or mad as a wet hen. Finally, when the clock in the main hall chimed five o'clock, she gathered her belongings and went to wait at the edge of campus where Papa had promised to collect her in the sleigh.

That night Stella helped her mother and sister clear the dishes from the table while Papa stoked the fire before settling into his big chair in the parlor. At supper, Papa had mentioned that he'd met Dr. Whitestone for tea that morning. She was anxious to find out whether they'd spoken of James. Perhaps Papa could shed some light on why James had failed to make their appointment.

The minute she came into the parlor, Papa put his newspaper down, leaned over, and patted the chair beside him. "Come. Sit for a minute, Stella. There's something we need to discuss."

Stella didn't like the sound of this. She watched her father's face closely as she settled in the chair that Mama usually occupied in the evenings. She heard Helen reading to Mama in the kitchen.

"Yes, Papa. What is it?"

"I had a visit with Arthur Whitestone this morning. He tells me that you and this James Collingwood have been spending a great deal of time together." He gazed into the fire, not looking at her, apparently waiting for a reply.

Stella didn't know how to respond. "You know we have, Papa. He tutors me each Tuesday and Thursday afternoon, and he's been walking me to the mill each evening for some time now. But you know all that."

"Arthur says you've come by his office on Mr. Collingwood's arm on several occasions."

She nodded. "Yes, Papa. I sometimes stop by Dr. Whitestone's office with James on our way to the mill. He. . . he offers his arm as any gentleman would."

Her father cleared his throat. "I learned some rather disturbing things about Mr. Collingwood this morning, Stella. I've asked Dr. Whitestone to assign you a new tutor."

"But, Papa, why?" She couldn't imagine what could have possessed her father to do such a thing.

He turned to her and looked her in the eye. "I don't believe an explanation is necessary, Stella, but I know you well enough to know that you will badger me until you find out the truth, so I'm going to do you the courtesy of telling you what I know, with the understanding that this information is to stay in this room."

Stella's curiosity about what Papa had heard almost overwhelmed her anger at his actions.

"Do you understand what I'm saying, Stella Mae?"

"Yes, Papa, but—"

He stopped her with an upraised palm. "I am not a man to judge another by the deeds of his past, Stella, and what I am about to tell you does seem to be in the past. Nevertheless, when it comes to my daughter, I believe a man's past is an important factor."

"Papa! What are you talking about?"

Marcus Bradford leaned forward in his chair, put his elbows on his knees, and tented his fingers beneath his bearded chin. "It seems that James Collingwood got into a bit of trouble a few years ago. The details aren't important, but it involved a serious crime—theft, if you must know. As I understand it, the young man has made restitution, and Arthur believes him to be rehabilitated. I trust Arthur's judgment, and I'm willing to let time prove Mr. Collingwood's sincerity. But until it has been sufficiently proven, I want you to have nothing to do with him."

"Papa! You can't be serious! Theft? James would never do anything like that!"

Her father was silent for a moment, gazing again into the crackling flames. When he finally spoke, his voice was soft, but Stella didn't miss the waver it held when he told her, "Then you have just proven your poor discernment where the man is concerned, Stella, because Arthur heard the story from James Collingwood himself. It seems that Mr. Collingwood was employed for a time at the hotel in Barton's Grove. He was caught stealing from the owner. Quite a large sum of money, as I understand it. I don't mind telling you that the fact that Mr. Collingwood has chosen to keep this information from you offers me no comfort."

Stella's mind was reeling. What Papa said couldn't be true! Yes, James had hinted at a rebellious period of his youth. But the things he had said implied the usual boyish tomfoolery—turning over privies and other harmless pranks, she had imagined. Not criminal activity!

But Papa said Dr. Whitestone had heard it from James himself. It must be true, then. And of course, this explained why James had broken their appointment this morning. Her heart lurched, and her face flushed as she realized what a fool she'd made of herself defending James to Papa. No, she corrected herself, it was *James* who had made a fool of her. Her hands began to tremble, and she wished James were here so she could give him a piece of her mind.

Instead, she stuttered, "Papa, I don't know what to say. I–I assure you, James has been nothing but a gentleman toward me."

Papa reached out and put a warm hand on her arm. "Stella, from what Arthur says, it appears that young Collingwood is making an effort to reform. However, this black mark on his past causes me to feel very cautious, particularly when I learn that my daughter is spending an inordinate amount of time with the man and, in addition, he has told her none of his story." Again, Papa cleared his throat noisily. "I have requested that Arthur assign you a new tutor. I trust that will relieve Mr. Collingwood of the opportunity to accompany you to the mill after your sessions, but should he persist, I want you to let me know immediately and I will see to it that the man leaves you alone."

"But, Papa—"

"I don't intend to discuss the matter further, Stella. If Mr. Collingwood has kept his record untarnished a year or two from now and if he still has an interest in pursuing a respectable courtship with you at that time, we shall revisit the matter. Until such time, I have asked Arthur to see to it that his assistant has no dealings with my daughter." Papa picked up his newspaper and turned his back on her.

Chapter 5

"Please, I'd like to speak to Mr. Collingwood."

The young girl behind the desk in the antechamber of Arthur Whitestone's office in Voorhaven Hall was preoccupied, sorting a stack of what looked like examination papers. She barely glanced up at Stella. "He's teaching this morning, Miss."

"Oh. Do. . .do you know which class he's teaching?"

The girl puffed out her cheeks with annoyance and put her work aside. She opened a drawer of the desk and took out a schedule. Running her finger down the columns, she said, "It looks like he's filling in for Professor Cramer in Room 201 Andrews. That class gets out at half past ten."

"Thank you." Stella hurried from the building and started across campus. Leaving the narrow brick walk, she tromped through the snow, taking a shortcut across the lawn. She paused for an anxious glimpse at the tower clock. Quarter past ten. She should be able to catch him if she waited outside the entrance to Andrews Hall. Brushing off the snow that had blown onto the bench in front of the building, Stella pulled her collar close and sat down to wait.

She stayed there, shivering, for twenty minutes. The carillon clock chimed the half hour, and the campus filled with students. But a few minutes later, the crowd of young people thinned, most of them inside again for the last class of the morning. And still no sign of James.

Stella stood, put her hands on her hips, and spun full circle to scan the pathways that radiated like the spokes of a wagon wheel toward the immense limestone buildings. Laughter drifted from a distance down one walk, and she spotted James Collingwood strolling her way. But Stella tensed as she saw the young woman at his side. The girl was flirting boldly and giggling, as though James were not only the best-looking man on campus but also the funniest.

A streak of jealousy shot through Stella, though she could hardly fault the girl. As the two came closer, Stella recognized Iva Mae Waxler, a first-year student who was in her English Grammar class—the same class in which Stella had met James. She started down the walk to meet them, and James greeted her with something like relief in his eyes.

"Hello," Stella said, looking pointedly at James. She suddenly realized that she had no idea what she would say to him. But she had to talk to him—alone. She forced a smile in Iva Mae's direction. "Hello, Iva Mae."

"Oh. . .hi, Stella," the girl said, as though she'd just noticed Stella's presence.

James gave Stella a look she couldn't interpret and glanced at his watch. "Well, I hope I've answered your questions, Miss Waxler," he said to the student. Then, turning to Stella as though he owed her an explanation, he said, "Iva Mae had some questions about the essay assignment."

Iva Mae bestowed an adoring smile on James. "Mr. Collingwood has been *so* helpful," she gushed, her voice revealing her Atlanta roots. "I don't know what I'd do without his help."

"Just doing my job," he said, tipping his hat and coloring slightly. "Well, good day, Miss Waxler."

The young woman's smile drooped, but she said, "I'll see you this afternoon for our tutoring session, won't I?"

James's color deepened. "Yes. . .yes, of course."

Iva Mae wished them good day and turned to walk slowly up the path toward Andrews Hall.

"How are you, Stella?" James's tone was polite but distant, exactly as it had been with Iva Mae.

"James? What is going on?"

He took a step back, as though he were uncomfortable being so close to her. Looking down at his boots, he said, "I assume your father informed you of his discussion with Dr. Whitestone?"

"Oh, James, it's all mixed up! He's forbade me to see you! Papa heard some things—awful rumors—that make him think you've done something terrible."

James ran his fingers through his hair, and when he looked up, she saw that his face had paled.

"Tell me what he heard, Stella."

His voice was a low monotone, and she almost imagined that he was trembling. Watching him, she knew it couldn't be true. Her James was simply not capable of the things of which he'd been accused.

"Dr. Whitestone told him you'd been arrested for stealing! From the hotel in Barton's Grove. Isn't that preposterous? You've probably never even *been* to Barton's Grove! I think Papa is just looking for any excuse to keep us apart. He didn't want me going to the academy in the first place, and now he's afraid someone is going to take his precious little girl away—"

James took a step toward her and placed his hands on her shoulders. "Stella, we need to talk."

Something in the tone of his voice frightened her, but she couldn't seem to stop babbling. "He's just an old ogre!" She stamped her foot. "I knew he'd try to keep us apart. I just knew it—"

Again, he spoke the words. "We have to talk, Stella."

"What, James? What is it?" Her heart was beating like a drum. After Papa had told her the news last night, she'd been angry with James. But now, seeing his kind face, hearing his voice, she knew that even if what Papa had said were true, anyone who knew James now knew that he'd straightened out his life. She didn't know a more generous, kind, upstanding gentleman. Perhaps he'd had some trouble in his past. He had told her that he'd been a bit of a rebel in his youth. Granted, he'd never given her the details. But that was all in the past. It didn't matter now. Papa just needed to give him a chance.

Silently, James steered her down a short sidewalk to the stairs that led into Andrews Hall. He slumped onto the top step and pulled her down beside him. "Your father is right, Stella."

"What? What are you talking about, James?"

His Adam's apple bobbed in his throat, and his words came out in a whisper. "I *was* caught stealing. In Barton's Grove. . . just like your father said."

Her breath caught. "But. . .why didn't you tell me, James?"

He tipped her chin, forcing her to look at him. "You must believe me, Stella. I didn't mean to keep it from you. I've never lied to you. You have to believe that. But neither have I told you everything. And that was wrong of me."

"I–I know you said you'd done some wild things, but James, stealing?"

He pressed his fingertips to his temples. Then as he stared at the ground, the story unfolded. "I was sixteen. Sylvia became ill, and Mother couldn't work any longer. Since I was the oldest, I was expected to provide for them. I took a job at the hotel. It was hard, going to school all day and working till late at night, but it was the only way to put food on our table. Except that Sylvia's medicine took almost every dime I made. I got to eat for free in the hotel's kitchen, and sometimes Mr. Browne—the owner—let me bring home scraps. But Sylvia and Mama were hungry all the time, Stella. It about killed me to see them near-starving like that."

James paused, and she waited in silence for him to continue.

"I–I made a terrible decision, a foolish, stupid mistake—one I'll regret for the rest of my life." He swallowed hard. "One night the cashier accidentally left the cash register open. I was dusting the front desk and the drawer just slid open and there in front of me seemed to be the answer to all my problems. I took the money, Stella. All of it. I know. . .I know how stupid it sounds now. And I intended to pay every cent back, truly I did. But of course I got caught before that could happen."

"Oh, James," she breathed. She didn't know whether to be angry or whether to cry for the foolish, desperate boy he'd been back then. "What happened? Did you. . .did you go to jail?"

"No. The owner of the hotel forgave me. In fact, he gave me a job in the dining room waiting tables at a wage almost twice what I'd made before—on the condition that I pay him half my earnings until I'd repaid what I stole."

"But if he forgave you, how did Papa hear about it after all these years?"

James picked up a clump of snow from the side of the walkway. He formed it into a hard ball and threw it forcefully to the ground. Anger and frustration were revealed in his action, but the look he gave her was one of adoration. "You're so innocent, Stella. Don't you know 'once a thief, always a thief'? The word was all over town about what happened. If Mr. Browne hadn't been willing to keep me on, I guarantee you I would never have worked anywhere in the county again. But God was with me, Stella. You have to believe that. After Mr. Browne forgave me, I dedicated my life to the Lord all over again. I prayed so hard that God would make a way for me to go to university. It seemed as though I were praying for the impossible. Then that Christmas Mr. Browne handed me an envelope—and inside was more money than I had ever dreamed of saving. From that day on, I never doubted God's care for me, and I knew He'd truly given me a second chance."

Stella wanted to offer some comfort, some comment on the things he'd confessed, but she found herself uncharacteristically speechless.

James took her hand in his. "I'm sorry, Stella," he said. "I should have told you before. And I don't blame your father for not wanting you to have anything to do with me. If you were my daughter, I'd feel the same way."

She looked into his eyes, and she could find nothing there that hinted of a thief or a scoundrel. All she saw was her precious James. Papa didn't know him. Papa was making his judgment based on cold, impersonal facts. But she knew her father well enough to know that he'd made up his mind about James, and nothing she could say or do would cause him to change it.

"Stella, I'm so sorry. I—I've grown to care for you deeply. But I can't ask you to go against your father's wishes. He's only doing what he thinks is best for the daughter he loves. I—I shouldn't even be talking to you now, but I couldn't leave things unsettled between us. I wanted you to hear the truth from me."

"Oh, James. I don't hold what you did against you. I know you've changed. From what you say, anyone could see that you had a good reason for what you did."

"Thank you, Stella. That means a great deal to me. But it doesn't change the fact that your father has forbidden you to see me."

She put a hand on his arm. "It's not fair. I have to convince him to get to know you. Can't Dr. Whitestone vouch for you?"

"From what I understand, he already did. But your father isn't thinking about me, Stella. He's thinking about his daughter. And that's only right. I certainly understand his concern."

Somehow she had to convince Papa to get to know James, to see the man she knew. The strong, loving, honest man who sat beside her now, his head bowed in defeat.

"I'll talk to him, James," she cried. "I'll convince him that you've changed. He has to see that—"

"Stop it, Stella." James stood abruptly and backed down the steps away from her. "I think it's best that we leave well enough alone. Perhaps what is between us"—his hand traced an invisible path from his heart to hers—"simply wasn't meant to be."

Tears sprang to her eyes and with them the vision of Iva Mae Waxler clinging to James's arm. She thought she understood then. Perhaps she had misunderstood James's intentions all along. Maybe she had read something into his kindness, into his warm smile that wasn't really there. At least not the way she'd imagined.

Feeling like a fool, she struggled to her feet and ran through the snow. She didn't stop running until she reached the sanctuary of the library. She hurried through the stacks until she found a quiet corner at the back of the massive room. There she silently wept until there were no more tears.

Chapter 6

James Collingwood stood in front of Andrews Hall and watched Stella run away from him. He knew by the slump of her shoulders as she fled that she was crying. Twice she nearly tripped as her skirt became heavy with accumulated snow. Everything in him wanted to go after her, take her in his arms, and comfort her. But what good would that have done either of them? It would only make the inevitable more difficult.

Dr. Whitestone had called him into his office that morning to inform him of Marcus Bradford's request for a new tutor for his daughter. Bradford wanted James Collingwood to have nothing to do with Stella.

"I don't understand," James had told his mentor. "Have I done something wrong?"

Dr. Whitestone hung his head. "James, I'm afraid I'm unwittingly to blame for this."

James looked at him, confusion in his eyes.

"Marcus asked me about you and I–I foolishly took it upon myself to tell the man your story. I had no right, James. I'm sorry. The man is a good friend of mine and an honorable gentleman. I promise you, I told him your story because I believe it to be one of the finest testimonies to the power of God to redeem a man that I've ever heard. But I didn't take into account that Marcus was asking after you because of his daughter's. . . um, shall we say. . .interest in you. He reacted in a way I never expected. "

James was stunned by Dr. Whitestone's revelation. On more than one occasion, Stella had warned him that her father was overly protective. That was one of the reasons he'd been reluctant to tell her his story. But he'd never expected repercussions of this magnitude.

Apparently Marcus Bradford had also requested that James not be allowed to substitute in any class Stella attended. Arthur Whitestone had drawn the line there.

"I informed Marcus that I would not allow his mollycoddling of his daughter to interfere with the way we conduct the department," the professor told James. "Having no daughters myself, I can't say that I understand the man's obsession. I'm sorry, James, but I did promise him that I would assign Stella a new tutor.

I apologize. What he's requested is not fair, but I know you'll understand that I need to accommodate the man as much as I possibly can. He's not only my friend and the father of a student of St. Bartholomew's, but he's a generous benefactor of the academy, as well."

James nodded and dared to ask his superior if he thought Marcus Bradford would ever change his mind.

"Well, I wouldn't hold my breath, Son." Arthur Whitestone sighed. "I'll be glad to put in a good word for you. Not that it will do any good. I already sang your praises when Marcus approached me, and you can see where it got me."

James had declined the offer. If he couldn't win Stella's father over himself, there was no use sending someone else to do it.

Now with the damage done, James sighed, brushed the snow from his pant legs, and retrieved his valise from the bottom step. He had papers to mark and a lesson to prepare for tomorrow. He'd always known that his youthful transgressions might catch up with him. No sense in being surprised and hurt over it now.

But his heart was heavy as he trudged to Voorhaven Hall. He gathered his belongings from the office and started across town. He would work in his room at home tonight. Maybe he'd talk over his troubles with Sylvia. His sister always had a sympathetic ear and a wise word for him.

❧

The following Monday, Stella walked into Dr. Whitestone's class to find James Collingwood substituting in the professor's stead.

He nodded a barely perceptible greeting as she entered the room. She took her seat and began copying the sentences from the board with trembling fingers. For the rest of the hour, she felt his eyes upon her. Looking at him made her ache with longing. Her emotions were so muddled that she feared she would burst into tears at any moment. When the class period ended, Stella stayed in her seat, meaning to linger until the room cleared and she could talk to James alone. But several students went forward with questions, and when fifteen minutes had passed and one young man still stood in line waiting to speak with the instructor, she began to feel awkward. She knew James was aware of her presence in the back of the room, for he glanced her way every few minutes. But she could not read in his expression whether he wished her to remain or was imploring her to leave.

Finally, she slipped out of the room, feeling lower in spirit than she could ever remember.

For the rest of the week, Stella merely went through the motions of living. She rode with her father each day to the academy, she attended classes, she even worked with the new tutor Dr. Whitestone had assigned. The young graduate student was a perfectly pleasant—and quite handsome—fifth-year student. But for Stella, the lessons had become drudgery.

She did not see James again that week. She was ever watchful, hoping to catch a glimpse of his broad-shouldered form striding across the campus grounds or huddled in a study carrel in the library. But it was as though he were purposely avoiding the places where he knew she might be.

She tried to put the vision of James and Iva Mae Waxler head-to-head in the study room at Robinson Library out of her mind, but the image refused to leave. When Iva Mae approached Stella after their English grammar class on Friday morning, asking if Stella knew what had happened to Mr. Collingwood, Stella became alarmed. "What do you mean?" she asked.

"I just wondered if you knew where he's been. You seem to have the inside track where Mr. Collingwood is concerned," she drawled.

"But. . .isn't he tutoring you, Iva Mae?" she asked the girl, ignoring the sarcastic dig.

Iva Mae shook her head sadly. "Some other gent showed up, and he's the one been coming ever since. You don't suppose Mr. Collingwood's left St. Bart's, do you?"

Stella didn't know, and she began to worry that something was wrong. If Iva Mae hadn't seen James, then that quashed Stella's fears that James's interests had turned to the Southern belle. But what had happened to him? Her thoughts churning, she extricated herself from Iva Mae's diatribe about the English department and hurried toward Dr. Whitestone's office.

A new girl sat behind the desk in the anteroom, and Stella took advantage of the fact. "I'm here to see Dr. Whitestone," she said, trying to make it sound as though she had an appointment.

The girl glanced at the ledger on the desk. "Why, I don't believe he's expecting anyone this afternoon. What did you say your name was?"

"I'm Stella Bradford. Please tell Dr. Whitestone I'm here."

Looking again at the schedule, then shaking her head in bewilderment, the girl went back to the office suite and knocked on Dr. Whitestone's door before opening it a crack. "Sir? There's a Stella Bradford to see you."

Stella could not make out the professor's reply, but the girl motioned for Stella. She slipped into the office, a sheepish smile on her face. "I'm sorry, Dr. Whitestone, but I had to talk to you. I'm worried about James. . .Mr. Collingwood. No one has seen him all week and—"

Arthur Whitestone interrupted her with a raised hand, then gestured toward the leather-seated chair in front of his desk. "Please, Miss Bradford. Have a seat." He gave her a smile that she knew was meant to reassure.

She sat down and waited while Dr. Whitestone seemed to scrutinize her face. Finally, he told her. "You were inquiring about Mr. Collingwood's absence?"

She nodded anxiously.

"James's sister was taken ill on Monday. He requested the rest of the week off to care for her."

Stella knew that her relief must have been written on her face. "Is Sylvia—is his sister seriously ill?"

"I believe she suffers chronic health problems. But James stopped by the office here midweek to pick up some papers to mark, and at that time he thought she seemed to be improving. I don't believe it's anything for you to worry about."

Dr. Whitestone had a strange look on his face, and for a moment Stella was afraid he was going to reprimand her for barging into his office to inquire after things that were none of her business. Instead, he cleared his throat and leaned forward over the desk. "Miss Bradford," he said haltingly, "I feel I owe you an explanation."

Stella's puzzlement must have been apparent because he held up a hand and promptly continued.

"I don't know what your father—or James, for that matter—has said to you regarding my part in. . .well, in your father's decision to have Mr. Collingwood replaced as your tutor. I suspect one of them has told you that I had something to do with all that."

He paused, and Stella could sense that he was hoping she would tell him precisely what she did know. She was grateful for his honesty and quickly reassured him. "I know you meant no harm, Dr. Whitestone. It's just that Papa is—"

The professor saved her from having to finish the sentence. "Your father is a good man, Stella. And I trust you know that I had no idea my telling him about James would have the effect it did. As I'm sure you know, he loves you dearly and would not see you hurt for the world. On the other hand, I happen to believe that there is a young man who loves you equally dearly, though in quite a different way."

Stella's heart began to pound. Had Dr. Whitestone just said what she thought he'd said? "I–I don't understand. . ."

The professor thought for a moment. "If you truly don't understand, then it's not my place to say more, Miss Bradford. Let me only say that I believe your father will come to his senses. I'm praying that he will. For James's sake."

As Dr. Whitestone rose and came from behind his desk, he muttered, "If I have to see that lovesick young pup moping around here much longer. . ."

"What did you say?" Stella asked. But she had heard the man's words perfectly well. And they set her heart soaring.

"Nothing, nothing," he replied. "I'm glad you stopped by, Stella. I'll give James your greetings."

"Y–yes," she stuttered. "Please do."

She practically ran from the building. Dr. Whitestone, James's confidant, had called him—what was it?—a lovesick pup. That had to be a good sign.

Chapter 7

As she guided the horses down the land, Stella waved good-bye to Mama. Helen snuggled close beside her in the sleigh, and the horses trotted onto the country road. It would only take a few minutes to get into town. At her feet, wrapped in newspaper and a heavy quilt, was the basket of fried chicken and brown Betty she and Mama had fixed for James and Sylvia. Mama had even added some of her home-canned peaches.

Papa hadn't been crazy about the idea, but Mama had worked her wiles with him. Mama didn't very often argue against Papa, but when she did, he usually listened. He had finally agreed that Helen would accompany Stella. They could hitch the team on the street in front of James's boardinghouse and deliver their offerings. "But you come directly home after that, you understand?" he'd warned. Stella didn't care. At least she would get to see James, if only for a minute.

The horses picked up their pace on the open road, and Stella reveled in the feel of the wind in her face. She had forgotten how free she felt riding in the sleigh. Though she was always a little nervous to have the team under her control, it was exhilarating to glide so smoothly along the road. So different from riding in the wagon, which seemed to emphasize every little bump and rut. Since the storm, sleds and sleighs that had traveled over the road had forged a fine path, and the sleigh and team seemed to obey the slightest sway of the reins. Stella began to relax and loosened her grip on the reins a bit. She didn't even mind the cold.

She glanced over at Helen. Her sister's face reflected her elation, her cheeks rosy from the icy bite in the air, her lips parted in a wide smile.

"It's fun, isn't it?" Stella shouted over the jangle of the harnesses and the clatter of the horses' hooves on the hard-packed snow.

"Can I drive, Stella?" Helen shot back.

Stella shook her head vigorously. "Papa would have my head! Besides, I was almost seventeen before Papa let me take the team out on my own. You'll have to be patient and wait until you grow up a little."

Helen pouted for a moment, but it wasn't long before the smile was back on her face and she was reveling in the ride again.

When the silhouette of Clairemore appeared ahead, Stella slowed the team.

345

As they came into town, she saw that the snow had been shoveled into tall heaps along the street corners. After standing through two bitterly cold nights, the piles of snow had turned into veritable icebergs. They made it more difficult to maneuver the sleigh, and Stella's muscles tensed as she watched the street in front of her carefully.

Fortunately, she didn't need to change direction until she reached James's house. They glided smoothly through town on Main Street, past the mill, until the older neighborhood where Sylvia's boardinghouse stood came into view. The street narrowed, and an avenue of icicle-draped trees formed a canopy over the brick pavement. The sun had begun to thaw the ice that encased each branch, and the air was filled with an odd popping sound as branches broke loose from their frosty cocoons, followed by the sound of shattering glass as icicles hit the brick. Occasionally, a spray of freezing water and ice shards would land on the blanket that covered their laps, and Helen would let out a little squeal of delight.

Carefully steering the team, Stella called a low "Whoa" and brought the horses to a halt along the curb. She jumped down from the sleigh and reached over the side to retrieve the wrapped basket of food.

"You wait right here, Helen," she told her sister. "I'll only be a minute."

"Why can't I go with you?"

"Because," she said evasively. "Now sit still. Don't scare the horses."

With her heart racing, Stella walked up to the front entrance and rapped the brass knocker against the oaken door. Within a few minutes, she heard footsteps. Her heart pounded in her ears.

The door opened slowly. She faced James. "Stella? Hello. What. . .what brings you here?"

She held out the basket. "I heard Sylvia was ill. We wanted to bring you some chicken and some other things—to help out a bit. I hope Sylvia is feeling better."

"She's improving, I think. Slowly." He took the basket from her hands, but his eyes never left her face. "Thank you, Stella. This is very kind of you."

"Well, I didn't make it by myself. Mama fried the chicken. I–I helped make the brown Betty. And there are peaches from Mama's orchard. She canned them this summer. We thought you might enjoy them. They're really quite good. Oh. . . and Mama would like to have the jar back." She was babbling like a flustered old woman, but she couldn't seem to stop herself.

"Thank you, Stella. It. . .it's so good to see you." She suspected that the expression in his eyes was much like what he must be seeing in her own. In that moment, all her doubts about James—his past, his character, even his relationship with Iva Mae Waxler—vanished. She knew that the man who stood in front of her, this man who had taken time away from a job he loved to care for his ailing sister, was as kind and generous and honorable as she'd always thought him to be.

"Oh, James, I've missed you so."

"I've missed you, too, Stella," he said softly. "You said your mother helped with the food. Does. . .does that mean your father knows you're here?" He looked to the street beyond her as though he half-expected to see Marcus Bradford waiting for her.

She inclined her head toward the sleigh. "Yes, Papa knows. He sent Helen with me—to chaperone, I think—and he gave strict instructions that I'm not to stay for any length of time."

His shoulders slumped. "So he hasn't changed his mind about us seeing one another?"

She shook her head sadly. "I don't think so, James." She stamped her foot on the porch. "Oh, I hate this!" she cried out in frustration. "I hate it that Papa has practically exiled me. I hate it that we—"

Her words were lost in a deafening *boom*. A few yards in front of the sleigh, a heavy branch had fallen under the weight of ice and snow, crashing to the ground and spraying ice and water in every direction.

Startled, the horses bolted, but the fallen branch was directly in their path. One steed veered to avoid the obstacle, but the other reared up on its hind legs, causing the sleigh to tip precariously.

Helen's screams pierced the air, and even from the porch, Stella could see that her sister's face was a mask of terror as the team dragged the sleigh over the curb and onto a sloping lawn. Narrowly missing the broad trunk of the sturdy oak from which the branch had fallen, one runner under the sleigh slid up over a rock-hard drift of compacted snow.

Stella stood paralyzed as the sled toppled over onto its side. Helen was thrown from the seat like a rag doll. The child flew through the air and landed in a heap on the snow with a sickening thud. Stella watched in horror as the overturned sleigh skidded across the lawn, shuddered, and came to rest on the very spot where Helen's crumpled form had landed. The dead silence that filled the air in the aftermath of the calamity caused Stella's heart to cease beating.

Chapter 8

Before Stella could cry out his name, James flew off the porch and raced to the neighboring yard where the overturned sleigh rested. He bent to peer under the body of the sleigh, then quickly placed his hands beneath it. Straining under its weight, he lifted the carriage a few inches off the ground.

"Stella!" he shouted. "I need your help! She's trapped underneath."

The urgency in his voice brought her to her senses, and as the meaning of his words registered, Stella ran to his side, her breath coming in short, painful gasps. Together, they lifted the sleigh, and when they got it a few feet off the ground, James wedged one shoulder underneath its frame to hold it steady.

One horse was down, forelegs flailing in an effort to stand. The other pawed at the ground, trying to free itself from the dead weight of the sled, which tethered it to the spot. James spoke low, soothing syllables meant to calm the beasts.

"Oh, please, God. Please don't let her be dead," Stella prayed through sobs.

"Crawl under there and see if you can drag her out," James ordered, breathless from bearing the heavy weight on his back. "Check for broken bones first."

Stella knelt in the snow and scrambled under the sleigh. Helen was lying prone on the ground, her red coat a startling stain on the pristine snow. Her form was as still as a hitching post on a windless day, and Stella feared the worst. She bent and put her head beside her sister's face. Helen's breathing was shallow and uneven, but Stella silently thanked God that the girl was breathing at all.

The canopy made by the sleigh blocked out what was left of the waning sunlight, but Stella did her best to feel Helen's limbs through the girl's heavy coat and boots. Gently, she rolled her sister's slight form over, and throwing off her gloves, she worked the large buttons on Helen's coat. The little girl gave a low moan.

"Helen! Helen? Can you hear me? Say something, Helen," she pleaded.

James's voice came from above her, muffled and tight with fear and exertion. "Do you think you can drag her out into the open, Stella?"

"I'll try," she panted.

Stella pulled the red coat snug around the little girl and fastened the topmost button. Then moving to huddle near Helen's head, she rose to her knees and grabbed onto the collar of the coat. She backed out, inch by painful inch, dragging Helen from beneath the precariously balanced sleigh.

All the while, his back to them, James held the thing steady, anchoring it upon one strong shoulder as he continued to speak softly to the frantic horses.

When Stella was sure she and Helen were clear of the sleigh, she shouted, "We're out, James. You can let go now."

"You're sure?"

"Yes, we're clear."

He lowered his shoulder and staggered back. The carriage dropped with a resounding *bang*. Stella saw him rub his shoulder and wince, but he turned and hurried over to where she was working over her sister.

"Is she breathing?" he asked, reaching up to lift each pale little eyelid.

"Yes, but just barely."

The commotion had brought a parade of neighbors from surrounding homes. Stella heard someone shout that they'd go for the doctor. A group of young men worked together to right the sleigh and get the downed horse on its feet.

James had taken off his vest and folded it into a pillow to place under Helen's neck. Together, he and Stella inspected the girl for blood and bruises, finding only the latter. Several times Helen's eyelids fluttered, but each time she gave a breathy sigh and drifted from consciousness again.

Stella suddenly realized that Dr. Pulliam and Papa were standing beside her. With deep relief, she left Helen's side to make room for the doctor. Even as Dr. Pulliam quickly examined Helen for broken bones and internal injuries, the little girl started to come around.

Stella ran into Papa's arms and he held her close.

"What happened?" he whispered, his gaze trained on Helen's piteous form.

"Helen was waiting in the sleigh while I delivered the food to. . .to Mr. Collingwood and his sister."

She looked around for James and spotted him helping with the horses.

"That branch fell and spooked the team," she continued, pointing to where the limb had landed. "The horses bolted and overturned the sleigh. Oh, Papa, it was awful! Helen was trapped underneath."

"Underneath?" her father gasped. "However did she get out?"

"James held the sleigh up so I could drag her out from under. I thought she was dead, Papa!"

"He held it up by himself?"

"Yes, Papa. And it took me a long while to get her out."

She told her father the whole story then, but before she could finish, Papa put his hands on her shoulders and looked her in the eye. "Wait right here," he said.

He spoke briefly with the doctor, then strode to where James was working to untangle a badly twisted harness. Stella watched with wide eyes as Papa shook James Collingwood's hand and spoke quietly to him. She couldn't hear all their words, but she knew by Papa's demeanor and the timbre of his voice that he was expressing his deep gratitude to James.

As he started to step away, Stella heard her father tell him, "I'd like you to stop by our house tomorrow evening if you could, Mr. Collingwood. I know my wife will want to offer you a proper thank-you."

≈

Though Stella had been waiting on pins and needles for James's knock, when it finally came, she began to tremble inside. "He's here!"

Helen giggled and ran to admit their caller. Stella was right behind her.

Helen opened the door. James stood on the porch, looking handsome as ever.

"Hello, Stella," he said, tipping his hat.

"Hello, James." They stood staring at one another, and Stella felt unexpectedly shy.

She felt a tug on her skirt. "Aren't you going to ask him in?" Helen's silvery voice cut through the fog in her brain.

"Oh, my," she breathed. "Of course. What am I thinking? Please, James. Come in."

She opened the door wider, and he ducked under the lintel, removing his hat as he stepped inside.

Papa and Mama came into the hallway and stood, waiting to be introduced.

James nodded in their direction, and Stella finally came to her senses. "Papa, you remember Mr. Collingwood?"

"Pleased to see you again, Sir," James said, extending his hand. The two men shook hands, then James turned toward Mama. "And you must be Stella's mother. I can certainly see the resemblance."

Mama blushed at what was obviously meant to be a compliment. As she took James's hand, her gratitude poured out, mingled with tears. "Oh, Mr. Collingwood, how can we ever thank you?"

"No need, Ma'am. I didn't do more than any other man would have done under the circumstances. Stella is the one who should get the credit." He gave her a smile that turned her knees to jelly.

"You were both very brave," Mama told him. "Stella couldn't have gotten to Helen if it hadn't been for you. We are mighty grateful, Son, mighty grateful."

James knelt beside Helen, who stood in the hall staring up at him with a gaze of absolute adoration. "And how is Miss Helen feeling this evening? Have you recovered from your little adventure?"

She gave him her sweetest smile. "Yes, Sir. I'm feeling fine." She bowed her head shyly. "Thank you for. . .for saving me."

"You are very welcome, Helen," James said, putting a gentle hand to her cheek. "I couldn't have done it without your sister's help."

Helen nodded solemnly.

"Please, come into the parlor," Mama urged. "I have cocoa on the stove, and Stella made a cake."

Stella and her mother served refreshments in the parlor. Papa and James seemed to have found several common interests, and the women could scarcely get a word in edgewise. Stella couldn't have been more delighted.

Later, as James got ready to leave, Mama surprised Stella by issuing an impromptu invitation. "James, we're having dinner at the hotel Saturday night. Why don't you come along and be our guest?"

"Well, Ma'am. Thank you, but that's not necessary. That cake and cocoa were plenty of thanks—"

Papa jumped in. "Please, James. We insist. We'd be honored to have you."

Stella could scarcely believe her ears.

James looked at her, then back at her father. "Well, thank you, Sir." He looked to Mama and nodded his thanks. "Ma'am, I appreciate the invitation. I'd be honored."

Mama beamed, and Stella knew that James had succeeded in charming his way into each of their hearts.

Chapter 9

The dining room was crowded, and the tinkle of silverware and crystal and happy voices made pleasant music to accompany the Bradford party as they dined. But Stella Bradford's thoughts were focused in one direction only. James Collingwood sat across from her at the table, and by the way his eyes had held her gaze throughout the evening, she knew that his thoughts were directed toward her as well.

She could hardly believe that Papa had not only *allowed* James to be here with them but had extended the invitation himself. Helen sat at a place of honor at one end of the table, and she giggled every time James looked her way. He was Helen's hero, but more importantly, James had become Papa's hero.

Mama turned to James. "I hope your sister is feeling better, James. Sylvia, isn't it? I'm sorry she could not be with us tonight."

"Yes, Ma'am. Sylvia is much better, thank you. She asked me to give her regrets. She would have joined us, but there was a special gentleman coming to call this evening."

Stella turned to James with a cry of delight. "Is it John Matthews?"

He nodded, a smile of satisfaction on his face. John worked for Papa at the mill, but he and Sylvia had met when James hired him to do some carpentry work on the boardinghouse.

"Oh, James. I'm so happy for her."

The young girl who was waiting on their table came with the coffeepot, and they fell silent. The girl refilled Mama's cup and began clearing empty dishes from the table.

"Thank you, Miss," Papa said politely as she took away his dinner plate. "Might I ask your name?"

The lass gave him a shy smile. "It's Mariette, Sir."

"A very pretty name," Papa said. "Thank you for serving us tonight. You did a fine job."

Stella could tell the young woman wasn't accustomed to having gratitude shown in such a genuine manner.

"You are most welcome, Sir. It was my pleasure," she said, bobbing her head in a tacit curtsy.

Stella smiled as she thought of the surprise that awaited the girl a few minutes from now.

As though he'd read Stella's mind, Papa reached into his breast pocket and slipped out a small envelope, along with his fountain pen. Before they had left for the hotel, Stella and Helen had watched Papa tuck a five-dollar bank note inside the envelope. Helen had been more fascinated with the intricate depictions of Christopher Columbus on the paper bill than she had been with the idea of what it could buy.

As was their tradition, the Bradfords had prayed at home for the then-unknown person who would serve them their meal. Having observed the girl during the evening, Stella knew that this gift would make a significant difference in the life of young Mariette. She was proud of Papa's generosity and elated—as she had been every Christmas for as long as she could remember—to be taking part in this family tradition.

Papa wrote something on the ivory parchment, then closed the flap and laid the envelope on the table, tucking one corner beneath the porcelain saucer that held his empty cup.

Stella watched from the corner of her eye. Sure enough, Mariette's name was spelled out across the front of the envelope in Papa's loopy scrawl.

Stella knew that Papa was trying to be unobtrusive for James's sake. He had always said that it canceled the deed to blow your trumpet about it. But Helen was watching, too, and her eyes lit up. "Can we stay and watch her open it, Papa?"

"Hush," Mama chided, shaking her head.

Papa smiled at his youngest daughter. "You know the rule, Shortcake."

Helen pouted, and James turned to Stella, his knit brows indicating puzzlement.

"It's one of our holiday traditions," she whispered.

"I don't understand."

Leaning toward him and lowering her voice, she explained, "There is a five-dollar note inside the envelope. Every year before Christmas, we choose a night to eat dinner at the hotel. It gives Mama a break from cooking during the busy holiday season, but the real reason we do it is to bless someone who might not be as fortunate as we are. We always pray before we come that God will send the person to wait on us who most needs an extra Christmas blessing. But the rule is that we can't stay to watch them open the envelope. We want it to be a good deed done in secret." Listening to herself, she realized that she sounded like Mama explaining the special tradition to Helen.

James had a strange expression on his face.

Stella put a hand to her mouth. "Oh, and now I've ruined the secret part by telling you about it, haven't I? I'm sorry, James. I don't mean to crow. But it seemed rude not to explain it to you."

He put up a hand and shook his head. "No, it's not that," he said.

Concern filled Stella's heart. His complexion was pale, and he looked as though he might be sick.

"James? What's wrong?"

Without saying a word, James Collingwood pushed his chair back from the table and hurried from the dining room.

Chapter 10

Papa and Mama exchanged worried glances and turned to Stella for an explanation, but she couldn't begin to offer a motive for James's strange behavior. She shrugged and excused herself from the table.

Weaving her way through the other diners, she went to the lobby. The expansive room was empty, save for an elderly couple waiting at the front desk.

Hurrying through the front doors, Stella stepped into the cold night. Wisps of snow blew across the boardwalk, and she shivered involuntarily. Looking both ways down the darkened street, she spotted a lone figure at the north end of the building.

It was James. He stood, leaning against the brick facade, his head bent against the bitter wind. Though the frigid air bit painfully through her light wool dress, she went to him.

"James? Is everything all right?" *What a silly question.* One glance at his face told her that something was terribly wrong. "James, what is it? What's wrong?"

Without looking at her, his voice a monotone, he asked one question. "Stella, how long has this tradition been going on in your family?"

"The tip, you mean? The five-dollar note?"

He nodded.

"Why, as long as I can remember, I guess. What on earth does that have to do with anything, James? What is going on here? Why—"

"Did your family ever eat at the hotel in Barton's Grove? At Christmastime?" he interrupted.

She wrinkled her brow and tipped her head to one side. "I'm sure we did. We lived there for several years while Papa ran the mill. But I was little. I–I don't remember for certain. Why?"

James stood straighter, and for the first time, he seemed to notice that she had come out into the bitter winter night without her coat. He quickly removed his jacket and wrapped it around her. Keeping his right arm around her shoulders, he gently turned her toward the hotel. "Let's go inside," he said. "I. . .there's something I want to tell you."

They went back inside, and James led her to a narrow settee in a quiet corner of the lobby. Her mind was reeling, unable to imagine what had precipitated James's strange conduct.

He took her hand and looked into her eyes, confusion and awe oddly mingled in his expression. "Do you remember when I told you about that Christmas when I was working at the hotel in Barton's Grove? How I prayed that God would make it possible for me to enroll in the academy?"

"Yes. It was when your boss gave you the envelope—the money, right?" A hint of a memory began to niggle at her consciousness. There was some connection here that she couldn't quite fit together. "That was at Barton's Grove?"

James nodded. "But the money wasn't from Mr. Browne, Stella. It was a tip, a gratuity left on the table in an envelope with my name on it—by a family who had dined there that evening." His words gathered steam as they spilled out.

Stella gasped, and a broad smile spread across James's face.

"Oh, James, are you thinking what I'm thinking? Do you really think it could have been us—our family—that you waited on that night?"

A faraway look came to his eyes. "You know, Stella," he said, "for the longest time I wanted so badly to know who my benefactors were. I couldn't imagine why anyone would show such generosity to a stranger. For a time, I suspected that Mr. Browne just made up that story because he knew I wouldn't accept the money as charity from him. But he always insisted that he knew nothing about it. Finally I just quit asking and accepted the money for what it was—a gift from a God who loved me more than I could imagine."

"James," she breathed. "This means that you and I met each other before—before I ran into you on campus."

"You know," he laughed, "the night I got that envelope, I was so bowled over by God's answer to my prayer that I could scarcely think straight. I wracked my brain to remember something—anything—about the people I waited on that night. But the only thing I ever recalled was this family—a family with a baby and a pretty little towheaded daughter who chattered like a magpie through the entire meal."

Stella didn't know if James was teasing or not. Neither did she care, but she gave his arm a playful punch for good measure. She was still trying to wrap her finite mind around the amazing possibility they'd just stumbled upon. "Oh, James, can we tell Papa? Can we tell the others the story?"

He thought for a moment. "I think it's only right that they find out—after all these years—just how much your little tradition blessed a certain young man."

He took her hand in his, and a little shiver of joy ran its fingers down her spine.

"Yes, Stella, I'll tell your father what he could not possibly have known on that long-ago winter night." A twinkle came to his eyes as he continued. "That the anonymous boy he prayed to bless with that envelope would someday come to him asking to become a part of his family."

It took a moment for his words to register, and even then, she wasn't sure she had heard him correctly. "I don't. . .what are you. . . ?" she stuttered.

He slid from the settee and knelt before her, gazing into her face. "Stella, I know we haven't known each other very long, and right now all I have to offer you are two feet to walk beside you and these hands to hold you." He held his hands palms up before her, as though they held all the promise of his offering. "But I have come to love you with all of my being, and if you will still have me when the day comes that I can provide you with everything you deserve, I intend to request your father's permission to ask you to be my wife."

At that moment, Stella knew in the deepest part of her soul that this was the man God had made for her. The knowledge filled her with joy. "Oh, James," she breathed. "Yes! A thousand times, yes!"

She bent to receive the tender kiss he offered as a promise of his love—a token of the thousands upon thousands of kisses they would share in the hopeful ribbon of years that spooled out before them.

Epilogue

Dakota Territory, 1876

T hat was a fine, fine dinner, my darling," James said, wiping his hands on the white linen napkin, then rubbing his midsection contentedly.

Stella laughed, looking around the elegant dining room of the Clairemore Hotel, where they sat at a small corner table. "Well, I certainly can't take any praise for the meal. But you are right. That new chef the hotel hired is marvelous." She patted her husband's hand. "Thank you, Dearest, for the break. It was nice not to have to cook tonight."

"Thank your father," he told her with a wry smile. "This little tradition was his idea."

"I will do that—when I see him at Christmas dinner next week." She intertwined her fingers with his across the table. "I think I might even have the house plans ready to show Papa by then."

"I certainly hope so." That familiar, endearing glint she knew so well came to James's eyes. "As much as I do love her," he continued, "I am growing a little impatient with my architect. I am very anxious to begin filling up all those carefully drafted bedrooms with children."

She smiled and squeezed his hand. "I'm nearly finished with the plans. Truly. But before I turn my drawings over to the builder, I want them to be perfect."

"Well, I couldn't say about the *design* of our house. . . ." He rubbed a warm thumb across the back of her hand, then brought it to his lips and kissed each fingertip. "But as long as you are living within its walls, it will be perfect as far as I'm concerned."

Their waitress came just then with a pitcher of water in one hand and a fresh pot of coffee in the other. They waited in silence while she served them.

The dining room was crowded, and the girl seemed harried and tense. Stella watched their waitress surreptitiously as she replenished their water glasses. The young girl's shoes were scuffed and worn, and her uniform was a size too small. Her hands were red and chapped as though perhaps she spent the hours after the restaurant closed scrubbing pots and saucepans in the kitchen.

James leaned away from the table so the lass could reach his coffee cup more easily. "Thank you, Miss," he said, then cleared his throat. "I'm sorry—what did you say your name was?"

"I didn't say, Sir. But it's Annie."

"Well, Annie, we thank you for your service this evening."

"Quite welcome, Sir," she replied. "You folks have a merry Christmas now."

"And you," James and Stella said in concert.

Annie gave a half-curtsy and, with a weary sigh, moved on to the next table to pour coffee.

Smiling at his wife, James reached into his breast pocket and withdrew a small ivory envelope. Stella watched as he lifted the flap and inspected the contents. Apparently satisfied, he sealed the envelope and placed it on the table in front of him. Withdrawing a fountain pen from his pocket, he wrote Annie's name across the face of the envelope in his fine, precise script. He put away the pen, but his hand returned and lingered for a moment over the name he'd penned, as though he were asking a blessing upon it.

Then he pushed his chair back from the table, rose, and held out a hand to his wife. "Come, my love. Let's go home, shall we?"

Christmas Cake

by Janet Spaeth

Dedication

For Megan and Nick, simply because I love you.

Chapter 1

Elizabeth smiled as she heard Joel's steps outside the door. He paused, and she mentally counted with him, *one, two, three, four,* as he stomped his feet on the wooden porch four times before turning the doorknob.

They'd only been married six months, and already she knew the rhythm of his daily life. He had to have a cup of steaming coffee first thing in the morning. When he ate, he started with the vegetables and worked around his plate, saving the meat for the last. And she could definitely count on those four stamps of his feet before entering the house.

It was a sign of his thoughtfulness. The early snow that covered their Nebraska homestead's yard was easily tracked into the house, and Joel conscientiously cleaned his feet as completely as possible before entering.

She looked up at him as he entered the room. His face was red from the cold, and he puffed on his hands as he rubbed them together briskly.

"Cold?" she asked unnecessarily.

"Yup." His monosyllabic answer was lightened by a quick grin. "But it's November so we can't really expect different."

She smiled at him. The past six months with him were wonderful and joy-filled. The other women in town had told her eventually those four stamps of his feet, the coffee, the pattern of his dining, and the predictability of his ways would drive her insane, but she doubted it. Not when she was this deliriously happy.

"Cat got your tongue, Mrs. Evans?" His eyes twinkled as brightly blue as the clear plains sky as he studied her.

"No," she answered. "Just thinking that I am undoubtedly the luckiest woman on earth to have you as my husband."

The corners of his mouth turned up in a lopsided smile. "Luck?" he repeated. "Luck, my dear wife, had nothing to do with it. I saw you, I lost my heart to you immediately, and determined you were the woman I wanted to marry. So I did."

"Oh, you did?" She nodded, pretending to be seriously concerned. "And what about me?"

He stood towering over her, his hands on his hips. "Yes, what about you?"

What about her, indeed? In her memory she revisited their first meeting.

She'd been leaving Sunday services at her grandfather's church in Omaha when another member introduced the young man accompanying him. "This is Joel Evans, the son of an old friend."

Her grandfather frowned slightly as the two young people's gazes met and locked, but his friend had reassured him, "Not to worry, Cal. Joel's just visiting from Boston. He'll be here two more days, and that's it."

That evening both Joel and his elderly companion dined with Elizabeth and her grandfather, and by the end of the evening, both Elizabeth and Joel knew he would not be going back to Boston, not in three days, not ever.

They married six months later, after Grandfather was convinced their love was real and abiding, and that Joel had in his heart the same love of the Lord Elizabeth did. Within a month, they moved to the prairie farm so that Joel could try his luck at his dream: coaxing crops from the rich mid-western soil.

Grandfather had been loath to see her go, but despite his misgivings, they traveled on with his blessings.

It had worked out remarkably well. Soon after Elizabeth and Joel's departure, Grandfather met a charming widow only a few years younger than himself, and they just declared their own vows last month.

He was no longer alone in the big house on Locust Street, which relieved Elizabeth's mind, and if she were inclined to confess the truth about it, it also made him less fretful about his only relative living so far away.

She didn't worry about whether he was eating enough vegetables, and he didn't worry about whether she was safe from the winter winds. Instead, they committed their cares to the Lord and went on with their private earthly duties.

Elizabeth returned to the question at hand. "What about me?" she repeated. "I saw a man I knew I could love. A man I knew could love me. And after that, well, as they say, it all was history."

"You went after me with a vengeance," he agreed. "I had no choice but to give in." He sighed and let his shoulders slump. "I didn't have the strength to fight you."

"Oh, you pitiful thing!" She stood up and wrapped her arms around his frosty neck. "And I've been torturing you ever since."

They kissed, her lips warm against his still-cold mouth. This, Elizabeth knew, would never get tiresome, this age-old symbol of love. Their lips had barely parted when Joel clapped his hand to his pocket. "Lizzie! I almost forgot! A letter from my mother came today."

He pulled out a wrinkled envelope. The corner was torn, showing the distance it had traveled, but the elegant script of the senior Mrs. Evans was distinctive.

"What does she say?" Elizabeth asked, unconsciously smoothing down the front of her dress. Joel's mother made her nervous. It wasn't that she was indifferent or spiteful to Elizabeth—not at all—but rather that in her presence, Elizabeth felt tongue-tied and awkward. Mrs. Evans was so. . .so elegant. And Elizabeth was. . .not.

"She's coming for a visit!"

"A visit? Here?" Elizabeth looked around her and sank to the chair. "Here? She's coming here?"

"Yes!" Joel slapped the letter against his leg. "Yes! She's coming all the way to Nebraska! She's taking the train from Boston. We'll pick her up in Omaha and drive her out here."

"Here?"

"What's the matter, Lizzie?" His forehead wrinkled. "Is something wrong? Don't you want her to come here?"

"Oh, no, I mean, yes. No. Oh, Joel!"

His face clouded. "I thought you liked my mother."

"I do, Joel, I really do. And I am anxious to see her again."

He smiled at her. "That's better."

"When is she arriving?"

"She'll be here in a couple of weeks! She's coming for Christmas!"

This time Elizabeth didn't dare let herself say it, but she thought it: *Oh, no.*

The house was still basic. It was simple. What it actually was, Elizabeth finally admitted to herself, was unfinished. The floorboards were planks of rough-hewn pine, covered with inexpensive rag rugs. She'd counted herself fortunate to even have flooring; many of the women she'd met in town bemoaned the fact that they still had dirt floors.

She'd seen the Evans house in Boston. There weren't dirt floors there, and the floorboards were highly polished oak.

This house, this dear house, would seem like a hovel to his mother. And if she hated it, then perhaps Joel would see it through her eyes: the spaces between the planks, the knots in the rugs where Elizabeth had inexpertly tied the rags together, the cheapness of the thin yellow-edged drapes that had earlier seemed so cheerful.

Could he still be happy here? Elizabeth formulated the only prayer she could: *Please, God. Please.*

Dimly Joel's voice floated back in. ". . .And caroling and roasting chestnuts over the fire, and oh, my goodness, fruitcake."

"Fruitcake?" Elizabeth asked, feeling stupid.

"It's all the rage on the coast. Has been for a couple of years now. Aunt Susan makes a fruitcake that would. . ."

His voice faded back out, and Elizabeth let the feeling of dread settle in her chest. Caroling. Chestnuts. And now, fruitcake. Her beloved husband was going to hate Christmas out on the prairie. They couldn't go caroling, not when the houses were spread as far apart as they were.

And they couldn't do it alone, just the two of them. She'd need an extra bolstering of other female voices. Hers was, bluntly put, as pleasing as a saw on metal.

The nearest chestnut tree, as far as she knew, grew in the park near her aunt's house in Indiana.

And fruitcake? Now that didn't sound too bad.

Elizabeth sat up straight. Her husband was *not* going to regret staying in Nebraska with her. If he wanted fruitcake, then he would have fruitcake.

Just as soon as she found out what it was.

Chapter 2

A tiny swirl of cold crept under the quilt, and Elizabeth burrowed deeper.

Stamp, stamp, stamp, stamp.

Joel had already been out to feed the animals. She opened one eye and peeked out cautiously. Daylight flooded the room, telling her she'd clearly overslept. Dawn came late in winter.

She had no idea how long she'd slept, though. When they'd moved to the prairie, Joel said they were not bringing any clocks with them. "What's the purpose of knowing it's four-thirty-two in the afternoon?" he'd said. "In Omaha, that may mean something, but not to us. We won't need a clock to tell us the cows need to be milked. Their lowing will let us know. We won't need a clock to tell us when it's dinnertime. Our stomachs will tell us."

She threw the covers over her head. She should get up, but she was so tired. She'd stayed up most of the night worrying.

Something icy cold snaked down into the burrow she'd made and cupped her face. She sat up with a start. Joel stood beside the bed, grinning at her. He held out his hands to her. They were bright red.

"Lizzie, my dear, I do believe it's winter."

She leaped up and took his cold hands in hers. "Oh, Joel, are your hands going to be okay?" She held them to her face and rubbed them, trying to warm them. Panic bubbled up inside her. She'd never seen hands so brilliantly crimson. "You poor thing. They're probably frostbitten!"

His body shook a bit, and she looked up suspiciously. She hadn't been married to him nearly five months without learning something about her husband.

Sure enough, his eyes danced with hidden laughter.

She dropped his hands and glared at him. "Joel Evans, you tell me the truth this instant. What is going on?"

He crossed to the stove, which was burning cheerfully with new logs, and picked up the mittens she'd knit for him.

She'd knit them from thick wool, intended to keep his fingers safely warm while he was out on the cold Nebraska plains. She specifically had chosen a merry red that would, she hoped, be a cheerful note when the prairie winter seemed endless, as she knew it would.

But now they dripped onto the floor, vivid scarlet drops pooling on the raw wood planking. "I'm afraid your wool wasn't colorfast, Lizzie."

She'd been so anxious to show him what a good wife she was going to be that she'd failed to prewash the wool, or at least rinse the mittens out with saltwater before giving them to him. Her eyes filled with tears. She had let him down. "Oh, Joel, I'm so sorry!"

"No problem," he said, coming to her to give her a hug. "If my hands have to be another color, red is as fine a hue as there is. Besides, it'll wash off." He smiled at her. "So what do you have planned for today?"

"I thought I'd go through the wedding trunk your mother packed," she answered. "There were some Christmas decorations in there, I believe."

Joel frowned. "She didn't try to pass off that set of glass ornaments on you, did she? The ones that came all the way over from England on a packet ship and managed to arrive unscathed, not a single one broken?" From the way he said the words, the box of ornaments were clearly a family tradition, and the story of their arrival was near-legend.

"I don't think so," Elizabeth answered. "But I can't be sure until I go through the trunk again."

"Well," he said, grinning at her, "if you do find them, do me a favor."

"What?"

"Drop them. They're hideous."

Elizabeth waited until Joel went back to the barn. He was worried that the increased cold might signal bad weather, and he wanted to make sure the animals were secure with food and dry hay.

She pulled the trunk out from the corner where it usually sat. Something tiny and dark scurried from the light, and she breathed a sigh of relief as it scuttled through the space under the front door, nearly flattening itself in the process.

It was probably a field mouse. By now she should be used to them. The trick was, as Joel put it, to encourage them to live elsewhere when the house was the warmest place around in the dead of winter. She'd tried not to shudder as he talked about the mice. She'd nodded knowledgeably and agreed that they were an unavoidable nuisance, but inside she shivered with revulsion. Mice.

Fortunately no rodents had gotten into the trunk. Everything was still packed as nicely as it had been when Mrs. Evans ordered Joel to put it in the wagon.

Somehow it didn't surprise Elizabeth that his mother could pack this well. Even the table linen remained unwrinkled. Joel had built the house well, but keeping anything clean, let alone white, was a never-ending task. Dirt seemed to sift through even the tiniest crack in the door. Wisdom borne of experience living on the prairie told Elizabeth fancy white linen was silly.

Or was it? She shook out the linen tablecloth and studied it. It would look pretty on their table. The least she could do was make their home an inviting place. She laid the beautiful piece aside and investigated further.

She had gone through the trunk when they'd first arrived, being careful not to disarrange anything that Mrs. Evans had so meticulously packed. Elizabeth had glanced through the recipes and found them to require ingredients not available on the farm, and she'd cautiously retied the ribbon around them and placed them back in the trunk, thinking one day she would use them. That day had arrived.

At last she found what she was looking for. Mrs. Evans had told her she'd placed them in there. Her fingers closed around the ribbon-bound packet. Even this, Mrs. Evans had prepared with her special touch. Ribbons!

And on the front of the bundle was, in Mrs. Evans' recognizable flowery script, "RECIPES."

Her hands trembled as she untied the packet. It had to be in there. It had to be. She began to pray in an undertone as she sorted through the recipes, "Please, God, let it be here. Creamed chicken on toast points. No, no, not it. I want this to be special for Joel, God, a Christmas that won't make him regret marrying me. Curried corn. How awful. Who would curry corn? Lord, please, oh, please let it be here. Here's apple bread. Close but I don't think that's it. Please, please, please. Fruitcake. Aunt Susan's fruitcake. Thank You, Lord!"

She sagged back in relief, the dear recipe in her hand. Here it was, the recipe that would make all the difference in the world to her. She scanned through it, her eyes widening at some of the ingredients, her head bobbing in agreement at others.

Such a recipe! She'd never seen anything like it before. Aunt Susan's spidery handwriting was clear and readable, though, so everything on it must be right. Candied orange rind? She shuddered. It sounded dreadful.

So this was fruitcake.

⁂

Joel banked the straw against the lower parts of the barn's interior walls. The wind whistled through incessantly, it seemed. He was using hay bales around the edge of the house. Here in the barn, where the planks didn't quite meet on the northeast side, he'd piled more bales, too.

Actually, with the animals generating heat, the barn was a fairly cozy place. A bit fragrant, perhaps, but warm.

He stroked the twin noses that poked through the slats of the stable walls. As soon as Joel had decided to stay on the prairie and try his hand at farming, he'd bought the two horses. He'd trained them himself, or, as he sometimes said laughingly, they'd trained him. They were like children to him. As inquisitive as children, at least.

"Come on, Day. You, too, Lily." The team followed the sound of his voice as they moved restlessly in their stalls and whinnied at him from the front where the gate was lower. "You need to get out and run a bit. Don't want you going soft on me."

The horses understood all of it, it seemed to him. He turned them into the corral and watched as they ran with the absolute joy of being outside.

He knew how they felt. He loved it there.

And he loved Elizabeth.

He didn't know anyone could be as blessed as he was at this very moment. He paused to thank the Lord for her and for all that she had brought into his life. She was such an unexpected gift.

Gift!

"Run all you want today, girls," he said to the horses. "Tomorrow we're going into town. We have some Christmas shopping to do."

What could he get her? He frowned as he kicked a clump of snow away from the corral's gate. He was not a creative man. But Christmas was Christmas, and it was almost there.

Whatever thinking he might have ahead of him, he'd better come up with something quickly.

❧

Their dinner seemed almost formal that night. Perhaps it was the embroidered linen she'd put on the plank table. Or perhaps it was the way that Elizabeth and Joel watched each other.

"You'd better give me that shirt tonight," Elizabeth said at last.

"What shirt?" Joel paused, his fork suspended midway between his plate and his mouth.

"The one you have on. Look how long the sleeves are! Why, they're almost to your knuckles!"

He glanced guiltily at his fingers and quickly popped the bite of meat into his mouth before hiding his hand under the table. He'd washed his hands before dinner—repeatedly. He'd even tried the strong lye mixture that he used in the barn, but the dye from the red mittens was stubborn. The last thing he wanted to tell her was that he hoped she liked red hands—because his were apparently going to be red for quite a while.

370

Chapter 3

Elizabeth tucked an extra blanket around the basket of eggs that were cradled on her lap. The air was still and crisp, with no hint of wind or storms, but on the prairie, it never hurt to take some extra precautions.

Besides, it was cold.

Apparently Joel thought so, too. He stopped and gazed at the front of the wagon, his mind clearly engaged on imagining something.

"You know," he said, "I saw some willow down by the creek. Come spring, I think I'll go down there and get some saplings. They might be flexible enough to build an arch over the front of the wagon. Then we could. . ."

He chattered on as he got into the wagon. With a light flick of the reins, Joel let Day and Lily know it was time to go.

Elizabeth only half listened to Joel. The gait of the horses on the frozen ground jostled the eggs, and she had to hold onto the basket tightly. Occasionally, though, her fingers strayed to her pocket where the precious recipe was safely nestled. What if she lost it? She should have made a copy of it, but there hadn't been time. She would just have to be extra careful with it.

How much the ingredients for the fruitcake would cost worried her dearly. Since the sunny days of August, she'd put aside some of her egg money in a credit at the store, planning to use it for Joel's Christmas gift. She hoped that she'd have enough accumulated to trade evenly.

". . .And that'll shelter us from the elements when we go into town. What do you think, Lizzie?"

Guiltily, she realized she had missed everything Joel had been talking about. Something about willow saplings, bending them, elements. . .

She took a wild stab at it. "It'll work quite nicely, I think."

He rewarded her with a smile. "You don't have a clue what I've been talking about, do you? What's up, Lizzie dear? Christmas secrets?"

Her fingers brushed the recipe. "Yes, Joel, Christmas secrets."

She loved this man so much, it seemed impossible for her heart to hold any more joy. All she wanted was to make him happy, to keep him smiling. And in return, she knew that he wanted the same for her.

It wasn't as easy as she'd dreamed it would be, though. In her adolescent reveries, she'd been the perfect wife, serving perfect meals. . .and knitting perfect mittens. Mittens that didn't bleed bright red dye over her husband's hardworking hands.

He wore his old leather gloves today, since yesterday's fiasco forced him to stop wearing the red woolen mittens. She hoped his hands stayed warm enough.

Maybe she could purchase some more yarn, and she could knit him some new mittens that wouldn't bleed on his skin. It was a good thought. She settled back and watched the dazzling winter sun create glitters of diamonds on the new snow.

Mr. Nichols, the owner of the general store, stood behind the counter patiently as she smoothed out the precious recipe.

"I'll need a pound of candied fruit peel, a pound packet of raisins, a small container of thick molasses, and a cone of brown sugar. I'll also need cinnamon, mace, nutmeg, and allspice."

"A tin of each?" Mr. Nichols asked, frowning slightly.

Elizabeth consulted the recipe. "I need no more than a teaspoon of each. Is it possible to get less than an entire tin?"

The shopkeeper rubbed his chin thoughtfully. "I think I can do that." He gathered the supplies and put them into the basket that had held her eggs. "Anything else?"

She looked at the recipe again. Eggs, flour, baking powder, salt, and lard she had. She shook her head. "I believe that'll be all."

"Good thing you brought in your eggs," he said. "Demand's high with Christmas coming, and not everybody's hens are laying as well as yours. Cold weather gets to them, I guess."

He licked the tip of his stubby pencil before he began totaling the charges. When he gave her the sum, Elizabeth almost lost her breath. She hadn't expected it to be this much.

She looked longingly at the wool she'd laid aside. She didn't have enough money to buy all of the ingredients for the fruitcake and still afford the yarn for new mittens for Joel. Sadly she pushed the skein of yarn aside. It was a terrible muddy, brownish-gray color, ugly but serviceable. Joel needed mittens, but perhaps she could set the color in his red ones. That way he could have mittens and his fruitcake.

She'd seen the reminiscent glow in his eyes as he revisited his Christmases in Boston. If there was anything she could do to recreate even a part of those Christmases, she would do it.

"Have you had fruitcake before?" Mr. Nichols asked as he slid the now-filled basket to her.

"No, I haven't."

He rummaged under the counter and pulled out a tattered magazine. She recognized the name: *Godey's Lady's Book.* "Here," he said, thumbing through it, "there's an article about it. The missus showed it to me the other night."

Elizabeth scanned the page he showed her. According to the article, fruitcake was a favorite food of Queen Victoria's, and now it was considered a delicacy of fashionable people.

"You're the first person to come in and get the ingredients for it," Mr. Nichols said. "You're quite a style-setter, Mrs. Evans!"

" 'Is there any thing whereof it may be said, See, this is new? it hath been already of old time, which was before us.' "

He gaped at her. "Excuse me?"

Elizabeth laughed. "It's from Ecclesiastes. This fruitcake that's all the rage in England and now the East Coast is actually an old recipe from my husband's family. What is old is new again."

A movement outside the store window caught her eye. Joel had stopped to talk to a few men, but he'd soon be in to pick her up. "Do me a favor, Mr. Nichols." She leaned across the counter and lowered her voice. "Do not say anything about this to my husband."

He nodded in understanding. "Prices a bit steep, is that it?"

"No, no, nothing like that." She paused and couldn't resist. "Well, except for that skein of wool. It shouldn't sell for a penny over forty cents, and you know it."

The door opened a crack, and she could hear Joel bidding one of his companions a Merry Christmas. "Don't tell him about this because it's a surprise. A Christmas secret."

Mr. Nichols straightened up and winked at her. "No problem, Mrs. Evans. No problem at all."

"Well," Joel said in a jovial voice behind her, "I probably should be worried that the shopkeeper is winking at my wife, but I'm hoping it means that she's getting a good price on her groceries."

Groceries! She'd totally forgotten about them.

"So what did you get?" Joel asked her, reaching for the basket and lifting one corner of the cloth she spread over the top.

Faster than she thought possible, she reached across and lightly slapped his hand. "Joel Evans, you know better than to go snooping this time of year."

Joel laughed and put his arm around her. "Let's go so we can get back home before dark."

As they left, Mr. Nichols called out, "Say, Joel, stop back by the next time you're in town. I've got some good liniment for those hands. I don't believe I've ever seen hands that chapped—and that red!"

&

The little farmhouse, with its plank flooring and raw white walls, seemed especially cozy that night. The wind had finally picked up, blessedly after they'd gotten Day and Lily stabled, the cows fed, and the chickens settled with fresh grain.

The tips of Elizabeth's fingers still tingled from the cold ride home. In her anxiety to leave the store before Joel saw the ingredients for the fruitcake and figured out her surprise, she'd left her gloves on the counter.

Joel teased her about her vanity in not wanting to wear the extra pair that was on the floor of the wagon—big, rough cloth gloves so old that the fur lining was patchy with age—but she couldn't tell him the real reason.

She didn't dare let go of the recipe. It was enough that she'd lost her gloves. If she lost the recipe, too, she'd be devastated. Too much was riding on it, so she'd kept her hands in her pockets, her fingers curled protectively around the precious piece of paper.

She turned her chair to the fire and opened her Bible to her favorite passage.

"Read it aloud," Joel said from the other chair, which also faced the fire. He was nearly asleep.

She barely needed to follow the printed words as she began her favorite chapter from the Bible. " 'Though I speak with the tongues of men and angels. . .' "

"1 Corinthians 13," said Joel, not opening his eyes. He continued with her drowsily, ending with, " 'And now abideth faith, hope, charity, these three; but the greatest of these is charity.' "

His head dropped to one side, and she studied his face. It was the face of a good, kind man, one whose love would indeed fail her not. She tucked the quilt closer around his shoulders and kissed his forehead.

When she counted her blessings in her evening prayer, she would include this night as one of them.

"Did I tell you I might not be back until after dark?" Joel asked, returning to the house for the fifth time since hitching Day and Lily to the wagon.

"Yes, you did, my sweet." Elizabeth turned him around and pushed him out the door. "Now go, or it'll be dark before you leave!"

She watched from the door as he walked to the wagon, put his foot on the sideboard, and then paused. She sighed as he returned to the house. "Joel, if you—"

Whatever she was going to say was silenced by his kiss. "There," he said when he drew back. "I knew I'd forgotten something. See you later tonight!"

This time she wrapped up in the thick shawl she kept by the door, and she accompanied him to the wagon. "Give Brother Jensen my warmest wishes for his recovery," she said as Joel slid onto the wagon's seat.

"Rotten luck for him, breaking his leg like this," Joel said, "although better now than during planting or harvest, I'd say."

"It will cheer him to see you, I know." She pulled the wagon robe tighter around his feet. "And I hope the cookies will be enjoyable for him. Don't eat them on the way."

Brother Jensen, the aging man who served as the pastor of their tiny congregation, had broken his leg in a fall from his barn loft. A widower, he had lain alone for thirty hours until someone stopped by and found him. The leg was slow in setting, and the church members were taking turns bringing him food and companionship.

Elizabeth was almost looking forward to Joel's absence. It gave her an entire day to work on the fruitcake. She tidied up the kitchen, made the bed, and swept the floors. Straightening the small house didn't take long. There were really only three tiny rooms: the kitchen, the living room, and the bedroom.

With a fresh apron tied around her waist, she set forth to make fruitcake. Joel had fed the chickens and gathered the eggs that morning. They were in a bowl on the table, with a note beside them. *Lizzie, where's the egg basket? Couldn't find it.* Elizabeth breathed a sigh of relief. If he'd gone looking for it, her secret would have been exposed.

The tins of flour, salt, and baking powder went next to the eggs. The tub of lard joined them. Then she reached into the far corner of the top shelf, where she'd hidden the ingredients she'd bought at the store. They were still tucked in the egg basket, where she was sure that Joel wouldn't bother to look.

As her hands closed around the woven handle, something small and gray and very quick scampered out of the basket, leaped to the edge of the nearest chair, and jumped onto the floor. Without a second thought, Elizabeth grabbed the broom and chased it outside, where it vanished under the woodpile.

The field mice were getting worse. Every morning she had to chase them out of the house. She'd have Joel look into traps when he went into town next.

This is the prairie, she told herself. *I'm not the only creature out here. I have to expect that there will be mice and snakes and—*

She broke off the thought before she could go any further with it. She was alone in the house for several hours, and the last thing she needed to do was start thinking about what could scare her.

What she needed to do was make a fruitcake.

She took the basket down and set it on the table. A clean bowl, a baking pan, a spoon—she scurried around the small kitchen, gathering the utensils.

At last it was all ready for her to begin. She reached into her pocket and unfolded the recipe, although she didn't need it anymore; she had read it so many times, it was etched in her memory. She took the brightly checked cloth off her egg basket and nearly fainted.

The mouse had been busy. Every single packet had been gnawed into. The candied fruit peel had apparently not been to his liking, for he'd chewed into the package and then abandoned it after one piece. The raisins were a mess, and the brown sugar had teeth marks all around the cone. Even the tiny envelopes containing the spices had been torn into.

Elizabeth sank onto the floor and buried her face in her hands.

How was she going to make the fruitcake now? And how was she going to make this Christmas as good as the ones Joel had had before? She should have put the supplies in tins. She knew about the field mice, and she hadn't taken the appropriate precautions.

Everything was ruined. Everything.

Joel pulled into his pastor's farmyard and was greeted by the familiar figure of Brother Jensen at the door, waving to him.

The man hobbled out onto the hewn rock step and motioned to him with a rudimentary crutch. "Come on in, Joel! You didn't have to come all this way, although I'm mighty glad you did. It gets a bit lonesome out here, being stove up like this with my bum leg."

The inside of the pastor's house was tidy, but the fire was laid awkwardly and burned too cold. Brother Jensen apologized for it, explaining that, thanks to his broken leg, he couldn't bend over far enough to get it done correctly.

Joel realigned the logs so they were slightly angled, bark side down. "Where's the fatwood?" he asked, looking around the stove for the soft wooden sticks that would get the fire going.

"I'm out," Brother Jensen admitted. "I'm using what's at the bottom of the woodpile."

"And how are you doing that?" Joel asked suspiciously. "You shouldn't be digging around there with your leg."

Brother Jensen waved his objections away. "I didn't. Well, not much. Earlier this week Karl Lund stopped by and filled a pail full of kindling. It's nearly empty now."

"I'll fill it before I leave," Joel said, smiling with satisfaction as the logs caught and began to burn cheerfully.

Brother Jensen passed Joel a plate of the cookies Elizabeth had sent over. "Would you like one? Your wife certainly is a good cook."

Joel accepted one of the oatmeal cookies. "Elizabeth is a wonderful cook. There isn't anything in this world she can't make if she sets her mind to it."

"She brings my departed Abigail to mind. Now there was another fine woman. You're a fortunate man, Joel."

"Amen to that, Brother Jensen. She is a godsend of a wife, and I am truly blessed."

The two men visited about the price of wheat, the usefulness of the new threshing equipment that had arrived in Omaha, and the impending weather.

Brother Jensen grinned broadly when Joel told him his mother was coming. "We'll pray, then, whatever winter storms are ahead for us will hold off until the new year is settled in," the pastor said. "That'll give you time for a visit and time for her return."

"I appreciate your prayers," Joel responded, "although I'm not convinced God always listens to what we order up when we talk to Him."

The older man laughed. "Oh, He listens, all right. What's hard for us to accept is we might, just might, be asking for the wrong thing, and He's simply fixing things for us up there in heaven."

"So," Joel continued, smiling, "are you saying if we pray for calm weather and He delivers us a blizzard, there's a reason?"

Brother Jensen nodded. "We don't always see it right away, sometimes not for years, maybe not for centuries, but the Lord never puts down His hand on this earth without good cause."

His voice was getting hoarse, and Joel realized the pastor needed some rest.

"I think I'd better get back," Joel said softly, rising to his feet. "Let me bring more wood in now. You're running low on logs."

"I'd appreciate it, Joel. You know what the Good Book says, 'Where no wood is, there the fire goeth out.'"

As he refilled the woodbox inside the pastor's house, Joel's thoughts turned to Elizabeth. The sun was starting to set, and he'd just make it home in time for dinner. What delightful meal would she make tonight?

❦

Elizabeth sat in the middle of her kitchen, the precious contents of the egg basket now relegated to the garbage. Outside, the sun set in a vivid blaze over the prairie, pouring liquid purples and vibrant crimsons over the snow-whitened land. Only when the glorious display was gone, swathing the land in darkest night, did she realize that Joel soon would be home, and she had nothing ready for him.

Even as she thought it, she heard the sound of the wagon approaching. She hurriedly sliced some meat and bread. It was not much, but it would have to do today.

Stamp, stamp, stamp, stamp. Joel walked into the house.

And her heart overflowed with joy.

Chapter 5

I have to go into town," Joel said the next morning.

"Again?" Elizabeth turned from the shirt she was mending, rose, and walked over to the window. The sky was a clear, promising blue. Not even one fluffy white cloud marred the scene.

He came up behind her and put his arms around her from the back. Together they stood, gazing at the prairie spread out before them, a vision of white snow and blue sky, all so startlingly clean and pure, it almost hurt to look at it.

"I doubt that it'll storm today," he said at last.

The prairie could, at any moment, turn menacing. They both knew that. A storm could blow in quickly, true, but she'd pack an emergency food bundle, and the buffalo robe would keep him warm and dry until the storm blew over.

"Anything I can pick up for you while I'm there?" he asked.

Her thoughts flew to the ingredients for the cake. She could hardly ask him to pick those up for her without arousing his suspicion. She turned to him and smiled winningly. "Can I go, too?"

"Uh, sure," he answered. "If you want to."

A flicker of something passed across his face as he said the words. Had she imagined it? It looked almost like—disappointment.

Her heart dropped like a stone. Didn't he want to be with her? Was he bored with her, with their small house on the plains, already? It had been his idea to live on the prairie. If he was tired of their life, if he wanted to be alone, she must be letting him down somehow.

She strengthened her resolve. She had to go with him to town. She had to make the fruitcake. It was a link with the home and the traditions he'd left behind for the flat Nebraska farmland.

Yes, the fruitcake. That would make him happy.

✥

Joel was quieter than usual on the ride into town, but Elizabeth couldn't read his expression or his thoughts.

Every once in a while he'd look at her and smile, and all her doubts would evaporate, no more substantial than the tiny puffs of snow kicked up by the horses' hooves as they followed the worn path through the snowy landscape. But for the most part, he kept whatever was going through his mind to himself. She would have given anything to know what he was thinking about so intently.

Fear, or maybe worry, washed over her, a feeling so overwhelming, she felt as if she were drowning in it. She had to do something to break into his thoughts.

"So what are you going to get in town?" Her words, unnaturally loud, rang through the still winter air like shots.

He glanced over at her and smiled almost guiltily. "Oh," he hedged, "something. Nothing."

"Well, is it something or is it nothing?" Her voice sounded more impatient than she had intended.

"It's neither. It's both."

She nodded. "Very well. Just as long as we're clear about it."

He laughed and let the reins drop onto his lap as he reached across the wagon seat and enclosed her in his arms. Day and Lily, used to the trip, plodded along methodically.

"You silly goose," he said as he held her closely. His lips were cold against her forehead. "Why do you think I'm going into town? It's not quite two weeks until Christmas."

How could she have been such a ninny? Of course he'd get her a present, just as she was making something for him: the fruitcake.

Curiosity caught hold of her. "What are you getting me?"

He shook his head. "Oh, no. You're not charming that secret out of me."

"Please?" she wheedled.

"No."

"Is it a hat?"

He shook his head.

"A new bowl."

"No."

"A necklace."

"No. You can quit asking. I won't tell."

"Oh, Joel." She sank back and pretended to pout.

"But you can tell me what *you* got *me*," he said as he picked up the reins and tched to the horses to go faster.

"I can't!" She tried to keep the panic out of her voice but was unsuccessful.

"Don't I even get to guess?" he teased.

"No. I mean, I'd rather you didn't."

He shrugged happily. "Then don't ask me any more questions about your present."

The remainder of the ride into town she spent half asleep, dreaming of Christmas secrets. The wagon rumbled to a stop, and she woke with a start. They were already in town, in front of Mr. Nichols' store.

"I'll be back pretty quick," Joel said. He glanced at the sky, and Elizabeth's gaze followed his. Along the horizon, thick white clouds were scudding toward them, the kind of clouds that carried snow, and lots of it.

"I'll hurry," she said.

They both stood beside the wagon uncertainly. "I'm going to Mr. Nichols' store," she said pointedly.

"Yes?" He grinned.

"If you, um, need to go in there, too. . ."

"Why would I need to go in there?"

It was indelicate, but there was no way around it. "For my. . .you know."

Her husband pretended surprise. "They sell you-knows in there? And all the time I thought they grew wild!"

She rolled her eyes. "My present, you lunatic. You said you were getting my present today."

"I am."

"But don't you need to go in there?"

"Not getting it there," he said, shoving his hands in his pockets and beginning to whistle.

"Where are you getting it, then?" she asked.

He lifted his shoulders and looked innocent, and at last she sighed and went inside the store, her curiosity still unresolved.

Mr. Nichols beamed at her as he hurried to her side. "Mr. Evans with you?" he asked after a surreptitious look around.

She shook her head. "He had some other errand."

"Then tell me—how did it turn out?" Mr. Nichols waited in anticipation.

Elizabeth twisted the ties of her bag in her fingers. "Not quite as I'd hoped," she said at last, her words so low that he had to lean forward to catch her answer.

He rubbed his hands together gleefully. "Even better! Then it exceeded your expectations?"

"Well," she hedged, "it didn't turn out at all the way I'd thought it would. It didn't. . .it didn't turn out at all, truth to tell."

He rubbed his chin. "Not at all? I've heard the texture of fruitcake is unusual. Perhaps that's the problem?"

She shook her head miserably. "I didn't get to make it at all. A mouse got into the supplies before I could."

"A mouse?" Mr. Nichols frowned. "Those miserable little creatures are certainly an annoyance. Everyone struggles with them invading their homes during the cold months of winter."

"I do the best I can," she said, looking down. "But there they are, no matter what I try."

"Well, I certainly wish replacing your ingredients were something I could do without extra charge, but I'm sorry, Mrs. Evans, I can't."

"I know." Her voice was almost a whisper. "I brought eggs."

She handed the basket to him. "There aren't as many as last time," she said. "But I'm hoping. . ."

"I need eggs badly," he told her as he lifted the cover of the basket. "Everyone in town is busily baking for Christmas, and I can't keep up with the demand. Let me do some figuring."

As he pulled a sheet of paper from the counter and did some quick calculations, Elizabeth picked up the hank of yarn from the display. *What a horrid color.*

"Interested in the yarn, Mrs. Evans?" Mr. Nichols leaned in, as if to close the sale.

"Is this the only yarn you have?" She knew she shouldn't even be inquiring; she didn't have any way to pay for it. She almost sighed with relief when the shopkeeper shook his head.

"No, I'm sorry. That's all I have left. The colorful skeins went earlier, for Christmas knitting, I assume."

"Well, then," Elizabeth said, giving the yarn one final pat, "I'll stay with what I have."

"It looks to me like we're about even, Mrs. Evans. I can replace your ingredients in exchange for the eggs."

"I can't pay for it," she said, "and I won't buy on credit."

"I'd be glad to extend you a line of credit," he said. "You're a regular customer, and your chickens are reliable. You can pay me later."

She paused. Mittens would be nice, but she could not bring herself to take something she had not paid for. "No," she said, "I can't, but thank you for your offer."

The sound of a cough behind them alerted them to the fact that Joel was there, too.

"Time to go?" she asked, gathering the ingredients Mr. Nichols hastily assembled.

He nodded. "Looks like we have a storm to outrun." His voice sounded cheerful, but she detected an undercurrent of worry.

Elizabeth gathered up the supplies, checked to see that they were nestled in the basket. This time all of the ingredients were in tins. They were her last hope for a good Christmas for her husband.

Then she went out to face the storm with him.

Chapter 6

The flakes swirled with increasing intensity as Joel and Elizabeth ventured across the prairie. Snow gathered in thick heaps and piles in the folds of the buffalo robe and quilts Elizabeth had tucked around them.

What had begun as an easy winter snowfall drastically increased in strength until it became a full-bore blizzard. The temperature dropped measurably, and although his legs and feet were warm enough under the covers, Joel had to drive with his elbows tucked tightly against his chest to hold the blankets in place as the wind increased. An icy finger of frozen air slipped its way in as a gust lifted the top quilt, and he shivered involuntarily.

Joel reached up to wipe away the icy whiteness from his eyebrows and eyelashes, and snow cascaded down his sleeve. He didn't dare take his eyes off the road to shake the melting snow from his arm. He had to move them forward.

"Hyah, Day! Hyah, Lily!" The team sensed the urgency in their mission and took off as if they were in a race, galloping in perfect harmony. All around them, the snow moved like a living thing, and the cold wrapped itself around him until his fingers became stiff.

The path of the well-worn road was becoming obscured as the wind-driven snow filled in the ruts, smoothing it out so it matched the rest of the endless prairie. The storm altered the landscape as the wind moved the snow into piles and drifts, making hills that hadn't been there before. Nothing looked the same as it had on the ride into town earlier that day.

It was perilously easy to get lost.

Joel tried to keep the landmark tree in his vision, the place that would tell him where he needed to turn to the east. If he could see it, they would make it safely; but the fury of the storm increased, and the horizon was disappearing into a blur. Suddenly, the tree vanished.

All around him, everything turned white. He could barely make out his own hands holding the reins.

Whiteout.

It was every traveler's worst fear on the prairie, this time when the wind took the snow, picked it up, and made it into a whirling cloud of white that took away a man's sense of direction and often drove him farther out onto the prairie.

There was nothing to do at a time like this but hold true to the course, trust in the horses. . .and have faith in the Lord. This was, Joel figured, as good a time as any to talk to God. And he did. *God, it seems like I come to You more when I'm needing You than when I'm thanking You, and for that I truly apologize. But I'm in a fix here, and if You feel that it's right to take me in this storm, do so, but save Lizzie. Save my love.*

He would have given anything to be able to take her in his arms and hold her tiny form to him. The winds paused briefly, and in this pocket of quiet he realized she was speaking. He couldn't catch every word, but he made out enough to recognize what she said. She was reciting from her beloved Psalm 100: " 'Know ye that the Lord He is God. . . .' "

What an odd choice, he thought. *A psalm of praise, now?*

The reins pulled in his hands, and he realized Day and Lily were turning. He tried to straighten them out, but they resisted.

"Day! Lily!" The wind tore the words from his lips and tossed them away with the flying snow. The reins slipped from his frozen fingers and flapped free. He couldn't catch them and watched as they disappeared into the white cloud that surrounded them. He had no choice but to give the horses their head and let them take them home. . .if that was, in fact, where they were going.

"Joel?" Elizabeth's voice cut through the wind, and he turned to look at her. Her next words vanished into the wind's roar, but the question on her face was clear. *Will we be safe?*

He smiled at her with an assurance he didn't truly feel. It was one thing to place all your trust in God; it was another thing entirely to be sure that you and God were of the same mind.

How did he know they would be safe on earth—when, in fact, the Lord might be planning for them to be safe in heaven? It was a theological question his wind-chilled mind could not fathom, but something crept through his numbed thoughts with lightning precision: he wanted to live—with Elizabeth.

The full measure of his love for her almost overwhelmed him. He'd always known he loved her. It was something he'd never doubted, not from the first moment he saw her on the steps of her grandfather's church in Omaha. He'd known then that this woman had his heart.

He was not one to believe in love at first sight, not at all, but what happened to him was different. Not that he could explain it, not then, not now. He was a pragmatist. He wanted proof, something solid he could point to and say, "This is real. I can see it. I can touch it. I can prove it."

But one thing became progressively more obvious to him: love was the one thing that could never be explained as he would like.

He smiled as Elizabeth reached for his hand and squeezed it. Even through the snow-crusted mitten, he could feel the warmth of her touch. Maybe this was the physical proof he wanted. Love was real in Elizabeth.

The horses stopped. He hadn't even realized they had slowed. The cloud of white that had been their nemesis dissipated somewhat, and he shouted with joy as he saw what was in front of him. "Elizabeth, we're home! The horses brought us home!"

He swung out of the wagon, nearly toppling when his deadened hand didn't grasp the edge of the wagon.

They were home!

He clumsily wrapped the reins around his wrist and led the horses to the barn, recognizing as he did so the irony of that. Here they were, just yards from the barn door, and he was leading in the animals that had brought them there.

The door was wedged partially shut with snow, and he kicked it free. Day and Lily trotted inside, their breath turning translucent in the warm barn.

Joel helped Elizabeth down awkwardly; his hands might as well have been wooden stumps. He blew into his mittens, his breath warming his cold hands. Experimentally he flexed his fingers, grimacing as his fingertips stung. The painful tingle was a good sign; the feeling flowing back into his hands meant that there was no frostbite. "The barn is safe. We will stay here and wait out the storm."

She nodded, and he noted how tired she was. Joel checked her hands and feet and even the tips of her ears to make sure she hadn't suffered any frostbite. He took a pitchfork and freed a bale of hay, releasing the sweet-smelling dried grass into a fresh bed for her, but she shook her head. "No. I'll help you curry Day and Lily. Then, we all will sleep."

Working together, they had the horses brushed and fed and in their stalls quickly. They tended to the cows and chickens, then collapsed onto the fresh hay.

They rested in each other's arms and were silent until Joel broke the stillness. "You were saying Psalm 100 during the storm, weren't you?"

She nodded drowsily. "It seemed appropriate."

"Why, though? Why were you praising God instead of pleading with Him?"

She glanced at him. "Is that what you were doing, pleading with Him?" She smiled. "I was, too. But through it all, I felt drawn to the Psalm. 'For the Lord is good; his mercy is everlasting; and his truth endureth to all generations.' No matter that there was a storm, Joel, the Lord *is* good."

He ran his hand over her hair, now tangled and matted with hay, and touched her cheek, wind-bitten and raw. He had never seen anyone as beautiful in his entire life.

The Lord was, indeed, good.

Chapter 7

*S*tomp, stomp, stomp, stomp.

The unmistakable sound of Joel's entrance to the house woke Elizabeth. She knew she had probably overslept again, but she had been bone-tired after the trip through the storm, almost as if she had pulled the wagon herself.

Joel grinned at her as she stumbled to the fire. "Good morning, sleepyhead." He planted a kiss squarely on her lips, laughing at her reaction to his icy cheeks against her face.

"Is it still snowing?" she asked, pulling back as a shower of snow cascaded down her neck.

He shook his head. "The storm blew itself out late last night. Don't you remember coming in here?"

"Only vaguely. Are the horses all right?"

"They're no worse for the wear. Actually, they seem rather proud of themselves, bringing home the mister and missus all by themselves."

Mister and missus. How she loved to hear that. "I hope you rewarded them well."

"Each of them got an extra apple this morning. That made them very happy. In the horse world, an apple must be the equivalent of a gold medal. Day and Lily came as close to smiling as I've ever seen."

The image of the two horses smiling was too much for Elizabeth, and she was still laughing as she returned to the fire, now dressed warmly. Joel stood at the window, looking out across the snow-swept plain. Something was bothering him, she could tell.

"What's wrong?" she asked, coming up behind him and wrapping her arms around his waist.

"I'm worried about Brother Jensen," he said. "He can't get around too well with that broken leg of his. The temperature has dropped so low that it would be dangerous for him to be out there, alone in his house, without a fire."

"Is it very cold?" she asked, already knowing the answer.

He nodded, his eyes not moving from the landscape.

"Then why must you go?"

It was then that he turned to her. "Lizzie, Brother Jensen is a man of God;

but even if he weren't, I couldn't rest with myself knowing I didn't try to ensure his safety."

" 'Insomuch as ye have done it unto one of the least of these My brethren, ye have done it unto Me,' " she quoted softly.

Elizabeth knew, then, that he had to go. She'd worry, she'd fret, she'd stew. But she would let him go on his journey because he was on God's errand. She had to trust in that.

Besides, a little voice in her head reminded her, *he'll be gone long enough for you to make the fruitcake.* She smiled up at him. "Give Brother Jensen my best, won't you, please?"

The thought of finally getting the fruitcake baked was almost heady. She wrapped Joel in two scarves, the old red mittens, and a thick fur-lined hat; packed three pairs of extra socks and a spare sweater; and bundled the wagon seat beside him with quilts, blankets, and the ever-present buffalo robe.

As he was set to leave, she added a heated brick, wrapped in layers of cotton flannel, to the floor of the wagon near his feet.

She handed him a basket. "I'm sorry I don't have something fancier for Brother Jensen, but here are the leavings of lunch and some nice new bread. I included a jar of raspberries for color. They might be tasty on the bread."

"He'll appreciate anything you send, Lizzie."

She kissed him and urged him into the wagon. "You'd better hurry along now."

Joel looked at her curiously. "You know, Elizabeth Evans, you seem mighty anxious to get me gone. What's going on?"

She widened her eyes innocently. "Why, nothing. The winter days are short, and I don't want you riding at night."

Joel didn't seem entirely satisfied by her answer, but he picked up the reins, and Day and Lily instantly became alert. "I will try to be back before dark, but if I'm not, put a light in the window to guide me through the prairie night."

"If you are late, my husband, I shall put a light in every window and all along the edge of the house and the barn, to bring you back safely." Her words were barely above a whisper.

With a click of his tongue to encourage the horses, he set off. Elizabeth watched him go until he faded to only a speck on the endless white horizon. At last a spasm of shivering sent her inside.

She took her ingredients down, congratulating herself on having had the foresight to place them in a metal container. They were, indeed, safe and fresh. Within minutes she had the table covered with the accoutrements of baking. One by one, she laid the ingredients out next to the bowls, the spoons, and the pan.

Then she tore into the bedroom and from the trunk where she had carefully hidden it, she took a piece of paper—the recipe.

The recipe seemed straightforward enough. It seemed a bit overladen with the flour and molasses, but Mr. Nichols had said that fruitcake was heavier than the usual cakes she was used to.

She creamed the lard and eggs to a frothy pale yellow, and then scraped the brown sugar cone until she had the correct measure. In went the sugar, the flour, the baking powder, the spices, and the salt, and she stirred and stirred until she was convinced her arm would drop clean off her body. The mixture was so dreadfully thick.

She consulted the recipe anew and checked her additions. Yes, it was right. Apparently, it was supposed to be this unyielding.

The recipe called for alternately adding molasses and the candied fruit. The molasses gave the batter some liquid, but it was still terribly thick.

Elizabeth frowned and studied the recipe again. She had done everything correctly. Perhaps it was one of those miracles of cooking that she had never understood. She sighed and put it in the oven and sat down to wait.

Elizabeth had never been a good waiter. She alternately sat and fussed around the tiny kitchen, popping up and down like an impatient sparrow. The cake had to bake for at least two hours, possibly three, and she'd drive herself insane if she didn't take care of her edginess.

Finally she took her Bible and settled before the fire. She knew exactly what she needed to read. The glorious opening lines of Psalm 9 had the power to ease her soul: *"I will praise Thee, O Lord, with my whole heart. . . ."*

They reminded her of her grandfather. He had read opening verses of it in her wedding service.

She missed him, but he had been so happy at his own wedding that she couldn't begrudge him spending Christmas with his new wife and her family in Lincoln. Besides, there was the very real fact that this house would be stretched to hold the three of them when Joel's mother came. Adding two more people would tax it beyond its limits.

Perhaps after Christmas they could ride into Omaha and visit her grandfather and his new wife. She'd suggest it to Joel.

The most heavenly aroma reached her nose, and she was drawn into the kitchen. She couldn't resist a peek in the oven. Taking a mitt from the table, she opened the black metal door. Heat blasted her face, and she blinked reflexively before leaning closer. She didn't like what she saw. It smelled wonderful, but it looked awful. It was flat with a sudden depression in the exact center.

No cake she'd ever made had turned out like that. What could be wrong with it? Was it underdone? Overdone? Or—and she shuddered a bit at the thought—was it perfect as it was? For the first time since they moved to the claim, Elizabeth regretted not having a clock. She'd never had to bake anything this long, and she'd certainly never had to bake anything like this.

She gave it an experimental poke. The edges were springy, no, spongy. The depression in the middle was gooey and clung to her fingertip. The hot batter burned and she stuck her finger in her mouth.

It tasted good, a bit strongly flavored, but perhaps it would mellow after baking.

Elizabeth shoved it back into the oven. She'd leave it in there a bit longer, at least until the center set, and then she'd take it out.

Her stomach clutched with anxiety. Joel's whole Christmas was riding on this fruitcake—and so was hers. She couldn't focus on anything, not even her Bible now. She flitted around the house, straightening neat pillows on the bed, wiping off spotless shelves, adjusting a perfectly aligned painting on the wall.

The house had never been tidier.

She couldn't stand it any longer. She opened the oven door and pulled out the pan. It was still soft in the center, completely undone, but the edges were becoming harder.

Maybe she was so worried, she'd temporarily lost her ability to determine how long two hours were. She put the cake back in the oven and threw her coat on. She might as well check on her chickens while she waited.

The barn was warm, although it was warmer when the horses were there. The cows mooed a greeting, and she freshened their hay.

Her chickens clucked in anticipation of the grain she spread out for them, and she chided them as they eagerly pecked at the hem of her dress in their zeal to get at the food. "Patience, patience," she scolded, realizing the irony of the words as she said them. She was certainly no one to lecture a chicken about patience.

There was not enough to do to fill up the empty minutes while she waited for the fruitcake to bake. At last she pulled a chair up beside the oven and waited.

Time after time she checked, and time after time the results were the same. The edges were getting harder and harder, and the middle seemed content to stay uncooked.

When she looked out the window and realized sunset was falling over the plains, she knew she couldn't wait any longer. Joel would be home soon, and he certainly couldn't find the cake there. . .not yet, anyway.

She took the cake out, amazed at its weight, and put it on the sideboard to cool. It looked even worse in the lamplight. Muddy in color, pebbled in texture, it was a dreadful sight.

Another problem presented itself quickly. The aroma of the cake permeated every corner of the tiny house. She stirred up some spice cookies and put them in to bake. They'd be warm when Joel got home, and they'd disguise the smell of the fruitcake.

When the cookies were in the oven baking, she tackled the fruitcake. It had hardened even more in cooling, and now she could not get it out of the pan. The usual gentle pat on the bottom of the pan didn't work. A butter knife around the inner edges of the pan didn't work. A whack on the edge of the table didn't work.

In desperation she took the sharpest knife she had and tried to cut it out of the pan. With a loud clunk, the cake fell out onto the table.

It was, indeed, a heavy cake. She picked it up. The cake kept its form, even out of the pan, and except for the still-soft middle, the cake was as hard as a brick.

Perhaps it was supposed to be crusty on the outside, and inside it would be moist and delicious. She stood at the table, the knife poised over the cake.

If she tested the cake carefully, perhaps a judicious sampling from the bottom, she could for once and for all satisfy herself that the cake was all right.

Elizabeth tried a cautious cut across the bottom with the knife, holding her breath.

The knife blade bent.

She pressed harder.

The blade bent more.

She put her weight into the cut.

The knife threatened to snap. It was then she knew her worst fear had come true. The cake was as hard as the frozen prairie. Certainly this was not the fruitcake that was the rage on the East Coast. This fruitcake was totally inedible.

She opened the door and, with all her might, hurled the fruitcake across the open land, startling a flock of winter-roosting birds to flight.

With a somber heart, she returned to the fire to wait for Joel's return. And, as she had done so many nights in the past, she turned to her Bible once again.

This time the book opened to Proverbs and her eyes were drawn immediately to the verse that had always meant so much to her: *"Whoso findeth a wife findeth a good thing."*

The words seemed to mock her. "A good thing?" How could she be a good wife if she could not give him the Christmas that obviously meant so much to him?

"I should give up baking and become a stone-mason," she grumbled to herself. "I seem to have a real talent for that."

She loved Joel so much, her heart ached with the joy of it all. More than anything she wanted him to be happy and comfortable, and now she had failed him.

The clop of hoofbeats and the creak of wagon wheels told her Joel was home. For the first time in their marriage, the sound made her cry.

Chapter 8

The sun was just peeking over the horizon as Joel put the last touches on the wagon. He and his mother would be riding quite a distance, and he knew how hard the seat of the buckboard could be. If they didn't get out frequently and stretch, they'd be numb from the waist down by the time they got to the house.

There was one stop he'd have to make on the way back, and he knew his mother wouldn't mind the delay.

"I'm going to stop by Brother Jensen's on the way back," he said, "and pick up the book he got us to give to Mother. It's a nice set of poems. She'll like that."

He had another reason for stopping there, one he couldn't share. He hoped Elizabeth would like his Christmas present.

She stood beside him, silently watching. She seemed almost sad, and he hadn't been able to get her to tell him why. She trailed after him like a shadow, not saying anything and yet full of unspoken questions. He almost jumped when she spoke at last. "Be careful."

"I will."

She didn't say more, and he paused before getting into the wagon. He turned to her. "Are you sure you don't want to go to Omaha with me?"

She shook her head. "No. Grandfather and his wife are away to spend Christmas with her family. And besides, I have to bake that lovely goose you brought back from Brother Jensen."

"Well, then." He stood and looked at her as if memorizing her face. She was so beautiful, his Elizabeth.

He wrapped her in his arms, and for the moment, time stood still. Together there was a power between them, much more than he had ever expected. This was love, but more than that, Elizabeth was his best friend. How did the Good Book say it? "This is my beloved, and this is my friend."

He tore himself away. "I have to go."

She nodded, and as he rode away, he heard her call, "Godspeed."

No clouds marred the clear blue of the sky. He couldn't have chosen a better day to travel, and even the horses seemed to anticipate the ride. They tossed their heads, their manes fluttering, as if to tell him, *Let's go.*

Joel arrived at Brother Jensen's house in good time. The pastor opened his door and limped to the steps, pausing to lean on his crutch.

"Brother Jensen, you shouldn't be out," Joel scolded as he leaped out of the wagon. He wouldn't unhitch the horses since his visit would be short.

"I heard a wagon coming," the pastor responded, "and my curiosity got the better of me. You heard that the book for your mother arrived?"

Joel nodded. "I can't thank you enough for suggesting it and then ordering it for me. I do appreciate it."

Brother Jensen beamed. "My pleasure. The book is charming, and I hope she'll spend many pleasant hours browsing through the poems."

The fire in the farmhouse burned brightly, and Joel noted that the woodbox held a considerable amount of split logs. He'd fill it to the top before he left.

"Lots of people have been by to visit," Brother Jensen said to Joel, "it being Christmas, you know. That woodbox has never been more than three-quarters empty. I know you're on an errand today, though, and don't have time to chat. You're picking up your mother, aren't you?"

"In Omaha," Joel agreed.

"I've got the book all ready for you." He handed Joel a small volume bound in rich green leather and edged with gilt.

"And the other—?" Joel prompted.

Brother Jensen winked conspiratorially. "The other? Now there's a gift that'll be appreciated. Everything's going to go just as planned, my son. Just as planned." He gave Joel a hearty pat on the back. "Now you'd better get on the road. You have a long drive ahead."

Joel left the house and climbed into the wagon. He paused long enough to wave at Brother Jensen, framed in the doorway, and then, with a click of his tongue, he was off to Omaha.

❧

Elizabeth had the entire day ahead of her. In this magnificent spread of hours, she somehow had to come up with a Christmas present for Joel.

Why hadn't she let herself take the wool for the mittens on credit? It would have been only a week or two before she'd have been able to pay it off.

"Because," she told herself out loud, "you are your grandfather's granddaughter." She smiled as she recalled his words, *There's no credit in credit*. She could almost recite the mini-sermon he gave on borrowing money. "A man should not take what he cannot pay for. It prevents him from being a foolish spender, and it keeps him from the poorhouse."

It was good advice, but for once, she wished she hadn't listened to it.

There was nothing to be done about it, though. The wool was still in the store, and she would purchase it with the next batch of eggs. Her husband would have his mittens, although not for Christmas.

She fed the chickens. They surrounded her with their usual anxious pecking and jostling. She loved her chickens. Her favorite part of tending them was reaching into the hay and withdrawing a newly laid egg, still warm from the hen's body.

They hadn't laid as many as usual, probably because of the cold weather, but she gathered what was there. "Now, my beauties, get to work. Remember, every egg you lay takes my Joel one step closer to new mittens." They didn't even look up from their feast. "Ungrateful creatures," Elizabeth said, laughing.

She returned to the house and did her morning tidying. A tiny brown field mouse scurried from behind the trunk as she moved it out to sweep behind it, and she chased the little creature outside.

The Lord must have had a reason for the mouse and the mosquito, Joel had said one August evening, *but why is truly one of His mysteries.* Elizabeth agreed. She'd never get used to either one of them.

The day sped by, filled with small tasks, and soon the time came to begin preparing dinner. The goose was truly beautiful. Elizabeth made the apple and raisin dressing that Joel liked, stuffed the goose, and put it in to bake. That, with the potatoes from the root cellar and the squash and the canned raspberries, would be their Christmas dinner.

If only the fruitcake had turned out!

It was too bad that the ingredients were so alien to the prairie. Now, if instead of candied fruit, there had been dried blackberries in the recipe. . .

"Neglect not the gift that is in thee." She could almost hear her grandfather's voice reciting the line from the Bible he used to remind her to be resourceful. She would improvise a dessert. She could do it; she did it all the time. But this one would be special.

A pinch of nutmeg and a heady dash of cinnamon were all that was left from her escapade with the fruitcake, but these remnants were added to a sweet batter she stirred up quickly.

A grated apple, a handful of chopped nuts, a scoop of dried berries. . .all went into the mix. The spicy aroma soon joined the crisp scent of the goose baking.

Stamp, stamp, stamp, stamp. The sound heralded her husband's arrival. The door burst open, spilling Joel and his mother into the tiny house. The welcome sound of her husband's feet was sweeter to her than his next words: "What smells so good?"

"Is my son always this forgetful of his manners?" Mrs. Evans swept over to Elizabeth and enclosed her in a tight hug before releasing her and holding her at arms' distance. "Let me look at you! I must say, the prairie agrees with you. You are looking every bit as lovely as when I last saw you."

"And you, Mrs. Evans. Let me take your wraps while you tell me how your trip was." Elizabeth helped her mother-in-law take off her coat.

Mrs. Evans looked around her at the small house, and Elizabeth held her breath. If her mother-in-law found fault with it. . .

But instead, Mrs. Evans beamed. "This house is absolutely charming! It's cozy and warm and quite obviously filled with love!"

Elizabeth exhaled in relief.

Mrs. Evans sniffed in delight. "I must admit, I'm hungry. My son may be rude but he has excellent taste. Whatever you are cooking smells wonderful!"

"Brother Jensen gave us a wonderful goose, but I'm afraid it won't be ready for a while," Elizabeth apologized.

Mrs. Evans shook her head. "No, that's not what I mean. Something smells warm and spicy and inviting."

"It could be the cake, I suppose. It's about ready to come out now."

"I know you probably have everything planned out, but could we please have a piece of it now?" Mrs. Evans smiled at her.

"Listen to my mother beg, would you," Joel said teasingly from the bedroom where he'd put his mother's belongings. "But she's right. It smells good, and I'm hungry."

Elizabeth laughed. "Well, that settles it, then."

She took the cake out of the oven and sliced it into servings. She watched anxiously as both her husband and his mother bit into it.

"This is delicious," Mrs. Evans said.

Joel grinned at her. "Don't I recognize some of our own raspberries and black-berries in it?"

Elizabeth nodded.

"So it's prairie fruitcake, then, isn't it?" Mrs. Evans's tinkling little laugh sounded like a hundred tiny bells ringing at once.

"Oh, don't you remember Aunt Susan's fruitcake?" Joel asked his mother, who smiled in return.

"Indeed. That was the first sign of the holiday season, when her fruitcake arrived at our door."

"When I think back on the Christmases of my childhood," Joel said, "I remember those fruitcakes."

"Weren't they something?" Mrs. Evans smiled at the memory.

"I think Lizzie's prairie fruitcake is better than Aunt Susan's," he proclaimed loyally.

Elizabeth felt her face grow warm. Was the terrible subject going to arise this early?

She pressed her hands to her heated face, and Mrs. Evans glanced at her.

"Elizabeth, are you all right? Look, Joel, she's flushed. Perhaps she has a fever." Mrs. Evans stood up and reached for Elizabeth's forehead.

"I'm all right. I just—I just have a confession to make. I wanted this Christmas to be special." She looked at her husband, who was watching her with concern. "It's Joel's first Christmas with me, his first Christmas on the prairie, and when he talked about his memories of Christmas, the fruitcake. . ."

"So you made this one?" her mother-in-law prompted.

"I made this one, but I wanted it to be like the ones Joel remembered." The tears began to flow as rapidly as her words. "So I bought the ingredients, and a mouse ate them, and then I bought more, but it turned out so awful that even the wild animals won't eat it. I threw it out yesterday, and I checked today: It's still there, with not even a tooth mark on it. Although," she finished, sniffling, "there are probably some broken teeth laying around it. It was like stone."

She blinked away her tears and realized that they were laughing at her. The man she loved and his mother were laughing at her! "It's not funny!" she protested. "It's all I have for Joel's Christmas present. I wanted to get him—"

Mrs. Evans hushed her. "There, there. We're laughing because we know what happened. You used Aunt Susan's recipe, didn't you?"

"Yes."

"Aunt Susan fancies herself quite a cook, my dear, but she is not. She's a sweet woman, but not in the kitchen. Her fruitcake is a tradition in our family, that's true, but we can—and do—live without it."

"Her fruitcake is like the Yule Log," Joel continued, "except no self-respecting fire will touch it."

"Joel!" his mother chided, but she laughed.

"Well, it's true, Mother. It's harder than brick, more unbreakable than steel, and totally impervious to any natural forces known to man."

"I have a suggestion," Mrs. Evans said. "Let's make a new tradition here. It will be something good, something wonderful, something wise. We will call *it* Elizabeth's Christmas Cake."

"Do you know what Aunt Susan's fruitcake reminds me of?" Joel asked.

The two women shook their heads.

"It reminds me of the stone which the builders rejected. Remember?" He crossed the room and got the Bible from the table. "Here it is. Psalm 118:22: 'The stone which the builders refused is become the head stone of the corner.' From an awful traditional recipe comes a wonderful new one. That is," he added, "if you will make this every year, Lizzie dear."

She was about to respond when something small and furry brushed her leg. She leaped up, ready to go for the broom, when Joel, to her astonishment, laughed.

"I see my Christmas present escaped."

He lifted up a tiny bundle of gray-striped fur. "This is your mouser. I know how much it bothers you when the field mice come to visit, and this fellow will keep them at bay. Won't you, Little Gray?"

Elizabeth took the kitten from him. It immediately began to purr, and Elizabeth lost her heart a second time.

"I hope you like him. Brother Jensen gave me the idea. He has a cat in his house, and it catches the mice for him. He told me the Larsens in town had a new litter of kittens, and that's what I was doing there the day we got caught in the blizzard—picking him out for you. They took it to Brother Jensen's house, and Mother and I picked it up today."

"So that's what all that intrigue was about!" Elizabeth exclaimed.

Joel laughed. "It was quite the plot."

"Well, I guess there's no reason to wait on giving you my present," Mrs. Evans said, "seeing as the kitten already brought it out to you."

Elizabeth noticed a trail of yarn from the kitten's paws all the way to the door of the bedroom. It was a beautiful blue wool, the color of Nebraska skies, the color of her husband's eyes.

She was speechless as Mrs. Evans rolled up the yarn and handed it to her. "Joel told me you had been looking at some yarn in the store but you hadn't bought any. I hope the color is all right."

"It's beautiful," Elizabeth managed to say.

Joel gave his mother the book Brother Jensen selected, and as they all chatted happily, Elizabeth took the goose out of the oven and placed it on the table.

Elizabeth noticed her mother-in-law touch the white linen tablecloth she'd sent in the wedding trunk. "I'm glad you're using this," Mrs. Evans said, almost shyly. "It was mine when I was first married."

"And you gave it to me?" Elizabeth asked in astonishment. She hugged her mother-in-law impulsively and was gratified when Mrs. Evans returned the embrace wholeheartedly.

"That tablecloth has seen many dinners served and eaten in love, and I'm glad it will continue to serve its purpose," Mrs. Evans said.

Joel grandly seated his mother and Elizabeth before taking his place at the table.

"The goose looks and smells divine," Mrs. Evans said. "God has certainly blessed this food already, but I believe we should give Him our thanks."

Elizabeth nodded. "Joel?"

She grasped the hands of her husband and his mother as they joined in the circle of prayer. She had never been happier, she realized, than she was at that moment. She'd been foolish to worry about recreating the traditions of Joel's youth.

The greatest tradition of Christmas was something that could not be roasted or knitted or baked. It was too big for any wrapping, except, perhaps, some swaddling clothes that enveloped the best gift of all.

Love transcended the unimportant boundaries of coast and prairie.

Joel began the grace. "For the gifts of Christmas—Your Son, Your love, and Your grace—we thank You. Your love is endless and magnificent, and what we feel for each other is only a portion of what You feel for us. May we be worthy of Your love, and may we love as You have taught us."

He paused and added, "Thank You for the circle of love we are enclosed in tonight, for bringing my mother safely to our hearthside, and I especially thank You for my dear Lizzie, who. . .Amen."

Elizabeth looked up in surprise and realized that the kitten had gotten up on the table and was making off with a goose leg nearly twice his size.

Their first Christmas together, their first holiday memories.

She imagined them sitting side by side fifty years from this night, remembering the fruitcake that didn't work and the one that did. She could see Joel in her mind, his hair as white as the prairie snow, his smile still charming its way into her heart. She would love him forever. That was a tradition that would never change.

This Christmas *was* perfect.

The kitten jumped off the table with a thump, the goose leg grasped in its tiny teeth.

"Amen," Elizabeth said happily.

ELIZABETH'S CHRISTMAS CAKE
(Prairie Fruitcake)

Elizabeth didn't have all these ingredients at hand, but make the best of your modern grocery store and try this newer version. By the way, Elizabeth used dried raspberries and blackberries, but this is also good with any dried tart fruit, such as cranberries or cherries.

½ cup shortening
1 cup white sugar
1 cup brown sugar
2 eggs
1½ cups applesauce
1½ teaspoons baking soda
1½ teaspoons salt
1 teaspoon cinnamon
½ teaspoon cloves
½ teaspoon allspice
Generous dash of nutmeg
2½ cups sifted flour
½ cup water
½ to 1 cup chopped walnuts
¾ to 1 cup dried fruit
1 cup chocolate chips (optional)
Extra brown sugar for topping, about ½ cup

Grease and flour a 9x13-inch pan.

Cream together the first four ingredients. Mix in the applesauce. Add the baking soda, salt, and spices. Blend in the flour and then the water. Stir in the remaining ingredients. Sprinkle additional brown sugar on the top.

Bake at 350 degrees for 45 minutes, or until the cake tests done.

Colder Than Ice

by Jill Stengl

Dedication

With love to my daughter and toughest writing critic,
Anne Elisabeth Stengl,
and to my sister, Paula Ciccotti,
who introduced me to prairie life in Iowa.

Chapter 1

Coon's Hollow, Iowa—1885

Hello! Sir, hello!"

As Frank Nelson jogged his horse past the Coon's Hollow train station, he noticed a strange woman waving a handkerchief from the sun-baked platform. At first he thought she must be beckoning to someone else, but a quick glance around ended that hope. "Ma'am?" He reined Powder in and halted near the steps.

Clad in black from her bonnet to her boots, the woman twisted the handkerchief between her gloved hands. A large trunk waited beside the empty depot office, and two carpetbags sat on the bench. "I'm sorry to disturb you, sir, but can you deliver a message for me?"

"Deliver it where?" After a sleepless night, he was in no mood to serve as messenger boy. He squinted, thinking she looked vaguely familiar. "Who are you?"

She drew herself up and stared at him down her long, narrow nose. Hot, gusty wind sent her bonnet flapping around her gaunt cheeks and ballooned her ruffled skirts. Soot streaked her forehead, and dust grayed her garments. "If you would ask someone from the hotel to collect my luggage, I shall be grateful."

That incisive voice rang a bell. "Have we met?"

"Never."

Squinting against the wind, he studied her face. Shadowed eyes, sharp chin, and prominent cheekbones. "Are you related to Paul Truman?" Certainty filled him. "You must be his sister from Wisconsin. What are you doing here?"

"I cannot see that it is your business," she began, then informed him, "I have been offered employment in the area."

"That was months ago."

"And how would you know?" Queen Victoria herself could be no more imperious.

"I'm Frank Nelson, the pastor. I offered you the job, Miss Truman. I hope you at least informed Paul and Susan that you were coming."

"*You* are the minister?" Chin tucked, she looked him up and down. Her shoulders squared. "Has the position been filled?"

401

"No."

He was tempted to tell her he no longer needed a secretary. Let the harpy go back to the big city and terrorize small children there. Coon's Hollow held its quota of odd characters. And he definitely didn't need another eccentric spinster in his life.

"Why don't you come with me to the parsonage, cool off in the shade, and have some lemonade, and I'll send someone to Trumans' with a message from you. It's only going to get hotter on that platform." His shepherd calling wouldn't allow him to leave even an ornery ewe to the mercy of the elements. She would be in no danger from wolves, that was certain.

She blinked. "Very well."

Frank dismounted, leaped up the steps, and grabbed her carpetbags. "They're planning a new depot with a covered waiting area, but it won't happen this year. Have you been here long?" *She must have arrived on the morning train.*

"What about my trunk?"

"It'll be safe here until Paul comes for it. The parsonage is just around the corner." He hopped down and swung the two bags up onto Powder's saddle. When he turned around, Miss Truman had descended the steps. She was tall, he noticed. And thin. Truly spindly.

"Miss Truman?" He extended his arm. She curled her gloved fingers around his forearm and fell into step along the dusty street. Powder followed behind, led by one loose rein. Now that Frank had offered lemonade, he remembered drinking the last of it yesterday afternoon.

He tried to recall details about Miss Truman. Upon hearing of their mother's death, Paul had offered his only sister a home with his family, adding the further incentive of a job as the minister's secretary. "Taking her into my home is the Christian thing to do," Paul had said with the air of a martyr. "And she could be a great help to you if she doesn't drive you to an early grave."

Frank gave the woman a side glance. She appeared more underfed and exhausted than dangerous. "Why did you decide to come to Iowa after all? When Paul had no reply from you, he assumed you weren't coming."

"My circumstances became. . .insupportable," she said in a flat voice. "If you no longer require my services, I shall find employment elsewhere."

"What did Paul tell you about me?" He felt awkward asking.

"He told me that you are attempting to write a book and need someone to transcribe it for you. Is your office in your home or at the church?"

"At the parsonage."

"I assume your wife will act as chaperone."

As if this woman would require one. "My housekeeper will chaperone; my wife died eight years ago."

"You have no family?"

"Not living with me. My daughter, Amy, is married and living in Des Moines. My son, David, recently bought a farm near your brother's and is fixing up the farmhouse. He is betrothed to your niece, Margie. They are to marry Christmas Eve, so you and I shall soon be related in a way."

"I see."

"Here we are." Frank wrapped Powder's rein around the post and pushed open the picket gate. Seeing Miss Truman examine his home, he scanned it himself. A riot of perennials overflowed the garden fence, invaded the weedy lawn, and sneaked across the walkway. Morning glories strangled the hitching posts and attempted to bind the picket gate shut.

A wide veranda wrapped around most of the house, offering shade and a breeze. Beyond the stable out back, cornfields stretched as far as the eye could see. A windmill squeaked out its rusty rhythm. Water trickled from its base into a huge tub. A swaybacked horse plunged its nose into the sparkling water and playfully dumped waves over the tub's far rim.

"The Harlan Coon family donated this house and the stable to the church twenty years ago. Those are Coon cornfields, but Bess there is mine. She's too old to work, but I keep her as company for Powder." A handy excuse for keeping an oversized pet. "The church is a good stretch of the legs up the road from here, but the walk gives me exercise."

The woman said nothing. These long silences seemed uncanny from a female. Perhaps she was tired. "Have a seat here, Miss Truman, and I'll find you something to drink. Mary should be around somewhere." It occurred to him that the simplest course of action would be to hitch up his own buggy and take the lady to Paul's house.

The screen door squealed, and Mary Bilge stumped onto the porch. An unlit cigar dangled from her lips. "Who's this?"

"Miss Truman, newly arrived from Wisconsin. Miss Truman, this is Miss Bilge, my housekeeper." He watched the two women eye each other and shake hands. "Miss Truman has agreed to assist me with preparing my manuscript for publication."

Mary's dark gaze pinned him. "How's the Dixons' baby?"

"Better, the doctor says."

"Humph. I'll bake them a raisin loaf."

He would believe that when he saw it. "Uh, do we have any of that lemonade left, Mary?"

"You oughta know, seein' as how you drank the last of it." She disappeared back into the house, letting the screen door slam.

Frank avoided Miss Truman's gaze. "I'm sorry."

"May I enter your kitchen?"

"Certainly." He opened the screen door and beckoned her inside. She peeled off her gloves, surveying the room, the largest in his house. To his surprise, she opened the firebox and added two sticks of wood, picked up the kettle, and nodded. "I can make tea, if you have any."

"Help yourself. I don't know what I have. People give me food sometimes.

Like the lemonade Mrs. Wilkins brought over."

Miss Truman searched through cupboards, canisters, and the icebox, producing a tin of tea, a sack of white sugar, and a small pitcher of cream. Frank watched her brew tea in an old china teapot. Whenever she glanced his way, he found himself standing straight and holding in his gut.

"You may summon Miss Bilge." The lady located cookies in the jar and laid them on a plate, loaded the waiting tray, and carried it out to the porch before Frank could stop her.

"Come and have tea on the veranda with us, Mary," he called, uncertain where she might be. "Then I need to hitch up Powder and take Miss Truman home."

He heard Mary thumping and muttering on the cellar stairs. What had she been doing down there? He didn't dare ask.

"Tea on a day like this? La-de-da! Give me coffee."

"But Miss Truman brewed tea."

"Coffee's good enough for me. Got some left from breakfast."

Frank grimaced at the idea, but Mary poured herself a cup and shuffled outside. In hot or cold weather, she always wore the same man's overcoat over a sack-like gown, heavy boots, and a broad-brimmed hat. She seemed about as wide as she was tall. Slumped into a rocking chair, she seared Miss Truman with her stare.

Serenely composed, Miss Truman perched in another chair, prepared to pour the tea. "Cream and sugar, Reverend Nelson?"

"Thank you." After pulling up a third rocking chair, he watched her prepare his tea and accepted the cup. Her remote gaze caught his once more. "Reverend Nelson, when do you wish me to begin work?"

He sipped the tea. Sweet, creamy—better than he had expected. "How about Monday? That should give you time to settle in at Paul and Susan's. I warn you, my papers are a disaster."

"Huh," Mary said, cradling her grimy coffee cup against her chest.

Frank started to grin but stopped when his lips quivered. He took a handful of cookies.

Silence lengthened. Frank wondered if the women could hear him chewing. No telling how long those cookies had been in the jar. Since spring maybe.

A large black cat strolled across the veranda, gave Mary wide berth, oozed between Frank's boots, and sat in front of Miss Truman. The lady moved her teacup to one side, and the cat flowed into her lap, curled up, and disappeared against the shiny black fabric.

"Dirty critter," Mary muttered.

Miss Truman stroked the cat, and Frank heard a rumbling purr. Again he met Miss Truman's gaze and, for the first time, saw in her pale eyes a fleeting emotion. "I like cats," she said.

Frank gulped down the last of his tea. "We have several roaming about the place. Belle is the queen cat and the best mouser. We used to have a dog, but he died a few years back of old age."

Miss Truman watched the cat as she petted it, and Frank watched her long hands caress its glossy fur. Abruptly she took a sip of tea. The cup rattled in the saucer when she replaced it, and Frank suddenly noticed the slump of her shoulders. The poor woman must be exhausted almost beyond bearing, yet he'd kept her drinking tea on his veranda and talking business. He hopped up, leaving his chair rocking wildly. "We'd best be off, Miss Truman. If you'd like to rest awhile longer, I'll take the buckboard to the station for your trunk first and return for you."

She nodded. "Thank you, Reverend Nelson." Rising, she gathered up the tea things and carried them inside. The screen door closed quietly behind her.

"You're gonna hire that woman? She's gonna be here every day?" Mary glowered.

"I'm hiring her as secretary, not replacement housekeeper. Your place is secure."

Scowl lines deepened between Mary's brushy brows. With another grunt, she set her empty coffee cup on the floor and rose. Nose high, she stumped down the porch steps and headed toward her little house across the road.

When Frank drove through town with Estelle Truman at his side, he encountered curious glances from townspeople. She shaded her face with a black silk parasol and sat erect on the bench seat. Polished boot toes emerged from beneath her gown's dusty ruffles. For the first time, he noticed the worn seams on her sleeves and a rip in the skirt, repaired with tiny stitches.

"We'll have you home in no time," he promised as they left the schoolhouse and one last barking dog behind. "So, Miss Truman, you have lived in Madison all your life until now?"

"I have. Reverend Nelson, I do not wish to confide my life story in you during this drive to my brother's farmhouse. I'm sure you will understand."

He deflated. "Of course."

"I overheard your conversation with Miss Bilge today—something about the illness of a baby?" She spoke quietly.

"Ben and Althea Dixon's first child. Only nine months old. He took ill last week. The doctor thought he would die, but he rallied during the night and seemed almost back to normal. I was on my way home from their house when I met you at the station."

"Were you with the family all night?"

"Yes. They asked me to come and pray, and this time God chose to restore little Benjamin's health. We lose a lot of children here. Paul and Susan's daughter, Jessamine, died of typhoid a year ago, and they nearly lost Joe, too."

"Paul never wrote of their daughter's death."

"Jessamine was sixteen. I believe the sorrow and strain have drained Susan's strength, yet her spirit is stronger than ever."

Miss Truman's chin tipped up. "I shall not increase Susan's burden. She will find me useful around the house."

"I pray you'll also find time to assist me in preparing my book for publication.

I often fear I should abandon the project and turn my mind to more practical pursuits, but then I feel as if God is pressing this work upon my heart and I must keep writing it." He looked down at her marble profile and wondered if she could make any difference.

"I shall assist you to the best of my ability, Reverend Nelson, commensurate with my pay."

Rather than respond to that baffling remark, he pointed. "Ahead is Paul's farm. All this corn around us is his. He also raises hogs. He's a good man. Good farmer. Good friend. I'm honored to have my son marry his daughter." He turned in at the Trumans' drive, wondering how the family would react to this maiden aunt's arrival.

The barn and the white farmhouse looked insignificant in the vast expanse of surrounding prairie. One large tree shaded the house. Chickens ran clucking from the buckboard as it rolled up the drive, and a cow bawled. Frank glanced at Miss Truman. Her expression revealed nothing.

"Hello, Frank. Who's that with—" The question cut off sharply. Paul jogged across the farmyard, his eyes locked with his sister's. "Estelle!"

"Hello, Paul. I came."

He stopped beside the buckboard, still staring. "I can't believe it."

"If you have changed your mind, I can take a room in town."

He seemed to start back to reality. "No, no. Here, let me help you down." He offered her a hand, and while she climbed to the ground, he turned his head to shout over one shoulder. "Josh. Alvin. Joe. Get out here *now!*

"I just can't believe it. You haven't changed much, Stell." Paul gave her a quick hug.

Frank saw her lips quiver before she stepped back to straighten her bonnet. "Twenty years, Paulie."

One after another, Paul's three sons appeared from barn and fields. Frank saw little Flora poke her head out the kitchen door, then duck back inside, probably to inform her mother about their visitors. Eliza, the farm dog, came running, tail wagging as she sniffed around Miss Truman's shoes. To Frank's surprise, the woman held out one hand to the dog and gave her a pat.

While Paul introduced his sister to the boys, Frank unloaded her trunk and bags from his wagon. She spoke to the boys politely and shook their hands. Frank caught an exchange of uncertain glances between Al and Joe. Josh unobtrusively punched the younger boy when he made a comment behind one hand.

Susan and her daughters emerged from the house, and Frank felt himself relax. A welcoming smile wreathed Susan's face, and her daughters were beaming. "Estelle! This is a wonderful surprise. My dear, please come inside out of this heat. The men will bring your things in. You can share Margie's room until she marries." Amid a spate of further instructions and welcomes, Susan took Miss Truman's hand in hers and led her toward the house. The three boys picked up the luggage and followed.

Paul met Frank's gaze. "I can't believe it," he repeated. "What are we going to do?"

"You invited her here," Frank said. "She came. Susan doesn't seem to mind. Why should you? She's *your* sister."

Paul still looked dazed. "How did you meet her?"

Frank related the scene at the depot. Paul kept shaking his head until Frank wanted to shake him. Miss Truman might be haughty and reserved, but she was no monster. "She agreed to start working for me on Monday, so she won't be around your house all day. I assume you thought of transportation."

"She can use the dogcart."

"She told me she won't be a burden to Susan."

Paul let out a huff. "Don't look at me like that, Frank. You don't understand. Stell and I were good buddies as children. But she changed during the war. When I came home...trust me: That woman has a block of ice in place of a heart. I won't let her destroy my home like an encroaching glacier."

"Do you want me to stay around this evening?" Frank offered. "Just for a while?"

"No, thanks. We'll manage." Paul gave Frank a sidelong glance. "But I'd surely appreciate your prayers."

Chapter 2

Without looking in their direction, Frank knew when the Truman family neared his position at the open double doors. He patted an elderly parishioner's hand, gazed into her eyes, and thanked her for her compliments on his sermon. "God's Word is my source, Mrs. Coon. A preacher cannot go far wrong if he sticks to his source. Bless you, ma'am." The widow of the town's founding citizen always had something kind to say.

For two days Frank had been wondering how Miss Truman was adapting to her new surroundings and how her family was adjusting to her. He both dreaded and anticipated introducing her to his dilapidated manuscript on the morrow.

Paul gripped his hand hard. "Good message. Supper with us this evening? David's already coming."

"Lately it seems the only way I get to see my son is to meet him at your house. Can't imagine why," Frank said, grinning. "Thank you. I'll be there." Anything beat Mary Bilge's Sunday stew. And the fellowship at Paul's house was always excellent.

"Pastor Nelson, thank you for that wonderful sermon." Susan's smile radiated inner beauty. "I always leave this church inspired to live another week in the Lord's presence."

Miss Truman stood nearby, hearing every word. Frank lowered his gaze, cleared his throat, and said, "It's the Holy Ghost, not me."

"I know, but you're His instrument. Come by at five o'clock tonight."

Susan moved on. Margie, Joe, and Flora each shook his hand in turn. Josh and Alvin had passed through the line earlier. Flora asked him, "You met Auntie Stell, didn't you? She likes cats."

He looked into the child's pale blue eyes, then up at her aunt's, noting the resemblance. "I know she does. She met Belle at my house the other day."

"And she is going to make me a blue gown for Margie's wedding."

"Indeed?"

"Today we're going to make pies from the blackberries Joe and I picked yesterday. I get to roll the crust, Auntie Stell says. Margie never lets me. You get to have pie after supper tonight."

"I can hardly wait."

Flora returned his smile and walked on, head high, shoulders back, without her usual bounce. Frank suspected imitation of her aunt, and the realization surprised him.

He turned to face Miss Truman. "I trust you are adjusting to your new home? Flora is evidently smitten with you."

"She is a sweet child." Yet no hint of a smile curved the woman's tight lips. "Thank you for your inquiry, Reverend." After barely touching his hand, she moved on.

Frank shook hands with the last few people, then walked around, straightening hymnals and picking up rubbish. Two calls to make that afternoon, then supper at the Trumans'. These next few weeks should prove interesting in many ways. Perhaps after all these years, he would begin to make headway on his manuscript.

"How are things going with your aunt?" Frank asked Alvin that afternoon as he stabled his gelding in the Trumans' barn.

"Not bad."

Hardly the informative answer Frank desired. "She gets along with your ma?"

"Yep. She's a good cook."

"And your pa doesn't fight with her?" Frank bent to pat Eliza, letting the dog lick his hand.

"Nope. She don't talk much."

A family trait, apparently. "See you at supper."

"Yessir."

Paul greeted him at the front door.

"How are things going?" Frank asked, hanging his hat on the hall tree. He ran his fingers through his damp hair and hoped he didn't stink of sweat and horses.

"Surprisingly well. My sister jumped right into the chores, cooking and cleaning. Even washed and ironed the family's laundry along with her own and started in on the mending. I didn't know she had it in her. Guess she's learned how to work since our childhood days."

Paul led him to the kitchen. "Pastor's here."

Miss Truman and Flora worked over at the counter. Neither one looked up.

"Hello, Dad." David sat at the kitchen table, conversing with Margie while she helped prepare the meal. "Good sermon this morning."

Frank reached across the table to shake his son's hand. "Thank you. How are things going?"

"Very well. If you have time this week, I could use help replacing the windows in the parlor. The frames are rotted, and two of the panes are cracked. I decided to replace them entirely. It's slow work, but I expect to have the house ready by December." David smiled at Margie, who gazed adoringly into his eyes.

"What about the harvest?"

"Mr. Gallagher put only three fields into corn and beans this year before I bought the place. Harvest should be quick. Got five hogs ready for market by next week. It's a great farm." Enthusiasm burned in David's eyes. Frank recognized himself at that age. So zealous for life, with a promising future and a lovely bride.

When David's attention returned to Margie, Frank allowed himself a look at Miss Truman. Wearing a calico apron over her black mourning gown, she laid a circle of pastry atop a mounded heap of blackberries, all the while chatting with Flora. Her sleeves were rolled up, revealing white arms. Silver laced the waves of dark hair around her forehead.

"Hello, Pastor Nelson." Susan's greeting from the pantry doorway jolted him back to reality. Holding up two jars, she said, "Estelle, I have pickled beets and dilled cucumbers. Which do you think?"

"With chicken pie, I would serve the cucumbers, but this is your home, Susan."

"Nonsense, sister," Susan said. "It's your home now, too. And it's your chicken pie."

"Hello, Susan. I didn't see you there," Frank said. "Can I do anything to help?"

She gave him an odd look. "You needn't shout, Pastor. My hearing is excellent."

Frank felt his face burn. Anxiety sometimes increased his volume.

"If you truly wish to help, you may carry the chicken pie to the table once it's baked." Susan moved toward the work counter.

Frank tried to make himself small to let her pass, but she stepped on his boot. "Excuse me, Pastor."

"Sorry." He shuffled back, colliding with Miss Truman. "Pardon."

Giving an exasperated huff, Miss Truman planted one hand between his shoulder blades and pushed away. He turned to see her brushing flour from her skirts and staring downward. Following her gaze, he beheld his scuffed, cracked brown boot toes emerging beneath striped gray trousers. Did his feet look as large to her as they felt to him?

Without a word, she returned to her pie, and Frank felt himself scorned. "I'd best remove myself from the kitchen before I break something." He laughed and saw Estelle wince. Another loudmouthed gaffe.

Before he could escape, Flora slid in close and caught his sleeve. "Auntie Stell made an extra pie from my berries for the Dixons 'cause their baby was sick. She made a chicken pie for them, too. Josh took supper to them, but he'll be back before our supper is cooked."

"How thoughtful," Frank said quietly. "I'm certain Althea and Ben will appreciate your kindness."

Flora beamed. Miss Truman did not even glance in his direction. Frank patted Flora's shoulder and tried to smile. He longed to slink away and lick his wounds.

At supper, the men discussed the town baseball team's latest game while Margie chatted about wedding plans with the ladies. Alvin, Joe, and Flora remained politely silent. Needing no urging, Frank accepted a second helping of chicken pie. Its crust flaked over creamy gravy and tender strips of chicken. He wanted to compliment the cook, but her expression discouraged light conversation.

Susan voiced Frank's thoughts. "Estelle, this pie is delicious."

"Where did you learn to cook like this?" Paul asked. "Not at the office of Blackstone and Hicks, I'm certain."

"Our great-aunt Bridget taught me to cook while she lived with us."

Paul chuckled. "Aunt Bridget! I haven't thought about her for decades. Remember the time we brought the litter of raccoons into the parlor while she and Mother were having tea?"

Joe and Alvin stared in silent disbelief.

"We truly did." Paul nodded. "Back in those days, we were a pair of rascals. Most of our pranks were Stell's idea. I was the trusting little brother."

Miss Truman's lips tightened. "Nonsense."

"Aunt Bridget, the ornery old buzzard." Paul leaned back in his chair and reminisced. "We called her 'the witch' when our parents weren't around. She always wore black, and she always looked disapproving. Aunt Bridget taught you more than cooking, Stell."

"She also taught me piano."

"That's not what I meant. You're just like her. I hadn't realized until you mentioned her name; then the resemblance struck me."

Frank heard several sharp gasps around the table. His chest felt tight, but not one beneficial word came to mind.

Miss Truman pushed back her chair and rose. "I must check the pie."

Paul glanced at Susan and wilted. Making a visible effort to amend the situation, he said, "You should hear Estelle play piano. She used to play the pipe organ at our church in Madison, too."

"Might she be willing to play piano for our church?" Susan asked, turning to watch Estelle remove the berry pie from the oven. "Estelle, would you? We've had no pianist for years. The old piano just gathers dust."

"She could give music lessons, too," Margie suggested. "Flora has always wanted to play piano."

Flora nodded vigorously, her eyes glowing.

"If Miss Truman wishes to play piano for the church, we would all be grateful. We have plenty of hymnals." Frank watched her work at the counter, keeping her back to the table. "Not that I wish to impose, Miss Truman."

"I shall be pleased to play the pianoforte for Sunday meetings." She laid down a knife and squared her shoulders. "This pie needs to cool for a time before I slice it."

"Let's go sit on the porch and enjoy the evening," Susan suggested.

Dishes clinked and flatware clanked in the tin dishpans as Margie and Estelle hurried to use the last minutes of twilight. Two cats plumped on the kitchen windowsill, tails curled around their tucked feet, yellow eyes intent on the aerial dance of fireflies and bats above the lawn. Stars already twinkled in the pink and purple sky over the small orchard of fruit trees.

Although barnyard odors occasionally offended Estelle's nose, she savored the stillness of a country evening. Perhaps Iowa was a small corner of heaven, for her new life here held an almost magical charm. She found the big boys, Joshua and Alvin, somewhat boisterous and intimidating, though they spoke to her kindly and complimented her cooking. Gangly young Joe seemed aloof, but she suspected he was merely shy. Marjorie treated her like a bosom friend, and little Flora hung on her every word. Susan seemed grateful for her assistance with the housework.

Paul was the only fly in her ointment. *Aunt Bridget, indeed!*

"Tell me what you think of David, Auntie Stell," Margie said, rousing Estelle from her reverie. "Don't you think he's handsome?"

She contrived an honest compliment. "He has kind eyes."

"Doesn't he? Bluer than blue, with those thick yellow lashes. And I love his golden hair and his dimples. He sunburns easily, but in the winter his skin gets white like marble. I call him my Viking."

"I had the same thought." David's parson father required only a Wagnerian opera score to accompany his clumsy swagger.

"Did you?" Margie gave a delighted chuckle. "The pastor looks even more like a Viking with his bushy beard. I was afraid of him when I was little because he's so big and has such a loud laugh, but I soon figured out how kind he was."

Recalling the pastor's sympathetic expression and obvious efforts to please, Estelle felt a twinge of guilt. There was more to the man than enormous feet and a forceful voice. His sermon that morning had been excellent.

Susan entered, carrying a lamp. "Why are you two working in the dark?"

"Our eyes had adjusted," Margie said. "It didn't seem dark until you brought in the lamp. But now I can see better to wipe off the table. We're almost finished, Mama. David had to leave, so I plan to spend the evening sewing."

"The rest of the family is in the parlor, absorbed in newspapers and checkers. Pastor Nelson said to tell you both good-bye, and he'll see you in the morning, Estelle."

"Isn't he nice, Auntie? I'm so glad you'll be helping him with his book. David says he had about given up on ever finishing it, so you're an answer to prayer. You should see the pastor's study—papers everywhere!"

"It will also be wonderful to have a pianist for our church," Susan said as she placed glasses in a cupboard. "We haven't had one since Kirsten Nelson passed away."

"Reverend Nelson's wife played the piano?" Estelle asked.

"The church piano was hers," Susan said. "You can set those plates back on the china dresser if you like, Estelle. I can never thank you enough for your work around the house. You're a godsend to all of us, and no mistake." She gave Estelle's shoulders a quick squeeze and returned to her task. "I can't recall the last time I felt so rested of an evening."

Estelle couldn't recall the last time anyone had thanked her, let alone hugged her.

"Mrs. Nelson was a nice lady," Margie continued, "cheery and friendly. I remember how she always played hymns so high that no one could sing them. And we sang the same five songs over and over. David says they were the only hymns she knew."

"Marjorie, that is unkind."

"I don't mean it to be unkind. I liked Mrs. Nelson. I sometimes wonder if Pastor should move in with David and me after we marry, to be certain he eats meals and gets his wash done. David says Mary Bilge causes more dirt and mess than she cleans up. She'd probably go back to drinking if Pastor fired her, so he keeps her on."

Estelle hung her apron on a hook and straightened her hair. "If you don't mind, I'll do some sewing tonight as well."

"Of course I don't mind! I want you to teach me how to make piping and those tiny ruffles." Margie caught her aunt by the hand and towed her upstairs.

Chapter 3

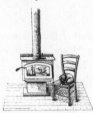

Frank shifted a stack of papers from one chair to another, then placed a second stack on top. No, that last pile needed to be separate. He moved it to the first chair and used a rock as a paperweight. When he slid a stack of books aside to search, it tipped. He grabbed at the sliding top book, but it eluded his grasp and landed open on his boot. Then the bottom half of the stack disintegrated and dropped to the floor with successive plops. He juggled two last books, caught one by its flyleaf, and watched the page rip out.

A morning breeze wafted the tattered window curtains, and notes fluttered about the room like moths. A horse whinnied outside. Hoofbeats passed the house. Frank ducked to peer outside. Estelle Truman, regal upon the seat of a dogcart, drove toward the barn.

Frank dropped the flyleaf and abandoned his study. Hearing the screen door slam, Miss Truman stopped her horse and looked over her shoulder. "Good morning, Reverend Nelson."

He took the veranda steps in two strides. "Good morning. I'll unhitch your horse today. Since you'll be coming regularly, I'll hire a boy to care for him from now on."

"You are kind." A hint of surprise colored her voice as she accepted his assistance to climb down. "Paul says Pepper can be difficult to catch. It might be best to stable him." She reached back to lift a covered basket from the cart.

"On such a fine day, I'll put him in the paddock with Bessie. Don't worry. If he gives us trouble later, we'll bribe him with carrots." Frank grinned, wondering if anything could make her smile.

"If you say so. Shall I begin work in your study?"

"Uh, you might want to wait for me. How about. . .how about you make tea again?"

She lifted one brow. "Most men prefer coffee."

"I like both," he said, stroking Pepper's forehead. The pony began to rub its face against his belly. Miss Truman's eyes followed the motion and widened. She tucked her chin, turned, and walked away, her swishing skirts raising a cloud of dust.

Once his new secretary had entered the house, Frank looked down at his blue plaid shirt and found it coated with horse saliva and white hair. "Thank you, Pepper," he muttered.

Freed of his harness, the pony bucked about the paddock, sniffed noses with the swaybacked mare, then collapsed to roll in the dust. Frank stowed the dogcart in his barn, hung up the harness, and rushed toward the house. Miss Truman must not see his study until he had a chance to pick up that last avalanche.

He stopped inside the kitchen door. The tea tray waited on the kitchen table. A basket of blackberry muffins and a bowl of canned peaches sat beside his filled teacup. Miss Truman poured hot water from the kettle into the dishpan, whipping up suds with her hand. The black cat rubbed against her skirts, purring.

"I brought muffins from home. Flora thought you might enjoy them. I found the peaches in your cellar. While you drink your tea, I'll wash up these dishes. Is Miss Bilge off duty today?"

"She usually shows up late. You don't have to do that." He waved at the dishpan.

"I cannot concentrate in an untidy environment. Tomorrow I shall come earlier to prepare your tea. The morning is already half gone. At the office in Madison, I began work at seven each day."

"And how late did you work?" Frank sat at the table, bowed his head to give silent but fervent thanks, and picked up a muffin.

"Until seven at night. I shall be unable to work that late here, however, for I must help with chores at home." She scrubbed dishes as she spoke. "My mother became accustomed to dining late."

"You prepared supper for your mother after working twelve-hour days?" He polished off his second muffin and took a sip of tea.

"When Aunt Bridget was alive, she cooked. After her death..." Her shoulders lifted and fell. "We lived simply." She wiped down the countertops, the stovetop, and the worktable. Sinews appeared in her forearms as she wrung out the dishcloth. Hefting the dishpan, she carried it outside. He heard water splash into the garden.

Only then did she take another cup and saucer from the cupboard and pour herself a cup of tea. "May I carry this into the study?"

He nodded and stood up. "I'll carry the tray." He didn't want to leave those muffins behind. But then, picturing the study as he had last seen it, he realized there would be no place to set a teacup, let alone a tray. "Wait."

When she gave him an inquisitive look, her eyes were almost pretty.

"Let me go in first and pick up. I...had trouble this morning."

"You hired me to make order from chaos, Reverend Nelson. Please direct me to the study and trust me to earn my pay, which, by the way, has not yet been discussed."

"Down the hall and to the right." To the left of the hall lay the parlor, which completed the house's main floor plan. Upstairs were two small bedrooms, and below the kitchen lurked the earth-walled cellar, where she had found the peaches.

Not much in this tiny parsonage to interest a cultured woman.

Estelle took a sip of her tea and set the cup and saucer on the table. With a lift of her chin, she swept past him into the hall, her skirts brushing his legs. Belle trotted after her, trilling a feline love song. The study door creaked open. Frank sat down, crossed his forearms on the table, and dropped his head to rest upon them. A silent plea moved his lips.

The screen door slammed, and his heart gave a jolt. Tea sloshed on the table from the two cups, and a muffin fell from the basket. Halfway to his feet, he gaped at Mary Bilge.

"You sick, Preacher?" Her dark eyes scanned the tidy kitchen, the teapot, and the muffins—and narrowed. "Eating sweets at this hour musta soured your stomach. What you need is strong coffee." She filled the coffeepot from the pump, poured in a quantity of grounds from the canister, and clanged the pot on the stovetop. "Reckon I'll put on beans to soak for supper before I start the laundry."

Frank nodded. Beans again. He took another muffin. "No coffee, thanks. I've got calls to make."

"She gonna be here all day?" Mary jerked her head toward the study. Beans rattled into a cast-iron pot. She dropped the empty gunnysack, placed the pot in the sink, and pumped until water gushed to cover the beans.

"Yes. Let me lift that, Mary. You want it on the stovetop?" Frank couldn't sit by and watch a woman heft such a load.

"Yup." Mary grinned at him. "I'll keep an eye out to make sure that woman don't cheat you."

Frank hoisted the pot to the stove. "Want this over the heat?"

"No, it's just gotta soak a few hours. You go on, Preacher. I ain't no city lady with skinny arms and a frozen heart. You can rely on me. I'll do your wash today."

Frank smoothed his hair as he approached the study. Still in the hall, he heard Estelle give a little cough, then the shuffle of papers. "Miss Truman, I have calls to make. I'll be back after midday. Can you cope alone until then?" He closed his eyes while waiting for her answer, feeling like a coward.

"Yes, Reverend Nelson. Remember to wear a clean shirt."

He glanced down at himself and brushed at the imbedded hair. "Of course." *If I can find one.*

Minutes later, he cantered Powder through the stable yard and out the gate. August sun baked his shoulders and wind whipped his cheeks, but for a few blessed hours he was free from controlling women.

First he visited the Dixons and their recovering baby. He prayed over the tiny boy, rejoiced in his increasing strength, and promised to return soon. Althea Dixon gave him a hug and a jar of tomatoes before he left. She reminded him of his own daughter, Amy.

While riding to his next call, he wondered about Estelle. Upon his return, would she resign her position and inform him that his scribblings could never form a book? Would her cool blue eyes mock his pretensions? A confusing blend of fears troubled his heart.

In a sunlit sitting room at the rambling Coon homestead, old Beatrice Coon talked with him at length about family concerns, particularly one great-grandson. "Jubal's boy, Abel, is shiftless and sly. I pray for him every day, as I do for all my loved ones, but I do believe the boy is deaf to the Lord's call. His great-grandfather surely turned in his grave when Abel left college." She dabbed tears from her wrinkled cheeks.

Frank sympathized, well aware that Abel had been expelled from the university. The young man was rapidly becoming a bane to the community as well as a sorrow to the honorable Coon family.

When Frank made noises about heading out, Beatrice protested. "Why so restless today, Pastor Frank? You can't be leaving without reading to me from the Good Book."

Although Mrs. Coon lived with her grandson Sheldon's large and literate family, any member of which could have read to her throughout the day, Frank couldn't deny her request. She rocked in her chair and knitted while he read, and when he did finally say good-bye, she handed him a blue stocking cap with a tassel. "Soon the snows will be upon us, and you'll find it useful to warm places your pretty yellow hair doesn't cover anymore."

His hand lifted to the thinning patch on top of his head, and he returned her grin. "Thanks, Mrs. Coon."

"I made it to match your eyes," she said with a feminine titter. "Can you blame an old woman for keeping a handsome man near using any means she has?"

Freedom from controlling women was a pipe dream. He chuckled, squeezed her gnarled hands, and prayed with her before he left. Being near the feisty octogenarian made him feel young and spry, a rare sensation since the passing of his fiftieth birthday last spring.

As he entered town and approached the parsonage, he noticed the rundown condition of Mary Bilge's house across the way. Mary's personal habits seemed unaffected by her profession of faith. True, she no longer inhabited the saloons, a mark in her favor. But her slovenly attire, cigar smoking, and lack of ambition persisted. Hiring her as housekeeper had been his daughter Amy's idea, a kind-hearted attempt to build up Mary's dignity. Instead of dignity, Mary seemed to have developed expectations Frank would rather not think about.

Pepper whinnied a greeting from the paddock. Young Harmon Coon, another of Beatrice's great-grandsons, should arrive soon to hitch up the old pony. Frank trusted the boy to keep his end of the bargain. Those Coons were principled people. A founding family to be proud of, despite their one black sheep.

Frank's laundry waved from the line behind the house, neatly pinned. Shirts, trousers, combinations, nightshirt, all looked. . .clean. Kitchen towels and dish-cloths gleamed white under the summer sun.

As he mounted the veranda steps, a pleasant aroma made him stop and sniff. Had Mary baked bread? Maybe the perceived competition from Miss Truman had prodded her into action. Brows lifted, Frank pursed his lips in a soundless whistle and let the screen door slam shut.

He placed the jar of tomatoes on the kitchen counter. "Hello?" Belle, curled on a kitchen chair, lifted her head to blink at him sleepily. Two towel-draped mounds on the countertop drew his attention. He peeked under the towel and nearly drooled at the sight and smell of warm, crusty loaves. Something bubbled on the stove. He lifted the lid of a saucepan to find not beans but a simmering vegetable soup.

Mary Bilge could not create such artistry if her life depended on it. Had she and Estelle fought for control of the house? How would two women fight? Flat irons at ten paces? Rolling pins to the death? The mental image of Belle the cat battling a mangy upstart to maintain her queenly status made him smile. No wonder the cat had bonded with her human counterpart. However—his smile faded—Mary had been here first.

The only way to find out for certain what had occurred was to ask. "Miss Truman?" He pushed open the study door and actually saw carpeting instead of books and papers. His gaze lifted to discover shelves full of books, papers stacked on the desk, and his flighty notes weighted by the rock. The file cabinet stood open, and Miss Truman appeared to be labeling files.

She had removed her jacket. A tailored shirtwaist emphasized her slim figure. No longer did she look scrawny to Frank. He knew her as a creative powerhouse. How had the woman accomplished so much in one day? And she still managed to look unruffled.

She glanced up. "Reverend Nelson, I require your assistance. I believe it would be helpful to create an individual file for each topic or chapter of your book. As I look over your outline, I see distinct categories which will simplify this task."

His heart thundered in his ears. "You do?"

"Yes. We should also file your published periodical articles along with their research material in case you decide to reuse any of them in your books. My suggestion would be to create a file for each doctrinal issue—eschatology, predestination, divine attributes, and so forth. You may discover a need for further breakdown of these categories, but this will give us a start."

"A start," he echoed. While she continued to describe her system, he moved closer and looked over her shoulder at the miraculous way his stacks of paper fit neatly into her files. She smelled of fresh bread and soap. Although her skin betrayed her advancing age, sagging slightly beneath her pointed chin and crinkling around her eyes and mouth, it looked soft to touch. She must be near fifty, since she was Paul's elder sister. Just the right age.

Her eyes were like diamonds with blue edges, keen and cool, focused on his face. He suddenly realized that she had asked him a question. "Pardon?"

"I asked if you were planning to work on your manuscript tonight. If you prepare a few pages, I'll transcribe them for you tomorrow. I do request that you attempt to write more clearly. Some of your letters are illegible."

"Can you. . .can you write from dictation?"

"Yes, although I find that few people organize their thoughts well enough to dictate good literature." She tucked one last sheaf of paper into the file, slid the drawer shut, and leaned her back against it. Her expression as she surveyed the room revealed gratification. "A promising beginning to our work, Reverend. Tomorrow I shall clean this room before we begin."

The thought of her returning in the morning warmed him clear through. "I noticed the bread and soup in the kitchen. Mary had planned beans for tonight. I don't see her around anywhere. What happened?"

Her long fingers rubbed the corner of the file cabinet, and her gaze lowered. Pink tinged her cheekbones. "I smelled the beans burning and went to stir them. Reverend, she did not rinse the beans, and they had not soaked long enough to soften before she set them to boil. You would have had crunchy beans for supper tonight, along with rocks and sticks."

It wouldn't have been the first time. "And the laundry?"

Her lips tightened into a straight line. "She was washing your clothes without soap and draping them over the line dripping wet."

"So what did you do?"

"I advised her to use soap. She dropped your...uh, garment in the dirt, called me some unrepeatable names, and walked away. I have not seen her since."

"So you washed my laundry, baked bread, cooked my dinner, and filed my papers, all while I was away for a few hours. Miss Truman, you will exhaust yourself at this pace."

Her gaze snapped back to his. "Nonsense. I enjoyed myself." Suddenly her color deepened. With a quick lift of her chin, she slipped around him and headed for the entryway. "I had better leave, since my chaperone is missing."

He followed her. "You won't stay for soup?"

Tying her bonnet strings, she glanced up at him then away. "They will expect me at home. The soup should be ready for you to eat. I made it with canned vegetables from your cellar and a bit of bacon."

She opened the front door. Pepper, harnessed to the dogcart, waited at the hitching rail out front. Afternoon light dotted the lawn beneath the trees, and sunflowers bobbed in a breeze. "Good day, Reverend Nelson. I shall return in the morning."

"You'll make tea?" He wanted her to look at him.

"Yes, but you need to purchase more." When she gazed into the distance, her eyes reflected the sky. "You need to bring in your laundry. It should be dry."

"I'll do that. Thank you, Miss Truman."

"It was my pleasure. I'll iron tomorrow." She hurried down the walkway and climbed into the cart. Frank watched her drive away. Almost as soon as she disappeared from view, he set out down the street toward the general store to stock up on tea.

∞

Later, after piling his clean laundry into a basket, he sliced bread and buttered it, then ladled out soup into a truly clean bowl. He spooned a bite into his mouth.

Slightly spicy, rich, and hot. Perfect with the tender bread. He ate his fill, then put the rest away for lunch tomorrow. Remembering Estelle at his sink, sleeves rolled up as she scrubbed, he rinsed his supper dishes and stacked them in the dishpan. In a happy daze, he sat and rocked on his veranda until evening shadows fell.

How could this be? A man his age couldn't be fool enough to fall in love with a woman for her cooking. He scarcely knew Estelle Truman, yet his heart sang like a mockingbird every time she entered his thoughts.

"Lord, what do I do now? I don't even know if she's a believer, though she spoke about doctrine with familiarity. She is so serious and. . .and cold." His brows lowered as he remembered Paul's analogy.

Although his memories were fading, he still recalled Kirsten's round, rosy face with its almost perpetual smile. Plump, blond, and talkative, she had been Estelle's exact opposite. No, not exact. Kirsten had been a good cook and housekeeper, too.

"And she loved me," he murmured. "I wonder if Estelle could love me."

Warmth brushed his leg, and a cat hopped into his lap. Belle, of course, purring and almost maudlin in her demand for affection. He rubbed her cheeks and chin, assured her of her surpassing beauty, and stroked her silken body while she nuzzled his beard and trilled. Of course, if he had picked her up uninvited, she would have cut him dead with one glance, growled, and struggled to be free.

"Is Estelle like my cat, Lord? Maybe she'll respond to undemanding affection. How does a man go about courting a woman who's forgotten how to love?" He sighed. "Why do I have the feeling I'm going to get scratched if I try?"

Chapter 4

C old seeped through the study windows as a late October wind moaned around the parsonage. Frank lifted the new calico curtain to reveal a gray early morning, then settled back in his desk chair with a contented smile. Soon Estelle would come and turn the cold, empty house into a home.

Since she had arrived in August, his life had exchanged confusion for comfort. Organization had never assumed a more appealing form. Even Mary now accomplished work around the house—sweeping, dusting, beating rugs, and laundering. Frank suspected the woman hadn't known how to keep house until Estelle trained her.

And music had returned to the church. From his seat on the platform, Frank could watch Estelle's profile as she played piano for the morning service each week. Since her arrival, people had started requesting a longer song service, Lionel Coon had led the singing with renewed enthusiasm, and attendance had increased until there would soon be need for two Sunday services unless the church could afford to enlarge the sanctuary. Whatever the board decided was fine with Frank. More people heard God's Word each week—that was the important thing.

He occasionally finagled a supper invitation out of Paul and had opportunity to observe Estelle in her brother's household. Frank sought evidence of thawing around her heart, but she seemed as detached and cool as ever. Flora obviously adored her maiden aunt. Did Estelle care at all for the child? Margie raved about her aunt's needlework; Estelle had helped design the wedding gown and the gowns for the attendants. Yet did she derive any pleasure from her accomplishments? Thanks to Estelle's help around the house, Susan had regained much of her strength. Although Susan rained affection and appreciation upon her, Estelle appeared to endure rather than enjoy her sister-in-law's attention.

Only once had Frank witnessed affection from Estelle Truman. Its recipient had been, of all things, Belle the cat. Returning early from a call, he had stopped at the post office, then entered his house quietly, examining his mail. Hearing talk in the study, he had approached and stopped outside the door, amazed to recognize the cooing voice as Estelle's. Loud purring plus an occasional trilling meow identified her companion. Another step revealed the tableau to his astonished gaze. Estelle cradled the fawning creature in her arms and rubbed her face against

Belle's glossy fur, wearing a tender expression that stole Frank's breath away.

The floor had creaked, revealing his presence. Two startled faces had looked up at him. Belle leaped to the floor and scooted past his feet. Estelle brushed cat hair from her gown and turned away, but not before he witnessed her deep blush. He could not recall what had been said in those awkward moments.

Would Estelle ever look at him with warmth in her eyes? After all these weeks, he still felt uncertain in her presence. While she no longer openly scorned him, neither did he receive affectionate glances from her. They frequently shared pleasant companionship, sipping tea while discussing the arrangement of paragraphs or catching up on community news. She pampered him with delicious meals and fresh-baked bread. Yet she maintained an emotional distance that discouraged thoughts of romance.

He entertained such thoughts anyway. Kirsten had often accused him of being a hopeless romantic; perhaps it was true. A more hopeless romance than this he could scarcely imagine.

Returning to the present, he flipped through notes for the final chapter of his book. The last chapter. How had it all happened so quickly? Estelle insisted the book had been complete before her arrival; she had simply put his notes in coherent order. He knew better. The book never would have been written without her. How had he survived before she entered his life? He never wanted to return to the colorless, disordered existence he had endured since Kirsten's death.

If he could convince Estelle to marry him, his problems would be over. Well, some of his problems. Actually, marriage often presented a new set of problems. Despite his prayers for God's leading, he hesitated when it came to proposing. Maybe God had been trying to show him that such a union would never work. Or maybe he feared rejection. Estelle might fix her keen gaze on him and question his sanity. His touch might fill her with loathing. With a groan, he crossed his arms and laid his head on his desk.

Oh, to be a cat.

"Reverend Nelson?" He lifted his head and turned, blinking at the embodiment of his dream. "I saw the lamplight. Did you spend the night here?" Estelle's gaze flickered across his manuscript.

He rubbed his stiff neck and rolled his head and shoulders. "No, I rose early to work. I never heard you drive up."

"It's windy today. Paul says a storm may be coming." When she approached to open the curtains and let in morning light, her full skirts brushed his left arm. "It's cold in here. I built up the fire in the stove. You'd better come into the kitchen until the house warms up. I'll make pancakes if you like, or oatmeal."

"Pancakes, please. And tea, as long as you drink it with me." He followed her to the kitchen. Belle greeted him, winding around his feet. He pulled a chair near the stove, let Belle hop into his lap, and watched Estelle work. Her every movement seemed to him graceful and efficient. Like poetry or music.

While whipping eggs for pancake batter, Estelle glanced at him. "You're quiet this morning. Did you accomplish much work?"

"No. I was thinking about you."

For an instant, her spoon froze in place; then slowly, she began to stir again. After greasing the griddle, she poured four small circles of batter. "Since the book is nearly complete, I imagine my employment here will soon end."

"I don't know what I'd do without you."

She swallowed hard. Once she opened her mouth to speak, then closed it. "I don't understand."

He wanted to stand up, turn her to face him, and declare his love—but he knew better. Like Belle, she would struggle and growl and resent his advances.

"You have become part of my life. Part of me. I can't imagine a future without you here in my home every day." He rubbed the back of his neck again. "If I have your consent, I want to ask your brother for permission to court you."

She looked like a marble statue: *Woman with Spatula.*

"The pancakes are burning."

Breath burst from her, and she flipped the cakes. "But why?"

He almost made a quip about things burning when they cook too long but thought better of it. "I think you're a wonderful woman, Estelle."

She sucked in a breath and closed her eyes.

Encouraged, he elaborated. "You are accomplished and creative and thoughtful. Out of the kindness of your heart, you have made my house back into a home, so much so that I hate to leave whenever you're here. You've trained Mary Bilge into a decent housekeeper, a miracle in itself. Your list of piano students lengthens daily. Without a word of complaint, you took a disastrous mass of scribbling and turned it into an organized manuscript, possibly worthy of publication."

She snapped back into motion, rescued the pancakes, and poured a new batch, scraping out the bowl. Quickly she buttered the cakes and sprinkled them with brown sugar. "Eat them while they're hot."

"Thank you." He bowed his head, adding a plea for wisdom.

When he opened his eyes and began to eat, she was staring at the griddle. "You don't really know me."

He finished chewing a bite and swallowed. "I want to know you better. Everything I see, I like. Is there hope for me, Estelle?"

She turned the pancakes. "I need time to think."

"Do you want to take the rest of today off?"

After a pause, she nodded. "I'll clean the kitchen first."

"When you're ready, I'll hitch Pepper."

Frank attempted to work on his manuscript, but concentration was impossible. He needed to be with Estelle, needed to know her thoughts. At last he gave up, saddled Powder, and rode to the Trumans' farm. Susan greeted him at the door, and Paul came from the barn. "What brings you out this blustery day, Frank?" he asked, wiping axle grease from his hands with a rag.

"Come inside out of the cold," Susan said.

Frank stepped into the entry. "I'm looking for Estelle."

Susan closed the door behind Paul and took Frank's hat and scarf. "She came home for a short time and left again. I thought she must have forgotten something; she never said a word."

"Did she take anything with her?" Fear shortened Frank's breath.

"I'll go look," Susan offered, then hurried upstairs.

"You might as well tell us what happened. I can guess, but it's easier to ask." Paul led him toward the kitchen, where Eliza left her warm bed by the stove and came wagging to greet him.

After patting the dog, Frank slumped into a kitchen chair and accepted a cup of coffee. "This morning I told her I planned to ask your permission to court her. She said she needed time to think, so I gave her the rest of the day off."

Paul set his own cup down and sat across from Frank. "You don't want to marry her, Frank. Trust me on this one."

Susan bustled in. "No, no, don't bother getting up; I'll join you in a moment. Estelle's trunk is open, and it looks as if she took something from inside, but her clothing and bags are all here. What happened, Frank? Did you propose to her? I know you're in love with her. I think everyone in town knows."

Heat flowed up his neck in a wave.

"Estelle is a good enough person, I guess," Paul said, "but she would make a poor choice of wife. She closed her heart to love twenty years ago."

"What happened then?" Frank asked.

Paul sipped his coffee and grimaced. "She was engaged to a ministerial student by the name of John Forster. A sober fellow with social aspirations. When the war started, he joined up as chaplain. Made it through the war unscathed, then died of a fever before he could return home. Estelle was furious with God."

Frank bowed his head. "Understandable."

"Yes, but she never got over it. She turned bitter and heartless. When I brought my wife home to meet the family, my only sister rejected her simply because she had worked as a maid."

Susan shook her head. "Now that's not entirely true, Paul. Estelle stood with her parents in public, but before we left, she secretly gave me that heirloom pin of your grandmother's. I think she felt bad about the way your parents behaved, but who could stand up against your father? He terrified me. I can't blame her for bowing to his will."

Paul huffed. "You're too forgiving."

"Can anyone be too forgiving?" Frank asked, turning his cup between his hands.

"Paul, tell about when you wrote to your parents," Susan said.

He sighed deeply. "Around two years ago, you preached a series of sermons on forgiveness, Frank. I wrote to my parents, trying to restore the relationship. Estelle wrote back to tell me that our father had died soon after Susan and I moved away, leaving them penniless. Estelle had been working at a law office all those years to support our mother and, for a time, our great-aunt. Mother never answered my letter."

"And you didn't contact Estelle again until she wrote to inform you of your mother's death," Susan said.

"Which was when Paul came to me," Frank finished the tale, "and asked if I would hire her as secretary. She's had a lonely, disappointing life from the sound of it."

"True, but she didn't have to freeze into herself the way she did," Paul said. "Many people endure heartbreak and disappointment without becoming icebergs. As a child, Estelle was lively, full of mischief, loving toward me. She wept when I went off to war, and she wrote to me faithfully. I told her about my new wife in my letters, and she seemed excited. And then to have her reject us so coldly. . ." Paul shook his head. "She's worse now than ever."

"I think she is afraid to love," Susan said.

"I think she's angry at God," Paul insisted.

"I think I need to find out the truth from her," Frank decided. "Thanks for the coffee. I'll hunt for her around town. I have an idea where she is."

Chapter 5

Frank let Powder gallop toward the church. Gray clouds scudded across the vast sky. With the fields harvested, a man could see for miles. A raucous flock of crows passed overhead and faded into the distance. Wind tugged at Frank's hat, trying to rip it from his head.

The church's white steeple beckoned as if promising refuge. As Frank expected, Pepper dozed in the shed out back, still hitched to the dogcart. When the wind shifted, tempestuous music filled the air.

Frank opened the church doors and slipped inside. The music increased in volume again when he opened the sanctuary door. Estelle sat at the piano, her sheet music lit by tapers in the instrument's folding candle racks. Her strong hands flew over the keys. Frank thought he recognized Beethoven, a violent piece. Its intensity covered his footsteps until he could slide into a seat four rows behind her. When the song ended, she turned a few pages and played a yearning sonata, then moved on to several complex and stirring works of art. After a pause, she performed a hauntingly romantic piece. The music flowing from her fingers brought tears to Frank's eyes.

As the last notes faded away, she clenched her fists beneath her chin and hunched over.

"I've never heard anything more beautiful," Frank said.

Estelle hit the keyboard with both palms as if to catch herself. Instantly she jerked her hands up to end the discordant jangle and glanced at Frank over her shoulder. "I didn't hear you enter." She checked the watch pinned to her shirt-waist, exclaimed softly, closed her book, and slid the felt keyboard cover into place. "How long have you been here?"

Frank rose and approached the piano. "Not long enough. Whatever you were playing there was powerful. Music for the soul."

Estelle avoided his gaze. "Thank you."

"I felt, while listening, that at last I was seeing and hearing the real Estelle."

"Your wife played. Does it bother you to hear me play her piano?"

He rubbed one hand across the piano's top, then brushed dust from his fingers. "Kirsten never played like you do. Her music was cheery and uncomplicated, a reflection of her personality. Your music is rich and passionate, a reflection of your soul."

With shaking hands, Estelle began to gather up her music. "That was Schubert, not me."

He lowered his voice. "Paul and Susan told me about John Forster's untimely death. Paul believes you're angry with God. Susan believes you're afraid to love. I wonder if both are correct."

She paused. "If they are, my feelings are justified."

"Tell me."

Her oblique gaze pierced him. "Why should I?"

"As I said this morning, I want to know you. And I think you need to talk. Anything you say is confidential; I will tell no one."

She breathed hard for a few moments, staring at the keyboard. "John didn't die in the war," she said with quiet intensity. "God took him from me. Then my parents rejected Susan, so Paul went away hating me. Then my father died of a heart attack, leaving behind debts that consumed his entire fortune. For twenty years, I slaved in an office to support my mother and my great-aunt, who spent the remainder of their lives complaining about my insufficient provision and warning me never to trust a man."

Frank could easily picture them, having encountered human leeches before. "Did your mother never work? I remember when Paul learned of your financial ruin—long after the event, I'm sorry to say. He told me how socially ambitious and dependent your mother was and wondered how you managed her."

"Mother took to her bed years ago, though she was not truly ill until last winter. Doubtless you will think me a monster, but I have shed no tears since her passing. Her death came as a blessed release, as did Aunt Bridget's demise ten years earlier. The last person I mourned was my father, the model husband and father, who betrayed us all by keeping a second family on the far side of town. The other woman made her claim after his death."

Frank's jaw dropped.

"I did not want to believe her assertions, but once she proved my father's infidelity, I did right by my five half brothers and sisters. They are all grown men and women by now; at the time, they were helpless children."

"Does Paul know any of this?"

"No. When it occurred, I was unaware of his location. He contacted us a few years ago. Mother refused to acknowledge him, so I wrote to him secretly."

"He told me what happened when he brought Susan home with him after the war."

"She had been a housemaid. Far too good for any of us Trumans, actually." Estelle closed her eyes. "At the time, I thought it my duty to uphold my parents' decision, but Paul will never forgive me. Oh, life is unpredictable and cruel!" Her voice broke.

"The people who should have loved and protected you failed you, Estelle." Frank spoke softly. "I understand your anger and your bitterness. I've had a share of heartbreak in my life, but unlike you, I've also had people who loved me faithfully."

"The only people who might have loved me, God took away."

"That's not entirely true."

She glared at him. "Now I'm to hear the sermon about God's faithful love."

Frowning to conceal his hurt, he rubbed his beard. "I didn't know I annoyed you so much."

He heard her sigh. "I apologize. That accusation was unkind and unfair. Your Sunday sermons challenge my mind, as does your book, yet often when you preach, I hear only riddles and contradictions. 'God's plan of salvation is simple,' you say, yet as I work on your manuscript, I am overwhelmed by the complexity of the Christian creed."

"I thought you understood."

Shaking her head, she watched her fingers fold pleats in her skirt. "Aunt Bridget told me that my salvation lay in religion and duty. I have done my best, but sometimes the loneliness is too much to bear."

"Good works cannot regenerate your sinful spirit or mine. Our righteousness is as filthy rags in God's sight. He must transform us from the inside out."

"But what if He doesn't?" The pain in Estelle's expression tore at his heart. "I do believe that Jesus is God's Son, sent to earth to die in my place, but my belief seems to make no difference. What if I'm not one of His chosen ones?"

Frank prayed for the right words. "Belief involves more than an intellectual acceptance of fact. It involves acknowledgment of your unworthy condition, surrender of the will, dying to self. If you come to Him, He will certainly not cast you out."

Emotions flickered across her face—longing, defiance, resolve. "You say God is love and God is all-powerful. If He is both, how can there be sin, deceit, murder, and ugliness in this world? Why do innocent people suffer? Why doesn't God allow everyone into heaven if He loves us all so much?"

"We're all sinners. One evidence of God's love is that He doesn't simply give us what we deserve—eternal damnation. Instead, He offers everyone the opportunity to love and serve Him or to reject His gift of salvation."

She nodded slowly.

Encouraged, he continued, "Each day of your life you choose between good and evil, as do the murderers and liars and adulterers of this world. Our choices affect the people around us, and the more those people love us, the more deeply they are affected. You have chosen a life of isolation rather than to risk the vulnerability that comes with love." As soon as the words left his lips, he knew he'd made a mistake.

Shaking visibly, she leaped to her feet and poked her forefinger into his chest. "You have no right to judge me!"

He bowed his head. "It's true. I have no right to judge; only God has that right. For a man who makes his living with words, I'm bad at expressing my feelings. Because I care, I want you to share the abundant life God gives, but the choice is yours to make."

She folded her arms across her chest and stared at the floor. "You ask me to risk everything by loving a God who has never yet shown Himself worthy of my faith."

"The request for your faith comes from God, not from me. He said a Savior would come to earth, and He did; we celebrate that kept promise at Christmas. He said He would die for us, and He did; we commemorate that sacrifice on Good Friday. He said He would conquer death and rise again, and He did; we rejoice in that triumphant victory at Easter. You can trust Him to keep His promises, Estelle. He desires your love and trust enough to die for you."

Estelle's head jerked back. "I need to go home."

Frank swallowed hasty words and bowed his head. "Yes, it grows late. I'll follow you home."

Outside, the wind knifed them with the chill of winter. Estelle clutched her shawl around herself and gasped. Frank closed the church doors. "You need more than a shawl in this wind. We can stop at the parsonage for blankets and coats. I think we might get snow overnight."

He took Estelle's hand and led her back to the shed where the horses waited. Without protest, she let him tie Powder up behind the dogcart, climb in beside her, and drive through the dark churchyard to the main road. Wind whipped trees and scattered leaves across the road.

"Hang on to me, if you want," he offered, raising his voice above the wind. She immediately gripped his arm and buried her face against his shoulder. He grinned into the gale.

When Pepper stopped in front of the parsonage, Frank heard Estelle's teeth chattering. "Come in for hot tea before I take you home." He rubbed her unresisting fingers. "Your hands are like ice."

"But it's nearly dark," she protested.

"Just for a moment." He helped her from the cart. Within minutes, he was stoking the fire in the oven and filling the kettle. Seeing Estelle shiver, he hurried to find blankets.

When he returned, she was pouring tea. Lamplight turned her eyes to fire as she glanced up. "I hope Susan doesn't worry."

"I told her I would find you. She won't worry." He accepted his teacup and pulled two chairs close to the stove. "Wrap this blanket around your shoulders and soak up that warmth. We can't stay long, you're right, but I want to feel heat in your hands before we head home."

She nodded and obeyed, huddled beside him beneath a quilt. "I shall consider what we discussed at the church," she said. "I plan to read the Bible while looking for the principles you laid out in your book. Until tonight I thought them mere dogma, intellectual pursuits, and I privately mocked your insistence upon applying scripture to everyday life."

He sipped his tea to conceal his reaction to the affront.

"I shall pray for insight as I read." She laid her hand on his arm and peered up into his face. "Reverend Nelson, I must thank you for taking time to hear my tale and offer your sage advice. I understand why your parishioners seek your counsel. You are a man of many gifts that were not immediately evident to me."

He swallowed the last of his tea and stood up. "We must be off. Wrap up in that quilt, and I'll bring another for your feet." She had met and exceeded his one criterion—warm hands. The imprint of her hand would burn on his arm for hours to come.

⸎

"Thanks for bringing Estelle home, Frank," Paul said while Susan poured hot coffee. The four sat near the glowing oven in Susan's kitchen. "You can sleep on the sofa tonight. I already told Josh to stable your horse. It's no night to be on the road."

"I appreciate the shelter." Frank studied Estelle in concern while speaking to Paul. "That wind held an awful bite. Wouldn't be surprised to see snow on the ground come morning." Would she take ill from exposure? He had tried to protect her from the wind, but she still looked pale.

Paul frowned. "Estelle won't be returning to the parsonage. You can bring work here for her. From all I've heard, the book is nearly ready to submit to a publisher."

Estelle's head snapped around. "I most certainly will be working at the parsonage. I need access to the files. Why should Reverend Nelson have to bring my work here?"

"Because your situation has changed. Frank is courting you; therefore, it is no longer appropriate for you to work in his house. A minister must observe proprieties, perhaps even more carefully than most people do."

Frank barely concealed his surprise and dismay. He had interpreted Paul's earlier discouraging comments as a refusal of his courtship request. When had the story changed?

Estelle met Frank's gaze across the table. "But what will you eat?" As soon as the words left her lips, she flushed and looked away.

"Eat?" Paul said, glowering at Frank. "Is my sister a secretary or a cook? I don't like the sound of this."

"Now, Paul, I'm certain they have behaved properly," Susan inserted gently as she handed out steaming cups of coffee. "Don't jump to conclusions."

Embarrassment and frustration built in Frank's chest. "Thank you, Susan. You can rest assured that nothing untoward occurred while Miss Truman worked at the parsonage, but I respect Paul's decision. I don't mind bringing work here until the book is complete. I can drop by each morning before I make calls, and we can discuss progress and objectives then. I'll still pay her to complete the job."

Later that night, Frank wedged his frame into the confines of the hard horsehair sofa. Between the effect of strong coffee and the discomfort of a chilly parlor, he knew sleep would be long in coming, so he prayed. *Lord, I know now why I had no peace about proposing to Estelle. I was wrong to blurt out my feelings today, but at*

430

least we had our first meaningful discussion of You, and I know where she stands. I can't say I'm happy with the situation, but knowing is better than living in the dark.

He rolled to his side, pulled a quilt over his shoulders, and felt a draft on his feet. *Much though I would like to, I can't blame my present dilemma on Paul. Today I, a minister of the gospel, declared my love to an unbeliever, and now we are officially courting. Calling myself all kinds of a fool also leaves the problem unsolved. What can I do? If I withdraw my offer of love, I'll be one more person letting her down. If I don't, she'll be expecting me to court her. . . .*

Chapter 6

Weeks passed, and Estelle's life again settled into a routine. Frank stopped by the Truman farm each day before beginning his round of calls or planning his sermons. He behaved like a pastor and friend; no hint of the ardent lover reappeared. Estelle began to wonder if he had changed his mind about courting her. Not that she intended to marry the man, of course. But as revisions on the book neared completion, she realized how much she would miss seeing Frank each day when he no longer had a reason to call.

Thanksgiving Day arrived. David joined the Truman family, but Frank traveled to Des Moines to visit his daughter, Amy, and her husband. Estelle helped prepare the Truman feast and took part in the family celebration, struggling to conceal her loneliness. When had Frank's presence become essential to her contentment? This need for him alarmed her. She needed to make a complete break if she was to maintain emotional independence.

One morning in mid-December, Frank dropped by as usual. Shaking snow from his overcoat, he let Estelle take his hat. "I brought out the cutter this morning. Winter is here to stay. Which reminds me, will you join me for the Christmas sleigh ride this year?"

Estelle hung his hat over his scarf. "Christmas sleigh ride?"

"You haven't heard about it? The sleigh ride is a Coon's Hollow tradition—when we have enough snow, that is. It's an unofficial event; people ride up and down the main streets and out into the countryside. Some of the young fellows have races, but us older folks prefer a decorous pace. My little cutter carries two in close comfort. I'll bundle you up with robes and hot bricks, and we'll put Powder through his paces." He looked into her eyes and smiled.

Despite the pastor's flushed face and disheveled hair, Estelle found him appealing. For the moment, her emotional independence diminished in value. "I shall be honored to join you."

His dimples deepened, and his eyes sparkled. He caught her hand and squeezed gently. "Soon we need to have a serious talk, Estelle." He glanced around, and Estelle became aware of Joe and Flora chatting in the kitchen. "Privacy is scarce these days."

Tightness built in Estelle's chest. Desperate to escape its demands, she pulled her hand from Frank's warm grasp and focused on the portfolio beneath his arm. "Did you make revisions on the final chapter?"

He blinked, and the sparkle faded. "I did. This next week I plan to read through the entire thing, and if no major flaws turn up, I'll mail it off to Chicago. My brother, who pastors a large church there, spoke with an editor who happens to attend his church. It seems this editor is eager to see the manuscript. I didn't seek these connections, but apparently God has been making them for me."

Hours later, Estelle lifted her pen and stared at the final page, revised as Frank had requested. After just over three months of work, the book was complete. She laid the paper atop her stack, selected a clean sheet, and dipped her pen again. The concluding chapter contained a scripture passage and application she wanted to keep for her own study. Reading Frank's words was the next best thing to hearing his sermons, and writing them down fixed them into her memory. Lately his explanations of Bible passages seemed clearer, though she still often found herself perplexed.

Eliza, lying across Estelle's feet beneath the table, moaned in her sleep and twitched as if chasing a dream rabbit. Estelle rubbed the dog's white belly with the toe of her shoe.

She paused to flex her fingers and stare through the kitchen window. Where green lawn had once met her gaze, blindingly white snow now drifted in gentle waves. She imagined skimming over the snow in a cutter, snuggled close to Frank beneath warm robes, and a smile teased her lips. Often lately she sensed a hazy, tantalizing possibility, as if someone offered a future of beauty and hope but kept it always slightly out of her view.

Rapid footsteps entered the kitchen. "Would you care for a cup of tea, Auntie Stell?" Margie offered. "How is the book coming?"

"Thank you, yes," Estelle said. "My fingers need a rest. Have you finished sewing on the seed pearls?"

"Almost. They are perfect on the headpiece. I still can't believe you gave them to me."

"I removed them from your great-grandmother's wedding gown years ago after moths spoiled it." Estelle gave her niece a fond look. "I can imagine no better use for them."

"A few weeks ago I despaired of finishing my gown in time, but now I believe we'll make it. Only two weeks until my wedding!"

"Fifteen days until Christmas. Flora's gown is ready, and mine needs only the buttonholes."

Margie left the teapot to give her aunt a hug. "You were wonderful to sew Flora's gown, and I can't express how excited I am that you will come out of mourning for my wedding."

Estelle patted Margie's hand on her shoulder. "It has been more than six months since my mother's death."

"Yes, but—" Margie stopped and returned to preparing the tea.

"You've heard that I've worn mourning since my fiancé's death twenty years ago?"

The girl nodded hesitantly.

Estelle pursed her lips and flexed her fingers. "I no longer believe it necessary." Abruptly she picked up her pen and began to write again.

"Here's your tea, Auntie."

Estelle accepted the cup and saucer, meeting her niece's worried gaze. "Thank you, Marjorie."

"You're welcome. Why are you frowning? Did I offend you?" Margie sat across from Estelle and stirred her tea. "I'm sorry if I did."

"No, child. I was preoccupied."

"Thinking about Pastor Nelson?" Margie clinked her teacup into its saucer and leaned forward, resting her chin on her palm and her elbow on the table. "So are you going to marry him? David told me about his courting you. Pa doesn't seem to think you ought to marry him, but I think it would be wonderful! You'd be my mother-in-law, sort of. David says he's been afraid Pastor would let Mary Bilge bully him into marrying her, so he would be thrilled to have you as a stepmother instead."

"Mary Bilge?" Estelle nearly choked. "I hardly think so."

Margie covered her mouth. Her hazel eyes twinkled above the napkin.

"She must be several years his senior." The idea turned Estelle's stomach. "Do you think he might marry her if I turn him down?"

"I hope not! But David says she has turned into a decent cook and bought herself some new clothes. He suspects she's hunting for a husband, and her sights are set on Pastor. Have you seen her at church recently?"

"No. I am usually at the piano before and after services."

"She comes late and leaves early. But no matter how well she cooks or how much better she looks, she's not the woman for Pastor. I think she scares him."

Recalling how he had overlooked Mary's shoddy work, Estelle was inclined to agree. "I taught her to clean and cook," she said, staring blankly at the table. "I felt sorry for her. She resented me, but I had no idea. . ."

"You had no idea he would fall in love with you," Margie said.

Estelle knew her cheeks were flushing. "Nonsense."

Margie chuckled. "And I think you're in love with him, too, though you don't know it yet. How sweet!"

Estelle gathered up her papers and stacked them. "With your wedding date approaching, you are in a romantic state of mind. Reverend Nelson considers remarriage for purely practical reasons."

Smirking, Margie picked up the empty teacups and carried them to the sink.

Falling snow sparkled in the light of Frank's lantern as he hiked home from church one evening humming a Christmas carol. Snug beneath its white blanket, the parsonage welcomed him with a warm glow. He climbed over the buried gate and slogged to the front door. The path would require shoveling come morning, but not even that prospect could dim his joy.

Ever since Estelle had agreed to join him for the sleigh ride, his hopes had been high. Although he seldom spoke with her in private, her questions about his manuscript told him she was seeking God's truth. He needed only to be patient.

Smiling, he burst into song as he stepped into the entryway. "Glory to the newborn King. Peace on earth and—"

"Take off your boots. You're messing up my clean floor." Mary appeared in the kitchen doorway, wiping both hands on her apron.

"Oh, you're still here?" He stated the obvious.

"I baked you a chicken, and it ain't done yet," Mary said and pointed at his feet. "The boots."

After hanging up his coat and hat, he obediently used the bootjack, but his mind rebelled. It was time, past time, to put Mary back in her proper place. Lately she had taken to spending entire days in the parsonage, rearranging and. . .

He didn't know what else she did all day, but he knew it wasn't cleaning. The woman behaved as if she regarded his house as her domain.

He set his jaw and padded into the kitchen. Mary was removing a pan from the oven. As she straightened, he observed pleats across the expansive waist of her white apron. Navy skirts swept the floor, and iron-gray fluff surrounded her head. "What happened to your coat?"

Lines deepened around her mouth. "Got myself two new gowns and warshed my hair nigh on a month ago, and you just now noticed?" Her dark eyes skewered him with a glance.

He floundered for a proper response. "You look cleaner. Quite unobjectionable."

She grunted, sliced meat from the chicken, and slapped it on his plate. "Want preserves on your bread?"

"Please."

She jerked her head toward the cellar door. "Down cellar."

He blinked, then picked up a lamp, lifted the latch on the door, and descended into the clammy hole. Canned fruits and vegetables, gifts from parishioners, lined the wooden shelves protruding from the frozen sod walls. He found a jar of peach preserves and climbed back upstairs. After placing the jar on the table, he folded his arms. "Mary Bilge, it's past time you and I had a talk."

A wave of feminine emotion flitted across her face. She reached up to pat her hair into place. "Yes, Preacher?"

The quick changes in her attitude and expression confused Frank. One moment she was a bad-tempered harridan; the next moment she became an amiable woman.

"I pay you to fix my meals and clean my house, not to tell me what to do. I don't expect a slave, but I do require respect. If my future wife decides to retain your services around the house, you will need to give her the same measure of respect."

Only her trembling jowls revealed life.

"Mary, I don't want to seem ungrateful...."

She turned around, picked up the pan holding the roast chicken, and dumped it upside down into the sink. Brandishing a wooden spoon, she approached Frank. He looked down into eyes like sparking flints.

"Next time I see that skinny icicle woman, I'll break her in half." With a loud crack, she snapped the spoon in two over her knee.

Stunned, Frank watched as Mary Bilge hauled on her tattered coat, hat, and overshoes and stumped outside through the kitchen door, leaving a rush of icy air in her wake.

⌘

Satin gowns in varied shades of blue were draped over armchairs around the parlor. Margie's gown enveloped the sofa, shimmering in snowy splendor. Susan stepped back and reviewed the finery once more. "We'll curl our hair before we leave home and hope the curl lasts until the ceremony. Estelle, I truly don't know how we would have managed without you."

Estelle rested in a rocking chair near the fireplace. "These months since I arrived in Iowa have been the best of my life. I'm grateful to be part of this family."

"My gown is glorious," Margie said, clasping her hands at her breast and closing her eyes. "I can scarcely wait until David sees me in it tomorrow!"

"And I can scarcely wait to see Auntie Stell in her new gown," Flora added. "We'll be twins." The girl wrapped one arm around Estelle's neck and leaned close. "And we'll be ever so beautiful."

Estelle kissed the child's soft cheek. "Beautiful we shall be, my dear. And humble, too."

Flora giggled. Tapping all ten fingers on a side table, she pretended to play the piano. "Wish I could play the wedding march tomorrow. I can play it really good. Can't I, Auntie Stell?"

"Indeed you do play well," Estelle said. "Your progress has been remarkable."

Susan smiled. "I imagine someday you'll play piano for many weddings, but not this one. Now off to bed, Flora. Tomorrow will be a busy day."

"And the next day is Christmas!" Flora exclaimed. "I hope it snows more and more. Joshua promised I could ride with him for the Christmas sleigh ride this year."

"Oh, did he?" Susan accepted her daughter's good-night kiss.

"He says this year I'm his best girl, and I'm light, so he'll win all the races."

"Ah, the truth comes out." Margie laughed. "Josh is determined to beat Abel Coon this year."

Flora skipped into the hall and thumped upstairs.

Paul entered through the front door in a gust of frigid wind, brushing fresh snow from his shoulders. His ladies shooed him away from the satin.

"I hope it doesn't storm tomorrow," Margie said, her face clouding. "Any other year I would be thrilled at the prospect of snow for Christmas Eve, but not now. People might not be able to come to my wedding if the weather is bad."

"All you really need is a minister and a groom."

"Papa!" Margie protested.

Paul chuckled. "Last night at home for our girl." He hugged Margie, blinked hard, and cleared his throat. "Best get some sleep, all of you. I'm heading up to bed."

"You're right, Papa. Good night, Mama. Good night, Auntie Stell." Margie followed her sister and her father upstairs.

Susan took Margie's empty chair. "It seems like a dream. My little girl will be married tomorrow."

"She'll make a good wife for David. She took me to see her house last week. Such a lovely home it will be." Estelle gazed into the fire.

"You needn't envy her, Estelle. You'll make the parsonage into a lovely home, I imagine."

Estelle fanned her face. She had never been one to blush, but everything seemed different since her arrival in Iowa. "I never intended to marry."

"I believe Frank never intended to remarry, but then he met you. And tasted your cooking."

Estelle met Susan's twinkling gaze. "You believe he wishes to marry me for practical reasons."

Susan laughed aloud. "Not for a moment. He loves you, Estelle."

"I understand practical. I don't understand love."

Susan stared into the fire and spoke in dreamy tones. "Does anyone understand love? Why do I love Paul? Sometimes he annoys me; often I irritate him. Yet we are devoted to each other. God calls Christians to demonstrate love to one another whether we wish to or not. The amazing thing is that feelings often follow actions. I was afraid to love you when you first arrived here, Estelle. Yet I resolved to demonstrate God's love to you, and to my surprise, I grew to love you dearly."

Estelle listened in silent amazement.

"Love is perilous," Susan continued. "God knows this better than anyone, for He loves most. At Christmas we celebrate His greatest risk of all. When I think of God the Almighty lying in a manger as a helpless baby, the chance He took for the sake of love quite steals my breath away."

"Chance? God?"

"Yes, chance. For love of you, Estelle, He was mocked, beaten, and brutally killed. Then He conquered death and sin and returned to heaven to prepare a beautiful home for you. He could force you to love Him in return; He has enough power to make you do anything He wants you to do. But He doesn't desire the love of a puppet, so He simply woos you as a lover and longs for you to return His love."

Susan's words burned into Estelle's soul like a hot iron. The pain finally propelled her out of the chair and upstairs, where she lay in bed and shivered for hours.

Chapter 7

Estelle smoothed a calico apron over the skirts of her blue satin gown and glanced around at the other women working to decorate the hotel dining room. Frank's parishioners had leaped at the chance to help prepare the wedding reception for their minister's son. Of course, many of these women had known Margie since her birth. Estelle found the townsfolk's loyalty appealing.

Of particular interest to Estelle was the plump, golden-haired young woman helping Susan arrange table centerpieces—Amy Nelson Syverson. Amy had greeted Estelle earlier with a twinkle in her blue eyes. She must know about her father's intent to remarry, and apparently she approved. The knowledge boosted Estelle's spirits.

Entering the kitchen to see if she could be useful, she discovered several ladies in a huddle. Their concerned expressions roused her curiosity. "Is anything wrong?"

"Nothing serious," Mrs. Isobel Coon said. "We need a few more jars of fruit for an after-dinner sweet, but I suppose we can stretch what we have here to feed fifty people. If only Loretta hadn't broken—"

"Plenty of fruit in the parsonage cellar."

Estelle recognized that gruff voice. Mary Bilge stood at the huge cast-iron stove, stirring a pot, the old slouch hat pulled down over her eyes. Her change in clothing style had been short-lived.

Mrs. Coon nodded. "Pastor Nelson is probably at the church already, but I'm sure he'd be willing to donate fruit for his son's wedding reception. And the parsonage is just down the street. Where is Amy? Someone ask her to fetch us a few jars of peaches or pears."

Mrs. Fallbrook shook her head. "I saw her and Susan leave. Mary Bilge, would you—"

"No." Mary turned her broad back.

The other ladies blinked at each other, obviously trying to remain pleasant. "Well then, I suppose we must do without." They bustled off to finish their preparations.

Estelle approached Mary. "I can stir that soup while you get the fruit. It'd be a shame to run short of food at David and Margie's wedding reception."

"La-de-da. If you want it, you get it."

Her lips tightening, Estelle nodded. "Very well. I shall. Tell the others where I've gone." She hung her apron on a hook and located her cloak and overshoes. She would have to hurry. Josh had promised to stop by and pick her up on his way to the church.

Estelle left the hotel by the side door closest to the parsonage. A light snow frosted her woolen cloak, but she was able to keep her skirts hoisted above the drifts lining the street. If her new gown became soiled before the wedding, she would never forgive Mary Bilge. The selfish woman! What had gotten into her lately? She seemed like the old Mary again, even smelling of cigar smoke.

Frank must have shoveled his walk that morning. The front steps were icy but clear. It seemed strange to enter the parsonage uninvited. Belle greeted her in the hallway. "So you are lady of the house today?" Estelle stooped to stroke the cat. A mildew odor from the rug told her that Mary's housekeeping enthusiasm had waned along with her personal cleanliness. Poor Frank.

The kitchen was warm and smelled of something burnt. Restraining her urge to tidy up, Estelle peeled off her gloves and lit a candle at the oven's banked coals. She lifted the wooden latch on the cellar door and stared down into darkness. Stale, frigid air wafted up the steps. "You stay up here, Belle. I don't want to accidentally shut you in. I'll be only a moment."

Her shoes clopped on the wooden risers as she descended into the hole, keeping her skirts from brushing the whitewashed earth wall. Shivering, she scanned the shelves and located two jars of spiced peaches and one of pears. To carry three quart jars and a candle while safeguarding her gown would be impractical, so she hunted for a tote basket. Candle lifted high, she spotted a dusty one on the end of a top shelf.

Just as she reached for it, something banged up in the kitchen and Belle let out a yowl. Dust sifted through between the boards overhead. At that moment, the cellar door shut and the candle extinguished. Estelle spun about and heard the thunk of the latch dropping into place.

"Oh, no!"

Above, the floorboards creaked, and Belle meowed. Maybe the cat had bumped the door, causing it to close. Feeling her way in the darkness, Estelle hefted her skirts and climbed the wooden steps. She pushed at the unyielding door, then felt for the latchstring. It was missing. A cat would not have pulled it through to the other side.

Someone had shut her in the cellar. Mary Bilge was the only person who knew she had come for the fruit. Mary must have done it. But why? What could she hope to gain by such a petty, senseless act?

Rubbing her upper arms, Estelle sat on the second step down. At least she still wore her woolen cloak. Her gloves lay on the kitchen table, and her overshoes were near the front door. Frank would surely find her soon.

Something furry touched her hand, and she yelped. A mouse? The something scrabbled at the door and gave a soft meow.

Estelle relaxed. "Belle?" She felt along the crack beneath the door and found a paw. The cat was reaching for her. "You scared me." Estelle slid her fingers through the opening and touched a warm, vibrating body, a shadow against the dim slit of light visible beneath the door. *At least I'm not entirely alone. Someone will come after me before the wedding starts. They need me to play the piano.*

She tucked her feet in close and huddled beneath her cloak, resting her cheek against the solid door. "It's cold down here, but I'm sure Frank will find me before I freeze to death, and you're here to keep my fingers warm, Belle. Why would Mary lock me in the cellar? The person she hurts most by doing this is poor Marjorie, who will have no music for her wedding if they don't find me soon." Her voice sounded thin.

Long minutes passed. Aside from Belle's occasional mew and rumbling purr, Estelle heard only her own thoughts. She considered calling for help, but who would hear? The cellar had no windows.

She tried to estimate the amount of time passing. The gray slit beneath the door finally vanished. Would they go ahead with the wedding? She pictured Margie in her gown, gazing up into David's adoring eyes. How lovely the bride would be, and how handsome her young groom!

Trying to ignore the cold, she hummed the wedding march. Outside, snow would sparkle in the lantern light, turning Coon's Hollow into a Christmas wonderland. At the wedding there would be laughter and rejoicing, yet for Estelle the night was silent.

"Why did You allow me to miss Margie's wedding, God?" Despite her disappointment, she couldn't rouse herself to anger. Her recent studies of God's ways and His nature assured her that He allowed nothing to happen without reason. Oddly enough, her soul felt peaceful as her thoughts drifted back over last night's chat with Susan.

"Lately it does seem that every conversation, every argument circles back to the subject of love. Your love for me and my lack of love for others." She spoke just above a whisper. "I arrived here in the heat and light of summer, yet my heart was colder than ice. Now I sit in frozen darkness and feel the warmth of Your love. Your presence, not my circumstances, makes the difference."

Music wafted through her thoughts, and she began to hum, then sing quietly. "Silent night, holy night. Son of God, Love's pure light." She hummed again, pondering the words. "All these years I have denied Your love. I struggled alone in despair when I might have rejoiced daily in the knowledge of You. Because my parents failed me, Paul left, and John died, I quit believing. You offered to share my burdens and ease my load, but I refused You."

Tears welled up in Estelle's eyes, overflowed, and burned her cheeks. "It's not too late for me, is it, Lord? I acknowledge my hopeless condition; without You I am nothing—a selfish, cold, meaningless woman. Love is painful—You know that better than anyone—but I want to live and love and hurt along with You. Forgive my anger and my unbelief, and truly be Lord of my life."

The walls of ice split apart and crashed into the sea of God's love. The flood-gates of Estelle's soul opened wide, sweeping away every icicle of bitterness and anger and filling her with living water. For the first time in more than twenty years, she wept cleansing tears of joy.

She must have slept, for the next thing Estelle knew, the door swung away and Frank lifted her into his arms. Still groggy, she felt his brushy beard against her cheek. He trembled as if he were cold, yet his embrace enveloped her in warmth. She rested her face on his waistcoat and patted his shoulder. "Dear Frank, is the wedding over?"

"How on earth did you get shut in there?" he asked, his voice breaking. "We've been looking everywhere for you! I knew something must be wrong when you didn't show up for the wedding, but I waited until after the ceremony to panic. How did you end up in my cellar?" He sat on a kitchen chair and settled her on his lap, rocking her like a child. His big hands pressed her to his chest, stroked her face, tucked her cloak around her, then hugged her again as if he could never bring her close enough.

Light from the lamp on the table glowed in Belle's golden eyes. A moment later the cat leaped into Estelle's lap to join the embrace. "Belle kept me company and warmed my fingers." Estelle tucked a fold of her cloak around the purring cat.

Worry still vibrated in Frank's voice. "I've got to let Paul know you're safe. First tell me what happened. Josh feels terrible; he was supposed to pick you up at the hotel, but when he arrived there, you were already gone."

Estelle told her short tale. "Mary Bilge is the only one who knew where I went. I suspect she shut me in the cellar, but, Frank, please don't confront her about it."

"Why ever not?" His eyes blazed in the lamplight. "You might have frozen to death down there!" He smoothed hair from her temple, and she felt his fingers shaking.

"Nonsense. It isn't that cold, and I'm sure Mary expected you to find me today. Her conduct was spiteful and childish, not vicious," Estelle said. "But poor Margie! Did she walk down the aisle in silence?"

To her surprise, Frank chuckled. "No. Your prize piano student played the wedding march with more animation than accuracy."

"Flora?" Estelle sat up straight.

"Yes, Flora. The child performed well, and Margie seemed as happy as any new bride despite the lack of refinement in her accompaniment."

Estelle laughed aloud. "I would almost suspect Flora of shutting me into the cellar, if she'd had any opportunity. The little sprite undoubtedly enjoyed her chance to shine."

Frank stared.

Estelle touched her face, wondering if she had smeared dirt on her cheek or nose. "What is wrong?"

"I've never heard you laugh before."

Suddenly conscious of her position on his lap, Estelle pulled away and rose. Belle squawked in complaint and jumped to the floor. "Would you like a cup of tea? I need something warm to drink."

"No, thank you."

She moved the kettle over the heat. "I must tell you something, Frank. You deserve to know."

He looked wary. "I'm listening."

Estelle busied her hands with setting out a teacup. "Although I'm sorry I missed the wedding, I believe the Lord wanted time alone with me."

When she looked up, surprise lit Frank's features. She glanced away, still trying to control her emotions, yet her voice trembled. "I finally understand about love."

"You do?"

A smile broke free and spread across her face. "Oh, Frank, how much I have missed all these years! You tried to explain, but only God could reveal the wonder of His love. I know I can never make up for the years I've wasted, but all the life I have left belongs to the Lord."

He covered his face with both hands. Emotion clogged his deep voice. "I'm so glad, Estelle. So glad." He pulled a handkerchief from his jacket pocket and mopped his eyes, avoiding her gaze.

Her hands formed fists. She hid them behind her back, sucked in a deep breath, and took the plunge. "I would gladly spend the rest of my life with you, Frank Nelson."

He pushed back his chair and arose but remained at the table. "No more anger?"

She shook her head.

"No more fear?"

"Actually, I'm terrified." Her legs would give out at any moment.

He sounded short of breath. "So am I. Dearest Estelle, are you certain you can endure living in this tiny old parsonage with a rustic boor of a minister? You're so genteel and elegant, and I feel like a buffalo around you sometimes. I know my loud voice annoys you, and I leave my clothes lying around and forget to change into a clean shirt or polish my boots. . ."

Estelle dared to look at his face. "Then you need me to remind you. I want to feel needed. The happiest days of my life were the days I spent caring for your home and preparing meals for you. I shall try to be gentle and meek instead of bossy and high-handed."

"And I shall endeavor to be considerate." He folded his arms across his great chest. "Often you remind me of Belle, the way she demands affection only on her terms."

Estelle translated his unspoken question. "You fear angering me with unwelcome attentions?"

He slowly nodded.

She lowered her gaze and pondered the matter. "I have never possessed a demonstrative nature, and adjusting to the demands of marriage may require time. If you can be patient, I shall accustom myself to fulfilling your needs." Her face grew hot.

"I promise the same to you. And now, much though I hate to end this moment, we must consider the needs of our family and friends and assure them all of your safety."

Estelle lost interest in tea. She moved the kettle off the stovetop. "I have no idea what time it is. Are we too late for the wedding reception?"

"Not at all. The wedding ended less than an hour ago. The food should be hot and plentiful. Let's join the guests at the hotel and announce our own news." He paused, and his brows suddenly drew together. "We do have news, don't we? You will marry me?"

Estelle smiled. "I shall."

His face beamed like a summer sunrise. "I confess I jumped the gun and told Amy about my hopes. She seems to approve of my choice."

"I suspected as much; she was particularly friendly to me. A lovely young woman, Frank."

"I think so." He glowed with pride.

Estelle drew on her gloves. "I hope Paul approves. I know Susan will. Oh! We mustn't forget the three jars of fruit."

"I'll fetch them. You stay out of that cellar until I fit it with a modern doorknob that doesn't lock." Frank tapped her cheek with one finger. His eyes caught her gaze and held. "I love you, Estelle."

"Frank," she whispered, then found herself wrapped in a mighty hug. Her arms slid around him, and she pressed her cheek to his chest. His hand cupped her head, destroying her hairstyle, but she didn't care.

Chapter 8

Christmas morning dawned clear and bright. "No wind yet," Josh announced as the men came in from chores for breakfast, red-cheeked and stamping snow from their boots. "It's a perfect day for a sleigh ride."

Flora squealed and danced a little jig with Eliza frisking around her skirts. "Did you see what St. Nicholas put in my stocking, Josh? An orange, and hore-hound candy, a penny, and a little doll with a real china head!"

Estelle smiled as she set a dish of fried potatoes on the table. She had pur-chased the doll head at a shop in Madison many years earlier, unable to resist its sanguine smile. Together she and Susan had completed the doll for Flora and cre-ated its miniature wardrobe.

Joe played with his new gyroscope until Paul reminded him that the breakfast table was an improper place for toys. Joe hid it beneath the tablecloth. "Did this really belong to you when you were my age, Pa?"

"It did. Your aunt saved it all these years and brought it for you."

"Thank you, Auntie Stell."

"You're most welcome." Estelle basked in her nephew's approval and his first use of her pet name. She sat beside Susan and passed dishes of food to the other ravenous young men. Not even Margie's empty place at the table caused sadness this glorious Christmas morning. Estelle imagined the young bride preparing breakfast for her young husband at their new home and smiled with satisfaction.

She met her brother's gaze. Paul reached over and grasped her hand. That one gesture expressed his forgiveness and acceptance. Her voice held a sister's lifetime love. "Merry Christmas, Paulie."

"And a blessed Christmas to you, Stell. Having you in our home and full of joy is the best gift I could receive today, I think." After one last squeeze of her fingers, he returned his attention to his breakfast. Noting his heightened color, Estelle let the emotional moment end.

Josh advised Flora to hurry if she still wanted to accompany him on the sleigh ride. Glowing with excitement, the little girl raced through her chores and ran upstairs. Estelle wondered when Frank would arrive. As soon as the kitchen was tidy, she did some primping of her own.

Along with the blue satin gown for Margie's wedding, Estelle had found time to add two new shirtwaists to her wardrobe, one white and one of gray calico with pink sprigs. They would enliven her worn black skirts and jackets until she found time and means to sew more colorful garments.

Regarding her reflection in the small mirror above the dressing table in her dormer bedroom, Estelle coaxed the wisps of hair behind her ears into loose curls. The mere memory of Frank's expression when she removed her cloak at the hotel last night brought a smile to her face. He found her attractive, she knew, and the realization pleased her beyond measure.

At the reception, he had kept her at his side throughout the evening. The most disturbing moment for Estelle had come when she met Mary Bilge's flinty stare. *That poor woman! Something must be done to help her. But what?* She was no worse off than Estelle had been upon her arrival in Coon's Hollow. God could bring joy and love into Mary's life, too, if she would allow it. With a nod at the mirror, Estelle appointed herself to pray for Miss Mary Bilge.

The pin-tucked white shirtwaist Estelle wore contrasted nicely with her black jacket, and a red ribbon at her throat gave it a festive touch. Hearing sleigh bells, she ran to the window. Powder trotted up the drive, blowing twin plumes of steam.

Lest she keep Frank waiting, Estelle hurried downstairs, tying a long scarf over her bonnet and tucking it around her throat. With the addition of her cloak, mittens, and overshoes, she considered herself ready to brave the weather. "Frank is here," she called, patting Eliza's silky black head.

"Enjoy yourself, dear," Susan answered from the kitchen.

Paul leaned against the kitchen door frame. "Be home before dark," he warned with a twinkle.

"Yes, sir." Estelle gave him a hasty kiss before bustling outside.

Frank tucked her beneath robes and furs, climbed in beside her, and clucked to his horse. "Can't keep Powder standing when he's warm." At first the horse kicked up a frozen spray, but once he settled into his stride, Estelle uncovered her face.

"How beautiful!" Sunlight glittered on rolling drifts of pristine white. Silvery bells jingled with Powder's steady trot. The cold tingled her cheeks and froze inside her nose.

Frank's eyes seemed to reflect the vivid sky as he returned her smile. "Yes, you are beautiful."

Estelle unburied her arm enough to link it with his, then leaned her face against his shoulder. "This is the happiest day of my life."

"So far," he said with a grin. "I passed Josh and Flora on my way."

"They're off to the races, no doubt. I think Flora will be the envy of every eligible young woman in the county. I wonder why Josh hasn't started courting a girl yet," Estelle said.

"I imagine he hasn't found the right one," Frank answered. "I'm glad I waited until you came along."

Estelle snuggled closer. "I approve of your hat. It matches your eyes."

"So I was told by the lady who knitted it for me."

"Lady?"

He chuckled. "Jealous? Beatrice Coon was the lady."

The cutter swept through town, around on a looping county road, then back toward the Truman farm. Estelle waved at each sleigh they passed, recognizing chapped and smiling faces. David and Margie waved a joyous greeting but didn't pause to chat. Josh and Flora stopped to visit. Their horses pranced in place, steaming with sweat but still raring to go.

"I'm guessing by your smiles that you whipped Abel Coon today," Frank called.

"We beat him by a mile!" Flora shouted back. "But Abel says Josh cheated because I'm his sister and can't be his best girl."

Josh grinned. "He thought up that rule too late to do him any good this year."

Frank laughed. "Are you on your way home?"

"Yup. Got to give Chester and Sandy a good rubdown and some hot mash. They earned it today. Merry Christmas, and congratulations, Pastor Nelson. My aunt will make you a great wife." Josh winked at Estelle and clucked to his fretting horses.

"Good-bye," Flora called, and Estelle blew her a kiss.

Frank jiggled his reins, and Powder trotted on. "Amy and Bradley chose to remain at the parsonage today," Frank said. "Their best gift to me this year was the news that I'm to become a grandfather next summer. I hope you don't mind marrying a grandfather."

Despite his teasing tone, Estelle detected a hint of anxiety underlying his question. "As long as I get to be a stepgrandmother, I favor the idea. I love babies. Since I can never have a child of my own, I shall treasure the opportunity to love your children and grandchildren."

Powder slowed to a walk. Estelle studied their surroundings. "Where are we?"

"Nowhere. I've been thinking and planning, but for the life of me I can't think of a place we could go today to find some privacy." Leaving his horse to set a moderate pace, Frank turned on the seat, caught her mittened hands, and brought them to his chest.

Estelle's heart thundered in her ears. Frost glittered in his eyebrows and mustache, but his expression warmed her face. His voice wavered. "This is our first Christmas together, and I want you to remember it always with joy." For a long moment, his blue eyes studied her. She saw his lips twitch with emotion and suddenly understood.

"I shall." She was too bundled up to move, so she put one hand behind his head and gently pulled his face toward hers. His frosty mustache tickled, but his lips on hers were surprisingly warm.

He sat back with a pleased smile. "Thank you."

"I love you, Frank."

His smile widened. Giving a little whoop, he snapped the reins and started his stalled horse off at a brisk trot.